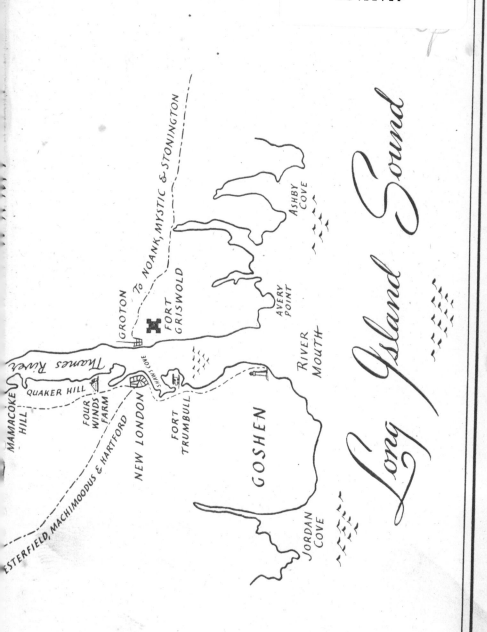

Long Island Sound

Long Island

To NOANK, MYSTIC & STONINGTON

GROTON

FORT GRISWOLD

ASHBY COVE

AVERY POINT

RIVER MOUTH

Thames River

QUAKER HILL

MAMACOKE HILL

FOUR WINDS FARM

SHAW'S COVE

NEW LONDON

FORT TRUMBULL

GOSHEN

JORDAN COVE

WESTERFIELD, MACHIMOODUS & HARTFORD

HOLDFAST GAINES

THE MACMILLAN COMPANY
NEW YORK · BOSTON · CHICAGO · DALLAS
ATLANTA · SAN FRANCISCO

MACMILLAN AND CO., Limited
LONDON · BOMBAY · CALCUTTA · MADRAS
MELBOURNE

THE MACMILLAN COMPANY
OF CANADA, Limited
TORONTO

Holdfast Gaines

by
ODELL SHEPARD
and
WILLARD SHEPARD

THE MACMILLAN COMPANY

NEW YORK · 1946

PRINTED IN THE UNITED STATES OF AMERICA

The log at the wood-pile, the axe supported by it,
The sylvan hut, the vine over the doorway, the space clear'd for a
garden,
The irregular tapping of rain on the leaves after the storm is lull'd,
The wailing and moaning at intervals, the thought of the sea . . .
The sentiment of the huge timbers of old-fashion'd houses and
barns . . .
The beauty of independence, departure, actions that rely on themselves,
The American contempt for statutes and ceremonies, the boundless im-
patience of restraint . . .
The blazing fire at night, the sweet taste of supper, the talk, the bed of
boughs and the bear-skin . . .
Spar-makers in the spar-yard, the swarming row of well-grown appren-
tices,
The swing of their axes on the square-hewed log, shaping it to the
shape of a mast . . .
The death-howl, the limpsey tumbling body, the rush of friend and foe
thither . . .
Roar, flames, blood, drunkenness, madness . . .
The hell of war, the cruelties of creeds,
The list of all executive deeds and words, just or unjust,
The power of personality . . .

—WALT WHITMAN

CONTENTS

vii

BOOK THREE

THE BLACK DRINK

BOOK FOUR

ECHOING GUNS

BOOK ONE

FOUR WINDS FARM

While I was musing the fire burned.

PSALM XXXIX, 3

LONG TOM SPEAKS

(New London, Connecticut—November, 1780)

"Br-OM-m-m-m!"

The roar of a great gun shook the rafters of the night.

One moment before there had been only a vague whisper of river-waves that felt the first embrace of the sea. A dull watchman, at any rate, would have heard no more than that, unless it were the rusty croak of a heron flapping over from the pools beyond Fort Griswold. To a drowsy sentinel it would have seemed that nothing could happen here on a night so black and still, with the placid Thames pouring down toward Long Island Sound as peacefully as ever in all its Indian centuries.

But Holdfast Gaines was watching tonight, and he was neither dull nor drowsy. Moreover, he had been warned. Almost half an hour ago the two tall sails of the ketch *Rebecca* had come breasting out of the dark, and while they glimmered by he had heard the voice of a friend from the deck, subdued but excited: "Ahoy, there, Fort Trumbull!"

"Hello!"

"That you, Holdfast Gaines?"

"Good guess, Sam Avery."

"How many with yeh?"

"One dog."

"What's that ye say?"

"I'm alone, Sam. Three o' the garrison are down with pox and three home on leave. The rest went off to a husking-bee. By this time they'll be drunk and asleep in the hay."

"Wal, what a way to fight a war!—But anyhow, stand by to give the 'larm iffen ye hev to."

"Alarm! What for?"

3

"I ben chased, Holdfast. British frigate. Left her hull-down at night-fall a league off river-mouth."

"Coming up, is she?"

"Sarting sure. Hell-bent to git me this time."

"By open boats?"

"Yeah. An' by s'prise attact, tonight."

"Surprise, eh?—Think they'll try to storm the fort, Sam?"

"Gawd, no! They don't want yer li'l toy fort. They're arter me, I tell yeh. I'll go on to anchor an' make ready fer 'em."

"'Li'l toy fort'! Say, look here, you weevil-eating pirate . . . !"

But it had seemed absurd to call out even the friendliest vituperations into the silent dark—absurd, and perhaps not in the best military tradition.

And then, as though some vast invisible bell had been lowered over the promontory of rock, every sound and sight was shut away. Even the tiny stone blockhouse close at hand, though covered with white-wash, was no more than a glimmer. He could move three paces to the left of his gun and then three paces back to its cold damp metal. His moccasins made no sound. Mostly, though, he stood still, keenly alert, listening intently, snuffing the wild odors of river-water, feeling up and down the long smoothly rounded iron of the great gun.

Badly flawed the gun was, and unfit for first-rate batteries. On the left-hand side of the muzzle-face there was the scar of an old wound made by the direct hit of a six-inch ball. That was the reason why, for all its gigantic girth and bellow, it was not riding the sea tonight on some great ship of the line but was standing here in the dark defending New London. It seemed almost a human companion. The fondness that Holdfast Gaines felt for the gun was partly due, also, to the fact that he had helped to place it here on the rock, and had himself hewed out the transom, breast-piece, cheeks, and bed of the carriage from chunks of Gungywamp oak. Moreover his cousin Mamohet, a Mohegan blacksmith, had hammered out the iron bolts, the holdfasts, and the side-tackle rings at his forge in Mohegan Village.—Once again, as he remembered these things, the young man swept a hand along the bulge of the barrel as though it were the arm of a friend.

More companionable still was the six-foot murdering-piece leaning there in the dark against the great gun's pommelion. Hunters called it a duck-gun because of the way it scattered shot, but the strongest

4

of them had to fasten its barrel on the gunwale of a boat or some other such support, because of its weight and fierce recoil. To old soldiers of the French and Indian War it was a "murtherer." Holdfast himself called it "Hobbomok" when using his native Mohegan tongue, and said that in English this name meant "Mischief Maker."

And then, too, it was comfortable to have the dog along—a dog not much to look at, certainly, but of a sterling character. There had not been a whimper out of him when the *Rebecca* went by.

Standing watch on such a night as this, Holdfast thought, was a little like deer-stalking—except of course that tonight he was not going to kill anything. His job would be, if the time came, merely to make such a frightful noise that the earth would seem to be torn loose from the sky. For that noise he could depend upon the great gun. Every townsman and farmer for miles around knew the voice of Long Tom, and was precisely aware what he had to do when it spoke its one huge word.

The tunk of an iron fluke against a wooden bow up there, a slight splash, and the rattling of a cable, told him that the *Rebecca* had come to anchor. He heard a low voice or two, and the thud of a spike on the deck. Of course they were trying to be quiet, but . . .

The *Rebecca* in danger! The British coming up-river to take, or perhaps to burn her! With that thought the lingering, distant, half-hearted war came home. For his boat she was, as much as Sam Avery's. Sitting across from Sam by the kitchen fire, three winters ago, Holdfast had whittled a half-model out of pine boards, and from this they had lofted her lines to scale, in chalk, on the barn floor. With the help of an old shipbuilder from Portersville and a few handy lads too young for soldiering, they had built her in partnership, at the river's edge under Quaker Hill. Being scarcely more than boys at the time, they had botched her, no doubt, in many ways, but not for lack of care, pride, or affection. There was plenty of good solid Gungywamp oak in her timbers. And a lucky sailor she had been too, the ketch *Rebecca*— beloved name! Three of the seven British prizes she had captured, all larger than she was, lay at anchor tonight in this very cove.

And now her foes were out to take her "by surprise attack," "in open boats," and "tonight!"

Into these thoughts there came creeping a little thin alien sound. Was it only a wandering breeze that feathered the wavelets—or some animal, a deer perhaps, swimming the river?

5

But no! Unmistakably he caught a faint rumor of oars, heavily muffled and stealthily moving, from far down the water.

He held his breath, and heard the quickening thump of his heart more loud than the beat of oars.

Steady, now! This was no time to act like an untried boy. After all, he was almost twenty. If he should fire the signal-gun when only a fishing dory was rowing back to harbor he would never outlive the laughter of the countryside.

Yet why should it come so cautiously, with no hail to the fort, in the dark of the moon, and under a blanket of cloud?

A minute passed, and another, with the dull beat of oars still advancing.

Reaching down to touch the little dog huddled against his leg, Holdfast Gaines dimly saw a shape of deeper blackness, the shape of a longboat, gliding by half a pistol-shot off. She was going by like a ghostly deer, heading into the cove.

He crouched to peer along the sights, and saw that if the muzzle had been slightly lower he might have hulled her through and through. Then, just as she was moving out of range, he had a glimpse of a pipe-clayed cross-belt.

British marines! And would there be another boat behind her?

He seized the three-tined iron crow that lay in the angle of the bulwark and, catching its claw under the gun's breech, slowly prized the butt upward until the muzzle was brought to bear upon the surface of the river close at hand. Then he thrust the wooden quoin beneath the breech.

Now . . . But when he saw a second dim shape swim directly into his aim he was sorry for these preparations. By one swift sweeping motion of his arm and hand he could blow that boat and all she held into a sudden chaos of blood and brains and slowly sinking splinters.

Why not? It was his duty. What held him back? Whose voice was that, calling from inside his heart, crying out against the deed? Why should *she* care?

So he paused and stood bewildered, torn two ways at once. And when he peered again along the sights he saw that those many lives had passed beyond his power.

In a way he was glad. The killing of men was different from stalking deer. He had never yet killed a man. It had been his hope that he would

6

not have to kill anyone in this white man's war. He drew his hand across his brow. It was damp with sweat.

But forty British marines had gone by the fort to attack the tiny *Rebecca* and her crew of ten—all friends of his. He must fire the signal at once.

Crouching again to lay fresh priming to the vent, he discerned a third shape growing in the gloom out there. By what right were they here, these thieves, invading his Indian river, the old beloved stream of his fathers? There leapt up in his heart a sudden and savage anger. That third boat, he knew, was doomed. Like a hidden hunter who watches a deer steal down through the woods toward a pool at midnight, he stared at its slow coming-on. His heart was pounding. Now the stem of the boat loomed just beyond the long dark barrel—now the fore-sheets—and now he had her exactly nailed amidships. Standing far to one side to avoid the recoil, he lifted his "murtherer" over the great gun's breech-vent and snapped the flint down against the frizzen. Instantly, with a blinding flash, Long Tom bellowed into the night.

Before the first echoes came rolling back from the opposite bank Holdfast Gaines had leapt the bulwark and was running up the cove toward the unseen *Rebecca*. He tore off his buckskin shirt as he ran. A small dog, barking furiously, was racing far behind him. He heard the screams of men from the water. Away to his right, in the cottage windows of New London, candle after candle was beginning to glimmer through the dark.

CUTTING-OUT PARTY

The flash of Long Tom brought an instantaneous and composite picture to the eyes of the *Rebecca's* captain and crew. Each man or boy on the deck, according to the chance direction of his gaze between those two heart-beats, saw a different object leap suddenly out of darkness and die back again.

For Tantaquidgeon the Mohegan there was only a large bird of night, perhaps an owl, spread out motionless on the air above him. To Nate Rogers came the heights of Fort Griswold and a few Groton house-fronts below it on the water's edge. Steve Denison caught a

7

glitter of little waves near at hand, with three sharpies tugging at their buoys. Aaron Cheseborough had a glimpse of Nathaniel Shaw's big stone mansion topping the warehouses. And Moses Packer read the name—*The Angel*—newly gilded on the transom of Shaw's fine sloop just home from the West Indies. In that moment young Bill Small saw nothing but his own bare feet, and they in need of a scrubbing. Right before the level gaze of Peter Fanning stood the distant but startlingly vivid figure of Holdfast Gaines, black against orange, with his huge "murtherer" thrown up across a sudden huff of flame. Captain Avery glimpsed that too, but what he chiefly saw was a long-boat packed with men—a boat torn in two amidships as one might break a long loaf of bread. Most of the marines in her had been standing up, and now they were caught by the light in staggering, crouching, clutching, and toppling attitudes as though shaken by earthquake. Two other boats, nearer by, uninjured and bristling with armed men, were rowing toward the *Rebecca,* taking utmost care to make no noise.

No noise? Had the world stopped?

But then it sounded—a huge body-hollowing roar that seemed to lift the arch of his skull. Most comforting it was to hear Long Tom's laconic comment upon the scene just passed.

There was no time in which to rig boarding-nettings. And, anyhow, why should he? His four three-pounders and six swivels were loaded with musket-balls. Three tubs of loaded pistols under the bulwarks, ten or twelve boarding-pikes and as many cutlasses at the foot of the mainmast, together with the muskets, tomahawks, knives, and blunderbusses carried by the men themselves . . . Besides, every man and boy on the *Rebecca* owned a lay in the vessel and would defend her as his very own.

From Groton Heights to Town Hill, from Shantok to Gungywamp, across and across the river the shout of Long Tom went echoing. People must have heard it up in Norwich by now, and down in tiny Noank on the Sound.—Indeed, why should those echoes ever cease? Why shouldn't they roll on through the coming years and out over the western wilderness? Long Tom had seemed to know that he had a country behind him, and perhaps the small beginnings of a nation. He had seemed to say: "This is ours, and we mean to keep it!"

As he leaned over the taffrail Avery heard the cries of wounded men from the water beyond Fort Trumbull, the barking of a dog, and a thudding of padded rowlocks close at hand. A low voice, hardly a hundred feet off the stern, was giving indistinguishable commands.

8

"Le's fire inter 'em right thar, Cap!" whispered Bill Small at his elbow.

"Sartingly not!—An' Bill, iffen ye're a-goin' ter git eggsited I'll shet yeh up in cabin afore fightin' starts."

"Aw, Cap, I wanter *shoot* somebody!"

"Ye'll shoot yerself, mos' likely. Gi' me that blunderbuss. An' now do ye paddle yerself up forerd an' stay thar, quiet 's a marlingspike, less 'n ye git summat to report. We ain't a-goin' ter hev' Mrs. Small's li'l boy gittin' hurt round hyar."

Bill shuffled away with his hands in his pockets, his head hanging. Avery told off two men to light the battle-lanterns and bring them from the galley. The others huddled about their captain on the quarter-deck. They could hear one another breathe. They heard the chuckle and sigh of the out-going tide. On the shore close at hand a dog was barking, shrilly. Candles were beginning to twinkle from the windows of the town. Here and there among the crooked lanes a lantern-light staggered drunkenly down toward the cove.

Then the *Rebecca* herself awoke—or so it would have seemed to a watcher on the shore. The men at the after rail were aware without looking round that their two battle-lanterns, iron-ribbed and horn-sided, had been hung against the masts. They shed a light like that of the thinnest moon overcast by cloud.

"Hold yer fire now, boys, till I give the order," Avery whispered.

He was answered from below by a sudden thudding hubbub of oars drawn in, trampling feet, and a boat's stem bumping the rudder. From twenty throats at once there rose a cheer that was half a yell, confusedly mixed with orders, oaths; and above the other voices rang out one: "Give me a back, there! One—two—three—*heave!*"

The head and shoulders of a man in officer's uniform showed above the transom, making a perfect mark for a pistol; but Avery threw his arms wide and backward to keep his men from firing and then with his cutlass knocked up the shaft of Tantaquidgeon's lunging harpoon.

Blue and white the stranger's uniform looked to be. That would mean a Lieutenant in the King's Navy. Young, tall, blond, his eyes flashing, he stood with one hand on the taffrail and the other jerking his sword from its sheath. It came out with a long dim glisten.

For half a second he stood there, swiftly glancing about. Then in one smoothly flowing motion he vaulted the rail and alighted on his feet, his sword-point up and steady, threatening.

There was a gallant folly in these boarding tactics that won the heart.

9

—Or was it contempt?—Anyhow, take him alive. Exchange him for a dozen New London lads now rotting in British prison-ships.

"Leave him to me!" Avery yelled. "Keep them others offen deck!"

Was it contempt? Well then, so much the better. A man who scorned you was half licked already. Seeing that his antagonist carried only a sword, Avery dropped his own pistol from his left hand. It exploded as it fell and was kicked by the recoil against the bulwarks like a live thing.

Chancy work this was, though, fighting by lantern-light in the cramped space of the quarter-deck, with the tiller, binnacle, and companion-hatch to dodge around, not to mention the mizzen-mast with its pin-rail, halyards, and shrouds, and that treacherous two-foot drop at the break of the poop. The Lieutenant slipped out of the corner between the bulwarks and transom with catlike ease. He fought with a blade a foot longer, an amazingly long blade, and certainly knew how to use it. But then there was the advantage of knowing one's own deck and being hidden in nut-brown homespun. Homespun was the wear for such work. The stranger's waistcoat, lapels, and cuffs were white. Keep him facing the battle-lanterns! Watch the swing and thrust of that right cuff! Watch it!

The two blades met and gnashed down clear to the hilts, grinding a spray of sparks. His own wrist, the Captain felt, was the stronger, but . . . And now, as he lunged and recoiled, taking a scratch on his cheek at one rally and a shrewd thrust in the thigh at another, he began to hear an uproar behind him of pistols, muskets, and swivels, thud of boarding-pikes, clatter of tomahawks, oaths, cries of pain and defiance and derision.

So this, he thought with half a grin, was their surprise attack.

But not all of it. At the moment when he was trying most desperately to keep out of that fatal angle in the stern-quarter he heard the shrill voice of Bill Small: "Go it, Cap! Slice his lights out! C'n I help yeh, Cap?"

"Git outer hyar!"

"But Cap," the lad screamed, holding a lantern high above his head, "I come ter tell yeh. They's 'nother boat come 'longside on t' fore-quarter, an' she's swarmin' wi' men."

"Keep off!" Avery shouted, seeing out of the corner of his eye that Bill was about to climb to the quarter-deck where, already, there was too little room.

"An' Holefas' he jes' now clum on deck start nekkud, an' he's a-goin'

10

fer 'em like a catamountain. Oh, will ye *look* at that Holefas'! He's a-luggin' a cannon, Cap—on his back!"

"Boy, git the hell out!"—And, on the instant, seeing that his foe's right cuff had fallen for a moment low and that he was standing with his back to the two-foot break of the poop, Avery lunged. The Lieutenant toppled backward over the break, striking his right arm between wrist and elbow against the sharp combing of the after-hatch. His sword fell, clattering.

Avery leapt down, put his foot on the long sword, and took the lantern from Bill. The young Lieutenant's face had gone paper-white.

"Will ye give me yer word not to try to escape 'less yer fellows take my ketch?"

"My arm's broken," was the faint reply.

"Then, Bill, take keer o' this man. He's our guest, 'member. I'll be back."

Running forward with the lantern, the Captain found that young Bill's report had been true enough. Holdfast Gaines—not quite "start nekkud" to be sure, but stripped to the waist, and his sopped leathern breeches showing almost the exact color of his skin—stood crouched by the bowsprit under the weight of a three-pounder gun which he had torn from its carriage and borne some ten feet on his shoulder. He was peering over the side. Then, with a heave that made the muscles of his bronzed back writhe like snakes, he sent the four hundred pounds of metal plunging.

Avery swung his lantern in time to see his precious gun crash through the bottom of a large boat packed with men. Black water welled in at the hole it left, and British marines were spilling out of her like peas from a split pod.

Holdfast straightened up, drew a deep breath, and shook the seawater from his long black hair. His eyes glittered in the lantern-light as he stood listening for a moment to the yells from the stricken boat. A wild exultation, such as Avery had never seen there before, shone for an instant in his face. Something hidden in Holdfast, something usually held down, had apparently broken loose in those few minutes of violence, slaughter, and carnage. It was as though his savage ancestors had been suddenly awakened. He was all but laughing as he looked down at his friend and said: "Well, Sam, that's two boats. How about the other?"

"Their Leftenant got aboard, but he's quiet now. The rest . . . Let's go see."

11

Lantern in one hand and cutlass in the other, the Captain ran aft with Holdfast striding beside him. Some five of the enemy had forced their way on board, but two of these were dead or dying. Avery felled a third with the flat of his cutlass. A fourth leapt overboard. The fifth, breaking away from Tantaquidgeon, made at the bare-bodied and empty-handed Holdfast with a boarding-pike. Holdfast laughed aloud as the fat, red-coated figure charged him. He caught the pole of the pike in mid-swing and snapped it. Then he picked up his furiously kicking assailant and dropped him over the side. Everyone heard the splash and the gurgling yell that followed.

Holdfast was still laughing as he came back into the glimmer of the lantern. Sea-water trickled from his long black hair and between the plated muscles of his chest. All the crew saw now in his eyes what was left of that savage glee which had surprised the Captain. "Great God o' the Mountain," he cried, "what a glorious fight!"

"Ugh! Nice one. Very damn nice one for Bear Asleep," agreed Tantaquidgeon, proudly gazing up and down his young chieftain's body.

"Sixty 'g'inst us ten, an not one of us hurt!" the Captain exulted.

"Look what I got, Cap," a voice shrilled at his elbow.

Bill Small was holding a little yellow dog, very wet and miserable, shivering.

"Sixty against eleven, you mean, Sam," said Holdfast, taking the dog in his arms. "We couldn't have done much without the dog."

"Nor withouten Holdfast Gaines, nuther. Iffen 't warn't for that fust god-a'mighty big bang we'd all ben fish-bait by now."

"Well Sam, make it twelve, then. Still, they had the odds.—Here, Bill, this little tyke is all tuckered out. You dry him off and let him go to sleep. I'd do it myself, but I've got to get back to the fort."

"That's all right for the dog," said Captain Avery, "but this hyar Leftenant needs more 'n I can do fer 'im. Holdfast, do ye carry 'im down to cabin an' splint his arm. I'll find yer shirt, pick up Hobbomok, git yer fort manned, an' be at Four Winds Farm by dawn to tell the folks ye're comin'."

"Do you think we ought to take the prisoner up there, Sam?"

"Whar the hell else is they to take 'im to? He's a gentleman, an' we got to treat 'im proper, like they never do us."

"But Sam . . ."

"Who's Cap'n o' this hyar ship o' the line? Whose pris'ner is this? Yourn?—No back talk!"

12

Holdfast Gaines turned slowly away and walked to the rail. They could just discern his great dusky figure there on the edge of the dark. His back was to them, but they knew he was staring out with eyes trained from childhood to see through the night. It seemed a long time that he stood so. The crew, clustered under the after-lantern, was grinning uneasily when he came back into the light and knuckled his brow to the captain in mock submission. "You are two years older than I am, Sam," said he, "and, as you say, you're the Captain. So have it your way."

"Wal then," said Avery, "Tantaquidgeon an' young Bill, do ye swab the deck down an' keep watch an' pull in any stray lobster-backs ye find floatin' round.—But no scelpin', unnerstand. It's too good fer 'em."

"Aye, aye, sir!" sang out Bill Small.

"Oh, an' Tantaquidgeon, iffen ye ketch this young hell-hound offerin' any hurt to them ye haul aboard, jest knock 'im cold an' bury 'im at sea."

Tantaquidgeon grinned—and so, after a moment, did Bill.

Moving then to the after-rail, but taking care not to offer a target for the muskets below, the Captain found that the fight there had degenerated into an exchange of blasphemous remarks.

"Now, gentlemen," he called, using his politest school-bred language, "the entertainment of the evenin' is a'most over, and you can take either one o' two tacks. Either you can row back an' report your success to your captain, or, if you really prefer, you can hang round here about five seconds longer and take a bag of canister from this here heavy-loaded swivel. I recommend a prompt decision. As for your Leftenant, he has accepted a pressin' invitation to remain with us."

There followed a murmur of sullen voices, a low curse or two, and then a splash of oars.

"Oh, an' gentlemen, since you feel you must leave us, pray remember to extend to your commander the greetings and felicitations of Captain Samuel Avery of the ketch *Rebecca*, together with those of the nine men and boys in her crew—by no means forgetting Mr. Holdfast Uncas Gaines, a Mohegan Injun."

"Yeah," piped a boy's piercing voice, "an' ye go tell yer fat-faced ole King George 'at this hyar Holefast is king o' the hull Mohegan nation! He comes down from ole King Uncas, he doos. An' our Holefast he says to King George 'Do ye git the hell outen our Thames River an' keep out o' hyar or he'll do things to 'im that . . . '"

13

The sentence was broken off as though a strong hand had been clapped over the boy's mouth; but then, to complete it, the dog in Bill's arms began a furious barking.

The sound of oars was growing faint.

"I'll send back the gig for yeh, Holdfast," said Avery. "Ye'll need it to bring in the Leftenant.—Good night."

"Good night, Sam.—And we'll fish up your little three-pounder tomorrow."

INWARD BATTLE

Lying motionless on the extra hammock in the cabin of the *Rebecca,* Lieutenant John Reid counted six bells of the second night watch sounding from the forecastle. And then, as though in confirmation, more slowly and farther away, there fell three deep tones from the tower of some church on shore. That would mean almost four hours of torment before the rise of the sun.

Through the tumult of his fever Reid could remember that he had been carried down here in the arms of—well, it did not seem probable, but he would have said in the arms of a naked giant. Then someone had bandaged a splint, not unskillfully, to his broken arm. Meanwhile there had been a good deal of shouting and calling on the water, and, later on, a splashing of water on the deck overhead. He knew what that would mean.

The tyrannous grind and crunch of pain made him fancy that his own body had been laid aboard and beaten under hatches. It was a rudderless ship, a derelict, rising and falling on a sea of pain.

He rehearsed the tales he had heard about these wild Yankees. They were said to fight like the Indians, with no regard to the code of civilized warfare. No doubt they tortured their captives in terrible Indian ways. Moreover, he had been told that some remnants of the old Pequot and Mohegan tribes still lingered along the Thames. It seemed to him that he had actually seen a redskin up there on deck, brandishing a huge barbed spear.

But at least as unpleasant to contemplate as death by Indian torture was the possibility that he might be penned up among foul diseases in the poisonous stench of a prison-ship. If England herself condemned

14

her prisoners of war to the slow corruption of scurvy and smallpox on board the *Jersey* prison-ship in New York Harbor, he thought he knew what to expect from these ignorant yokels.

Of course there was a chance that he might be exchanged. He saw himself a free man once more, rowing out to the frigate *Amazon* and standing before his captain to report.—Ah, but what words could he hope to find? With what face could he stand before even that kindly man with such a tale to tell? No! Rather than such humiliation he would choose the Indian stake.

But the question was, what to do? He had yet some hours of darkness. Through the open window of the cabin he could see no lights on shore. There was no sound of footsteps, no call, from the deck, to show that a watch had been set there. A faint rubbing and bumping from below the window told him that the Captain's gig had not been taken away.—But the Captain's hammock, side-by-side with his own, blocked his way to the cabin window. The Captain himself was evidently sleeping there. Crippled as he was, Reid knew that he had no chance of climbing over or under that hammock without waking his enemy. These Yankees had a way of getting results, apparently, with a minimum of effort and paraphernalia.

All at once Reid remembered that, before binding his arm, the naked giant had given him a long stiff swig of some fiery liquor— "apple-jack," had he called it?—from a flask in the Captain's cupboard. In remembering the flask and how it had looked in the dim light he recalled another glimpse that had come at the same moment. He had seen a glitter of steel, of cutlasses, ten or twelve of them, ranged together somewhere in this cabin. Ah, yes! They were hanging on a rack attached to the butt of the mast. They must now be within four feet of his hand.

Well, then?

Yes, it would be a remotely possible thing. At least it would be a thing to do, instead of lying here in this dreadful silence with hell bursting loose in his brain.

By a violent effort Reid lifted himself upon his left elbow. His hammock's edge, he found, touched the edge of the other man's. When his own body swayed by as much as half an inch the other man's swayed also.

Yet he pulled himself to a sitting posture, and then for some time sat still, resting, listening, trying to think. Once again he heard the gig bump against the stern and the cluck of wavelets along the water-

15

line. What else he heard was the low even breath of the man lying close beside him.

During his years at sea, reaching back into boyhood, John Reid had killed at least a score of men. Killing was in some sense his profession. But to kill a sleeping man . . . ! In sleep, because of its trustfulness and its hint of death, there was something holy. Hitherto, moreover, he had been sustained by the heat of battle. Now he had to think, alone, in the silence. And while he sat thinking, gripping the hammock's edge with his left hand, feeling the tides of heat and cold sweep through his veins, a doubt grew up in him whether this deed would be an act of duty or one of crude selfishness. Certainly he would never care to mention it to his closest friend. It would be a thing to forget, laboriously, and to wash his mind of—if possible.

Notions came to him, perhaps out of his fever, which at another time he would have thought fantastic. Hitherto, he told himself, he had killed men's bodies only. Now he was planning all at once to freeze the current of a man's thoughts forever, to wreck the airy fabric of his dreams, and to bring the stored knowledge and wisdom of his years to a pinch of dust. This was different. This was horrible. In such a deed he would be acting as God's enemy, irretrievably changing the total pattern which the Hidden Weaver had imagined. How could he dare to set a bar across every path which this unknown man might have followed, to stifle his words unspoken, and to shut him away from his future deeds? Considering the numberless ways in which every life flows into every other, he thought, the murder of this man would amount to a treacherous assault upon all mankind. It would slay something precious and never to be replaced in the life of Lieutenant John Reid himself.

Reid could not recall whether he had given his word not to attempt an escape; but this complete trust in him, this kindly treatment, was enough to bind a gentleman. Not only, then, would the deed he had in mind be wicked; it would violate the code of honor.

Pausing for a moment upon the one word "honor," Reid's thoughts began to emerge from the mists in which they had been wandering. Chivalric honor was a thing about which he, as a proud descendant of King Robert the Bruce, had clear convictions. One of these was the belief that a gentleman's code was binding only in his relations with members of his own class. Now, the Captain of this pitiful thieving privateer was obviously no gentleman. He did not wear a uniform. His own crew stood little in awe of him. His language, as Reid

16

vaguely recalled it, was that of some coarse uplandish bumpkin. In the sword-play up there in the dark he had won not by skill with the weapon but by a most ungentlemanly trick. To be sure, he had been lucky in slipping in and out of the river-mouth at a time when the Sound was swept almost clear of rebel sail. His clever little craft had become, in fact, decidedly troublesome. That was why three boats carrying sixty men had been told off to take and destroy her. Yet it was scarcely in his favor that he had for so long been a nuisance to the King's loyal subjects. Neither had he earned any special consideration by compassing the deaths this night of many British marines and, perhaps, of two or three naval officers. No one would ever ask how he had met his end, but many a Tory of New York and Long Island, and at least three captains of British men-o'-war now riding in the Sound, would be glad to learn that the Captain of the ketch *Rebecca* would trouble them no more.

Thus the whole problem came clear at last, and Reid saw that it was his duty to cut the sleeping man's throat. Just this, so to speak, was what he had been sent out to do. If he failed to do it, he might as well cut his own.

With extreme caution, so as to avoid any chance of bringing a blade with a clatter to the floor, he reached out his left arm, groping. In a moment his fingers came upon a cold edge of steel. Now, to get that cutlass by the hilt, to lift it from the slot, and . . .

"I'm sorry, Leftenant," said a gentle and yet strangely deep and powerful voice beside him, "that your arm gives you so much trouble. —But which arm is it now?"

Reid felt something turn over in the region of his stomach. Could this man see in the dark?

"I—I must have a fever," he managed to stammer out. "I think I must have been dreaming."

"Ah, yes. No doubt of it. And no man can control his dreams when a fever is on him.—But is there anything I can do to help you sleep better?"

Though most quietly spoken, the words filled the tiny cabin as the sea brims a tide-pool.

"Nothing more just now, I thank you," said Reid, sinking back with a sigh of relief into his hammock.

"Not another sip of apple-jack? It's good. Captain Avery and I froze it down three winters ago.—We froze it three times."

"Aren't you the Captain?"

17

"No, no. I'm Holdfast Gaines, the man who bound your arm. The Captain has gone ashore."

"Oh."

"But now try to sleep a little, Leftenant. Night's nearly over, and when day comes I'll take you to a place where you'll like to be. I tell you so."

It was a voice, Reid felt, that one could rest down upon—a voice just now as musical and low as a western breeze crooning among the sails, yet somehow holding reserved within it the power of a storm-wind. Was there anything this unseen man could do to help him sleep better? Well, yes: and it had been done merely by speaking a few sentences of an English pure and simple as rain-water.

John Reid closed his eyes. He had been conquered twice, completely, in one night. That seemed to matter less and less. His fever cooled and the pain in his arm subsided. Long before dawn tinged the hills across the Thames he was asleep.

FOUR WINDS FARM

Colonel John Chester heaved himself up from the settle, limped across the kitchen floor, and peered into the storm through the small greenish panes.

"What a 'nation big storm for Thanksgivin'!" he boomed. "Must be eight inches on the level, Mother."

"My stars!" his wife exclaimed, closing the door of the bake-oven. "Mought hev a winter like the old folks tell 'bout, back in 'forty."

"Eeah. Rec'leck that un myself. My granfer chilled his cider with ice from the ledges, that year, up to middle o' June."

"Aw, yer granfer! Thar he is agin."

A young Indian rose from his huge oaken chair by the fire and strode to the window, bending to avoid the beams of the ceiling. His hands and face had the hue of old bronze. His straight black hair brushed the shoulders of his buckskin hunting-coat. He moved noiselessly, yet with a hint of speed and power.

"Where's Becky?" he asked, peering out at the Colonel's side.

"Over to Bolles Wood, arter greens."

"But it's steep and rocky over there, Father—and with all this snow . . ."

18

"Aw, hell now, Holdfast, do ye rest yer neck an' ears! She tuk all the sarvints with her, an' Sam Avery besides.—Whar 'd ye git the turkey?"

"Over in Gungywamp, out of a big oak."

"Larrabee Oak, mos' likely."

"You know that tree, Father?"

"*Know* 'm! Old friend o' mine. Oldest friend I got. Yer father uster call 'im the Uncas Oak, an' he had a right to know."

Holdfast's face brightened. Evidently he had not known that fact before.

"And Gungywamp, what sort of place is that?" asked a fair-haired young man sitting by the fire, his right arm in a sling.

"Wal, it's a darn place, iffen y' ast me."

"Darn?"

"He means full o' ha'nts, Leftenant," said Mother Chester. "Folk say the old Pequots useter hold their powwows in thar, an' mebbe they left a few ghostes hangin' round."

"A *few* ghostes, d' ye say, Mother? Whar ye s'pose all the sperrits o' them burned Pequots went to? Thar's a good four hundred jest to start with, not to mention all the Injuns were killt in the Swamp Fight and King Philip's War. Why, Mother, there's Injun sperrits an' ghostes an' ha'nts all over Gungywamp, from Thames side spang to Narragansett Bay. I'd bet they's a dozen of 'em at least in Larrabee Oak alone—an' I mean good sperrits, o' course, like the ones Holdfast talks with over thar. That's how it got so powerful big an' old. That tree, it ain't the dyin' kind.—An' then too, they's snecks a plenty, in Gungy, an' wild-cats, an' thunder-pumpers, with mebbe a few b'ar. Old Gungywamp, acrost Thames thar in Groton, she's prob'ly the darnedest place in all Connecticut—less'n mebbe Devil's Hopyard an' Cochegan Rock."

"Oh, yes, I remember now," said Reid. "I've heard that word 'darn' in Scotland, too. It means weird, uncanny, eldritch."

"H'm. Mebbe so. But iffen ye wanter know 'bout Gungywamp, ast Holdfast hyar. He loves the place, and all the b'ars an' catamountains in it. Allus did."

"I wouldn't say there was much bear in there, Father."

"No; not iffen they was ten thousan' ye wouldn't. 'Cause b'ar, Mr. Reid, they b'long to Holdfast's fambly—or tother way 'bout. An' I s'pose he wouldn't say they was ary a Pequot in thar, nuther."

"Not nowadays," the young Indian quietly answered.

"Good reason why. Y' oughter know, Mr. Reid, that way back we

19

whites cotched 'bout a hunnerd of 'em over thar in the swamp an' sold the squaws an' young uns for slaves. Danged iffen I know why. They ain't no sprawl to an Injun slave—no gimp, no gumption, nor yet no spezzyrinctum. Injuns jest nachally don't take to 't.—But anyhow, all the braves we rowed out into Sound, fur 'nough so's they couldn't swim back, an' dumped 'em overboard. Sence which they ain't guv us much more trouble."

"Now Father," broke in Mrs. Chester, dusting flour from her hands, "Holdfast an' me don't like that story. That's enough of it."

"You don't mean to say that isn't all!" Reid exclaimed.

"Plenty more same kind," the Colonel went on, nudging Holdfast and winking at his wife. "Jest afore that these same white Christians, all of 'em overflowin' with milk o' human kindness an' brotherly love, they tuk an' burnt up four five hunnerd Pequots over to Mystic, six or eight mile east o' hyar. Burnt 'em all to cinders, I say, men an' women an' children, in one night."

"My God!" said Reid under his breath.

"Eeah—although I ain't *quite* sartin God was thar at the time."

"But was this done by regular American soldiers, or by rabble off the streets?"

"Huh! I reckon it was done by 'bout the best people we had them days—pious church members an' founders o' what some call our 'best famblies.' I hear, too, they tuk a preacher along to ask the blessin' for 'em—afore an' arter meat, so to say. But as for 'reg'lar 'Merican sojers,' I don't reckon they was sech a thing them times. 'Cause all this happened way back, Leftenant, at the very beginnin'. Consekence is, every damned man o' them baby-burners must 'a' ben borned an' brung up in Old England."

Mother Chester wiped her face with her apron. "What I don't unnerstan'," she burst out, "is how a man so lovin'-hearted as you be, John Chester, can delight to tell turr'ble tales the likes o' that un. Y' oughter know it hurts our Holdfast to hear them things, an' what hurts him hurts us. Yeah, an' then bringin' in 'bout Old England with Mr. John Reid a-settin' by yer own kitching fire!"

"Oh, I'm not English, you know," Reid spoke up quickly. "I'm Scotch."

"Wal, what the hell!" shouted the Colonel, "Cain't a man hev a little fun in his own house Thanksgivin' Day?"

"Fun! Ye call it 'fun,' makin' people feel bad!"

"Makin' *who* feel bad?"

20

"Holdfast an' Mr. Reid, talkin' 'g'inst Injuns an' English like ye hated 'em."

"Mother," laughed the Colonel limping hurriedly across to his wife and putting his arm about her waist, "do ye take that back. Leftenant an' Holdfast, they both know better. I 's jest tryin' to—wal, git 'em started, touch 'em up a bit."

"Huh!"

"Eeah. 'T is true I hev killt my share of Injuns in my time, an' also p'r'aps hyar an' thar a few English; but as for *hatin'* 'em, I do not, an' never did. How 'n hell c'd I hate the English arter sailin' round the world under George Anson when I was a lad? How c'd I hate Injuns when I rec'leck how the father o' Holdfast Gaines guv his life for mine at Detroit in sixty-four? Mother, ye must try to be more sensible!"

"Besides all that," Reid put in, "let me say again that I'm Scotch, and the Colonel has certainly shown that he doesn't hate me."

"Course," said Mother Chester, "I don't reely b'lieve he never hated nobody. It's jest his way o' talkin'."

"Talkin'! Me? Hardly ever say a word. A man don't git a chanct in this house."

"Oh, wal," his wife replied, wiping her eyes and laughing at the same time, "now we got that settled, I'll be 'bleeged iffen some o' ye strong men 'll flax round an' set the board.—But not you, John Reid. Do ye stay sot an' nuss that arm."

"An' ye want me to be keerful o' my game leg, doucher, Mother?"

"No fear o' that. An' so all the work 'll fall to Holdfast, as us'l."

The Colonel stumped to the hearth and took a long-stemmed clay pipe from a pewter pot on the mantel-piece. He looked down at Reid with a merry smile as he packed tobacco into the pipe-bowl with his little finger. "Y' oughter know, Leftenant," he said, "that on Thanksgivin' Day Mother don't reely wanter be holped. Rises up long afore red o' dawn, she does, an' tells all the slaves an' sarvints to git out o' the house. Then she turns herself into the sarvint an' slave of us all. I dunno why. Jest a queer notion o' hern."

"Why, John Chester, I've told yeh a thousan' times I like to hev this day like it was when they was only you an' me.—That's how 'tis, Leftenant, an' he knows it well 'nough."

The Colonel was lighting his pipe with a burning twig he had taken from the fire. His face was obscured by puffs of blue-gray smoke, but the little flame lighted up the kindly wrinkles at the outer corners of his eyes. Keen eyes they were, and humorous. Their color made one think of the deepest-hued wild asters that blossom on the verge of frost. His hands and face were deeply tanned even now, in late November.

At length the dottle which he had taken from another pipe and laid upon the fresh tobacco was aglow. He tossed the still burning twig back on the fire. "Wal, mebbe I do know, Mother," he said with a poor pretense at gruffness. "An' then too, mebbe I like to hear you say it over every year."

At that moment the kitchen door flew open, letting in first a few snowflakes and then the seventeen-year-old daughter of the household. Her cheeks were glowing. From under her riding-hood of blue camlet a strand or two of vividly auburn hair had escaped. Her light-blue eyes sparkled in the fireshine.

"Well, good evening, Holdfast!" she cried, pulling off her hood and then shaking the snow from her petticoats. There was a momentary glimpse of blue hand-knitted stockings above her shoes of stout cowhide.

"Morning, Becky."—And indeed it did look, while the young man crossed the room and spoke these two words, as though for him the day were just beginning.

Rebecca's hair, burnished by the firelight, tumbled loose to her shoulders as she put both her hands in one of Holdfast's and looked up at him. "Feel how cold they are!" said she.—"And why weren't you up for breakfast, sir?"

"Huh!" the Colonel growled. "Ye wanter stunt the lad's growth, Becky? Even Holdfast cain't watch all night an' then traipse round all day in the woods with a good-for-naught baggage of a gal."

"'Baggage,' you say, Father?—But I did miss you, Holdfast, this morning. You'd have loved those old twisted hemlocks over there on the ledges, with the snow on them and more coming down. Like Indian ghosts they were. I was afraid, without you along. S'pose a wolf had got me. Wouldn't you have felt terrible?"

"Becky, hyar's Leftenant. Y' ain't seed him this mornin', nuther."

The girl turned at her mother's voice and made a formal curtsy to John Reid, who had risen from his settle when she entered the room. He bowed from the waist. His face was flaming. "Good morning, Miss Chester," said he.

There was a sound of stamping feet at the door, and in came Captain Sam Avery, Rebecca's cousin, with two bundles of glistening laurel sprays. Behind him were Injun Jim and Joe Nonesuch, the

22

Mohegan servants, with streamers of ground-pine. Three black slaves
—Governor Trumbull, his wife Nancy, and young Pompey—brought
up the rear, all but hidden by branches of hemlock and leafy white
oak.

Under Rebecca's direction, Holdfast began to wind ground-pine
round and round the queen's-arm musket that hung over the mantel.
The girl issued her commands in a tone of friendliest authority. John
Reid, who had returned to the settle, did not once take his eyes from
her. Red light streamed from the fire along her lissom body. Her face,
slightly freckled, looked all but translucent. One could fancy that a
flame was dancing inside her.

Grand in stature, dark, taciturn, Holdfast Gaines made the strongest
imaginable contrast with the slight and volatile girl. To her incessant
chatter he answered hardly a word, and it was clear that she did not
expect, need, or want that kind of answer from him. To a close observer it would also have been clear that her present tone of authority
was merely playful, and that in matters of any real importance Holdfast would inevitably take command. If she was a dancing flame then
he was the rough and weathered rock that shelters the fire from the
wind.

There were eleven of them standing round the board as they sang
the Doxology to the tune of Old Hundredth. At the Colonel's left was
Mother Chester. At his right was John Reid, then Rebecca, and Holdfast Gaines beyond her. Across the board stood Sam Avery, Captain
of the ketch *Rebecca*. Below the great standing salt-cellar came the
slaves and servants, black and red.

The Colonel, still on his feet, began to talk before the others were
well seated. "Now what d'ye cal'c'late 'd be jest the right word for
carvin' a turkey? Up to Norwich my rich friends never tech a knife
to their victuals—only o' course they use forks up thar—'thout finding
out the right word. Makes 'em shudder to hear a plain man like me
talk about 'cuttin' up a chicken.' What they say is: 'thrust that chicken'
—'break that goose'—'pierce that plover,' an' 'spile that hen.' But 'bout
a turkey, now, I never did hear 'em tell."

"Ye'll spile that turkey, Father, iffen ye go on talkin'," said Mother
Chester.

It was a thing she could not patiently endure, to see her husband
pause in this way, knife in hand, before he began to carve. So many
different things that hand must have done with knives on very dif-

23

ferent occasions. He had never told her much about his far-away doings in the French and Indian War, but she had heard other old Indian fighters talk. She knew Israel Putnam.

Yet a kinder man than her husband had never, she believed, existed. Good-looking he was, too, at fifty-five, with his long iron-gray hair combed back like Ben Franklin's—he had never been able to endure a wig—and his powerful shoulders, broad chest, strong hands. Some people might think that his square mouth and eyes of frosty blue gave him an air of sternness, but he had never been stern to her. To say the worst of him all at once, he was what she called a "dretful tease." He tried to tease his closest friends, his daughter, his wife, and even Holdfast. But with Holdfast, at any rate, he never had the slightest success.

There could not be a more perfect kindness, she thought, than that which he had shown during these last four weeks to John Reid. Treating him always as an honored guest, never reminding him that he was really a prisoner and worth a good deal in ransom-money to his captors, providing him with funds and clothing and the best surgeon in New London, he had always stood ready to negotiate an exchange whenever the young man said the word. For that, however, the Lieutenant seemed to be in no haste.

Hospitable treatment of captured British officers was not, she knew, uncommon. All over Connecticut, and especially in the seaboard towns, these gentlemen had been taken into private homes as the Colonel had taken John Reid. She understood that as a rule they had been given almost unlimited freedom and that few or none of them had abused it, yet she doubted whether these arrangements had anywhere produced so warm a personal regard as that which had grown up between John Reid and her husband.

The main reason was, no doubt, that Lieutenant Reid was decidedly a likable young man. Mother Chester felt that herself, and so, she knew, did Holdfast. She suspected that even Rebecca did not dislike him so much as she sometimes pretended. But there was another reason, which only the Colonel's closer friends could have guessed. Few knew that in spite of his fiery American patriotism, in spite of the fact that he had fought and been badly wounded at Bunker Hill, he was, and had always been, fond of the British people. For most of his life he had been a loyal, indeed an enthusiastic, British subject. He had fought side by side with the British through several hard campaigns of the French and Indian War. Many a time she had heard him say with pride, even since this new war began, that he himself had once been a British soldier under General Wolfe. And then too, what was more important, she

24

had heard him boast to John Reid that his own great-grandfather—the man who built this farmhouse—had been a Captain in the King's Navy. Indeed he might have made some shadowy claim to membership in that Navy on his own account. While hardly more than a boy he had gone to England in one of his father's vessels, taking with him his friend Jonathan Gaines, the father of Holdfast, and there had shipped with Commodore George Anson on a four-year voyage that took them round the world. The Colonel seldom mentioned that old adventure nowadays, but his wife was aware that it had made a deep impression on him. Among other things, it had left him with an admiration for the men of the British Navy which no hostilities could erase.

What pains the Colonel had taken to make John Reid like Indian corn, whether it came to the table as hoecake, journeycake, samp, suppawn, hominy, appones, succotash, rokeage, or hasty-pudding! Indian corn in sufficient quantities, he insisted, could turn anyone into a good Connecticut citizen. And another thing that hastened this desirable transformation was plenty of Connecticut cider, preferably "hard."

At times the Colonel seemed to assume that Reid's conversion was already complete, or recalled his foreign birth only with humorous compassion. These were likely to be the occasions when he was relating what a mort of trouble he had been to in building and arming Fort Trumbull.

No sooner had he finished carving and sat down to the huge wooden trencher which, on Thanksgiving Day, he shared with his wife, than he began to growl on this favorite theme. "Why, sir," said he, "d' ye know that thar fort was built by nothin' but a passel o' boys an' a few old hulks like me, too bruk down to fight in Cont'nental Army?—an' that means bruk down consid'able."

"You surprise me, sir."

"Fact, sir. All the able-bodied men had been tuk off somers to run away from the British, leavin' me an' Holdfast to git in the craps, defend Thames Valley, an' build a fort atween whiles.—Why, hell, ye must 'a' seen yerself, comin' up Cove a month back, our Holdfast was the only man we had to sarve on the reception committee."

He was interrupted by a vigorous nudge from his wife.

"Eh? What say, Mother? Aw, nonsense! He don't mind. Wal, as I was a-sayin' . . . Whar was I? Oh, yeah. (That's a good ale we got thar, Mother.) Wal, Holdfast an' me, we c'd 'a' built the fort fast enough iffen it hadn't 'a' ben for all the help we had to git from Legislater an' Congress an' Council o' Safety.—Hev s' more turkey, Leftenant?"

"No, thank you, sir."

25

"I'll cut it up for yeh."

"You are very kind, Colonel. Thanks. I will, then."

"Help yerself to another pot of ale.—Wal, afore a single cripple can spit on his hands the word has to go from Hartford to Lebanon—that's whar Jon'than Trumbull lives, Gov'nor o' Connecticut—an' then back to Council o' Safety. Then the Council sends down hyar to Colonel Saltonstall to ask how 't looks to him, and Nate Shaw must ride up to Hartford an' give the Council a lot o' much-needed advice."

"All this must have taken some time."

"*Time,* d' ye say?—An' all the while they was talkin' the left hind leg offen a cow up to Hartford, thar was them two British frigates, *Amazon* an' *Niger,* a-layin' spang off river-mouth, an' not a battery, nary a gun, nor yet so much as one blind watchman to keep 'em from comin' up-river an' burnin' every stick in town!"

"Don't forget, Father," said Rebecca, quietly, "that Leftenant Reid was on the *Amazon* himself, and that he *did* come up the river."

"Wal, so ye war, Leftenant. So ye war. An' a fine clean-cut frigate she 'pears to be, lookin' at her through my glass from the hill hyar.— Hev 'nother bait o' turkey, Sam?"

"Not another dite, Uncle. But iffen ye got any apple-jack . . ."

"Hev we *got* any! Nancy, git the winkum.—But meantime, what's a-goin' on? Wal, Legislater says we oughter hev a few guns for the fort—iffen so be we ever git one. Good idear. So I writes to Congress axin' can we have some o' them pieces tuk at St. Johns. Answer is, three months later, no we cain't. Wal, then, can we hev a few tuk by Com'dore Hopkins at New Prov'dence? Same answer. An' so, with six months gone an' ten enemy sail in the Sound, Connecticut starts out to make her own guns."

"Oh, Father, you do make such a long story of it," sighed Rebecca.

"Not so long to hear as to live through, my gal.—Now sir, the only place for makin' guns was up in Sal'sb'ry, a good hunnerd mile off through the woods, whar we hev an iron mine, a good un. But Richard Smith's furnace up thar ain't big 'nough an' Smith hisself turns out to be a Tory what's run off to Boston, so then Committee o' Safety goes an' gits thisheer Colonel Joshua Porter an' he builds a new furnace fer makin' hand grenades, salt pans, sulphur pots, six hunnerd army kettles, an' mebbe a few cannon. Wal then, next Porter he gits him a lot o' green hands what know 'bout castin' cannon jest like I do 'bout combin' a cat's whiskers, but howsomever Porter he trains 'em an' we folk hyar in New London git to thinkin' mebbe we won't hev to set out on our

26

ridge-poles with fire-buckets in our hands only a two-three year longer an' mebbe we'll hev a gun that'll go off an' say 'bang.' But no: we mustn't git onpatient. Jest when them hands was ready to begin they find out Sal'sb'ry woods is all used up, so's they cain't fire the furnace. Jest think o' that, sir! Twenty British sail off river-mouth an' a hull year gone! So Porter he takes an' builds a new furnace up in Colebrook an' starts all over agin with 'nother green set o' hands."

The Colonel laid down his knife, leaned back from the table, and gazed at the Lieutenant with an expression of blank despair.

Rebecca, after one glance at her father's face, was suddenly seized by a fit of laughter. She laughed until the tears ran down her cheeks, her shoulders shaking. "Oh," she cried, "he's going to start all *over* again!" Young Pompey was the first to catch the infection. "Yas'm, he's *bleedzed* ter staht all ovah agin," he called in his mellow tenor. He too began to laugh, and the other slaves and servants with him. Captain Sam, who had been plying the jug of winkum, hitched the words to the tune of a sea chantey. Mother Chester began to laugh, and her husband. Although somewhat bewildered, John Reid allowed himself to smile. But Holdfast, seeing that Rebecca's laughter was verging upon hysterics, took her hands from before her streaming face and held them down on the table. After a succession of little sobs, she grew quiet.

"And yet you did finally get at least one big gun," Reid went on when the merriment had subsided.

"Ah, so ye tuk notice of 'im, did ye?" said the Colonel, wiping his eyes.

"Was that piece cast in Colebrook, sir, or in Salisbury?"

"Nuther, sir. An' iffen he had ben th' ain't 'nough oxen in the hull o' Connecticut Col'ny to 've drug 'im down to tide-water. 'Cause he's a god-a'mighty whopper, that Long Tom, an' throws a forty-two pound shot.—But no man knows who made 'im, or when, or whar. He's a myst'ry, so to say."

"Like Melchizedek," Reid suggested.

"Prezackly. Borned 'thout father nor mother. Anyhow, I bought 'im, up in Boston. One raisin I got 'im good cheap, the British had ben afeared to mount 'im on a fust-rate man-o'-war even, but I figgered we had one tarnation big gunner in Holdfast an' so oughter hev one big gun. I bought 'im an' made a present of 'im to Connecticut an' Continental Congress, 'thout axin' Council o' Safety mought I."

"That was generous of you, sir."

"But we did hev one everlastin' hell of a time—eh, Holdfast?—git-

27

tin' Long Tom down hyar an' then parbucklin' them four ton o' stubborn iron up the rocks o' the Battery. Oh me, oh my! Tuk us a long hard week o' sufferin' like a thole-pin. But howsomever, we wrastled 'im, we got 'im sot thar; an' now we're tarnal glad we did.—Ain't you, Leftenant?"

"I can think of things to be said on both sides of that question, Colonel."

"Wal, but iffen 't warn't fer that old gun ye wouldn't be settin' hyar this minute eatin' this hyar turkey an' Injun puddin'. No, sir. Ye'd be eatin' weeviled biscuit an' leathery salt horse this day, like I done all the way round the world with Comm'dore Anson."

"What's 'weeviled biscuit,' Father?"

"Why, my gal, thunk ev'ybody knew 'bout that. But, now—wal, now, ye know what biscuit is, don't ye?"

"Of course I do."

"Then weeviled biscuit is biscuit what's got weevils in it."

"That's all right when ye're jest startin' out on a v'yage, Colonel," said Captain Avery, "but arter ye've ben out a year or two it's weevils with the biscuit inside 'em."

"But what I want to know is, what are weevils," Rebecca insisted.

"Oh, them!" said her father. "Wal, I'd say weevils is the foundation o' King George's throne an' the support o' the British empire. The only fresh meat the Navy ever gits to fight England's battles on is weevils. Only real livestock they ever take aboard.—Ain't that so, Leftenant?"

"And even that, sir, the men of the Navy don't really appreciate."

"Not by no means. Most onthankful 't is, Becky, to see 'em knockin' four five big an' juicey weevils outen every biscuit arter all the trouble British Admiralty went an' tuk to put 'em in thar. Nachally, in the course o' nater them weevils they'd climb up the ropes the mess-tables are hung by an' drap back into the biscuits ag'in, but danged iffen the officers don't work four five tossels into them ropes so's the pore critters cain't climb over an' jest nachally go an' starve to death!—Hev s' more ale, Leftenant. Holdfast, how's the blackjack? How's the winkum, Sam? Mother, y' ain't eat 'nough to keep a peckerwood alive. Hyar's the wish-bone, Becky, fer you an' Leftenant."

"But Father," cried the girl, blushing, "even now I don't know what weevils are!"

"Wal then, may the Lord help yeh, for I done my possible.—But hyar's a quare thing, now: chances are Long Tom must 'a'ben made in Old England, an' sartinly they 'd of liked to use 'im for killin' 'Mericans. 'Stead o' that, the blessed old gun has banged a British Leftenant spang into our kitching at Four Winds Farm whar we're all right glad to hev 'im. Long Tom has taught that Leftenant to eat Injun corn an' like it. He's taught 'im to drink an' keep down a quart o' Connecticut hard cider an' be damn thankful 't ain't tea. Why, God He knows, Long Tom might make a good Connecticut citizen o' Leftenant John Reid yet.—Hyar's success to Long Tom!"

Reaching far down the board, the Colonel seized the huge blackjack of ale that stood by Holdfast's trencher and drank, copiously. From his hand to his wife's it went, and on to her nephew Sam. Then it was lifted across the table to Rebecca, who passed it, untasted, to Holdfast. When young Pompey had finished his draught the bottom pointed at the ceiling.

"Good friends," said Reid, rising from the bench and going red to the roots of his curly blond hair, "I am not practiced in making speeches, but now you have given me a chance to say a thing I have long been feeling. I came to this house as an enemy. You took me in as your guest. I came as a prisoner, and you have treated me as a friend. You have taught me many things that I could not have learned anywhere else in the world. You have given me a home, and that is what I have never had since I was a child. It would take me more lives than one to pay back all that you have given and taught me.

"Of course you do not forget that some of the men who died four weeks ago were my comrades. I cannot help mourning for them. Yet I begin to hope—I do not yet know why—that some great good may come to me, perhaps to us all, out of that defeat and destruction. Already there is this much good, that I can say to so many new friends, white and black and red, from the bottom of my heart I thank you!"

THE NEW HOME

More and more deeply, as winter wore by, John Reid felt that Four Winds Farm was the very place he had so often dreamed of, hopelessly, while tossing at night on restless seas or idling about in strange harbors and ports of call. Often it seemed to him that he had always lived here on Quaker Hill, and would never have to leave it. In most

29

respects he was treated as a member of the family, and as his arm grew stronger he began to do what he could of the work on the farm. For days at a time he forgot that he was technically a prisoner, subject to ransom and exchange. Although the Colonel continued to make jesting references to the *Amazon* and the *Niger,* still apparently waiting for him down there at the river-mouth, no one ever seriously suggested that he might try to escape. He went and came freely, often on day-long excursions with Holdfast, and also, when he liked, alone.

Realizing that he was in some sense their property, worth a considerable sum to them—or at any rate to Captain Sam—in ransom-money, Reid could scarcely tell the Chesters that leaving the farm would now nearly break his heart. Such a confession would scarcely have been becoming in an officer of the British Navy, and his Scottish dislike of emotional display would have been enough by itself to keep him silent. Even if he had tried, moreover, he could not possibly have put into words his ever-deepening affection for these new friends and the place in which they lived.

For he had fallen in love with the place as well as the people. This had been an easy and natural process because the very look of the tilted Connecticut acres, rock-bestrewn, together with the sharply indented coast, the frith of the Thames, and the salt-laden breath of the sea, recalled his childhood memories of Scotland. The pimpernels, pinks, and daffy-down-dillies of Mother Chester's garden were very like those he had learned to love as a boy, and so were the "worts" and "yarbs" of her "sarse-patch." Smells and sights and sounds of the barn-yard revived his recollections of croft and byre. The amphibious life of Thames Valley—"one foot on sea and one on shore," as Shakespeare had put it in one of his songs—was in no way strange to a Scot. Neither was the frugality of that life, its decent and sober dependence upon labor, its self-respect flourishing upon poortith. The sight of Holdfast, bare to the waist, mowing in the meadows with his six-foot scythe, all the slaves and servants round him vainly striving to keep the swing and pace of that huge blade, and then the dew on the salt-grass at dawn and the scent of the wind-rowed aftermath at sunset, with the calls and the laughter and the songs, went home to the British prisoner as though he had known them all before he was born. In the thumping round fruit of apple-harvest, russet and red and golden, Reid tasted again the flavors of twenty years gone by, strangely mingled with tangs of the woodland, the forest, the backwoods, which no Scottish or English apple had ever held. Old apples they were—as old, perhaps, as the

30

Romans and Goddess Pomona—but crossed now and fired with the wine of some western Bacchus, some Indian blood. They were taking a new start, these apples that England and Scotland and Europe had known for twenty centuries—renewing their youth, rooting down with a patience and tenacity learned through the ages into this untamed soil.

In the old farmhouse itself, proudly guarded by its two centenarian elms, he had come to see a spare, ascetic beauty, trimmed to the quick, worn, used, and lovely as an aged and richly experienced human face. Solid and wide and low, it rested down upon the hill-top and clung to the soil like a natural growth; and yet in certain lights there was something almost ethereal about it too, befitting its airy and uplifted station. Honest craftsmanship had done much to make it beautiful, but mainly it was a creature of the sun, the wind, rain and snow, helped out by the patience of time. Its unpainted clapboards had been damped and dried and rubbed and silvered by the weathers of more than a hundred years.

The Chester homestead was a "salt-box" in shape, gambrel-roofed, with a wide overhang and a huge-throated central chimney. It faced toward the River Thames, which ran broad and blue two hundred and fifty feet below it at the foot of an eastward-plunging hill. Looking up at its dignified eastern face from the Chester Store at the water's edge, one might have guessed that the house belonged to some prosperous merchant with several sloops on his string and large accounts in the West Indies involving shad and mules and slaves and rum. Such a guess, however, would have been made in ignorance of Colonel John Chester and of the important ways in which he differed—always amicably enough, and yet violently—with his "rich friends up to Norwich." His great-great-grandfather, really a merchant, had built the house in 1646, facing it eastward, so that it could not fail to be seen and admired by sea-captains going up or down the river. It was his grandfather, a man of sense, who had added the lean-to kitchen which extended the full length of the western side, with its small-paned windows looking north and south but mostly westward. Colonel John preferred the kitchen to any other part of the house, for several reasons: because it was low and humble and fit for a man coming in from work in his farm-clothes; because even on stormy days when his game knee forbade his venturing out he could still survey some part of the farm-work from its windows; and because the light of evening lingered there longest. After all, he was accustomed to say, most of America lay to the westward—a fact of

31

which his Norwich friends seemed to be unaware. And finally he liked this room best because of the fire, almost sacred to him, that burned night and day throughout the year in its cavernous hearth.

The true character of the house was best seen and felt, therefore, in the kitchen, which did service also as work-room, dining-room, and parlor. During most of the year the Colonel and his wife slept in the kitchen, on a turn-up bed near the fire. Rebecca's room was adjoining. The second story, unfinished, was given over to the household loom, miscellaneous lumber, and the Mohegan servants. The slaves had their quarters in the long ell connecting the house with the barns and sheds. Holdfast and Reid slept on cots laid side by side between the queen-posts in the attic. Bitterly cold it was up there on winter nights, and yet delightful. Reid often fancied that he was in a ship at sea as he lay listening to the fumble of the wind on the shingles and the tiny tramplings of the rain. And then he would wonder again at the strange fortune which had brought him through defeat and disaster to such peace as this, such friends, such a home.

The treatment accorded him in this household, so different from what he had expected, remained a puzzle. Was Colonel Chester trying to pay his debt to some old British comrade-in-arms? That seemed plausible because he had apparently acted with a like motive in adopting Holdfast Gaines. But then perhaps this kindness was nothing more than would have been shown to any human derelict within reach of the Colonel's hospitality. The still simpler explanation that he was liked for his own sake did not often occur to Reid.

And that was partly because of Rebecca, whose bearing toward him was, for the most part, painfully unlike that of her family. To be sure, there were moments, hours even, when she treated him with an almost bewildering friendliness. Once or twice she had even joined him in his lonely pacing up and down the rocky summit, a little higher than the house and to the west of the barnyard, from which he could overlook the river's mouth, the sails there, and Long Island Sound. Such occasions, however, had been few and brief, and after them she had always gone back to a behavior which made him feel that to her, at any rate, he was an intruder. She avoided his glance, speaking to him as seldom as possible. To this he could think of no response other than a strong effort to avoid gazing at her when she might be looking and to address her only when politeness demanded at least a word.

There were times when he thought her cruelly unjust, and not to himself alone. Even her parents suffered—as it seemed to Reid, with amaz-

32

ing patience—from her uneven temper, her sudden veerings from tears to laughter and from gentleness to tempestuous wrath. The wind that filled her sails, Reid said to himself in his nautical language, seemed never to shift through less than ninety degrees. But when Holdfast was present it never shifted at all. With him she was always cheerful and serene, like a wide blue day at sea with a following wind and sunlight glinting from every wave-crest.

Holdfast Gaines was a puzzle of another sort. The fact that he had spent his childhood in an Indian village helped to explain his athletic prowess and his remarkable knowledge of woodcraft. The further fact that he had been taught by the learned Mohegan Samson Occum and by Nathan Hale made his occasional references to books and his command of English speech less surprising. And yet a mystery remained. What was it that Holdfast brooded upon during the long hours of friendly silence they spent together in the woods or beside the kitchen fire?

Setting himself to find out all he could about the young man who more and more drew and held his fascinated attention, Reid soon learned that Holdfast was the "Malagah" or Leap Dancer of the Mohegan Indians, whose central village lay a few miles north of the farm on the road to Norwich. This meant that he was also their titular chieftain, although on account of his youth and his other duties he had delegated his powers to his uncle, Samson Occum. Holdfast's mother had died at his birth, and his father had been killed in battle while he was still a child. The first ten years of his life had been spent in his native village, but at the age of ten he had been taken into the Chester household, apparently as a companion for Rebecca. That, assuredly, he had been, and still was. What more he might be to her, or might wish to become, Reid would have given much to know.

But Holdfast never talked about himself, and Reid, although the elder by seven or eight years, shrank from venturing upon personal questions. He learned from others about the young man's growing fame as a wrestler, swimmer, and long-distance runner. Little by little he came to realize the respect in which Holdfast was held by the canny, hard-headed townsfolk and farmers round about. Because of their confidence in him they saw nothing at all "out of the way" in the complete freedom of his relations with Rebecca. And yet they too were puzzled. More than once, at stone-bees and house-raisings, Reid overheard the neighbors asking what had recently happened to Holdfast to make him so thoughtful and silent. The only answer offered

33

was that he might be anxious about the situation of the Mohegans, once a proud and powerful tribe but now dying out.

Thus the question about Holdfast led back to Holdfast's people. They were still intensely proud, Reid found, and they showed this perhaps chiefly by a firm refusal to allow any mingling of their blood with that of the whites. They were proud of Samson Occum, who knew Latin and Greek and Hebrew and had books in his library that had been given him by the King of England. They were even more proud of their young Leap Dancer, lineal descendant of King Uncas, feeling that something of their ancient prowess was revived in his feats of skill, strength, and endurance. A few of them, it was said, had at first resented his going away to live in a white man's home and attend a white man's school. At first they had not accepted or understood the reasons that Occum gave them for this departure, and it had not been enough for him to remind them that in his youth he had done the same thing. Probably they did not understand even now, but all resentment had long since been wiped out by the young man's unquestionable fidelity to his tribe. Nothing, they now felt, could ever change that. Whatever else he might do or become, he would always be their chieftain and champion, their Leap Dancer—or, to use the name his father had given him in his infancy, their Sleeping Bear.

Proud they were, then; but they were powerful no longer. A century and a half before, when the white man had first come among them, their hunting-grounds had comprised at least one quarter—or so they said—of what was now Connecticut. Their tradition was that in those days the Mohegan sachems had controlled the valleys of the Quinebaug, the Shetucket, and the Thames all the way from the Sound to the holy lake Chargoggagoggmanchauggagoggchaubunagungamaugg on the Massachusetts border—a rich and mighty domain. Such were their claims and contentions about the past; but now . . .

On a sunny day in December Reid walked up the Norwich Road with Holdfast and spent several hours in Mohegan village. He met some of the head men there—the Tantaquidgeons, Mamohet the blacksmith, the Ashbow brothers, Henry Quaquaquid, Joe Nannapoon, Joseph Joquib, Simon Choychoy, and, most notable of all, Samson Occum. Thus it was made clear to him that the tribe could still produce a vigorous and intelligent manhood, but on the whole he was saddened by the visit. Holdfast's friends and relations, among whom were several playmates of his childhood, were living in a hopeless poverty which was saved from squalor only by the wild and beautiful surroundings of rock

34

and hill and forest. Vice, drunkenness, disease, and slow starvation had left their mark on not a few of the faces he saw. The children, especially, were a pitiful sight.

Leaving the village a little before sunset, Holdfast took Reid up a great hill, close at hand, to see the ruins of the cabin in which, tradition said, King Uncas had spent his last years. A wind from the northwest was hurrying fleets of crimson clouds across the sky as they climbed, and all the world below looked wild and strange in the red reflection. Near the village a few scattered and spindling shocks of corn were a-shiver in the lurid light. Farther up, a grove of old oaks, black against red, made a mournful music in the blast. Then came a wide slope of hillside darkened by juniper, bayberry, and dwarfed cedar. No paths of beasts or men were there, and no sounds except the wail of the wind overhead and its whistling among the stiff stems of the bushes.

The sun's last ember was quivering down among the woods of Chesterfield when they reached the crest and stood gazing out over a tumbled country, rock-strewn, shaggy, primeval, weirdly illuminated by the conflagration in the sky. The tangled wilderness of Gungywamp stretching far away eastward, beyond the river, was all aglow. Every pond and pool was a clot of crimson. The Thames looked a river of blood. Dragon Hill, across the river in Groton, was flushed as though by fever. Four Winds Farm on Quaker Hill, eight miles due south, was a spot of rosy red.

After gazing down for a few moments into the shallow pit, half-filled with rough foundation stones, which marked the place of Uncas's cabin, Holdfast began to speak. The King had chosen this place, he said, for its good look-out. From here he could see the twelve-mile stretch of the river, and could keep some watch on the Pequots across the stream. Fort Shantok, at the river's edge, lay northeast, the village northwest, and a second fort on Mohegan Hill a mile toward the sunset. Hidden among the woods near Mohegan Hill was the huge rock called "Cochegan" where Uncas had held his councils and talked with his gods. Mamacoke, Kittemaug, Massapeag, and Poquetanock were his outposts on the river. It would have been hard to take him by surprise. He never was surprised, Holdfast said, but held his own throughout his long lifetime against Indians and white men alike.

Having thus begun to talk, Holdfast went on in a rising torrent of words. He described the Great Plains Fight which had furiously swept, one hundred and forty years before, across and about this very hill. The Narragansetts, he said, had come a thousand strong against the two

35

hundred warriors of the Mohegans. Their chieftain, Miantonomoh, though by no means a coward, had worn an English corselet to ward off arrows. But Uncas and his men had beaten them utterly, both by stratagem and in open fight; had driven them headlong to the cliffs above the Yantic, where thirty of their braves had taken the death-leap; had collected a huge pile of scalps, and, chiefly through the skill and courage of the Tantaquidgeon of those days, had captured Miantonomoh himself. Uncas had split his enemy's skull with a tomahawk and then had eaten, raw, a piece of his shoulder.

It was not the darkening afterglow alone that made Holdfast look, while he told this tale, like a man on fire. His eyes were burning, and in his voice there was a tone of wild elation. Reid felt that he did not know this man in whom a quite unsuspected gulf of savagery had been suddenly uncovered.

Darkness had fallen and the stars were bright by the time the young men returned to the road. And then all the long way home, striding southward at a furious pace that kept Reid almost on the run, Holdfast poured forth the story of his people's wrongs and the white man's treachery. He narrated the history of the Mason Claims, the thefts of the younger Fitch, the false bequest of Attawanhood, and the other devious and shameful ways by which the Mohegans had been pushed back and back from their once ample patrimony into these rocky acres which no white man would deign to plow. His magnificent voice, mournful and bitterly indignant by turns, was the human counterpart of the wind in the branches above them.—It was with a sigh of relief that Reid heard the distant barking of the farm-dogs and saw the gleam of the candle set in the kitchen window.

Here was matter for long reflection. No doubt Holdfast's spells of brooding might be explained by the situation of the Mohegans alone —at any rate if one added the young man's sense of responsibility toward them. Besides that, however, there was the fact, discovered almost by chance up there in the fiery light, that Holdfast was not, after all, the serene and gentle person that he seemed. At least, he was not that entirely. Although it was held under stern control, there was in him also a savage delight in violence, carnage, and slaughter—and, it might be, a savage thirst for revenge. Two natures, sharply contrasted, were struggling for mastery in Holdfast. On the one hand there were the basic passions and instincts of the man of the wilderness, scarcely modified in coming down the generations from the half-cannibalistic King Uncas. Contending with these were the superimposed restraints and decencies of civilization. Which of the two was likely to win out, considering Holdfast's resentment at the wrong that had been done his people?—And then, too, one could not forget how grandly the young man had been equipped to take by force whatever he might want.

Inward struggle, then, might be the cause of Holdfast's brooding, and this was a matter about which Reid himself had recently learned a good deal. Yet he remained unconvinced. He thought there might also be something else, and of another kind. He watched Holdfast and Rebecca more and more closely, trying to catch and interpret every look of theirs, every gesture. He listened intently when either one spoke to the other. Since he could not or would not ask, he tried to find out for himself the answer to a certain question which had come to seem the most important in the world. It was not that he spied upon them. He merely made the most of every small daily incident which anyone might have witnessed or overheard. And he scarcely knew his motive. Certainly it was not a personal hope. His feelings for these two had no tinge of jealousy, no taint of self. They, so to speak, were unconscious actors upon a stage, and he was their spectator.

What Reid learned was little more, he felt, than anyone might easily have found out. For quite clearly these two were hiding nothing. Their frank, open glances and manner showed that much at once. So did the firm authority, often hardening at need into sternness, with which Holdfast restrained and strove to correct Rebecca's volatile nature. Like her mother, the girl was highly emotional, romantic, sentimental even, and her easily excited feelings often carried her to the verge of hysterics. At one moment she would be gentleness incarnate, and at the next swept away in a tempest of wrath. Often she acted like a spoiled and ungovernable child, but that would be only when Holdfast was not at hand to check her with a glance of the eye or a quiet word.—On the whole, then, Reid found that he could not improve upon the metaphor that occurred to him early in his stay at the farm: if Rebecca was a dancing flame, then Holdfast was the rough and weathered rock that shelters the fire from the wind.

But would not the rock be warmed by the flame?

Reid could not doubt that there was love of some sort between them, but neither could he make sure what kind it was. Why did they so often seem to be living in a world of their own, harking back to some hoard of memories which they and they alone held in common, sending signals to each other too swift and fine for any other eyes or ears? Was it the passionate love of man and woman or only a long-established

37

companionship of girl and boy that set them apart and bound them together? Watch and listen and ponder as he might, John Reid could not make quite sure. There were times when he thought it must be both.

CO' PEEG!

The winter was long and hard. Nearly all the news of the distant war was discouraging. Taxes, always heavy and steadily mounting, were taken cheerfully enough at Four Winds Farm so long as they could be paid in money, but when they called for grain, horses, mules, and cattle, the Colonel himself looked grave. He was proud to have General Washington call Governor Trumbull his "Brother Jonathan," and to know that Connecticut was the "granary" of the Continental Army, but he was beginning to doubt whether there would be enough seed-corn to produce another crop.

A main trouble, he said, was that whatever the tax-collector might leave the Tories of Long Island came over and stole. All winter the tales rolled in of their liftings and reavings at Saybrook, Lyme, Mystic, and Stonington. For a while they let Quaker Hill alone—probably, the Colonel suggested, because they had heard of Holdfast Gaines—but after a raid near the mouth of the river he decided to post a night-watchman. "Feed bein' what 't is, or ain't," said he, "we gotter let the hawgs run in the woods o' nights, an' them oak-woods are jest nachally created fer hawg-stealin'.—Same time, we gotter keep every damn tusk an' whisker. Cain't afford to let a single grunt escape."

From New London steeple there traveled the sound of twelve leisurely strokes. The river, a hundred feet off, sent up vague indistinguishable murmurs. Perhaps the tide was turning. Far away to the south, riding low, two dim red lights marked the moorings of the *Amazon* and *Niger*.

For a long while, lying in the sandy hollow left by an up-torn oak, John Reid stared at those two lights. Drowsily, he was trying to recall the whole series of events which, during the past half-year, had altered his location by some five miles and had changed a Lieutenant of the Royal Navy into a hog-ward.

38

The night was strangely warm for the month of April. There was no moon and the stars were overcast, but the soft contented sounds of rustling, pattering, grunting, and crunching that came from far and near told him that the herd was holding well together. The deeper grunt of a sagacious old boar, leader of the herd, proved that all was well.

Once he thought he heard a voice from the direction of the river. A few minutes later there came the unmistakable bump of an oar against a boat-side. He rose to his feet and peered down toward the water. Last year's leaves hung so low on the white-oaks that he would have been able to discern little even if there had been more light.

But the hogs farther down were beginning to squeal and scamper. Someone coming up through the dark must be driving them. Patter-patter went the little hooves here and there across the dry leaves, with a noise of snapping sticks and rattling brush as they ran. The herd was in stampede, rushing straight for the hollow where Reid stood. A sow plunged headlong over the edge and lay on her back, half stunned, at his feet. Other dark forms dashed by near at hand, all going down hill. And then a voice called, not loudly but from close by: "He-e-re pig-pig-pig-pig-pig!"

"Dang yer lungs, Ben!" another voice interrupted fiercely. "Shut up! Old Chester's house ain't half a mile off, an' Holdfast Gaines c'd toss us all back to Montauk with a turn o' the hand."

"Wal, but good God, Joe, how 'n hell we goin' to git the beasts 'thout givin' the call?"

"S'round 'em, ye lunkhead!"

"How ye goin' to s'round suthin' ye cain't see hide nor hair of?" the first voice objected. Then there came the noise of a crashing fall in the brush, with imprecations and low laughter.

Reid had heard enough. Resting the barrel of Holdfast's huge "Mischief Maker" on the edge of the pit and aiming in the general direction of the voices, he pulled the trigger. The recoil sent him reeling backward, and before he recovered balance the woods were resounding with yells, squeals, and echoes. He dragged himself up the slithery side of the pit and started out for the farmhouse as fast as the darkness and the weight of "the murtherer" would let him. Pausing for a moment after he had gone a hundred yards, and listening intently, he made sure that the marauders were retreating.

The Chesters were setting candles, he saw from far off, in the kitchen windows. Colonel Chester was in the doorway, fully dressed, with his wife in her linsey-woolsey gown behind him. The old Indian-fighter

39

was fresh-priming the musket which he had taken down from its pegs on the wall. Rebecca came into the kitchen as Reid entered the door. Here face was pale in the light of the candle she held. He saw that she looked at him for a second with almost startling intensity.

"Did ye git 'em, Leftenant? Did ye wing any of 'em?"

"I can't say, Colonel. It was too dark. But they were close by, and I may have."

"An' did they git away with any hawgs?"

"No. I'm sure of that."

"Good. Now I only wish 't we could smell out whar they come from, an' we 'd larn 'em how hawgs really oughter be stole."

"Oh, they come from Montauk."

"Eh? How d'ye know."

"I heard one of them say so—or as good as that."

"Wal now, ye really *are* a watchman! Montauk, eh? An' not Montauk Point, I reckon, but the village—a reg'lar nest o' thieves, pirates, cut-throats, an'—wust of all—Tories!"

The Colonel limped toward the mantel to find his pipe, though he still grasped the musket as though it recalled friendly memories. His face was beaming. "H'm! Eeah!" he exclaimed. "Pleasant li'l place, Montauk. Danged iffen I wouldn't like to row over thar, one o' these nights, an' take a look 'round."

Besides the Colonel and Holdfast Gaines there were six "praying Indians" in the first of the two big long-boats going down river. The second, commanded by John Reid, carried also the three Tantaquidgeon brothers, Injun Jim, Joe Nannapoon, Mamohet, and young Pompey.

Now and then a grumble of thunder was heard from below the sea-rim, like the sound of guns in some distant and desultory battle. Apparently a storm was working up, of the kind that usually came at midsummer.

John Reid was glad that this night was even darker than the night before. Otherwise there would have been grave danger of discovery by the watch on the *Niger* of the *Amazon*. He brought his boat close up to Holdfast's as they stole round Avery Point, wishing not to lose the sound of the other's oars.—And a queer thing it was to be so cautiously avoiding those British ships, one of them his own vessel for years, while going on such an errand!

The Indians were at home in these big, powerful long-boats, which

40

were much used on the Thames for getting merchandise up and down the river. Between river-mouth and Race Point they made good time through the chopping waves. A light breeze sprang up just beyond the Point, and the sprit-sails were hoisted. Reid and Holdfast stood in the stern-sheets and swung on the tillers, shaping a course due south.

Reid could hardly see his own boat's bows. Following the faint phosphorescence of the wake ahead, he kept wondering by what mysterious faculty Holdfast could find his way without chart, compass, or landmark. The men rested on their oars, and for a while there was no sound except the delicate crackling of waves at the bow and the croon of the sail. Then Pompey began one of the songs he had brought from the southern plantations:

> Mah dog did bark an' Ah went to see—
> Carf 'im to de heart!
> An' deah was a possum up dat tree—
> Carf 'im . . .

"Shut up, Pompey!" the Colonel commanded.
"Yassuh, Massa John."

Reid's sail flapped slack. He saw that the wake ahead was now much wider. Ordering out his oars, he told his men to row softly, and struck his sail.

Ten minutes later the phosphorescence disappeared. Reid shipped his oars and floated, silently, until he heard Holdfast's prow slice into the slushy sand of a beach. Soon he too was standing on the beach with his six Indians and young Pompey round him.

Injun Jim whispered that this was Fort Pond Bay, with Montauk Village near at hand. Samson Occum, he said, had once lived here, so that the region had long been familiar to all Mohegans.

Colonel Chester took charge. He let Holdfast keep "Mischief Maker," but to each of the others he gave only a club and a gunny-sack.

"But Massa John," Pompey whispered, "what iffen they'se a dog?"

"Do ye let Master Holdfast take keer o' that. An' boys, I'll stay hyar an' hev the boats ready iffen ye hev to run. But keep still as a mink ketchin' trouts, an' ye won't hev to."

"Big barn full o' corn to sta'board," Ben Tantaquidgeon whispered to Holdfast.

"Burn house in woods fai side road," advised Nannapoon.

"No burning!" Holdfast replied. "Joe Tantaquidgeon, you stand by

41

the door of the house and handle anyone that comes out. Pompey, bring on those sacks."

For twenty minutes they staggered from the barn to the boats with bulging corn-sacks and went back for more. Reid could not guess how the others found their way, but he followed close behind Holdfast and made good time. Meanwhile the Colonel was hugely delighted at the loot coming in. "Godfrey, boys! Godfrey!" he exclaimed as the fat bags plumped at his feet. "This 'll feed Washington's Army another year!"

But the hogs? Although the air was rank with the smell of them, near the barn there was no sty.

"Bill Tantaquidgeon," Holdfast ordered when nearly all the sacks were loaded, "go find pig."

The strangely unseasonable storm was now close at hand. Except by the lightning flashes Reid could not see the faces of the men who stood nearest. When they were instantaneously lighted up, those faces were grinning, one and all.

Suddenly there rose a clamor of hogs let loose and running free in the night. Hundreds of hogs were screaming at once as though each several throat among them was about to be slit. Then the muffled barking of a dozen dogs, evidently from within the house, was added to the tumult. A window was violently thrown open and out of it sounded the spiteful bang of a musket.

Reid saw in the flash the side of an unpainted house, and, near it, a large pig-sty. Inside the sty stood Bill Tantaquidgeon with a struggling pig under each arm.

"Take hold of my belt, John Reid. And Pompey, you grab the Leftenant's. All the rest the same way. If a hog comes along, scoop him up and lug him down to the boats. Now—forward, *march*!"

Holdfast, Reid thought, had not spoken so gaily for months. There was in his voice a tone of rollicking laughter.

Another musket-shot rang out as the line of men went up the slope toward the narrow road.

"They won't hit us," Holdfast called back. "But if they don't stop it I'll give them a dose with 'Mischief Maker.'—Hello, Bill! Carry those two pigs down and come right back."

Could Holdfast actually have seen Bill Tantaquidgeon? But while Reid was asking himself that question some furiously rushing creature knocked his legs from under him and he fell heavily forward. Only his firm grip on Holdfast's belt kept him from striking his head on the ground.

"Are you hurt, John?"

"No; but I lost that hog."

"There 'll be plenty more. And men, don't let them knock you down. Keep ready for them."

Reid heard a terrific squeal careering, as it seemed, straight at him. He braced himself and reached down with his left hand as though groping for the ears of an unseen hog. There was a thud of impact just behind him, followed by the voice of Pompey raised in exultation: "Ah got one, Massa Holefas'! Ah got a peeg, sho' 'nuff!"

A third musket-shot rang from the window. Pompey screamed. Reid heard the thump of a body to the ground. Yet he could still feel the slave's hand at his belt. It was trembling, violently.

"You aren't hit, are you, Pompey?"

"Yassah, yassah, Ah's . . . Oh, no sah! *Ah* hain't hit, but mah peeg, he's daid, an' Ah's all oveh blug!"

The roar of laughter that followed was broken by a blast from "Mischief Maker" and the crash and chankle of falling glass. Then the hogs began to scream as though they had before been silent. The dogs inside the house were evidently going mad. A donkey brayed from somewhere off in the night. The door of the house banged open, and half a dozen men, followed by as many dogs, took the stairs at a leap. The men had flaming pine-torches in their hands. They were yelling "He-e-re pig! He-e-e-re pig-pig-pig-pig-pig!" in a high and piercing wail. Their dogs rushed round the corner of the house toward the intruders. From up the road eight or ten more torches were now bobbing and flaring to the cry of "He-e-e-re pig!" From down the road that same cry came also with a lurch and joggle of many torches.

Then Holdfast began to call "Co' peeg! Co' peeg!" with a curious clucking sound at the end of each upward inflection which the hogs evidently found most seductive. Clearly many of them had heard that call before. Soon all the men from Thames Valley were giving it, and a hundred hogs were dashing here and there as though striving to obey all the cries at once.

"We're going to have trouble, aren't we, Holdfast?" said Reid. "Most of these men have fire-arms."

"Yes; but they think we have too, and they don't want to unload their guns before they know our strength. They can't see us, remember, and

43

can't guess how many we are. We ought to be making a noise like a hundred men."

The torches were huddling now by the pale house-front fifty feet away. The men under them, those twenty-five or thirty heads and faces reddened by the flare, were apparently gathering for a charge— or, perhaps, for a concerted volley. Their aim might be guided by the sound of Pompey's song, now defiant and taunting:

> De possum meat am good to eat—
> Carf 'im to de heart!
> Ye'll allus fin' 'im good an' sweet . . .

"Aw, shet yer face, ye damn nigger, or I'll . . ."

Reid felt his hand suddenly released from Holdfast's belt. Then a huge voice, barely recognizable, shouted from twenty feet off in the dark: "Down with that musket! Drop it!"

There was a moment of hesitation.

"Dat's Massa Holefas' Gaines a-talkin' to y'-all naow," called Pompey. "Ye betteh not git ouah Holefas' riled up. 'Mischief Maker' he nevah keel less 'n ten men to one bang."

"Drop it, I say," commanded the great voice again, from farther off but even more loudly.

A musket thudded to the ground.

Reid was startled a moment later by a terrifying shout from the darkness by the corner of the house and within a few feet of the torches: "I have you all covered. Every man will drop his musket when I say the word. *Now!*"

Would they obey? Not unless they were demoralized by that stentorian voice, by its bewildering way of darting about in the darkness which made all shooting futile, and also by their fear of the man from whom they knew it must come. But—yes! One musket fell, then another, and then three or four. Then a dozen clattered down together.

"Just pick 'em up, Joe Tantaquidgeon," Holdfast said a moment later at John Reid's side, "and take 'em down to the boats. I'll watch our Tory friends while you're doing it. The rest of you boys can go on catching hogs."

But the gods had other plans. A flash of lightning from overhead was instantly followed by a crash of thunder. A blast of wind from off the Sound tossed the flames of the torches and bent them level as though striving to tear them loose from the tarry knots of pine. Then rain swept in, at first with a few large scattering drops but soon as a

44

lashing torrent, a cloud-burst. The torches reeked and were doused, one by one, until the two groups of hostile men faced each other on the equal terms of total darkness.

"Every man keep his hold on the belt before him," Holdfast shouted. "And call the hogs."

"Co' peeg! Co' peeg! Co' peeg!" rang out from fifteen voices on the Patriot side, and "He-e-re pig-pig-pig-pig-pig!" from many more on the side of the Tories. The hogs, driven frantic by the storm, the calls, and their own efforts, outdid themselves in blind and headlong speed.

"It's like Election Day!" Holdfast shouted to Reid.

Reid crouched to clutch some approaching porcine noise—and missed it. Those sleek drenched bodies were now as hard to hold as so many four-legged eels.

> Ah reached daown fo' to pull 'im in—
> Carf 'im to de heart!
> De possum he begun to grin . . .

The sky was filled with a dance of leaping light. Reid saw in one flash that the opposing groups had merged into a confused huddle. Clubs were lifting and falling there, and faces were distorted by unheard yells. He saw three men go down before one charging hog. At the next flash he himself was down, with a dog's teeth snapping in his face and Holdfast near-by at the sty-gate whirling his murtherer with one hand and dragging out a hog with the other. A moment later Holdfast was in the middle of the sty, and several Tories round him were beginning to throw large billets of fire-wood. Reid groped his way in there along with three or four Indians. He pulled down one of the assailants, leapt to the top of the wood-pile, and began to throw billets himself. He could hear Holdfast laughing. Out of the darkness came Pompey's battle-cry, "Oh, ca-a-rf dat possum, chilluns!" Then Reid's foot slipped, the wood-pile collapsed, and he bumped down into a writhing, grunting, swearing and biting mass of white men, red men, black men, hogs, dogs, and frightful filth at the bottom.

"One trouble with them ignernt Tories," the Colonel was saying when Reid came to himself, "they don't even know how to call hawgs. Didn't ye hear 'em say 'He-e-re pig-pig-pig-pig-pig'? Wal now, no self-respectin' hawg's a-goin' to pay no 'tention to a call the like o' that thar. Leastwise not iffen he's a hawg that's had any advantages, he ain't. An' some o' these we're a-takin' back home, Holdfast, they're eddicated.

45

They've traveled. Seen the world. I bet some o' these old boars must 'a' ben back'ards an' for'ards atween the shore an' Montauk a dozen times. Wal, hawgs the likes o' them, they's pertic'lar. They got a fine ear fer music. Ye gotter call 'em proper or they won't come."

Evidently the Colonel was in high humor. And so was Holdfast, to judge from the quiet laughter that answered the Colonel's sally. When he lifted his aching head for a moment from the sopped gunny-sack on which he lay, Reid could see why. Except at the midship thwarts where the rowers sat, the long-boat was piled high with bags of grain under tarpaulins, and under the thwarts were a crowd of recumbent forms, some of them still struggling against their bonds but for the most part resigned. The boat swam low in the smoothly heaving water. From far in the west came a reminiscent rumble of thunder. A quivering line of palest pink was broadening on the eastern horizon.

"Too bad 'bout the Leftenant, though," said the Colonel. "Mought kinder put 'im offen pig-parties, a bump like that un."

"Oh, John'll be all right, Father. His eyes are open now."

Reid put up a cautiously exploratory hand. His head seemed to be about twice its normal size.

"I'll be ready for another party by tonight," said he in a faint voice.

Rolling over the waves from the boat behind came a rollicking song:

> Ah carr'd 'im home an' Ah dressed 'im off—
> Carf 'im to de heart!
> Ah hung 'im dat night in de fros'—
> Carf 'im to de heart!
> Oh, ca-a-rf dat possum, chilluns!
> Carf 'im to de heart!

VIEW FROM A HILLTOP

John Reid never knew what it was that woke him so early on the fateful sixth day of September, 1781. In later years he was to guess that it might have been some obscure sense of a duty unfulfilled, or the silent call of old companions. At any rate, he found himself lying broad awake before the attic walls were gray, staring out at the sign of the Great Bear. Holdfast had not yet come in from his night-watch.

With a sailor's quick notice of every change in the sky, Reid saw that the wind had gone about in the night and was now blowing straight down the valley. That would explain the amazing brilliance of the stars, and also the chill of the air that was pouring through his window such unnamable odors of swamp, forest, river, and field. His blood tingled as though at the sound of a bugle.

Hastily dressing, he groped his way down the narrow stairs to the second floor and then to the kitchen. At the lower door he heard the cords creak in the turn-up bed.

"That you, Leftenant?" said the voice of the Colonel, whose years of Indian fighting had trained him to waken at the slightest unusual sound.

"There's no light yet," Reid whispered. "But I can't sleep."

"No more can I"—and there was the thud of bare feet on the floor.

Stepping out into the dark was like a plunge into cold black water. For a moment, looking up into the depth beyond depth of a sky all afoam with stars, Reid fancied that he was gazing once more from a ship's main-top at a phosphorescent sea. What keels might plow and plunge among those heavenly meridians? If a man could draw a net from Orion to Cassiopeia, what monsters of the celestial deep might he not capture! Between Betelgeuse and the Thighs of Boötes what Virgins and Fishes and Bulls, what Scorpions, Lions, and Archers!

Thus the breath of the Great Bear worked in his veins, exciting his Celtic fancy. His heart was filled like a tide-pool with the night's beneficent beauty—and with it there came a confidence that his long struggle between divided loyalties was nearing its end. Somehow on this day that was coming, or soon, the chart of his life would be shown him. Soon now, he felt sure, the Commodore of the star-fleet would break out his signal-flags.

Reid strode past the silent barns, past the shed where the oxen were audibly munching, and breasted the slope of the rock-strewn summit rising steeply toward the western stars.

Up here he had been many times to see the dawn redden over the Sound. Here Rebecca had once lingered beside him while the sunset crumbled behind the hills of Chesterfield. He had been lonely here as a crippled gull tossed on the midmost wave of an empty ocean. By night and by day he had suffered here, in the Colonel's beautiful phrase, "like a thole-pin." And largely because of that suffering he had come to regard this bleak outcropping of granite as a place of revelation—like Holdfast's Mount Machimoodus over westward and the huge rock called Cochegan, King Uncas's shrine.

47

The stars, when he reached the top, were still dripping liquid light, but the old worn moon in the east was fading. Such dreadful scenes it had shone upon in its time, that pallid battle-lantern!

He paced up and down, waiting. A cow lowed in the sheds. A cock crowed, drowsily. At the kitchen window a candle was burning, and behind it the room grew ruddy with the brightening light of the fire.

Never before had Reid so surely known that this place and no other was home. Tears sprang to his eyes as he pictured the faithful house-father moving about in there, lighting the candle, renewing that old fire from the embers on the hearth, making ready for one more day.

And then, faint tinge by tinge and hue by burning hue, the vast room of the sky was ruddied. Reid stood still and watched and waited, deeply stirred by some mysterious excitement. He waited and watched until on the farthest sea-rim there rose a quivering sliver of fire—God's candle!

It made the world new, he felt, with its mantling flush and soft up-welling of colors washed in the day-spring, of hues that sprang from the drench of the dark and were rinsed in an infinite distance. The soiled and sinful earth, blown clean of its yesterdays, was now like an opal flashing with crimson and gold and blue held high in an Almighty Hand to be filled with the light of the sun.

The Sound was one wide shimmer, with Long Island a whale of silver and green asleep upon it. New London's two steeples loomed up from the dusk. Town Hill and Manwaring Hill stood forth with their clusters of small white houses. Fort Trumbull, beyond, jutted darkly into the river. Across the Thames in Groton the grassy earthworks of Fort Griswold were edged with vivid light. Up-river in Norwich the window-panes were flashing.

Cleared fields, stone walls, tilted pastures, low white houses under their wine-glass elms, villages and hamlets and twisting roads and slender tapering steeples—all at once Reid saw these things as a human treasure won from the wilderness by a hundred and fifty years of toil. Unspeakably beautiful they looked to him in the early light, and fragile as the quail's nest that Rebecca had shown him last May by the rail-fence down in the meadow.

And they were all in danger. Reid saw that it would be an easy thing for the British forces, leagued with the envenomed Tories of the region, to lay waste this entire valley in one windy day. For the two forts were absurdly under-garrisoned. Few able-bodied men had been left behind by the recruiting officers. The river towns had no organized fleet. Even

Sam Avery's *Rebecca* was now on her way to the West Indies. New London Harbor was crowded with prize-ships which the British would give much to regain. The *Hannah* alone—and there she lay clearly visible in Winthrop's Cove—had been valued by Nathaniel Shaw at a hundred thousand pounds.

If Sir Henry Clinton in New York only knew what the British prisoner on the rocky crest of Quaker Hill could so clearly see!

Reid paused in his pacing and looked steadily southward. Those dim gray specks just beyond the mouth of the river, twenty-five or thirty of them . . .

He rubbed his eyes. It might be that all this dreaming about divine beneficence and the Commodore of the star-fleets had a little obscured his vision.

But unmistakably they were sail. They must be vessels of the British Navy sent up from New York on a special mission. And those smaller objects moving off from the larger ones and in toward the shore could be nothing but British long-boats laden with soldiers.

He stared and stared while the light grew.

So this was what those signal-flags in the sky had meant!

A two-gun signal boomed from Fort Griswold, across the river.— Good! They were awake over there, and were calling out the militia. —But that signal must have been understood by some one in the British flotilla, for there followed soon a puff of smoke, and then, much later, the report of a third gun, heavier, farther away, rebounding from hill to hill.

That third gun had sounded from the *Amazon,* his own ship!

Turning to run down to the farmhouse, Reid saw the Colonel already hurrying stiff-kneed across the barnyard. He had his long brass-mounted spy-glass in one hand.

"The British! The British are landing at river-mouth!" Reid yelled.

"Wal, don't I know it, lad? Cain't I figger 't out? But next time we'll hev three guns for danger an' two for good news. Then see how them Tory spies can twist that!"

He reached the top. "How many of 'em?" he asked, breathing heavily.

"I make out thirty-two sail, most of them transports."

The Colonel's hands shook as he strove to adjust the spy-glass. "How many men that come to?"

49

"Nearly three thousand, I'm afraid."

The old soldier went white in the face. He slipped his glass under his arm.

"Three thousand!" It was pitiful to see his face crumple. "An' we, iffen we had time, we mought muster three hundred old men an' boys to stand 'em off.—Oh, mighty an' marciful God!"

Reid could not answer.

"They've got us, Leftenant. They can do with us what they want. An' they'll do—wal, what they did over to Fairfield an' Danbury. They'll burn us!"

Again no answer.

"Say suthin'! Won't they?"

"I fear so, Colonel."

"I know they will. These ain't the men I fought beside in the old French War," said the Colonel, more softly. "These 'll be Hessians an' Tories that damned traitor Arnold's been gittin' ready for months up to New York! He was born hyar, an' knows jest what to burn!"

"I'm going down to them, Colonel," said Reid. "Maybe if I tell them how kind you've all been to me . . ."

"An' git a dozen Hessian bagnits stuck inter yeh? That ain't no way to treat a good Connecticut man like you, Leftenant," said the Colonel, looking straight into Reid's eyes. Then the old soldier threw back his head and squared his shoulders. "John Reid," he said in a firm, clear voice, "ye're our prisoner; an' ye're a-goin' to stay up hyar this day an' keer for them that love yeh. Hear that?"

"I understand you, Colonel."

"Wal, partly ye do. But now hyar's a thing ye don't know, an' ye hev a right to. Mebbe I oughter told yeh afore, but fack is we never did let the British know ye were hyar. They prob'ly think ye're dead."

"Oh, Colonel . . ."

"Mebbe we did wrong, John. But Mother didn't want—an'—wal, we tuk a likin' to yeh, an' I put it off. Holdfast, he said, 'Don't tell 'em, Father,' an' course we allus go a lot by what Holdfast says."

"Holdfast said that? And Rebecca—did she . . . ?"

"Oh—ah—Becky?" The Colonel was trying to adjust his spy-glass. "Why, Becky, she didn't—ah—make no ruckus, fer's I rec'leck."

Overwhelmed though he was on his own account, Reid was amazed at the speed and precision of the Colonel's orders and acts after he had stumped down the hill into the kitchen. Without a word to his pale-

50

faced wife and daughter, or even glancing at them, he took his queen's-arm from the wall, blew into the barrel, and felt the edge of the flint with his thumb. While reaching for his bullet-pouch and powder-horn he began to speak.

"Nancy," he said to the young negress, "run over to Mr. Raymond's house tight as ye can scamper. Tell 'em to hev all their men an' boys down to Smith Cove in less 'n pig-squeal. Then run to Mr. Otis an' say same thing. Say I'm goin' down river to-oncet by long-boat, an' everybody be thar. Tell 'em British comin' up, both sides.—Now, run like all hell's arter yeh!"

The door slammed, and Nancy was gone.

"An' Injun Joe, do ye bring all the Injuns down from Mamacoke in the whaleboat. Say bring tomahawks, harpoons, knives. Send a runner up to Mohegan Village an' roust out every fightin' man. Go!"

The Indian slipped from the room.

"Mother, we're a-goin' to hev sech a tarnation big eatin'-bee up hyar today, an' mebbe all night long, as ye never did see. Mought be back fer 't an' then agin I mought not, but anyhow do ye git ready to feed all the folk in New London. They'll be a-comin'. An' Becky, help yer mother.—Help her all her days, my gal."

The two women started toward him, but were checked by his upheld hand. " 'Member now," said he, forcing a smile. "This 'll be a grand old day for Four Winds Farm. Wish 't I could be hyar, but—goodbye Mother. Becky, goodbye."

A moment later, outside the kitchen door, he spoke again. "John Reid, ye'll be the man o' the house. Take my pistol. Now—but ye've seen sojers arter a fight with drink in 'em an' women about. Ye're my friend.—No, damn it, boy, arter Holdfast ye're the only son I got; an' Holdfast he'll be busy elsewhars. Un'erstand? Goodbye! God help us all!"

Reid wrung the Colonel's hand, finding no word, and watched him go, half running in spite of his bad leg, round the corner of the house.

Reid became aware of a large pistol tightly clutched in his left hand. Cocking the hammer, he saw that it was unprimed. Then he recalled that the Colonel had taken with him all the powder and ball in the house. He let the pistol fall. His head pained him. Things seemed to be whirling. With one hand against the back of the house he staggered a few steps and sat down on the well-curb.

Was it hours, or perhaps only minutes, later that he heard Mother

51

Chester calling from the door? "Leftenant," said she, "please bring us a bucket of water."

As he dropped the bucket into the well and heard it rumbling and splashing down there in the dark he realized that these two women, although they had their own suffering, had also their steadying work to do.

"How else can I help you?" he asked, setting the bucket down in the kitchen.

"Wal, fust off ye can mend the fire. Next, ye can bring in 'bout half a cord o' wood. Arter that ye can milk the cows, iffen ye really think ye've larned how, an' drive all the creaters into upper pasture with no bells on."

"But Mother," Rebecca protested from the kneading-board, "Leftenant Reid is only one man, and a Britisher."

"Huh. Only man we got. So when he gits through with all that he can fill the fire-buckets an' lug 'em up in attics whar they'll be most wanted."

"Wanted for what?"

"Puttin' out fires, o' course."

"And why should the Leftenant put out fires his own comrades have set?"

"You hold yer sarsy tongue an' work on wi' that dough. This ain't no time to git spunky at Leftenant."

"I think it's the best time of all, just when his friends are coming to burn our house down."

"Why, Rebecca Chester! Iffen ye give us a little more o' yer lippiness I'll spat yer skirts, my gal. Yeah, an' mebbe more 'n skirts I'll spat, too. Ye think 'cause Holdfast ain't hyar ye can say what ye please, but ye mought be s'prised. A woman what acts like a child 'll git a child's treatment round hyar this day."

Rebecca turned to her work, the tears coursing down her cheeks.

His own work, filling the next hour, restored the young man to some steadiness of mind. When it was done he went to the barns and woodsheds and there gathered up every edged or pointed tool that might serve as a weapon. He looked to the fastenings of all the doors and windows in the house. He saw that the fifteen-gallon kettle over the fire was full of boiling water, and asked the women to keep it so.

"Now next thing," said Mother Chester, slamming the door of the oven upon a dozen loaves of bread, "I want fer yeh to take Becky an' me up thar with the spy-glass an' show us what's a-goin' on."

52

Reid himself had longed, and yet feared, to know just that; but when the glass was finally adjusted no remarkable change was discernible. The men-o'-war were riding somewhat farther off-shore than they had been at dawn and the clumsy bluff-bowed transports were close in-shore, their long-boats and barges plying slowly to and fro. Half of these were making toward Eastern Point on the Groton bank and the others were grounding at Brown's farm, two miles below Fort Trum-bull.

So much Reid saw while he for a moment held the glass; and when he turned it over to Mother Chester it was as though he still saw the scene with her eyes. Together with her he watched the men massed on the long-boats and their slow disembarkation. It seemed absurd that those painted dolls, stiffly jerking over the gunnels and wading up either bank, could think of harming the wide green country.

Rebecca's mood too he could share when she put the glass to her eye, and it was a mood of swift anger. By what right were these red-coated strangers trampling the fields of Brown's farm, spoiling the corn and hay? What right had they on the Groton side among the Avery meadows and wood-lots? Had they driven the savages out, or fought the wolves away? Had they cleared the stones from the fields, laid the walls, or built the small white houses?

"Here," said she, roughly handing back the glass. "Take it. Perhaps you will be able to recognize some of your friends."

His face was crimson. "There's probably not a man down there," he said, "whom I should know by sight."

"Why not? Aren't they your old comrades?"

"No. They are soldiers. I was a sailor. Many of them are hired Hessians, from Germany, who have never seen the coast of England. Many more are American Tories."

"Aren't they doing England's work?"

"As they see it."

"And won't they burn the town?"

"I fear so."

"You fear it, but . . ."

He saw that her face was dead white. Her mouth was twitching uncontrollably. A blast from the north whipped her hair across her eyes, and she threw the strand back with a violent gesture. The wind tossed her petticoats over her knees. She paid no heed.

"But what, please?" he asked.

"Rebecca!" warned her mother.

53

"But you stand here and watch what they do through a spy-glass. You will watch while your friends burn the town where our friends live. I don't see how you can bear it!"

"Neither do I. But I must."

"Why?"

"Your father told me to stay here."

"Because he feared you would run away?"

"I don't think so."

"You know the British would shoot you."

"Or hang me. To them I am a deserter."

"And to us, too!"

"Rebecca, stop this!" Mother Chester broke in. "Ye're sayin' ye don't know what, to a man that's broken-hearted. Ye've ben a cruel an' wicked gal. Now march yerself back to the house."

For a moment Rebecca stood still, as though dazed. Her head was hanging and her mouth open. Her breath came in sobs. And when at last she did look up at him Reid could see that her passion of anger had blown itself out.

"Oh," she cried, "I *have* said terrible things! I don't know why. Believe me, John Reid, I did not mean them all. Perhaps not any."

"Wal, I should think not," her mother agreed.

"But I'll remember them, always."

"So shall I," said Reid.

She held out her shaking hands as though in some inexpressible appeal. Then she said in a voice that choked: "Ah, don't! I beg you to forget them. I have been wicked and cruel, as Mother says. But never think, don't you ever dream, that only you have suffered—for weeks, for months, but, most of all, today."

She started down the hill, staggering a little, sobbing violently, her mother holding her close about the waist.

VIEW FROM A HILLSIDE

When John Reid began to think somewhat more clearly, and to look about him, he found himself on the old Mohegan Road half-way between Four Winds Farm and New London.

Mother Chester, he remembered, had sent him down here to get

54

what news he could of the Colonel, of Holdfast, and of how the day was going. There was no more need of him back there, she had insisted, unless and until the British came. Only let him keep between the invading troops and the farmhouse.

All this had seemed clear and true when she had said it, yet probably her motive had been to give him something to do—and to keep him away from Rebecca.

Standing now on the slope of the last long hill above the town, he heard the meeting-house clock strike eleven. The full deep tones came to him precisely as he had often heard them on still summer evenings at the farm. They spoke to him in their habitual accents of peace, exactly as he had heard them for the first time months ago in the cabin of the ketch *Rebecca.*—But that clock, he knew, might never strike again.

The day had been so scoured, burnished, and hollowed out by the north wind that objects far away looked almost within reach of his hand. Even without the spy-glass which he still carried under his arm Reid could see with startling clearness the two long lines of red-coats winding up either bank of the Thames. They were moving rather slowly along the crooked sandy roads, yet on the western bank, below New London, they had already come to Green's Harbor. Unopposed as they were, they would soon reach Fort Trumbull where it lay open and undefended on the landward side.

What chance for Holdfast and his twenty-three men against that solid lock-stepping thousand? Holdfast would do well if he turned his great gun to fire one blast into their steady ranks. He would do miraculously well if he escaped with his bare life.

Two British sloops had managed to beat up the river against the wind. Escape by water to Fort Griswold would be cut off by their fire.

Against Fort Griswold on the opposite bank a somewhat longer line was steadily climbing, like blood soaking upward through green cloth. To meet that force, Reid knew, there was a garrison of some fifty men and boys, ill-armed and untrained, eked out by such volunteers as might have straggled in from surrounding farms.

The river itself was a scene of frantic toil. All the Yankee vessels and the prize-ships, having lifted anchor at the first alarm, had been blown southward by the wind and sucked downward by the tide until they now lay just below Winthrop Point in a tangle of ropes and yards and thrusting bowsprits. Twenty open boats—and no doubt Colonel Chester's among them—were striving to drag them up-stream before the

55

town was taken. Twenty hawsers, cables, and tow-lines were straining taut. But human skill and strength were matched by the might of wind and wave. The shipping stuck, as though rooted to the bottom, while the line of marching men came steadily up the west bank with fife and drum. A few sailors were still at work among the billowing bulges of the canvas. Reid saw that they would be falling soon, when the British muskets came within range, like dead flies from a ceiling.

And yet in these same vessels, so desperately caught and entangled, lay for many the only hope. While they hung there in midstream, yawing, a dozen gangs of men, like ants bearing eggs and larvae out of a broken ant-hill, were packing and piling them with merchandise from the warehouses of the water-front. In and out, back and forth, wove the bobbing dories and yawls and gigs, absurdly tossed about by the wind on the dancing glitter. From Shaw's warehouse alone, farthest off, they crammed the deck of a sloop. To the watcher on the hill rose a hubbub of calls and curses, orders, yells, wild laughter.

A few scattered musket-shots from far away, on the southern edge of the town, added their mite to the confusion. They sounded like the high-pitched barking of little dogs. And then—yes, it was smoke! And soon it was flames, flapping!

Ah! So the Colonel had been right. New London, like Fairfield and Danbury before her, would soon be undergoing the ordeal of fire, deliberately set, on a day of high wind.

In other such scenes as this John Reid had been an actor, scarcely able and often unwilling to be anything more. But now, as in the cabin of the ketch on the night of his capture, he was obliged to think and to feel. Helplessly looking on, he was compelled to see each event as a part of a larger pattern, and woven into that pattern there were certain poignantly human elements for which he had never before allowed enough.

The Colonel had been right when he told his wife that all New London would soon be climbing toward Four Winds Farm. At any rate, that had been a pardonable exaggeration. For as far down the hill as Reid could look, the sunlit road was cluttered with women and children. They came by twos and threes, sometimes in companies of eight or ten, occasionally one at a time, dragging or pushing or bearing the most grotesque and pitiful burdens. Among them were a few old men, too weak or crippled for fighting. Some of the fugitives walked as fast as they could, with panting breath, as though they could hear the tramp of the foe behind them. Others took their time, and paused now and then to look back. But on the faces of them all there was one monotonous expression of dazed bewilderment.

Here came a cart laden with furniture and drawn by slow oxen. A young woman with an infant at her breast sat on the trundle-bed that topped the crazy pile. She was leading a brindled cow with a frayed rope tied around its horns.

An older woman followed, riding a large and well-fed farm-horse, with a feather-bed for a saddle. An assortment of brilliantly burnished pots and pans dangled and clattered.

A small brother and sister were driving a cow. The boy had a heavy sword stuck in his belt. It tripped him now and then in his walk. His sister carried a loaf of bread in her two arms, and behind the loaf, snuggled close to her bosom, there was a wooden doll. When the cow stopped to browse the lad kicked her with all his might and poured forth his whole stock of vituperation. The sister was visibly impressed.

Then came an old woman, daggle-haired and thinly clad. With one bony hand she was clutching a fine cashmere shawl beneath her chin. In the other hand she carried a bird-cage of wicker. The bird was singing shrilly as the old woman hobbled by.

And here was a lad barely five years old, stumbling wearily up the hill. His face was blubbered. An old stocking apparently stuffed with paper hung round his neck. He looked lost.

"What's wrong, my boy?" asked Reid, drawing him to the side of the road.

"Grampaw's got a hole in his head. Somebody—thombody thot—I mean, shot him. I know who 't wath."

"Who was it?"

"I—I forget."

The child suddenly broke down into uncontrollable sobbing. Reid took him in his arms and sat, holding him close, under an elm by the stone wall edging the road. A dozen fugitives went by, blankly staring. The boy's body shook with his sobs. His eyes were haunted.

"He shot him—dead—my grampaw!"

"Yes, my boy," Reid answered in a colorless tone. "That's so. And do you see how hard those men down there are trying to pull their ships up-stream? Do you think they 'll make it?"

The lad glanced at the turmoil on the river.

"I—I dunno."

"If you and I were down there we could be a great help. Don't you think so?"

57

"Oh, yes.—I mean, yethir."

"But what is this that you have in the stocking round your neck?"

The look of fear came back into the child's eyes. "Granny put money in 'tockin'," he stammered, "an' then the thay 'go get lotht in woodth.' But thereth bearth in woodth."

Reid considered this. Then he said: "I suppose there are a few. But do you know what I think a bear would do if he saw a big strong boy like you coming?"

"No. What?"

"I think he would run away."

The child's face also was deeply serious as he said, "You do?"

"I certainly do. What's your name, boy?"

"Perthy."

"Oh! That's a grand name! Do you know what it means?"

"No."

"Well, 'Perthy' is the name of one of the bravest families that ever lived. They lived near Scotland, where I come from, and fought against kings. They had much trouble, the Perthies did—some people call them the *Percies*—but they were so big and strong that those kings could never beat them. Every bear that didn't run away—well, they killed him. And usually, I suppose, they killed him with a knife, because 'Percy' means a piercer, a man who sticks a knife right through the things that are bad and cruel. Do you understand me, Perthy?"

"Yethir! An' I *got* a knife—a big one. With a green handle."

"You have? Where is it?"

"Home. My father brung it for me. He's dead now."

"That so? And where's your mother?"

"She's dead too."

"H'm. I see.—Why do you lisp, Perthy?"

"Cauth I like to."

"That's a good reason. Just the kind of reason I'd expect from a Perthy. Have you lisped before today?"

"No thir."

"And do you like maple sugar?"

"Oh, yethir!"

"Well, then, suppose you just walk straight on up this road until you come to the top of Quaker Hill, and then you go into Mrs. Chester's house and she will give you all the maple sugar you want. Do you understand me? Mrs. Chester's house on Quaker Hill."

"Yethir. Mithith Thetherth houth. Maple thugar."

58

Then the lad trudged on.

Reid's private trouble was imperceptibly melting into the bewilderment of all these other lives. He forgot that if the British should take Four Winds Farm this day he would probably be hanged as a deserter. He forgot Rebecca. He forgot even his sense of personal shame.

A woman limped past him carrying a pillow-case filled with pewter. Another woman was lugging a large copper kettle, and in the kettle was a maltese kitten, vigorously mewing. A third, very old, had nothing with her but a large black book, perhaps her Bible.

An old man, dressed in his Sunday black, sat for a few minutes beside Reid on the stone wall. His breath came short. His face was nearly as white as his hair.

"She died last night," he said, in a quavering voice. "Six year old. So when I clum the hill an' seen the red-coats a-comin', I went an' got me a box I had in the barn. Made o' good oak, 't war, an' jes' long enough. I never did know afore why I'd ben a-savin' that box so many year, but I do now. Divine Providence made me save it, ever since afore Mercy war born. Yes, sir; the Lord will pervide, as the good book says. An' so I put her in the box an' nailed the kiver down. I say I put her in thar an' nailed the kiver down, not an hour ago, with these two hands."

He held them out in the flickering shade and stared at them as though with surprise. They were gray old hands, and bony. They had done much hard labor in their time, but now they were shaken by palsy. The man's lips were trembling too, but his eyes were deeply considerate. They seemed to ask some question, though not of Reid.

"An' then," the patient voice went on, "I tuk the box on my shoulder —an' that was easy 'cause Mercy she never growed much—an' I got a pick out o' the shed an' I went an' buried her."

A sly look came into his eyes as he laid a hand for a moment on John Reid's knee.

"I buried her whar they'll never find her. I put a big rock on the place, out o' the old stun wall. It made me dretful tired, wrastlin' that rock. I feel all beat out."

"But I suppose you have some other—ah—grandchildren," said Reid.

"No, sir. Nuther chick nor child. Mercy 's all I hev."

"Ah, I see. And so that is why you are wearing your black coat today."

"Yeah."

Then the old man walked slowly on, up the hill, alone and empty-handed.

From the column marching up the western bank four companies had been deployed at the cross-roads just below the town. They made a brave show swinging across the tidal flats with fife and drum, their bayonets glittering.

Reid held his breath. He gave up trying to adjust the glass. During this next minute he would not need the glass to see whether Holdfast Gaines was to live or die.

Gorgeous, gay, marching as though on parade to their own shrill music, the four companies detailed to take Fort Trumbull were filing in close ranks through the gate on the landward side which Holdfast for some reason had not closed. Near the little block-house at the outer end of the rock, pitifully few and dull-hued in their home-spun and buck-skin, the defenders were working in a frenzy at their one great gun. They had prized him round to face landward. They were loading him, double-loading apparently—and, if they were wise, considering that one discharge was all they would have time for, with canister. Old men and boys and Mohegans those defenders would be, with a few battered hulks, as the Colonel had put it, "too bruk down to sarve in Cont'nental Army—an' that meant bruk down consid'able."

Twenty-three against, say, three hundred; and Holdfast among those twenty-three looming head and shoulders above his fellows as a mark which even a British musket had no right to miss.

The distance between the great gun and the front rank of the red-coats, all of them now inside the gate and still steadily stepping onward, had narrowed to about one hundred feet.

A flash, pale orange in the sunshine—a slow puff, pallid, rounded—and then the gigantic well-remembered roar of Long Tom thrusting at the noon's blue roof.

The men of the garrison spiked their gun and leapt for their whale-boats floating near and were out, well out, on the river before the echoes had ceased to roll. The thing had been bravely, brilliantly done, no doubt under orders, and had left a wide swath of slaughter behind, but there was broad rough water for them to cross, those racing rowers, and wind and tide were against them. Before they had gone half a pistol-shot the bullets from behind were splashing, scooning, slinging up tiny momentary fountains. Holdfast's boat, though it had started last, was leaping ahead. The British on the nearest sloop were using their muskets now, but could not reach the distance. And yet—yes, an oarsman two thwarts behind the blown black banner of Hold-fast's hair dropped his oar and clapped his hand to his shoulder. The

60

sloop was running a long gun through her bow-chase port. Yells, screams, thinned by distance, came up the wind, and the angry barking of muskets. The sloop's first shot, too high, tore a long white seam through the blue waves. Holdfast's whale-boat went plunging on, untouched. The report of the gun, belated, stabbed unexpectedly into the uproar. Another puff at the sloop's forward port, and the last of the whale-boats splintered amidships and filled and sank, circling slowly. Her seven men, toppled out, were bobbing black dots on the water. Holdfast was nearing the opposite bank. There were six dots now. There were five. Two spreading spots of red floated down the river, gradually fading, merging into the blue. Holdfast was landing below Fort Griswold.

The rest of the British column had gone on into the streets of the town, a winding ribbon of red among the white houses, with here and there the glint of a bayonet. Reid had to guess what the column might be doing from glimpses and sounds: a boom from Fort Nonsense, a crackle of musketry, quick spurts of flame, wisps of smoke in the upper town.

The old field-piece on Manwaring Hill spoke thrice, in solemn protest. Black smoke gushed up from Manwaring's house, then a streamer of fire. Far out on the Colchester Road the house of Pickett Latimer, one of the Colonel's oldest friends, blazed briskly. A talon of flame clutched at the hay-stack, clambered the roof of the barn.

Much nearer, from behind the dark red head-stones of the Ancientest Burying Ground, a dozen or fifteen chance-gathered citizens were firing down the hill at the British line. They were clearly visible through the spy-glass as they lay there on their bellies, half in shade half in shine, their gray-stockinged legs spread wide, biting their cartridges, sprinkling their powder in their priming-pans, and ramming their charges home with cool deliberation as though they were only out after snipe in the river meadows. Each of them, having loaded, rested his elbows on the ground, braced his barrel against a grave-stone, pressed his cheek to the gun-stock, and squinted along the browned barrel with an unmistakable intent. Every time one of them snuggled a trigger he meant, Reid saw, to kill one particular man.

At first this looked to him like murder. All his active life he had been accustomed to the British method of firing by platoons, to eight or ten orders, according to the direction explicitly set forth in a manual based upon Prussian drill. This method made the individual soldier a mere

61

cog in a machine. He aimed scarcely at all, but merely "presented his piece." At the moment of firing he might actually turn his face away from his sights to avoid the huff from the pan. He fired in the general direction of the enemy, no more; and whatever injury his ball might do under such circumstances would certainly not lie upon his conscience—if, indeed, it even came to his knowledge. It was so, according to the Colonel's story, that the British had fought at Bunker Hill, and also under Braddock on the Monongahela. In both places, and of course on hundreds of other fields, they had fought bravely, even gallantly, as men do when they think of warfare as partly a profession and partly an arduous and dangerous game with strict rules like the game of chess. For the most part, in Europe at least, they had fought without rancor against other men of much the same sort who knew the rules and obeyed them. They had fought there as though both sides knew and acknowledged that England and Europe had too many men to support, and that therefore an occasional thinning of the human crop—if executed with dignity and decorum by men splendidly garbed and accoutered for the sacrifice, and to the accompaniment of martial music—was a thing warranted as much by reason as by precedent and tradition.

But over there in the steeply sloping grave-yard among those drab-suited citizens of the town—all of them church-goers no doubt and some of them probably clerks in Nathaniel Shaw's warehouse—there was, Reid felt certain, a positive, perhaps even a personal, rancor. The sound of their muskets and fowling-pieces, he thought, had a spiteful ring as they fired not to orders at all, and not by platoons of course because after all they were very few, but raggedly, one by one, as each man, taking his time, got ready. They were shooting, clearly, to kill—and that, in a way, was dreadful. Yet the thought occurred to Reid, as he watched, that these citizens were fighting for their town, their church, their homes, their families. That, he considered, ought to be kept in mind as a mitigating circumstance. Some of them might actually be firing from behind the grave-stones of their own grandparents, or of their children. Nathaniel Shaw himself might be among them, trying to defend his warehouse and shipping. Why, then, should they not act somewhat differently from professional soldiers fighting for a few pence a day three thousand miles from home?

These men, although they must have had some elementary drill on "training-days," simply did not know the ancient and honorable rules of civilized warfare. Probably not one of them had ever read or heard about Bland's "Treatise on Military Discipline." In Connecticut, moreover, and in America as a whole, men had never been too many but always too few. Over here in this new land, therefore, the individual amounted to more than he did in a crowded country. He had to. Perhaps that was one reason why each of these men was, so to speak, his own officer, issuing orders to himself. Perhaps, too, that might suggest a reason why, when one of them fired, he aimed at a single individual among the red-coated strangers now striving to drag a field-piece up the steep hill. One ball to one man—it was a simple equation. One pinch of powder in the pan to snuff out one human life.—For those citizens on the hill, whatever else one might say against them, were not in the habit of wasting powder and lead.

The British on the slope below the graveyard made no reply whatever to the slow, selective fire of the citizens. Here and there, as they climbed, dragging their field-piece, one of them suddenly threw up his hands and fell, or sank into a sitting, a crouching, or a recumbent posture as though he had been reminded of some problem not yet thought through. Yet the red line as a whole kept moving upward, until at length the gray-stockinged townsmen rose from the ground, stepped over the wall, and disappeared among the trees. They went away in no order and no haste, as though, having exhausted the possibilities of that good place, they now hoped for better occupation elsewhere.

Reid watched the red-coats plant their piece among the graves. The wind had veered, however, and the tide was making, before they began to fire on the shipping below. The American vessels, large and small, were by that time half a mile above Winthrop Point. The first ball splashed far short of its mark, and from the still struggling whaleboats there rose a faint derisive cheer.

The clock in the meeting-house steeple began striking twelve, as though rudely awakened.

A man on a coal-black horse, in the uniform of a British general, rode out on the graveyard hill. A large man he was, powerful, and a good horseman. He looked out over the town, the shipping, the harbor, Fort Trumbull, Fort Griswold, shading his eyes with one gloved hand. Then Reid saw him turn to a mounted officer at his side, pointing toward Winthrop Neck. The officer's horse wheeled and plunged down the slope.

"Thet thar gin'ral on the black hoss, thet's Benedick Arnold," said an old fisherman who had paused to peer through Reid's glass. "I know 'im, the son of a . . . Knowed his father afore 'im. Borned an' brung up in Norwich he war, the God-damned traitor!"

From roof to roof on Main Street the flames were leaping like squirrels from tree to tree. On the Parade they caught the courthouse, the jail, the church, the shops. A dozen houses were burning there. The wind, now coming from the south, brought up the crash of falling timbers, the smell of burning wood, the roar and crackle of the flames. Saltonstall's mansion was ablaze. Along the roof of Shaw's house on Bank Street flames flickered for a while and then were extinguished. Explosions of powder on the water-front shook the air.

John Reid had seen enough for years of thinking, for a lifetime of suffering. Yet he stayed there. It seemed his duty. The farm was not in danger. The red lines on the western bank were tending southward. And some furious action was just beginning at Fort Griswold across the river.

Even with his glass Reid could see little of that action because the embankments of the fort hid nearly all that went on within. But he could imagine enough.

A gun spoke from inside the southwest bastion, disputed at once by a score of opposing muskets. Behind the muskets rose a company of red-coats striving to scale a rampart of pickets that bristled outward. A few of them remained impaled, as though frozen. Others were trying the same thing on the eastern side, and also on the north, where the gate was. Their yells were faint in the distance. The wrangle of guns and muskets was barely distinguishable from the crackling of fires in the town below. Then someone was opening the northern gate of the fort from the inside. A crowd of red-coats rushed in. Then more firing —more yells—and silence.

The small garrison must have surrendered. And that, of course, was the right thing for such a hopeless handful of men and boys to do.

But again, louder, and more continuous than before, there sounded a steady rattle of musket-shots. Reid knew, with a sense of personal shame, that the British must be firing under orders, by platoons, after their foe had surrendered.

And Holdfast Gaines was inside the fort.

For a full minute that firing went on and on—regular as clock-work, deliberate, calculated, and delicately beautiful in sound as exploding puff-balls. The glass in Reid's hands was shaking.

64

He saw a man, tiny with distance, leap the parapet on the western side of the fort with a long duck-gun clutched in an up-thrown hand. At a bound this man cleared the pickets of the fraising. Half a dozen red-coats were firing at him from the parapet as he ran, dodging, head low, still clutching his piece, along the outer ditch and burst into the open and came with huge strides down to the water, his hair streaming like a black gonfalon behind him as he ran and leaped and plunged.

Though the wind had fallen, a waft of heated air brought up from the burning town the taste and odor of wood-smoke. Two hawks were circling upward on the rising column of heat without flapping a wing. Across the river a flock of crows, gathering up with vague clamor from the woods of Gungywamp, black-peppered the eastern horizon. The guns and muskets were still, at last, in Fort Griswold. Little jerk by jerk, holding his murtherer over his head to keep it dry, Holdfast Gaines was swimming back across the Thames. Beauty and horror merged into one like the two sides of a coin.

Reid was thinking, feeling, nothing at all. He would have said that nothing could wring from him one more spasm of pain.

But suddenly he raised the telescope to his eye. A large ammunition wagon, dragged by some twenty red-coats and apparently filled with wounded men, was bumping through the northern gate of Fort Griswold. And now there appeared more red-coats, two and two, bearing more wounded between them or dragging them out by the legs. These were dumped into the wagon like sacks of potatoes. Then, slowly, and retarded at first by soldiers before and behind, the wagon started down the slope toward the river.

But the descent was steep and rough. The small bushes of laurel and blueberry, stumps of trees, and outcropping granite, gave no effective check to the burdened wheels. The wagon, Reid saw, was getting out of control. After some effort to stay its course the soldiers in front broke away, and those behind let go their hold. The wagon leapt forward.

It lurched over a ledge of rock and trebled its speed. The stump of a tree, struck sidelong, sent it into a drunken spin. For a moment, half-way down, it came almost to a stop, and two or three bodies were joggled out on the ground; but then, with thills crazily dragging and bumping and stabbing, it began to go again, moving faster at every yard, moving swiftly as a sled on snow, until it struck the trunk of an old apple tree at the foot of the slope and recoiled and slewed round and stood still.

Half a dozen men fell out of it, sprawling. Above the clamor of the crows and crackle of flames Reid could hear the screams of wounded men still crowded deep in the tumbril. The red-coats came lumbering down the hill. Two paused near the bottom to fire into the writhing mass. One of the wounded, a large man, shaken out, pushed himself up to his hands and knees and was crawling slowly away. A red-coat strode after him with uplifted musket and clubbed him over the head several times, not leaving him until quite certain that he was dead.

NOCTURNE

When Reid got back to Four Winds Farm he found the barnyard crowded. Horses and oxen from the other side of town were nibbling in the cart-way, and strange cattle stood in the byre. The hay-loft, as he peered up into it by the light of a lantern, seemed to be packed with children. Crop-full of the morning's milk but too tired and excited for sleep, they were chattering there in the dusk like so many fledgling sparrows.

Through the half-open door he looked in at the kitchen. It too was crowded. Three or four women, strangers to him, were helping Mother Chester prepare a meal. A brisk consumption of cider and beer had loosened many tongues. The main difference between this gathering and any ordinary stone-bee or house-raising, Reid thought, was that here he could see no men of fighting age.

Ah, but the warmth, glow, safety, and human kindliness of that room! As never before he yearned toward it, now that he felt more than ever unworthy. Hardly knowing what he did, as though drawn by a magnet, he took one step forward and stood in the doorway, wistfully gazing in.

"Leftenant Reid," called the comfortable voice of Mother Chester from the fireside, "will ye jest come in an' shet that door an' make yerself some use? We ben a-waitin' for a real man of his hands 'round hyar for Heaven knows how long."

Could she have seen his hand tremble on the door-jamb? Did she know that his lips were twitching? Not likely. Not with his back to the after-glow. And yet some women, evidently, could see without looking. Some of them could understand without being told. Mother Chester might even have guessed how doubtful he had been whether he ought ever to cross that threshold again. Yes; and possibly her calling out to him in so motherly a tone had been meant to show the roomful that he was still welcome in her house.

Rebecca, carrying a pot of beer to old Mrs. Hempstead, walked past him as though he were not there. Her lower lip, he saw, was fiercely caught between her teeth. Light-headed as he was from the strain of the day, it seemed to him somehow pitiful and wrong that she should bite her lip like that. It might do her harm. And he felt, too, that she ought not to be allowed to work so hard, lugging beer for toothless old women until her brow was damp and her blue eyes desperately weary.

John Reid, who had eaten nothing all day, greedily drank off the nipperkin of apple-jack that Mother Chester had brought him, asked for and drank another, saw the room begin to whirl, and then started in lugging beer.

And even though his wits might be turning, he could not help thinking it a ludicrous thing for John Reid of Glasgow, son of the Laird of Glasgow, scion of The Bruce, and once a Lieutenant in the King's Navy, to be drawing and lugging beer in a Connecticut farmhouse for these remarkably bibulous old women. Still, as someone in Shakespeare had said, one man in his time plays many parts. Anon! Anon, sir!—or rather, Madam! Score a pint o' bastard in the Half Moon. And Tyb my wife that as her life loves well good ale to seek, full oft drinks she till you may see the tears run down her cheek.— And if there had to be tears, dear God, there had to be beers to make them!

Reid felt fairly sure that he was losing his mind, and he did not care.

Another thing that made this gathering different was that all the persons present were discussing the same topic. As one composite mind they were gathering facts and fancies. Already, though the sky was not yet dark in the west, the events of the day were being caught up and transformed into legend and myth. To the picture of what had happened each was contributing some detail of outline or splash of color. History, that wondrous fabric of truth and fiction, was growing here on the loom of imagination.

One woman said: "My old neighbor wanted to see the red-coats go by his house—mebbe 'cause he'd fit 'long-side 'em back in French Injun War. Anyhow, nothin' would do but he must git on his hat an' stick when he heard the drums beatin' at top o' street an' potter out to gawp at 'em over the fence. 'Hooray!' he yells, seein' 'em go by, an' waves his stick. I seed 'im from up-stairs winder. Then they war some shootin', but 'cause o' the noise an' burnin' everywhars I kinder slunk back into the room. Howsomever, arter things got quiet I went out an' tuk a look, an' sure 'nough thar the old man lay with 's pore old face a-bleedin' into the bull-briars. His gramboy 'd run off into woods an' his old woman tuk on turr'ble."

"Did he have a rake in his hand?" Reid asked. "Was he raking leaves?"

"Wal, mebbe 't war a rake an' not a stick. Mebbe ye war thar an' not me. A body can't take notice o' them things a time like that. All I know is, he war dead as a stun. An' then they tuk an' burned his house down."

"This town's been all clemmed up with Tories today," said a woman whose hands trembled so that her beer spilled down the sides of her cup. "Red-coats knowed eggzackly whar to go an' what to burn, like they war all born'd hyar."

"Yeah! That's Bible truth!" exclaimed an old fisherman, grizzle-bearded and hawk-nosed, still dressed in the garb of his craft. "Take that Benedick Arnold, now. I seed 'im, the young son of a . . . Anyhow, I seed 'im a-settin' his big black hoss up top o' graveyard. I'd 've guv an eye to put a bullet through 'im."

He glanced about the group to see whether this was considered an exaggerated statement.

"An' young Bill Pertwee, he war thar too. Ye know, the Pertwees what useter live on Town Hill an' we druv 'em out to Long Island."

"H'm. That young jackanapes, Pertwee. I 'member 'im well 'nough, but I don't 'member no good. Hope he had a nice day bangin' down an' burnin' up his old neighbors!"

"But did ye hear tell 'bout ole Miss Jenkinson over Bank Street way? No? Wal, I swan! When she heerd red-coats war a-comin' what she go an' do but lay herself down in her best bed, in her best bib an' tucker, she did, an' begin to groan like she war expectin' right off 'most any minute. Groaned like all god-a'mighty she did. An' so red-coats come in an' hear her groan like thataway an' o' course they all goes tip-toein' out ag'in, very respeckful an' well-wishin'.—But ole Miss Jenkinson, now, course she couldn't reely expeck nothin' much iffen she war to groan a thousan' year."

"No, 't ain't in nater," went on the old fisherman. "But, I dunno, the way 't is, a body cain't hardly tell who's which these times. Tories an'

68

Patriots, old maids an' expectin' mothers, an' I dunno but even male an' shemale—they's a-gittin' mixed. Course a man wants to be free an' independent an' all sech, but same time he don't want to go bangin' away in the dark an' mebbe shoot his mother's own head off."

Hearing no demur, he continued: "Way I see 't is, they's a mort o' folk in thisheer town was borned an' brung up under King George. Most on 'em, in fack. Ain't that so? An' a mort on 'em, like me, war nigh onto seventy year afore they ever heerd tell o' no one but King George what wanted to lay down the law fer 'em. Wal now, they don't give a . . . What I mean say is, they don't care a hoot who lays the law down fer 'em, iffen only ye give 'em time to find out who 't is. But all thisheer 'bang-bang' an' burnin' the town down with 'God Save the King' still echoin' in yer whiskers—wal, I dunno, but I'll persume to say it's enough to make a man feel peevish."

He raised inquiring eyebrows and then, apparently satisfied that he had voiced the general sentiment, took a deep draught of cider.

Well after nightfall they heard the voice of the Colonel out in the dark. He began calling for food and drink before he entered the room.

Mother Chester met him at the door. She had a pot of beer and a chunk of cold meat in her hands.

"John," said she, "be ye all right? Y' ain't hurted?"

"Sartinly I'm all right," he answered with scornful emphasis after drinking off half the beer. "Why wouldn't I be?—But thar's them that ain't."

"Yes, I—I s'pose. Whar's Holdfast?"

"I dunno, Mother."

"He ain't . . ."

"Ain't *what?*"

"*You* know."

"Holdfast? Mother, you must git a holt on yourself! Who in tarnation could kill him? He ain't the dyin' kind."

"Oh!" was all she said, but her hand dragged hard for a moment on his arm. He was staring right past her as he ate and drank. Never before had she seen his face so haggard, his eyes so haunted.

"But John, ye're all beat out. Ye ben workin' hard all day, an' . . ."

"Yeah; an' I'm a-goin' to work hard most o' the night, too. Jest come up to git some tools. Do ye feed the boys an' send 'em back to the boat on the run. I must git back to Griswold. Thar's suthin' tarr'ble down thar. I can't tell yeh now, but—suthin' tarr'ble."

Mother Chester looked deep into her husband's eyes. She kissed him on the cheek.

His eyes brightened. He squared his shoulders. "I'll try to be back by midnight," he said. "Gran' big eatin' an' drinkin' bee hyar, I see. Wal, ye got the Leftenant, an' the British ain't a-comin'.—All right, Mother?"

"All right, John." The words came soft as a sigh.

"I must git down thar."

And with that he was gone. The empty beer-mug was in her hand. Through the open door she saw some vivid western star burning down among the hills of Chesterfield.

The hours wore slowly by. Everyone was tired to the bone, but few could sleep. There were too many bed-mates absent. There was too much that they had to guess, and to fear. Why, after all these hours of silence, had no one come up from the town? Looking out from the southern windows of the kitchen, or from the barnyard, they could see the broad Thames aglimmer with a star or two on its bosom; but no boats cut across that glimmer and no voices rose through the still night air.

It grew cold. John Reid helped to build a fire in the pasture. Ten or a dozen old men stood round it in the dance of the red light. They had little left to say. The stars grew larger, brighter, like thousands of answering camp-fires in the pastures of the sky. Nine, ten, and eleven o'clock were counted out by the meeting-house belfry far below. Near midnight Reid went into the kitchen.

He found that all the women from New London had somehow been put to bed. Holdfast was sitting by the fire, talking in a tired low voice to Rebecca and her mother.

But tired? Holdfast? Yes. And as he looked for a moment into the young man's eyes Reid saw that here was a companion in the brotherhood of pain.

"No, Mother," he was saying. "I'd like to. I'd like to sleep all winter, like a bear. But I mustn't sleep. I'd see things, hear things."

"What things, Holdfast, my boy? You can tell me. You must."

He looked at her almost hopefully, but the light died in his eyes. "Ah, no!" he cried. "I must never tell—even you!" He rose, suddenly, and made two strides toward the door. "Hobbomok" fell with a clatter.

"Young Holdfast," said Mother Chester's calm and kindly voice, "do ye step yerself back hyar this minute an' set yerself down in yer cheer."

He paused in the doorway, looking back.

70

"An' don't ye never say ag'in thar's a thing in the world ye cain't tell to the woman that brung yeh up. Thar ain't—an' cain't be."

Holdfast came back from the door, rested his two hands on the mantelpiece, and stood gazing into the fire. "This thing 'll break your heart, Mother," said he. "You don't know at all what it is."

"Mebbe not, but I'm a-goin' to, tonight. Becky, git our Holdfast 'nother tankard o' beer; an' then, iffen ye don't think ye can stand whatever 't is, ye can go to bed."

Rebecca went to the beer-barrel in the corner. "I think," said she, turning the spigot, "that a woman can bear to hear about 'most anything that a man can bear to live through."

"Well spoke, my gal!" the mother answered, quietly smiling. "But oftentimes it's the *not* hearin' that's hardest of all—like waitin' from dawn to dark this day not knowin' whether our men were alive or dead."

Holdfast, manifestly touched, set down the tankard Rebecca had brought him and went back to his chair. He picked up his "murtherer" and sat bending forward, tense, his elbows on his knees, clutching the long brown barrel. One expected to see the iron dinted by the force of his agonized fingers.

Rebecca was standing at the side of the hearth with her left arm resting at full length on the mantel. Her gaze was downcast and her face very pale. Mother Chester sat in her wicker-bottomed chair just before the fire, rocking a little, with her hands in her lap. Great weariness had brought out in her face the lines that would show there when she was an old woman. Turning her head to the right, she was gazing straight into the dark-brown eyes of Holdfast.

Reid felt, looking on, that time stood still.

"Now then, my dear," Mother Chester went on, "do ye jest begin an' say all 'bout what 't is that won't let yeh sleep. So then mebbe thar 'll be the two on us a-layin' awake in this house tonight."

"Well, Mother, I'll make it short. At Fort Trumbull, when the red-coats came up this morning, we gave them one charge of canister. Then we ran for the boats. Most of us twenty-three got across and into Fort Griswold alive. In there we found about a hundred and fifty, mostly—mostly friends o' mine."

"Yes, Holdfast. O' course. Go on."

"There were hundreds more in the woods outside, but they wouldn't come in. You can't blame 'em. I'm glad they didn't. Besides, they weren't soldiers. Inside and out, they were only farmers and hunters

71

and boys—good shots at a squirrel or a turkey but bad at shooting down men to a 'one-two-three!' They never had done that."

"No. Naterally. Go on."

"Then the British sent up a white flag, demanding instant and unconditional surrender. Our Colonel Ledyard, speaking for us all, told 'em we wouldn't. 'Lige Avery, Amos Stanton, and John Williams took back our reply—all of 'em good friends o' mine, and all dead now."

"Go on, Holdfast."

"So they came up the hill from south and east, marching in quick step and solid column. It seemed a foolish way to come, as if men's lives weren't worth much. We gave 'em the muskets from eastern battery and then two bags o' canister from the old eighteen-pounder. Some twenty fell and their column broke, but they came on from the south and the west. Another division—because, remember, they had over a thousand to our hundred and fifty—came round and hit us hard on the east, where we were weakest. They brought five hundred against our forty. I was one o' those forty. They got into the ditch, where we killed a good many. They got up the ramparts, and there we killed more. They began to climb the pickets. I set those pickets. We fought them with all we had—guns, muskets, pistols, swords, knives, harpoons, stakes, scythes, pitchforks, crow-bars, and stones. Joe Woodmansee loaded and fired his nine-pounder until it jumped from the carriage. Jake Twaddle cut a red-coat in two with his scythe. John Stallion stood on the rampart in the thick of their fire and threw down cold shot like big black hail. I saw a man's head split open under a cannon ball. His brains . . . ! The Latham boys, and all the Averys of course, fought like wild-cats caught in a corner. I swung old 'Mischief Maker,' maybe bruising a few, but still they came on over the pickets, and got in.— For what could forty do against five hundred? We couldn't stop 'em. I tell you, we *couldn't,* Mother. If you'd been there you'd have seen we couldn't. No forty men on earth could have stopped that rush, and —oh, Great God o' the Mountain!—forty were all we had."

"Do ye jest go on from right thar, now, Holdfast."

"It was while they were breaking in that Joe Nannapoon went down, right beside me, shot through. I can see his eyes on me now as he died. I'll see them forever. 'Don't forget, Sleeping Bear,' he said in Mohegan, and smiled, and died.—'Don't forget!' "

"We won't none of us forgit, Holdfast, not ever. An' the hist'ry books in the schools, they won't forgit it, nuther."

"Books! But the thing I've seen today could never be written out—

to say nothing of those I've done with these two hands. You take one thing I remember—and not the worst. I saw that black Jordan Freeman drive his whale-lance right through the body of the Major leading their charge. Jordan put his bare foot on the body and pulled the lance out with a jerk. I heard it come."

Rebecca turned from the mantel and sat down in her chair. After a moment, "Go on, Holdfast," said she.

"Well, they rushed over us and opened the northern gate to let in all the rest. Up to that time we hadn't lost many, and they a good number. But when Colonel Ledyard saw that the fort was taken and they were ten to one against us he yelled for every man to throw down his arms. We did throw them down—all except ten or twelve in the southwest bastion who couldn't hear him."

"You did right," said Reid.

"We did what we had to, under orders from our commander. But then, the next I knew, the British were shooting down those ten or twelve in the bastion while we stood helpless. We had surrendered. Our arms were on the ground."

"Who did that?" Reid sharply asked. "Hessians?"

"Leftenant, you can make sure for yourself. I know the town was burned today mostly by Hessians and Tories, led on by a scoundrel who used to live in Norwich. But to the best of my belief . . . Well, you can make sure for yourself."

"Thank you."

Holdfast got up from his chair and replaced a brand that had fallen in the hearth.

"Haven't I told you enough, Mother?" he asked while his face was turned.

"You ought to know whether you've told it all."

"Oh, no! Great God, I haven't begun it!" He sat down again and buried his face in his hands.

"After they'd shot down those ten or twelve in the bastion," he went on, "they began firing at us."

"What's that?" Reid called out, leaping to his feet. "After you had thrown down your arms?"

"Sir," Holdfast replied, looking up now and speaking in a voice that shook the pewter plates on the dresser, "I said so! They began firing by platoons, with the corporals calling off the orders. Our men went down like hoppers caught in a grass-fire."

Holdfast drew his buckskin sleeve violently across his brow.

73

"I was standing close to Colonel Ledyard. Then up comes an officer —I don't know his name—and 'Who commands this fort?' he yells out. Our Colonel draws his sword, lowers the point, turns it round, presents the hilt to that officer, and bows. 'I did, sir,' says he, 'but you do now.'"

"Like the gentleman he is, that William Ledyard," Mother Chester interrupted.

"You mean, Mother," said Holdfast, "like the gentleman he *was*. Those were his last words. That officer grabbed the hilt, and drove the blade through Colonel Ledyard's body."

For several seconds there was nothing to be heard in the kitchen except the flapping of little flames on the hearth and the ticking of the clock in the corner.

At last, in a dull monotone, Holdfast continued: "The Colonel died in our arms. We laid him down. When we knew he was dead I closed his eyes. What next I knew was a half dozen of those wolves out of hell rushing up and trying to stab his body with their bayonets. We drove 'em off. Then they stood away and shot at us. They killed Peter Richards at the first volley—Peter Richards that I used to go to school with. He and I've been out after trout many's the time."

"Yes, Holdfast. I remember Peter, of course."

"And many others fell that I can't bear to name over now, and you couldn't bear to have me. There were some of your family, Mother, but I'm going to let Father Chester tell you about them."

"Oh, Holdfast!—Do you mean . . . ?"

"He will tell you, when he comes. But fifteen or twenty Mohegans are gone—all four of the Ashbow boys and Joe Nannapoon and . . ." Holdfast's voice broke.

"That's dretful!"

"And they killed them for sport, remember—for *sport*, I say, after they'd laid down their arms."

"But you?"

"They tried to. I wish to God . . . But by that time I felt like twenty men, as though all the strength of those dead young Mohegans had gone into me. I picked up my old 'Mischief Maker,' and he mows a wide swath."

"Aye, that he doos!" boomed a voice from the door. "Wish't we'd had a thousand murtherers like that un in New London an' Groton today, with a thousan' such men to swing 'em."

The Colonel came up to the fire. His hands, face, and clothing were foul with blood and grime. He seemed to have aged, since the morning,

74

by ten years. His hand trembled as he took the pot of ale Rebecca brought him.

"Get on with yer tale, lad," said he. "Ye must know things I ain't heerd 'bout."

"Well, by that time," Holdfast continued, "we could see that they meant to kill us like rats in a barn. There's no block-house up there, o' course, and so most of our men that could crawl or stagger got into the power-magazine. There were fifty of them jammed together there in a solid mass, and they had no weapons.—Now, don't believe this if you can help it, but I saw twenty red-coats crowd up around the door o' the powder-magazine and fire in on 'em, taking turns. I heard the yells and screams from inside. Then, all at once, I knew I'd had enough. I caught two red-coats and jammed their heads together. I grabbed them by the collars, caught up 'Mischief Maker,' and ran for the rampart with those two dangling so that if anyone did get in a shot it wouldn't hurt much. At first the others were too busy or too much surprised. Anyhow, I got away. Just beyond the rampart I dropped the two bodies and jumped the fraising and ran down and swam the river. Since then, on this side, all the way to the Sound, 'Mischief Maker' and I have been doing what we could. You don't want to hear about that. I'll never tell anyone about it—except that we missed Benedict Arnold. We couldn't find him."

"Too bad, that," said the Colonel. "But they was some ye didn't miss —eh, lad?"

"That's what I'm not going to talk about, Father. It's my burden, not yours, and not Mother's either. You have both done your best for me, but it hasn't been enough. I'm a savage still, and today I acted like one."

"Wal, why the hell not, arter what ye ben through? 'T was the right way to act."

"No, Father, it was wrong. It was dreadful.—I should have gone home to Mohegan Village tonight instead of coming here, but I couldn't bear to."

As the young man covered his face again with his hands, Mother Chester leaned over and laid a hand gently on his arm. "Now that's prob'ly the most tarr'ble story," said she, "that ever a man had to tell, or a woman to listen to. But for tonight, anyhow, let's all try to think it's suthin' that happened a long while ago."

"But my friends, Mother! Nearly all the friends I have in the world! The Mohegan tribe is broken, lost. They died for nothing. They were butchered. And I was their chief. I couldn't save them.—Why couldn't I at least have died with them today?"

The Colonel, trying to introduce a lighter tone, cut in: "It's like I told yer mother this evenin', lad. Ye ain't the dyin' kind."

"Well, then," Holdfast cried out, looking with a wild appeal from face to face, "what kind am I? What's left? Who needs me? I have to know."

"I do," Rebecca promptly replied. "You've always known that, Holdfast."

"An' *I* do an' we *all* do," added Mother Chester. "Ye mustn't talk nonsense, my dear."

"Needs yeh! Huh!" snorted the Colonel. "Oncet we git these murtherin' lobster-backs licked, I cal'late to find a few things we need yeh fer. How 'bout the stun wall round upper paster whar the cows go through like herrin' through a busted net? How 'bout roofin' the barn afore it falls down? How 'bout dreenin' Upper Swamp an' rootin' the ivy an' lamb-kill outen Old Medder?—Who *needs* yeh! My good Gawd!"

A small yellow dog—ill-conditioned, lame, and blind in one eye—slid in at the door and, after a moment of hesitation, ran three-legged across the room to Holdfast.

"That your dog, lad?" the Colonel asked in a tone of humorous commiseration.

"He's anybody's dog that needs him most, Father; but we two have been going round together quite a bit these last few weeks.—Hello there, Wash. What you doing up so late?"

"He don't hev to sleep more 'n half so much," Colonel Chester suggested, "hevin' only one eye."

"But look how he's worritin' them strings o' Holdfast's moccasins!" exclaimed Mother Chester. "Whatever d' ye s'pose he means by 't?"

Holdfast stood up. "I think," said he, "that we'd better find out. Samson Occum says that one eye is better than two for taking good aim.—Come on, Wash."

And then, as soon as the kitchen door had closed, Mother Chester began to weep, holding her apron to her eyes. "Oh, John," she sobbed, "the boy's heart's broke. All those friends o' his gone—an' ye know how he allus did need his friends. He'll never be the same boy ag'in."

"Mebbe not; but he mought be a man, iffen ye give 'im a chancet."

"I mean, he'll never laugh an' joke an' play like he useter would."

"Stint yer yammer, now, Mother, an' let the lad grow up. Keep a-smilin'—or, iffen ye cain't, then make 'im think yer cryin' fer yer own folks gone, which ye got a right to."

"Hush, John! He's a-comin'!" And the little woman, hastily dabbing at her eyes, forced an unconvincing smile.

"Oh, the dear!" she exclaimed a moment later, lifting the candle high to look at the sleeping boy Holdfast held in his arms. "Whar'd ye find 'im?"

"Down by the cattle-gate. He was asleep there, under the old lilac. Wash took me."

"He's been crying," said Rebecca.

"He's had something to cry for," Reid answered.

"And he's cold," said Mother Chester. "Jest feel his pore little hand. Oh, the beautiful dear! Holdfast, you lay 'im down in the middle o' the turn-up bed an' we'll put the warmin'-pan in an' cover 'im up 'thout his wakin'."

"Like we did young Holdfast," laughed the Colonel, "when I brung 'im in from the Village ten year back come Christmas. Rec'leck, Mother?"

"Do I rec'leck! But this is a good un too.—Did he say anythin', Holdfast?"

"He only said 'Mithith Thetherth houth. Maple thugar.'"

"Wel, marciful God!" boomed the Colonel. "We got *bar'ls* o' sugar!"

COIN OF THE REALM

John Reid was least miserable, during the weeks that followed, down in the general store on the river-bank below the farmhouse. The Colonel's two long-boats were tied up there, and close at hand were the ruined ways on which the ketch *Rebecca* had been built and launched. The deep cushion of dubbings, chiefly oak chips, that covered the bank recalled the ship-builders of earlier generations. In the shadowy structure of the old store itself, weather-worn, gray as a hornet-nest, jutting out from the bank on moss-grown piles and lulled day and night by the lisp of the river, Reid found a charm that soothed if it did not solve his trouble. The breath of the sea mingled there with odors of cinnamon, cloves, mace, pepper, molasses, and rum. The past lingered on there in many a cobwebbed relic of the time when the

77

Colonel's great-grandfather, needing a place of deposit and sale for the goods of his West India trade and for pelts brought in by Mohegan and Pequot hunters, had fitted these pine and oaken beams together to make a warehouse.

King Uncas himself might have trodden this puncheon floor in the dim antiquity of a hundred and twenty years gone by. Attawanhood might well have been here, and even the noble Canonchet. John Winthrop the Younger, founder of New London and Governor of Connecticut, had certainly come here often to consult with old Samuel Chester the prosperous merchant, formerly a Captain in the Navy of King Charles.—It was no slight relief to John Reid to escape from thoughts of the present into such cool distances of time.

And even the present was less painful to him there than in other places. While selling sticks of mohair, barrels of pork, and gallons of rum he could move away from his own concerns and into the lives of others. The customers who came in from Quaker Hill, from Groton, and from up or down river, no longer held it against him that he had once been an enemy. Most of them knew, apparently, that he had resigned his commission in the British Navy immediately after the massacre. If anything now set him apart it would be the peculiarities of his speech, and these he was making strong efforts to overcome. For the first time in his life he was beginning to feel that he belonged to a settled community and had some part in its affairs.

Moreover, there seemed to be a chance of making himself useful. Colonel Chester hated the work of the store, and said so. Rebecca had little taste for it, and less ability. As for Holdfast, he had recently been spending days and nights together away from the farm—for no reason that anyone, with the possible exception of Mother Chester, could guess.

Reid took delight in keeping the store-book exactly and up-to-date. He kept it as he had kept the *Amazon's* log-book, figuring the day's work and the store's position in neat columns. In-so-far as the Colonel would allow he made the store a place of business rather than a center for the more or less disguised distribution of charity. His many years of moving from port to port had made him acquainted with most of the foreign coins that were current in the chaotic monetary conditions of the time—ducatoons of Flanders, écus d'or and silver louis of France, johannes and crusadoes of Portugal, old rix-dollars of Germany, Spanish doubloons and dollars and pieces-of-eight. He never confused the pound sterling with the far less valuable New England pound, or the

78

pine-tree shillings of Massachusetts Bay with the real shillings of His Majesty's Mint. Deliberate confusions of that sort, he more than once affirmed to the Colonel, had nothing to do with patriotism. Neither, he said, had the desperate plight of Connecticut paper money—or, for that matter, of Continental currency, which he firmly refused when the Colonel was absent to accept at more than one-sixtieth of its face value.

The Colonel, convinced that the deterioration of American paper money had been caused by Tory intrigue, was inclined to combat this coldly mercantile attitude. He wanted to know how America was ever to get a sound money unless a few people who believed in the country stood by the money they had. The technicalities of Reid's answer were beyond him, but he could not fail to understand that Connecticut was really repudiating her own paper currency when she insisted that certain taxes be paid in gold and silver.

Reid told the Colonel a true story about a Connecticut soldier who, on his journey homeward after his discharge from the Continental Army, had been obliged to spend a night at a tavern in the town of Danbury. He attempted in the morning to settle his bill for food and lodging by offering, in Continental currency, all the money, amounting to forty dollars, which he had received for five months of military service. This was refused, and he was finally obliged to pawn his rifle, in addition to paying the forty dollars, to satisfy the demands of the landlord.

What finally brought the Colonel round, however, was the young man's unquestionably accurate statement that General Washington himself, while in Connecticut a few months before, had paid two hundred and fifteen paper dollars for the help a certain Patriot had given in pulling his horse out of Bull's Falls in the Housatonic. In fact Reid quoted the General directly, to the effect that a wagon-load of Continental paper would not buy one wagon-load of good provisions. The Colonel fumed and swore at these home-thrusts, but had no answer.

Having won his way to this extent, Reid went on to master the more difficult local valuations governing barter. He learned, for example, that one bushel of shelled Indian corn was the equivalent of four dozen breeches-buttons or a yard of the best black shalloon. He discovered that a pound of good clean brimstone was exchangeable for a New Testament or two copies of Isaac Watts's *Metrical Psalms*. Nine skins of musquash brought in by a Mohegan called for a gallon of the best Jamaica rum, and a quart of yokeage ground by hand in a Gungywamp quern had to be accepted for a pint of cheap gin. When dealing with the Indians Reid took six beads of white wampum or three of black, if they were well strung, as equal to one English penny; but he tried to make them realize that this old custom could not be much longer maintained. Beads of roanoke, from Virginia, he refused altogether.

And yet with all his care, and in spite of the sharp distinctions he learned to make between "pay," "pay as money," "country pay," and "hard money," it grew clear that the store was not prospering. The occasional contributions brought in by Captain Sam Avery did not help much because the people of the neighborhood had as little taste as they had coin for the exotic luxuries acquired by privateering. Moreover, the Colonel positively would not permit the refusal of further credit to certain old customers far in arrears. When Reid pointed out that Hannah Higginbotham was already in debt to the store for seventeen gallons of rum and had yesterday come in for another, the answer was that the Colonel had known Hannah all his life, that she was a miserably poor old widow whose sole comfort and happiness consisted in getting drunk and staying so, and that he, Colonel John Chester, would be everlastingly damned if he was going to snatch that one pleasure from her.

Little by little Reid came to see that the Colonel could not possibly be, as he thought himself, a wealthy man. He considered himself so by mere force of habit, and because he had neither the patience nor the ability to look into his own affairs. He could not, or would not, take into account the effect of the eighteen different taxes that Connecticut had levied during the past year alone, several of them requiring payment either in hard money or else in beef, pork, flour, cloth, or live cattle. He persisted in the opinion that paper money would soon be as good as gold, even though he was discovering that so old a friend as Nathaniel Shaw would not accept it in payment of a debt. When it was pointed out that even hard money would not buy half as much as it had before the war, he merely damned the Tories and went on charging three pounds for a barrel of good salt pork, as his father had done before him. A bushel of clean salt, he insisted, simply was not worth more than four shillings, and it did him good to hear that the people of Norwich and New London, where the store-keepers charged ten shillings and twelve, were traveling miles to buy his salt.

Not often could the Colonel be brought to face the evidence of his

80

own accounts, and when he did so the resulting interviews were often vociferous and heated. He loathed the sight of the store-book even more after Reid had begun to make it reveal the truth. Less than ten minutes it usually was before he threw down his goose-quill, swore volubly at the man who was trying to help him, and stumped out of the store in dudgeon.

Once, however, and once for all, he gave Reid "a piece of his mind." He said, in substance, that if that young man was trying to make it appear that he, John Chester, was pretty soon "going on the town," why then all he had to say was that he, John Chester, still owned the store and all there was in it, together with a mill on the Yantic up in Norwich and a good share in Winthrop's old grist-mill down in New London and several lays in the ketch *Rebecca,* not to mention his twenty-eight cows, two bulls, six farm-horses and a good riding-horse, four yoke of oxen and two other yokes in training, a score of mules ready for shipment to the West Indies, over two hundred acres in tilth, a good three hundred in cleared pasture, plenty of meadow, a dozen wood-lots, five hundred swine, six or eight slaves, *and* the barns *and* the out-houses *and* the farmhouse itself. Furthermore, he had the good will of all Connecticut, and General Washington did not exactly despise him. If General Washington did despise him, then why had he so cheerfully spent the night in that same hovel of a farmhouse back in '78? Could John Reid answer that? And that same Connecticut owed him, John Chester, about—well, say about twenty thousand pounds. Connecticut would pay him back, in solid coin, when it got good and ready.

But one thing he wished John Reid distinctly to understand—namely, that he, John Chester, washed his hands of the store. John Reid could *have* the place, lock, stock, and barrel, and there he could skimp and gouge and dicker to his heart's content, keeping his dirty little store-book right up to the minute so as to be sure to the penny at the end of every day just how much he had lost, and always feeling poor as Job's turkey. But as for him, John Chester, he had other things to think about—far more important things than haggling over a bushel of salt and trying to squeeze a few filthy pence out of the Widow Higginbotham.

Thereafter the Colonel kept his word fairly well, and seldom appeared at the store. One brilliant morning in early autumn, however, Reid saw him coming down the hill with a strong, handsome stranger, deeply bronzed as though by tropic suns, whom he introduced as "Mr.

John Ledyard, of Groton." Reid had already heard that name more than once. He said so.

"Holdfast anywhars 'round?" the Colonel inquired.

"He's down the bank, patching his canoe."

"Call him in, will you, John? Hyar's a friend o' hisn he'll be glad to see."

Reid saw that this was true when Holdfast came in, blinked for a moment in the gloom, and then eagerly grasped the visitor's hand. The two had been comrades together, he found, before the war, and had not met for eight years. During that time, apparently, Ledyard had been adventuring all over the world. He had come home chiefly to write a book and to get it published in Hartford.

"What the hell ye want to write a book fer?" asked the Colonel. "Dangdest thing, John Reid—last time I heerd 'bout John Ledyard he ben floatin' down Connecticut River in a dugout with a *book* for cargo. Seems like he cain't do nothin' 'thout a *book* to 't."

"Yes," laughed Ledyard. "I was running away from Dartmouth College at the time—just beginning my education, so to speak—and so I took a copy of Homer along."

"Homer, eh? Oh, yeah. Ye war a-comin' back *home* to Connecticut. Good idear."

"And now I'm writing a book about the greatest sailor and explorer that ever lived."

"What's that? Ye mean Commodore George Anson o' the *Centurion?*"

"Of course he was a great man too, but I mean Captain James Cook."

"Oh, yes, Cook of the *Resolution*," said Reid. "The man who found a cure for scurvy."

"That's the man. I was with him on his last voyage. I saw him killed at Hawaii."

"Ha—what? What ye say thet place was?" asked the Colonel.

"Hawaii, out in the middle of the Pacific."

"How-ah-ye, huh? Damn queer name, that. Injun, I s'pose. An' in the Pacific, eh? Ye ben out thar, John?"

"All over it, Colonel. Up and down and across."

"All over it, eh?—Same as I did with Anson forty year back, chasin' that 'ar Spanish galleon, an' takin' her crammed with gold.—But what ye go for, John?"

"Well, Colonel, I think you had more to do with it than any other man."

82

"Oh, come now, John Ledyard. I ain't never no more 'n heerd tell o' How-ah-ye."

"No, but don't you remember that when Holdfast and I were boys you were always talking about the Charter that Governor Winthrop brought back from King Charles, and how it gave us all the land running west to the South Seas and the Islands thereto adjoining? Didn't you say a hundred times that when we grew up we ought to go out there and see how big Connecticut really was?"

"Wal, o' course. An' I do think so, today."

"But, Colonel, I *have* been there. Where it says 'South Sea' in Connecticut's Charter it means the Pacific Ocean, and Hawaii is one of the ten thousand 'islands thereto adjoining.' I was with Captain Cook when he discovered that Connecticut island."

Ledyard's three listeners gazed at him intently, as though trying to gain from his physical appearance alone some hint of those mysterious lands and seas.

"But John," said Holdfast at length, "Father Chester never said anything about going by water. He'd done that himself. I always thought he wanted us to *walk* out there, and 'beat the bounds of Connecticut.' "

"That's what I had in mind, Holdfast, when I sailed with Cook from London. I wanted to start from the western coast and walk back. But when we got there the Captain couldn't spare me; so I'll have to find some other way."

"But why not start from this side?"

"Because then I might never get home again. Besides, I want to send back a cargo of furs. It would pay for the voyage ten times over."

"I see.—It would *pay* you.—Yes."

"Queer thing," said the Colonel, "talkin' 'bout furs in thisheer warehouse. Place used to be full o' pelts in my grandfer's time, an' *now* look at it!"

"But the pelts of all New England would be nothing to those you could get in the West. For a few barrels of glass beads a man can get enough furs out there to make him rich as Croesus."

"Not to mention what a few glass bottles might bring in," the Colonel suggested, "iffen filled proper."

Holdfast stepped to the open door looking out on the shimmering Thames. The light in his eyes had grown dim.

"Yes, Colonel," Ledyard went on, "there are a thousand fortunes to be made in the West. I want you to have your share, and I know you'll

83

be interested when we have time to talk it over. Today I came over to learn how my Uncle William was killed at Fort Griswold. Holdfast was there, I know, and he must have learned the facts."

"William Ledyard," the Colonel replied, "was killed with his own sword by the man he was giving it up to."

"I'm afraid that's so, John," said Holdfast. "I was close by and saw it all."

"That's what I've heard," Ledyard replied. "I wanted to make sure."

"But let's remember, Holdfast," Reid interrupted, "that the criminal who did that murder wasn't a British officer at all. I hear that he was a blackguard by the name of Bromfield, a Tory, born and brought up in New Jersey."

"Of course some say it was Captain Beckwith," the Colonel added. "But then he's a Tory too."

"You gentlemen are really not very helpful," said Ledyard. "My business is to find out what particular Tory it was who killed my uncle. I want to have a serious talk with him."

"Not a long talk, I hope," laughed the Colonel.

"No. Not much longer than his with my Uncle William.—I'll find that fellow somewhere, if I have to go to England after him. When I've finished my little business with him, I plan to start an expedition to the Western Coast after furs. Rich men 'll go for the money in it, but I hope to find that Northwest Passage to the Pacific that everyone's been talking about. I reckon it's probably on Connecticut land. Anyhow, I'm going to call it 'Connecticut Straits.'"

COCHEGAN

"These autumn leaves!" sighed Rebecca.

She was walking with Holdfast along an Indian trail that plunged and clambered beneath tall trees. Vivid leaves of chestnut, maple, sycamore, and oak fluttered before them, or raced in little sibilant companies along the trail. Rebecca's hair was blowing loose in the wind.

"They make me think," Holdfast answered, "of the bonfires we used to have at the farm when you were small."

"You weren't a giant yourself, those days. Only just a long-legged

Mohegan boy.—But yes; that's one thing they bring back. One of ten thousand. And now they're all saying 'goodbye.' Everything is."

"Humph!"

"Well, aren't you going away?"

"Yes."

"And isn't that why we had to come up here today?—Oh, I bet you feel just the way I do, only you're too much an Indian to show it."

"I thought, Becky, that you'd been brought up a good enough Indian so you wouldn't spoil a day like this by going soft."

"I'm not. I'm as tough as a—well, as a wild-cat. All I said was, these dead leaves make me think of the times we've had. They do."

"But those times have been good ones. I've seen to that. Kindly see that this is a good day too, and nothing to weep about."

"Ah, but they're all in the past; they're gone by, like these leaves."

"The leaves of its own past," said the young man, "are what a strong tree feeds on. Just so with a man and his memories. They may be all he has, or is."

"And how 'bout a woman?"

"Do you mean a grown-up woman?"

"You know what I mean. I mean a woman like me."

"Oh, she may have her—hopes. And they're nothing to cry about, either."

A gang of bluejays set up a raucous clamor, soon augmented by a score of crows. "Yank-yank, yank" came the nasal call of a nuthatch spiraling up the bole of a beech-tree. Young partridges blundered off into the thicket.

The trail was narrowing now, and the woods were wilder. This was pure Indian country, so unfit for plow or axe that no white man had ever tried to wrest it from the Mohegans. The blunt, writhen hemlocks bristling here and there on the ledges were primeval.

"Well, anyhow," said Holdfast, breaking a long silence, "here we are again."

Rebecca looked up, as he was looking, to the crest of a slope that rose on the farther side of a shallow brook. The westering sun, though it dazzled her eyes, could not hide the huge boulder recumbent on the top of the hill like some incredible prehistoric monster that had clambered up there from its den to bask and brood.—She caught her breath, and moved closer to her companion.

85

Even in childhood, when she first began to come here with her Indian playmate, Rebecca had wondered why Holdfast chose the most terrifying spot in all the region for their game of "playing house." His reply had always been that if she really wanted to be a good Indian this rock, once the council-house and fort and shrine of King Uncas, was the best place in which to learn how.

Something in her, she felt, must have changed since that had seemed a sufficient answer. Perhaps it was that she no longer wanted, above all things, to be "a good Indian."

Since her childhood, she vaguely felt, she had grown softer, more subject to emotional whims and caprices, to sudden inexplicable laughter and tears, while her companion had grown steadily more stern—or, if not quite that, then stronger, ever more like a man of stone.

Never before, at any rate, had the rock seemed so hostile. High above the gold and crimson of the surrounding trees its blue-gray bulk heaved against the sun, formidable, daunting, and demonic, as though it harbored a stubborn and sinister purpose. It lay on the hill like the burden of the knowledge of death on the human heart. After its million years in this one wild place it still looked a stranger, a wanderer out of unimaginable distance, pausing here for a while to meditate, prone in the sun, on its way from the ages before man was to the ages when earth would forget him.

"Yes," she said, faintly. "Here we are—for the last time."

"I say, Becky, that here we are *again*. I'll ask you to keep to that."

When he saw that her lashes were wet his tone grew sterner. "One of the rules from the very start," said he, "has been 'no sniffling.' I won't have it."

She darted a glance at his face. His firm-set jaw, his mouth drawn down at the corners, his darkened brow, were almost convincing. He had been gruff with her, and commanding, a thousand times before, but never so cold and withdrawn. Almost she felt afraid. He seemed to have taken his stand against her on the side of the rock Cochegan.

But this, she knew, was absurd. If Holdfast was sometimes as cold as the rock he was also as firm, as unchangeable. She felt a sudden impulse—and it came as much from the growing woman in her as from her frank and gallant girlhood—to show this dark-browed man how little his present mood could shake her fondness. She laid her hand on his shoulder and looked steadily into his eyes, smiling, and yet frowning a little also, in perplexity.

He looked down into her eyes, as steadily.

86

Thus they stood for several seconds without a word or motion. The wind, although they could hear it roaring among the woods, did not reach to this sheltered meadow. The crows and jays had flown far off. A woodpecker tapped at a dead branch close by. The brook made a weary murmur.

Yet there was nothing that the blue eyes could see in the brown which had not always been there. Perfect fidelity there was, and the firm authority as of an elder brother, but no yielding to any tenderness of farewell, no weakening of any sort.

But then, suddenly, and with a shock that ran through her like a spasm of pain, she understood. Ever so slightly, yet unmistakably, his shoulder was trembling under her hand as the trunk of a great oak trembles when its branches are lashed by a gale.

"Oh, Holdfast!" was all that she dared to say. She lowered her eyes, dropped her hand, and moved a little away from him.

He made no answer, by word or look or motion.

She was overwhelmed with pity, and with despair at the tangle in which three lives had been innocently caught.

Slowly moving onward to the bank of the brook, she knelt there on a flat rock with her back to him and looked into the water.—It was something to do.

Eyes of sky-color looked up at her, utterly different from the dark eyes with glints of gold into which she had just been gazing. They looked up from a proud, passionate face, with a nose high-arched, and round the face was a wind-blown riot of auburn hair. Its untamable strands, writhing and intertwisting, made her think of something that Nathan Hale had once said about a beautiful woman with snakes for hair who turned men's hearts to stone. Whether the mirrored face below was beautiful, like Medusa's, she did not ask herself, but certainly it was the face of a broken-hearted woman.

The reflection in the water was blurred by a falling tear, and then by another. The shoulders of the mirrored woman were shaking.

"Stop it!" she heard him say from close behind her, in a tone of command.

She struggled to obey.

"Now wash your face."

She did that, submissively, scooping the water up with one hollowed hand while she leant on the stone with the other. It was his perfect right to issue orders in this place—or, for that matter, in any. And it was his unquestionable right, because therein lay his only safety,

87

to maintain their old hard and cool relationship of friendly boy and girl. She hated herself for weeping, and slapped the brook-water against her eyes with vicious dabs, as though wishing it to hurt.

"And now," said he, pointing with his foot to the haversack he had unstrapped from his shoulders, "pick up this bag and go ahead."

She slung the load to her back and buckled it on with hasty fingers. The sternness of his tone rejoiced her. She was glad to know that love had not unstrung him. It had merely bent the hickory bow.

She found it hard going, with her burden, among the sharp-edged stones of the slope.

"Stop toeing out like a white woman! Have you forgotten how to walk?"

"Almost I have," she agreed; and then for the next few steps the toes of her moccasins pointed inward.

Aunt Lucy Tantaquidgeon, she remembered, had made those moccasins. They were of moose-hide, dear-bought. Their blue and gold beads showed Holdfast's Clan of the Bear and the totem of Uncas. In shape and hue and texture they made one think of the moccasin flower. They smelled of hickory smoke.

And Lucy, too, had made this Indian tunic and skirt. She had toiled for a month and more over these ten skins of the doe, making them as delicately clean and soft and gay as the painted trillium. And oh, years back, in the dusk of the smoky wigwam, how the old woman's eyes had shone when she brought these garments from the cedar chest and drew them over the pale body of a girl!

For Lucy had hoped, fond soul, that this girl would be a daughter of the tribe. Never had she quite accepted the proud determination of her brother, Samson Occum—and, indeed, of Holdfast himself— that the blood of King Uncas should be kept undefiled.

But why, feeling so, had Occum allowed Holdfast to live for ten years at Four Winds Farm? Rebecca could not regret, even now, that strange arrangement; yet she thought that Occum, so wise in most ways, should have foreseen the sorrowful thing that had happened. In fact, he *must* have foreseen it. And why, then . . . ?

But here, at last, was the top of the hill. Rebecca turned, panting, to lean for a moment against the huge rock.

"You can rest," said Holdfast, "after I have eaten."

She moved on, fingering for support the rough damp granite and stepping cautiously. With Holdfast behind her she went down and down along the narrow path centuries old, until she reached, at the lower face of the boulder, a shelter, a shallow cave, made by the upward tilt of the rock's underside and the downward slope of the hill.

Some twenty feet in depth and as many broad, the cave was flooded with the sunshine of late afternoon. Leaf-shadows danced on its floor. In the middle, surrounded by large flat stones, was a heap of ashes, and seven feet above that heap the underside of the boulder was black with the smoke of many fires.

Holdfast gathered wood and started a blaze from the clamshell packed with smoldering punk which he had lighted that day from the hearth at home. Then he lay down in the sunshine and watched Rebecca's preparations.

He saw her take their single wooden trencher from its hiding-place, together with their table-knives and spoons of pewter, two of each. He watched her stretch on sticks before the fire the two rabbits he had shot with his bow at the farm that morning. He surveyed her baking of small flat corn-cakes in the embers, as Lucy Tantaquidgeon had taught her. Also he saw her dash the tears now and then from her face with the back of her hand; but he was willing to suppose that the wind, blowing under the western edge of the rock, had carried smoke into her eyes.

At last, having set their stone table and adorned it with four fringed gentians he had brought up from the meadow, she rose to her feet and called him.

"But where are the others?" he asked, also rising.

"What do you mean?" said she in a low voice, not looking at him. "There's only you and me."

"You know better."

There was a sad appeal in her glance as she almost sobbed: "Oh, no! Not that, not that!"

"Get them, Becky."

She hesitated for a moment, but then, with a despairing gesture, walked to the inner wall of the cave where the under-surface of the boulder sloped up from the rubble and red earth. There, after some digging with a strong pointed stick, she drew forth a wooden box wrapped in cow-hide. This she opened, clumsily, as though she could not see very well, and lifted out two images carved in wood, one of them painted white and the other red. She brought them to the table and propped them there against stones, one on either side.

89

Holdfast's smile as he gazed down at the crudely wrought figures was both amused and fond. "I don't see," he said, "that they're anything to be ashamed of. I was only twelve when I carved them, and I had nothing but a jack-knife to work with."

"I'm *not* ashamed of them, and you know it!" was Rebecca's reply, spoken in a tone which no true Indian squaw would have dared to use.

Finding that he did not chide her, she came closer. "And now, Holdfast," said she, "I've done what you wanted and I—I have a thing to ask."

"Well?"

"Of course it's not the way we've always done here, but I'd like it if—if I could eat with you today."

"What!"

"Yes, out of the same trencher, like father and mother at Thanksgiving."

He frowned a little and shook his head; but then, seeing that she was once more on the verge of tears, he gruffly said: "Very well. Only you must not count upon it hereafter."

Whether to laugh or to cry she did not know—to laugh at his solemnity in carrying through their old childish game or to weep at the bravery with which he ignored the fact that they were playing it for the last time. But of one thing, while she gazed up at him with swimming eyes, she was certain: he would have made a magnificent lover. Seeing now as a woman sees and not as an unripe girl, she realized for the first time his wild masculine beauty and the headlong force he had held in check. So easily and irrecoverably, if only his self-control had been by a particle less, they might both have been swept away long since into unimaginable gulfs of passion. For she had nothing in herself, she knew, that could have withstood him—not even the thought of that other, that stranger from the sea with the curly blond hair and the frosty eyes.

For a moment Rebecca let her fancy race into the life that might have been as she watched Holdfast bend over their rude stone table with his straight black hair falling forward, and saw through the slit of his hunting-shirt the slope of his great bronzed chest. She saw him take on the point of his knife four slivers of rabbit-meat. These, according to his Indian custom of returning thanks, he dropped one by one into the fire, saying reverently: "There's for Becky, for Holdfast, and for each of the others."

Then they sat down together and began to eat from the same trencher.

The cry of the wind and the calls of wind-blown birds went farther away among the woods until there was nothing but the faint throb of the brook to be heard. Although the sunshine still paled the flames of the fire at their side, blue shadows were gathering in the meadow below. The day was visibly waning.

"You know, Holdfast," said Rebecca, shivering slightly, "I wouldn't dare to come up to Cochegan alone, or with anyone else but you."

"Why not?"

"Well, I used to think it was because the rock might slide downhill and crush me; but now I know it's because this place is haunted."

He looked slowly round the rock-strewn shelter with eyes that were woe-begone.

"You are right," he said, simply.

"Oh, Holdfast, I'm sorry!"

"And it's not only the ghosts of the men who used to crowd round this hearth when Uncas was King. You must add those of twenty Mohegans killed in this white man's war. Many nights we have sat here together. I was their chief. I am still, though they are dead. All my life I shall be a leader of dead men."

Though quietly spoken, the words reverberated under the arch of the rock as though Cochegan were speaking. And Rebecca, listening, felt that this was not her familiar comrade who sat gazing with haunted eyes toward the back of the cave, forgetful of his food and of her. Neither, certainly, was this man a broken-hearted lover. He was a stranger, with heights and depths in him at which she could only guess. He made her afraid.

"Down at the farm," she stammered, "we—we've always thought you belonged to us."

His gaze returned, slowly, to her face. "I've had two homes," he said. "Two tasks. I've tried to be both red and white, like the images here. But now, that's over."

"How d' you mean?"

"It's like this, Becky. Ten years ago the Colonel thought he needed someone to care for you, especially on the long walk to school in New London and home again. He was right. In a town like that, where there are always sailors just in from sea, he did need someone. Of course he had other things in mind too, but that was the main thing —anyhow, at first. Well now, let's say that I did that job fairly well.

Nathan Hale used to say so. But it's over, and I can turn to something else."

"You mean," laughed Rebecca, "that you don't have to protect me any more against the sailors?"

After a second or two in which Rebecca's laughter suddenly died, Holdfast glanced at her face. It was crimson. Clearly she too had realized that her words could bear more than one meaning.

"Exactly," said Holdfast, and bit into a corn-cake.

Rebecca pretended to busy herself at the fire. At length she said: "O' course there are things I don't understand; but what I know is that I'm losing the best friend I've ever had, and it's going to break my heart."

"I don't think so," he answered, calmly. "You are going to be happy before I leave you, and also after I'm gone. If I weren't sure of that I might not go at all."

She laid down her knife and spoon and considered what his words must mean. Her voice trembled when she spoke: "Holdfast, it isn't the right thing for an Indian woman to say, but—but you're—I guess you must be the grandest man that ever lived!"

"This rabbit," he coolly replied, "is well cooked. I couldn't have done it better myself."

"Huh! Glad you like it!"

"And as for going away—well, I'm a wandering man. That's one of the things you don't understand. During the last year I've been a wanderer even here in Connecticut, whenever I could get away from the fort and the farm. One night I'd sleep here under the rock, the next over in Gungywamp by Larrabee Oak, and maybe the night after that in the big cave near Machimoodus, twenty miles west."

"Yes, we've known about that, a little, and about the races you've won, and the wrestling matches. Everyone knows about those things. But isn't Connecticut large enough for you to wander in?"

"Father Chester says it reaches clear to the Pacific Ocean."

"I don't care if it runs round the world. That's no reason why you should. Your place is where people need you, and love you, and always will."

"That's so," he said, still gently. "I must always have a place like that.—But now, we've had ten good years together. Nothing has spoiled them. Whatever may happen, they'll never change. No one can take them away."

She suddenly laid her small hand upon his great one. "Nobody," she said, with deep earnestness. "Nobody in the world! I'd like to see him try!"

It was strange how her eyes could brim with tears while they were also flashing with indignation at some imagined insult. It was amazing how she could be possessed by two violently clashing moods at the same moment.

One tear spilled over and began to trickle down her cheek.

"Cry-baby!" said Holdfast, drawing his hand from under hers. And then he went on: "Of all the things a white woman does, crying is the very worst."

For a moment they both laughed. Then Rebecca sat silent, with her hands lying open on her lap. Her look was less sad than dreamy. One would have said that she was listening to the voice of the brook below.

At last Holdfast rose to his feet. "The sun," he said, "is almost down. It's time for you to get the dishes washed and put the others to bed." He began to stamp out the fire.

But Rebecca sat still, gazing at the ground. In her face there was some new and tenderer expression.

"Now Holdfast," said she without looking up, "I don't think we ought to leave them here. You know we'll never come back, and—oh, it feels so lonesome to think of them lying under the rock and turning to dust year after year."

"They won't turn to dust so soon as we shall," he answered. "They will be young still when you and I are old. And we shall come back. You and I will sit at this table and eat at this trencher again. On that day we shall want them to be here, waiting."

"I don't see how you know such things," the girl replied.

"But I do. And where I am going I can't take them with me. As for you—well, Becky, you won't need them. Or not for long."

"Why won't I need them?" she passionately demanded. "Why shouldn't I want them always, to—to remember things by?"

"You will forget them. I know that, too."

And now she was on her feet, facing up to him, her cheeks aflame and her eyes blazing.—"How can you bear, how can you dare to say . . . ?"

"Wrap them carefully, Rebecca, so that no damp can get into the box, and put them back to sleep. Before you and I are wrapped and laid away we shall see them here once more. And I like to think they will see us too, and know how the years have used us."

93

WHAT SHALL I DO?

Almost as familiar to Holdfast Gaines as the kitchen at Four Winds Farm was this upper room which Samson Occum called his library. Here as a child Holdfast had learned to read, standing by the western window at the good man's knee. Until he was ten years old this little house of the famous Indian preacher had been his home, more dear to him than even the wigwams clustered near at hand beneath the oaks and maples.

While waiting for the Preacher's return he allowed himself to wonder how life might have gone with him if he had never left this place. He would scarcely have known the Chesters, and Rebecca herself would have remained a stranger. He might have fallen in love with some Mohegan girl, might have been by this time a father, and the active chieftain of his tribe. Or else, having gone to school in Lebanon Crank, he would have proceeded from there to Dartmouth College, founded by Occum's old teacher upon funds collected by Occum in England. After that there would have followed a mission to the Indians and a useful, perhaps a heroic life. Certainly it would have been a happier life than the one now stretching before him, less lonely by far and less tormented by conflicting loyalties.

Holdfast had never clearly understood why the Preacher, so rigid a stickler for the purity of Indian blood and custom, had allowed his own nephew, unquestionably dear to him, to grow up in a white man's home. How could so wise a man have failed to realize that an upbringing half barbaric and half civilized could only produce a mind, a heart, a character tragically divided and at war with itself? And what had the Preacher thought would result from an arrangement in which a youth and a maid were to grow up in the daily companionship of work and play, wandering freely together, sitting by the same fireside, and yet held asunder as though by a wall of flame? Had he ever heard the sorrowful story of how Tristram and Iseult had lain through the night together with only a long bright blade between them?—and did he, because of his age or for some other reason, think such things easy?

Colonel Chester's part in that arrangement had been more comprehensible. He had really felt the need of a companion and protector

94

for his only child. Moreover, he had never forgotten that he owed his life to Holdfast's father. Somewhat illogically, the Colonel considered that this obligation carried with it the right to adopt the dead man's son—an opinion which the people of Mohegan Village had by no means shared. Little by little, the Colonel had descended from proud demands to the covert offer of bribes, and then to requests and pleadings that continued year after year. For once he had been forced to ask a favor of Indians and to treat them with polite consideration. Yet the main thing was that he had finally got what he wanted, not only from the tribe but from Samson Occum—a man so much wiser, deeper, and in all ways stronger than he. Just there lay the mystery.

The solution must lie in the heart and mind of the Preacher himself—by no means a man to be seen through at a glance. Sitting in that familiar upper room and gazing at its oddly assorted furnishings, Holdfast was coming to realize that Occum also had striven to follow the white man's ways without sacrifice of his Indian strength, wisdom, and pride. Of that long effort, and of its triumph, this little room held the proof.

The Preacher's snow-shoes, made by his own hands, were leaning in one corner, together with two or three bows, a quiver, a Tower musket, and certain small fishing-nets of home manufacture. The empty rum-bottle, with a London label, hanging by a thong from the middle of the ceiling, was a souvenir of struggles long gone by. In strange contrast with these implements and weapons were the several hundreds of books on the plain pine shelves, some of them gifts from King George and others from the Earl of Dartmouth and the Countess of Huntington. There were books here that would scarcely be found in the library of any other New England minister, white or red. The Greek and Latin and Hebrew dictionaries were of course common enough, but not so the huge "Breeches Bible" lying open on the reading-desk. Holdfast could well remember how this pig-skinned volume had fascinated him in his boyhood, and how he used to stare at the date "1560" on its title-page, scarcely able to believe that any book could be so old as that.

Samson Occum had never talked much with Holdfast about the long visit he had paid to England in the year 1765. Except for these books, the empty rum-bottle, and the fame of the Preacher's success in collecting ten thousand pounds for the founding of Dartmouth College, nearly everything about that daring journey had been left to conjecture. Yet certainly such an experience, coming to a man born in a wigwam, must have made a deep and enduring impression. It must have contributed not a little to the wisdom that Occum now had, to the dignified courtesy of his bearing, and to the beneficent power and authority that he exerted upon all who knew him.

While he was glancing through the familiar pages of *Pilgrim's Progress*, gazing once more at its crudely powerful old pictures of Apollyon, Giant Despair, the Chained Lion, and Doubting Castle, Holdfast heard the outer door opened at the foot of the stairs and the tread of the Preacher, mounting. At once he turned to the first page of the book and began to read the opening words in a carrying voice: "I dreamed, and behold I saw a Man clothed with Rags standing in a certain place with his face from his own house, a Book in his hand, and a great Burden upon his back. I looked, and saw him open the Book and read therein; and as he read he wept and trembled; and, not being able longer to contain, he brake out with a lamentable cry, saying *'What shall I do?'*"

Here the Preacher entered the room—a man of some sixty years, powerfully built, with a mane of black hair streaked with gray falling to his shoulders and a strong, kind, open face. He was dressed, like Holdfast, in a hunting-shirt and leggings of tanned buck-skin. At first glance no stranger would have guessed that he differed at all from any other clean and self-respecting Indian of the village who lived by hunting, fishing, and occasional labor at some simple handicraft.

"Welcome, nephew!" said he, speaking Mohegan, as he stepped swiftly and silently across the room. The eagerness of his motion and the tone of his deep full voice showed the warmth of his affection.

The two men clasped hands and stood silent.

"I heard you reading those words," said Occum at length.

"Yes, Uncle. Those were the first words that you taught me to read. And I wanted you to hear them."

"Why?"

"Because they give the reason for my coming here today. I am like the Pilgrim standing with his face away from his own house and with a great burden on his back. And I come to ask you, Preacher, 'What shall I do?'"

Occum's face was grave as he turned and seated himself before the reading desk. "Sit down, dear boy," said he, motioning to a chair by the open window.

Ah, what a comfort to hear once more, and to speak, one's native

96

tongue! Always that language of his childhood would make Holdfast think of the jay's cry, the scream of a circling hawk, and the harsh acrid tang of cranberries eaten knee-deep in a bog. Always it would bring back the smell of the wood-smoke that had whirled from the wigwam tops on windy November mornings. It was a hidden and secret speech, this dying Mohegan, known to so very few. Somehow it was like that spring of water in Gungywamp, bubbling up under ferns in the hemlock shadows among the rocks, so small that the grasshopper could leap across it and yet very deep and cold. This language came from a darker, more mysterious world than the sun-lighted smooth-flowing English. And in a hundred years, more or less, it would be utterly lost and forgotten.

For a long minute, while the rustle of maple leaves came in from the vivid day, no word of any language was spoken in the room. At length Occum leaned forward and laid a hand on Holdfast's knee, his eyes showing a deep concern. "You come to ask me what you shall do," he said, gently; "but you would not bring me that question if you had not already done the hardest thing."

Holdfast did not reply.

After another long pause, during which he packed and lighted his cherry-wood pipe, the elder man went on: "Yes; I can see that you have done the hardest thing of all. You have given her up—and not because you could not have had her. Nothing that you will face in the coming years can be so hard as that. You begin your life, my boy, with a victory."

Again the soft lisping of maple leaves at the window. A breeze from the west was keeping them a-flutter. Holdfast, looking out from his chair, could see now and then a single scarlet or golden leaf, suddenly released from the twig on which it had grown, drop away out of sight. No sounds arose from the Indian village. The highway two hundred yards down the slope of the hill was deserted, now that the last of the groups going up from New London to the annual merry-making in Norwich had passed by. John Reid and Rebecca must by this time have reached the falls of the Yantic. At this moment they two, alone together, might be crossing the foot-bridge above that loud foamy water embroiled by great rocks, or else climbing the slope of the wild ravine toward the grave of King Uncas.

"Does Rebecca know," asked Occum, "how you . . . ?"

"Since yesterday, yes. I could not keep it from her."

97

"No. And her mother?"

"She has known for months, and has been unable to understand why it cannot be."

"Ah, she has always understood, though not with the heart. And now, your Aunt Lucy tells me, Rebecca is in love with John Reid, and perhaps he with her."

"That is true; and both have been unhappy."

"How so?"

"Their trouble has been of my making. I might have told John Reid long ago that I did not stand in his way, but I let him suffer. Mother Chester would not tell him, and of course Rebecca could not."

"But their trouble will soon be over?"

"Yes. It will end, I think, today."

"While yours will go on and on."

"Yes."

"And that trouble of yours—I suppose you would say I have caused it."

Receiving no audible reply, Occum rose from his chair and stood looking down at Holdfast. "Do you remember," he asked, "how I taught you, when you were a boy, to harden your arrow-points in the fire?"

A slow nod of the head made answer.

"Think of that, then, if ever you try to understand my reasons for letting you live among strangers. I foresaw at least some of the pain that decision has brought you, and will bring. Anyone could see the likelihood that you would fall in love with this dear and beautiful girl. The Chesters must have seen that, and they would have been proud to have you for their son. It was clear to me, too, that in finding a second home and having Nathan Hale for your teacher you would come to think in part like a white man, so that never again would you be simple and straight-grained and all of one piece. Thenceforth, I knew, there would be two natures struggling within you, two loves at strife, and your heart would be like a whirl in which two winds meet."

"That is so," said Holdfast.

"All this I foresaw. Many a time I thought it through, praying for divine guidance, during the years when the Colonel was pleading to have you. Often the plan to let you go seemed merely cruel. But then I said to myself that even if you remained with us your life would be hard. Here too, as chief of a dying tribe, you would find sorrow. Even here such strength as yours would attract danger and difficulty as iron

98

draws the lightning. Because you were strong already I wanted you to be stronger still, with a power of the spirit to match those bodily powers at which all men wonder. I said that a man who can eat and digest his trouble makes it over into a greater strength than any success can bring. That was why, finally closing with the Colonel's offer, I set in your way such trouble as I thought you could learn to bear.—May God forgive me if I was wrong, but I meant to make you ready for your task, to harden your arrows."

"My task?" said Holdfast, looking quickly up.

"Yes. But before we speak of that let me say that I do not know, and I may not live to make sure, whether I acted wisely. One thing, however, you will not doubt: I acted out of the best wisdom I had, and with great love."

"I know that, Uncle."

"And there's another thing. I should never have let you leave us if you had not already shown that you would be true to Mohegan Village —as you will be now, also, to Four Winds Farm—all your life. Thinking of that, I suggested to the Chesters that your Christian name should be 'Holdfast.' It suits you well. And I like also the Indian name, 'Sleeping Bear,' that your father gave you before he went out to die. He was thinking of our totem and the Clan of the Bear, but also of the fact that during the few weeks that he knew you, his only child, you were mostly asleep. To me the name means that you will bide your time, though it be long."

Again Holdfast looked up as he said: "In all that you say you seem to know what my task should be."

For the first time the elder man failed to meet his nephew's gaze. After a momentary hesitation he moved to the window and stood there looking out, with his hands behind him. "During your boyhood and youth," said he, "it has been right for me to direct you; but I hold that it is a teacher's final duty to set men free, even from himself. You must do what you will, be what you are. You must answer your own question. What a man is to be is always pulling at what he now is, and you must feel that pull. Yes, and it pushes, too. The thing he will do tomorrow, or fifty years hence, is like a drawn bow-string behind what he does today."

"I came," said Holdfast, quietly, "to ask what you think I should do."

If his back had not been turned, Holdfast would have seen that his uncle moved uneasily at this urging of the direct question, and that his hands, strongly clasped behind him, grew pale at the knuckles. His

99

voice, when he spoke, had lost its ring of authoritative decision. It had a new tone of almost wistful pleading.

"Ah, well, my boy," said Occum, "you must always have known, without being told, what has been my dearest dream for you. I could die happy, with assurance that my life had not been quite a failure, if I knew that the strong, wise, and deeply good man whom I have loved beyond all others, whom I tried to teach in his childhood, was giving his life to our people and striving as I have done to bring them into the Christian fold."

"That is, you would like to have me go out like David and Joseph Fowler, like the Brainard brothers, and like you, as a Christian missionary to the Indians."

"Yes. If I have not urged it, then that is because I have wanted it too much, and because I have feared that there might be something selfish in asking you to continue the work of my own life."

For a while, then, they heard only the sound of the soft western wind among the maple boughs where, now and then, some vivid leaf let go its hold and fell.

"Then, Uncle," Holdfast answered at length, rising from his chair, "here is something that will be hard for you."

Occum faced slowly round. His look, as he gazed up into the dark, compassionate eyes of the younger man, was that of one who squares himself against a blow.

"I will give up all that I have known and loved," said Holdfast, speaking even more quietly than before. "I will give my life to our people. I will strive as you have done to save them from the white man's cruelty, deceit, and greed. But the white man's religion, which you call Christianity, I will not preach. There must be something better."

Without turning his pain-stricken gaze from Holdfast's face Occum moved from the window to his chair and, as though he felt all at once weary with age, sat down.

"I am sorry, Uncle, to hurt you," Holdfast went on, "but this thing had to be said."

"Yes. Yes, my boy. If true, it had to be said. And I do not complain. I only ask what it means. Have you lost all the faith I taught you? Has the Colonel . . . ?"

"Ah, but it's not Colonel Chester. He's as good a man as most Christians. I mean, he's far better than most. But haven't you ever thought of this, that it was Christians who did that slaughter at Fort Griswold? It was a Christian who drove Colonel Ledyard's sword through his body after he had surrendered. Yes, and it was a band of earnest Christians who burned four hundred Pequots at Mystic without one tear of pity. They took a Christian preacher along to ask God's blessing upon their deed; and after it was done they knelt down among the smoldering huts and blackened bodies to return thanks to their Christian God. Do you ever think of these things?"

"Of course, Holdfast!—even though I strive to forget them, and to forgive. But have I not taught you that it is one of life's darkest mysteries, how the best is tangled with the worst?"

"And do you ever recall that even here, in the old days, while the Reverend Fitch was preaching to the Mohegans his Christian brothers were filching our hunting-grounds from us when they had made us drunk?"

"Often. But 'Vengeance is mine; I will repay, saith the Lord.'"

"He takes a long time, Preacher, and often He seems to forget. However, I am not thinking of vengeance today but of what I have to do. And one thing I cannot do is to stand before those who once owned all this land and ask them to accept the religion of those who took it from them, by force and lies and fraud and the poison of strong drink."

Occum glanced up, involuntarily, at the empty rum-bottle that hung from the ceiling. "Do promise me, at least," he groaned, "that you will leave drink alone."

"I do. I will."

"And women, Holdfast. For there will be many . . ."

"Preacher, a man who is in love with one woman is in no danger from many."

A faint smile, perhaps of triumph, hovered for a moment on the elder man's lips and was gone.

"And as for religion," Holdfast continued, "of course I shall never forget what you have taught me out of the Bible. I only mean that I must have something deeper, stronger, harder, and more Indian than what I have seen in most people who call themselves Christian."

"You will find it in the Bible itself, my boy," Occum replied, laying his hand on the Book.

"At any rate, I must find it in an Indian way, and live it as an Indian can."

"That is well said," said Occum. "And now I must try to answer the question you have brought me."

From a drawer of the reading-desk he brought out a tobacco-pipe of reddish stone, filled it with powdery leaves from a bag of buck-skin, and then sat for several minutes quietly smoking. Holdfast also, having returned to his chair, sat in perfect silence.

"Whether you call yourself a Christian or by some other name is perhaps no great matter," said Occum at length, speaking still in Mohegan. "And certainly I shall not insist that you continue my work if you continue that of my Master. His work you will do. I know it. Since your childhood, like Jonathan Edwards of Podunk, you have rested in the Everlasting Arms, you have listened for the Voice that says: 'Be still, and know that I am God.' You seek an eternal meaning in every event of time. You live in two worlds at once. To your comrades, white and red, you are a good companion, a tireless runner, a mighty wrestler. Only I, perhaps, know what has been your highest companionship. I know the real race you are running, and with whom you have wrestled, for what a prize, like Jacob in the night. If this be not Christian still it is certainly religious, and it is the most Indian thing about you.

"For we Indians, Holdfast, as you know already, are more religious by nature than the white man. Though our faults are many, and our sins are scarlet, we do not make a mock of things holy.—I remember at this moment a man whom I knew in England, a clergyman, a gentleman of high birth and admirable abilities, whose life was ruined by a deeply ingrained irreverence. Unusual charm he had, wide knowledge of the world, but within he was hollow if not false. I mention that old friend now—Parson Blandison, he called himself—because he was so utterly different in his hard worldliness from what you are and will be. He was unstable as water, and you are like Cochegan Rock. He pretended to religious beliefs which he did not really hold, but you hold deep and strong beliefs which few of your closest friends even suspect.

"Now you say, as I knew you would, that you will give your life to our people. But who and where are they? Even you can remember the time when, from the windows of this house, we could count the smokes of eighty wigwams rising among the trees. Today there are not thirty fires in the village. Nearly half our number have gone, by my counsel, to live among the Oneidas. Twenty of our young men have died in this war, slain by the soldiers of the King who once took my hand and called me his friend. We are dwindling like snow in May. We can no longer hunt unhindered in the forest that was our birthright. We have scarcely ground for growing the two holy plants, tobacco and maize, that we gave to the white man. Every year the palefaces crowd more closely about us, and in spite of all our care we have not held to the ancient ways. The blood of Uncas we have indeed kept pure, but certain of our young women . . ."

"Yes, Uncle. I know."

"Well then, Holdfast, while thinking deeply for years about these things I have come to understand that when we say 'our people' we should mean far more than our own small tribe. Though we are dying, not all of our kind need die also. We are hundreds at most, but of American Indians there are hundreds of thousands. Their campfires twinkle at night like the stars of a fallen sky from the Hudson to the western sea. And I say that all this multitude, speaking many diverse tongues and worshiping the Great Spirit under a thousand mistaken names, are 'our people.' "

Holdfast gazed at his uncle with glowing eyes.

"I think also what a heroic life there would be, what a gigantic wrestling-match for the man who should go forth to save these people of ours, with God's help, from the ruin that threatens them all. For they too will die, like us, unless they are saved in your time. Their lands will be filched away like ours, and the treaties they sign in good faith will be broken by force and guile, even as Connecticut has broken her treaties with us. They too will be blamed and punished for crimes the white man himself has committed. I do not say that they will always be without fault. Perhaps they will often need to be saved not only from the whites but also from their own violence and childishness. Yet all just men know that they are more sinned against than sinning. And they must have help. They must have a Moses to lead them out of captivity into their own land."

Occum's voice rang in the little room. He was leaning forward over the great Bible now as though in a pulpit. Holdfast, deeply stirred, went again to the window and stared out into the flame of the maples.

"I myself," Occum continued, "have led nearly half our number across the Hudson. But that was not enough. Already they are overtaken there by the cunning and vice and greed of their white neighbors. I see now, when nearing the end of my strength, that nothing can be done for Mohegans which is not equally done for all Indians. And I see also that the task requires not only a younger man but one far stronger, wiser, and in all ways better than I am."

"If such a man could be found," said Holdfast, "how would he do his work?"

Occum rose to his feet and stood with his left hand, slightly trembling, on the Bible. "I have in my thought," he said, "and I often think

103

I see in what is coming, a man who, having been deepened by pain and heightened by sacrifice, has taken into his heart the woe of his entire people. The love he once felt for a few, or for one, reaches out to embrace a great many. Though quiet, self-forgetful, and a friend of the humblest, he is no common man but a hero sprung from a royal line. In strength of brawn and thew he will find no equal. He can bear long hunger and thirst, fatigue and cold and loneliness. He is at home in the forest at midnight and in the heart of the storm. So close he lives to the earth, our mother, that one might think him kin to the boulder, cousin to the bear, and a child of the giant oak. He has learned the secrets of wind and weather, of birds and beasts, and of the stars. There lies in his mind a map of all the trails he has traveled from coast to coast of our country. His fame outruns his feet."

Occum paused a moment, moved a step or two nearer to Holdfast, and then went on to speak with increasing intensity of utterance: "But what would all this be worth if the man had no purpose, no goal, no task? Others may think him an aimless wanderer, but he knows the end of his journey. Never for a day, for an hour, during all the years in which he will take apparent defeat for his wages, does he forget the work he has set himself to do. He can bide his time like the sleeping bear, but also he can strike like the thunder-bolt. He can be silent as the midnight sky, yet at need he can command strange powers of speech. Having loved one woman well, and given her up, he holds himself a virgin from all women until his task is done. And always he will be seeking something better, more lofty and deep and true, than the religion that was taught him in his childhood. If such a thing can exist then I do believe he will find it."

Holdfast drew a deep breath. His eyes, though fixed upon those of the elder man, seemed to be gazing far away. "Uncle," said he, "how could one who knows little and has done nothing make himself ready for such a life?"

The Preacher smiled. "Speaking as a Christian," he answered, "I can only say that he must be born again."

"And for me that would mean?"

The reply was not ready. After relighting his pipe Occum paced thoughtfully up and down the room, looked out of the window, took a book or two from the shelves and put them back again. At length he said: "There is an Indian way, and, I think, a very old one, which is said to create in a man a clean heart and renew a right spirit within him. The little that I know of it was told me years ago, in the country

104

of the Five Nations, by a wise old chieftain, an Iroquois, who had gone many campfires toward the setting sun. He had been among powerful tribes that dwell to the west of the forest, riding horses and hunting the buffalo. These tribes, he said, have taken no taint of the white man. It would seem that they have deeper thoughts than ours, that they know more than we of divine things, and that their heathen beliefs are in some ways lofty and noble."

"So I also have heard."

"And this Iroquois told me that no young Indian of the great plains is thought to be yet a man, he is not fully a member of his tribe, nor can he know what his manhood's work is to be, until he has had his vision."

"His vision?"

"That, as I remember, is what they call it, using of course their different tongue—although I do not clearly understand what they may mean. It may be what a Christian means when he speaks of an answer to prayer, for these Indians believe it is a converse with the Great Spirit. And they say that before his vision can come the young man must live alone, fasting, in some high place, for long days and nights. He must not return to the campfires of his tribe until his vision is granted. He must be quite willing to die while waiting, if that is what the gods require."

Holdfast's eyes were shining with strong excitement as he suddenly stepped across the room to the Bible on the reading-desk. He turned to the Gospel of St. Mark and began to read: "And immediately the spirit driveth him into the wilderness. And he was there in the wilderness forty days, tempted of Satan, and was with the wild beasts; and the angels ministered unto him."

"Yes," said Occum. "It is indeed strangely, wonderfully like. And then again in the Old Testament—where is it?"

He turned the pages for a moment.—"Oh, yes. In First Kings, the nineteenth chapter. It says of Elijah: 'And he arose, and did eat and drink, and went in the strength of that meat forty days and forty nights unto Horeb the Mount of God. And he came thither unto a cave, and lodged there; and, behold, the word of the Lord came to him, and he said to him, What doest thou here, Elijah?' "

"I remember," said Holdfast. "And a little farther on there is something about a great wind and an earthquake."

"Yes. Here it is: 'And, behold, the Lord passed by, and a great and strong wind rent the mountains, and brake in pieces the rocks before

105

the Lord; but the Lord was not in the wind: and after the wind an earthquake; but the Lord was not in the earthquake: and after the earthquake a fire; but the Lord was not in the fire: and after the fire a still small voice."

"And Moses too," said Holdfast, "spent forty days and nights on the Mount of God before he had his vision."

"Of course.—How can I have failed for so long to see that our Indian way is the way of Elijah, of Moses, and of my Master, also!"

Holdfast closed the book. All the pain and perplexity was gone from his eyes as he looked down at the Preacher. "Thanks, Uncle," he said, holding out his hand. "This is hard, and Indian. It takes a man down close to death to find out how he shall live. This is what I shall do."

"My boy, it is your way."

"And what does the young Indian do when he knows that the Spirit is near?"

"I was told that he strips off his clothing and stands naked before his Maker. He has with him only his tobacco-pipe, packed and lighted, for a burnt offering."

"And then speaks the still small voice?"

"So that Iroquois chieftain told me."

"But do you believe him?"

After only a moment of hesitation Occum said in a firm clear voice: "I believe that the Lord reveals himself in many ways, and that in all ways and forever He is the Lord."

PRISONER FOR LIFE

To John Reid, riding up among the neighbors on the road to Norwich, there came a mood of sheer inexplicable joy. Perhaps it was the beauty of the autumnal morning, he thought, that made him so long to shout, sing, laugh aloud, or, at least, to spur his veteran plowhorse into a brisker pace. As yet there had been no frost, and the maples lining the rutted way, all gently and continuously astir in a steady western breeze, were trooping their gala colors. Myriads of wild asters, pure white, pale blue, and ultramarine, clustered and jostled against the gray stone walls of Quaker Hill to watch the company go by. At

Oxoboxo Brook a multitude of gentians crowded the sunny bank to make a pool of azure. The hickories towering above Fort Hill at Mohegan Village were pyres of yellow flame. Across Trading Cove a score of slender wineglass elms were reflected in the water of the Thames as sheets of beaten gold. For mile after mile both sides of the way were glorious with the bannered hosts of the golden-rod parading up the hills and down the dales as though to a music of elfin trumpets.

Glancing now and then at his companions, and listening, Reid tried to make out whether they too felt the exultation, the confidence of impending triumph, that was making his own heart beat so fast. Apparently they did not. With impassive faces and only an occasional remark about the excellence of the weather, they plodded stolidly forward on foot and horseback, in carts and wagons, under arches of leafy splendor which would have made an emperor's pomp look tawdry. And he felt that they must be hiding deep in themselves, holding it firmly down, the same ecstasy that sang in his heart. Surely they could not be so purblind as they pretended to the scarlet of the maples that shook him like a shout of trumpets marching by.

Clearly, however, they were no longer oppressed by the horror of the recent massacre and fire. In spite of what they might still be thinking and feeling against Old England, they did not hold him off. At Raymond's Tavern, at Bradford's, and again at Houghton's, he moved freely among the groups on the lawns and shared their gossip of crops and weather, of deaths and births and weddings, of ships that were home from sea and ships that had gone down.

Reid kept his gladness to himself—for one reason, because there lurked at the heart of it a kind of fear. Just the same mood of unreasoning ecstasy, he could not forget, had swept through him, less than six weeks ago, at dawn of the most dreadful day he had ever lived through.—What comparable ruin might this present joy portend?

He thrust that question away, and his thoughts went back to Holdfast and Rebecca. So deeply they were rooted in this beautiful land, like an oak and a birch that had grown in the same wild earth, the same rain and sunshine! Their love, Reid felt, was as natural and foreordained as the contrasting harmonies between the spun-gold of the birch and the oak tree's manly scarlet.—On his own account he had never hoped for much, and now, drawn forth into the beauty of the day, profoundly grateful for the goodness of his life, he murmured again the words of the Psalmist: "My cup runneth over!"

He caught only glimpses of Rebecca as she rode far ahead or behind, or stood on the edge of the crowd talking with girls and women he did not know. And Holdfast was nowhere to be seen. He had started with the company at Four Winds Farm but had disappeared on the way—perhaps at Mohegan Village.

Near the end of the road Mother Chester beckoned to Reid from the wagon-seat. Her kind voice was trembling a little as she leaned over and spoke. For once, she did not meet his eye.

"Ye know, John, Holdfast couldn't come along with us today.—Ye didn't? Wal, anyhow, he ain't hyar. An' so I'd take it kindly iffen ye'd go 'long with Becky an' some o' her friends up to that old Injun buryin'-ground whar they allus go for butternuts this time o' year."

"Why, certainly," said Reid, "but . . ."

"It's kinder wild an' steep up thar, with mebbe a few rattlers on the ledges; an' so, Holdfast not bein' 'long, why, wal, I thought mebbe . . ."

Reid, to conceal his surprise, pretended to be having some difficulty with his horse. Then he said: "Why, of course! Only, should I ask her permission, or . . . or is it understood?"

He flushed at the wild conjecture that Rebecca might already know about this arrangement—might perhaps even have made it herself.

But Mother Chester dodged the implied inquiry. "Oh," she quavered, with a smile that could not hide the tears in her eyes, "I guess ye better jest happen 'long. They won't send yeh away.—That is, I mean, Becky, she won't."

And indeed she did not. More than once, while crossing the narrow foot-bridge above the Yantic, she reached out to him her slender nut-brown hand. Yet he knew her to be as nimble and sure-footed as a deer.

Farther on, after they had begun to climb the slope of Uncas Ravine, there came a breathless moment when her hand lay, no heavier than a robin's feather, on his arm. He clenched his fists.

And higher up, while they were resting and listening to the roar of the falls, there was another moment, longer, even more bewildering, when she smiled into his eyes as though she knew all that he did and then something more, something quite mysterious and altogether wonderful. He bit his lips, resolving again with all the might of his manhood to speak no word. Holdfast, the Colonel, Mother Chester—he

108

clung to their names as though to the futtock-shrouds in the blast of a gale.

She glanced away, and threw a pebble down the slope.

But was it not unfair that the blue of her eyes should be deeper today, that the hue of her cheeks and throat should be warmer, and that the very tint of the oak-leaves should match with her wind-blown hair? The spirit of the place where they sat was in league with the girl's young beauty to puzzle his brain, to tamper with his will, and to break down all his resolves. The breeze ruffling up from the gorge embraced her delicately rounded body. The leaves wove a flickering nimbus about her head. With all his strength he strove not to look at her, but his strength was not enough. She was strong as a taut bowline. She was clean as dew of the dawn. She was lighted by inward fire like the cardinal-flower in the shine down there by the water.

"If you are rested now," he said, "—shall we go on?"

She flushed at his words, but rose at once and went on ahead of him. Although the slope was now much steeper, she did not reach him her hand again, or look back, or pause for breath. Apparently he had insulted her, as he had so often done, in some way he did not understand. Once more, and for the thousandth time, he had to reflect that his long years at sea had kept him ignorant of women.

And yet at the top of the long ravine she did not join her companions scattered here and there in the yellow woods, the young men high in the trees and the girls gathering nuts into sacks and baskets. Some of them called from the distance, but she made no reply. As though escaping into a world of her own dream, she walked slowly to a small enclosure near the head of the ravine, a place heavily shaded by tall oaks, and sat down there on the ground among the waving golden-rod and asters.

Reid felt that he ought not to intrude upon her meditations; and yet, surely, although she had deliberately walked away from him, he was still her companion. Her mother had asked him to stay with her and—and protect her from "rattlers."

He sauntered awkwardly toward the enclosure, within which some twelve or fifteen reddish headstones, rudely cut and inscribed, stood up among the flowers. This, he realized, must be that Indian burying ground which Mother Chester had mentioned. The stately woods about it and the roar of the falls below made a nobly appropriate setting, but in itself the graveyard was a forlorn little place, long neglected, and apparently all but forgotten.

109

Having nothing better to do, Reid began to decipher the names of the dead—Uncas, Owaneco, Attawanhood, Mamohet, Joquib, and the rest. On the most carefully worked stone of them all he read:

Sacred to the Memry of Jon
athan Uncas Gaines Grate
Grandson to Uncas Grand
Saychem of Mohegan He Dyed
in Battel A.D. 1764 at De
Troyt beeyng thenne Cheef
tan of his Trybe gretter
Love hath no Man than that
He give his Lyf for his Frend.

Reid turned to Rebecca. "Is this," said he, "the grave of Holdfast's father?"

"Not his grave. They buried him where he died. But Father thought he should have a headstone here with his people."

"And were all these others, buried here, descendants of Uncas?"

"Of course. Descendants of the first Uncas, 'King of the Mohegans.' He was a great man in his time—but cruel."

"How do you mean?"

Rebecca reflected for a moment before she said: "Well, perhaps he wasn't so very cruel, after all. Once he ate the shoulder of his dead enemy, Miantonomoh, and said it was the sweetest food he had ever eaten; but white men go far beyond that."

"I suppose they do; but—are you thinking of what happened at Fort Griswold?"

"No, I'm not! And you know it."

The words were so violently uttered that he could only stammer "I'm afraid I—I don't understand."

But now she had sprung to her feet and stood facing him. Her hair had fallen loose from its ribbon, her mouth was twitching, and in the eyes that had looked so deeply into his not ten minutes ago he saw only a flame of anger. Once again, as on that morning of the New London fire, she seemed possessed by a fury.

"What is it to shoot men down in cold blood?" she cried. "At worst, they die. And what is it to eat their dead bodies? They do not suffer. But cruelty is torture of the living. It breaks the heart, and then—oh, then it pretends not to understand what it has done!"

"Yes; but of what, of whom . . . ?"

"Of you! You! You!—As if you did not know!"

110

"Of me? But, Miss Chester . . ."

"Oh! 'Miss Chester'! After we've been living under the same roof, sitting by the same table . . . And then never to speak to me, never to listen when I speak, never to look in my direction, always to remember what I said that day, and to make me *see* that you remember!"

Daunted by the girl's flaming beauty even more than by her anger, he could only cry: "Never speak? Never look at you? I don't know what you mean."

"Then you must be the stupidest man on earth. You must be even more stupid than cruel. Yes; I think you are."

"Of course I know that I must be very stupid, but . . ."

"Oh, you are! But it's worse than that. There's not a red or a black servant in my father's house that you haven't been kinder to than to me."

"Do you say that I haven't been kind?"

"Not even polite. I say, sir, that you have been brutal."

Bewildered though he was, Reid almost broke into laughter. His heart, in spite of all, was gay as he said: "Brutal to you? Unkind to you? And remembering evil against you?—If your mother should swear it to me I could not believe that you have ever knowingly done wrong. And I could not hurt you in any way if it were to save my life."

"Words! Words!" she answered, bitterly. "But all these months of silence speak louder on the other side."

"Rebecca, let me speak now. And if you must think me a liar, at least hear the lie to the end."

At the sound of her Christian name, and hearing herself for the first time commanded by him, she stood suddenly silent. Her body was trembling.

"You have given me the right," he went on, "to tell you now, at last. If I never see you again I shall be glad to have told you."

"Never see . . ." Her hands fluttered up to her throat.

"But even then I shall see you always as I do now. If I never again hear your real voice, it will be in what the wind says to the pine and in what the ocean will whisper."

Her lips were parted. She stood very still.

"You say I have not looked at you, or listened when you have spoken. But I do not need to look to see you everywhere. When you are not in it, the house is empty. When you are there, it is home. And your voice, when you speak, comes from inside my heart."

She took a step toward him. "Then why . . . why . . . ?" she breathed.

111

"Why, then, have I not spoken? Is that what you mean?"

She nodded.

"But surely—why need I say it? Because I am not a traitor, a thief. Because your father has trusted me. Because your mother has been like mine. Because you have all made an enemy into a guest and a friend."

"Is that all?"

"No. Most of all it has been that Holdfast—one of the noblest men alive, a man who has always loved you and whom you must love . . ."

"Oh, I do! I always have and I always shall; but . . ."

"Of course I know that, and so . . ."

"But he's like my brother!"

"And so how could I speak?" said Reid, seeming not to hear her. "How can I even now? But I'm going away. You will forget what I have said, and it will not matter."

"You're going away?"

"Of course. But the words I've longed to say have burned in me—while we walked to town and back, while we were rowing home from Groton, that time we watched the sunset from the hill."

And now again he saw in her eyes that same deeply penetrating gaze, as though she knew all that he did and something more. She was coming nearer.

"What are those words?" she asked, almost in a whisper.

"You know them. I love you, Rebecca."

The cheek that lay against his own was wet with tears, and yet the slender body in his arms was shaking with incomprehensible laughter. Probably he would never get to understand this girl.

"Oh!" she cried, and her voice rang under the arch of leaves like the cry of a bird. "A British prisoner!"

"Yes. And now a prisoner for life."

"For many lives," she softly answered. "For a thousand American years."

THREE COURSES

One might have thought that it was the Colonel who was going to be married. Against all opposition he carried through his plan to combine his daughter's wedding with the festival of Thanksgiving Day and

112

the celebration of victory in war. And he it was who insisted that in the inviting of guests there should be no discrimination along lines of political opinion.

"We'll show them pizen Tories," he had exclaimed with a thump on the table, "that now they're trounced we can't spare the time to go on a-hatin' 'em. We'll hev 'em in to dinner, the hull king-an'-bishop-worshippin' lot. We'll git the Robertsons an' Tom Leffingwell an' Ben Butler down from Norwich. Let 'em bring 'long their own forks iffen they can't feed with honest knives an' spoons. We'll send over to Lebanon arter Colonel Fitch an' fill 'im spang up to the wig. I'd invite the Reverent Sam Peters o' Hebron iffen he hadn't been rid out o' town on a rail an' gone back to England. Why, Mother, I'd ask Bishop Sam Seabury hisself iffen I knew whar he's a-hidin' out these days."

"Oh, John!"

"I would. I feel jest that neighborlike an' Christian. What the hell I care whether he buttons his collar fore or aft? He was brung up in Groton an' New London, wa'nt he?"

"Whar was Benedick Arnold brung up?"

"Hey? What's that?—Oh wal, Mother, I allus did say women was the most vindicative. But anyhow, let's give them Tories a dinner 'll bust their silk weskits right up the back."

More and more, as the days passed, the Colonel seemed to identify Rebecca's betrothal to John Reid with the glorious victory of the American Army at Yorktown, news of which was driving New England wild with joy. "We got to make these King's people unnerstand," he shouted one night, lying beside his wife in the turn-up bed, "that they're knocked down, rolled over, an' stamped on. Wal, an' best way o' doin' that is—marry 'em. What's all this 'bout Washington an' Lafayette capterin' eight thousan' men? Hell's hinges! That don't decide nothin'. But our gal has gone an' captered an' hawg-tied a British off'cer so's he'll never raise hand or foot 'thout her say-so; an' right now, b' God, is the time to let the world know it."

"Now John, don't ye start swarin' an' eggsite yerself so 's ye cain't sleep."

"Swarin'! Who's a-swarin'?—Say, Mother, iffen ye ever reely did hear me start in to swar onct . . ."

"Some other time, mebbe. But John, what ye want to hurry the weddin' so fer? 'T ain't only 'bout three weeks sence these children found out 'bout lovin' each other. Course I'd knowed it fer months, an' so 'd pore Holdfast, but—only three weeks!"

"Wal, an' 'bout three weeks more, iffen we don't git 'em married

113

come Thanksgivin', we'll hev a young bastard on our hands, I wouldn't wonder."

"Not but what I wouldn't enjoy that," sighed Mother Chester. "More 'speshly iffen 't war a boy."

"Me too. An' o' *course* he'll be a boy. Ye don't think I'd go to all this trouble jest fer a gal, do ye? Course, gals is good to hev while they last; but soon 's ye git 'em house-broke, so to speak, ye got to go an' give 'em away."

"I'm afraid we're goin' to lose Holdfast too, John."

"Yeah"—and the Colonel sighed.

"He says he'll leave on the night o the weddin'; an' the way ye're a-plannin' it that 'll be the night o' Thankgivin' Day."

"I know, Mother. Not much to be thankful fer thar. The lad's got some fool notion that one son in the house 'll be enough. Seems to think John Reid can take his place. Not in a thousan' year, he cain't. But we've had Holdfast a long time, Mother; an' now—wal, we can be thankful fer that."

For several minutes the Colonel heard his wife weeping softly. After a while she spoke again: "John, be ye awake?"

"Sartinly I'm awake. What's wrong now?"

"What 'bout the gal's clothes?"

"*What* gal's clothes?"

"Oh, ye ain't! Ye're sound asleep."

"I am *not!*"

"Wal then, Becky's, o' course. We cain't make 'em afore Thanksgivin'."

"Clothes!—Mother, how can a sensible woman talk 'bout *clothes* a serious time like this? Y' oughter know 't when a gal gits married clothes is eggzackly what she don't need none of."

"Wal, of all the ignernt men!" his wife exclaimed, flouncing over and turning her back to him.

" 'Ignernt'!" he chuckled. The bed shook with quiet laughter.

John Reid's suggestion that, to save trouble, they might have a civil wedding down in New London was over-ridden by the Colonel almost with violence. His daughter, he declared, was to be married like a Christian, and not by any snuffling lawyer. He averred, moreover, that during the war Christianity had almost died out in New London, where there had been no settled minister for years. Its Congregational Church, to which he still legally belonged, had always been hateful to him for what he considered its brutal treatment of the Rogerene Quakers—a local group of zealots among whom he had many friends and whom he respected for their courageous honesty if not for their opinions. Since the Reverend Mather Byles had fled to Boston years ago to escape the gentle arguments of the Rogerenes—and had there become a rank Tory —the Colonel had gone to church in Norwich when he went at all. So his father had done before him, largely for reasons of personal friendship with the Norwich minister, Dr. Benjamin Lord. Both father and son had been well aware, however, of the advantages they gained by affiliating with a church some nine miles away, which, of course, they could not be expected to attend very frequently.

Not a few of the Colonel's Quaker Hill neighbors, together with most of his numerous acquaintances among the inland Connecticut towns, believed that he had no "religion" whatever. By this they meant that he took far less interest than they in the soul's eternal destiny. Theological debate left him cold—or, at most, amused—while others grew hot. He had been known to break out into scornful laughter during an earnest discussion of free-will and predestination. Mother Chester recalled a painful occasion when, having been asked by a visiting minister whether he considered himself one of "the Lord's elect," he had replied that he rather hoped he was not, if the persons he knew who did so consider themselves were a fair sample. If young Pompey and the Widow Higginbotham were going to be saved, he had said, then he would consider the matter seriously; otherwise he was not interested.

In extenuation of such outbreaks the Colonel's friends could only point out that his whole life had been one of steady beneficence and loving-kindness. They well knew, however, that no salvation was to be expected on account of mere "good works," and that in matters of doctrine and dogma their friend was deplorably unsound. It was even whispered that he, like Israel Putnam, had doubts concerning the Trinity. This was what came of association, during the French War, with British officers who had read Voltaire. It was the result of roaming about the world in youth, associating with unbelievers. Therefore the Colonel's friends did not precisely blame him, but neither did they confidently expect that he would join his voice with theirs, throughout eternity, in hallelujahs and hosannas round the Great White Throne.

Although Colonel Chester shared these doubts concerning his spiritual destination, he felt sure that he knew a good preacher when he heard one. And he could give his unqualified approval only to Dr.

115

Lord, a man now almost ninety years old and nearly blind but still able to preach and pray with the eloquent sweetness of an angel.

"When a man's ben preachin' in the same town for sixty-five year," he pointed out to Reid, "an' has baptized an' married an' buried more folks than the town holds today, why that means suthin'. 'Mongst other things it means ye c'n drap off to sleep an' be sure he won't try to work off no new doctrines on ye onsuspectin'. Ye feel a confidence in 'im; that's how 't is. Now, I've heard every one o' Dr. Lord's sarmons—or parts of 'em anyhow—sev'ral times over, startin' in when I warn't no bigger 'n a pint o' cider; an' damn good sarmons they be, iffen I'm any jedge. What I mean, they ain't jest Sunday-go-to-meetin' sarmons, but they got sentiments in 'em the which a man c'n bite down an' chaw on when he's mendin' wall, drivin' oxen, scelpin' Injuns, or 'most any time."

"They last you through the week," said Reid.

"Oh, a year mebbe, like a bar'l o' good salt pork, so 's ye don't hev to go to church more 'n jest on Easter Sunday iffen y' ain't wasteful.—An' hyar's 'nother thing: Dr. Lord c'n pray prob'ly the longest prayers of any man in Connecticut—mebbe in all New England. Never knowed 'im not to turn the hour-glass at least once in a real full-dress Sunday-mornin' prayer, an' I dessay the Almighty ain't nuther. Course I s'pose most any preacher could keep it up that-away iffen he jest said same things over an' over like most on 'em, but the Reverent Lord's prayers allus has a lot o' news in 'em that mebbe a man wouldn't hear 'bout iffen he warn't a church-goer. 'Most 's good 's the *Connecticut Courant* they be in keepin' yeh up to the times—not to mention all the information Heaven must git out 'n 'em."

"They do you good in two worlds at once, then," suggested Reid.

"Yeah. An' that's allus good bus'ness, as Poor Richard says. But 'bout their bein' long, rec'leck one time I had a bet with Old Put whether his man over to Pomfret would pray 's long 's mine, come next Sunday. Wal sir, mine beat his'n thirteen minutes by the watch. Fack, sir. I got thirteen new clay pipes out'n that bet.—Wal now, ye cain't lay down on a man like that."

"No. Certainly not. Let's have him."

"An' then too, what's mebbe more to the p'int, when the Reverent Lord marries folks they know suthin's happened to 'em. Look at Mother an' me.—Wal, he done that to us!"

And now the famous Dr. Lord of Norwich was in mid-flight through

116

a grace before meat evidently meant as a special effort. A small and feeble man, yet of a noble presence, wearing an elaborate wig in the style of fifty years gone by, and clad in a long black coat, black knee-breeches, black woolen stockings and shoes with silver buckles, he stood by the hearth with his tremulous hands clasped before him and spoke to his God as to an old and valued friend. He had already been going, the Colonel calculated, for some ten minutes, so that Mother had been wise in not serving the main dishes until he was through.

"It is well known to thee, O Lord," the gravely sweet old voice was saying, "that by thine aid thy people have recently won a magnificent victory over the benighted soldiers of King George. The news of this victory reached Connecticut almost a month ago, but still our hearts are filled with gratitude and our mouths with hosannas unto the Lord of Hosts.

"We would name no names, O Lord, at this season of neighborly rejoicing, and yet we do pray, if there be still lingering among us any who yet hanker after the ways of the past, any stiff-necked and un-repentant Tories, that thou wilt make plain and smooth to them the paths that lead forth from this our land. Let them not tarry to perplex our councils. Let them await no more signal mark of thy divine purpose than that vouchsafed at Yorktown on the nineteenth of last month, when no less than eight thousand British troops, O Lord, laid down their dishonored arms.—And yet far better were it for us all if thou shouldst awaken in them before too late a sense of those American liberties which they would be leaving behind, together with a due respect for the authority of the Continental Congress.

"May such men learn a lesson, we pray, from the interesting occur-rence of this morning, on which thine unworthy servant has joined in holy wedlock the hand of thy beloved daughter Rebecca to that of John Reid, once a Leftenant in the Navy of King George. May this union of two young lives that began in hostile houses teach them, and teach us all, the prevailing power of that human love which dimly shadows forth the love divine."

Yes, thought the Colonel, the good doctor was in form this morning. He certainly was telling those Tories off in a way they would not soon forget.

"And now we earnestly pray for thy special blessing upon this marriage. Of John Reid we have seen but little, yet of him it may at least be said that he has recently resigned his commission in the

117

King's Navy. But Rebecca, his wife, we have known through all her few years. Most dear hath she ever been to this ageing heart, and lovely as a young birch tree in the rains of April. It seems but yesterday, Lord, that thy servant held her, weeping, in his arms at thy baptismal table. Yea, and to him it seems but a little longer ago that he baptized her mother, Mary, then herself an infant, and also her father, John, now the stalwart warm-hearted master of this hospitable house, who doth thy work with no less of a will because he knoweth it not. And if it be thy pleasure that this thy servant may yet baptize also a son of Rebecca, verily the cup of his happiness will overflow. Less and less may it be truly said of her that she is quick to anger, and ever more may it be known that she is faithful and true and good. Teach her, we pray, to submit her fiery and headstrong will—hitherto, it may be, too little restrained by her parents—to the will of her husband. May she live long, and prosper, and be justified in her children.

"Dear also, and more than dear, is the foster-son of this household. Lord, thou knowest our Holdfast well as a man mighty of limb and thew, framed like the giant sons of Anak of whom thou hast spoken in Holy Writ. Greatly excelling in manly sports, in the hunt, and in feats of battle, he has won for himself already, though still but a youth, a resounding fame throughout this region. We need not remind thee that he springs from the dark wild children of the forest, or that in his boyhood he learned their lore from Samson Occum, that wise and holy Mohegan who has toiled so long in thy vineyard and is one of this company today. Lord, we thank thee that in Holdfast Gaines thou hast made manifest unto us the invincible vigor, the courage, and the beauty of this young land. He is like an oak, rooted deep in American earth, that will some day lift up a hundred arms to the stars and scatter the seed of numberless generations. Deeply wise is he also, and still. He has listened long in the silence out of which cometh thy voice.

"We know not, Lord, how such wisdom and strength may fail; yet man looketh only upon the outward parts. And therefore if at this hour thou seest in him a sorrow for which even our love may not atone, do thou grant him a grandeur of heart according to his need. Though the beloved voices he has known grow faint now and cease, give him to hear the music of thine eternal quietness. May he learn that no deep devotion can ever go wholly astray. Let him cheerfully leave to others all comfort, ease, fame, worldly wealth, and even that boon of human companionship which those who never let go thy fatherly hand can do without. Do thou walk beside him among the mysterious moun-

118

tains, by distant and unknown rivers, and along the dim paths of the forest. Let him never be afraid for the terror by night nor for the arrow that flieth at noonday. Though a thousand shall fall at his side and ten thousand at his right hand, let not destruction come nigh him. Oh, prepare a table before him in the presence of thine enemies. And let him never forget that wherever he goes our thoughts will be with him, our trust, our pride, and our lifelong love."

The Colonel, who had expected to be amused, forgot to look at his watch when the company sat down at the long tables with a rattle of heels and dragging of benches. Something in what the good old man had said, and especially in that part about Holdfast, had made him want to blow his nose—if only his handkerchief had not been of the finest silk, just brought in by Captain Sam from his latest prize. And that about Rebecca probably having a son pretty soon was good, too. Thinking of this he grew cheerful again, forgot his nose, and managed to be gruff with Mother when she returned to the table, several minutes late, with her eyes redder than ever.

Dog-rat it, why couldn't the woman make up her mind whether she really was the happiest woman on earth, as she insisted, or the most miserable and broken-hearted? One minute she would be all smiles and chuckles, as a wife ought to be, and then the next he would find her crying into her apron out in the pantry, the barn, or the sarse-garden. Sun and rain, rain and sun—like an April day she was, a good planting day with a soft wind up off the Sound.

To be sure, she hadn't spent quite all her time, lately, just crying into aprons. Take this dinner, now, for fifty people, not to mention those who were eating out in the barn. Mother it was, mostly, who had prepared this three-course dinner, the like of which neither New London nor the purse-proud town of Norwich had ever seen or heard of. Four long tables full there were, and every table loaded until you couldn't see the cloth. The oaken boards were positively sagging with the first course of cod's head, pea soup, venison, roast chicken, boiled ham, baked beans, yokeage, beef collops, buttered parsnips, celery, jelly, half a dozen kinds of jam, seven kinds of pie, and marrow pudding—not to mention the pickles and preserves and spices and a few things to drink, mostly alcoholic.

Probably these Norwich and Lebanon Tories, these delicate fork-feeders, would think that was all. Well, in the second course they would have roasted partridge poults, one for each of them, shot by

119

Holdfast in Gungywamp, together with scalloped oysters, steamed clams, wild duck, roast squirrel and rabbit, suckling lamb, haricot, smelts, onions, three kinds of tarts, and stewed pippins. Also a small dish of pigeon-tongues. On the whole, then, a good solid second course, especially if you took on enough of the Jamaica rum and Madeira that Captain Sam had bought from the prize-ship *Ranger.*—A providing boy, that Sam Avery. In fact, he had provided the bridegroom.

And then the third course would be—ice-cream! Let the Tories think about that, and wonder. Yes, let them try to imagine how any man could afford such a dinner as this, for seventy people, after an eight-year war and eighteen taxes in one year and all they had done to the paper currency. Let John Reid think about it too, and ask himself whether he still thought Four Winds Farm was going bankrupt.

Anyhow, three courses; and a week it had taken to prepare them. For a solid week Mother had been up early and down late, planning, overseeing, directing, ordering the slaves and servants about, doing half the work herself, thinking where to get this baked and that broiled and something else boughten, sending out to ask whether Mr. Hillhouse would let them use his bake-oven and Mr. Sam Bolles his fire-place and the Hempsteads a few frying-pans. The fact was that Mother had done nearly everything.

Colonel Chester reached under the board-cloth and patted his wife on the knee.

And so she might perhaps be a little tired. That might be one reason for all this unseasonable weeping. Certainly there couldn't be any other reason for it—or none that a man would care to think about. The main thing was to take on plenty of food and drink so that one might be strong enough to talk to Holdfast, later.

Large as it was, the old kitchen could not hold fifty guests at dinner without some crowding. But the company was in too jovial a mood to mind that. The hubbub of voices drowned out the clatter of spoons and knives. The servants and slaves, padding swiftly up and down between the benches or darting out to the barn to serve the overflow, passed dishes, often dropped them, laughed and talked with the guests, and strove to keep the glasses and tankards full. In the corner by the ale-barrel a left-handed fiddler was adding all he could to the din.

Colonel Chester found a moment to rise from his chair and look, with deep satisfaction, about the room. Then he seized his silver tankard and raised it high.

120

"Friends an' neighbors!" he shouted, in the voice of a man going into battle, "hev ye all got summat to drink?"

He was answered by general laughter.

"Then hyar's the first toast, an' we'll make it bottoms up!"

"Bottoms up 't is, Colonel."

"All these years we good neighbors ben hatin' each other, stealin' pigs back an' forth, an' ridin' one 'nother on rails with tar an' feathers on. That so?"

"Yeah. Lots o' fun."

"Mebbe. But we've all heard the news from Yorkto'n. What that means is that ridin' on rails is out, at least for the time bein'. Means that all of us, Patriots an' Tories, b'long henceforth to the finest kentry on arth. Means King George can *keep* his tea an' we'll drink what we please, like friends, together."

"What's the toast, Colonel? We're dyin' o' thirst!"

"Let's drink to 'Mericans All!"

Fifty cups and goblets and leather bottles and tankards and delicate glasses went tilting up and upward. There followed a dozen hurrahs.

"Fill again," called Captain Sam from his end of the table, "an' drink to our friends the Tories. May they work as hard to make us good Americans as they fought to keep us all English."

When this had been duly honored there rose in his place a florid New Londoner whom the Colonel had pointed out to John Reid, less than three months ago, as a traitor who ought to be hanged from the nearest tree. He would have made a good subject for a portrait, Reid thought, standing there in the light of the western window with the snow sifting down outside, his glass held high and the costly lace dropping from his wrist. "If this is America," he said, "—this fireside, this ample board, this warmth of heart and hand, then who could wish to belong to any other country? Let us drink to the health of our hosts—the Chesters, the Reids, and Mr. Holdfast Gaines."

It was done, with noisy enthusiasm.

"And now to the bride alone! To Mrs. Rebecca Reid!" quavered Dr. Lord from the fireside. Again there was a general uproar while the servants and slaves moved about with jugs and bottles and decanters. Again there followed a general gurgling.

But when Holdfast quietly rose and stood, every voice was suddenly hushed. Every eye was fixed upon him. He made the room seem small. Clear to the ceiling he lifted his huge leather blackjack and

121

said: "In water brought from the Spring of King Uncas I drink to the bridegroom—once my enemy, for more than a year my friend, and now my brother, forever."

Mother Chester slipped from her stool and hurried out of the room.

Returning five minutes later, she found her husband deep in talk with Eleazer Fitch, the famous Tory from Lebanon who sat as guest of honor at his right hand.

"Yeah," the Colonel was saying. "Plenty o' folks useter ask that same question. Course round hyar they all know who Holdfast is well enough, but over in Hartford an' places like that they 'd stop an' stare at 'im on the street an' then try to dig it out o' me whar sech a man come from."

"No wonder."

"Wal, anyhow, they'd guess the damndest things. Useter ask me iffen *I* warn't his father! Ain't that so, Mother?—Wish to God I war."

"Oh, I didn't mean that, Colonel."

"No. Sartinly not. Ridic'lous.—But one thing I never did try to deny."

"And that was?"

"The story that I'd found 'im over in Gungywamp an' tuk 'im offen an old she b'ar."

"And why didn't you deny that?"

"Wal, take a look at 'im. Wouldn't ye say he's got b'ar's milk in 'im?"

"But, Colonel . . ."

"What do you say, Mother?"

"Oh, it don't sinnify whar Holdfast come from. God sent 'im, an' now he's a-goin' back agin."

Hearing the tone of sadness in Mrs. Chester's voice, Eleazer Fitch politely paused for a moment before he said: "This is a good Madeira you have here, Colonel."

"Ah, glad ye like it."

"Reminds me of a wine I've been gettin' for thirty years from a London firm. Fact is, I missed a consignment of it a few months ago while I was, ah, visitin' up in Canada."

"What ship?"

"The *Ranger*."

Colonel Chester slapped the board with his open hand. "*Ranger*, eh? With six bar'ls o' the best Madeira comin' from the West Indies?"

"Exactly."

"Then prob'ly ye ain't heard that while ye war 'visitin' up in Canada,' the *General Putnam* o' this hyar port tuk the *Ranger* off Montauk Point an' brought her in as a prize."

"No, sir. I have been out of touch with the local news lately."

"Jest so. Wal, this was to 'a' ben yer wine. I admire yer taste, sir—although I us'ly stick to ale an' winkum myself. Hev 'nother glass."

The two men rose, bowed, clicked glasses, and drank to each other with looks of mutual respect and liking.

"Now, sir," said Colonel Chester as they sat down again, "seems y' oughter hev suthin' to celebrate yer home-comin' with. The good folks o' Lebanon, Patriot an' Tory, they're goin' to be damn glad to see yeh back. They'll call on yeh by the scores an' hunderds an' ye'll want to offer 'em a cheerful glass. Wal then, thar's five o' them bar'ls ain't yet ben broached, an' iffen the snow holds out so's I can use the sledge they'll be over to yer place by this day week."

"Sir, Colonel Chester . . . Sir, we could make a grand country here with a few more men like you."

"Oh, God's sake, jest two o' my kind's one more 'n enough. *Two* more, mebbe.—But now, to git back. I ain't so damn pious as some o' my friends among these hyar Rogerenes round about, but I do b'lieve in a few things. Fack is, I see the hand o' the Lord in how John Reid was tuk captive by our Sam an' Holdfast an' brung up hyar so's to fall in love with my gal.—An' did ye know that John Reid s'rendered to Becky the very same day that Cornwallis did to Washington down to Yorkto'n?"

"I hadn't heard that, no."

"Wal, it's a fack," the Colonel went on, speaking with deep earnestness. "An' what I want to say is, the Lord must 'a' ben busy that day. He must 'a' ben a-layin' plans, do ye mark my words. 'Cause not even our Becky—an' she's got spunk enough when her mind's made up—could 'a' forced John Reid to speak up that day 'thout the help o' Divine Providence. Wal now, stands to reason the Lord don't work a miracle like that jest fer the fun o' the thing. Suthin's bound to come of it. You follow me?—A *boy* 'll come of it; that's what."

"I do hope so, Colonel."

"An' he'll be a boy—wal, I dunno; but he ain't a-goin' to be jest any ord'nary boy. He'll be a boy that can lick sixteen British redcoats jest by lookin' cross at 'em."

"I see. Quite a remarkable young man."

"Yeah. I'm a-goin' to hev Old Put baptize 'im with fire-water, an'

123

from the day he's born he won't be fed on nothin' but apple-jack and b'ar meat."

"H'm. Seems unnecessary to drink to the health of a boy like that, but yet I should like to wish him success in life."

"Ye mean, why not drink to 'im in 'nother glass o' your excellent Madeira?"

"Why not?" said Eleazer Fitch, filling his glass and rising.

THE FIRE-BAG

Perhaps it was not quite hospitable for them to be sitting at the fireside all by themselves, merely watching Holdfast. Yet surely they had earned a rest. The dancers out in the barn would not miss them for a while, and the left-handed fiddler had instructions that would last until well after midnight.

Rebecca had let it be known that if Holdfast was not going to dance, then neither would she. That remark had cast a certain chill. Now that she had the man she had wanted, after tearing everything to bits to get him, wasn't it just like a woman, the Colonel asked himself, for her to mope and pule because she couldn't have the other one also? He pulled hard at the slug that had lodged half-way up the long stem of his pipe, softly cursed it a little, and decided that Rebecca was not being fair to John.

"You folks rec'leck last year's Thanksgivin'?" he asked. "We only had our John with us then, 'stead of all these seventy. An' even he wa'n't much of a guest, but a'ready one of us."

"I 'member John's arm war in a sling that day," said Mother Chester.

"So 't war. But tonight he might be puttin' it to better use, iffen he wa'n't so damn shy—eh, John?—An' oh, how it snew that day!— though not so bad as tonight. I had to tie Holdfast down to keep 'im from goin' out to clear the road."

They listened to the cry of the wind at the door—a desolate sound, and yet somehow a comforting one. Nothing, they knew, had put out this fire during many a year.

For a while, staring at the fire, Reid wondered where his old ship, the *Amazon,* might be tossing tonight in the rain and sleet and snow. He seemed to see her stumbling back toward England, lonely, beaten, forlorn, sheeted with ice on ever rope and spar. A single lantern glimmering at her binnacle was the only light she bore. He imagined the groans of her labor as she plunged stem-down into the troughs and heavily wallowed up the rollers of the wind-angered sea. Little more than a year ago that ship had been his only home, but now, by the grace of God, he had the love, the warmth, the safety, the old established peace, of this fireside. The Colonel's wedding-gift of a small house in Norwich and the paper-mill on the Yantic had provided him with a home of his own and prospect of a competence in worldly goods. And he had—oh, wonder!—a wife. Beyond all hope, expectation, or even reason, Rebecca was his and not another's.

Reid found himself gazing with quickened curiosity at the man who deserved all this, who had held it within his grasp, and then had voluntarily given it up in favor of something else, unnamable, or at any rate unnamed. He saw that the Colonel and Mother Chester were also gazing at Holdfast, apparently forgetful of their many guests and even of the bride and groom. Rebecca too seemed to have forgotten that there was any one else in the room. For her also it was just now the only important thing in the world to watch, to study, and to memorize the face of the young man sitting in his great oaken chair on the other side of the hearth, now and then looking up with a light in his eyes that did not come from the fire but steadily sewing all the while at the woodchuck-skin he was making into a bag.

Massive his face was, as seen in the elvish firelight, and yet finely, even delicately drawn. Although by no means sad, it was already penciled by thought and pain. Framed and shadowed by the long black hair that fell to his shoulders, it somehow gave an effect of mystery. The high cheek-bones and aquiline nose showed the marks of race. It had the hue, Reid thought, of the coppery earth on Mamacoke Hill up the river, or that of the water in Bolles Wood Brook where it flowed all tawny and with glints of gold from the year-long shade of the hemlocks. In the eyes there was a visionary look as though they were more accustomed to gaze at distant horizons than at objects close at hand. The jaw was powerful and the mouth large and firm.

Force held in check, fire smoldering, power drawn back and held like a bow by the bow-string—that was what John Reid discerned in the face of his friend. He saw that it was a proud face, but with no hint of arrogance. He saw daring there, with a will to match it. No woman, however thoughtless, could ever forget such a face. A thoughtful man,

125

remembering it, would ask himself: "What have I missed in life, never known, or passed unheeding by?"

Here Reid paused, feeling that he was on the verge of extravagance. He reminded himself that Holdfast Gaines, born in a wigwam, with no great advantages of education or travel or acquaintance, was still a very young man, untried, unknown. Not only had he done little as yet but he seemed to have no ambition for money, fame, or power. Whatever might be his potentialities, there was still the question where he would find the motive to bring them into play. Apparently he had been happiest when hard at work on the farm—or, during recent weeks, in wandering rather aimlessly about the countryside, often with young Perthy. Reid felt obliged to ask himself, therefore, whether he had not somewhat over-estimated his friend, misled perhaps by an appearance of power which did not in fact go beyond the physical man.

Yet why, in that case, were they all watching him tonight with such fascinated attention? Had Dr. Lord been entirely wrong in all that he had said and implied about Holdfast in his prayer? Had Eleazer Fitch of Lebanon, that shrewd judge of men, been deceived? And why had it happened, at dinner, that when Holdfast stood up in his place, and before he had spoken a word, the whole noisy roomful fell suddenly still?

No doubt the young man's sheer bodily magnificence, if that was the right word, played its part. His amazing manly strength, and something about the look of him that made Reid wish there was a precise and unspoiled name for masculine beauty—such gifts were not to be ignored. Yet Holdfast's athletic prowess, though it had brought him local renown, would not explain the feeling that people had for him throughout Thames Valley and beyond. Something more than the body, more than deeds of any kind, was involved. People honored Holdfast for what he essentially was—or rather, perhaps, for what they believed he might become. In their feeling for him there was a faith, an expectation, not unlike that aroused by the thought of their young country.

At this point in his musing Reid recalled certain phrases of Dr. Lord's prayer: "In Holdfast Gaines thou hast made manifest the vigor, beauty, and daring of our young land. He is like an oak rooted deep in American earth that will some day hold up a hundred arms to the stars and scatter the seed of numberless generations."

Yes, there was the clue. Unconsciously, no doubt, but with an instinctive confidence, the people who knew Holdfast Gaines had chosen him as the incarnation of their patriotic hopes and wishes. In so doing they had satisfied the deep human need for heroes, and also for hero-worship, which the ancients had met by their tales about the beneficent Heracles and the wandering Odysseus. And to Reid it seemed right that this hero of the Thames Valley should belong to a race deeply wronged which yet, in some of its representatives at least, was still noble under the stroke. It was right and necessary, if Holdfast was to stand for America, that he should be strong beyond the needs of any present task, vague in purpose, dreamful, pulled two ways at once, a homeless lover of home, living on two levels, dowered with the strength of a giant to do the work of the soul. It was fitting that he should not be a famous and finished man, a Washington or a Franklin, but young, untried, uncertain, leaving much to surmise. Of his future one could only guess. Such a man, like such a country, might more than possibly fail. One only knew that his failure, if it should come, would be grand, noble, and tragic.

Thus, on the night when he was to bid his friend perhaps a final farewell, John Reid began to understand what that friend essentially was—or, at least, what he stood for. Though substantial and real enough as a physical presence, Holdfast Gaines was, to Reid as to many others, also a symbol. And that would be why the effect he made was both vivid and vague, like the effect of America upon a new-come stranger. That was why, though the image he left on the senses was startlingly clear, he remained to the mind somehow shadowy, hidden, withdrawn. As with America so with Holdfast, what he might become all but overpowered the realization of what he now was. Yet even now there was in him that fierce coupling of dynamic vigor with inveterate idealization, that conflict of fact and dream, which Reid had come to recognize as the quintessential American trait.

Let the beaten *Amazon* toss and plunge eastward, then, through the blinding storm, but to John Reid the benedict, safe and warm and dry beside this undying fire, the image of a lonely man walking westward into the American mystery, searching for the heart of that mystery as the key to his own nature, bidding a long and perhaps a final farewell to all he had known and loved, cheerfully giving up the good things that most men mainly cherish, bearing all that he owned in his two hands and on his back, facing danger and darkness and storm as his native element, confronting the terror that walks by night and the arrow that flieth at noonday, wandering among cloud-hung moun-

127

tains and by unknown rivers and along the intricate trails of old forests, sitting by solitary camp-fires winking alone in the waste like the single star that peers out from a skyful of cloud, drinking with the duck, couching with the deer, listening for his music to wolf's howl and scalp-dance, hearing instead of these beloved voices of the fireside and the timed talk of New London steeple only the rutting cry of the elk and the Homeric thunder of buffalo-hooves—that image, growing every moment clearer as Reid gazed at his friend, was by far the more compelling of the two.

And yet was not this conclusion also somewhat "enthusiastic," inclined to "extravagance," and therefore unworthy of a cool-headed Scot, son of the Laird of Glasgow, and scion of the Bruce?

In many a port and capital city of the Old World John Reid had met the cynics of his time who for some reason—could it be jealousy?—preferred to think of human grandeur as confined to the remote past, chiefly good for boys to read about in the pages of Plutarch. They could accept the assertion of Genesis that "there were giants in the earth in those days," but were convinced that the titan breed had died out long ago, leaving only little people, dwindled hearts and minds, ignoble motives, and an ever-lowering level of mediocrity. But Reid's years at sea had kept his heart young. They had shown him that the exceptional is quite as "real" as the ordinary. Let it be granted, he said to himself, that hardly one oak in a million lives beyond five hundred years; still, the Larrabee Oak in Gungywamp was twice that old. That tree was a fact. John Reid had seen it. And also he had seen Holdfast Gaines.

Reid heard the faint simmer and hiss of water-drops on the burning chestnut logs, and the howl of the wind down the chimney. The snow would pile in deep drifts tonight. Colonel Fitch, on the road to Lebanon, would be glad of his bear-skin coat. From the barn came a strain of music and the nasal chant of the fiddler calling figures.

Rebecca stirred in her chair. She did wish that someone would speak, but she would not be that one. Partly it was that she could not trust her voice.

The church clock in New London, heard in a lull of the wind, struck ten.

At length, having finished the last crude seam and knotted the end of the sinew, Holdfast rose from his chair, took a large quahog shell from the pocket of his hunting-coat, and stooped beside the hearth.

128

John Reid and the Colonel could see that the shell was half filled with a soft yellowish substance, apparently punk, which he was igniting with a coal from the fire.

"What ye got thar, lad?" asked the Colonel, unable to restain his curiosity.

"Oh, just a way of carrying fire that Samson Occum taught me."

He closed the shell, bound the two halves together with deer-sinew, and then put it into the bag of woodchuck-skin.

"Wal, what an idear! I never did see the like o' that all the years I fit the Injuns."

"Probably not," Holdfast agreed, slinging the bag from his belt. "You don't find out quite all there is to know about Indians, Father, just by killing them."

He had scarcely returned to his chair when the door of the kitchen was violently thrown open, letting in a blast from the north. Ten or a dozen red-skins, brandishing tomahawks and yelling, leapt into the room.

The two women rose, screaming, and fled to a far corner. John Reid, starting up, felt for the place where his sword-hilt used to be and then stood, white in the face, looking helplessly about for a weapon. The Colonel, instantly on his feet, reached the mantel in two strides and snatched down the queen's-arm musket.

"You red devils," he bellowed, "git the hell out o' my house afore I blow yer bleedin' hearts to quiverin' shreds!"

But five or six of them had already darted across the room, torn Rebecca from her mother's side, and were now dragging her back toward the open door. The Colonel, unable to fire, stood hesitant, the musket's muzzle shaking in his hands.

"Holdfast! Shut the door!" he yelled.

But Holdfast, still quietly seated, only looked up from the fire for a moment and then looked back again.

"Gi' me a tomahawk! A knife! An ax!" the Colonel cried.

John Reid seized a red-skin by the neck with his two hands, flung him to the floor, and reached for another.

"Wal, then, this 'll do!"—and the Colonel clubbed his musket, stumping toward the huddle of intruders by the door as fast as he could go. But before he got within striking range they had escaped, the door had slammed shut, and Rebecca was gone.

"Arter 'em, Leftenant! Ye c'n track 'em easy through the snow."

Reid threw a glance at Holdfast, but—and this was the most shocking thing of all—Holdfast only smiled, and shook his head. Reid reached for the loaded musket, but the Colonel drew it back. Then, with a gesture almost of despair, the young man tore the door open and ran into the night. Mother Chester ran after him.

The Colonel limped back to the hearth and hung the queen's-arm once more on its bracket. He was laughing a little, but silently, and there was no real merriment in his eyes.

"Cap'n Sam an' his Injun friends," said he, "done up that little job neat 's a pig's tail. Nary a hitch.—Not but what it moughtn't be summat hard on John Reid, though. White 's whey, he was."

"Yes; very hard on John Reid," answered Holdfast.

" 'Pears like he never did hear o' the old custom o' bride-stealin' back in the old kentry. That boy's got a lot to larn."

"M'm."

For half a minute the two men listened to the boisterous shouts and laughter that sounded, on gusts of wind, from the barn. In trying to fill his pipe the Colonel managed only to snap the stem. He threw the two fragments violently into the fire.

"Wal," he exploded, "why the hell cain't ye say suthin', lad?"

"Say what, Father?"

The elder man sighed as he took a fresh pipe from the pewter mug.

"Guess ye're right," he replied, clipping his words and using the coldest tone he could command. "Most of it's ben said a'ready; an' anyhow 't ain't a thing fer words. But thar 'll come days, an' long nights too, when we'd give our best eyeteeth fer a word with each other."

"That's so."

"Every time I lug in a load o' hay, take down a tree, or try to lift a heavy rock offen a stun-boat, I'll be thinkin': 'Whar the hell ye s'pose that damn loafer's got to by now?'"

"I'll be missing that work."

"Fact is, I'd git 'long better 'thout my own right arm than with you away."

"Don't make it too hard, Father."

The Colonel stooped, took a red coal from the fire, and lighted his pipe. He made as long a business of it as he could. Then he stood silent again, puffing vigorously. The deepened furrows of his face suggested that he was making a strong effort to comprehend something beyond the range of his experience.

130

"I useter think," said he at last, "that mebbe I c'd teach yeh a few things; but now fer years ye ben a-teachin' me.—Same time, hyar's suthin' ye mebbe don't know 'bout a b'ar."

"That so?" said Holdfast, looking up.

"Yeah. Damn quare thing 'bout a b'ar, that iffen ye don't hit 'im fust off whar he cain't git at it why then he'll take an lick the ha'r all round whar ye hit 'im an' plug up the hole.—Jever hear tell o' that?"

"No," said Holdfast, as though this apparently trifling information meant much to him.

"Wal, it's a thing ye got a right to know, seein' ye sartinly hev got some b'ar nater in yeh. I say, iffen ye give 'im time so's he c'n git away in the bresh, an' he c'n git at it, he'll plug it up with his tongue so's he won't bleed to death; an' then, b' God, he c'n run a thousan' mile."

"I see what you mean. And I'll remember it."

The Colonel turned suddenly half-way round, brought his elbows down hard on the mantel-piece, and hid his face between his hands. "Ah, dear God!" he groaned. "So *that's* all I c'n give yeh, all ye'll take —jest that damn-fool story! An' I've wanted for yeh to hev all I own in the world."

Holdfast rose from his chair and laid his hand across the Colonel's broad shoulders.

Eleven strokes sounded from the steeple in New London.

The two men were standing by the fire with their right hands locked when, a few minutes later, the kitchen door was flung open.

"Aha, John Reid," said the Colonel, speaking in his heartiest tones but with his back for the moment turned, "so ye got yer Becky back arter all."

"Yassah," sang out young Pompey, "Mistah John Reid he suhtinly did git 'er back. Allus 'cep' Massah Holefas', Ah nevah specs ter see no man fight so tur'ble hahd. Tored inter Cap'n Sam, he did, like a passel o' wildcats, so's puhty soon they wa'n't no mo' Injun feathahs lef' on 'im, an' hahdly no mo' paint."

"H'm. Sarved Cap'n Sam right fer breakin' the Leftenant's arm a year gone by."

"Oh, Holdfast," Rebecca called, "I have a letter for you."

"For me, Becky?"

"Yes; it's from Russell Bean. An old peddler gave it to me out in the barn. Said he'd brought it all the way from Tennessee."

131

"Tennessee!" exclaimed Mother Chester, incredulously. "Don't b'lieve they is sech a place. Not in 'Meriky."

"Read it out, my gal," the Colonel boomed.

"But it's for Holdfast."

"That means it's for all of us, Becky. Read it."

Going to the mantel, on which her father set a lighted candle, Rebecca untied the thongs that bound the awkward bundle, unrolled the soiled wrappings of deer-skin, and disclosed a smoothly planed slab of pine, one foot square, with awkward writing on both its sides.

"Wal!" said the Colonel. "It's a forest letter, d'reck from western woods! I bet Russ Bean made his own ink, like I useter, outen oak bark, an' wrote with a wild-goose quill.—How long ye s'pose it tuk a-comin'?"

"Over a year, the peddler said, Father. The writing isn't very good —and the spelling . . . !"

"That Russ Bean wa'n't never a scholard; but read on, Darter."

Rebecca shaded her eyes from the candle-flame with one hand. She looked frail, spirituelle, refined almost to the breaking-point by alternate joy and grief, as she stood there in the high-waisted wedding gown of pearly silk which had been her mother's. Holdfast was watching her so intently that it seemed doubtful whether he was even trying to make sense of the halting, hesitant syllables. And Rebecca herself missed the meaning more than once as she strove to decipher these words:

Deer Holefast how air ye I amm wel an hev ben. I leff Pensilvaynay sune as the gunne bizniz them parts was bad accownt all them duchmenn thar maiks tenn thousan poppgunns kant cill a mous lessen he crawlz doun the barill but all pore fules bys them cauz thay be shepe. I head onne furder west throo Cumberlan Gappe & amm nowe in betwix 2 set of montings on a mudy river cald Holsten an bildin flattbotes to flote us westward still thar hant ben nary whitt mann heer moren 12 yere butt now fillin upp an I sez Gif me Elbo Rume lik Dan Boon an west for me Holefas. Wee hant got no tru karpinteers so bild ower botes lik cabins bote bildin is a rippin traide so I quitte bildin riffles for a spel an turn karpinteer an howe the gals an young Injun squawz do stare when histin a 40 foote logge in plais withowt nuther man layin a hand too her thay wd lik yow to Holefas cum onn owt heer. Sune we shal be reddy flote west nyne men an Cap Robbertson wente over land to ffrennsh lick to bild cabinz last yere we shal taike thr famblys by rivvers holsten an tenessea an hoape tha gott thar butt hev nott yit heerd. Kernel Donelsone is leedin owr partie an I stear his bote aventure U owt too sea his gal Raichell what a gal Holefas what a gal. Evvere yrs to commande

132

dere Holefas an pleeze to gif my best regars to all the gude fokes atte 4 wins farme an speshuly Rebeka an hoapin shee is missus Holefas Gaynes buy now well must clos yrs afecktionaly

Russell Bean.

PS. Holefast cum onn owt heer this kentry nedes a man lik yow.

"H'm! Who ever see the beat o that!" the Colonel exclaimed as Rebecca handed him the strange wooden letter. He held it at arm's length for a moment, squinted at it with far-sighted eyes, and passed it on to Holdfast.

"Must be three year now sence that Russ Bean come hyar," said Mother Chester to Reid. "Jest a boy he war then, for all his traipsin' round with the gals; but my stars, what a scallywag!"

"He come hyar, John," the Colonel added, "to git some good Connecticut iron for his rifle-locks. Course his fambly, way back, come from Bean Hill, up Norwich way. Rec'leck ridin' all the way to Sal'sb'ry with 'im, arter iron. Tuk us a week out an' back. An' every time we come to a tavern he'd fall in love with the gal at the bar."

"An' she with him, I wouldn't wonder," put in Mother Chester. "'Cause he sartinly was a boy mighty easy to look at.—But I s'pose he's all growed up by now."

"Whar's that he says he's a-goin', Becky?" the Colonel asked.

"He said something about French Lick, I think it was, on a river called Tennessee."

"Iffen thar be sech a river, which I don't b'lieve," said Mother Chester, firmly, with a swift glance at Holdfast.

"Oh, I dunno, Mother," her husband replied in a tone of tolerant laughter. "It's an all-fired big kentry we got hyar, once ye git walkin' out into her. Thar's room in 'Meriky for all kinds o' places, with the dang'dest names to 'em. Rec'leck when I was out with Old Put back in sixty-four an' we came to Detroit, why, thinks I, this must be the end o' the kentry; but right thar I talked with a man had ben clar to the Miss'sip', an' he said no man oughter pertend he'd ever seen a real river 'til he'd sot eyes on that 'n. Yeah; an' said the Injuns told him the Miss'sip' wa'n't half-way 'crost."

"Ah, well, Father, out thar in the bresh they'll tell you anythin' comes in their noddles. Anyhow, River Thames is good enough fer me."

"I like it too," the Colonel agreed. "I ben round the world with George Anson an' I ben to Detroit with Israel Putnam, but I like our little old Thames whar I was borned and brung up best of all. Same

133

time"—and here he also shot a glance at Holdfast—"iffen I war a young man, or even as old 's I be but with two good laigs, I bet I'd go an' find out how big that other river is, an' likewise what lays t'other side. Rufe Putnam—that's the cousin of Old Put, John—he's ben out thar. So's Moses Cleaveland o' Canterbury. So's Moses Austin o' Durham. Grand kentry they all say 't is, with black 'arth ten foot deep an' nary a rock in a day's travel. An' thar's a man up Stafford way, fergit his name—oh, yeah, Peter Pond, that's it—claims he's figgered how to go from Detroit spang to P'cific Ocean by water. Think o' that, now. 'Northwest Passage,' he calls it.—An' o' course we know how John Ledyard o' Groton is allus a-talkin'."

"That John Ledyard," opined Mother Chester, "ain't too strong in the haid."

"Wal, mebbe not, but thar's suthin' to 't. An' what we got to 'member, it's all Connecticut, 'cordin' to the Charter from King Charles."

"Thought we'd kinder ben a-gittin' rid o' kings," said his wife.

"Ain't ben a-gittin' rid o' nothin' kings ever guv us! An' oh, how I'd like to go see how much 't is!"

Again the Colonel glanced under his bushy gray brows at Holdfast— not, to be sure, as though he were advancing an argument but rather as one who confirms and applauds a decision already made. That much he could still do for Holdfast. For his wife he might at least postpone a final thunderstorm, coming after so many a shower, of tears. Furthermore, it would do John Reid no harm to be reminded that Holdfast was by no means slinking away as a rejected suitor, but was going forth of his own free will to see the wonders of the earth.—Thus it was for the common good, including his own, that the Colonel went on talking of cool and distant matters, striving to hold their thoughts away from the past, the future, and the merciless ticking of the clock.

"Connecticut," he continued, "she gotter send somebody, an' he better be the best she has. 'Cause why? 'Cause iffen he ain't, then he won't last long. They got varmints in them western parts—not jest now an' then a b'ar or a catamount, mebbe, but—wal—critters o' the damn'dest kinds. Hear tell they got unicorns out thar, like the one I see on the State House up to Boston. Allus did wonder whar that beast come from. An' Injuns? Oh me, oh my! Make these hyar Pequots of ourn look like suckin' lambs. Call theirselves Chockters an' Cherrakies—suthin' like that. Anyhow, every man of 'em is a real blood-an'-thirsty scelper."

"The dirty beasts!" Mother Chester exclaimed, with a shudder. "That scelpin' gives me the grue."

Her husband smiled indulgently. "Yeah," he said, "see how ye mean, Mother. 'T ain't comf'table. Same time, it makes things more int'restin' like, scelpin' does. Kinder stirs yeh up, more 'n jest settin' round hyar listenin' how long the Reverent Lord c'n pray."

"Not but what one o' his prayers mought do 'em a heap o' good!"

"No. True 'nough. But, Mother, you women don't git it. Ye cain't unnerstand how 't is with a man—how he gits to longin', times, jest to step out an' far away from all the fine-lady fuss an' feathers.—Scelpin'? What's scelpin' 'mount to, long-side o' what the Ladies Aid S'iety c'n do to yer rep'tation at one sewin'-bee? They go in to kill, the ladies do; but scelpers, they jest wanter lift yer ha'r—an' iffen ye die arter, wal, it's yer own look-out."

Yes, Mother was laughing, though perhaps not very heartily. And then she said: "All right, John; ye say women don't unnerstand. Wal, s'pose ye take an' tell us how 't is with men."

The Colonel looked at her sharply, trying to see whether he had really succeeded beyond his hope or whether she was merely pretending to be absorbed in his talk so as to spare him the full weight of the blow about to fall. Deciding to give her the benefit of the doubt, he replied: "I c'n tell yeh how 't war with a boy, iffen that 'll do any good."

"It mought," said his wife, as though she did not know what was coming.

"Wal, the boy I'm thinkin' 'bout, he was born in thisheer house, an' he loved the place—house an' barns, field an' paster, medder an' wood-lot—like the youngest angels must fall in love with heaven. Git it, Mother? Ye say Four Winds Farm is good 'nough fer you, an' that 'ar boy felt same way. Same time—an' hyar's suthin' even I don't unnerstan'—he felt jest the offset. Times he'd go down to Winthrop Cove with his dad an' mebbe go aboard a sloop jest in from the Indies or parts beyond an' talk with the sailors thar—some on 'em not much older 'n he war—'bout whar they ben an' what seen an' done in them furren kentries. Anyhow, when he got 'long 'bout twelve or fifteen year old he couldn't stand it no longer, an' axed his dad could he go to sea. Course his dad was a man o' sense, an' said 'yes.' Then thisheer boy tuk his best friend with 'im—a Mohegan boy he war by name o' Jon'than Uncas Gaines, an' them two sailed to England with a friend o' the boy's dad an' were sicker 'n hell most o' the v'y'ge an' half-starved the rest, an' so tarnation homesick the hull o' the time they wished they war daid, an', to make a long story short, had a grand an' glorious time."

135

"Humph! Sounds like it!"

"Hear me out, Mother. Ye mought larn suthin'.—Wal, thar in England them two boys found Com'dore George Anson o' the *Centurion* was jest fittin' out for a cruise ag'in' the Spaniard down 'long the coast o' South 'Meriky, an' right thar they forgot all 'bout bein' homesick. Anyhow, they signed up with 'im an' went along. They chased the Spaniard down past River Plate an' round Cape Horn an' up an' acrost the P'cific Ocean. Arter some two year they caught him out somers in the Phil'pine Islands an' tuk away all his gold an' come back home t'other way round—'cause the world *is* round like an apple, ez I've told yeh many's the time, Mother, an' ye never will b'lieve me."

"Did those two boys from New London git any o' the gold, John?"

"Not a pennyworth. But that ain't the p'int."

"What did they git, then?"

"Manhood, that's what. They went away boys, an' come back men.—'Sides that, they'd ben round the world, which is mebbe the only way o' makin' sure that home is the best place of all."

Mother Chester still seemed to be really interested. "An' now tell us 'bout men, John," said she.

"Oh—an' I s'pose you mean real he-male 'Merikins. Wal, they come 'long into fresh kentry, kinder take a shine to it thar, chop down all the trees, kill off all the Injuns, clar the fields and plow an' plant 'em, build the houses an' barns an' schools, beget a few thousan' childern, an' then they up an' say: 'Aw, let's git the hell out o' hyar! We cain't stand this place no longer! It smells bad!'"

"But how 'bout the women, John?"

"The women? They say 'Naw; let's set hyar a spell longer. Let's jest set an' listen how long the Reverent Lord c'n pray."

"Dear! Dear! It don't seem right, arter the men 've ben to the trouble o' begettin' all them childern.—But then what happens?"

"The women stay whar they be, an' all the old battered hulks with game laigs they stay with 'em an' build up tame little woman-towns like Norwich an' Hartford to keep 'em in."

"What ye mean, 'woman-towns'?"

"Towns whar all the old she-cats snoop an' sneer an' ask how much money so-an'-so's got an' who his granfer was an' why don't he eat with a fork. A woman-town is whar folks jest set like a hen on an addled egg an' keep what they got, forgettin' how to dream. They git to thinkin', these old she-cats, that dreamers are fools. Their faces grow hard an' their hearts grow cold, an' they mostly turn into Tories."

136

"S'pose ye never did hear oł an old *he*-cat, did ye, John?"

"Naw. All cats turn she-male when they git old, an' so do old towns too. That's why a real man has to walk away into the wind an' snow, back to the wild things that kill clean an' suddent.—My God, don't I know? Hain't I done it a score o' times when I had two good laigs— tuk my musket an' horn an' walked out o' New London into God's weather?"

"But ye allus did come back."

"Why, sartin sure! I don't hold wi' them that only jest keep on a-wanderin'. They're s'archin' fer a cold Wilderness Stone that mebbe ain't thar, an' all the while their own hearthstone with the old fire on it is kep' warm fer 'em night an' day.—Yeah, an' 'sides the fire on the hearth thar 'll be a candle kep' burnin' every night an' all the night in the window-place, too."

Mother Chester's face suddenly crumpled. "Oh, John," she cried, "I know ye done yer best, but I cain't bear it! You can talk all you want 'bout scelpers an' wilderness stones an' she-cats, but it's lonesome, that candle, an' they ain't no sense to 't, an' . . ."

She stopped there because her husband, after a swift glance at the clock, had risen from his chair and laid his hand gently on her shoulder. "Mother," he said, "d' ye 'member that tale our Holdfast was readin' out to us, a while back, 'bout the big man 'mongst the little people? Gunniver, wa'n't it? No, Gulliver, that's the name. Anyhow, the little folk tied 'im down with sewin' thread or some sech she-male thing. He c'd 'a' picked up a good ten of 'em in one fist an' dashed their damn heads off; but they tied 'im down jest same, whilst he was asleep. Most pitiful tale I ever did hear.—Wal now, that's what you an' me ain't a-goin' to do. We won't tie our Holdfast down."

In a lull of the wind there came from the barn a burst of laughter and a lilt of "The Girl I Left Behind Me." A dog was whimpering out- side the door. The great clock in New London's steeple began to speak, turning the days that had been into the days to come. Everyone in the kitchen counted the deep slow strokes, from one to twelve.

Holdfast's hands convulsed into fists. His face changed. The look in his eyes as they swept round the little group was no longer distant and dreamy. He rose, twitched his belt a notch tighter, and took a long stride toward "Mischief-Maker" and the haversack standing in the corner.

But Mother Chester, already on her feet, rushed between him and the door. "Holdfast!" she cried, "whar ye goin'?"

137

"To Mohegan Village, Mother—for tonight."

"But it's midnight! It's tar'ble cold, an' snowin' hard! Hear the wind!"

"Mother," he said, one arm about her waist, "you know about this. You agreed to it, months ago."

"But now it's . . . Ye comin' back hyar?"

"Sometime, yes."

"Oh, 'sometime'!—I cain't bear it."

"Now, Mother"—it was the Colonel's voice—"I guess we'll hev to. 'Member ye never bore this boy; an' all the pains ye mought 'a' had doin' it, wal, we can bear 'em now, together.—'Cause right now he's a-gittin' borned agin."

"But how 'bout Perthy?"

"He's up at the Village. He wants to go with me. Samson Occum agrees. We'll take the dog along."

"Why not leave 'em both with us? We c'n take better care of 'em."

"No," the Colonel again cut in. "Danged iffen we're a-goin' to hev any more boys round thisheer house—allus 'ceptin' what nater pervides. Nor dogs nuther. Jest tear yer heart out, dogs an' boys do."

He laughed, ruefully, and drew his wife to his side.

Holdfast looked round the room. "Goodbye to you all," said he.

John Reid came across from the fire and shook his hand, saying nothing. Mother Chester, even the Colonel, could speak no final word.

But Rebecca?

She was still standing by the hearth with her left arm resting on the mantel, her hand shading her face.

"Goodbye, Becky." The words sounded like a deep-toned bell in the hush of the room.

She dropped her hand and looked at him. For a long moment they stood thus. Then he turned, slowly, toward the door.

But before he crossed the sill her hands were on his shoulder, drawing him back and down. Still she could not speak. She kissed him on both cheeks and on the brow.

He did not return her kisses. "Be happy always," he said. "Goodbye. And remember!"

Then, hastening to the door, they saw him stride away. Mysterious and dim he looked to them out there, half-hidden among the whirling flakes, and not as one they had known for so long and cherished. He was singing as he strode, some marching-tune. Behind him the little

138

yellow dog, hurrying to catch up, anxious, whimpering, floundered through the snow.

They saw him reach down and lift the dog and take him inside his hunting-coat.

After that there was only darkness and the cry of the storm.

BOOK TWO

WESTERN WATERS

*Can a man take fire in his bosom, and
his clothes not be burned?*

PROVERBS VI, 27

CARRYING WEIGHT

(April, 1788)

At the crest of a low hill looking out over Salisbury, North Carolina, Russell Bean brought his pack-train to a jingling halt and let the animals crop the young shoots of flowering dogwood and azalea growing beside the trace. They had come eight miles since dawn, and had earned a rest.

As seen from this hill-top, Salisbury was a sightly town, with its two wide roads of red clay meeting at right angles, its court-house, jail, tavern, store, and almost a hundred houses, most of them built of sawn timber. For some reason the townsfolk had taken to planting little trees at the roadside. To Russell Bean, a child of the forest, it seemed a queer thing to be bringing trees back into the very place from which they had been so recently, and with so much toil and trouble, expelled.

He was rather fond of towns, at any rate for brief visits, and he liked this town more than most. Charleston, from which he had just come, was of course the metropolis and mart of all the region, full of fine mansions and rich old men and ladies fit to knock your eyes out; but somehow he always felt more at his ease in Salisbury. For one thing, it was nearer to the mountains and the great woods. For another, he never came here without being pleasantly reminded of a visit he had paid, years ago, in the company of Colonel John Chester, to the not wholly dissimilar town of Salisbury in far-off Connecticut. And then, too, it was a good place for trade, with the pack-men climbing up to it from tide-water all year through and the long-hunters continually dropping down from the Blue Ridge beyond. Civilization, government, law and order, reached just this far. Everything to the west was wilderness.

One proof that Salisbury was civilized could be seen in its neat quarter-mile race-track on which, as a runner, Bean had won several prizes

143

and considerable local celebrity. A certain white girl lived here whom he had by no means forgotten, and he had no fear that she had forgotten him. He liked white girls, as he did white men's towns, for a change. And finally, Salisbury had a comfortable rambling old tavern, delightfully riotous, noisy, down-at-the-heel, and beloved by good companions far and near.

Too handsome to be interesting at all, an intelligent woman would have considered Russell Bean as he stood there leaning against the neck of his Seminole horse and gazing idly at the town below. No depth of thought and little refinement of feeling was evident in his reckless blue eyes. His features, though boldly chiseled, did not suggest strength or depth of character. Indeed it was not his face so much as the shape and poise of his entire body that drew the eye. Moderately tall, with broad shoulders, narrow hips, sinewy legs, and a deep chest, he approached perfection as a human animal.

One would have guessed that the young man was well aware of his physical advantages and meant to make the most of them. Somewhere in the woods this morning he must have doffed the frayed and muddied garments in which a pack-man struggled through swamps and briars and slept upon hemlock boughs beside the trace. His hunting-shirt of buck-skin, dyed a bright yellow and hanging almost to his knees, was drawn in at the waist by a broad belt of wampum, moon-white with vermilion streaks, and was decorated with fringes of red and black. He wore a necklace of wolves' teeth clasped by two turkey talons. His long leggings and moccasins were of elk-skin. When the skirts of his hunting-shirt blew aside one saw that he wore an Indian breech-clout instead of breeches. The carved handle of a tomahawk was thrust into his belt under one arm, and under the other glittered a broad-bladed hunting-knife. From his shoulders hung a brilliantly painted powder-horn and an embroidered shot-bag. His rifle-gun, entirely of his own manufacture, was almost exactly of his own height as he rested its butt beside him on the ground.

A close observer would have seen that Indian women, for one reason or another, had contributed much to Russell Bean's adornment. He was a walking exhibit of their handiwork.

In one hand he held a large hat, reddish in hue, with a loose brim. A breeze from the Blue Ridge was ruffling his curly blond hair. All expression left his face as he stood there for some ten minutes, resting, immobile, while the mocking-birds and cardinals tried to out-sing one another in the spinney close at hand. But at length he drew himself

144

erect and gazed more intently. He had seen that little groups of men and boys were gathering on the fresh grass inside the circular race-track just south of the town. Other groups were straggling in that direction. It grew clear that something of importance was going on down there from which the swiftest runner in North Carolina ought not to be absent.

Bean slipped the bridle of his horse over his left arm, shouldered his rifle, whistled to the boy at the rear of the train, and then, accompanied by the clank-a-tonk of many bells, started down hill toward Rowan House. He laid his left hand, as he went, on the bulge in his capacious hunting-shirt made by the paper-money he had taken recently, down at Charleston, for his east-bound load of furs, ginseng, and hickory-milk. Over a thousand dollars he still had left, after buying all his salt and iron and lead for the return journey. Oh that the good Lord would help him to lay a bet on himself, this day, against some green-horned Yankee who had not heard how he could run!

And as Bean went down the hill the woods were set ringing once more with a song that had lightened many a weary and lonesome mile:

"How wonderful, how glorious, how marvelous I am,
How wonderful it is to be me . . . !"

"What's up?" Bean asked the gate-keeper.

"Dang'dest go y' evah see. They's a quahteh-mile on, an' the fellah 't tuk the handicap—a god-awful big fellah he is, tew—he's a-carryin' weight. Hit's a fool business, 'peahs to me, but they's a mort o' money up.—Say, looky heah; hain't ye Russ Bean?"

"What iffen I be? I wanter see thisheer race. See you later."

The crowd was too nearly wild with excitement to resent the unceremonious vigor with which Bean elbowed his way to the front row. And it was no wonder. Several years of foot-racing had given him no preparation for what he thought he saw at his first glance up the track. A hundred yards away and still round the curve but thundering down at him at amazing speed there came a monster that looked at least nine feet tall—probably human because it ran on two legs, but tapering at the top into a head so small and so violently shaken that it seemed to have no relation to the body underneath. The face that went with this head was convulsed with laughter, and the arms, grotesquely high up and disproportionately small, were flailing like those of a jockey who lashes his mount up the home-stretch.

145

Ah, yes; one man was carrying another. He gripped the rider's legs and ran with his head down. Long black hair, shaken loose, hid his face. The rider turned, looked back, then bent and yelled in the ear of his mount. The runner's strides lengthened. He was pulling away from the slender youth with bristling reddish hair who ran, stripped to the belt, a few feet behind him. There were fifty yards left to go. The crowd was in a frenzy. Hats were thrown up. Three or four pistols were fired. Encouragement, advice, imprecations, and threats filled the air. A little yellow dog, barking furiously but quite unheard in the clamor, was coming full tilt at the forward man's heels. "That ain't fair!" said Bean to himself. "Might trip 'im up." But now there were only twenty yards—fifteen—ten, and the gaunt youth with the bristling hair was two strides behind. Bean could see in his eyes a strange hard glitter. He was gathering every muscle and nerve to hurl himself at the line.—But there was no hope for him, still a stride and a half behind and with so few feet to go. The man ahead plunged on with the momentum of a charging horse.

And yet—yes, there was a chance! The little dog, having taken a short-cut across the grassy enclosure, now darted directly into the path of the forward runner. For an instant he paused there, six feet from the finishing line, and turned to look up as though with a welcoming smile. To avoid crushing the dog the huge man broke his stride. The youth shot ahead.—The race was over.

While the crowd swarmed into the track Bean saw the losing runner help his badly shaken rider to the ground and then scoop up the yellow dog. He saw him rise to his full height, saw the arch of his heaving chest, saw him shake back his straight black hair, heard him laughing.

"Holdfast!" Bean yelled.

"Who's that calls me?" the words carried easily over the tumult.

Bean went through the crowd as though no one else were there.

"You—you, Russell Bean? Great God o' the Mountain! Where 'd you drop from?"

"All over. An' whar 'd ye?"

"The same."

The two men shook hands, heartily, and looked each other up and down.

"Git my wooden letter?" Bean asked.

"I certainly did."

"When?"

146

"Thanksgiving Day in Yorktown year."

"Ah. An' so ye come, jest like I tole yeh."

"I came right off, Russ. Started that same night."

"Wal! I be damned! Seems like ye tuk yer time on the road, though. Hit's seven year, a'most."

"I had a few odds and ends to do on the way."

"Sech ez?"

"Oh, exploring 'round. But mostly I've been raising this boy.— Perthy, this is my old friend Mr. Russell Bean. I've told you about him —all that's fit to tell."

Perthy regarded Bean's splendid attire with evident admiration.

"And Russ, this is Perthy. He's my pardner."

"Perthy, eh?—and Bean took the boy's hand. "But hell, Holdfast, I thunk hit war a man ye war a-totin'."

"And maybe you'll think so again when you see how he throws a knife. We don't know when his birthday is, but we guess he must be getting on toward twelve."

"H'm," Bean mused. "Son o' yourn?"

Holdfast laid his hand for a moment on the boy's blond hair and then drew one of his own black locks through his fingers. "Only in a manner of speaking," said he in a serious tone.

"Oh," Bean replied, embarrassed. "I didn't know. Thunk p'r'aps . . ."

"And this," Holdfast went on, holding up a bedraggled paw of the yellow dog still panting on his arm, "is General Washington. We call him 'Wash' for short."

"Becauth he never doth," explained Perthy, speaking for the first time.

"I see," Bean answered, smiling at the dog and then at the boy. "He's the tyke that lost the race for yeh."

"Ah, well, that's good for us. But here, speaking of races"—and Holdfast reached out for the shoulder of the young man with the bristle of hair—"I want you to meet a friend of mine. Mr. Russell Bean, Mr. Andrew Jackson."

The two shook hands, glancing swiftly and appraisingly into each other's eyes and then away.

"I saw yer race," Bean drawled with a hint of condescension.

"Wal?"

"Wal, seein' 's y' ax me, ye got good laigs but don't use 'em right. Ye don't use yer haid. Stride's too long. Ketch yer tail on fire, ye do.— Hain't nobody never tried to larn yeh how to run?"

147

"Hell, no," Jackson replied with a strained and humorless intensity. "All *I* know is, how to win races."

"With the help of a dog?" Bean pleasantly inquired.

Young Jackson's face flamed. A long scar on his brow went livid. He stepped instantly forward with his bare right shoulder hunched, right arm bent, and his fists clenched. "No, by the 'Tarnal," he snarled in Bean's face. "I don't need *no* help of a dog—nuther durin' a race nor yet arter, axin' questions."

For several quiet seconds Bean gazed into a most remarkable pair of eyes, exactly on a level with his own and about six inches away. Intensely blue they were—steel-blue and steel-hard. How suddenly this fury had leapt up in them!

This young man had a long narrow face, with a chin strangely elongated and sharp, like the prow of a plunging ship. Even while gazing so fixedly into his eyes Bean saw exactly where he could place a blow on that chin which would send its owner into oblivion for about half an hour. And yet . . .

The face was slightly pock-marked. Young as it was, it bore the marks of suffering. A long white scar, perhaps of a sword-cut, crossed the upper brow and was lost in the stack of hair. The vivid face, the furious eyes, the working mouth, the tinge of red in the hair, suggested a man on fire.

Russell Bean began to feel vaguely uneasy. He felt a stirring of respect, also, for this hungry-looking hard-bitten youth, mostly gristle and bone and freckles, whom he could have swept aside with his left hand. Yet of course it would by no means do for him to show any such feeling. His smile of faint amusement, mingled with boredom, was meant to suggest that he had encountered any number of young hot-heads of this sort and had quite easily destroyed them all.

But what to do? What to say? At least fifty men had gathered about, all of them happily expectant. Several conventional expressions, suitably insulting, had occurred to him. His fists were clenching. The only trouble was that he rather liked this young man—it was hard to say just why.

Then a large strong hand was gently laid on Bean's shoulder and another on Jackson's, so that, without any apparent exertion of force, the two found themselves standing at a more ceremonious distance apart.

"I'm right glad to see you two friends o' mine taking to each other this way," said Holdfast, smiling down at them both. "Of course I knew you would. And about the dog getting mixed up in the race, that was my fault. I should have kept him tied. But now, Mr. Jackson, I owe you a hundred dollars."

What was left of Jackson's anger suddenly turned in a new direction. "The hell you do!" he ground out. "I won't touch your dirty money."

"Oh yes, I think you will."

"I think I won't.—What the jedges say?"

"They say you won it, fair and square."

"Then damn the jedges. I'll run you ag'in for the same money."

"Not today. Perthy couldn't stand it. He's all shaken to a jelly now."

"Theemed like my head wath a-comin' off," reported that young man. "Onth more an' it would, too."

"Mean to say ye 're a-goin' to let me walk off with a hundred dollars jest 'cause a yaller dog runs in front o' yeh?"

"Something like that," Holdfast replied, thrusting a bundle of paper into the young man's breeches pocket. "Why, man, it's only Car'liny money. It's won't buy you more than a few drinks."

"Wal, then," said Jackson—and a swift appealing smile lighted up his face as he spoke—"we'll have them drinks down at Rowan House, tonight. Me an' some friends o' mine were a'ready a-thinkin' we ought to do somethin' 'bout my jest gittin' through with my law studies, so this here comes in handy. Gen'lemen, what say? Will you honor me as my guests? Landlord mixes a good flip."

"Many thanks," said Bean. "I'll admire to be thar, but I won't drink."

"You won't . . . what's that you say?"

"I won't drink."

Once more Andrew Jackson surveyed Russell Bean with care, taking particular notice of his gorgeous attire. There dawned in his eyes an expression of moral pain.

"You tryin' to come the gen'leman over me?" he snarled.

"No, no," laughed Holdfast. "He won't drink because he thinks it spoils his good looks. Better leave him out, Mr. Jackson; and me too. I *can* drink, but I don't."

After a brief effort to assimilate this information Jackson replied: "All the same, I'll be expectin' you two old maids down to Rowan House for five o'clock dinner. An' I'll tell landlord to make you a nice pot o' good hot gruel. Hope it won't kill yer kidneys."

He swaggered away through the crowd, throwing his butternut shirt over his sharp high shoulders as he went, and ramming the tail of it

149

inside his belt. The tangled thicket of his hair flopped up and down as he strode. Young, bitter, cocky, and completely unlicked he was, thought Holdfast and Bean, watching him.—And how an Indian would go after that tossing scalp!

The two friends were at first somewhat shy of each other as they strolled up and down the red roads of Salisbury, talking. They had been scarcely more than boys when they had last met, and now each of them was uncertain what sort of man the other had become.

Russell Bean tried to bridge the years by a compendious account of his adventures among women, red and white. Finding, however, that Holdfast made no return in kind, and did not even express an adequate appreciation of his narrative, he went on to a voluble discussion of his own prosperity as a pack-man, trader, and gun-smith unsurpassed. He named the handsome prices that rifles of his making had brought him, and the profits of a round-trip journey with his pack-train from Western Waters to the sea. Trade with such and such a tribe was good, he said, because that tribe was still "fresh," but with such and such another it was falling off on account of the excessive distribution of fire-water by his unscrupulous rivals. He was opposed to letting the Indians have any fire-water whatever, on the ground that it was bad for trade. He himself did not drink, for the same reason. It wasn't his looks at all that he had in mind, as Holdfast had absurdly suggested to that young red-head, but business. Some of his best customers among the tribes actually took a dislike to traders who drank too much themselves and tried to make the Indians do so. He knew a large town out in the Creek nation where the Miko had ordered his braves to knock the bottoms out of ten kegs of whisky sent to him as a gift by a French trader.

"You mean the town of Tukabahchee, I suppose," said Holdfast.

"Yeah.—But ye don't know that town, do ye, way out thar on Tallapoosa River?"

"I've lived there. That Miko is a friend of mine. What's more, I'd like to think I had something to do with their destroying that whisky."

"Tukabahchee Miko told me 't war an Injun called 'Sleepin' B'ar,' put 'em up to 't."

"Well, that's my name."

"Hey? What say?—Hev a keer, now, Holdfast. That Sleepin' B'ar he's a famous man. Injun gals, they cain't talk 'bout no man else, seemin'ly, an' I hear a power o' talk, one way an' 'nother, from Injun gals."

"Have you ever seen him?"

"Wal, no; cain't say 's I ever hev. An' that's a damn queer thing, too. Must 'a' slep' in sight o' Sleepin' B'ar's camp-fire a score o' times, an' often ben within a whoop an' a holler of 'im on the trace."

"That may be so, Russ, but you've known him for ten years and you're talking to him now. 'Sleeping Bear' is the name my father gave me. It's the only name I go by among the tribes."

"Great jumpin' jack-rabbits! Wal, but my good God, Holdfast . . . !"

"Take it easy, Russ. Sit down to it, if you want to. But, after all, why shouldn't I have that name?"

"Oh, I dunno, but . . . My good God!—But then, o' course I know a lot 'bout yeh, Holdfast. I know 'bout you all I know 'bout Sleepin' B'ar."

"A good deal of which may not be true."

"Yeah, they do lay it on, them gals. Only thing ye don't never ketch 'em sayin' is y' ever had nothin' to do with none of 'em. But anyhow, ye must be a trader."

"I have been; but Perthy and I made so much money at it that we lost interest."

"Hey? Anan? I don't git that."

"In a few years we made enough to keep us in all we want for the rest of our lives. We don't need much. Wherever we go nowadays the tribes want to take us in and adopt us.—And so we turned to more important things."

"Sech ez?"

But Holdfast's answer to this question was, in Bean's opinion, quite unsatisfactory. Something there was about learning many Indian languages, sitting at many council fires, and getting a map in the mind of all the criss-crossing deep-rutted trails that ran through forest and swamp from the Atlantic to the Mississippi.

At last Bean burst out: "Holdfast, hit don't make sense!"

"What doesn't, Russ?"

"The way ye're a-livin', a man the likes o' you, with all the chances ye got. My God, course I ain't a ridin' preacher; but hit's *wicked*, Holdfast, you wastin' yer life this-away. Hit's slack-twisted. Be damned iffen 't ain't."

Holdfast laughed aloud. "But didn't I tell you, Russ," said he, "that Perthy and I have enough?"

151

"Aw, 'enough'! What kinder way's that fer a man to talk? Y' oughter be gittin' rich hand over fist, like Robert Morris. Th' ain't nothin' c'd stop yeh. Ye're eddicated, ye don't drink much, an' all the tribes 'twix' hyar an' Father o' Waters think ye're prob'ly an Injun god. They'd work fer yeh like they never did work fer Alec McGillivray or even Jim Adair."

"But I don't want them to work for me. I want to work for them."

"My God!" Bean continued, hardly hearing. "Hain't ye larned yet ez thisheer's the land of opp'tun'ty? Don't ye know 'bout the rollin' stone an' the early worm? How ye gonter feel when ye git an ole man an' ye see other fellers not half so good ez you be wuth a thousan' times as much, an' you still walkin' the woods with a brat an' a yaller fice-dawg?—I bet y' ain't got so much as one square mile o' yer own on the ye'th."

"That's right, Russ, I haven't."

"Look at that, now. Ye ben out hyar seven, eight year, an' y' oughter salted down 'bout half o' the State o' Franklin.—But ye don't hev to go on this-away. All ye need is a leetle more spezzyrinctum—ain't that what the ole Colonel useter call it?—an' mebbe a pardner like me. Then, afore ye know it, ye won't hev jest only *enough;* ye'll hev a *plenty!*"

"I'll be glad to have you for a partner," said Holdfast, but in a tone so charged with negative meanings that Bean felt he had made no progress.

Several minutes went by in silence. At length Bean asked, obviously making a lunge at a topic he had long postponed, "An' how 'bout the folks at the farm?"

"Mother Chester and the Colonel? They're both well. That is, I saw Sam Avery down in Charleston two years ago and he said they were about as usual. The Colonel's game knee still troubles him, but that's about all."

Bean hesitated, then asked in a colorless tone: "Becky all right?"

"Yes, Becky keeps well too, so far's I've heard. She has a boy, Sam told me. They call him Samuel Chester Reid."

"Hold up thar! *Who* called him that?"

"His mother and father, naturally.—Rebecca and John Reid."

"John Reid?"

"That's so; he came after you left. Well, he used to be a Leftenant in the Royal Navy. Sam took him prisoner on the *Rebecca,* and we kept

152

him at the farm without exchanging him or taking ransom money. So now he's—what I told you, and my good friend."

Russell Bean's mouth hung open. Having long been convinced that Holdfast was in love with Rebecca Chester, and also that Holdfast could certainly take and have whatever woman he might desire, he made no sense of this.

"Becky married?" he stammered.

"I said she had a son."

"When 'd that happen?"

"She was married the day I left home."

"But how 'bout—how 'bout you?"

"I'm not married."

"Oh.—Ye don't wanter talk 'bout it, eh?"

"What more is there to say?"

The two men walked the length of the road in silence, with their heads bowed. Women peered out of the windows as they went by. Children at play by the roadside grew silent at their approach. At last Russell Bean summarized his reflections: "Wal, I'll be damned to ever-lastin' hell-fire!"

THE PLUMPER

"From the length o' time you're takin' on that punch, Landlord, a man might think it one o' the major works o' creation. And the evenin' and the mornin' made up the eighth day.—Zebulon, sixty-three, five."

It was a drawling, indolent, and not quite sober voice that spoke, yet clearly a cultivated one.

The landlord of Rowan House looked round from his crouching position beside the open fire, in which he was heating a long poker.

"Pahson," said he, "I s'pose ye hain't tuk notice o' these heah spots o' red on the floah an' walls, an' a few on the ceilin'."

"No," said a handsome bob-wigged gentleman lolling at the table, "can't say I have. One doesn't take special note of every spot in a foul old groggery like this."

"Huh! Groggery, eh? An' foul, is it? But jest same, them spots is reely kindah partic'lah. Them spots, iffen ye'd like ter know, is human goah, suh."

153

"So? Your own, I take it. Some guest o' yours, more energetic than I am, or else more prone to righteous indignation, has been giving you what you deserve, you old rascal. Thus the dwelling-place o' the wicked shall be brought to naught.—Balaam, fourteen, four."

The landlord's fat shoulders shook as he turned to the fire. "No," he chuckled, "them spots is from the last man what tried to make me hurry makin' a pitcher o' flip."

This witticism, evidently a favorite of the speaker's, was greeted with appropriate guffaws by most of the eight men seated round the table. A huge dinner of wild turkey and venison-pasties, considerably enlivened by brandy, metheglin, cider royal, and kill-devil rum, had induced a disposition to be pleased with any well-intentioned efforts for their entertainment. And now they were waiting for that noble potation for which Rowan House was famous as far away as Richmond or Charleston itself.

There was something mysterious and secret about the way their host mixed his ale, rum, eggs, and molasses. Eight pairs of eyes were fixed upon him as he stood up now before the fire and began pouring the dark creamy liquor from one huge pitcher into another, then back again. At last he stooped before the fire, took up the white-hot poker, and carried it with the full pitcher to the table. The iron, plunged into the liquor, hissed. A quick steam and a strong sweet fragrance arose. Eager hands reached out for the pitcher.

"By Gad, gen'lemen," called out the Parson, smacking his lips, "this really *is* a major work. It's well worth a long journey through forest and swamp. And the Lord tasted of it and behold it was very good.— Gamaliel thirteen, nine."

At this remark the oldest man in the room, a dignified figure in snuff-colored coat and breeches, wearing a tie-wig, rapped loudly on the table with the silver knob which took the place of his right hand.

"Parson Blandison, sir," said he, "why is it that you never quote Gospel correck, an' never name the right place for what you do try to quote? A man o' your cloth ought to know the passage you just now blasphemed ain't in Gamaliel. It's in Deuteronomy, sir."

"That so?" laughed the Parson, taking another delighted sip. "But even an old soldier and lawyer ought to know, Colonel Stokes, that Deuteronomy ain't in the Gospels. It's in Scripture, sir!"

The Colonel rapped again, with stern emphasis. "Objection not sustained!" he shouted. "Answer the question, sir."

"Moreover," the Parson continued, "the most brilliant legal mind in

154

all North Car'liny must be aware that *mis*quotin' Holy Writ ain't blasphemy. It's just an ami . . . just an amiable weakness, sir, the which I hope my friends will condone."

"Hooray!" shouted a gangling youth already half-seas-over. "Jest a . . . a . . . well, anyhow, jes' a weakness." And he shoved his empty glass in the general direction of the steaming pitcher.

"Tom Searcy," said Jackson, "ye're shot in the neck."

"Don' give damn. 'S a weakness."

The last rays of the sun were striking now through the small panes of the western windows, bringing into the long low room a strange romantic glow. They glittered on the bellies and stems of the wine-glasses, found the blue bulge of the flip-pitcher, and gilded the round of the silver knob that took the place of a hand. The faces of the diners were ruddied. The flames on the hearth grew pale. The drifting wafts of tobacco-smoke that floated above the table took on a few tints of a sunset sky. Thus into the midst of carousal there descended a moment of glory, unheralded, undeserved, like a gift of divine grace.

Parson Blandison, though feeling strongly that he ought to return thanks, was not sure to which of the two or three deities in whom he still believed his prayer should be addressed. Obviously it would not do to ignore the claims of the great god Bacchus, whose beneficent presence was unmistakable; but then neither should one forget Fortuna, goddess of luck, either now or at any other time. Could those two, working together, produce out of sun's rays and smoke and flushed faces such a wonder as this? Or was there, perchance, some Other, more potent than chance or strong drink, who gave these glimpses through heaven's gate?

He postponed that question, by no means for the first time, and drained the contents of his glass to retain the moment. But even Bacchus could not stay its flight. The rays of the sun grew dim, and the moment was gone. The landlord set lighted candles on the table.

The Parson found himself wishing that some good painter—say Thomas Gainsborough or Sir Joshua Reynolds—had been there. Then, at least, the world might have had a record. And yet he thought it probable that a really great painter such as Rembrandt would have used the golden glow and all the objects and faces it enriched merely as a background for the noble head and shoulders of the man with the coal-black hair who was sitting so quietly, drinking not at all, just across the table. Hitherto he had been sitting with his back to the light,

155

but now that the candles were brought on his eyes—those dark brown pools illumined by tiny camp-fires—were the Parson's center of attention.

A corpulent young man, expensively attired, leaned forward, wagging a persuasive finger. "Parson," he said, "that there 'amiable' an' 'condone' are damn hard words, but we know what you mean. 'Tain't blasphemy to misquote round here. You got the law on your side—an' we'll stand by yeh."

"Law's a damn dry subjick," said Searcy, gulping at his refilled glass.

"Thanks, Judge McNairy," the Parson answered, bowing from the waist. "The learned professions should stand together."

"H'ray! Larned perfessions!" from Searcy. "Le's have a toast."

The youthful judge joined in the cheer that followed. "Yes," said he, "an' that distinction you make about *mis*quotin' is worthy, if I may say so, Parson, of a fust-rate lawyer. It may save your neck some day."

"H'm. Yes, if I ever go up into Connecticut, where I hear they hang a man for what they call blasphemy."

"Not so far as I've ever heard," said the deep voice of the man across the table.

"Never heard of it?" asked the Parson. "You never read the Gen'ral Hist'ry of Connecticut by the Reverend Samuel Peters?"

"No. But I remember when the good people of Hebron, Connecticut, came near to riding the Reverend Peters out of town on a rail."

"What for?"

"Mostly for being a Tory, but also for being a liar."

"You don't say!"

"And after that he went home to England and wrote this book—a book, they say, which proved he was a liar anyhow."

"Ah. Lie upon lie and decept upon decept, eh?—Azazrael three, six."

"There he goes again," said Colonel Stokes indignantly.

"And how do you know so much," the Parson continued, "about Connecticut?"

"I come from there."

"Oh"—and the Parson took refuge behind his tall flip-glass.

"Hah, so you come from there, do you?" young McNairy shouted. "Well, a sensible thing to do. Why, sir, if half the things I hear up in Virginny are true, Connecticut can't be a fit place for dogs, sir!"

"Ah, come now," laughed Russell Bean with a wink at young Jackson, "hain't we heered 'nough fer one day 'bout dogs?"

Jackson lifted his glass, smiled at Bean, and drank.

"An' 'sides all that 'bout one gen'leman not callin' 'nother gen'leman a dog," spoke up a neatly dressed man of middle age from the far end of the table, "these heah Col'nies, or whatsomever we're a-goin' to call 'em, have got to larn not to call bad names."

"Heah! Heah! Verb sap!" agreed Colonel Stokes, banging his silver knob on the table-top. "That's how to tell the young men, Spruce McKay."

"Yes, an' *ole* men too," groaned Searcy, now supporting his head on his two fists. "It's *ole* men makes all the trouble, an' speshul the damn ole Tories."

"What you want to bring Tories up for?" snapped Colonel Stokes. "We're havin' a good time tonight. Let sleepin' dogs lie."

But Searcy was not to be deflected. "I say," he went on, "the gawd-fersaken Tories, which is a-drawrin' it mild."

"That's enough now, Tom Searcy," said Jackson, master of the feast. "No more of it."

Searcy looked about the table for a moment through half-open eyes. "Ver' well," said he with extreme dignity. "Andy says no more of it, an' so ver' well, ge'men. What mean say is if thar be any low-down ra'lesnake of a Tory has wormed his way inter our mi'st ternight—an' mind yeh I say if thar *be*—well then, what I say is, let 'im refleck I *don't* mean him."

"Heah! Heah! He don't mean him!" Colonel Stokes exclaimed in tones expressive of great relief.

"An' ge'men, more 'speshly I mean say if any no 'count Church of England pahson has ben run out somers up in Virginny an' squirmed his way in heah ternight to listen to our sober delib'rations . . ."

"Tom Searcy, you're drunk," called Spruce McKay. "You mean *libations,* don't you?"

"P'int well taken, yer Honor. 'Cep' c'rection. But what I mean to say is to say any sech mis'rable Tory pahson why don't let 'im think I 'lude to him, 'cause he's a frien' o' mine an' I love 'im like a brozzer. Is 'at distinck, ge'men? 'Nited we stan', 'gezzer we fall!"

"But don't let's fall just yet, Mr. Searcy," said the Parson. "I want a few more drinks before I join you under the table."

Several brotherly hands shoved the pitcher in his direction. He poured, drank, smiled benignly, leaning back in his chair with the look of a man completely at his ease. "The s'picion," he said, "was just crossin' my so-called mind that my honorable friend might be alludin' to me—and then I heard him deny it. I'm glad he did."

"Oh, so yer glad, eh?" sneered Searcy. "An' why ye so damn glad? I demand answer, sir."

"Because if my s'picion had grown that you were callin' me a runaway rattlesnake and a few other such things, I should have felt obliged to take you out in the court-yard and horse-whip you, sir, as you would then so richly have desarved."

"Oh! Is that so!"

"And that would have cost you pain, and it would have meant some exertion to me, and for us all it would have been a temp'ry int'ruption of a pleasant evenin'."

These remarks, perhaps especially because of an unmistakable charm and grace in the speaker, were well taken by every one except the young man to whom they were ostensibly addressed. Tom Searcy hardly heard them. He was falling asleep.

"I sometimes wish," the Parson continued, "that my friends would take me for what I am, good and bad, in the present, and cease to concern themselves unduly with what they suspect I may have been in the past."

Unmistakably this was interpreted as a plea for elementary justice. Murmurs of approval grew into cheers.

"If that's how you feel about it, Parson," McNairy called, "better come out to Western Waters with the rest of us. No man has a past out there—and not much of a present. Land o' the future, Western Waters is."

"Where's that, Judge McNairy?"

"Huh!" Bean interrupted. "Thunk everybody knew that. Western Waters is down Nolichucky, Holston, Tennessee, an' up the Cumberland, out t'other side o' Washin'ton County. 'Bout six hunnerd mile off Western Waters lays—an' them miles mostly up an' down."

"It sounds big and cool and fresh," the Parson answered, his blue eyes gleaming in the candle-light. "Any Indians out there?"

"Injuns! Hain't nothin' else but—or not hardly. Fresh Injuns they be, too. Reg'lar ole ha'r-lifters."

"H'm," the Parson mused, and refilled his flip-glass. "Well, gentlemen, I thank you for the inv'tation an' I admit that I'm int'rested. The very name 'Western Waters' has a kind of magic. It reminds me of the things my friend Thomas Gray, an English poet, used to tell me

158

about the Lake District in England—only, I think, we have no 'hair-lifters' there."

"You better go, Parson," said Colonel Stokes. "These young men 'll see ye get properly scalped. No trouble 'bout that."

"Kindly observe, sir, that I wear a wig. But in other respects the proposal suits my plans well enough."

"And they are?"

"For the present purpose I can indicate them s'ficiently, sir, in the el'quent words of your own American poet, Mr. Philip Freneau:

"From Europe's proud despotic shores
Hither the stranger takes his way,
And in our new-found world explores
A happier soil, a milder sway,
Where no proud despot holds him down,
No slaves insult him with a crown."

Uttered in suitably grandiloquent tones, these lines were greeted with loud applause, augmented by the banging of the silver knob on the table. Tom Searcy, half awakened, grumbled out: "Potery! Wha' hell wanter lug in potery nice comf'le li'l time like 'is?"

"You better come on out, Parson," urged McNairy. "You'd be the only preacher in ten thousan' square mile. Think o' the weddin's you could do!—that is, arter we git a few women. Think o' the fun'rals!—if and when we c'n find 'nough parts o' the dead bodies. And what's more to the point, how are we goin' to work up any law practice without somebody to maintain the sense o' sin?—The larned perfessions must stand together, as you said."

"Am I to understand I have the privilege of addressin' the future members of a firm of—ah—solicitors?"

"I don't know about 'solicitors,' but if you mean 'lawyers,' then that's right. Thar's Andy Jackson, future Districk 'Torney o' Western Waters. Thar's Tom Searcy, future Clark o' the Court if ever he sobers up. And here, sir, at your service, is John McNairy, future Judge o' the S'perior Court o' Nashville, for the want of a better."

"All of 'em graduates o' the Sal'sb'ry Law School, Messrs. Stokes and McKay," added the second of those gentlemen, bowing.

The Parson took a small note-book from his pocket and appeared to be making a calculation.—"And what," said he, "might be the average age of the members of this distinguished corporation?"

McKay, after a moment, replied: "It seems to work out to about twenty-two years."

Parson Blandison sighed as he returned his note-book to his pocket. "Eheu! fugaces labuntur anni!" he murmured.

"Hey?" said Jackson, looking up sharply.

"I was just tryin' to re'lize, sir, that I've lived in this wicked world almost as long as all three of you taken together."

Jackson stared at the speaker between narrowed eyelids for several seconds before he grated out the words: "Take me for a spring-chicken, do ye? Wal, don't fool yerself. I ben through more different kinds o' hell than ye'll ever see till arter ye die."

"That may be so, sir, although I hope not," the Parson gently replied. "But every heart knoweth its own bitterness.—Jehoshaphat, fifty, ten.— And so you are going out to Western Waters with your friends?"

"Hell, no! I got to work up a law practice this side o' Blue Ridge."

"Ah, now, Andy, we ben thinkin' 'bout that," said McNairy. "When we get out there we c'n get you appointed public pros'cutor or somethin'. Not much money in it, but prob'ly a lot o' land."

"Yes, land! An' what 'd that be wuth? Hear tell Gin'ral Washin'ton owns four hunnerd thousan' acres, an' they wouldn't bring 'im in 'nough to light his pipe."

"He better wait a while," Bean suggested. "Mought go up some."

"No," said Jackson. "I'd admire to git out thar like blazes, but I owe debts. I owe thisheer landlord hisself only God an' him knows how much."

"And yet," said the Reverend Blandison, pulling hard on his long-stemmed pipe, "I have obsarved, Mr. Jackson, that you ride an excellent hoss."

"Why not? A gen'leman has to."

"True. And on this hoss I have obsarved an admirable saddle."

"Nachally."

"Now it happens that I am in need of a good hoss an' saddle, as you are in need, you say, of money—with a small quantity of which I am at present provided."

"My hoss, sir, is not for sale."

"Ah, no, no; I quite understand. And a really excellent animal he is, at least for North Car'liny."

"He's from Virginny. Son o' Diomed."

"What's that? Diomed that won the Darby back in eighty?"

"That's right, sir."

"Aha! He smelleth the battle afar off.—Hobab seven, two."

"Cain't say. But if he does smell it he c'n git thar. I'll say that fer 'im."

The Parson drummed with his fingers on the table. The easy nonchalance of his attitude did not change, but in his face, and especially in his narrowed eyes, there was a new expression, speculative, calculating.

"Besides the money that I spoke of," said he, "I have in my pocket two small objects of bone, called dice."

Every man at the table except the slumbering Searcy looked up. Colonel Stokes, McKay, and McNairy edged forward on their chairs. Their eyes brightened. Holdfast Gaines and Russell Bean, the only quite sober persons in the room, glanced at each other with a smile. The landlord was rubbing his hands.

"Don't play 'im, Andy," whispered McNairy. "We don't know 'im well 'nough. We'll manage some other way."

But Jackson sat silent, frowning darkly at the candle flame. His two fists—thin, sinewy, freckled—showed bone-white knuckles on the table-top. He seemed to be listening, waiting for some inward voice.

At last, "What's my score come to, landlord?" said he in the tone of a man in a trance.

"Oh, not much. Not much, Mr. Jackson. Say 'bout—aw, say 'bout three hunnerd, countin' tonight."

"Three hunderd, eh? An' I got one hunderd.—Wal, fer gawsake don't set thar jest gawpin'! Git us 'nother pitcher o' flip, cain't ye?"

As the landlord waddled off to the tiny bar in the corner Parson Blandison took two diminutive dice from his waistcoat pocket and laid them on the table. "How shall we play?" said he.

"Dunno's I'll play 't all. That hoss is nigh 'bout the only good thing I got in the world."

"All the more reason, I should say"—and the Parson blew a languid smoke-ring toward the candle-flame—"for playing. If you win—well, then comes the chance o' Western Waters and all that may lie before you in that wide, new, wonderful country. You should consider, sir, that these two trifling bits o' senseless bone may lift you up out o' the afflictions of Egypt into a land flowing with milk and honey.—Manasseh, seventy, nine."

"Don't play 'im, Andy," McNairy whispered again.

"Ah, but he thinks I'm drunk, John. I ain't. Never git that-away.—

161

Or mebbe he thinks I think he is. I don't. If I play, I'll watch 'im like a hawk."

"I say, don't play 'im, Andy. You can see he's an old hand at this game."

"Not wishin' to interfere," said Spruce McKay, "an' sartinly not alludin' to any gentleman o' the present comp'ny, I just now call to mind a remark once made by a Gov'nor o' Virginny anent the clergy o' that same Old Dominion."

There was an expectant pause.

"Well, what he say 'bout 'em?" asked Colonel Stokes.

"He said—and, mind you, this is the Gov'nor speakin', not me—that the clergy o' Virginny were a pack o' scandalous fellows much given to vices an' riotous conduct not agreeable to their coats, and greatly addicted to swarin', drunkenness, and fightin'. If I remember rightly, he went on to speak about their surprisin' skill in games o' chance—a skill which made it impossible for ordinary players ever to beat 'em.—O' course all this was a long time ago, and no doubt there's been a great change, but—well, I thought I might just mention it."

"Merely, I suppose, as a contribution to historical knowledge," said the Parson.

"Precisely, sir. Merely that."

Jackson did not appear to be listening. His eyes were two slits of metallic glitter as he stared for ten still seconds straight into the candle-flame. Then all at once he spread his hands open on the table and his eyes grew large and strangely bright. He seemed on the verge of some painful kind of laughter as he cried out in a shrill, ringing voice: "By the 'Tarnal, I'll *beat* yeh, Parson!"

Sitting back in his chair, Parson Blandison studied the young man's flaming face with care. "What makes you so sure?" he finally asked.

"Why, hell, 'cause I *got* to win. Ye don't think I'd play if I wa'n't a-goin' to *win,* do ye?"—The words were shot from between clenched teeth.

The Parson bent forward and laid down his pipe. "Oh, as to that, let's see," he said. "What rules?"

"Let Colonel Stokes make the rules. I never played the dice afore,—an' I'll never play 'em ag'in."

"Yes, suppose you do, Colonel."

"Well, then, what I say is, the game o' hazard is too comp . . . too compelcated, considerin' our present happy condition. So s'pose—I say s'pose we jest say the highest number o' spots wins every throw, an' all ties played off as part o' the throws in which they occur."

"I accept those rules. They're like what the ancients called 'Venus and the Dog.'"

"Damn the ancients!" said Jackson. "How many throws, Colonel?"

"I'll say fifteen throws for each player, not countin' in the playing off o' ties."

"Agreed," said the Parson. "Fifteen throws to each, and stop there, however we stand."

Jackson nodded.

"These dice all right?"

Jackson picked them up, looked closely at them, shook them in his palm, and made an experimental throw or two. "We'll see," said he. "Depends how they behave."

"Now, first bet, gen'lemen," called out the Colonel, rapping hard.

"I lay one hunderd dollars 'g'inst one hunderd from the Parson," said Jackson.

Finding his bet accepted, he threw a five and an ace. The Parson threw eight spots.

"Your money," Jackson said, drawing a bundle of paper from his breeches pocket and tossing it over. "Now next, what ye offer 'g'inst my saddle?"

"Fifty dollars."

"Wuth more. But throw."

Parson Blandison threw a double six.

Jackson's thin-lipped mouth twitched in a nervous grin, showing his long, sharp, irregular teeth. His throw was a four and a three.

"Saddle's yourn," said he, brusquely. "So now we come to the hoss. What ye lay?"

"Say three hundred."

"Hoss 's wuth a damn sight more 'n that, an' ye know it."

"I lay three hundred."

Jackson drank off half the glass of flip which the landlord had set at his elbow. Then he said: "Wal, seein' ez I'm a-goin' to beat yeh anyhow, three hunderd 't is." He set the dice spinning from his right hand. When they came to rest they showed a three and a five. The Parson's throw, in which the dice rolled scarcely at all, was a double five.

Young Jackson gulped what was left in his glass. His hand trembled a little. Several drops of the liquor ran down his long sharp chin, unnoticed.

"Your hoss," said he. "That is, for a while. An' . . . let's see now. I still got a shirt. What lay?"

"I don't really need it," the Parson replied with a critical glance at the young man's well-worn upper garment, stained with butternut juice, "but, just to keep up the game, I'll lay five dollars."

He threw a three and a four, and Jackson a five and a six.

"Now," said the Parson, "I'll lay you five dollars against the five you've just won."

Jackson lost with four spots against ten. On the next throw he lost his shirt. He insisted, against the courteous protest of the Parson, upon stripping the garment off at once and laying it on the table. His shoulders were high and bony, his chest almost pitifully narrow, and his collar-bone threw dark shadows against his scrawny neck in the candle-light.

"Now, o' course," said he, looking downward, "thar's my breeches; but they ain't wuth much."

"Oh, don't say that, man. They sarve the purpose."

"What I mean is, they ain't wuth much to you."

Jackson thought a moment, and then his face brightened. "But I got a plumper," said he, "that is a dandy. The man I won it offen, down in Charleston, he told me it was made by Paul Revere, out of elephant."

"Elephant, eh? But what in creation *is* a plumper?"

"A plumper," said Jackson, reaching with his index finger far back into his mouth and producing a rounded object, half an inch long and made of ivory, "is this here."—He held it out into the light of a candle for close inspection.

"But what's it good for?"

"Wal, for me, it takes the place o' two big teeth a British corp'ral knocked out o' my head when I was a boy—jest for the exercise, seemin'ly. I dunno what good it mought do you, but it helps me bite my victuals until I c'n do suthin' back to the British."

"Heah! Heah!" murmured Searcy, now half awake again. "Sounds pa . . . patriotic."

The Parson examined the plumper closely. "Seems to be just what I need," said he. "I have several places where it ought to fit fairly well. Yes; I'll lay the shirt against it."

"But before we throw," said Jackson, "I call for a change o' dice."

"What's that for?" the Parson asked. "Don't you like these?"

"I ain't fond of 'em.—Landlord, ye got any dice in the house?"

"Any number, Andy."

164

"Umpire," the Parson called, "are you going to allow changes like this in the middle of a game?"

"Any player," ruled the Colonel, "may call for a change of dice, or for a dice-box, at any time."

"But surely he must give a reason."

"He may, but he don't have to."

Jackson regarded his antagonist with steady eyes. "Any man," said he, using the correct English which he reserved for occasions of some formality, "is welcome to my reason. I reckon, though, that Mr. Gaines and Mr. Bean know it already, because they haven't been drinking."

"What is it, Andy?" asked McKay.

"It is that this Parson here has a way of palming his dice and then throwing 'em out so that they don't roll. It's pretty to watch, but I've never had the time to practice."

The Parson's right hand slid swiftly to the place where, had he not been a gentleman of the cloth, he might have expected to find a sword-hilt. He rose half-way from his chair.

"You mean to say, you . . ."

"Sit down!" said Holdfast Gaines, not loudly but in a tone that made the whole room seem to tremble.

The Parson resumed his chair.

"I mean to say," Jackson continued, "that we'll play for my plumper and your butternut shirt with a fresh pair o' dice and a dice-box.—Is that all right, Colonel Stokes?"

"Quite correck," said the Colonel.

Jackson passed the fresh dice and one of the two dice-boxes provided by the landlord across the table. "Now," said he, "let's see how you roll these."

"A five," the Parson reported, without enthusiasm.

"A five for me, too."

At the second try the Parson rolled seven and Jackson nine.

"My shirt. An' my plumper still. Now I'll lay them both 'g'inst your small red game-cock."

"What! That bird's worth fifty dollars."

"So's my plumper—not to mention the shirt."

"Then why did you . . . ? Oh, very well. I lay the cock."

Jackson won the cock with a throw of eight against five.

"Now," said he, "the cock is ready to win back that saddle o' mine."

"He usually wins what he goes after," the Parson ruefully replied.

165

Jackson lost the cock on the next play and was reduced once more to his shirt and plumper, but with the following throw he won it back again. In playing off a second tie he won back his saddle. Then he paused to put on his shirt and to light his clay pipe with a coal from the fire. On the next throw he bet the cock and saddle against a hundred dollars, and won. Laying a hundred dollars against another hundred he won again. Every man in the room except young Searcy was by this time on his feet, eagerly bending over the table.

"What a run o' luck!" McNairy exclaimed.

"Don't ye say it!" Jackson replied with a fierce upward glance at his friend. " 'T ain't luck 't all. It's needcessity!—An' now, Colonel, how many more throws?"

"Two more. Only two more throws, gen'lemen."

"Wal, then, I'm ready to win back that thar hoss, an' I'll lay two hunderd dollars an' the cock an' saddle aginst him."

"That hoss," the Parson remarked, "if he really is a son o' Diomed, is easily worth five times two hundred."

Jackson looked again into his opponent's eyes as he answered: "I *said* he's a son o' Diomed *an'* I said I'll lay against him two hundred dollars *an'* the cock *an'* the saddle."

"Oh, well"—and the Parson palmed his dice, drawing back his long carefully kept white hand for the throw.

"Put them dice back in that box o' yourn an' roll 'em from thar!"

"My mistake. Force o' habit." Parson Blandison rolled a five and a four from the box, and then leaned back with an expression of mild satisfaction.

They could see that Jackson's hand was trembling slightly as he took up the dice. He looked down into the box and addressed them in tones so earnest that no one thought of laughing. "I need that hoss," said he. "Fact is, I got to have 'im. Ye unnerstand me? I wouldn't throw dice aginst 'nother man's hoss, but when 'nother man wins mine offen me —wal, I *got* to have him back."

He rolled a double five.

"Western Waters!" yelled McNairy.

"My hoss!" Jackson whispered.

"One more throw, gen'lemen. Better make it a good one."

The Parson drew from his breeches pocket a large bundle of paper money. This he laid on the table. "Shall we say the hoss and saddle and cock," he asked, "against—ah—say four hundred dollars?"

Jackson puffed at his pipe until a cloud of smoke surrounded his head and blue-gray streamers floated above the candle-flames. Once more his eyes were reduced to blue slits.

"Say a thousand."

"What's that? Why, man . . . !"

"Yeah. Ye heard me right, I reckon. Didn't ye jest now say yerself that hoss o' mine is wuth five times two hunderd?—Wal then, fergit the cock an' saddle an' jest say one thousand dollars, even, aginst the hoss alone."

"Look here, Mr. Jackson, did I hear you say that you've never played dice before?"

"Fergit that too. I'm playin' 'em now, anyhow. D' ye take my lay?"

The Parson hesitated a moment longer but then "I take it," said he.

The long scar on Jackson's brow had all but disappeared, so pale was his face. He lifted the box and whispered into it: "I *got* to win! I dunno why, but I *got* to. Unnerstand?"

The faces of the men bending over the table were tense with excitement. Even Holdfast Gaines was waiting for the next turn of the two bits of bone as though he felt it would determine destiny.

Jackson threw a three and a four.

The Parson smiled again, faintly. He also raised the box to his lips, and whispered: "How have I seen the wicked flourish like unto the poison ivy!—Beelzebub, thirteen, thirteen."

Then he rolled a double deuce.

A huge shout went up. McNairy, beating his friend hard on the back and shoulders, shouted: "Andrew Jackson and Western Waters forever!"

"Hey? Who said 'water'?" Searcy grumbled, still half asleep.

"Western Waters!" breathed Andrew Jackson, with a look of pure wonder, and then, still more softly: "Saved with a plumper by God!"

SHADE AND SHINE

They took their time and traveled at their ease, climbing slowly upward beside the amber brawl of the Catawba under huge oaks and chestnuts and hickories that were just beginning to cast a flicker of shade.

The narrow, deeply worn trace ran close to the water's edge. Sunsparkle struck up from the hurrying waves, lighting every leaf with a tremulous glimmer. Young ferns uncrumpled their silvery fiddle-heads, dabbled with spray. Vivid moss and violets yellow and white and blue bent down to sip of the stream. Here and there the arching leap of a trout from the thread of the river made a momentary rainbow. Again and again, as they rounded a bend, does and fawns standing on little peninsulas of sand raised dripping muzzles and stood irresolute whether to bound away or to stand and stare. Woodchucks shook their corpulent sides down the path three rods ahead. Raccoons waddled out of the way like fat old women. Aimless vari-colored butterflies rambled and floated about them. A half-grown bear kept them in sight for a long way, until he could no longer endure the vociferations of the dog Wash and plunged disgustedly off into the thicket. The morning air was haunted, enchanted, by odors of wild-grape, honeysuckle, and sweet-fern. Azalea blossom, pink and orange and gold, lighted the woods as with candles of colored flame. The river had learned its song in Paradise. Voices of mocking-birds, cardinals, and thrushes rallied them on from glade to glade.

There was no need of haste. A runner had come through the town before they left Rowan House, bringing news that Governor John Sevier of the State of Franklin would not reach the mountain village of Morganton for his trial in less than a week. They were determined to witness this trial, but even at the lagging pace of Bean's pack-train the journey could easily be made in the time they had.

Andrew Jackson rode ahead on his excellent horse, often shouting back friendly jibes at the slowness of his companions. Parson Blandison, miserably mounted, rode as far behind—like Geoffrey Chaucer, he said, on the pilgrimage to Canterbury. He had doffed his three-cornered hat. His bob-wig, newly dressed by the barber of Salisbury, was crazily jiggling before him on the pommel. His eyes, continually darting, resting, and then steadily fixing here and there, had evidently been charged to reap a harvest of beauty from every wild acre of this new land. They were missing not one hue of a cloud or a tree or a wave, no contour of a rock, no gesture of a wind-tossed bough.

Rather handsome eyes they were—large, light blue, and highly intelligent. They were the eyes of an experienced man who now, on the verge of old age, though perhaps somewhat disillusioned and even slightly cynical, had by no means lost the faculty of wonder and admiration. And they suggested not only that he was now looking forward

168

to better things but that a good deal lay behind him in the way of tradition, breeding, privilege, and even of power. Unlike his present companions, he seemed to have inherited more than he had earned, and one felt that he had been to some extent a spendthrift of his patrimony. One guessed that he had not lived up to the strongly carved features, the graceful hands, the tall and shapely figure which had come down to him through many generations of gentlemen. His gaze, though utterly fearless, was somewhat evasive. His slightly florid complexion spoke of long indulgence, never gross but habitual, in wines and fiery liquors: One saw at first glance that the Parson was not what is conventionally called "a good man," but even after long study of him one could not make sure wherein, if in any way, he was a bad one. And, clearly, his defect or flaw—whether one decided that it was sensuality, weakness of will, loss of ambition, or some deep wound that his pride had once suffered—had not made him unhappy. On the contrary, one judged that he had always been much entertained by his own thoughts, much amused by the human spectacle, and often moved to keen delight by beauty. Goodness and truth, one felt, would have to come to him in the guise of things lovely, fair, majestic—although he would certainly discern beauty unheralded and hidden where others did not guess its presence.

Today he looked a gay and joyous man as he rode the narrow trace on his raw-boned nag, quite oblivious of whatever might have soiled his yesterdays, warmed to the heart by the glory of the passing day, and bravely confronting a mysterious future.

Young Perthy, perched astride the leading mule of the pack-train, was obviously enjoying himself also, and was proud of his promotion to the rank of Bean's chief assistant. Russell Bean, on horseback, drove the train, using a whip with an extremely long and accurate lash. After him came the three gentlemen of the law—Spruce McKay riding first and then the juniors, McNairy and Searcy. Holdfast Gaines, on foot, ranged up and down on either side of the trace. It was the opinion of Spruce McKay that when it came to a difficult bit of going Holdfast ought to carry at least one mule.

Released for a time from the tension of nerves and senses that most of them would have felt in a wilder place, they enjoyed the morning keenly, each in his own way. Bean had said that he could move along here at midnight as easily as his tongue could find its way among his back teeth. It was a country of friendly Indians, he said, in which a

169

man did not have to worry even about shooting and cooking his own victuals. If there was anything one had better keep his eyes peeled for along the Catawba, it was snakes.

"Take a squint at thet crooked stick, Pahson," Bean drawled, reining in his horse to let the lawyers pass by.

The Parson could make out something of the sort, lying across a flat stone by the trail-side.

. "Wal, thet 'ar," Bean went on, snapping the lash within an inch of the object, "is prob'ly the most piz'nous varmint in these hyar mountings."

The crooked stick coiled instantly, like a watch-spring, its head hideously flattened and its crimson tongue vibrating like a tiny flame.

"Charming sight!" exclaimed the Parson, starting to dismount. "I should like to scrape an acquaintance."

"It'll be the last thing ye ever scrape. That varmint c'n roll arter yeh like a hoop goin' downhill, an' when he cotches y' up . . . ! See the leetle horn in his tail?"

"Can't say I do."

"That's 'cause ye spile yer eyes readin' so much prent. But anyhow, he's got one, an' that's whar he keeps his sting."

. "Oh. He stings, does he?"

"Stings? Say, d' ye see these hyar dead trees all 'round? Wal, them's the ones got in his way."

The Parson laughed pleasantly. "You do the honors of the wilderness, Mr. Bean," said he, "with a grace. I see it will not be your fault if I have one tedious moment all the way to Western Waters. And how many horns has this 'varmint'?"

"Only one. But that leetle one horn it is a dandy, iffen only ye c'n git a-holt o' one. Most as good as a madstun, that horn is."

"See here, young man, let's take one thing at a time. What is a madstone?"

With a visible effort Bean curbed his amazement at this abysmal ignorance. He laid open his otter-skin pouch with a jerk and showed its contents.

"What's the deer's hoof good for?" the Parson inquired.

"Why, hell, to help me run good, o' course, an' give me good huntin'. But thisheer 's the madstun."

He held up between thumb and finger a dun-colored globular object,

170

apparently composed in part of coarse hair and about as large as a pigeon's egg. The Parson stared at it with a look of faint disgust and asked where it came from.

"Guts of a buck. Only 'bout one buck in a million has one, an' so it costs like smoke; but every trader an' long-hunter he can't do much 'thout a madstun in his pouch. Good fer dog-bite, wolf-bite, snake-bite, scratch of a wild-cat, fever 'n' ager, woman's disease, mumps, smallpox, pizen ivy—an' sech."

"I see. That's a bezoar. Queen Elizabeth had one. She depended upon it a great deal."

"Mebbe so; but she didn't call it right. That's a madstun, I tell yeh, an' don't let yer Queen 'Liz'beth tell yeh no differ'nt."

"H'm. And now about this one little horn of the—ah—of the 'varmint'. What's that good for?"

"Oh, good fer snake-bite—that is, other snakes. Good fer belly-ache, any kind. Drop it in water an' make a girl drink that water an' she's yourn. Good fer most kinds o' pizen. Keeps off witches an' ha'nts an' rheum'tiz. One o' the best things fer gittin' over a drunk. Y' oughter hev one, Pahson."

"But I never get drunk."

"No? Wal, then mebbe ye got one a'ready, 'cause ye seemin'ly take plenty o' chances. All the old grog-bruisers 'round these parts hez one on a string 'round their necks; an' they do tell that iffen thar's any pizen in the drink they're a-makin' ready to guzzle, then thet 'ar wizard horn 'll bust out into a sweat so's they leave that drink ondrunk."

"So!" mused the Parson, pursing his lips in a silent whistle. "You interest me extremely, Mr. Bean. Nearly everything you say recalls the well known virtues of the unicorn's horn."

"The which?"

"Unicorn's horn.—You don't mean to say you've never heard of unicorns!"

Bean looked puzzled for a moment. Then, a sudden light shining in his eyes, he exclaimed: "Ah! You mean those men—wal, that *ain't*! Yeah. But I never *did* hear tell they grew horns!"

The Parson, hugely delighted, reined in his horse and stopped, wishing to make this important matter quite clear. Bean stopped also. The sunny river chuckled past them among the sycamore roots as though it too were enjoying the jest.

"No, no," said the elder man, "Not *eunuch horn*. UNICORN!"

"Oh, yeah. I see," Bean replied, making it perfectly apparent by his

171

puzzled expression and by the way he scratched his handsome head that he did not.

"I mean a beast, a wild animal, very wild in fact, like an elk, say, but with only one horn—a remarkable one, long and tapering and moon-white—springing from his brow.—Ever see one?"

Russell Bean, his self-confidence now considerably reduced, was not quite sure that he ever had. There might be a few of them up in the higher mountains, he thought, but seemingly they seldom came down along the trace.

"Yes, they are shy," the Parson admitted, "and hard to catch. Unicorns are 'kittle cattle,' as they say in Scotland. In fact, the only known way of catching one is to seat a virgin under a tree and then drive the beast toward her, with dogs, through the woods. When he sees the virgin—or smells her, for authorities differ on that point—he advances and lays his head in her lap. Then the hunter steals up behind and kills him."

"Huh! Damn'dest kind o' huntin' I ever heerd tell of! Fust thing is, whar ye goin' to ketch yer virging, leastways 'round these parts? An' then too, the bait's wuth more 'n the beast.—Or ain't she?"

The Parson's tone was serious and matter-of-fact as he replied: "Well, on the whole, I shouldn't say so. A good unicorn's horn, like the one I have seen in the Tower of London, and others in the Cathedral of St. Mark in Venice, is commonly valued at about one hundred thousand pounds, sterling. And I submit that with such a sum one should be able to secure, in the open market, several desirable virgins."

"A hunderd thou . . . ! Great jumpin' jack-rabbits! Ye don't say so!"

"I do indeed, Mr. Bean. And when I was a boy every apothecary in London was obliged by law to keep in stock a sufficient quantity of powdered unicorn's horn. It sold for its weight in gold."

"My God! That's better 'n salt!"

The Parson was not a little pleased with himself as Bean went back to his pack-train, evidently pondering deeply. With all the elaborate lies, hoary superstitions, and beautiful myths of the Old World at his command, he hoped to hold his own against these rather boyish western prevarications. Europe and Asia had been lying such a great while longer.

And yet, did they not come to much the same thing in the end, these lies about hoop-snakes with single horns in their tails, yarns about unicorns and virgins, myths about blind Homer and Ossian and one-eyed Odin, fables about Christian saints and Indian medicine men, together with the wondrous and dreamy backgrounds of all the world's religions? Tall tales they seemed to him now, chiefly good because they served to beguile the tedium of life's journey. And a wise man, neither credulous nor scornful, would hear them all with a certain tenderness because of the pathetic things they hinted about the human heart, so lonely and lost and bewildered. Such charming lies men had told to one another beside the myriad camp-fires of the world—fires that could throw their light only a little way into the surrounding darkness! And what benefactors of mankind, he asked himself, had ever served their fellows better than the tellers, early and late, of lies?—of the glorious, free-soaring, fearlessly creative lies that one often longed to believe, they were so lovely.

Russell Bean, after some minutes of deep thought, paused again to let the Parson overtake him.

"Think mebbe I could scare up a virging," he remarked in a casual tone. "But what I wanter know is, d' ye mean all that 'bout—what ye call 'em?"

"Unicorns?"

"Yeah."

"Why should I deceive you, young man?" said the other with a look of mild surprise. "All that about unicorns is a matter of ancient belief. You will find several unicorns in the Bible."

"Mebbe; but what I wanter do is, find 'em round hyar."

"Naturally. And of course in what I told you I wished to make a fair exchange for your information about the snake that rolls like a hoop and stings trees to death."

Russell Bean's eyes wavered.

"And then, too," the Parson added, "as My Lord Hamlet once remarked, ' 'tis the sport to have the enginer hoist with his own petar.' "

"H'm. Yeah. See what ye mean," said Bean, riding away again, still thoughtful.

But now there was heard a faint clamor of barking dogs, and Wash went promptly forward to investigate. Bean told the company that they were approaching a village in which they would almost certainly dine.

Rounding a final bend of the trace, they saw a number of bark huts and two or three approximations to log cabins. Naked children scam-

173

pered back along the trail, squealing, and squaws disappeared behind the buck-skin flaps of the doorways. The dog Wash was being given a vociferous but not hostile reception.

Inside the enclosure of stakes to which they soon came, the grass had been bitten short. Evidently, then, these Indians kept some sort of domestic animals. But the grass could never have amounted to much because it was clear that this particular piece of land was one that the river rolled over in every freshet, leaving it chiefly gravel and sand. The sun of high noon beat down upon the pebbles and sand-grains, edging with gold the gnawed bones there, the ordure, and the wings of the crows and jays that uneasily fed on the offal.

Russell Bean took the lead, putting Jackson behind him. At the edge of the village he stopped, dismounted, and laid his rifle on the ground.

"I calc'late," he said to the group of men as they gathered, "we-uns is a-goin' to eat hyar."

"What? Dog?" asked McNairy.

"Naw. Dog is fer bankits. Ven'son, mos' like. Mebbe a hunk o' b'ar. —What d' ye make it out, hangin' yender from a branch?"

"It looks to me like a swarm of bees," said the Parson.

"Naw. Flies. Shows it's good, thet does. When flies won't tech a piece o' meat, better leave it alone."

A sturdy round-faced youngster of about Perthy's age, dressed in breech-clout and moccasins, came out from behind a tree a hundred yards off. He stood still, facing the strangers, holding an arrow on the string of a small bow. Clearly he felt responsible for the safety, or at least for the dignity and decorum, of the entire village.

"Hullo thar, young feller! I'm Russell Bean, trader, an' thisheer is Sleepin' B'ar, hisself."

The lad stood still for a moment, and even at that distance the strongly controlled amazement and delight in his face were visible. Then he laid down his bow and arrow and came slowly forward, holding himself straight and tall, gazing all the while at Holdfast alone.

"How!" said he, at fifty yards, raising his right hand, with the palm forward, above his head.

"How!" replied the visitors, with the same gesture.

"What?" asked the lad.

"We come see my friend New River," Bean answered.

Holdfast added a few words in a language which, so far as any one in the group could tell, might have been the rare and difficult Catawban itself. At any rate, the young sentinel replied in kind. Then he led the

174

way, stalking proudly, to the largest cabin in the village and knocked at the door, using a peculiar rhythm evidently agreed upon as a signal.

Half a minute passed before the door was opened, slowly, from within. An aged Indian, tall, clear-eyed, with iron-gray hair falling to his shoulders and massive silver bracelets on his arms, stood in the doorway, supporting himself on a pair of crutches. His face, colored like mahogany, was a wilderness of wrinkles. He looked at his guests man by man, gazing longest at Holdfast Gaines.

"How!" he said at last, raising a tremulous hand above his head. "How!"

He gave a command to the boy, who darted off. Then he hobbled down from the door-sill and stood to one side, bowing. His guests laid down their arms, left their animals under the superintendence of Perthy, and entered.

New River's cabin, of crude Indian construction but modeled upon the frontier dwellings of white men, showed a roomy and long interior which could be divided at need, by a partition of skins. Across from the doorway there was a makeshift chimney of clay and sticks, and on the hearth a tiny fire was burning. Square port-holes that could be blocked in time of danger took the place of windows. Against one wall stood the chief article of furniture, a huge couch or bed covered with a splendid blanket of turkey-feathers.—And it would be on that couch, one saw, that the aged chief now spent the greater part of his nights and days, not sleeping much probably, but remembering many things.

While the guests were seating themselves on the earthen floor Searcy remarked: "They tell me New River's a king. That means this must be a palace."

"What I know is," McNairy answered, "it's a camp-ground for fleas."

"Bring in that yellow dog o' yours, Holdfast," suggested Searcy. "Soon as the fleas smell him they'll hop, and then we can drive him out and shut the door."

"White man," said New River, surprising them all, "white man, he love to bite; but he do not love to be bited."

Yes, a very surprising remark indeed, the Parson thought to himself. Holdfast Gaines, to judge from his smile, was enjoying it not a little. And there was the question why New River, understanding and using English as well as he did, had not hitherto spoken a word. The only answer seemed to be that he had not cared to exert himself.

Meanwhile the aged chieftain had limped to his couch and begun to

175

fill, from a rabbit-skin bag, a large red pipe of stone, exquisitely worked.

Cherokee, Bean said, a pipe so fine as that would have to be, although the stone itself would have to come from hundreds of miles beyond Cherokee country. A good workman might spend a year on the wooden stem alone, writing out the career as a fighting man of the warrior who owned it. Bean thought it would bring a hundred dollars down at Charleston.

From the stem of the pipe, covered with picture-writing throughout its three-foot length, there dangled on deer-thongs several small bits of copper kettle, hammered thin and brightly burnished. Together with these there hung many blue, red, and green glass beads, a silver shoe-buckle, a finger-bone or two, and also a human scalp painted red and neatly stretched on a frame of twigs. On the bosom of the bowl the savage artist had depicted a naked man and woman, standing, with no undue concern for the modesty of the delineation.

New River with his stiff old trembling fingers stuffed the bowl with golden leaves as though all the gods were watching. Then he took a coal from the hearth, lit the tobacco, blew a puff to the north, another to the south, a third to the east, and a deep-drawn fourth to the west. His gestures were deliberate, thoughtful, and nobly dignified.

And just why, the Parson would have been glad to know, was there such unmistakable emphasis in New River's offering to the western quarter? Did he too feel that there was something mysterious and therefore holy in the realms of the sunset, "that undiscovered country?" —Ah, this ancient and everlasting abracadabra of priestcraft! Always it had been largely make-believe; and yet it had pointed back always to something deeply true, elemental, which all men had known—perhaps on Plato's sunken continent of Atlantis.

Now Holdfast Gaines was rising to take the pipe from New River's hands. First he held it high, looking upward, and said "To the sky, my Father." Next he turned the bit downward and said "To the earth, my Mother." Then he turned in a full circle while holding the pipe at arm's length, saying "And to all the four winds, for each is my Brother." Finally he blew a puff upward, one downward, and one to each quarter of the sky. The puff he sent westward was a large slowly moving smoke-ring.

"Ugh!" grunted New River, obviously impressed.

Holdfast stood for a moment trying to study out the hieroglyphics carved on the stem and bowl. His look expressed astonishment at the wonders he surmised there. Then the pipe was passed on to Russell

176

Bean and so about the little circle, each man in his turn puffing and wondering. In the meanwhile New River looked quietly down at each smoker in turn, with eyes that poured contempt upon every human achievement, including his own.

Shortly after the storied pipe had returned to its owner's hands a young Catawban threw open the door. He had been running. His dark face and figure had almost a feminine grace.

"Welcome, white men!" he gasped, sitting down beside the Parson.

After a decent pause, so timed that the young man might catch his breath, Bean said: "We come for talk with the great chief New River."

"Good. I say over all talk you tell me."

"Your English is good," remarked Parson Blandison.

"I learn him William Mary College. I lose him very damn quick." There was a meditative pause.

"Chief New River damn big man," Russell Bean ventured at length.

"Yao. Hunner year ole. Very damn."

"We have seen his tobacco pipe," said the Parson. "Will you read it to us?"

The young interpreter spoke with his chief for a moment in Catawban and then rose from the floor. "New River say these men hungry. Feed."

He strode to the door and bawled something to the squaws in the distance.

"I told yeh so," Bean whispered out of the side of his mouth to Searcy.

Returning from the door, the young Indian took the pipe from the couch and examined it closely while the white men crowded round him.

"You say read pipe New River," he began, pointing with a long brown middle finger at the first of the figures on the stem. "I read him like white man piece paper. Once many winter long time New River young man go hunt. Many Seneca come find. New River run like hell. Stop kill one-two-three-four-five-six-seven Seneca no time take off hair. Other damn many Seneca come catch New River in swamp. Make ready burn. Take off clothes. Take off moccasin. Only leave New River. Make run white man call blockade. Hit New River many time. New River laugh, call bad name. Bimeby grab club kill one-two Seneca jump damn quick in lake swim under. Other side New River climb out, laugh long time. New River turn backside slap him yell 'Whoo-Whoop!' Then run all day all night like hell. Rest some. Many Seneca very damn tired go sleep. New River come find. Creep up take

177

tomahawk take one-two-three-four-five hair. Then chop five Seneca very damn small. Run back dig up take one-two-three-four-five-six-seven hair. Chop small. Then run home dance Ha! Ha! Other many Seneca come see many small piece Seneca. By God feel very damn sick. Go back home. New River very damn big man."

At the end of this heroic recital each of the white men turned to the aged Indian now standing with folded arms by the hearth and bowed. He returned their courtesy with a slight inclination of the head. One could see that it now mattered to him very little what a person of his name might have done on the war-path so many years gone by; yet this tale of his greatest exploit was probably a tradition of the tribe, and, as such, deserved some attention even from him. Besides, it might help him to understand the figures carved on his beloved and precious pipe. Might not one of the twelve scalps he had taken on that adventure be the very one now dangling from the stem? Probably he was not quite sure.

Someone knocked at the door, and the young interpreter, going to investigate, came back into the circle dragging a small wooden tub half-filled with dark-colored meat. In his left hand he held a jug of red earthenware.

"Aha! B'ar ven'son!" exclaimed Bean. "What 'd I tell yeh? An' corn-water!"

Jerking his hunting-knife from the sheath he hacked off a generous chunk and carried it, on the point of the knife, to New River. All the white men in the group set to as well, each carving for himself. Hold-fast carved first for Perthy and the dog, and then, having cut his own portion, he rose and carried a small bit of it to the fire. New River, the young interpreter, and Russell Bean made their offerings also.

They could hear the brawl of the river as they ate, and the calls of cardinal-birds in the tree overhead. The flies circled nearer.

"These ain't bad victuals," said Searcy, with his mouth full.

"Why should they be?" asked Bean, similarly impeded. "Hung victuals is allus better 'n victuals jest shot. An' these here, they ben cooked good."

"Do you mean to suggest," said the Parson, "that anyone has actually tried to *cook* this—ah—this flesh?"

"Wal, it's warm, ain't it?"

"Yes; because it's been hanging in the sun."

"An' sun-cookin'," said Bean, "is the best cookin' thar be. Sun an' plenny o' flies—that's all good b'ar-meat wants."

178

"Here, Parson, have a swig o' corn-water," Jackson suggested. "It'll make you relish your victuals better."

"Corn-water? How old is it?"

"Made yes'day, I wouldn't wonder."

"Ah, so I feared. No thank you."

"Parson, it's what we all have. Don't make New River feel bad."

"No, Mr. Jackson. Time alone, and a great deal of it, can change a poor and trivial thing into something excellent."

"This corn-water," said Andrew Jackson, stressing every word, "is a damn good drink. I like it."

"Naturally you would, Mr. Jackson, because you are rather young yourself. You too, if I may quote you, were 'made yes'day.' But when you reach my age . . ."

"Naow, Pahson," drawled Russell Bean, "course 't ain't respeckful fer to take an' tell The Cloth to shet his trap; but iffen I war to say jest that, why then that thar 'd be 'bout what I mean."

"Oh?"

"Yeah. An' 'cause why? Wal, 'cause they ain't nothin' corn-water needs, whilst ye're a-drinkin' of it, like jest bein' a gen'leman. Ye be s'prised how it helps the taste, more 'n all the time in the world."

A close observer would have seen a faint flush, possibly of shame, mantling the Parson's neck and face. He sat quite still for several seconds, staring at the floor, and then said: "Mr. Bean, I have to thank you for a sound lesson in good maners, and for a friendly rebuke, well desarved."

"Aw, hell . . ."

"Thanks, Russ Bean," said Jackson.

Parson Blandison was glad to find himself alone when the horses and mules of the little cavalcade were once more picking their way along the trace. Holdfast had stayed behind for a talk with New River, and Perthy was either with him or, more likely, was being entertained by the young sentinel. Russell Bean rode ahead, driving the pack-train with his long lash and occasionally breaking into those paroxysms of profane abuse which he seemed to think essential to the management of mules. Now and then, still farther on, Andrew Jackson came into view as he rode his mettlesome "son of Diomed" through a pool of sunshine left by an opening in the sycamores. Rather absurdly, Jackson insisted upon carrying his newly acquired fighting-cock, Little David, on the pommel of his saddle. He had grown inordinately fond of the

179

bird, and held long conversations with him as they rode. Young Searcy averred that Little David often answered back in a gruff throaty language of his own, probably saying something about bloodshed. And, indeed, why should there not be a natural affinity between the man and the cock—both of them red, lean, young, utterly fearless, and always looking for battle?

When starting out from Salisbury, three days before, Parson Blandison had expected little more than amusement from his companions. He had meant to maintain, without effort, the easy superiority of a scholar, a gentleman, and a citizen of the world associating with a group of crude youngsters. Well, the amusement had not failed him, but in other regards matters had not gone according to plan. The standards by which he was accustomed to judge his fellows did not exactly apply to these young men. Russell Bean, for example, now clad in old worn buck-skins colored like a dead leaf, would have cut a queer figure in a London drawing-room; but here on the banks of the Catawba he, and not the Parson, was the man of learning, experience, poise—yes, and even of decorum.—There was a matter that called for thought.

The fact was that Bean's rebuke had considerably shaken the Parson's complacency. Not for years had he felt such a sense of shame. No doubt it would have been appropriate on many other occasions, but hitherto he had been protected by a conviction that, however, he might err in other matters, he was at any rate well-bred. And now to be lessoned in deportment by a backwoodsman, a muleteer!

For most of his other derelictions the Parson had his excuses ready. Thus, there was nothing in his code that made gambling for high stakes dishonorable. If one gambled, one wanted to win—and what could be wrong, then, about assisting the goddess Fortuna by such expedients as ingenuity, daring, and painfully acquired skill might provide? The use of such devices might lead to charges of dishonesty which no gentleman could afford to tolerate. Duels might follow—and if in one of these a man should be killed, so that his opponent had to flee to a distant land, that was rather a misfortune than a burden to his conscience. Similarly, it was a misfortune to be caught for life in a profession not of one's own choosing, a mere repository for younger sons, which imposed quite unreasonable standards of creed and conduct. Under such circumstances the Parson had not done worse than many others. Living in a time of religious and theological laxity, he had encountered little trouble as a clergyman in England, and still less in Virginia. Perhaps that was because, by virtue of his family and his education, he was thought to be at least "a gentleman."—But now Russell Bean, a mule-teer, had as good as told him that he was not even that, or at any rate had not acted as one while accepting the hospitality of New River. Moreover, Russell Bean had been right.

The situation would have been less painful if the young man had spoken only for himself. But he had been the spokesman of all the others. Holdfast Gaines had heard him, and undoubtedly had approved.

At this point in his meditations the Parson began to realize that Holdfast, from the start, had been the real leader of the group, giving it whatever cohesion and character it might have. It was to him that the others deferred, perhaps unconsciously, and it was his good opinion, not Bean's, that they sought. Probing down farther than he usually cared to go into his own conscience, the Parson recalled the faint sense of guilt that had come to him at the dinner in Salisbury when he had caught, and for a few seconds held, the steady gaze upon him of Holdfast's remarkable eyes.—Perhaps, then, his tutor in gentlemanly conduct was not to be a muleteer after all, but a full-blooded American Indian!

At any rate, he was going to learn—and to that end he resolved to discard the mask of a disillusioned worldling which he had worn for too long. It had never, he knew, suited a nature so eager as his, so easily moved to admiration. Old Horace's maxim, *nil admirari,* might have been sound enough in ancient Rome, and might serve fairly well in modern Paris or London, but here on the Catawba, in the midst of such a boundless Eden . . . ! Could Horace himself have stood before one of these gigantic blossoming magnolias without a catch of the breath, a quickened heart? Could he have sat by a camp-fire in the forest at night beside Holdfast Gaines without some glimpse of a human grandeur unguessed before?

No; for Horace had been a poet. And besides, that phrase *"nil admirari,"* so commonly misinterpreted, was really a counsel against thinking too much about material possessions. Horace would not have disapproved even an enthusiastic admiration of magnolias, but an envious admiring of Andrew Jackson's fine horse would have seemed to him a different and reprehensible thing.

A strange place this, truly, in which to be remembering the poet of the Sabine Farm! And yet there ought to be some continuity from age to age. One should not entirely abandon the old and tried in reaching toward the unknown. The Parson felt that he would rather lose even his precious wig than the little green book in which Russell Bean had yesterday spelled out the words "Quintus Horatius Flaccus" and had

181

got no further. He felt about that book much as Holdfast Gaines seemed to do toward the never dying fire in his clam-shell.

Russell Bean had expressed a stubborn doubt whether such a person as Quintus Horatius Flaccus had ever existed, or, indeed, such a language as Latin. He had suggested that the Parson made up names like Shakespeare, Plutarch, and Plato out of his own head. And this was the man from whom Parson Blandison, Oxford Master of Arts, was now setting himself to learn new ways, new thoughts, new manners. He saw that his recently acquired humility would be kept in vigorous and regular exercise.

Most of the young men were by this time in the habit of laughing at the Parson a good deal. Snapping up the term from his own talk, they had nicknamed him "The Cloth." They never tired of ridiculing his sharp-angled and senescent nag. His habit of pulling out the little green Horace as he rode along, reading a line or two, and then replacing it in his pocket, seemed to them deliciously absurd. They thought him ridiculous also when he stopped to stare at a large or shapely tree, at azalea or rhododendron blossoms, at waterfalls and dark green pools in the river, gazing at such common things as though he had never seen their like before and never would see them again. His fine black clerical garb and splendid bob-wig were to them an inexhaustible source of laughter.

It was clear that the Parson enjoyed the friendly banter of his young companions, often going out of his way to give them openings, but he did attempt some defense of his attire. He said that if he should tell them the history of his wig—as he certainly did not mean to do lest they should try to take it from him—they would be astonished. His present clothing, he said, was of precisely the same material and cut as that in which he had once dined with Horace Walpole at Strawberry Hill in company with Mr. Thomas Gray, and neither of those rather exacting gentlemen had seen in it anything ludicrous. He was aware, of course, that he would never be able to satisfy the sartorial taste of such an *arbiter elegantiarum* as Mr. Russell Bean, but he did hope that the Cherokees and Chickasaws over the mountains would, out of courtesy, look upon his garments if not with favor at least without disdain.

He found it a comfort and a joy to be laughed at by these young men. Their laughter showed that they had accepted him, made him their fellow, and meant to give him the chance he had asked for to outlive his own past. Never the least reference had any of them made to his somewhat questionable conduct in the dice game with Jackson. He doubted whether they had forgotten, but—well, the likelihood was that Holdfast had spoken some quiet word.

Very different this journey was from the one the Parson had taken, many years before, as tutor of several young Oxford graduates on their tour through the Alps and into Italy and Greece. Those well-bred English youths had not laughed at him—at any rate in his presence. They had even shown some respect for his classical scholarship and close knowledge of Hannibal's campaigns. But in the eyes of his present companions even a smattering of Choctaw would win him more regard than all the Latin and Greek he had ever known.—An odd thing, that! All those long years ago he had been thought a learned man, and now, at three-score, he was beginning to con a new alphabet.

In that earlier journey he had led his charges over the Alps to study an ancient and defunct civilization which, in some degree, they expected to imitate. These young Americans, on the other hand, were stepping confidently westward to help in the creation of a country entirely new. They would imitate nothing—for one reason, because they had no models in mind. Always excepting Holdfast Gaines, they were ignorant both of the past and of the present. What was it in them, then, that compelled respect? Should one call it audacity, a gambler's faith, a willingness to stake upon one throw all they had or hoped for?

At any rate they did not feel, like those Oxonians, that they were living in the sunset of time. Rather, they seemed to move and have their being in the dawn's early light. They made one think of mythical and legendary begetters of nations, like Cecrops, Deucalion, and Aeneas.

That evening they pitched their camp beside the stream where it went racing down a succession of rocky slides into a great round pool, emerald-green and deep. Driving the butts of long sycamore branches into the sandy soil, they bent the tops down and threw blankets over the arches thus made. Four such flimsy tents they set up in a few minutes. Hemlock twigs thickly strewn on the ground would serve for mattresses.

For supper they had several small trout which the Parson had taken from the pool with his jointed fishing-rod, using an artificial fly of his own manufacture for the lure.—On the whole, he had thought it best not to tell Andrew Jackson that one red feather used in making this fly had been tweaked, in Jackson's absence, from Little David's top-knot.

Cooked and eaten within a few minutes after they were drawn from

183

the water, these trout were a welcome change from the diet of journey-cake, wild turkey, and hog-an'-hominy on which the travelers had fared since leaving Rowan House. Perthy, Bean, and Holdfast drank from the stream, but the Parson had his flask of brandy and the three men of the law shared a jug of kill-devil rum.

After supper they lounged about the fire that Holdfast kindled, not saying much but listening as they smoked their pipes to the rush of river-water and the tankling bells of the pack-animals and riding-horses browsing close at hand. The Parson asked the name of the bird that sang at dusk from the dark of a hemlock near camp. Each clause of its song began with a long-drawn note, ethereally pure, suddenly bursting into cascades and cadenzas of clustered tones as though some distant lofty lake were breaking loose down a mountain-side. At one moment it seemed to be coming from far away, and in the next it sounded from within the listener's own mind and heart. The solitary singer was improvising, patiently meditating, upon one persistent theme, expanding a single note into a world of meanings. And one knew that he sang not at all to be overheard but for his own ear alone.

"Swamp angel," said Bean; but Holdfast called it a "hermit thrush." After several minutes of quiet listening the Parson asked: "What makes his song so sad?"

"'T ain't—fer's I see," Bean answered.

Holdfast made no reply.

The Parson listened again, and then "I think it is," he went on. "The poets over in Europe, ever since Petrarch, have tried to make out that the nightingale is extremely melancholy about something or other—and, considering the human ages he has had to live through, one might say that he ought to be. Yet this hermit thrush, always singing here in what my friend William Cowper calls 'a boundless contiguity of shade' and quite ignorant of our human sorrow, has the sadder voice of the two.— I don't understand why that should be."

Holdfast looked up and said: "Have you ever heard the mourning-dove, Parson?"

"Ah, yes, indeed. He sings only one syllable, but loads it with heart-break."

"Well, my people in Connecticut have a legend that in the old days the mourning-dove sang like the bobolink and wren. He changed his song, they say, when the Pequots were destroyed by their white neighbors—hundreds of them, old men and women and children, burned to death in one night."

184

"Ah."

"Yes. And that kind of thing has happened here many times. This is an old country, Parson. We have had much sorrow here too. I tell you so. The hermit thrush may have overheard."

"I think I see what you mean."

"Aw, hell," Russell Bean broke in, rising. "You two fellers gimme the belly-wobbles. Whut ye want is to hear some real music what won't make ye so damn down-hearted."

He disappeared into the darkness for a minute and returned with a battered fiddle and bow. Then, standing in the firelight and keeping time with his left foot, he scraped out half a dozen burly and rollicking tunes, evidently trying to atone by the energy of his performance for certain technical deficiencies. Dance-tunes, he said they were. One of them, "The Girl I Left Behind Me," he played twice over, by request. The Parson said he had known it since his boyhood, and Holdfast recalled, speaking in a low, grave voice, that he had heard it once before.

"Yeah; an' back in eighty," said Bean, "I played it all the way down the rivers to Nashville—played it a thousan' mile, b' God, an' jest 'bout kep' us alive.—Not all on us, I don't mean, but some. Arter we 'd ben a day an' a night, mebbe, tryin' to shove a flat-boat offen a rock, I'd come up outen ice-water an' wring my shirt-tail an' slam-bang inter 'Gal I Lef' Behind Me' so 's purty soon we-uns all felt warm an' dry an' full."

He stared for a while at the fire.

"But mostly I rec'leck," he continued, "how Rachel Donelson useter dance to that god-a'mighty grand ole chune. Cap'n's darter she war, an' only sixteen, but a-roundin' out a'ready an' with snappin' black eyes an' long black floatin' hair on her ez 'd make a man lay awake nights. Oh, I mean to say!—An' when it come to dancin', b' God she war the all-fired leg-shakin'est gal what ever went down the middle. Times, I'd give the fiddle to ole Cap'n so's I c'd dance her myself. I 's the only man aboard c'd whirl her off her feet. She liked that."

"Oh," said Jackson, drowsily. "So you 's the only one, eh?"

"I said so. An' I bet that gal's got more heft to her 'n 'bout thirteen Andy Jacksons."

"That so?—Rachel Donelson, eh?—Wal, mebbe we'll hev to see 'bout that."

"Huh! Mebbe we won't, too, 'cause she's gone an' got married to a jealous skunk 't won't let her dance 't all.—Spiles everythin', gittin' married does."

185

For a long while after their companions had crawled into their improvised tents for the night, Parson Blandison and Holdfast Gaines sat by the fire, silent, each apparently absorbed in his own thoughts or else listening to the rush of the river. Now and then they heard the hoot of an owl, or caught the green-gold reflection of some wild animal's eyes from the thicket. The boughs that arched high above them, faintly laced with young leaves that let a few stars shine through, loomed ruddy and boldly rounded in the flickering light. Beams and pencils of firelight groped out into the surrounding forest like tremulous fingers.

This was the third night in succession on which the Parson had sat thus with Holdfast, neither man saying more than a few words. On the first occasion he had been decidedly uncomfortable, accustomed as he was to the quick give-and-take of polite conversation in which each party strives above all to make "points," like a fencer, while carefully guarding his own heart. But that ancient and honorable art of the drawing room, in which the Parson modestly considered himself an adept, now availed him not at all. What else was there, then, he could not help asking himself, which two men alone in the whispering dark could fall back upon?

The second night had been even worse. Holdfast's determined silence had been like a wall excluding all intrusion and approach. It had felt, indeed, like a stern rebuke, and had left the Parson baffled and humble.

But tonight there was a difference, subtle but profound. For one thing, the Parson was now coming to realize that his companion's silence probably had no reference to him whatever—or that, if it had, it was meant as a courtesy rather than a reproach. It seemed to assume that he, the Parson, must also wish to spend at least one quiet hour of every day in converse with his own innermost self.

Tonight, according to his inveterate habit, the Parson was ranging back through his literary recollections to see how the past might illumine the present. He recalled the occasion, reported by Plato, on which Socrates had stood for many hours motionless and silent in full sight of the armed camp, listening, no doubt, to his "daimon." He remembered how Seneca, Nero's tutor, had insisted in his letters to Lucilius upon the necessity of hearing often, and clearly, from oneself. There came to mind the strangely thrilling words of some old Spanish mystic —was it Miguel de Molinos?—about the differences between the several kinds and qualities of silence, one of which he had called "the inward road to the treasure-chamber of peace."—Could it be that this American

186

Indian, now sitting on the other side of the fire wrapped in a huge and shaggy buffalo robe, had found that path without the help of any such guides? Had he discovered it without a hint from any old book, with no assistance from the slow accumulation of human knowledge and wisdom? Was he following such a path at this moment through the hushed crepuscular mountains of the mind? For, if not, then what was he doing? If not, why was this present silence so different from any mere abstention from speech? What made it so warm, friendly, and eloquent? This silence of Holdfast's somehow went beyond even the speech of the same man, uttered as that was in a voice that ranged all the way from the whisper of a dry oak-leaf to the shock of crashing thunder. This silence, the Parson felt, did not shut him out. It engulfed him. It supported him. It made him think of the noble sentence, "Underneath are the everlasting arms," Deuteronomy thirty-three, twenty-seven.

The Parson was beginning to wonder, hesitantly, whether he also might discover such an inward road, and whither it would lead him. Inevitably, he saw, it would take him directly down into a hell of memories which it had long been a main purpose of his life to avoid, evade, and as much as possible forget. Still it lay there, he knew, waiting. Drink, games of chance, scholarship curious and wide-ranging, playful fondling by the mind of its own hoarded treasures, even the ministrations of art and the glories of nature—none of these had ever permanently availed to keep down the voices and fumes that rose from that place of torment. But now the thought came that if only he could somehow manage, like Dante, to wade through those pits of despair he might come, on the other side, to a path that would lead to some region of calm.

Yet even Dante had needed a guide, and one thing that the Parson knew about himself was that he could do nothing without the support and authority of example. Hitherto he had depended largely upon the written words of men long dead. That habit of dependence could not now be thrown off, but perhaps he might transfer his allegiance from the monarchs of European wisdom to this son of the forest who was blazing his own trail westward.

The fire was waning now, and Holdfast was no longer feeding it from the small pile of sticks at his side. The few stars that looked down through the roof of boughs moved on and were replaced. The quietness deepened.

At last the Parson heard himself speaking, simply, naturally, and in so quiet a tone that his words made scarcely a ripple on the midnight air. It was almost as though he were talking to himself.

"Mr. Gaines," he said, "I think you said the other night, down at Salisbury, that you come from Connecticut."

"Yes."

"And Mr. Russell Bean has told me that you belong to a tribe of Indians called Mohegans."

"That is so."

"Does this tribe live near a town called New London?"

"Yes, Parson," Holdfast replied with quickened interest, "it does."

"And that tribe—is it small or large?"

"It is very small."

"Ah, then, I am almost sure that you have seen, perhaps known, an old acquaintance of mine, a close acquaintance—at one time I should have said a close friend. For he too was a Mohegan from the region of New London. He came from a place he called Mohegan Village, not far from New England's River Thames."

"But his name, Parson! What was his name?"

"Samson Occum. The Reverend Samson Occum, to be more precise. —You have known, or seen, him?"

"He is my uncle—my father, almost," said Holdfast, unable quite to curb the excitement of his tone. "I lived in his house until I was ten. He taught me most of the little I know. He told me what I had to do."

"Mr. Gaines, what a marvelous thing! It makes me think—it's like something out of Judge Fielding's 'Tom Jones' that you and I, both owing so much to one man, should be sitting here tonight in this wild place! For Samson Occum used to tell me also what to do. More than that, he *showed* me, by example. In that regard the main difference between us is that I haven't done it."

"Where did you know him, Parson?"

"In London, at first."

"In 1765, I think that must have been."

"Yes; or, perhaps, a year later. One dark night, at about that time, he saved me from a gang of cut-throats who were bent on killing me, just outside a gaming-house in London. I had never seen him before, but he happened along at the right moment and dispersed them, using only his cudgel."

"Ah, yes; I remember that cudgel. It was cut from a Gungywamp oak."

"Well, at any rate, we struck up a friendship there and then—a

188

friendship as oddly assorted, to outward appearance, as one could imagine. He was engaged in collecting funds to found a school for American Indians, and, with such talents as I had in the collecting of funds, I helped him all I could. It was in some sense a missionary enterprise, and therefore more worthy than most of the efforts to which I have given my time and strength. It took us all over England. We met many interesting people and had adventures of many sorts, ludicrous and romantic, which a man like Henry Fielding might have made into a fascinating book. Samson Occum, as you probably know, became a famous man. What is more to the point, we did collect those funds, to the amount of ten thousand pounds. That money was used in the founding of Dartmouth College, 'for the education and instruction,' as the Royal Charter said, 'of the Indian tribes of this land.' 'Holy plunder' I called it, having in mind both the end in view and also some of the means that were used without Samson's knowledge."

"I know something about that journey," said Holdfast, "although I was only a child at the time, and my uncle, for some good reason, has seldom spoken of it.—And yet, now that I know of your acquaintance, I think I have heard him mention your name."

"Not favorably, I fear."

"With liking, certainly; but I seem to recall that he thought you a scoffer at holy things."

"Ah, yes; he would say precisely that. He would say it even today— and perhaps things worse. In the years since I last saw Samson Occum I have by no means followed either his precept or his example. There is one reason why, when I found it advisable to come to America, I chose not to go to the region where he and I might have met. I came to Virginia instead. And when you said the other night at the tavern that you were from Connecticut—well, you may have seen that I was not unimpressed."

"And now," said Holdfast, staring at the last dwindling flame of the camp-fire, "you are leaving even Virginia."

"For reasons which, though I do not name them, seem to me good and sufficient."

After this relapse into his earlier manner the Parson sat silent for half a minute. Holdfast, in the meanwhile, made no effort by word or gesture to decide the struggle that might be going on in the heart and mind of the elder man.

"But the strange thing is," the Parson at last burst out, "that just now, when I need it most, I find myself thrown by the goddess of good luck

189

into companionship with the nephew of the only man who has ever thought me worth saving from perdition."

"I am glad, Parson, to hear you call it 'good luck.'"

"Samson Occum would have said 'Providence,' and he might be right in so saying. However, here is my point, Mr. Gaines, and my excuse—if I have one—for keeping you awake so far into the night: I do believe that your uncle, if he were here, would urge you to take up the task at which he failed, through no fault of his own. It would be a harder task now because I am now confirmed in the habits of thought and action which he deplored. Yet perhaps I am a little wiser. At least I see, now, that my life has been, and still is, little better than a purposeless drifting from one amusement to another, one excitement to the next. I have never before admitted that much to any man, and perhaps if we were not sitting alone here in the dark I should not now say it to you. You must not think that I have failed utterly, for at least I have enjoyed my life. I have seen the glories of this world and have understood that they are glorious. Yet there is something, and something essential, that I have missed."

"Perhaps it is," said Holdfast, "that you have never had your vision."

"Yes—or something like that, if I understand your meaning. No task or duty which I recognized as binding and my own, has ever been laid upon me. If I have done one thing with complete devotion, then it was that same gathering of funds for the education of American Indians; and even that I did out of gratitude, friendship, and a kind of admiration."

"The American Indians are still in great need of education, Parson Blandison."

"And so am I.—But let me add, taking advantage of the darkness, that I have recently found for the second time in my life a man whom I should like to help in any way that I can. That he also should be a Mohegan Indian, and the nephew, almost the son, of the man with whom I worked in a good cause years ago—why, that I should attribute to the beneficent intervention of the Goddess Fortuna."

The last little flame of the camp-fire died down, revived for a moment, and then disappeared. The figures of the two men sitting beside the embers were swallowed by the dark. Once more, and for several minutes, they sat in silence, listening to the roar of the waterfall. From far off among the hills came the howl of a wolf.

The Parson felt a touch on his shoulder and knew that Holdfast had risen to his feet. He also rose, stiffly. Then "Parson," said a quiet voice

190

at his side, "one of the hardest things we all must learn to bear is loneliness."

"Yes. Loneliness."

"Some of it is good for a man, but you and I have had more than our share."

"At any rate, I have."

"During the last few years, when Perthy was not with me, I have sat by thousands of camp-fires alone, listening to the howl of the wolf. Hereafter, I hope, you will sit there with me often, and many times."

"Mr. Gaines, you are a man who says much in few words. At present I can only say that I share your hope, and that I thank you."

Then the two men shook hands, warmly, and parted for the night.

THE PAISLEY SHAWL

Dawn was gilding the tops of the tallest trees when Parson Blandison awoke. From near at hand he heard the calls and songs of a hundred birds. A clangorous gobbling of wild turkeys came from up the hill. Under all these voices and the sough of the morning wind ran the strong bass note of the river.

He shrugged his blanket aside and worked his way, feet first, out of his narrow tent. The ashes of last night's fire were gray and cold.

A splash and a shout from the pool below the camp told him that some of his companions were awake. He saw a circle of water widening there, and soon, within the circle, Russell Bean emerged, snorting and blowing, scattering drops from his hair. On a rock at the pool's farther edge stood Holdfast Gaines, his arms folded, looking into the swirl.

To the Parson, gazing, there came a mood of humorous self-reproach. "You go about staring at trees," he murmured. "You admire birds, horses, streams, mountains, and sunsets. But the fact is, Reverend Sir, that the human animal at its best is the most glorious of God's creatures. That is what the wise Greeks knew and Christianity has made us forget."

Russell Bean stepped out of the pool, dripping. He called something derisive to Holdfast and went leaping toward him from stone to stone like a springing panther. For a second the two stood side by side. Shorter by a head and far slighter in build, Bean had another kind of physical perfection. His skin had the healthy pallor of a man who has spent most of his life in the forest. Holdfast's body, as seen in those deep shadows, was dark brown, and his hair dead black.

Quick as the flash of a flint-lock Holdfast caught his friend by the waist with both hands and tossed him far into the pool. Then after him he went, and caught him again and soused him. Next he too sank, pulled down from below, in a froth of blue bubbles and violet foam. Darkened ivory groped and fumbled about down there on the pool's bed. At last, struggling upward, twisting and turning like otters at play, the pearly and bronze-hued bodies came back to the air, broke apart, and floated, panting, laughing. Their shouts resounded from the rocky banks under the arch of leaves.

The Parson sighed, turned away, went back to his tent, took his clerical bands from a hickory twig, and began adjusting them about his neck. He did not once look up when the swimmers returned from the pool.

After breakfast, mostly composed of a great golden trout which Holdfast had speared in the pool before dawn, Perthy led the animals in from the woods. He unfastened their hobbles of hickory withes and tied down the clappers of the bells they wore on their collars of woven corn-husk. Upon each of the beasts, as it came to hand, Bean loaded two bags, each containing one bushel of alum salt which weighed, he said, eighty-four pounds.

"Not much of a load, is it?" the Parson asked.

"Wait an' ast me ag'in arter ye've clum a few slopes tother side o' the Ridge."

"Steep, is it?"

"Wal, I dunno whut ye mought call steep, but ye c'n bite the ground in front o' yeh 'thout bendin' over."

"Yes," said McKay, who was looking on, "and in some places, going down, a man would like to have hob-nails on the seat of his breeches."

"Out west o' the Ridge, Parson," said Searcy, his face preternaturally grave, "the mountains crowd so damn close together that all the dogs living in the valleys have to wag their tails only up and down."

"Is that so?"

"Fact, sir."

"Yes," McNairy put in, "and the folks out there have to look up their chimney-flues to see their cows come home."

"But tell 'im what kind o' cows they be," said Bean. "Ye know—

them with all their four laigs growin' all on one side so's they c'n graze on the slopes 'thout fallin' over. Queerious lookin' critters they be."

"And of course," added McKay, "the boys have to drive them clear around the mountain to get 'em home, because, naturally, the animals can't turn back."

"Most interestin'," the Parson replied, with a sigh of pure enjoyment.

" 'Sides all that," Bean went on, "the trace ain't never more 'n wide 'nough fer a good fat snake. Load yer brutes half an inch too much one side an' over they goes, salt an' all, mebbe a thousan' feet down. That ain't good fer the salt."

"And how much will a bushel of salt bring out there?"

" 'Pends whar ye be. Down Watauga way, now, a good clean bushel brings a fresh young cow an' her fust calf; but I seen the time over in Cumberland when a man c'd sell a bushel fer two cows.—Useter come mostly from N'orlins, salt did, them days."

"And how much is a cow worth?"

"A cow? Aw, not much. She don't give no milk to speak of, an' then too she's allus gittin' kilt off by the b'ars. Best thing a cow is good fer is smellin' out fer Injuns.—She c'n smell an Injun a week away, a good ole wise cow kin."

"No; but how much? Because you see if your cow is your unit of value, why then . . ."

"Oh, ye mean how much a cow!" Bean paused for a moment in his loading and scratched his head. "Wal," said he, "a good young cow, 'bout to freshen, she'll bring twenty beaver, or, say, forty gallon o' red-eye, second run."

"And how much is a gallon of red-eye worth?"

"H'm—how much a gallon o' red-eye? Wal, lessee now. Wal, ye c'n git a gallon o' good red-eye fer one coon-skin—with the tail on, o' course."

"I mean, how much in money?"

"Money? Hell, I dunno. Folks don't valley money much over thar. Ye got to offer 'em suthin' useful."

"Such as?"

"Wal, The Cloth, ye suhtinly be purty damn igner'nt! But cowbells, now, an' axes—they're useful. Knowed a man oncet out Cumberland way—right nigh to Nashville his piece was—an' he guv a six-hunnerd-forty o' good bottom-land jest fer three axes an' two cowbells. 'Course that was back at the beginnin'. But brandy's good, too. So's powder an' lead, or salt, or any old piece of iron. They got 'most every-

193

thin' else out thar, but they'll give their eye-teeth fer iron an' salt. So that's what I tote over."

"I thought they had salt enough in the old buffalo licks."

"Yeah, but dirtier 'n hell; an' takes a day to bile down a fistful."

While he explained the monetary system of Western Waters Bean was fastening to the backs of his mules long bars of iron so bent as to fit close to the animals' bodies. To these he added, for the Indian trade, certain leather sacks of highly colored beads and bits of copper. He strapped on a few crooked bars of lead, a dozen bags of gun-flints, and as many bags of gun-powder. Dan'l Boone, he told the Parson, could make gun-powder out of the materials of the wilderness, but then Dan'l Boone . . .

"And what is the price of iron," the Parson asked, "beyond the Ridge?"

At that moment the mule on which Bean was working lashed out with his heels and tried to throw off his load. Bean instantly seized one of the beast's flopping ears, clamped it between his strong white teeth, and gnashed at it fiercely. The creature stood still, trembling.

After a few appropriate remarks to the mule, Bean returned to the Parson's question. "Two shillin' the pound," he said, "speakin' in tarms ye c'n unnerstan. 'Course I mean King's shillin's, hard money. But they ain't no sech shillin's over thar, an' mighty little iron excep' on the plows. Ain't nary a nail nor yet an iron latch to no man's cabin west o' Watauga. Never will be, I reckon."

"Never?"

"I said 'Never.'"

"Jest the same," said Jackson, overlooking Bean's labors from the back of his horse, "I bet they'll hev iron a plenty over thar some day. And soon."

Bean looked up with a smile. "A young greenhorn like you," he said, "he'll bet on most anythin'—speshly when he don't know nothin' 'bout hit."

"And what's more," added the Parson, "he'll win, too."

Yet the Parson's frequent efforts to lure Andrew Jackson into another game at dice had been unavailing. Jackson averred, with unaccustomed humor, that he had "got religion." Dice-playing, he said, was a form of gambling, and therefore a thing to which no gentleman of The Cloth should lend his countenance. The Parson, in his opinion, could put his

194

time and skill to better use in communicating all that he knew about the care and feeding of game-cocks.

Little David was a constant anxiety to Jackson. Was he feeding the bird too much or too little? How much water and exercise did he need? At night came the fear of foxes, wild-cats, and other such vermin—a fear which the cock did not seem to share in the least, for he often awoke in the darkest hours and set up a clamor that might have been heard for miles through the still mountain air.

Partly for the pleasure of badgering Jackson, Bean expressed a strong dislike of these vocal performances. " 'T ain't so dangersome right now," he admitted, "but by time we-all start down Nolichucky Path we'll be in tiger kentry, an' that chicken 's gotter be soup."

"Oh, he will be," said Searcy. "Andy's goin' to match him at Morganton, an' a puny li'l banty-leg like David won't make a bite for one o' Judge Avery's stags."

At these and other remarks Jackson bristled in a way wholly delightful to his companions. Apparently it was impossible for him to accept, or even to comprehend, the most good-natured jest leveled at himself. And in his tantrums, which came often and lasted long, he seemed to feel, like his own little red game-cock, that life was made for fighting.

Up and ever upward wound the cavalcade. The huge magnolias in full flower, before each of which the Parson had felt obliged to halt his horse and to stand in mute adoration, were giving place now to highland trees no less majestic—to enormous black oaks, tall pillar-stemmed tulips, and hemlocks of gargantuan girth. All the Parson's companions except Perthy and Holdfast laughed aloud at his amazement when for the first time he looked out from a bald eminence across many tumbled miles of blossoming rhododendron. The scarlet and crimson azaleas that blazed like a forest fire on every hand set him to muttering poetry in three or four languages. This must be the very region, he said, that had been so incredibly described to him by his friend William Bartram, a Quaker, of Philadelphia.

The trace was steep, now, and rugged. Waterfalls and small cataracts came scattering down at every bend of the dwindling river. The air blew cool at noon-day from the western ridges. Every spit of sand by the stream showed the hoof-prints of deer. Turkeys gobbled in the distance or ran for cover among the fern. Man after man dismounted and walked ahead of his horse.

"What's a hoss good for on a path like this?" the Parson called to Bean.

"Wal, iffen we run into Injuns they mought take the hosses an' leave us our h'ar."

"Not *your* hoss, though," laughed McNairy. "They'd take almost any suit o' hair before that hoss."

"Do they take white hair?" the Parson inquired with the pretense of a quaver in his voice.

"Next to red, it's the best of all," Searcy shouted back. "Always brings next to the highest price from the British."

"But they's wuss things 'n scelpin' out thar, The Cloth," said Bean. "Fack is, scelpin' don't hurt hardly 't all 'long-side o' gougin'.'"

"Gouging! What's that?"

"Whut! Mean to say y' ain't heerd 'bout gougin'? Wal, time ye did! Now, gougin' is takin' yer thumb an' puttin' it in a feller's eye an' jes nachally shovin' thet 'ar eye-ball out o' whar it b'longs an' walkin' off with it."

"But is this a custom of Western Waters?"

"Custom? I dunno. But hit's a habit anyhow.—'Course some fellers goes in fer bitin' off years an' noses, but eye-balls is more pop'ler, so to say."

"You mean they collect them?"

"Yeah, 'c'leck'; that's the word. Kinder sport, like birds' eggs. When things git so tarnation slow they cain't stand it no longer out in Western Waters then some feller ups an' says 'Aw, hell! Le's go gouge a few eye-balls!' An' then when they gits back f'm a gougin'-party they'll mebbe give a few to the babbies to play with an' the rest they strings up on a thread over the fireplace, like birds' eggs."

The Parson considered this information with a slow appreciative smile. At length he said: "Apparently, then, I shall be picked entirely clean before I even reach Western Waters. I do hope, however, that the inhabitants will leave me my teeth, such as they are."

"No use for teeth over there," McKay assured him.

"Why not?"

"Nothin' to eat, o' course. That's why Andy bet you his plumper."

"Ah, well, the sound of the grinder is low. Anything to drink?"

"Red-eye, pine-top, bald-face, and forty-rod lightnin'. Also a little Jersey lightnin' thrown in now and then, for a treat."

"Nunc dimittis!"

"How's that?" asked Jackson.

"I mean to say that I may as well stop right here."

"No; cheer up, Parson!" said Bean. "Less 'n a mile to camp, an' ye c'n use yer teeth tonight."

At last the trace dipped downward. Between the tree-tops they could see the valley of some tributary stream with open meadows and signs of cultivation. On the right there was a deadening of a hundred acres where a host of corpse-like oaks and hickories held up rigid arms against the blue. A herd of razor-backs was rooting and quarreling there. A snake-fence ran round it. Next came a field of young corn, full of weeds. Beyond, in the middle of a stump-scarred clearing, stood a large and rambling cabin. Smoke was wisping up from the crazy chimney of mud and sticks.

"Hurray!" shouted the men, and were answered from below by a chorus of eight or ten dogs and hounds. Perthy's yellow dog, pausing not an instant for reply, sprang down the hill as an arrow leaves the string.

"Wash! Come back here!" called Holdfast.

The dog came back so promptly that he scarcely seemed to have been away. Holdfast scooped him up and carried him on his shoulder.

"D' you know these folks, Russ?" asked he.

"Some. Ben past here afore. They'll take us in."

"What!" the Parson exclaimed. "Seven men and a boy—not to mention the dog?"

"Suhtinly. Glad to git the chanct."

A stub of a man, in buck-skins black with wear, bare-footed and bare-legged, was scrambling down from the ladder on which he stood to rearrange the slabs of bark that took the place of shingles on his roof. He waved a hand in greeting, although at two hundred yards he could scarcely know who his guests were. Cursing and kicking among the dogs, he came as fast as he could. He straddled in his walk. He wore a coon-skin cap without a tail. There was a long red scar, perhaps of a bear's claw, running from the corner of his mouth to his neck and narrowly missing the jugular vein. His face was deeply pock-marked.

"Wal, whar in the tarnation y'-all drap from?" he called.

"Sal'sb'ry," Bean replied. "The hull kit-'n'-bilin'. But we didn't drap; we clumb."

"Whar ye gwinter?"

"Morganton."

197

"Whut fer?"

"Jack Sevier's trile."

"Oh, don't say that, man!"

"Why not?"

"Ev'y time I hear tell o' thet trile I hev to set daown an' laff."

He came close. "Name's Jake McNab," he said. "What's yourn?"

"Russell Bean."

"Wal, dog my cats, so ye be! I must be goin' blind.—Git *daown* thar, Honey-Mouth, an' stint yer yip!—Oughter knowed yeh. Know yer paw an' maw tother side. Trader, ain't ye?"

He spat, vigorously, at a daisy-top some six feet off. The daisy turned brown, trembling.

"Not much of a trader. Rifle-man an' pack-man mos'ly. But thisheer's Holdfast Gaines. He useter be one."

McNab thrust his head far back to look up at Holdfast and thrust out a short grimy paw. "Wal, my godly! An' I reckon he *is* a trader, tew. Must be the reg'lar rooster of all traders sence the time o' Jim Adair. Praoud ter meet yeh, Mr. Gaines. Heerd tell o' yeh oftentimes, but never b'lieved it afore."

He was almost equally proud to meet all the other members of the company, including Perthy and the dog.

"Wal, naow," said he, rubbing his hands together, "what a grand ole tell we-uns be a-gwinter hev! 'Pears like it don't never sprenkle humans raound hyar but whut we git a freshet. Me an' Maw we looks up the trace an' we squints daown the trace fer six months, mebbe, an' never a soul in sight; but then all of a suddent-like hyar 's *seven* of yeh by godly, *with* a dog *an'* Mr. Holdfast Gaines!—Haow be ye, Wash? Thisheer's ole Honey-Maouth, an' she don't mean nothin' by 't. She won't bite yeh."

"Seven of us, Mr. McNab, are too many," said the Parson. "We know that. We'll just camp outside, somewhere along the bank of the river. We have our own . . ."

"Whut's thet? Ye'll jest camp aoutside 'long the river-banks o' hell! My good sufferin' . . . ! An' so naow, gen'lemen, we'll jest go anti-godlin daown thisheer hill an' s'prise Maw. 'Cause when folks creep up on her onbeknownst in her ole clo'es, so ter say, then she don't hev no time to put on no comp'ny manners."

"Oh, I see, Mr. McNab," said McNairy. "By 'antigodlin' you mean crisscross or slantindicular."

"Yeah—slaunchways, like. Ain't thet haow you fellers say 't?"

"Yes, yes; we all say 'antigodlin,'—or, anyhow we always will hereafter," the young man replied with a wink at his companions.

" 'Course I *hev* heerd fellers say suthin' like 'weewaw' an' 'skwywise,' but thet 'ar ain't eddicated talk an' it's reely 'antigodlin' all the time."

"Yeah," Bean agreed, " 'ceptin' o' course when hit's 'skewgee' or 'kitty-cornered' or 'whopper-jawed' or mebbe jest plain 'squowed.' "

"Up along the Connecticut shore," said Holdfast, surprising them all, "I've heard the old ship-carpenters say 'snied-off.' "

"Ah, well, o' course, Holdfast," Bean indulgently replied, "way up thar in them back'ard parts ye cain't expeck their talk 'll mean nothin' much, no more 'n that li'l green book o' the Parson's."

The cabin they were approaching was quite twice as large as most habitations of the frontier. The loose slabs of bark on the roof, held down by long split saplings, had evidently been there not more than one year. A bear-skin, stretched to dry in the sun, was nailed to the logs near the door. Three or four skins of wolves were similarly impaled against an out-shed. The flayed carcass of a deer, almost black, was hanging by the hind legs from the only tree close at hand. Large collops had been cut from the haunches. The flies were leaving it now, as the sun declined.

Three or four young brats, dirty-faced, with fingers in their mouths, eyed the strangers suspiciously from the corner of the shed, obviously ready to run at a moment's alarm. Farther off, near the barn, two gawky youths pretended to busy themselves with a wooden shovel and a pitchfork.

"Sightly cabin you have here, Mr. McNab," said McKay, gazing about.

"Ah, glad ye think so. But to me she don't hev no seem to her. Me an' the boys hed to do her alone a two-three year back, 'caount o' not havin' no neebors, an' we mammicked her. But the ole one got too small. Too many childern—an' then the gram-babes kep' a-poppin' till she a'most busted."

"How many children have you, Mr. McNab?" the Parson politely inquired.

"Aw, 'baout nine, near 's I c'n figger—not caountin' the one's a-comin'. But they ain't a-gwinter be no more. Thet's the *lot,* so ter say."

"Why, man," Bean exclaimed, "ye wouldn't stop with on'y nine, would ye? Don't ye think ye oughter help popperlate the kentry?"

"Nope. Ain't a-gwineter. An' anyhow, figger I done my share a'ready."

"How ye make so damn shore ye ain't a-gwineter?"

"Wal, fack is," replied McNab, darkening another daisy in mid-sentence, "me an' Maw's done faound aout whut's a-causin' it."

A shout of manly laughter circled out through the quiet woods, sympathetically joined by Perthy and Wash and all the dogs of the McNab establishment. Mr. McNab himself, however, did not even smile. He looked modest, but firm.

"And did I correctly understand you to say," asked the Parson at length, "that you also have grandchildren?"

"Any God's quan'ty of 'em, sir. Slews. Squirmin' all over the place. Ev'y time I turn raoun' an' look be damn iffen thar ain't a new one I never set eyes on afore."

"But Mr. McNab, you don't look . . ."

"Old 'nough? Jes' same, I'm a-risin' forty, an' folks 'laow ez Maw looks a dretful sight older 'n thet.—C'm on raoun' an' meet Maw."

But Maw McNab had made her escape, having correctly interpreted the outcry of the dogs. To show that she had recently been at the back of the cabin there was only a bucket of dirty suds and a pile of wet linsey-woolsey. Her husband, somewhat discomfited, called his two gawky sons from the barn and introduced them.

"Naow then," said he, "d' you boys take aour critters aouten stalls an' put thesen in, fur's they'll hold.—You Hunter thar, *daown,* sir. Jest give 'im a good kick in the slats, Perthy.—An' so, gen'lemen, will ye kindly step in an' rest yer ear-flaps?"

Russell Bean insisted upon tethering his animals beside the stream, and Jackson tied his horse to a tree. These arrangements completed, McNab stood back from the cabin door with a sweeping gesture of welcome and waited until the last of his guests, with their game-cock and their dog, had entered. The only one of his own dogs that tried to go in he sent sprawling.

"Naow, make yerselves to hum," he said. "Hyar's two hick'ry cheers an' a good staout bench. I allus set on the floor m'self."

Holdfast, Perthy, and Russell Bean also sat on the floor. Wash curled up by the fire on the hearth and closed his eyes. Little David, firmly held by the legs in Jackson's fist, peered belligerently about the room.

"Yeah, we hev a fire 'most all summer," said the host. "Helps ter fend off fever 'n' ager.—Thet is ter say, helps some; but Maw, she gits it, dretful. Course 't ain't so much right naow, but when she's a-goin' good folks 'll come from miles 'raound jes' ter see Maw shake."

In spite of the fire the room was already dim. Through the panes of

200

paper smeared with bear-grease at the two loop-hole windows there came only enough light to show how little the room contained. Half a log, eight feet in length and resting on rough stakes, served as a table. The floor was made of split logs. From pegs driven into the walls hung the family wardrobe, mostly made of the skins of wild beasts. A crude ladder at the far end of the room gave access to the pitch-dark loft.

While his guests were finding seats McNab took a woman's garment from a peg and gave it to one of the children crowding at the door. "Hyar, Babe," said he, "I wancher run find granny aout in woods an' give her thisheer gaown." He paused a moment, thinking, and a smile both fond and humorous ennobled his face. "Oh, an' yeah . . ." He walked to the corner, took certain articles from an upper drawer, and added: "Ye better take her shawl an' teeth 'long too. She'll be a-wantin' 'em."

"Her teeth?" exclaimed the Parson.

"Yeah. Teeth. Ye never did see such a tooth-praoud dummern ez Maw be. 'Pears she kain't bear ter hev strangers see her 'thaout her teeth in."

"But what kind of . . . ?"

"Aw, or'n'ry kind, whuttled aout o' saourwood root wi' my jack-knife two winters back. But they bite good. Maw, she c'n chaw 'most anythin' but b'ar-meat with 'em. B'ar an' biled eel.—An' anyhaow, she never did cotton to eel."

McNab was fumbling, while he spoke, at a loose puncheon in the floor. Presently he pulled it out and brought forth a large earthenware crock. This he shook, and listened. " 'T ain't more'n quarter full," he apologized as he handed the crock to Russell Bean, "but hit'll mebbe keep aour whustles wet till supper. Then we'll hev s' more."

"Mr. McNab," the Parson protested, "we brought our own suppers with us. All we want is a place to eat them in."

The host was now lying flat on the floor and groping with his right hand far under the puncheons. "Wal," he grunted, "we hain't got no sech place. But we *hev* got a place whar y'-alls a-gwineter eat *aour* supper, an' thet's right spang whar ye set."

"But there are too many of us."

"Hell! They's 'nough saow-belly 'raound hyar to feed a hull army, an' 'nough good dry floor to bed a hull army daown, tew."

"But . . ."

McNab's face brightened. He drew up a long slender bundle carefully wrapped in buck-skin. This, when opened, was seen to contain

201

two well-made white candles. He held them up for admiration. "Bought 'em offen Bill Gomme," said he, "fer only one mink. Maw, she dunno 'baout 'em. I kep 'em hid, savin' 'em up. Never knowed why. Never reckoned I'd be a-burnin' 'em some night with Mr. Holdfast Gaines in aour own cabin."

He rose, softened the butts of the candles at the fire, and carefully stuck them erect on the stone of the chimney-piece. Then, after a moment of esthetic contemplation, he sat down again beside Russell Bean. Finding that the crock had come full-circle, he finished off the contents and set it beside him.

"An' so y' all 's a-gwine up ter the trile," said he, wiping his mouth with the back of his hand.

"We hope to," Bean replied, "iffen the good folk 'long the trace don't kill us off with kindness."

"Wal, hain't it the damn'dest go, axin' a man like Jack Sevier ter stan' trile afore a passel o' lawyers!"

"Huh!"

"Mought 's well ax a maounting tiger won't he please ter come daown an' play wi' the rats in yer barn."

"My great good God," Bean exclaimed, roused to eloquence by the unaccustomed lift of the raw whisky, "iffen on'y these hyar tide-water lawyers c'd a-seed how Jack grabbed us up, eight year back come October, an' shoved us up along through wind an' rain fer thirty-six mile o' marchin'!"

"Whut ye mean—to King's Maounting?"

"Sartin shore. Whar else?"

"Thet so! Wal, ye must 'a' ben jest a slick-face them days, not cleverly growed."

"Boy or man, thar I war, howsomever—half asleep fer the heft o' the time an' the rest asleep ez a stun. But the cuss o' thet Jack Sevier— 'git along thar, ye sons o' bitches!'—come a-snakin' round my years like the snap of a mule-man's whup!"

"Yeah, thet Jack, he c'n cuss when he wants ter. But 'baout King's Maounting, naow, I war thar m'self, under Shelby. I rec'leck haow it rained—a reg'lar ole goose-draownder—an' haow ole Pahson Dook said a prayer afore we fit. 'An' speshly, O Lawd,' sezee, 'hev regards to these hyar damn Tories; fer they will need all thy help, O Lawd, an' prob'ly hit won't be 'nough.'"

"Yeah," Bean agreed; "an' he says 'Git ye ready fer 'em, Lawd, fer they'll be a-comin', ternight.'"

"An' haow they *did* come, by godly, daown hill wi' them home-made bagnets, like they'd los' the tas'e fer livin' an' bullets was good ez drink!"

"'Oh, these be the damn yellin' boys!'—'member thet, McNab, when we guv 'em the 'whoo-whoop'?"

"Shore do! Afore, they'd called us mongrels, but thet yell changed their chune."

"It must 'a' shuk their guts, that yell us thousan' guv 'em."

"Yeah. So them we didn't shoot, why, them we hung—or mos'ly."

"You say you hanged them, Mr. McNab!" the Parson exclaimed.

"Naw. I said we *hung* 'em. Hurts wuss."

"But what kind of treatment is that for prisoners of war?"

"Pris'ners o' war, nothin'! Didn't ye hear us say they was *Tories?*"

"But even so . . ."

"Lookee hyar, Pahson," said Bean severely, "iffen ye got any Tory blood lef' in yeh, better leave it thisheer side o' Blue Ridge, 'cause tother side hit won't last yeh long.—I advise yeh as a friend."

Parson Blandison walked toward the fire. "Oh, as for that," said he, "I always accommodate my political opinions to the company I'm with."

There was a silence until McNab remarked: "An' so we come back hum, an' ended thet thar war."

"Like hell ye did!" said Jackson, with startling ferocity.

"Whut ye mean? Didn't Cornwallis run yelpin' back ter Yorkto'n with his tail 'tween his laigs? Didn't he s'render arter King's Maounting?"

"Ah, but they was other things in atween."

"Sech ez?"

Turning his head so that the firelight fell upon his left cheek, Jackson traced with his finger the livid scar running up into the mop of his hair. He held out his left hand and showed another scar between the first and second fingers.

"Saber cuts?" asked McNab.

Jackson nodded.

"Haow come?"

"Refusin' to black a British off'cer's boots."

"H'm. Whut ye do to 'im?"

Jackson sprang from the bench and took three or four swift paces across the room, the fluttering game-cock still clutched in his fist.

"I lost 'im, that's what—bein' only thirteen at the time. I never even heard his cursed name. I'd go round the world to find 'im, but he's lost."

The young man had reached the open door and stood staring out, his back to the company, when they heard him say: "But I s'pose thar's more British off'cers somewhars, an' I'm on the watch fer 'em!"

"I'm looking for a man too," piped Perthy, "and I know hith name. I'm going to find him and kill him."

Several began to laugh at this outburst, but Holdfast's face was too grave and the lad's eye shone too brightly in the firelight.

Jackson went back to the bench, apparently blushing a little.

To fill the awkward pause, Bean said: "Thar ain't nary a man nor yet a woman west o' the Ridge what don't owe Jack Sevier more 'n they'll ever pay back. I'm the fust white man ever borned out thar, an' I oughter know. I owe 'im my mother's life."

"Ye don't say so, Mr. Bean!"

"Yeah. Back in seventy-six, 't war, an I on'y a shaver, when Draggin' Canoe an' Ole Abraham o' Chilhowee come rushin' down Nolichucky Path with three hunderd Cherrakies all war-painted an' honin' fer ha'r. Wal, my Paw, that's Cap'n William Bean, he was over to Watauga Fort, an' I had to take Maw an the younger childern thar. I tried, but one o' them childern ain't never ben found, an' 'nother one, 't would 'a' ben jest as good iffen we never had found her. Them Injuns tuk my Maw an' said they wouldn't kill her iffen she'd teach their squaws to make butter an' cheese. Then arter while a brave walks up an' snaps a musket in her face, on'y the powder was wet. Next they build a fire an' bind her arms an' begin to dance an' sing."

"H'm. Thet so! Awk'ard!"

"Yeah. Wal, Jack, he hears 'bout this an' sends a runner to Nancy Ward—her that's B'loved Woman o' the Cherrakies—an' Nancy she says this thing must stop. It did stop. An' so that's how my Maw . . . B' God, I'd swash through flames o' hell for that man Sevier; an' so would hunderds more."

"Same time," said Spruce McKay, "when it comes to breakin' the law . . ."

"Same time, nothin'!" cut in McNab. "When a man's saved a man's Maw's life, thet's all they is to 't."

The head of Spruce McKay, well stored with legal learning, bowed to the great American heart.

McNab went on: "Danged iffen I c'n figger aout why in the tarnation a man like thet 'ar bug-tit of a John Tipton ever was borned fer."

204

"Oh, I don't know," said McKay mildly. "Skeeters like him."

"Mean ye're a-gwineter speak up fer a slew-footed, buss-eyed mother's mistake the likes o' Tipton?—What hell's he got ag'in' Jack Sevier, anyhaow?"

Spruce McKay leaned forward and spoke with quiet emphasis: "Now, Mr. McNab, you prob'ly know very well what Sevier has been up to. He pretends to be the Governor of a State, just over the Ridge, that calls itself the State of Franklin. Now that so-called State—and I've been over there more than once—belongs by rights to North Car'liny, and she ought by rights to pay North Car'liny taxes like you do here."

"Not so's ye'd notice it much, I don't. An' iffen ary meachin' tax-c'lecter comes a-snoopin' raound arter the bit o' shoat-bacon he mought git offen me, then by godly my dawgs has their instructions, sir.—Yeah, an' my ole rifle-gun 'Honey Bee' she don't like taxes nuther."

"Well, I'm not a tax-collector myself, I thank my stars; but I fail to see how we're going to make a country without somebody paying a few taxes."

"Spoke like a clay-faced Tory!" McNab exploded. "An', what's wuss, like a penny-pinchin' tide-water lawyer—axin' yer pardon an' meanin' no offense."

"Oh, no!" laughed McNairy. "Lawyers are never offended. They can't afford it."

"Wal, ye ain't a-gwineter arsle aout of it thetaway.—Jever hear tell of a war we fit 'g'inst England, not s' many years back? An' whut fer? Jest fer tryin' ter c'leck taxes an' never doin' nothin' fer 'em. An' State o' Franklin's all same as the Col'nies back in seventy-six."

"Maybe so," said McKay, holding up a placating hand. "Fact is, I don't deny it. But we're talkin' about Jack Sevier, not taxes. Sevier's laid siege to Tipton's house down at Sinkin' Crick, which is an act o' violence."

"Sarved Tipton good damn an' right fer runnin' off with Sevier's niggers."

"An' Sevier's killed the Sheriff o' Washington County."

"Sarves the Sheriff right, 'cause o' him bein' in rebellion 'g'inst his own Guv'ner."

"Oh, come now, Mr. McNab! I don't like to disagree with a man in his own house, but do be reasonable. Shootin' Sheriffs is bad business, Mr. McNab. It ain't at all what we have a right to expect o' Governors."

205

"Aw, I dunno. Seemin'ly somebody's gotter do it. 'Better the man, better the deed,' ez Pore Richard says."

"No, sir; that's no way to talk," said Jackson firmly. "We can't run the country that way."

"Verb sap," McNairy agreed. "Governors must not shoot Sheriffs."

"What 'd you say, Mr. McNab," urged McKay, leaning still farther forward, "if someone was to tell you that Jack Sevier is plotting right now to turn the State of Franklin—yes, and the Cumberland Settlements, with all o' Western Waters—over to Spain?"

"Say? To a man 't tried to feed me thet 'ar hog-wash?—Wal, course I'd say he was a damn liar."

"You wouldn't b'lieve him, I s'pose, even if he showed you proofs?"

"Huh! Suhtinly not! Proofs is fer lawyers. I go by common sense."

McKay threw his hands over his head with a whimsical grimace. "I begin to fear," said he, "that you don't like lawyers as a class, Mr. McNab."

"Ez a class, no—iffen I ketch yer meanin'. Soon's they come in, a kentry starts daown hill. Arter the lawyers comes the doctors, which is mebbe wuss. An' then on the heels o' the doctors comes the ridin' preachers, arter which all decent folk hez to sell their betterments dirt cheap an' move aout a thousan' mile an' start all over ag'in.—Wal, I've moved aout twicet a'ready in my time, an' I don't cotton to them folks."

"I can't see what you want to lug in doctors for," said McNairy. "There ain't any doctors here."

"Eh? What say?—Oh wal, thar will be.—But whut I say is, hit all comes o' payin' taxes. Iffen ye don't start that, then ye got some chanct."

"Yes, but chance o' what?" McNairy wished to know. "A good chance you'd have, without the things taxes bring, of having your grand-children all scalped and your razor-backs eaten up by tigers."

McNab sank back against the wall. "Never lost a gram-babe thetaway yit," he drawled, complacently. "I don't never hev no Injun nor yit no tiger trouble. An' ez fer razor-backs, y' oughter see them fellers sky-hoot! Oh, haow they kin squander!—Naw; iffen ye give me my druther I'll take my chanct w' tigers an' Injuns stiddier 'n lawyers."

There was a hint of social frost in the air.

"May I ask what you mean by 'tigers'?" inquired the Parson, hoping to make a diversion.

"Up in Virginny," said Bean, "I hear tell they call 'em 'painters,' an in C'neckticut folk useter say suthin' like 'cat-o'-mount'in, or mebbe now an' then 'catawampus'; but o' course they be reely tigers all over."

"Most int'restin'," the Parson replied. "I didn't know that tigers belonged to the American fauna, and certainly I never expected to have a chance of seeing one."

"Ye won't see 'im, Pahson. He'll see you fust.—I ben livin' in tiger kentry all my days. Borned an' bred up in tiger kentry. Heered 'em yowlin' o' night an' follered their trace all day, but hain't never yet laid eyes on one.—Ever any you fellers seed a tiger?"

"Yeah, onct," said McNab. "Not a bob-cat nor yit a link he warn't, but a real he growed-up tiger, wi' whiskers on him mebbe a foot long. 'Baout gloamin', 't war, an' I jest a-slinkin' through the tall timber 'thaout my 'Honey Bee' nor yit even a dawg, which is a damn fool way to go—an' all of a suddent, like, by godly thar he war, 'baout ten foot off up a tree, with his tail a-swishin' an' claws a-gittin' ready an' two big eyes a-glaowerin' daown at me like he was all on fire inside.—H'm. Awk'ard."

"What ye do then?" Bean inquired.

"I lit aout from thar. I went somewhars else—I fergit whar, but a long ways off. Reckon thet tiger war kinder s'prised how quick they wa'n't nothin' o' Jake McNab left raound thet place a-tall."

"And yet," said McNairy, when the laughter had died down, "you like tigers better 'n lawyers."

"Wal, suh, yes I do—allus 'ceptin' present comp'ny, o' course. Tigers mind their own bus'ness an' leave yeh go 'baout yournses. Same goes fer skunks, copperheads, ra'l'snakes, cotton-maouths, toad-frogs, an' all the rest o' them good clean critters. But lawyers an' tax-c'lectors—wal, whut ever did the good Lawd take an' create the wilderness fer iffen 't wa'n't ter git away from them fellers in?"

"I think I see what you mean, Mr. McNab," said the Parson.

"Course ye do. Way 't is, thisheer's a more maountaynious kentry than whar you fellers come from, an' whar they's plenny o' maountings folk ain't so easy put upon. Thet's haow I figger 't.—But thisheer tell is a-gittin' dry."

McNab rose, strode to the door, and called out: "Hey, you Bill! Hank! Whar's yer Maw?"

"Aout in woods, Pap, gittin' dressed up," answered a distant voice.

"Wal, fer the Lawd's sake, tell her to git a hustle on. We wanter eat. An' fotch us thet 'ar biggest jug o' red-eye aouten barn. These men's perishin'."

He let himself down again to the floor with a look of extreme exhaustion.

"But while we're waiting for the red-eye, Mr. McNab," said the Parson, "won't you have a nip o' this old brandy?"

McNab reached up for the flask. "Brandy?" he said, his eyes shining. "Hain't hed a drap o' no sech a drink fer goin' on ten year."

He seemed to be making up for lost time. His head fell back. There was an expression of esthetic delight in his eyes as he returned the empty flask to its owner.

"Thet 'ar," he said, audibly smacking his lips, "hain't got no bad taste to 't. Makes a man wish 't he hed a throat a mile long."

He reflected for a moment.

"Goes daown good an' stays daown good," he reported.

More reflection.

"An' whut's more," said he, looking up with a grateful smile, "thar's a kinder fare-ye-weel to 't, like it left a leetle camp-fire a-burnin' in yer goozle."

"I'm glad you liked it," said the Parson, replacing the cork and privately wondering what sense the word "nip" might bear in these western wilds.

"Hyar's Maw," said McNab, hurriedly rising to his feet. He went to the fireplace, selected a burning twig, and lighted the two tall candles.

She was standing just outside the door, looking in, timidly. One hand was fluttering over her mouth. Coming so silently out of the dusk, saying no word, she was like a wraith in the half-light.

"Wal, whyn't c'm on in, Maw? We-uns ain't a-goin' ter bite yeh. We ben waitin' fer yeh Gawd he knows haow long."

She put one bare brown foot across the door-sill and moved toward her place by the fire, trying to speak but as yet unable.

Holdfast rose, then Perthy and the Parson, then all the others.

"Men," said McNab, looking ill at ease, "thisheer's Maw. An' Maw, hyar's Mr. Holdfast Gaines hisself, big ez life an' not sayin' nothin'. Hyar's Pahson Blandison, Mr. Andrew Jackson an' his fightin' cock, Mr. Russ Bean son o' Cap'n Bill, Mr. Spruce McKay talks like he mought be a lawyer but aour guest jest same, Mr. John McNairy an' Mr. Tom Searcy which is lawyers likewise, an' Perthy an' his dog by name o' Wash."

For a moment her shy glance was caught and held by the eyes of Holdfast, and then she looked at Perthy. She had on a shapeless gray garment of linsey-woolsey and a long apron of clean white doe-skin. Her figure, or what could be guessed of it, had nearly lost its feminine

208

outline. Her sweet, weary face was scored with the record of many toils and privations, many desperate child-births. Too much of woman's work and hope and daring, the Parson saw, had left her, in appearance, hardly a woman at all. Yet over her graying hair she had drawn a Paisley shawl of vivid beauty. It was fastened under her chin by a silver brooch, very old and delicate—French, perhaps, or Italian.

"Whut ye wanter git yerself tangled up in all them dew-dabbers fer?" her husband asked, an odd mingling of rough banter with affection in his tone.

"Why, Jake, ye sent 'em to me."

McNab chose not to pursue this phase of the topic. "Huh!" said he, accurately squirting tobacco-juice at a tiny flame in the fire. "Y' ain't wore thet leathern apern sence Bill Gomme drap by; an' naow ye hear we got Holdfast Gaines ye go an' git aout the shawl.—Don't I know yer tricks?"

The ghost of a girlish smile lighted her face. "I'm glad ye got aout the candles, Jake," said she. "They's beauchyus! I ben a-wonderin', ever sence Bill Gomme drap by, when ye war a-gwine ter burn 'em. An' ternight's the best time of all, naow we got Mr. Holdfast Gaines."

"Wal . . . wal, thar ye go, changin' the subjick!—But, Maw, we-uns are hollower 'n gourds. Whut ye got?"

"Co'n-pone," said she in a flat low voice, "an' razor-back, burries, trouts, b'ar-ile, hick'ry-ile, pickle-suckers, eel-meat, saour-buzzum, sad bread, red-eye, an'—an'—reckon thet's 'baout all, Jake."

"Wal, then, thet's prob'ly 'nough. Go git the gals ter help yeh, an' look spry. An' ye c'n put the red-eye fust, so's t' won't sinnify whut else we hev."—And once more Mr. McNab exhibited his marksmanship.

His wife unpinned her precious silver brooch and lifted the shawl from her head. Stepping softly to the corner, she reverently laid them both away in the top of the walnut chest. Then she moved toward the door.

"Aw, hell," said McNab, not ungently, "I ain't a-faultin' yeh, Maw. Y' ain't never hed too much ter be praoud on, an' I know it."

A moment later, when she had gone, he became still more confidential. "Thet 'ar shawl an' brooch," he said, "they was guv her the day we got married. They b'longed to her granny, fotched over from Scotland. —Fack is, she ain't sech a bad dummern, reely. She's heavy-footed jest naow—thet's how 't is. An' she's hed 'baout nine a'ready, like I told yeh."

LITTLE DAVID

Thirteen game-cocks, red and black, white, gray, and barred, were fighting a battle-royal in the pit, twenty feet across, under the great sycamore at Morganton. All incessantly leaping and flapping to over-top their opponents, they looked like rebounding hail, or pop-corn jumping in the popper. Their close-cropped wings as they rose with a clap made explosions as of tiny umbrellas suddenly opened. With long lean necks outstretched, breast to breast, beak to beak, they fought as though each of the thirteen knew that only one could survive. Not an eye, a muscle, a nerve, that was not straining. Not a beak, heel, or claw that was not questing for blood.

Some two hundred men, mostly in buck-skins, stood round the fight-ers, encouraging, imploring, yelling them on. They stood three-deep, the innermost leaning over the two-foot barrier and those on the out-side shoving for better positions. Already there had been promise of several fights among the men, but the counter-attraction of the cock-fight had thus far proved too strong. The shorter and weaker men had been sifted into the rear rank, where they could see nothing of the contest, or else were trying to climb the sycamore.

Landlord McKniff, looking on as well as he could from the doorway of his tavern, was thinking that here was a great day for Morganton, or at least for him. Two hundred thirsty men from the backwoods, and many of them drunk already, though the sun was not three hours high! He was beginning to doubt whether his four small barrels of bumblins would stand the drain. Certainly his bear-bacon and sow-belly would not. A deficiency of food would be no great matter, but he must be careful not to run short of drink. A little more watering of the bum-blins, now—could that be managed so as to escape detection?

How the crowd was roaring over there! Such a burst of yells must mean two or three chickens gone down at once—fallen down and dragged out by Russell Bean's long-handled hoe. Even some of the betting became audible: "Six to one on Avery!" "Take yeh fer five dollars Car'liny!" "Seven to three on McKinley!" "Take yeh at . . ." "Four to one against Jackson!" "Good, that's mine!"—And then all other sounds were suddenly quieted by the crashing of the lower branch in the sycamore on which seven or eight spectators had tried to perch.

210

A little cloud of feathers was floating above the cock-pit. Fluffs of vivid color settled slowly downward upon heads and shoulders, some of them rocking like tiny boats as they sank. A splash of bloody red came to rest on the long black hair of the huge man talking over there to Waightstill Avery. Someone had said that this man was Holdfast Gaines, but McKniff was not one to believe everything he heard. And yet, what shoulders! What a chest! Like an oak he was. If not Holdfast Gaines, then who could he be?

From the way the bets were made and taken one could see there was plenty of money here. Times might be hard, and money of any sort might be difficult to come by, but that was not interfering with pleasure. Already the pile of pelts traded in for drink stood three feet high under McKniff's counter. There was a bulge in his hunting-shirt just above the belt, made by a wad of current and legal paper from Virginia, Maryland, the Carolinas, and Pennsylvania. He even had a little from Massachusetts and Connecticut. Its actual worth in good second-run whisky was beyond his calculation, and so he took pleasure in jingling the silver coinage of Spain, France, and England in his shot-pouch.

"Four to one against Jackson!"—Parson Blandison had called that bet; and Jackson, hearing him from the other side of the pit, had shouted back "Good! That's mine!" Then, a moment later, he had added: "One hundred dollars, Virginny?" To this the Parson had nodded assent, making a note of the wager on the fly-leaf of his little book called "Quintus Horatius Flaccus."

At first thought one might call that even money. There were still eight stags in the fighting, of which Andrew Jackson owned two. So far as he could see, his big white Virginian—acquired only the night before in a card-game—and his little Jamaican red were holding their own. The white, to be sure, had suffered an ugly slash in the shoulder and had been badly punished about the head, but the same thing, or nearly, might be said of every bird in the ring excepting Little David. That vivid red streak of lightning had saved himself, thus far, from any dangerous hurt. He danced and flapped and ducked and towered as fresh as though just beginning. Small and light he was—scaling only three pounds ten at the weighing-in, while every other bird of the lot had weighed at least four pounds—but already he had killed two cocks nearly twice his size. One of them, to Jackson's deep satisfaction, had belonged to Waightstill Avery, the Morganton lawyer.

But the Parson had said, "Four to one against Jackson." After all, it was not encouraging to have the man who had owned the better of

211

these two birds now betting against both of them. The Parson probably knew, as Jackson did not, where and when and by whom Little David had been bred, fed, and walked; he knew whether Little David had been through the roup, and what earlier fights he had lost or won. Moreover, Jackson had accepted the Parson's offer to clip and trim the cocks before this battle. Perhaps that had been unwise. A man who would cheat at dice would scarcely hesitate at crippling a game-cock. Anyone could have seen, as the small scissors snipped in and out, that here was a department of learning in which the Parson had long been a master.

The Parson himself was taking small pleasure in the battle. Whose stag, after all, except for the turn of a die, was this that young Jackson was playing? Who knew Little David's points and pedigree? Not Jackson. And who, among all these ignorant muleteers crowding round the pit, knew the slightest thing about the history of cocking as it went back through England to ancient Rome, to Greece, to Persia, and was lost in old Cathay? No one. Even the sports of these western ruffians were crude, ignorant, and dull.

Why thirteen cocks—an odd number? A battle-royal required forty. And then, the gross and stupid irregularity of allowing any man to enter as many cocks as he liked! Mr. Avery, over there, had no less than six birds in the ring. They would be fighting each other, and that would confuse all the betting.

Moreover, even when properly conducted, a battle-royal was a coarse and sanguinary game. As compared with a main of cocks, the sport of kings, instituted by Themistocles, it gave no more opportunity for real excellence than the new-fangled "democracy" that Thomas Jefferson was bringing home from France. The better the bird the more likely he was to exhaust himself in his first encounter, and so to be struck down by some common dung-hill fowl.

The Parson's eyes went roving round the circle of flushed, unshaven faces. What these men wanted was gore. For the game-cock's fire, beauty, courage, and indomitable spirit they cared, he felt sure, nothing. Undoubtedly they would have put long heels on their birds if they had been able to secure and shape the necessary materials.

How different all this from that terrific match, thirty years back, in the yard of the Golden Cross at Oxford! Desperado and King Cole the birds had been, each of them a veteran and a feathered knight.

212

Three hundred undergraduates, in spite of the rules against cocking, had crowded the courtyard, the galleries and roofs and doorways, and the windows renting at a guinea an hour. Waiters in white and blue aprons went plunging here and there in the crowd with foaming mugs of porter and ale. The gates into Cornmarket were shut and barred, and the town boys struggled to squeeze through. And then the cockers coming, with the kicking birds in large white bags. "Four to one on Bingham's bird!" "A hundred pound on Blake's!" "Cuck! Cuck!" from the bags —"Cuck! Cuck!" And oh, the murderous look of Desperado as the cocker drew him forth—slim, trim, magnificently male, with a gleam on his bronze and golden feathers as though the sun were seeking them out alone! His neck lunging out of the bag was sinuous, snake-like, terrible. His pouncing body, his iron-blue sinewy legs came forth. With the fierce pride of an eagle he peered about. His beak was an eagle's. He was enormous on a small scale. His eyes were pools of blackened fire.

And then the elaborate ritual—some of it ancient, probably Greek, certainly religious in origin—gone through by the feeders and walkers, the weighers-in, the handlers, the masters, the setters-to. There had been a decorum about it, a deference to old tradition in the hoveling and chopping, the exact measuring of spurs, the moistening of bandaged ankles, the taunting and pampering, and at last the breasting of the birds. Ah, how the two glittering stags themselves had crowned and mantled at the first fierce glimpse of one another, as though they felt that the embattled cocks of three thousand years were looking down upon them!

Back there had been a disciplined beauty, a learning. It had made a savage game almost into an art.—But now! And here!

"Now do tell me," said Waightstill Avery, "how my old friend Colonel Chester is getting on."

"I'm sorry to say I can't tell you much," said Holdfast, "but to the best of my knowledge he's alive and well. Of course he has a bad knee, from a wound he got at Bunker Hill."

"Ah, is that so? I hadn't heard. But he's hearty. John 'll live to a good ripe age. And oh dear, oh dear, what times we two 've had together! One o' the kindest-hearted men on earth, John Chester is. A heart of gold."

"Yes."

"There goes another cock o' mine. Reg'lar little demon, that stag of Andy Jackson's. Just like his master.—But let's see, they had a daughter, didn't they—John and Mary?"

"Yes. One daughter."

"Her name was . . . ?"

"Rebecca."

"That's right. Now I recollect. But they never did have a son."

"Ah—well, no."

"Too bad, that. John would have loved a son. Oh dear, oh dear! Seems like yesterday. Up an' down Thames we'd go, over into Gungy-wamp, out along the Yantic, over in Brooklyn to see Israel Putnam—I know he's a famous man now, but just a jolly farmer and our Major in those days. Oh dear, oh dear!—Well, there goes another cock o' mine."

The old gentleman took Holdfast by the arm and walked him away from the crowd. "Tell you what 't is, my boy," said he. "Things haven't gone so bad for me down here, as you may judge for yourself; but I've known for years that I'd have been a happier man if I'd stayed where I was born, growing old among the friends I used to know."

"I understand," said Holdfast.

"O' course you do. But now, I'm thinking of you. Why don't you go home and stay there? Connecticut needs you. And you'll never find a better place on earth."

"No. I'm not looking for one."

"Well, then? You tell me you've been wanderin' about for years. What good is it? Why not build your life into one place? Why not take root like an oak tree up there among those Connecticut rocks?—My good Lord, just to see the Thames go sliding down into the Sound again, to smell the ocean up there by Cochegan Rock, see those Connecticut maples in October . . . Oh dear, oh dear!"

"Let's go back and watch the cock-fight," said Holdfast, turning.

"All right. But let me advise you, Holdfast. Go back and live and grow old with the people you knew when you were a boy. Why don't you?"

"Colonel Avery, five o' the boys I'd be thinking about—well, they bore your name. They wouldn't be there now."

"You mean the—massacre?"

"Yes."

"Ah, I see. And I s'pose that wasn't all the friends you lost there."

"No. There were the Ashbow brothers, four of them; and then 'Bijah and Riley Tharpe, and many more. No; I can't go back."

214

"That's true. I see it."

The old lawyer brooded, poking hard at the ground with his ivory-headed cane. "Holdfast," he said at last, "you and I are lonely. We're lost. America's too big for us. I have enough and—and I haven't anybody. My dear wife has been gone these many years, and all my children have left home. And so—see what I mean? Why not come and live with me, be my son for the little time I have left? You could get rich— oh, easily, Holdfast—if that would interest you at all. And we could have good times."

For a moment Holdfast's hand rested on the old man's shoulder. "Thanks, Colonel," he said. "I thank you a thousand times. But I—we'll talk that over."

Jackson's Hercules was failing, moment by moment, in his duel with the tall black cock belonging to Waightstill Avery. Half his glossy white plumage was soaked in gore. He staggered, panting. His wings hung limp. Just managing to follow his adversary's head that darted like a snake's up and down and from side to side, he could no longer make the least leap into the air to strike or to ward a blow.

"Seven to one against Jackson!" yelled a voice. Jackson did not hear. The black cock sprang again, slashing with both spurs at the white cock's prostrate head. When Hercules came out of that flurry of blows he had lost an eye. A shout went up.

"Ten to one against Jackson!" But still the young man paid no heed. He was leaning over the barrier, his bony fingers clutching the plank. The scar on his narrow brow was throbbing.—Yet not a muscle of his face quivered when the black sprang for the last time and sank a spur to the heel in the brain of his foe.

Hercules reeled and fell, rolled over twice, legs twitching, and came to rest with his polished toes clutching upward. Then, like an Indian taking a scalp, the black cock deliberately pecked out his one remaining eye.

Russell Bean reached out with the hoe and dragged the quivering body to one side. He seemed to be smiling.

Jackson straightened up and looked about him. "Did I hear ten to one against Jackson?" he yelled.

"Ten to one against you, Mr. Jackson!" called back Waightstill Avery. He was standing on the other side of the ring, with his three-cornered hat and cane under one arm. His long hair was iron-gray. He had a little betting-book in one hand, a pencil in the other. A flowered

215

waistcoat he had on, knee-breeches of satin, and silk stockings. Jackson could have hated him for these prosperous habiliments alone.

"One hundred dollars, Virginny?" Jackson snapped out.

"Agreed," Avery shouted back.—And yet he did seem to be somewhat surprised at the amount. He made a note of it in his little book.

Jackson felt that ten to one against him was surprisingly favorable odds, considering that only eight birds were left in the ring and one of them was his own Little David. Others might think that bird too small and light, but that only meant that the fire there was in him had so much less crude flesh to burn through. He was red all over. He might have been boiled in red. Already he had killed three birds, and still stood right as a trivet. A little blood here and there, perhaps not his own, but—ah, and there was the fourth! David ducked under the lunge of a big barred gray, leapt to his back in a flash, and drove a spur through his throat.

Drag him out, Russell Bean, and let's see you smiling now! Let's see a smile from old Avery—*and* the Parson!

David glanced round him—not so much to catch his breath, apparently, as to find the thick of the battle. Another cock went down, so that only six were left. Seeing that three of these were engaged in an irregular combat, David rushed into the midst of them. He tried to cut out a single opponent. Instead, he found himself facing three foes at once.

Jackson groaned. This was what he had feared. He leaned against the barrier and clutched the plank again. His face was white.

Someone tapped him on the shoulder. The Parson.

"Twenty to one against your winning?"

"Hell, yes!"

"How much?"

"Hunderd. Virginny."

The Parson gravely noted this wager in his little green book. Damn him! Everybody noting things down in little books! The world seemed to be filling up with little note-takers!

But almost before the words could be written Waightstill Avery's Black Demon, leaping at David from behind, had got him down!

He was slashing at David's head with vicious backward kicks.

Little David lay still.

Russell Bean dragged him away with his hoe. David's wings quivered as they were hauled through the bloody dust of the pit.

Jackson stared at the palpitating bundle of feathers lying so small and helpless beside the barrier. It was not credible that such a kernel of fire had now gone out.

No; but nevertheless he had lost his two birds. He had lost all the money he had in the world. He would have to sell his horse, his saddle, his clothes—everything.

Out of the corner of his eye he was watching Russell Bean's face. If that young man should show the slightest sign of happiness now, he would make himself a lifelong foe.

But Jackson could not make sure that Russell Bean was smiling. Neither, apparently, was Waightstill Avery. Why not? Was he thinking of something else? Damn him!

The battle was going to Avery's Black Demon. He killed one more contestant with ease, and faced down another bird. There followed a ragged encounter with his only remaining rival. Black Demon staggered off as victor, though badly wounded.

A cheer went up for Waightstill Avery.—Ah, this had been a battle that men would remember for years to come!

Russell Bean put one leg over the barrier, about to enter the pit and announce the victor.

"Git out o' thar!" yelled Jackson.

"What for?" Bean asked, going red in the face. "Battle's over, ain't it? An' I reckon I'm referee?"

"Ye don't know 't all them cocks is dead."

"Want me to go round an' feel their pulses?"

"You git out o' thar!"

Bean stepped back over the barrier. In spite of the fact that he was arrayed for the occasion in his most gorgeous Indian finery, his self-confidence was obviously shaken.

Black Demon, dragging one foot after the other, was tottering about the ring and pecking out the eyes of his late foes as he went. Jackson watched him, fascinated. Would David—those fiery eyes . . . ? Standing twenty feet off, he could see that David's eyes were not closed nor even glazing. Some ember of life might still be lingering there.

David's turn came last. Black Demon limped up to within a foot of him—but then seemed to forget what he had to do there. Perhaps he had now his glut of blood. The last tiny drop of his strength might have left him.

The two hundred spectators were quiet now. A mocking-bird was singing in the sycamore. A horse whinnied in the stables behind Mc-Kniff's.

217

Black Demon took one more step—a short one. His head was hanging low, and his eyes were almost shut. But Little David's eyes, wide open and burning, were fixed upon him. Thus for ten breathless seconds they gazed at each other. Then Jackson's bird, using his one uninjured wing, hunched himself into a sitting posture and slowly rose to his feet and stood, swaying.

A breeze stirred the leaves of the sycamore. Parson Blandison felt that his eyes were slowly filling with tears, as they were wont to do in moments of perfect beauty.

To Jackson, Little David now looked unconquerable. A bird that had touched rock-bottom an' nad been raked aside as dead and done for —well, what was there left for him except victory?

Thrusting his sharp chin forward, Jackson called out in a piercing voice: "Any gen'leman like to take one to a hunderd aginst Andrew Jackson?" He looked earnestly all round the circle, giving special attention to the Parson and Waightstill Avery; but no one answered.

The black cock and the red were swaying sullenly, beak to beak. Their heads all but touched the ground. For half a minute this went on, and then Little David lunged heavily forward, throwing all his weight against the black cock's body and toppling him sidelong.

Avery's bird lay inert, gasping.

At the sight of a prostrate foe new strength, it seemed, surged up in the small red body. David took another step. With one sure backward blow of the heel he kicked this spur into Black Demon's throat. Then, with minute and calculated precision, he turned and pecked out an eye.

He lifted his head, but in doing so threw himself off balance and sank back upon his close-cropped tail. Yet his head stayed up. It was thrown high, and backward. From his torn and bloodied throat there came, almost in a whisper and yet unmistakably triumphant, the cry "Co-cori-cu!"

Andrew Jackson did not hear Russell Bean's announcement. He scarcely knew that two hundred men were shouting his name and Little David's as though they had not shouted that day before. The tears were streaming down his face and he was laughing as he beat the planks of the barrier with clenched bony fists until the blood came. "By the 'Tarnal," he was saying over and over as though it were a chant, "By the 'Tarnal Lord God o' Creation, that's the bravest, beautifullest thing I ever will see!"

218

"A fine chance they have," said McNairy, "of givin' that man fair trial in this town today. Place is full o' Whigs, and most of 'em fought under Jack Sevier one time or 'nother."

"Wal," Russell Bean cheerfully inquired, "whut ye want? Tories? 'Cause iffen ye do whar ye gwineter git 'em in County Burke, 'cep' offen the gallus-tree? An' iffen ye're lookin' fer sech as hain't fit under Jack Sevier, try the chile unborned."

Bean was rubbing the nose of his horse with a wisp of grass. With half his mind he was speculating whether it would be better to leave his animals here in the shade of the pines, where they would not be so much pestered by flies, or to take them out into the deadening where the forage would be better. They had not been well fed of late, and the worst of their journey lay ahead.

"D' ye ever hear tell of a crime called 'high treason'?" young Jackson suddenly inquired, looking sharply at Bean. He had been so quiet during the last few minutes, earnestly prodding at a pebble lodged under the left hind shoe of his horse, that the others had nearly forgotten his presence.

Bean laughed, good-humoredly. "Seems like I hev heered some sech lawyer-talk," said he, "but it don't sinnify nothin'.—Not out hyar it don't."

"Well, we got to *make* it mean something!" exclaimed Searcy. "And damn soon, too. Treason's the crime Jack Sevier is charged with."

Bean threw away the handful of grass with a gesture of mild disgust. "Ah, hell," he growled. "You lawyers! I c'd a'most git to dislike ye iffen I hed to take yeh serious."

"You'll find high treason is serious enough, I reckon," said Searcy.

"All right, then—treason. Purty word. What's it mean?"

There was a pause.

"Why, ah, treason, Russ," said McNairy, "now, treason is a—a serious crime."

"So I jedge. Leastwise, ye lawyers don't think us other fellers oughter do it. Same time, do ye jest take an' tell me what 't is, so's ye won't be a-ketchin' me at it."

"Why, hell," said young Searcy, coming to the rescue, "guess everybody knows what treason is." Phrases recently memorized out of Coke and Blackstone fell glibly from his tongue as he went on: "Treason is to violate the king's companion, his eldest daughter, or the wife of his eldest son and heir."

Bean heaved a mock sigh of relief. "Wal, anyhow," he drawled, "Jack Sevier hain't never done that yit, I swar my bottom oath. An' afore he does he'll wanter git a good look at them ladies."

"No, that ain't right," said McNairy.

"Wal, figger 't out, young men. Ye reely oughter know what treason is afore ye convict Jack Sevier this day."

"Treason," McNairy recited, "is to compass or imagine the death of the king, the queen, or their eldest son and heir."

Bean stroked the mane of his horse with a happy smile. "No," said he, "thet thar lets Jack out too. He's ben too damn busy compassin' an' imaginin' the deaths o' Tories, Creeks, Cherrakies, an' Chickasaws to spend any brain-power on furren kings an' queens, let alone their Gawd-fersaken sons an' heirs."

But now Andrew Jackson set down the hoof of his horse. He was sitting with his narrow back toward Bean, and he spoke as though to the adjacent woods. "Treason," he said, "is to levy war against the King in his realm, or to be adherent to the King's enemies in his realm, givin' 'em aid and comfort in the realm or elsewhere."

The pleasant smile grew on Bean's handsome face as he realized that here was a chance to get even with this young whipper-snapper for an extremely embarrassing moment in yesterday's cock-fight.

"I'm glad to see," he said, "thet all you leetle boys hev yer lessings so nice this mornin', but Andy Jackson he hez hisn best an' so he c'n go to the head o' the class."

Jackson was on his feet. He walked very close to Bean and stared at him through narrowed lids. Bean had a strong sense of having been in just this situation before.

"You tryin' to insult me?" asked Jackson in a low, grating voice.

"On'y tryin' to larn ye suthin,' " said Bean, sweetly smiling. "But, 'sides thet, 't ain't easy to insult a damn traitor—an' thet's what you be, 'cordin' to yer own fool words."

Jackson's fist had gone not more than half way toward Bean's jaw when it was stopped as though against iron. His arms, at almost the same instant, were bound against his sides.

"Now listen, Mrs. Jackson's little boy," said a suave and fatherly voice, "I like yeh all right. We all do. We think ye mought grow up to be a nice big man, iffen ye don't git cut short by somebody takin' yeh too ser'ous, like. On'y, ye gotter larn *not* ter ketch yer tail on fire."

"Oh? An' who's a-goin' to larn me?"

"An' 'nother thing is, either ye ben guilty o' high treason or else ye're a damn Tory."

"Thet so?"

"Hell fire, hain't ye allus done all ye kin, ever sence ye clumb outen cradle, to levy war agin King George in what he calls his realm? Iffen I di'n' think so I'd jest natch'ly stomp yeh inter the dirt. But no; ye're a traitor all right. All decent folks is. An' the biggest traitor o' the lot is the man over thar in . . . Wal, damned iffen hyar don't come Doc Cosby!"

Feeling his elbows released from that invincible grip, Jackson turned and busied himself with the troublesome pebble in his horse's hoof. It was a blessed relief to Searcy and McNairy to have his flaming face turned away.

"Whar in Jeeroos'lem ye come from, Doc?" shouted Bean, striding down the path to shake hands with the slowly advancing horseman.

"Western Waters," replied the little man, wearily lifting his right leg over the horse's neck. He reached down a red-haired hand that somehow gave the impression of gentleness for all its stubby strength. A smile swept over his puckered face, twisting his mouth and brightening the blue of his eyes.

"What ye ben up to?" Bean asked.

"Oh, deliverin' one more o' your bastards, mos' likely."

Bean was too much interested in the magnificent mare the doctor was leading by the bridle to greet this familiar jibe with more than a perfunctory smile. Speaking in a tone that could not be overheard by the young men behind him, he inquired: "Hain't I seen thisheer mare afore somers?"

New and unsuspected wrinkles appeared on the left side of the doctor's face, and the sunny blue of his left eye underwent a brief eclipse. "No, ye hain't," said he, softly. "Never."

Bean's head went slowly backward. His eyes opened wide and his lips rounded in a long but silent whistle. "Thet's so, Doc," said he. "I hain't."

"Nice lookin' piece o' hoss-flesh, though, ain't she?" asked the doctor, raising his voice for the benefit of the others. "Doctors don't git sech fees round hyar every day!"

221

"Ye're a damn lucky med'cine man, Doc," assented Bean in the same tone.

"Whar's Jack?" Cosby whispered.

"Jail."

"Ironed?"

"Naw. Sheriff said he warn't goin' ter hev no gentleman ez mought be a Gov'ner a-settin' in his jail thet-away."

"Good ole Harrison.—When's the trile?"

" 'Bout an hour. Court-house is packed a'ready."

The two men looked across the clearing at the square building, somewhat larger than most of the other log-cabins of Morganton, round which there was a considerable gathering of men, boys, horses, and highly excited dogs.

"Any of ours come in?"

"McGimpsies, McDowells, Alexanders, an' sech. Sixty on 'em. Come in last night."

"Good. Then we c'n do it."

"Anythin' I oughter know?"

"Nothin' ye cain't figger out."

"Thisheer mare be a-comin' back purty soon, mos' likely?"

"She mought. An' damn fast, too."

"So's the trace oughter be kep' cl'ar?"

"Yeah, you betcher back teeth!"

"But arter she gits by, then 't ain't so important to keep it open, eh?"

"Naw. Not by no means."

The two men smiled in friendly agreement.

"These fellers know anythin'?" the doctor asked, with a slight jerk of the head.

"Not much. Jest young lawyers goin' out from Sal'sb'ry to Western Waters."

"Lawyers, eh? An' goin' out to Cumberland! My Gawd!"

"Oh, they'll larn, iffen on'y they keep their scelps on."

"That red-headed one over thar, studyin' his nag's hoof—that reely *is* a scelp!"

"Yeah. An' the luckiest damn scelp ye ever see. He jest pulled down 'bout ten thousan' in yist'dy's cock-fight."

"Hell ye say! Any sense?"

"Naw. But he's a powerful spunky boy, that Jackson."

"Jackson, eh?"

"Yeah. Andy."

222

"Never heered tell of 'im."

"He's young yit."

"Wal, Russ," the doctor said in a carrying voice, feeling for the stirrup, "I'll be gittin' 'long naow. Saw yer Maw t'other day, daown to Boone's Crick."

"Thet so? How's Maw?"

"Peart. Little fever'n'ager, 's us'l; but I jest tole her not ter git behind on her red-eye an' she'll be all right come high summer."

"Wal, keep yer ha'r on, Doc."

"Keep yer ha'r on, Russ."

Doctor Cosby clucked at his horse and jerked the halter of the led mare.

To Parson Blandison, who had been standing for nearly an hour in the heat and stench of Morganton's court-house, the legal arrangements of this western country were not commending themselves. What use, he asked Holdfast Gaines, in trying to uphold the majesty of the law in a place unfit for swine? He said it was a comfort to recall that Justice was usually represented with a blindfold over her eyes, and he thought that in Morganton she ought to be holding her nose as well.

A hundred men, heavily armed, unwashed, most of them smoking or chewing tobacco, and nearly all redolent of McKniff's whisky, were fast making the court-room intolerable to a man of the Parson's sensibilities. He was pushing toward the door when he heard an uproar from the direction of the jail—"Hooray for Chucky Jack!" and "We'll see yeh through, Jack, boy!"—that indicated the approach of the prisoner. At the same time a passage was forced through the crowd so that Judge Waightstill Avery and three or four lawyers could reach the low platform. A few moments later John Tipton, Sevier's enemy and accuser, also walked to the platform through a deep and significant silence.

Then a huge shout went up from those at the door, followed by another from the men in the room. A tall, powerful man in buckskins, remarkably good to look at, was striding down the aisle, shaking hands and smiling and calling out first names as he came.—So this, the Parson knew, must be John Sevier, the unrivaled hero of the West. This was the public official who had been accused, among other things, of having shot a Sheriff. The crowd seemed to love him for it.

After Sevier had seated himself on the platform there followed several minutes of vociferous cheering. Judge Avery and Sheriff Harrison shouted and hammered in vain for silence. The Parson, who had known

223

the decorous court-rooms of London, was asking himself whether this was a trial or an ovation. Was it the prisoner who had been brought before the bar, or the whole system of civilized law and order? He could only say that political society and the wilderness were standing face to face, and did not like each other.

No sooner had the clerk of the court begun to read the charge than the clamor started anew. It was evident that the crowd did not intend even to hear the accusation. Choleric John Tipton and his ten guardsmen, though they stood frowning on the platform with their guns cocked, were helpless before this good-natured mob.

Several more minutes passed, and the machinery of the law did not begin to move. The prisoner—to call him that—sat beside the Judge and looked about the room like an amiable hawk, occasionally nodding to an acquaintance.

A short, sandy-haired man, his face a wilderness of kindly wrinkles, was forcing his way forward through the crowd. At last he stood close beside the Parson and within ten feet of the prisoner. He caught Sevier's eye. A nod, a wink, and a smile passed between the two. Then the Parson saw, unmistakably, a jerk of the newcomer's head toward the outer door. Sevier—perhaps at the Judge's request—stood up. He was looking out over the heads of the crowd, a sudden light in his eyes.

The sandy-haired man, with one hand raised high to attract attention, took two long strides toward the Judge's chair.

"Yay! Doc Cosby!" yelled a dozen voices.

"Judge Avery," he called out above the din, pointing at Sevier, "hev ye done with that thar man?"

But the Judge was not given time to answer. While Tipton and his guards had their eyes on Cosby, Sevier leapt into the crowd. It opened before him like a school of minnows before the rush of a pike—and closed at once behind. Tipton's men could hardly see their prisoner as he plunged toward the door. They dared not fire. Laughter, calls, cries, curses, rang from every corner of the room. In the milling of the crowd the Parson was pushed to the platform, and he mounted it just in time to look back and see the fugitive leap upon a bay mare that was standing by the court-house door. A moment later he saw the short man with sandy hair, also mounted, shoot past the doorway in the same direction.

"Yes, Jedge," called a voice from the crowd, "I persume ter guess, by Gawd, ye *air* done with 'im!"

As soon as he was alone, having seen the three young lawyers move off toward the court-house, Bean set fiercely to work. Acting with practiced precision and speed, he dragged his iron, lead, salt-bags and ropes from the brush and began loading his animals. He seemed to be working with complete absorption, oblivious of all other things. Therefore it was the more surprising to hear him suddenly call out: "You, Jim Sevier, do ye c'm out from ahint thet thar tree an' holp me load these jolt-heads."

A youth of seventeen, with bristling hair and handsome aquiline face like his father's, came forward, flushing slightly.

"Oh, ye'll larn, young feller. Whar's yer brother?"

"Over in the bresh, Russ."

"Thunk so. Wal, git 'im!—An' who else?"

"Major Evans."

"Good. On'y we cain't ast 'im ter pack a mule."

"Thar's Jack Gibson an' Jesse Greene."

"Git 'em hyar, damn quick. Nobody 'll see 'em now."

In less than a minute there were four or five hurrying pairs of hands tying ropes, buckling straps, and pulling at surcingles. The boys braced their feet against the flanks and pulled with a will, grunting.

"What ye goin' do, Russ," asked young John Sevier, "lightin' out this-away?"

"Goin' 'bout my business, course. I'm a pack-man. Cain't hang round hyar all day jest 'cause yer Paw's a-gittin' tried fer high treason."

"What'll they do to a man convicted o' thet thar, Russ?"

"Will ye stint yer gawpin' an' git on with yer work iffen I tell yeh?"

"We c'n work an' listen too."

"Wal, jest afore ye two come a-stompin' by, makin' all that horrible noise, I was a-discussin' with two-three young lawyers. All crammed up wi' book-larnin' they war, so's it stuck outen their years. An' they tole me a man convicted o' treason, why, they take an' drawr 'im on a hurdle, whatever thet is, ter the place of ex'cution. Thar they hang 'im, but not ontil he be daid . . ."

"D' ye mean they kill 'im fust an' hang 'im arter?"

"Brace up, young-un. Thisheer's jest lawyer-talk. But they say they hangs 'im fust, till he's sorter half-daid, an' then they disembowel 'im —which is, they take his insides out, an' him a-lookin' on meanwhiles. Arter that they slice 'im up an' send his head to the king."

"What king?"

225

"How do I know? 'Most any ole king."

"But what does the king do with it?"

"Cain't say," said Bean, pulling hard on a belly-strap. "P'raps kings cornsiders heads a del'cacy, proper cooked. How 'n hell I know? Never knowed a king."

"They won't do all that to Paw, will they?" asked John.

"Not iffen ye git 'long wi' thisheer packin'.—But damn it all, boys, don't talk s' much. Give a man the he-cups, the way ye talk!"

"Yes, Russ—I mean, no; we won't."

"An' pack 'em big. We're a-goin' to cram this trace so tight wi' salt an' iron an' lead an' mule-meat so's a good-sized snake can't slide by 'em."

"When ye say 'snake' ye mean John Tipton, I s'pose," suggested Jesse Greene.

"Naw. I said a *good-size* snake, an' likewise I mean a snake 't ain't ben borned out o' holy wedlock, so to speak. I ain't got nothin' agin nice snakes."

For the next five minutes the men and boys worked in a fury.

"An' now," called Bean, "ev'y one ketch holt of a peg-tail an' bring 'em down to the trace on a trot. Iffen they starts kickin', jest take a club an' try ter kill 'em. No danger."—He was already astride of his own horse with the halter of the leading mule in his hand.

They heard a yell from the direction of the court-house, and a clatter of swift hooves on stone.

"Hyar comes yer Paw, boys!" Bean shouted back. "Bring 'em 'long now!" He kicked his horse in the ribs and dragged his loaded mule down hill.

A hatless rider, his long hair blowing free in the wind, was careening down the rocky path as though borne on a hurricane. The bay mare under him was coming on the dead run, her head down, her mane flying, the reins flapping low on her neck. "A' right, boys! Thanks, Russ!" yelled the horseman hurtling by the group of struggling men and mules. A rifle cracked behind him and something sang through the air like a hurrying bee. The rider turned in his saddle, laughing, waved his hand, and disappeared among the thick-set bushes of the trace. Doc Cosby followed close behind. The clatter of pounding hooves died suddenly away.

"Now then, boys," Bean shouted, "we gotter git these jolt-heads down thar an' squatter 'em out afore the Sheriff comes!"

226

Sheriff William Harrison sat his horse squarely in the middle of the path and stared down at Russell Bean with disillusioned eyes. "Wal, Russ," said he, "I allus thunk ye knowed haow ter drive yer own pack 'long a straight an' open trace."

" 'Pears like I don't, though," was the cheerful reply. "Same time, ye c'n see I'm 'temptin' to larn."

"Why 'n hell ye git 'em snarled up thet-away right whar the trace is the on'y way o' gittin' by?"

"Jest my bad luck, seemin'ly."

Bean's long-lashed whip sang and barked among the clustered ears as he spoke. It snapped among the huddled haunches. He beat and kicked and cursed and banged in a frenzied cooperation with the arm of the law. But he only made confusion worse confounded.

"Wal, what the hell!" he exclaimed at last, sinking down exhausted on a tussock of fern-frond. "Ye know what mules is, Bill Harrison."

The main trouble seemed to be that the leading mule was determined to go directly across the trace rather than along it—and this, too, at a place where the lie of the land made a detour of any sort impossible. He would kick and rear and jerk and show his teeth, but turn to the right he would not. Neither would any of his followers. They stood by their leader. And, what was most unfortunate, the whole pack-train had been tied together by a long stout rope running from the leader to the hindmost. This rope, in the confusion of the moment, Bean had found impossible to untie.

When he looked up again there was another horseman to be placated —or, if that should prove impossible, to be borne with. He had a red face, with fiery carbuncles on his brow, a bull-neck, and a bullet-head. He was the kind of man always threatened with apoplexy whenever he gives way, as he is prone to do, to paroxysms of rage.

"Git them goddam jolt-heads aouten thar!" he yelled, the whisky-fed crimson of his face darkening to a dangerous purple. Half a dozen other mounted men pounded up behind him and joggled to peer over his shoulder.

"Do the best I kin, Mr. Tipton."

Bean rose from the tussock and once more poured a rain of kicks, blows, and vicious whip-snappings upon the bellies, rumps, ears, and noses of his miserable pack-train. But the results were not commensurate with the effort.

"Russ Bean," called the new-comer in a voice that seemed to gurgle up through quarts of bear-fat, "iffen I hedn't 'a' knowed yer Paw . . ."

227

and there he hung silent, as though on the verge of some interior eruption.

After a decent pause Bean drawled: "Yeah. On'y ye *do* know 'im, *don't* ye! An' so?"

"An' so I won't hev ye 'rested, like ye oughter be, iffen ye cl'ar aout thet trace in 'baout two barks of a red fox."

"H'm. Useful man, my Paw!"

But a devil had got into the mules. Bean found it necessary to detach each animal from the train and to lead him some distance into the brush before returning for the next. It was a tedious process. At each return he glanced deprecatingly at Harrison and Tipton, but, in spite of all, they eyed him with suspicion.

When Tipton and his guard lumbered by, Bean figured that Jack Sevier had been glimmering down the trace for at least twenty minutes. He collapsed on a rotting stump, took off his hat, and fanned himself.

"Wal, now," he said to young Sevier as he and his brother and Greene and Evans returned from their hiding-places in the brush, "I don't reckon as no king's a-goin' ter chaw yer Paw's head fer supper.— Not tonight, anyhow."

STEPPING WESTWARD

(October—1788)

"Oh Shannydore, I lo-o-ve yer darter;
    Awa-a-ay, my rollin' river!
I'll take 'er daown the windin' warter;
    Ha! Ha! Ah! We're baound awa-ay
    A-daown the River Holston."

Russell Bean's full, firm baritone rolled easily out into the morning air above the roar of the river. Clearly, he liked that old song, coming from no man knew where, arousing memories and hopes of vague adventure, distance, danger, and the welcoming warmth of woman's arms. Feeling that it belonged to every man, he made little changes in the words and tune to suit his fancy. On the word "awa-ay," his voice

swept a full octave upward like a yodler's, giving the whole performance an effect of reckless abandonment to the moment's whim.—Some
singers, he knew, made a dirty song of it; but although such variations
were often amusing he did not really like them. After all, there were
some things . . .

> "Oh Shannydore, I lo-o-ve her trooly;
> Awa-a-ay . . ."

"Aw, shet up, will ye?" shrilled a voice from one of the blanketed
forms lying ten feet behind him on the ground.

That would be young Jackson, who did not care for music and was
on no account to be encouraged. Somewhat more vigorously, therefore,
Bean trolled out the second stanza:

> "Oh Shannydore, I lo-o-ve her trooly;
> Awa-a-ay, my rollin' river!
> An' for her I will pay yeh dooly;
> Ha! Ha! Ah! We're baound awa-ay
> A-daown the Tennessee-ee."

"Shet up, I tell yeh, Russ Bean! I kep' my watch, an' this here's
my time fer sleepin'."

"Hit hain't. Sun's up, an' ye've hed yer six hours a'ready, young
Jackson—

> "Oh Shannydore, her ha'r's like midnight!
> Awa-a-ay, my rollin' river!
> Her eyes is two all-night-long camp-fires;
> Ha! Ha! Ah! We're baound awa-ay
> Along the Cumberla-and."

Andrew Jackson, yawning, blinking at the dazzle on the waves, his
tawny hair flapping, came forward and sat on the log to lace and tie
his cow-hide boots. "Who the hell is that Shannydore ye're a-bawlin'
'bout?" he asked in a surly tone. "Gal o' yourn?"

Bean's limber hickory ram-rod slithered and sang in the rifle-barrel.
Extremely careful he was, one could see, with this beautiful weapon
made by his own hands. With him it was a regular morning ritual, a
kind of matin service performed while fasting, to draw out yesterday's
charge, make sure that his powder was dry, and see that every inch of
metal within and without was clean as a willow whistle.

"Shannydore ain't a gal," he answered at last. "Thet's her Paw."

229

"Wal then, who's he the Paw of?"

But Bean did not like Jackson's tone. "Try to find out," said he.

"Oh, now, gentlemen"—it was the Parson's voice behind them—"let's not have any hard feelin's before breakfast. Consider the beauty o' the mornin'! See what God hath wrought!"

The speaker stepped over the log, and sat down between the two young men. Meanwhile his glance swept up and down the glisten of dancing waves, took note of the splash of scarlet made by the maples across the stream, and lifted to the tender blue of the sky and the pearly clouds there sailing.

"Cain't see nothin' special 'baout the mawnin'," Bean drawled, looking up for a moment and then back at the bit of oily buck-skin with which he was rubbing his dull-hued rifle-barrel. "On'y I *will* say hit's purty damn differ'nt from when I come by hyar back in eighty."

"How was that?"

"Cold. Thet's how. So tarnation all-fired cold a man's hands stuck to the steerin'-bar."

"And you came by this place?"

"Wal, this the Holston, hain't hit?—an' wharsomever the damn river went we jes' nach'ly went 'long too."

"In boats?"

"Why, suhtingly, Pahson!—Ye see that shiny patch o' smooth up yender a piece? Thet thar's Pore Valley Shoal; an' thar we stuck, I rec'leck, all one long winter night—Boyd's boat, Rounsifer's boat, an' the good flat-boat *Adventure,* builded an' steered by Russ Bean hisself. All night long it blew an' snew like the end o' the world. Not a whisker grew that night, an' ev'y word we tried to speak hit fell down daid, friz."

"Oh, yes," the Parson mused with a faint reminiscent smile. "And next morning, when the sun shone on them, those words thawed out again. Is that it?—And did you have a little sour-faced Greek aboard by the name of Lucian, or perhaps a pot-bellied German called Baron Munchausen?"

Bean turned and glanced at the Parson suspiciously, somewhat as he had done while listening, on the Catawba Trace, to an account of the virtues and worth of unicorn's horn.

"Naw," said he, coldly, at last. "Never heered tell of 'em. An' next mornin' nothin' thawed out, but jes' same we got down inter water— 'bout thutty men an' wimming on us—an' pushed them flat-boats offen Pore Valley Shoal."

230

The Parson's smile disappeared. "I should think you would have died," he said.

"Some did. Mos'ly wimming. Tothers didn't hev time. They was lookin' for'ard, prob'ly, to Reedy Crick, whar we stuck fer a solid month o' blow an' snow an' wolf-howl an' Injun whoo-whoop. Or mebbe they didn't die 'cause o' honin' to see the Whirl, whar Jennings went on a rock an' his wife got out an' pushed whilst the Injuns shot her sopped clothes full o' holes. Yeah. Thar was a sight wuth a-waitin' fer. Maw Peyton—her 't hed a babe the night afore—she holpt to push. Babe died same night. Friz, mebbe, or got smashed, shot, drownded—I dunno. Maw Peyton, she come through all right. Jennings, he lived ter git scelped next year in Western Waters."

But the serene and bountiful grandeur of the morning grew as the sun rose higher. Up the stream every quivering wave-crest was edged by a tremulous rainbow. Down-stream the maned and broad-shouldered waves were huddling headlong westward on some momentous errand. Across the river the lifting fog disclosed depth after depth of scarlet foliage, purple hills, and dim blue distance.

Parson Blandison gazed for a while, and then asked: "But why all this in winter?"

"I fergit. Donelson's idear. Mebbe thunk we'd git to Nashville fer corn-plantin', which we done. Mebbe figgered Injuns mought leave us go by easy 'count o' bein' too cold to fight, which they did *not*. Fired on us from one side or tother, an' oftentimes both, all the way from Chickamauga Town to the 'Hiah, they did. Night an' day they fired. Times they come out arter us in canoes an' clumb aboard wi' tommy-hawks. Kilt half o' Jennings's fambly. Kilt young Payne in Blackmore's boat. All the folks in Stuart's, which hed the small-pox, they kilt or scelpt or tuk. M'm. An' then thet pox, hit run through their towns like a forest fire. Nashville—they never wouldn't 'a' ben no sech a place 'thout the help o' thet 'ar pox."

"Did ye hev a map?" asked Jackson.

"Had a no-'count map was drawred by Chief Tassel o' the Cher-rakies—like turkey-tracks in mud. C'n see ole Cap'n Donelson a-settin' thar now, up to Fort Patrick Henry winter o' seventy-nine, a-scrouchin' down over that smudge of a map in the firelight, an' we-uns axin' 'im how to git thar."

"How many miles?" the Parson asked.

" 'Bout a thousan', way we had to go.—An' him a-settin' thar p'intin' wi' that stump of a finger left from whut was friz off at Valley Forge

231

an' a-sayin' easy-like: 'Wal, naow,' sezee, 'we hez to go daown Holston to the Tennessee, an' daown thet thar to the 'Hiah, an' then up Cumberland to Ole French Lick. Boone's ben thar,' he says, 'an' so's Clark. Best land thisheer side o' Paradise,' he says, 'with all the salt ye want right thar in the Lick jest fer the b'ilin',' sezee."

Bean rested his rifle against the log and gazed up-river into the dazzle. His hands hung slack and his voice sounded weary, as though the ache of that by-gone toil had not yet left his bones.

"Easy to say but hard to do," he went on. "No white man ever ben that v'y'ge. Didn't know how fur 't war nor yet whut lay in atween—like Muscle Shoals an' Nickajack Cave an' that hell-hole called 'the Suck.' Didn't know we war luggin' down a boat-load o' pox; an' likewise them four-five wimming whut was expectin', they never said a whisper ontwell their pains come on. All we knowed was to *git* thar, come corn-plantin'; an' b' God it'll do my soul everlastin' good when I come to die, we *did* git thar."

There was a pause until Jackson said, "Seems like a damn fool time to start."

"Wal, God A'mighty an' ole Cap'n Donelson they made their plans 'thout axin' yeh. Anyhow, we drap down Holston the coldest damn winter the oldest Injun ever heered his gramp tell about. They was floatin' ice bigger 'n a barn in this hyar water, an' four-foot snow in the woods. The wind went in yer belly an' out yer back like 's iffen ye warn't thar 't all.—An' *hungry?* We c'd see the deer by the dozen a-layin' smoored i' the snow, but couldn't git at 'em 'count of Injuns an' wolves an' sech. One mawnin' we cotched a swan hed a wing bruk, an' never stopped to kill or cook 'im but jes' natch'ly tore 'im apart an' eat 'im raw.—Ye c'd a'most 'a' heered 'im squawk whilst he was a-goin' down."

For a while they listened to the many voices of the river, hurrying eagerly westward.

"But what drove those people?" the Parson asked.

"They warn't druv but drug," Bean replied.

And for once Andrew Jackson agreed with him. "That's right, Parson," said he. "Those that went down in the boats nine year ago, an' all these hunderd we're takin' out now, they got a notion suthin' big's a-goin' to happen out thar purty soon, an' they want to git thar on time. —So do I."

But Russell Bean was not to be deflected from his duties as a disciplinarian by a momentary agreement on the part of his pupil. "Don't ketch yer tail on fire, youngster," said he, "ez I've told yeh afore. Nashville c'n wait till ye git thar, an' when ye do heave in sight prob'ly they won't all come a-runnin' an' yell 'Hyar comes Andy Jackson!'"

"Now, gentlemen, not before breakfast!" the Parson pleaded. "If you must quarrel, do have some nourishment first."

Pretending to have discovered a flake of rust on his rifle-barrel, Bean set to work anew with his bit of greased buck-skin, chanting meanwhile a portion of the song he had made for himself as an Indian brave makes his personal song and dance:

> "How wonderful, how glorious, how marvelous I am!
> How wonderful it is to be me!"

"That song o' yourn gives me the belly-ache!" Jackson burst out.

> "I think I am the greatest man in all this wondrous land!
> Why sartinly I'm positive I be!"

Jackson suddenly stood up. He jerked viciously at his belt as he snarled: "I'm a-goin' to larn yeh, Russ Bean, to sing a differ'nt chune."

"But don't do it here, if you please," said the Parson. "With all of Western Waters to fight in, there's no reason why you two gentlemen should spoil my morning's contemplation."

"Then I'll do it up the bank a piece, iffen Russ Bean ain't afeared to go thar."

"Oh, so ye're callin' me out, like ye done ole Waightstill," Bean laughed. "Wal, seein' 's I ain't got much else on hand jest now, I c'n spare a few minutes fer tannin' yer young hide."

Bean rose, leaned his rifle carefully against the log, yawned, stretched, and said "Come 'long then, youngster.—Only, stiddier 'n hitchin' away at thet 'ar belt ye better be lettin' yer breeches down."

Parson Blandison sat alone on the maple log gazing out over Avery Trace at the headlong rush of the river. Breakfast, it seemed, would have to be postponed until the dove of peace flew back with the olive twig in her beak.

He had foreseen the probability of such altercations as this when Bean and Jackson had been detailed to keep watch, a mile or so up the trace from the main camp, against possible Indian marauders. Those two young men would continue to quarrel until one or the other of them—Russell Bean by main force and greater experience or else Andrew Jackson by luck and indomitable will—got and held the upper

233

hand. In the meanwhile it was somewhat amusing to see them continually cresting and crowning at each other like two green game-cocks. Serious bloodshed, the Parson thought, was not likely. On the present occasion neither of them had taken a weapon with him. Jackson could scarcely hurt Bean in physical encounter, and Bean did not want to hurt Jackson.

The company of those two was nothing much, of course, as compared with what the Parson might have had in Holdfast. He had gone with them partly because their outpost was thought to be somewhat dangerous, but also because it would provide quieter sleep and pleasanter smells.

As for Holdfast, his movements were as unpredictable as those of a summer cloud or a bolt of lightning. One seldom knew why he went or came—or, indeed, whence and whither. On his present journey he might be engaged in serious business among the northern tribes, or he might be merely avoiding the crowd that had been gathering all summer long at Jonesboro and was now setting forth over the new trace to Western Waters. Quite as much as the Parson himself, Holdfast had detested the petty spites and bickerings of that small frontier town, and especially when they had led to a farcical duel between Andrew Jackson and Waightstill Avery. The quiet of the wilderness would now seem to him like a bath under a water-fall.

During the five months in which Jackson and the other young lawyers had been "drumming up a practice" at Jonesboro, Holdfast had spent much of the time away. On two occasions the Parson had gone with him—once through the numerous Cherokee towns to the southward and again on a prolonged visit with a remarkable young Shawnee chieftain called Tecumseh. The Parson had greatly enjoyed these journeys, opening up to him as they did a world utterly strange, astonishing, and in some respects beautiful. He had tried to pay his way, so to speak, by telling Holdfast all that he could remember about his adventures with Samson Occum in the Old Country, and there had been a delicious incongruity in talking about London and Bath and Tunbridge Wells while camping under the boughs of a primeval forest beside some river with an unpronounceable name. Without asking any questions, he had been able on these journeys to make a shrewd guess at what, in Bean's phrase, Holdfast was "up to." But he was not telling any one. Among the things he had learned during this summer not the least was the art of holding his tongue. His friend's purposes and plans, he believed, were wholly beneficent. They involved great difficulties and dangers. The Parson wished to help them forward in every possible way.

He had made some progress, though slowly, in two or three Indian tongues—especially the Choctaw, which Holdfast said would take him farthest among the western tribes. He had learned the Indian names of birds, beasts, trees, rivers, mountains. A vague notion of the general lie of the land as it sloped toward the Father of Waters, interlaced by a thousand streams, criss-crossed by hills, and seamed by intricate traces and trails, was beginning to form in his mind. The improvement of his health and the rapid increase of his bodily strength had surprised him. With every week in the wilderness he seemed to shed a year of his age. He was actually learning to enjoy the taste of water dipped in his two hollowed hands from a brook or a woodland spring, and he had discovered that Indian corn-water one day old was really, as Jackson had asserted, "a damn good drink." Little by little he was acquiring wood-craft. Already he could lay sticks for a fire in the cautious Indian fashion and kindle it from Holdfast's clamshell. He could follow a well blazed trail through the forest even by moonlight. Very awkwardly at first, and greatly to the amusement of his companions, he had begun to learn how to load, aim, and fire Bean's rifle. The time might come, he thought, when he too, Parson Blandison, an Oxford Master of Arts who knew most of the Odes of Horace without book, would be able to bring down a gray squirrel—not for sport, to be sure, but for food—from the top of the loftiest tulip tree.

He had laid aside his clerical garb, preserving it for ceremonial occa-· sions, and had taken to wearing buck-skins fashioned by Russell Bean's "Injun ladies." For the most part he went on foot now, in moccasins, trying to walk like Holdfast with no toeing-out. Occasionally he tried to smoke the pipe that Holdfast had given him, made of a soft red stone brought from far to the north-west and packed with the acrid, strangling Indian weed grown by the Cherokees. Once, but once only, he had taken a tentative draught of the Indian "black drink," villainous in taste, powerfully purgative and emetic, which was able, Holdfast said, to drive out evil spirits. After he had partially recovered the Parson had replied that he did not doubt Holdfast's assertion in the least, but that it seemed to him wiser to "bear those ills we have than fly to others that we know not of."

But these were negligible matters in comparison with the magnificence, the daily wonder and the hourly charm of the summer's passing and the autumn's coming-on. Although the Parson had found his human surroundings drab and sordid enough in Jonesboro, the flowers and grasses and trees, the majesty of the mountains and the illimitable sky, had atoned for all. Disregarding the severe admonitions of the frontiersmen, he often rode or walked far abroad among the hills, alone, or with Perthy and the dog Wash. Better to him than any human companionship, at least when Holdfast was not available, was the huge rock-maple that he found one day ten miles from town and the sycamore that he saw letting fall its broad plates of gold into the pool below.

He came to mighty earthworks—tumuli, cirques, and serpentine forms—that made him think of Stonehenge, Karnak, Ur of the Chaldees, and Baalbec of the Waste. What unknown men had built them? What gods or demons had they worshipped here? He saw that this was indeed an old, old country, as Holdfast had said, and that it must have known much tragic sorrow. The song of the hermit thrush was explained.

And America's antiquity, he found, was not exclusively human. Pure mystery chilled and thrilled the Parson to the heart as he stood beside "big-bone licks" where monsters of an unimaginable age had fought and died and sunk and slowly rotted in marshes of salt. Hannibal's elephants had been ludicrously small in comparison. Noah's flood had been inadequate to drown them. He could only think of some young god trying his 'prentice hand in a frenzy of improvisation. Merely to gaze at such bones, he felt, would be enough to wreck the neat little theologies of Alexander Pope, Thomas Gray, George Whitefield, John Wesley, and Dr. Johnson.—But then a mocker like Voltaire would not find much comfort in looking at them, either.

A man needed some kind of faith, he discovered, while going out into this country. His own superficial irreverence of the old days began to look absurd. He was coming to feel that simplicity, of the deeper sort which he at least could have attained only by the long discipline and disappointment of skepticism, was for him the real crown of wisdom. Day by day it grew clearer to the Parson that the complexity of his life, his learning, his range of experience, his wit, his cultivation, could be really helpful only in the degree that he penetrated them, put them in some sense behind him, and came out as it were on the other side into the clear sunshine which he had known as a child.

One morning, on the heights above the Holston, he witnessed an enormous flight of passenger pigeons moving southwest through a

236

cloudless sky. They came in successive columns eight or ten miles in length, filling the day with the roar of their numberless wings. For an hour the sun was darkened as though by eclipse in their transit. And when they had gone by, the Parson quoted Scripture, for once, as correctly as he could: "Then Job answered the Lord and said 'I know that thou canst do everything. . . . I have heard of thee by the hearing of the ear, but now mine eye seeth thee.'"

One effect of his growth in simplicity was a deepened interest in ordinary people. He found himself looking at men and women, even children, with something like the concentrated gaze which his younger companions had thought so ridiculous when trained upon trees, blossoms, birds, beasts, and wild water. He was uncovering beauty from beneath many an unpromising human surface. Over and again the recollection came back to him of Maw McNab as she stood for a moment at the cabin door and then stepped shyly in, of her treasured brooch and shawl, her white doe-skin apron, her delight in the two tall candles, her worn and weary yet somehow beautiful face. To Parson Blandison, a connoisseur in feminine pulchritude who had seen and known many of the most celebrated fair women of England and Europe—dandled darlings of the court and stage, creatures of the cosmetician and the wig-maker—that had been a moment of revelation.

And so, what was he to think and feel about these fellow-travelers of his on the way from filthy Jonesboro to Western Waters? Many of them, no doubt, were vulgar enough—if it was not a vulgar thing to feel and say so. Frankly speaking, a good many of them smelled bad, for lack of sufficient washing. Thomas Gray and Horace Walpole would have held their noses at them. Coarse in manners and habits, slovenly in person, ignorant of all that lay outside their pitifully limited experience, disdainful of law and order, contemptuous of everything unfamiliar, greedy and lustful, violently profane, they often made one think of the good clean beasts with a yearning admiration. So Holdfast undoubtedly had felt when, after a week or two of breathing the stench of their sweat, he broke away into the wild and went back to blue asters, the howl of the wolf, the scream of the hawk, and the rutting buffalo. More than once, on their journeys together, the Parson had seen his friend lay a large dark patient hand on a lichened rock with a gesture that could not be mistaken.

But perhaps it would be fairer to look at these people with the tolerant eyes of an Englishman, seeking whether there might be a potential Falstaff among them, a Mistress Quickly, or at least a coarse-

237

grained Nurse destined to fail some future Juliet.—Or, say, with the eyes of that little paunchy man with the forked beard who, four hundred years gone by, had looked through and through the "nine and twenty in a company" that gathered one night at the Tabard Inn, and had let hardly one of them escape with his or her secret unguessed, untold.

Anyhow, here they came, now, at last. From far up the trace the Parson heard a faint lowing of cattle, barking of dogs. That would mean that the whole company was on the move, having made an early start, and that he would probably have to do this day's march at the malodorous rear of the procession instead of well to the front as he preferred. Still, there would be some compensation in sitting here within twenty feet of the newly-cut trace and watching the crowd go by.

The sun, now half an hour above the eastern ridge, was glorifying a cloud of dust raised by many horses, mules, cattle, wheels, and walkers on the first mile of the day's journey. Dim figures began to emerge from the golden nimbus, all moving at the slow pace of the cattle. They kept no order of march but came straggling, on foot, on horse-back, and in wagons, some with loads of household goods and others with no more than their hands could carry. Here and there the sun found out a well-scoured pot or pan, a burnished rifle-barrel, but for the most part they were a dingy lot with little instinct or opportunity for cleanliness.

A confusion of sounds spread out through the hills and along the trace before them: cries and curses of the muleteers, whinny and neigh of the horses, crowing of cocks, lowing of cattle, clatter of dangling tinker's-ware, rumble of wheels, creak of harness-leather, and the patient plod, plod of the hooves of oxen and cows. Strange sounds they were to this place which had known for ages only the songs of birds, the howl of the wolf, and the hoarse voice of the river. And after them came the smells of man and beast, equally strange to the wilderness, assaulting the Parson's sensitive nostrils. For the moment he felt himself entirely on the side of the Indians who, he knew, had deeply resented the intrusion of this wagon-wide trace into their ancient domain.

That resentment of theirs had been wise and prescient, for along the broad trace were rolling and rumbling now the first wheels that had ever trodden this virgin soil. Wheels, immemorially old in the Old World, had never been known to the aborigines of the New. But now that they were here they would bear down all before them, like Juggernaut, and leave nothing behind but the smooth shining track of their fellies.

238

Yet the wheel, after all, was hardly more than a symbol of the white man, with his steady purpose and will pushing on and onward out of Asiatic mountain passes and over Europe, over the sea, over these western lands, taking his dogs and his cattle with him, his horses, and always his doughty servant the wheel. What chance had the flitting and dreamy red man before such coherent force, mobile, determined, and driven by insatiable greed? This present company starting out for Western Waters, for example, though it might be small in numbers, ill-organized, ignorant, and inexperienced, was yet irresistible. If all the members of it should be slaughtered on the way there would be another company starting out from Jonesboro before their flesh had been eaten by the wolves. They were like the first drops of a flood spilling over a dike, as yet only a silver trickle but with a huge weight of water behind.

First rode Martin McGary, leader of the guard, on a tall and raw-boned horse. Four or five of his ten guardsmen were with him. The others had evidently been sent to the rear.

Next, side by side, on horses bred for the hunting-field, came two middle-aged Virginians ruined by the late war. The Parson knew them as hard drinkers, terrific swearers, and shrewd antagonists in a card game. Both were "gentlemen," and one a graduate of Oxford. Each had with him a valuable slave and rode an excellent horse. A speculative look came into the Parson's eyes as he watched Mr. James Greer and Mr. Herbert Gosse ride by.

Three villainous fellows followed close, on foot. Jail-birds, the Parson made them out to be. One had lost an eye—perhaps in the vigorous American sport called "gouging." There was not a boot, shoe, or moccasin among them.

Then there came shuffling up out of the dust a figure which the Parson could already recognize as typical. It was that of a "black" Scotch-Irishman, Crockett by name—a gangling and slab-sided man, long-nosed, long-lipped, with a greasy complexion, elf-locked hair, and a beard which left one in doubt whether it was due to intention or neglect. In an otherwise inexpressive face his little eyes glittered like glass beads. Clad wholly in the skin of the deer he slouched along, making his observations in quick little side-long glances, self-centered, canny, by no means humorless, and determined, one could see, that nothing and nobody should get the better of him. Long discouragement and perhaps even sudden disaster had tried to beat him, one guessed, but had finally turned aside, baffled. At present he was simply walking away

239

from them, by no means down-hearted, having reduced his impedimenta to a minimum. He carried an old flint-lock musket over his right shoulder and in his left hand held the bridle of a lumpy-kneed horse. On the horse were his wife, his youngest infant, a few filthy blankets, a frying pan, and a small dangling sack of meal. His two elder sons, ten and eight years old, walked behind the horse and carried an axe and a hoe. Next came a daughter, perhaps thirteen, pimply, with a boy-child in her arms too young to go on his own legs but with a voice already well-developed. A miserable dog, his hair full of burrs, skulked at her heels.

And so they came on, the hundred and odd of them, shuffling and strutting, talking and laughing, singing and quarreling, everyone already acquainted with everyone else and all of them feeling, in spite of diverse origins and occasional bitter dissensions, that they belonged together as a flock, a herd, a social group, with common rights and interests which were to be maintained, if necessary, against all the alien world. Considerations of social rank which on the other side of the Appalachians would have seemed of huge importance were coming to look ridiculous. The past had dropped away; the present was mere transition; it was the future—unknown, mysterious, beckoning, and still hundreds of dangerous miles to westward—upon which their thoughts and hopes were fixed.

A thorough re-shuffling of the human pack of cards was going on before Parson Blandison's eyes. He watched it narrowly, as a veteran gambler should. In the very fact that the three former jail-birds followed so closely upon the two once aristocratic planters he discerned a portent of things to come. Whether he personally would like these things was not now the question. The fact was that they were coming, ineluctably —or rather, were here. His wealthier tide-water acquaintances had been alarmed, when he last saw them, at the wild political and social scheme —"democracy," was it called?—that Thomas Jefferson was said to be bringing back from the seething cess-pools of France. But here, without any help from Jefferson, Rousseau, or even Tom Paine, was the very thing they had feared.

The Parson, however, was not a politician, and his early acquaintance with the aristocracy of England and Europe had left him almost indifferent to the niceties of social discrimination. No man of his time had a better reason than he to know how swiftly the buckets rattled up and down in the social well. Moreover, he was a man to whom, for better and worse, the sharply single and colored details of nature and art meant far more than any bloodless theory. Just now the main thing was to see these particular people exactly, vividly, as Geoffrey Chaucer had taught him to do.—How well that Martin McGary enacted Chaucer's Host of the Tabard Inn! Hearty, coarse-grained, swag-bellied, a confident master of men, he ruled his little troupe of backwoodsmen with a friendly firmness, ready at any moment to knock any one of them down, lift him up, slap him on the shoulder, and send him off laughing. And here were three of Chaucer's Millers—salty full-blooded men, well-stocked with wicked stories. To keep them company in laughter at God's ancient and somewhat monotonous jest of sex there were also two bulbous, redundant wives of Bath, for the time being unattached.

Lawyers, merchants, farmers, tinkers, maidens and wenches, widows and wives, perhaps a physician or two, here they all came riding or walking, a little more gaunt of body and sharper of face than the people Chaucer had known, far more nasal in their pronunciation of the King's English, but in essentials of the same old stock. Here too, in the Reverend Francis Asbury—he who so ridiculously called himself a "Bishop" —was Chaucer's "povre Person of a toun," really a good man to the core in spite of his Methodistical pretensions, abounding in charitable works. And finally, "a Clerk there was of Oxenford also," soon to climb astride of a lean and broken-winded horse, with an Elzevir copy of Quintus Horatius Flaccus bulging his buck-skin pocket.

Yes, the likeness was somewhat striking. But how much there was to be seen here, and more to be conjectured, of which Dan Chaucer had never distantly dreamed! That fork-bearded, book-minded old poet had done remarkably well in hinting the pearly charm of an English April with a foam of blossom in the hedges and voluble birds on the bough, but what could even he have done with these hues of October lighting a land of which he had never heard the name—with maple leaves glowing like gleeds and armies of asters massed on the hills? What had Chaucer known or guessed about the strangeness out yonder, the hope at the heart of a fear? What did he know of the shuffling bear, the stealthy panther, the wolf that smells human blood from miles away, the war-whoop, and the scalping-knife? After all, Chaucer had taken his little company safely back into a hallowed past, enshrined, safe, and familiar; but these modern pilgrims, dingy with dust, were confidently thrusting forward into a leaf-hidden future, with blood-sprinklings thick on the leaves and little but danger for lure.

241

McGary doubled his guard at Campbell's Station, where the French Broad and the Holston twisted together to make the wide Tennessee. From here on, he said, they would be going up into the country of Old Tassell, Dragging Canoe, Bloody Fellow, and Hanging Maw.

A dozen or more new families, some in Conestoga wagons and hailing from Virginia, joined the cavalcade at Campbell's. There came in also a score of redemptioners—German, Irish, English—who had tramped down the trails from Philadelphia. Along with these arrived a dozen unmistakable convicts recently shipped from English or West Indian prisons and jails. Altogether, the Parson estimated, there must be a hundred and fifty persons now taking the westward road. Such a crowd would probably intimidate the Indians, but the smells would be frightful.

Russell Bean came riding up to McGary as he was sitting his horse just within the station gate, the Parson beside him, counting the procession as a shepherd tells his flock. Bean's face was red, as though with anger. He pulled up so close to McGary's mount that for a second the Parson feared a collision.

"How 'bout that chicken o' Jackson's?" said he, clipping his words.

There was no reply for several minutes while McGary went on counting; and Bean, his face now crimson, jerked viciously at the bridle of his horse. Not until the last wagon had rumbled through the gateway did the guard-leader turn and say: "Naow, whut's a-bitin' yeh, Russ?"

"I say how 'bout thet puke of a game-chicken Andy Jackson thinks he's a-takin' out with 'im?"

"Wa-al?"

"Wakes up in the middle o' the night, he does, an' crows like all hell bust loose. Thet chicken oughter hev his neck twisted afore we all git scelpt."

"Aw, naow, ye know better 'n thet, Russ Bean. You an' Andy jes' ben hevin' 'nother one o' yer starin'-matches, an' Andy he stared yeh daown. Hain't thet a fack?—Annyhaow, I'm in chahdge o' these hyar scelps."

"An' I'm tellin' yeh thet 'ar cock is dangersome."

"Not s' much ez Andy 'd be iffen ye try an' take it offen 'im. I've knowed Andy Jackson, oveh in Waxhaw, sence he cut his fust tooth, an' he ain't my notion of a man to banter. Andy ain't never hed much, but what he r'aly wants he gin'ly goes an' gits—an' keeps."

"Aaron, twenty-nine, eleven," murmured the Parson.

"Ah, so ye're 'feared on 'im, air ye?"

242

For a few seconds the two men glared at each other over the tossing necks of their horses. McGary was the first to bring his temper under control. "Iffen I war," said he, "I'd be showin' more hoss-sense 'n a slack-twisted ijit whut don't even know his bettahs when he sees 'em."

"Betters, eh?"

"Yeah. Sartin shore.—An' I hain't a-gwineter choke thet chicken."

"Then I'll do it myself," Bean almost shouted, reining his horse toward the gate.

But McGary blocked the way. Putting two fingers to his mouth, he whistled shrilly. One of his guardsmen came cantering up.

"Know thet li'l red chicken Andy Jackson's totin' aout?"

"M'm. Make good soup."

"Not yet he won't. I want fer you boys to watch thet chicken night an' day, like 's iffen he war yer own bantling. Watch his feed an' wateh, keep his feathahs combed, an' see 't his toes don't git cold o' nights. An' iffen ye ketch any low-daown no-'caount chicken-thief tryin' to do 'im any dirt, jes' shoot the man daid an' report to me arter.—Thet's all."

The guardsman, somewhat astonished, made a perfunctory salute and rode away toward a group of his companions.

Russell Bean reined close to McGary. "I'm leavin', then," was all he trusted himself to say.

McGary stifled a good imitation of a yawn. "Wa'al, hit's yer own life," said he. "Free kentry, thisheer—an' plenny of hit."

"That's rather too bad," said the Parson as he and McGary watched Bean spurring up the trace after Perthy and the pack-train. "I shall miss Russell Bean."

"So 'll I—speshly naow we hain't got Holdfast Gaines. Same time, we cain't hev 'im tellin' me haow to run things an' all time squarin' up to Andy. A good scaout he may be, an' a reg'lar tore-daown killer wi' the wimming by all he says, but no more idear o' disciplyne in 'im nor a toad-frog."

"Do you really think Little David is dangerous?"

"Naw. An' Russ he don't think so nuther. Injuns don't need no cock-crow to tell 'em whar we be. They c'n smell a craowd the likes o' this-un ten mile up wind."

"Even I could do that, I think.—But then they must know we're coming."

243

"Huh! Nach'ly! Way daown in McGillivray's kentry the young red-sticks prob'ly sayin' right naow: 'Hyar comes hunnerd forty-seven pale-faces over the new trace to Nashville. Le's all go lift ha'r!'"

The Parson smiled, hopefully. "Then you think," he said, "that we may have trouble?"

"Hell, no! Not with a guard o' twenty men, we won't."

"I jest ben tellin' young Perthy," said Bean to Paw Crockett, "thet he's a-gwineter take my pack-train clar to Nashville. Course I mean him an' Wash' an' both o' them is all swole up wi' pride. Course, too, my reg'lar helper 'll do most o' the loadin' an' sech; but 't won't do no harm iffen a growed-up man war to give 'em a look now an' then."

"Suhtingly, Russ. I'll admire to do thet fer yeh."

"Good. An' so when we gits to Nashville I'll give yeh a bushel o' clean salt an' a hefty chunk o' lead."

"Aw, hell. Guess we all gotter help one tother, hain't we?"

"An' we will, too.—Say, what's eatin' thet 'ar brat o' yourn?"

"Cal'late he must be yellin' fer whisky, but we ain't got none. Anny-haow, Maw says 't ain't good fer 'im. I tell 'er give 'im a chaw o' terbaccy then. She won't do thet, nuther."

"He c'n beller like all out-doors. Y' oughter send 'im inter pol'ticks, or mebbe make a ridin' preacher of 'im."

"Wa'al, I dunno, Russ. Don' wanner waste 'im. He's got brains, thet brat hez. Iffen I war to say to 'im naow jest the one word 'Injuns!', he'd shet his gab tighter 'n a bear-trap.—Wan' me try 't?"

"Naw. Let 'im yell. Whatcher call 'im?"

"Times, we calls 'im 'the gawdamn brat,' or mebbe 'hell an' destruction'; but then other times we calls 'im suthin' more—ah—fambly-like."

"Y' oughter put a real name to 'im."

"Yeah; but thar's never a parson raound when we hev idears. Iffen we c'd git an idear an' a parson hooked up, then mebbe we c'd name 'im proper."

"An' tell yeh 'nother thing: a bantlin' with a beak like his'n—like a pin-feathered hawk he looks now, don't he?—wal, he's a-gwineter want a good rifle-gun, come purty damn quick."

"Yeah."

"An' not one o' these hyar Deckards or Gresheims I don't mean, but made o' good C'neckticut metal from Sal'sb'ry mine."

"I s'pose. But think my name's Robert Morris o' Philadelphy?"

"Hell, I'll build 'im a rifle-gun Bob Morris couldn't buy with all the money in his bank—a Russ Bean gun, rifled right, wi' sights o' pure gold from North Car'liny."

Paw Crockett looked overwhelmed. "W'y, Russ," he exclaimed, "then they won't be nothin' kin keep the boy daown!"

"Not wi' thet beak an' a rifle-gun o' mine, they won't," Bean agreed, reining his horse off the trace.—"Keep yer ha'r on, Paw."

Confident though he was, McGary at first took no chances. All day long he kept his scouts beating up and down in the cane-brake bordering the trace. He chose the camping-ground at Crab Orchard, on the first night out from Campbell's, with care. A sentinel watched through the night, or was supposed to do so, beside each of the four great fires. At the openings of the tents of buffalo-skins the grown men lay with their arms beside them.

To the Parson, always a light sleeper, the romantic shadow and shine of the midnight scene was powerfully exciting. What a subject for Salvator Rosa, those young men in buck-skins tramping up and down before the fires with shouldered rifles, the circle of tents dully glimmering where the firelight caught the gloss of buffalo-hair, and, best of all, the somber gold of maple, tulip, and hickory leaves far overhead! For an hour he lay awake, watching the silvery stars swim from bank to bank of gold. A bull-elk called once from the river.—And soon he would hear the Homeric thunder of the buffalo!

VIGIL AND VISION

"Are you sure, Russ, that McGary's camp is behind us?"

" 'Bout a mile, I'd say, Holdfast. An' all beat out, they'll be tonight. Must 'a' come thutty mile sence yes'dy, tryin' to git over the wust o' the kentry all to-oncet."

"If they're tired they may not be keeping a good watch, and this is bad country still."

"That's McGary's look-out."

"Yours too, Russ. Didn't you tell them back there that you would be watching both sides of the trace?"

"Mebbe I did say suthin' like that, but not to McGary."

"He's heard of it, though; and he'll be counting on you."

"Aw, hell, I'm tired. They hain't more 'n made camp by now, an' by time they're asleep I'll be down thar."

Holdfast laid another stick on the fire. "I'd go myself," he said, "if I hadn't agreed to wait here for Tecumseh."

"Who's he? Never heered tell of 'im."

"Never heard of Tecumseh, the Meteor, Chief of the . . . ? Oh, well, he's young yet, and his country lies north of your beat. But already he's a man of power, I can tell you. If they don't tell you about him it's because he has plans that the whites aren't supposed to know."

"Sech ez?"

"Plans that won't do anyone any good. That's why I'm waiting here for a talk with him—and it's one reason why you ought to be down watching the trace. Tecumseh may not have come alone."

It was clear that Holdfast did not mean to share any Indian secrets with even the closest of his pale-faced friends. An intense, withdrawn, recollecting look was coming into his face. His eyes were two deep caverns with little fires far back. Sitting perfectly motionless, his hands clasped round his knees, he might have been the image of some Indian god carved in stone.

Several minutes passed in silence. Bean watched the huge flickering shadow cast by his friend's body on the trunk of a chestnut-tree. He listened to the rippling of the two rivulets that flowed past the tree on either side toward their junction a few rods farther down. There was no other sound in the forest. The last light of day was fading overhead.

Russell Bean had been living alone, more and more resentful toward the persons who in his opinion had driven him away, for more than a week. He had not seen Holdfast for a longer time still, and now he was pining for talk. Holdfast, however, had refused to discuss either the iniquities of Andrew Jackson or the still more absorbing topic of women. Bean was growing impatient. He resolved to draw his friend back by the magic of a name which, he had come to feel, was all but forbidden.

"All this 'bout gals," he heard himself say over the pounding of his heart, "I s'pose thet's 'count o' . . . Becky."

Holdfast did look up for a moment with a slow half-smile, but he made no audible answer.

Bean gathered courage again, and at length said: "Ever hear from her?"

"No."

"H'm.—An' so that's whut's changed yeh."

246

"Changed?"

"Hell, Holdfast, ye know damn well ye ain't the same man as back at the Farm ten years gone by."

"In ten years I may have grown up."

"Ah, it's more 'n that. It's more 'n not takin' no int'rust in drink an' money an' cyards an' gals. Fer days ye listen to nothin' 't all, an' look at what ain't thar. Ev'y time ye hear 'bout the whites shootin' up the red-skins ye go offen yer feed, an' then when the Injuns do suthin' proper back at 'em, why, seemin'ly, ye wanter die.—Rec'leck the time we come on a white child layin' dead in the bresh up Holston way? Scelpt, she war, an' cut up some. Injun work. Wal, fack is 't wa'n't a purty sight, but fer a month there-arter ye went a-punin' roun' like yer heart was to-bruk, the ontalkin'est man alive."

There could be no doubt that Holdfast had come back from that cave of the mind in which he so often took refuge. He was paying attention now, as the look in his eyes bore witness. Even now he did not speak, but he drew one hand across his brow like a man overborne.

But Bean went on, determined at last to speak his full thought. " 'T wa'n't thet-away 't all," he said, "in them ole days I fust knowed yeh. 'Course even then the only gal ye c'd see in the world war Becky, an' ez fer drink—'t war wasted on yeh. Same time, ye c'd laugh an' dance an' sing them days. At huskin'-bees, stun-bees, house-raisin's, wrastlin's, frolics, 'lection-days, clam-bakes, turkey-hunts—wal, nothin' r'aly got started ontwel Holdfast Gaines got thar. But now ye set tother side o' the fire an' never open yer face."

"I'm sorry, Russ. I know I'm not much of a companion, these days."

"Wal, whatcher gwineter do 'bout hit?"

"What would you suggest?"

"Huh! Iffen it's Becky, then they's two things. One is, ye c'n go back home an' knock thet John Reid over an' jes' nach'ly walk off with her. Tother is, ye c'n find some other 'ooman jes' as good, which the world is a-bulgin' with, an' all on 'em a-honin' night an' day fer Holdfast Gaines."

"But suppose it isn't about Becky."

"Wal then, I dunno. Mebbe ye tuk religion or suthin' in one o' them sarvices the Reverent Asbury got up back in Jonesboro. They ain't no cure fer religion, prob'ly, 'cep' gittin' tarnation drunk.—But whut I *do* know is, ye're changed, Holdfast. An' I bet Becky she'd say so too."

"Changed"—the word echoed in Holdfast's thought after Russell Bean, foiled and disgusted, finally went away in the direction of the trace. Did it tell, in any degree, the truth? Would the folks at home, by whose fire he was sitting tonight a thousand miles away in the wilderness, agree? What would Samson Occum say, supposing that he was still alive and knew all? And Becky—would she "say so too"?

The main thing that Russell Bean had found fault with was a loss in his friend of gaiety, laughter, play. That charge could not be denied. One might say, of course, that Bean did not allow for the fact that some boys grow up, that he himself had never felt the pain of exile, and that the day-and-night longing for places and faces forever dear was apparently unknown to him. No such searing experience as that of the Groton massacre had he ever suffered. Bean's homeless wanderings in the forest had been made easier for him by—well, by his squaws. Nevertheless, there really had been a change, a loss. Russell Bean could see the results and name them, however blind he might be to their causes.

It was amusing to recall how Bean had plunged at the name of Becky, and yet even there he had not been entirely wrong. That girl, for ten years a care and for eight years more a shining memory, was still, Holdfast gladly acknowledged, the center and focus of his backward-looking thoughts. The farm, the river, the school, the town, the woodland, Larrabee Oak, Cochegan Rock—all shone for him now in the light of that one slim burning candle. It was she who had kept his youth alive through toil, strife, and horror. For her he was still a virgin. Hundreds of camp-fires had been less lonely and numberless miles of trail less toilsome because of her ghostly companionship. Even tonight she sat here by this little fire in the middle of Tennessee—not, of course, as Rebecca Reid, mother and matron, but as Becky Chester, the awkward auburn-haired girl of fifteen, freckled like a tiger-lily, vivid as daybreak, honest and hard and brave. There could be no mourning for the loss of her, because she was not lost, and could never be. Let John Reid mourn, if he must, the death of a girl into a woman, but in one man's memory her girlhood was immortal. He, Holdfast Gaines, had loved that girl, and he loved her still, though in a way which Russell Bean, a "come-and-go husband" in twenty tribes, would scarcely comprehend. In that regard, at any rate, there had been no change.

He had meant not to change at all but to be faithful, to be worthy of the good name "Holdfast" given him by Occum and the Chesters when he left the Village for the Farm. Certainly he had striven to be true to both of these, to represent them both, to resolve their disagreements and unite the best of each in one triumphant life. But that task, as

248

Occum had foreseen, had proved a hard one. Indeed it might be that the "change" of which Russell Bean complained was a sadness brought on by almost inevitable failure.

In trying to be true to both sides he had never been able to put forth his full strength for either. Right hand and left hand—both were powerful, but doomed to use most of their force in struggle each against each. He had been like a strong man locked, pent, walled-in by his own straining muscles, mightily pulling and pushing, but not at the outer world.—Meanwhile the mind looked on at the outward conflict, and on every field saw defeat.

Tecumseh was late at the rendezvous.—What might he be doing elsewhere?

Holdfast laid another stick on the fire.

And what would Russell Bean make of an acknowledgment, simple and frank, that the Indians were almost as much at fault as the whites in this dreadful struggle? He would probably say that he had always known it, and would express astonishment that Holdfast had ever thought anything else. Quite meaningless to him, and incredible, would be the pain of that long, slow discovery.

And what would he say if told that the blood-lust of Uncas was still alive in his descendant, often terribly tempting him to a savage violence? —That much, perhaps, Bean could understand, but not the shame which always followed such outbreaks.

Could he comprehend the restraints that kept a man silent while others were voluble, and held his hands down as by fetters of iron while others were acting?—Ah, how enviable, in a way, were the headstrong men who saw one-half the truth so clearly, ignoring the other half, that they might strike with their total power like chain-lightning! Young Andrew Jackson was convinced that the red-skins must be swept out of the white man's path, if necessary by extermination; and young Tecumseh was hard at work on a plan—perhaps involving British assistance—for the slaughter of all whites west of Blue Ridge. Both, of course, were terribly wrong; but at least one of them was already acting, and the other soon would be, while Holdfast Gaines only watched and listened and suffered.—Was he really weaker than they, less able or less determined, or was it that the task laid upon him was harder than theirs, dividing him against himself, exhausting his strength before he

249

could strike a blow, making his heart a battle-field of which his mind was the helpless spectator?

But then, too, Russell Bean had mentioned "religion," somewhat scornfully, as a possible cause of this alleged "change." Though shot at random, that arrow had hit the mark.

Occum's study—"What shall I do?"—a vague answer involving vigil and vision—the Breeches Bible—a hand-clasp—the wedding—snow-storm—the Village for one night—twenty miles through the snow—the Cave . . . Thus, step by step, while he sat by his fire in the forest waiting for Tecumseh, now and then adding a dry stick to the fire, Holdfast began to follow an old worn trail of recollection. For the thousandth time he lived through the forty days and nights which had divided his youth from his manhood and had, to that extent, "changed" him. The images that rose before him were as vivid, almost, as though he were watching the nights and days of another man. And to these he added, unconsciously, a wealth of symbolic interpretation, the natural growth through the years of his own mind.

During the first week of his vigil, when often he could not help remembering, he had been lonely, there in the Cave, almost beyond endurance.

In boyhood and earlier youth he had been alone in the woods for days and nights together, in places far wilder than this. More than once he had built his fire at midnight under Cochegan itself and had slept peacefully in that haunted place until the dawn. Often he had lain for hours in the woods of Chesterfield waiting for deer, so still that the mink and the black-snake had come within reach of his hand. Often on summer nights, deep down in the rocky jungles of Gungywamp, the fox-fire and wandering will-o'-the-wisp had been his only companions —unless it were for those small brown people, the muckowheese, brothers of the whip-poor-will, who dance on the lily-pads of the swamp and make their moccasins of lady-slipper.

But all that had been only solitude. This was isolation. That had drawn his thoughts outward; this shut them in. That had been in a world warm with love, with the confident expectation of return to hearth and home and someone there to greet him. Now his home was a savage cave sloping far back and up toward the heart of a giant hill; and whoever might dwell there had made no sound, no sign.

He had known this cave, in a dim and wondering way, since his boyhood. Even as a child in Mohegan Village he had heard what the younger men said of it, and had tried to guess why it was that the elders said little or nothing. Clear in memory, still, was the day when he had first stood for a moment before the cave's frowning entrance—and then had hurried away. Sinister, mysterious, at once forbidding and luring, it had haunted his thoughts for days and weeks. Half of him had yearned to go back and make sure that it looked just so, but the other half—for he had been only twelve at the time—had refused to look again lest it should be in fact as strange as memory averred.

All that had been boyish enough. Since then he had more than once slept in the little room, eight feet high, just within the frowning entrance—to show that he could. A few days before this present vigil began, moreover, he had laboriously dragged his firewood back into the womb of the hill—dragged it log by log through the narrow eighty-foot throat of the cave into the large pear-shaped room, all of rock, at the inward and upper end. In one sense, then, he might say that he now knew the place entirely; yet knowledge of its physical shape had not in the least diminished that old sense of awe. He did not know what those subterranean waters were that made a continuous rumor of ruffle and flow far down the chasm that yawned at the back of the room. He could not interpret the picture-writings dimly seen in the firelight high up on the walls, or guess who had made them.

For the first time in his life there came over him the terror of desolation. Often as he lay by the little fire that held aloof the darkness of night and of day in the innermost cave, he shook with a fear that had no meaning, no object.

Were they right, then—those who held that this cave had been a temple of devil-worship through all the Indian ages? Something of that sort might explain the reticence of the elder Mohegans. And was it not confidently asserted, among the whites, that the witches of all Connecticut gathered here on Hallowe'en to adore their obscene lord? Mother Chester believed that. So did many people of Norwich and New London—as well, no doubt, as many in Middletown, Higganum, East and West Haddam, much nearer at hand. They named a young woman of Wequetequock who had ridden, they said, her broom-stick hither. They suspected an old Rogerene of Jordan Cove. They were watching the gigantic Negro, Venture Smith, who lived down there at Haddam Neck, two miles away. Still more closely a few of the boldest had watched the graves in the Old Cove Burying Ground a mile down the river.

Many times he had smiled at these tales. White people, he had long been convinced, were not spiritually minded. For the most part they were merely superstitious. But now, why such terrible dreams at night and such convulsions of fear in the daytime? What horrors had these granite walls witnessed? Who had been here before him, worshipping whom?

Grandfather Nannapoon had told him, long ago, that this cave was the strong-hold of Hobbomok, King of Evil. And he had said also that the wild rocky hill called Machimoodus, a mile to the south-west, was the favored dwelling-place of Kiehtan the Holy. Therefore the subterranean uproar so often heard in the region could be nothing, Nannapoon thought, but the sounds of conflict between these inveterate foes.

In Mohegan Village, to be sure, the names had been "Maundu" and "Djibi." Samson Occum had called them "God" and "the Devil." But what of that? When one came into new territory, even though it were only twenty miles from home, one wished to call them by the names they had always been called in that place. Call Him "Kiehtan," then, as the men who once lived in this cave had probably done. And if one must name that Other at all, then call Him, with bated breath, "Hobbomok."

The strange thing was that these two should dwell so close together, as though friends and not foes. The entrance to the Cave of Hobbomok faced directly out across the narrow valley toward the Mount of Kiehtan, called Machimoodus. How then might one know the two apart? Was it not possible that adoration of the One might really be a service of that Other? How could a man be sure that in his strong effort to raise himself toward heaven he had not merely descended into hell?

Thus, in the midst of his fears and his loneliness, he was assailed by doubt. How much, after all, did he know about this holy vigil, its purpose, methods, and history? Only what had been dimly suggested in an ancient Hebrew book and in the little that Samson Occum had said. But Occum himself had never kept the vigil, nor did he even know a man who had kept it. And how could there be any guidance in the far-away, half fabulous lives of Jesus, Moses, Elijah? All three had been chosen out for a special mission, and it was no wonder therefore that the spirit had driven them into the wilderness, there to fast and wait and listen during forty days and nights. It was not strange that Kiehtan had spoken directly to them, for He had need of their service —but why should He speak to one whose claim was only his own great need and who knew not where else to turn?

In the loneliness, hunger, and silence of those first days his vigil often seemed to him merely insane. Again and again he caught himself thinking of it as Father Chester would think, and heard his scornful laugh. Nay, for that matter, what would John Reid think of it, or Mother Chester, or even Rebecca? What would be the opinion of any sensible man in Norwich, New London, or Hartford? One and all, they would be convinced that he was losing his mind and throwing his life away. And did it seem likely that all such sensible people would be wrong in so thinking, while he alone was right?—Just why, in fact, had he come here? What was he really doing, except slowly starving to death fifty feet below the groping roots of the laurel, hard-hack, and huckleberry? Why should he not immediately leave this fearful place while he still had the strength and prudence?

And then, to meet these incursions of what most men would have called common sense, he would laboriously recall the motives which had at one time seemed sufficient. He would remind himself that he had come here not in sorrow, not in defeat, but with the strong hope of finding a deeper, loftier, more strenuous, and certainly a more Indian purpose in life than the Christianity about him appeared to offer. He had come because he was about to undertake a life-long task which he felt to be far beyond his unaided human powers. Moreover, a man whom he honored and delighted to obey had suggested this quest. It was hard, dangerous, bold, and unworldly. It spoke to the athlete in him, calling for the utmost powers of body and mind and spirit. It forced him to confront the fascinating mystery of the Cave and the Mount—to find out, if he could, once for all what was dreadful in the one, what consoling in the other, and how they were related each to each. And finally this vigil would test the truth of the mighty sentence in Deuteronomy: "The eternal God is thy refuge, and underneath are the everlasting arms."

These, and others of the like sort, had been his motives. They endured while the winter deepened and the sterner cold came on.

There were things that he strove not to think of, remember, or even imagine.

At night, lying sleepless in his long narrow blanket on the innermost cave's rocky floor, he often seemed to hear the ticking of the Chester clock as it had come up the stair to him in his attic chamber.— And that same clock was still measuring out her days, his nights. "Tick-tock," said the clock on the shelf. "Tock-tick." Were they listening now, she and he?

But oh, great God o' the Mountain, slow down this pulse and chill its fever in ice and snow! Slow it down though it be with the finger of Death! Give me now the pulse of a sleeping bear that beats but once in a minute! Fill me now with the stillness of dawn and of dusk, with the strength of stars rising and falling. Oh, now for a quieted heart that is fevered no more for its own but gives back all it has taken!

In the Devil's Hop-yard, while walking over from Mohegan Village to the cave, he had killed a turkey with a well-aimed stone. Since then he had been able to bring down four partridges and a ruffed grouse, all of them with stones and sticks. His "murtherer" stood unused at the mouth of the cave, with the same charge in it that he had brought from Four Winds Farm. After all, it was a white man's weapon.

For the rest, his sustenance had been boiled lichens of the sort easily found on the rocks of the hill and called by the whites "rock-tripe" or "famine food." This would serve to keep him alive for weeks, though not to sustain his strength. It provided a means of starving slowly.

He smiled at times, with a cool and detached commiseration, to see how frail he was becoming. The strongest runner in Connecticut would totter now on his feet, his knees would knock and his head would swim, when he tried to climb the steep hill that rose above the cave's mouth. He had to contrive and study before hoisting a ten-pound stick to the top of the fire.

Yet this was what he had wanted. It was for this self-imposed and sought-out weakness, in part, that he had come here. The strength of a man must go, Samson Occum had said, and his pride in his strength must be humbled, before the Strong Ones could help him at all.

Little by little his fears left him. Perhaps he was growing too weak to feel them. Perhaps he was finding the peace of those who have nothing but life to lose and no longer care greatly about that. There were Presences still, he felt, in the cave, in the boulder beside it, and in the white oak that rustled its withered leaves above the boulder; but they meant him no harm.

All haste and anxiety went from him. He was no longer impatient for his summons from the Holy Mountain. Waiting and listening had become a sober joy. A strange new happiness rose in his heart, like the dancing sand-grains he had seen once, shining in the sun, deep down in a woodland spring. That imagined ticking of the Chester clock died away, and with it all sense of the white man's time. His time, henceforth, seemed to drip from eternity's store. It moved to a statelier music. Dark and dawn, noon and dusk were its measure, with the come-and-go of the winds, of the birds, and of clouds across the sky.

Day by day his affection grew for all fellow-creatures. Merely to rest his hand on the sun-lit bark of the white oak that stood near the cave's mouth was enough for happiness. How deeply chasmed and roughly grained it was—slightly warmed by the sun on the south-west side and tinged with faint green on the north-east! Most beautiful it seemed to him, that gray-green bark.

The sight and sound of a bevy of chickadees among the branches of the oak filled him with delight. What tameless courage, what daunt-less freedom, in those tiny scraps of valor! Ah, that he had even a crumb of bread to give them! As he stood near the oak one windy morning one of them alit for a moment on his shoulder.

On another morning he saw a fox loping easily through the snow fifty yards down the hill. He went gracefully over the drifts as a gold-finch bounding from wave to wave of the air.

Once or twice he heard the baying of a hound from far away among the hills, full and deep as the tone of a grand old bell.

Such events were welcome, but he did not need them now. The grain of the rock in his cave, the flame of the fire on the rock, the wood that he burned, the snow-flake on his sleeve, the sunlight striking across the snow—all were charged with a beauty which overflowed into his heart. Falling from the silence of the upper air, there sounded all night and day a vast ethereal music.

Already, then, his vigil had been justified. Even in the Cave of Hobbomok itself, and before his summons, he had found peace, com-panionship. His doubts and fears, not the vigil, had been absurd.

He saw that before the mind and spirit could soar they must sink deep, and that before a man could serve others worthily he must gather his strength and wisdom alone. Two symbols there were for every fulfilled life—the Cave and the Road; and the Cave must come first for the spirit and mind as it did for the body. In every rounded life there had to be a time of departure, exile, and seeming defeat. The coiled spring must be pressed down. The arrow must be drawn back. The solitude of Elijah, Jesus, and Moses had been normal, necessary.

Here was a law which the Christian world had forgotten, but the Indian not quite. One reason why the so-called Christian life was often scarcely distinguishable from a smug respectability was that Chris-tians had forgotten this law. So seldom were they driven by the Spirit into the wilderness, there to dwell among beasts and to be tempted by Satan.

Temptation and salvation, departure and return, the Cave and the Road, grief and joy, body and spirit, female and male, the falling leaf and the bursting bud, Hobbomok and Kiehtan, the transverse beam of the Cross and the upright beam—yes, however intricate God's blanket might appear, it was really nothing but woof and warp. The Hidden Weaver had only one way of working. From the beginning until now He had always thrown a strand of dark across every brighter yarn.

Thus his thoughts ranged on and on into a region of dim conjecture. All solid stuff of the senses became to him transparent symbol. He saw the material world as God's inexhaustible metaphor, charged with meaning in every part. The world, he saw, was God's way of darkening and yet shadowing forth his own Presence, so that its glory might be borne. Every laurel and hard-hack and huckleberry bush that grew on the hillside he came to see as a burning bush. God was in it.—Or, rather, it was in God.

So much he could discern even from the Cave of Hobbomok, the place of darkness. But as yet there had come no summons—perhaps for the reason that his human strength was not yet exhausted. And more and more, by night and day, he heard one quiet sentence resound in his heart and mind: "Ye must be born again!"

By late December he had peeled off all the rock-clinging "famine food" to be found within a mile of the cave, and that was the utmost distance to which he could walk with any confident expectation of a return. His larder, if one could give such a name to the means of retarded starvation, was exhausted. Possibly there might be a dozen of the gray-green crinkle-edged plants down there on the bleak northern scarp of the Holy Mountain itself. There they had been, at any rate, in late November, and the deer might have left them. The exact look of those rich-hued lichens, as he had seen them at dusk of a November evening while his strength was still in him, came now before the eye of the mind. "Communion bread" he had called them then, seeing how they were set ready at the top of a stern black altar of rock, hard to climb, where desperate men and lonely gods might meet. And now, perhaps, on the verge of death, he might not be thought unworthy of that communion—if only he could go so far to make it!

Three nights ago there had been a great circle round the moon, enclosing three stars. Last night the moon had been half-blinded, as though floundering through deep snow. Early this morning he had heard the mauls and mallets of ship-builders ringing clear from Abel Shepard's ship-yard up the river three miles away. He smelt the breath of oncoming storm. From the cave-mouth he saw a black flag in the northern sky, swiftly advancing.—Well then, a blizzard; and, after that, no more famine food to be found anywhere. After the blizzard, or during it, death would come.

And so, why make the effort? Why not meet Him here beside the fire brought from home? He would come gently. The pangs of hunger were past now. A few more days, a few more nights, and his vigil would be over.

He waited a day and a night.

On the next morning, looking out, he saw nothing but snow furiously driven out of the north. Earth, sky, rock and tree, the near and the far, were erased by whirling snow.

He crawled back to his fire in the pear-shaped womb of the hill. He sat by the fire for an hour, trying to think. While he still could, he laid a dozen sticks on the fire. The flames towered and flapped toward the high rocky roof, striving to be free through the tiny hole that gave vent to the smoke.

So this was the end. The summons had not come. He had kept his vigil faithfully, but the vision had been denied him. He had not been found worthy.

The flames lighted up a crude calendar which he had scratched with his knife on the wall of the rock. He stared at it, trying to count the days he had been there. Though his sight was by no means clear and his head was giddy, yet after the third or fourth effort he made sure that this must be the fortieth day of his fasting in the wilderness and that tomorrow, therefore, would be Christmas.

For a while he brooded upon that. Christmas had always been a day of festivity at Four Winds Farm—no doubt because the Colonel was not, after all, much of a "Christian." It was celebrated quietly, so as not to affront the more pious neighbors, but still with an air of rejoicing suited to the birthday of a great and beneficent Person.

He saw them, one by one, sitting at the Christmas board. The firelight was on their faces. They were thinking, talking, of him. Whatever toasts they might drink, he would not be forgotten. Whatever prayer they said, he would be in it. And they would know that he, if alive, would be thinking of them.

At every moment this picture in the mind grew warmer, nearer. He heard their voices, the tick of the clock, the flap of the fire on the hearth.

He took his clam-shell from the bag of woodchuck-skin at his belt, undid the thong with fumbling fingers, sprinkled a handful of fresh punk on the smolder, and then, tying it up firmly again, replaced it in the bag. From his shoulder he slung a small iron pot, his only utensil. Then he rose, painfully, and swayed in standing. There was a roaring in his ears.

With his long oaken staff he drew the fire together. Craftily husbanding his strength, he rolled the largest log he had, brought in for this purpose, to the edge of the fire. In old times, he remembered, he had easily carried logs thrice the weight of this into the kitchen. "Yule logs," the Colonel had called them.

And then, slowly, painfully, he crawled back to the mouth of the cave.

At one step beyond the protecting wall of the rock the north wind took him, shook him in violent glee. At once it snatched his breath away, beat tears from his eyes, and battered his lean frail body back and down. It meant to kill.

Round the edge of the rock it came with a scream and leapt upon him, a breath of pure hatred, a power of envious evil. By what right, he heard it cry, was this alien spirit, this human will, wandering here? To throttle it now, to crush it, blot it out!

But not yet! He fell to his hands and knees, caught a breath, and began to crawl, to creep. Keep going downward; let the hill, let the wind help him. It was so that a bear would go, shuffling, sidling, choosing the easier slopes and shielding his snout with his shoulder. So birds flew, fish swam, streams ran, resting, sliding, sinking, down-going always.

"Scree-ee!" yelled the wind its war-whoop. It surrounded him, battered him, entered him. It beat back the breath of his life and plucked at his will. But the crafty deep-down will of the man, harboring its own purposes, answered only to itself: "From the foe find the force to fight him!"

The snow flew level. It stung. There was no glimpse of Machimoodus. The valley was gone, the trees, the rocks, the ground, leaving only those furred moving hands below and the long white arrows that filled the world pelting thick from the bow of Hobbomok.

Yet he knew the way. It was south-west to Machimoodus—south-west whence the warm winds blew and the way all spirits go. He had always known the way to Machimoodus.

He had gone ten rods, now, of that long mile; and it was against all odds that a man so starved should make ten yards in the teeth of such a storm. Well, then, to keep on going for as long as the whip of the will could swing and sting. After that—ah, to rest, soft-sunk in the snow, and to sleep the winter through with his face toward Machimoodus.

Ah, the goodness of sleep, that deep dark mothering breast!

He sank down for a moment and rested and slipped toward sleep.

But tomorrow the sun would turn. Tomorrow Jesus was born. Tomorrow at Four Winds Farm they would feast and think of him.

And so once again the sting of the lash of the will and the left hand fumbling forward, the right knee jerking as much, and the mound of white moving downward and onward a little farther toward Machimoodus.

It was as though some snow-burdened fragment of sod were stirring there, moved by a purpose more sure than sod can feel. It was as though some hill-side rock had determined to sleep in the valley. Something moved on the whirried slope that was not moved by the wind.

It would have looked a pitiful, and yet somehow a gallant and dauntless thing, that moving shape, scarcely human. Feathered and furred with snow, it was often crushed down by the weight it bore or flattened out by the wind. Often it paused, for so long that one would have said it could never move again. But then once more, slowly, sleepily, the wonder of its weird white motion was renewed.

At dusk he came into a little vale, thirty feet across, muffled on either side by mounds of bending hemlocks. They were like old women, those trees, bearing huge burdens of white. The wind was less tyrannous here and the snow was deeper, softer. He sank to his elbows now. Far in toward the stem of a hemlock he found a plant of winter-green, and another. He ate them, root and all.

The vale ran in between the steep scarp of Machimoodus and a lower mount that shut off the wind. A man might sleep here, with a log to his back and a fire at his feet, with some expectation of waking.— Well, waking was not his concern; but certainly, and soon, he would sleep.

He found a rotten log beneath a hemlock tree, close in against a northern bank. With his hunting-knife he hacked off a few branches, feebly, and laid them in a hollow scooped beside the log. Dry sticks of hemlock and resinous billets of pine lay all about under the snow. He dug them out and heaped them, working as rapidly as he could because the light was failing. He worked with a kind of glee at having beaten the storm's malice. He began to feel stronger.

The wind had blown itself out. The snow was ceasing and the air grew colder. Through the trees, looking out over Salmon Cove and Connecticut River, he saw the embers of sunset.

So now he would eat, he would feast, before he—before he slept.

But not one of the leathery plants could he find on the lower ledges. Perhaps the deer had taken them all, or the snow had covered them over.

Well, then, he must climb.

Peering up through the gathering dark he could see a thirty-foot wall of gray layered granite, with here and there a dim glitter of ice. On either side no path, no trail. Most jealously the red gods had guarded their sacred mount! They chose their companions nobly. Only for those who had come through the valley of the shadow of death did they keep their famine food on these bleak ledges.

Here and there, as he started up, he found cracks and crevices in the rock, but the ice lapping smoothly over gave treacherous support to his frozen moccasins. Starved muscles and nerves did their work with agony under the bull-whip of the will. His frozen finger-ends were soon bleeding. Blood trickled with the sweat down his heaving chest, and froze there.—But all this he hardly knew, because of his growing giddiness and a great longing to plunge back headlong to the foot of the cliff.

Yet he kept his gaze upward. Twenty feet he had climbed. There were hardly ten more to go. Already he thought he could discern half a dozen plants of rock-tripe on the edge above him. Three feet more, and he would be able to reach the nearest.

Yet he found no foot-hold to lift him those three feet. For as far as he could reach on either side with his hands and feet he groped, and found no niche. Almost bolt upright, with arms and legs straining, he stood facing the cliff, rigid, bathed in sweat, and slowly freezing. He could move neither up nor down. His brain was numb with cold. He forgot why he had come there.

So for two minutes he clung as though nailed to the rock, with his arms out-spread. Deep night came down upon him. He felt forsaken by men and gods: He felt that he was alone.

His will let go, his fingers relaxed, his knees went loose, and he fell back into the snow.

* * *

260

He thought that it must be the voice of Long Tom calling.

But who could be firing the gun only he could handle?

Ah, but let them try! This was his time for sleep. He was off duty now. His bed was soft and warm.

But there again that gigantic roar went abroad, beating back and forth from hill to hill like the voice of his gun across and across the Thames. Only this voice came from under the ground.

He opened his eyes. Over him in the midnight sky the stars were keeping their ancient watch. Under his hands, his head, his shoulders, he felt the warm soft snow.

And then again for the third time, just as his eyes were closing, but now far louder and longer than even the call of Long Tom, there rose a vast roar from under the ground and into the darkness. It was as though Earth herself were calling. He heard the echoes sounding on like cannon-balls gone bounding down gigantic granite stairs. His bed of snow unmistakably trembled and shook. Cascades of snow came plunging from the hemlock boughs above him, and the delicate topmost twigs of the hemlocks were violently waving in no wind against the stars. The forest about him awoke. Foxes barked. A buck, near at hand, snorted with fear as he rose from his lair and went crashing down toward the river. A great owl, shaken out from the darkest pine, was swooping in wide circles among the stars with "Who-oo? Who-hoo-oo? Who-oo?"

He knew now. This was Machimoodus calling. This was his summons.

He sat up. He rose to his feet. His limbs felt strong and light. He started once more up the face of the cliff. At once his hand fell on a long slender root of hemlock snaking down from the top. He swarmed up it hand over hand, and then from the top he ran on through the dark under shaking trees—stumbling and staggering, falling and rising, but hastening on toward the summit.

From the fringe of the uppermost trees he could see it, at last. It was bare, black, rocky, over-topping the trees, all snow blown away.

At the edge of the woods he paused and tore his clothes from him. So Occum had said one must do. He kicked off his moccasins. From the pocket of his hunting-shirt he took his tobacco-pipe, ready-packed. From the woodchuck-skin he drew his clam-shell. The first deep draught of smoke made his head swim. He staggered drunkenly up the black jagged rock, holding the reeking tobacco high as an offering.

For a moment, then, he stood still, taut, naked, with head thrown back. Toward the North Star he blew a puff of smoke. Another he blew to the East, and to the South, and to the holy West.

"I am here," he cried. "Thou hast called me. I have no name, no people, no task. But Thou who knowest the inmost heart, speak now! I have waited long. I am waiting."

Holdfast Gaines returned to himself in the forest of Tennessee. With no stars or moon to help him, he could not guess how long a time had elapsed during his journey of the mind into the past. He saw, however, that his fire had burned down to a few glowing embers. How late Tecumseh was! Gathering a handful of dry leaves and then a few twigs, he fed the fire little by little until it was ready for sticks and billets.

Certain things had been vague and dim among the events of that night on Machimoodus. Whether all, or any, of them had actually occurred in the outer world of the flesh and the senses he would never certainly know. Some of them might have been added, or at least magnified, in the imaginings and recollections of later years. What of that? Did it matter how truth came, if truth itself arrived? Somehow, somewhere, somewhen those wonderful things had happened, perhaps in a world of reality to which the five senses could not reach. They had happened in the core of his heart. Whether facts or not, they were true.

That vision on the summit, of a huge man carrying a child across a rushing stream—had he seen it with his bodily eyes or in some other way? If sent by Indian gods, why should it be identical with the old legend of Saint Christopher the Giant which Nathan Hale had told him long ago? Why was it so close in meaning to the thing Father Chester had often said: "A man like you, 't ain't fair fer him to be so damn strong without he carries weight"?

His vision had told him nothing new, but had merely re-affirmed a truth long familiar. And no doubt it was thus that the true gods had always spoken, saying not new things but everlasting, and things less clear than deep. Moreover, it was not surprising that the Indian God of the Mountain had used a Christian symbol to shadow forth his meaning. Had not Occum prophesied something of that sort? Could there have been a better way of indicating the dual task that was imposed?

Concerning another faint memory or hallucination of that night on Machimoodus he was even more uncertain. Had he actually found a sleeping bear in a shallow cave just below the summit and crept in beside that shaggy shape and warmed himself and so saved his life?—But what matter? It was enough that this too had happened in some realm of unquestionable reality. If he had dreamed or imagined the event, it had none the less of meaning. Indeed the bear might have been the purely Indian phase of his vision, meant to balance the Christian.

Yes; for the true gods, if only one waited for their whole message, never spoke on one side only. That real or pretended contempt for the flesh which had always enfeebled Christianity was not from them. "In the beginning God created the Heaven *and the Earth.*" The gross and blundering bear was his handiwork as much as the humming-bird. Saint Christopher the burly giant was God's beloved, and so too was Old Grandfather Bear, head of the Bear Clan, grumbling among the huckleberries and clawing for honey high up the bee-tree, sagacious, tenacious of life, feeding where he could and fasting where he must, patient of all weathers, shielding his breath with his shoulder, sleeping the winter through in a cave snuggled close to Earth's mothering breast with his heart beating once in a minute.—"An' iffen ye hit 'im whar he c'n git at it an' give 'im time to git away in the bresh, he'll take an' plug up the hole with his tongue so's he won't bleed to death, an' then, b' God, he c'n run a thousan' mile!"

Holdfast Gaines once more mended and fed his lonely fire in the forest of Tennessee, half a mile above Avery Trace. It must be nearly midnight. Tecumseh was late indeed. What ought one to think of such delay on just this night, with over a hundred white travelers encamped so close below? When Tecumseh had named this rendezvous, the great chestnut between the rivulets on the Shawnee Trail to the Creek Nation, it had seemed appropriate enough—but now . . . ? How much did one know of that young chieftain, noble in bearing, powerful of mind and body, consummately skillful in speech, but yet certainly harboring a dreadful purpose? If he could break a tryst, what else might he not do? Why that persistent calling of owls, too many owls, down by the Trace an hour ago?—Ah, well, Russell Bean was down there watching, and he knew every Indian wile that a white man could find out.

Nearly all the rest of that strange experience eight years gone by was stuff of the five senses. For most of it he could call human witnesses,

263

at need. On the morning after his vision he had been found up there, wandering half crazed, by Venture Smith, the famous gigantic Negro—son of an African king, for many years a slave to white men, and now a prosperous farmer and ship-owner living at Haddam Neck. This black Saint Christopher, mighty as a bear, had gathered him up as though he were a child, had borne him gently down the mountain and across Salmon River, had nursed him, fed him, made him sleep, listened to him, understood him, and—greatest boon of all—believed him. Venture had said that in Africa too, when he was a boy, every medicine man and chieftain had to keep his vigil and talk with the gods before his real strength came upon him. He agreed completely and at once that no man can drink from the deeper wells of happiness and inward power who has not been broken, brought low, cast out, and dried to the last drop of his merely human force. He supposed that this must be known to everybody in the world except the whites, who were, of course, amazingly ignorant.

Only think, Venture said, what the whites had made of their own man Jesus! They talked about him, swore by him, preached and prayed and lectured in his name, on Sundays told him what they wanted of him, locked him up through all the week in their icy-cold white god-boxes so he wouldn't see what they were up to, called him a god even, praised him for being poor and a virgin while they went on with their fornication and grabbing for gold, and thought that he ought to take them to Heaven because they were white and respectable and rich.—But would he? That man who had dwelt forty days and nights in the desert and talked there with Satan? Venture Smith thought not. "Any man," said he, "whut's talk' wid ole Satan, dat spunky ole son-of-a-bitch, he git kinder choosey whut kinder white man he gwineter talk wid. Yassah. Ah s'pose so. Dat's way Ah does annyhow."

Venture had thought a good deal about "dat man Jesus" in an oddly independent, completely non-theological way. In a world almost wholly given over to success, Jesus was the best example he could name of the advantages enjoyed by those fully acquainted with failure, disappointment, and grief. And yet he made clear his opinion that his own life was a fair example also. To almost any other listener some of his talk would have sounded blasphemous—especially in his frightful tale of the time when he had voluntarily let himself be suspended for an hour on a cattle gallows. His "imitation of Christ" had gone strangely far. Though born a savage, he had converted the enfeebled and effeminized white man's religion into a way of life fit for a black man of amazing muscle and thew. Though he still kept a royal pride, he had somehow

264

gained or maintained, while suffering the grossest injustices, a sweetness, a patience, a simple grandeur, an inward peace, which passed understanding.—Holdfast felt that he had met this black Saint Christopher just in the nick of time.

Good days and nights those had been at Venture Smith's fireside in the comfortable house at Haddam Neck, resting, gathering strength, listening to Venture's wise illiterate talk and easy laughter, smoking deep-bowled pipes of Indian clay, remembering backward and planning forward and hoping a little.

On the morning of New Year's Day he left the farm-house, crossed Salmon River, skirted Mount Machimoodus, and easily climbed the long steep hill to his cave. The fire was out and the ashes cold, but in a few minutes he had a fresh flame prospering in that innermost uterine room where he had waited for nearly forty days and nights to be born again. On this morning he sat there for only an hour, as though saying farewell. Then he rose, folded his long narrow blanket, packed his duffel-bag, took his "murtherer" from a dark corner, looked about him for a moment, and crawled back into the light of day.

The morning lifted a tall blue tent above him as he stood at the cave's mouth—a tent with a glittering floor. The Holy Mountain, which had once seemed so unattainably far away, was shining close at hand. A thin column of smoke was rising over the Mount's right shoulder, perhaps from Venture Smith's unseen chimney. The sound of mallets and mauls came to him again from Abel Shepard's ship-yard below Chatham Landing. The Connecticut River was a long white winding street. Hill after hill, pure white or lilac or amethyst, lured the sight away to the heights of Higganum and Chester. In all the outspread landscape there was not a breath of breeze. It was a perfect day, heaven-sent, for smoke-signals.

From a pocket inside his hunting-coat he drew a small sheet of paper, carefully wrapped in dressed deer-skin, and read:

"At Noon New Year's Day or first clear day thereafter—
"One smoke—All's Well
"Two smokes—Come I need you
"Three smokes—Go and God Bless You Holdfast
"Becky"

And she, he knew, had another such paper, written and signed by him. They had exchanged the two on her wedding day, just before she was married. Smoke-signaling was an Indian game, taught them by an aged Pequot, which they had often played together in childhood.

265

"At noon"—and what was she doing now, twenty miles over there to westward? Had she already climbed the hill above the farm-house and laid her bundle of sticks, making sure by sprinkling snow on them that they would give forth a good volume of smoke? What blanket had she brought along? That oldest one, probably, with the moth-holes, which Mother had said might be used in the stables.

And surely she would be alone on the hill. At this time, certainly, and for these few minutes, her thoughts would be only of him.—Yet why "certainly"? How could he be sure of her now that so great a change had come into her life? Perhaps she had forgotten all about their agreement, being so happy now with her husband. She might decide not to come at all, lest John Reid should dislike it. She might be ill. The old life might have died entirely out of her heart.

Hastily then he sprang up the rocks and climbed the hill above the cave, with a bundle of sticks under one arm and his blanket under the other. He could see by the sun that the hands of the clock on the kitchen shelf must be coming together, and that soon she would hear twelve deep mellow notes welling up from New London.

He topped the hill, and for the first time in weeks looked out toward Four Winds Farm.—Ah, there already, thin and faint in the remotest distance, he discerned a column of smoke. Straight as a prayer it soared into the azure.

She had remembered. It was she. Her fire, like his, had been lighted by a coal from the hearth of home. She was with him once more, and alone. This was their moment.

He fumbled open his clam-shell, set fire to a handful of leaves and then to a few shavings. In less than a minute his smoke was answering hers. He fastened the farther end of his long narrow blanket, beyond the fire, beneath two stones.

But the sun seemed stuck in heaven. How to wait for these last few minutes, not knowing what she would say? It would mean much, nay all, her message. For years he had been carrying weight, and now soon he would learn whether that beloved burden had been lifted entirely to another man's shoulders, leaving him free.

He piled wet wood on the flames until his smoke rose almost black. A few seconds later he saw that she was doing the same.—So swiftly, as in the old days, their thoughts flew back and forth, needing no word! The hills they stood on, twenty miles apart, were like two small volcanoes fed by one subterranean fire.

He dampened his blanket with melting snow, as she would also be doing. He held his breath. There came a billowy puff, slowly rising. "All's Well."

Thank God!

He drew his blanket above the flames, held it there a moment, threw it off, and pulled it back. One round cloud of smoke went slowly up.

But surely she had more to say. They had agreed that there should be two messages. He gazed eagerly eastward. A minute passed before she began again with one smoke, "All's Well"—and then sent another, "Come, I need you." Would there be a third?—for the rest of his life hung upon that. Yes, yes a third cloud, tiny and dim, was rising, floating, fading away. "Go, and God Bless You, Holdfast."

He too sent up three puffs, vaguely wondering whether the sudden dimness of his eyes was due to the smoke or to the fact that his strength had not fully returned.

"Go, and God Bless You, Becky!"

Then for several minutes he stood and scanned the horizon. But the East had no further message, and no more need of him.

He smothered his fire in snow, took his blanket under his arm, and went down the hill, westward.

Holdfast Gaines, in the forest of Tennessee, replenished his fire and drew his blanket more closely about him.

On the whole, then, it seemed likely that Russell Bean was right in saying that there had been a change. And Becky might say so too.

There came a faint sound—not from the brook or a breeze or any bird. The man by the fire sat perfectly motionless for half a minute, listening, peering into the darkness, while his great shadow rose and fell on the trunk of the chestnut tree. Not for an instant did his gaze shift from the dim object he discerned out there on the edge of the shadow.—At last he rose, held his right hand high, and spoke: "How, Tecumseh!"

A young Indian, tall, handsome, walking with an elastic step and gracefully erect carriage, came forward. He was dressed in well-fitting tanned buck-skins. On his head there was a turban of blue wool. His oval face in the firelight showed a light brown complexion and his eyes were hazel. In one hand he carried a tomahawk, in the other a bow. He might be some twenty years old.

"How," said he, "Sleeping Bear!" His Choctaw was musically spoken.

"Sit. You are late. We have much to say."

267

TOO MANY OWLS

At Crab Orchard, within a short day's travel from Campbell's Station, four sentinels had watched through the night; but at Caney Fork, where the danger was twice as great, there were but two, and one of these lay down and went to sleep as soon as McGary had curled up beside the fire.

Andrew Jackson, to whom the Parson confided his doubts, was openly contemptuous. "Martin McGary," said he, "allus did hev a heart softer 'n a babe's. He sees a guardsman lookin' kinder tired an' says to 'im: 'Naow do jes' go hev a nice long nap, an' pleasant dreams to yeh!'— But, b' God, if I war a-runnin' this here guard I'd stand the fust man went to sleep up agin a tree, an' load 'im full o' lead."

"It sounds harsh, but I suppose you're right."

"Know damn well I am. Lead 's law out here; or leastways they ain't any law good for a damn that ain't got lead behind it."

It was evident that Jackson's legal education was progressing, and that he had already reached conclusions quite different from those inculcated by Messrs. Stokes and McKay. In time he might even come to see the propriety, which he had once sternly denied, of Governors—on suitable occasions—shooting Sheriffs.

His opinion had been delivered before dawn of an October day, on the first mile of a thirty-six hour march that took the company from Caney Fork to the Cumberland Plateau. McGary hoped by this rapid push to traverse the most dangerous part of the Indian country, in which Dragging Canoe and Turtle-at-Home had taken a score of scalps during the construction of the new road.

Well over forty miles they had gone between that start in the darkness and sunset of the next day, with no sleep whatever, with little to eat, with rifles ready and every sense alert. Therefore it was no wonder that nearly everyone went to sleep immediately after the hasty supper of half-cooked venison and parched corn had been dispatched. Men, women, children, and beasts were bone-tired, and weariest of all were McGary's guardsmen.

Andrew Jackson, declaring that he could go without sleep for any necessary number of days and nights, prepared to take the place of the guard. From Paw Crockett he borrowed a fistful of tobacco— rank enough, he said, to keep an ordinary man awake for a month—

and lay down between the Parson and Searcy with his head on his saddle. His rifle, his fine black horse, and Little David in a wicker cage, were close at hand.

The most wakeful topic of meditation that Jackson could hit upon was that of girls—of simple-minded girls he had known in the Waxhaws, ornamental and sophisticated girls encountered at Charleston, girls nondescript and more recently acquired at Salisbury and Jonesboro, and girls hoped for at Nashville. He feared that in the last of these towns, hardly ten years old, the species would be sparsely represented, and that most of the few examples they had there would either be married or else in some other way ineligible.

Who was that girl that Bean was bawling about the other morning, the daughter of Shannydore? Her name was . . . ?

Because of his own monogamous tendency, Jackson naïvely supposed that Bean had been celebrating one and the same anonymous fair both in his song and in a certain enthusiastic prose description delivered some time before. Vivid phrases of that description now came back to him: "Black snappin' eyes," she had, "an' sech long black floatin' ha'r on her as 'd make a man lay awake o' nights." H'm! Just the kind of girl for him to be thinking about on the present occasion. Besides that, Andrew Jackson, whose own hair was reddish, had a decided preference for girls with black hair. This particular girl might perhaps be a little old for him. Eight years ago she had been fifteen, and, according to Bean's expert testimony, "roundin' out a'ready." Oh, well, a year or two wouldn't make much difference if she was lively. At this point he recalled the declaration: "When it come to dancin' she war the all-fired leg-shakin'est gal whut ever went down the middle."

Jackson knew that it was unwise to believe anything that Bean said about women—except, to be sure, when he confessed about one of them that he had failed with her completely. Such confessions, though rare, were likely to be true. Well, now, Bean certainly hadn't boasted of any success with this daughter of Shannydore. That must mean that he had failed. And a girl that Bean had failed with was just the girl that Andrew Jackson, now twenty-one and a man of some amatory experience, would like to have a try at.

But her name?—Why, Donelson, of course. "Cap'n Donelson's darter," Bean had said. So then what in hell had he meant about "Shannydore"? And her first name still evaded him. He grew more and more drowsy in trying to recall it.

There was no sound in the night except that of the river, not far off, rumbling low in its rocky bed. "Must be nigh 'leven o'clock," Jackson muttered as he sat up to fill his corn-cob for the third time. Some day he must get himself a watch to tell the time by when there were no stars. He crawled over toward one of the waning fires for a light.

The thought came to him as he glanced about that this faintly lighted scene would not be much different if a band of Shawnees had stolen up ten minutes since and slaughtered every living creature in the camp. The only motion was that of a wise old dog that raised his head for a moment, twitched his ears, and then laid his muzzle again between his hind paws. Even Martin McGary slept like a dead man. And Jackson felt a thrill of pride that he should be the one man left awake, the single guardian, upon whom all depended.

Crawling back to his saddle, he wrapped his buffalo-robe more closely about him. Rather cold and hard the bed was.—And so about girls, in Nashville . . . But even the third pipeful of Crockett's villainous tobacco, although it was making his mouth feel like the inside of a kiln, could not keep him awake. His thought became one huge and empty interrogation about the name of that Nashville girl. And a voice from far away seemed to echo his question as it called "Whoo? Whoo-oo? Whoo?" Then another voice, farther off, called the same exasperating word.

"Why can't one o' them damn owls give the right answer?" he thought, just as he fell asleep.

But then, deep in the country of dreams, the owls changed to game-cocks.—Or rather, it was Little David answering the question the owls had asked. "Who? Who?" he cried out in Jackson's dream at the shrill top of his lungs. "D' ye wanter know who I be? Li'l David is my name, an' I don't give a damn who knows it. An' I want fer *you* to know, Goliath, thet I'm a-layin' fer yeh an' honin' to tear yer heart out."

Jackson struggled back to consciousness with a sense of strong apprehension mixed with shame. So this was how he kept watch! The game-cock two feet from his head was making what seemed, in the stillness of the night, a terrific clamor—just as Bean had foretold!

With one low word he stopped that noise. He sat up. No one was stirring. But the owls! On all sides of the camp, and near at hand now, they were hooting and calling. There were too many owls by far! An uncontrollable shiver thrilled up his spine.

"Searcy!" he hissed, leaning over and shaking the dark form at his

270

left. "Injuns! Git yer rifle-gun! Call the Jedge! Stand up! Don't say a word!"

Reaching then for his companion on the other side, he found the place empty. A moment later he saw the Parson arousing McGary and moving on to other members of the guard.

"Make a ring round the women an' childern, every man facin' out," Jackson whispered to McGary. "Then git 'em all back in the dark, away from the fires."

McGary did not pause to argue the question of authority. In less than two minutes the whole company, still heavy with sleep and ignorant of the reason for this night alarm, was on the move. Several wagons and a score of pots and pans were left behind, but a hundred and fifty men, women, and children were stealing quietly away into the dark with the firm cohesion of a swarm of bees.

Andrew Jackson, the last man to leave the circle of the fires, walked away leading his horse and carrying the wicker cage, a proud and happy young man. He and Little David—or rather, Little David and he— had not failed the company after all. They two were unmistakably the heroes of the occasion, and would be named for such as long as the occasion should be remembered.—A little more of this kind of thing, Jackson saw, and he would begin to be famous.

Panting up the last long hill above Stone River, Russell Bean saw that Holdfast was still two hundred yards ahead and going strong. For thirty miles Holdfast had kept that unvarying Indian pace, hardly a run but certainly not a jog-trot. It was a calculated, heady, experienced way of running, and a way that could eventually kill any white man ever born.

Bean's rifle—carried now in his left hand, now in the right, and then for a few yards bumping on his shoulder—had come to weigh, he felt, at least a hundred pounds. He longed to cast it from him under some bush, and would have done so had it not been for the shame, far worse than appearing naked, of letting the company see him unarmed.

Yet he told himself that he would not be tuckered at all but for the brief pause he and Holdfast had made at last night's deserted camping-place and what they had found there. He had seen dead bodies in great plenty before, and some of them had been hideously mangled, but one look at the four corpses lying among the still smouldering ashes of last night's fires had made him feel tired and old. It had spoiled his wind.

And what, he could not help asking over and over, had been his own

271

responsibility? Of course no one, not even Holdfast, would ever know, yet the question would not lie still in his mind whether this ghastly thing had happened during his stolen sleep last night, while Holdfast thought he was watching.—Well, of course it *must* have happened then. He had gone directly down to the camping-place as Holdfast had told him, but had found it deserted, though the fires were still dimly burning. There had certainly been no corpses there then. But this morning, going back again with Holdfast in the gray dawn, he had come upon that dreadful sight.

Stop thinking! Run!—Yet those four dead men must have been members of McGary's company, perhaps guards who had tried to resist overwhelming odds. They must have been brought back to the fires again after the main party had been captured and taken away into the woods. Or perhaps the four had been wounded, and the Shawnees had simply used the ready fires. . . . ! And if such a horror could happen to them, then what of the others—the Parson, Jackson, Paw Crockett, all the women, and that nameless child with the fierce peering look of a meat-hungry eaglet? Had they only been reserved for torture back in the Shawnee villages?

But run, now! Stop thinking about that! Blame Jackson and the crowing of his damned game-cock. Blame McGary. Throw all the blame on them. Here at last was the top of the hill and his breath coming in gasps and the silvery Cumberland looping far away—but nearer, right at the foot of the hill, where a little creek crossed the trace, McGary's company standing together, all in a huddled crowd by the stream!

Ah, what a joy to see them there, apparently all of them, alive, safe, and with not one Indian about! The mystery of the four blackened corpses, thirty miles back there among the cooling embers, could wait.

Russell Bean pounded down the hill at top speed, seeing quite clearly what he had to do: to find Jackson, now, call him a few suitable names, knock him down perhaps, and then grab Little David and wring his neck.

But—what . . . ? There was the Parson wading out to his middle in the creek with a kicking, yelling brat in his arms. The dogs were going wild on the bank, with Wash in the midst of them, and all the company standing silent, the men with their hats off. Holdfast had come to a stand at the edge of the crowd, his back heaving. And wasn't that Paw Crockett's boy in the Parson's arms? One couldn't mistake

272

that beak, that infernal yell. And then came the Parson's clear mellow voice above the purl of the stream: "Little David, I baptize thee in the name . . ."

"Little David!"

Bean came panting up to Holdfast's side just in time to see the Parson souse the Crockett boy completely under in the pool. The child spluttered when lifted out and began to scream and kick more violently than ever.

But "Little David"! Why that fool name? Surely this must be young Jackson's doing, meant to get him, Russell Bean, on the raw. Unmistakably, it was an intentional sneer, an expression of contempt, not for a moment to be tolerated by a famous runner and rifle-builder, one of the founders of Nashville, from a red-headed upstart and newcomer of whom no one had ever heard!—Young Jackson would have to be dealt with at once, and once for all, before they entered the town now but ten miles away.

A few seconds of irate elbowing and thrusting brought him before Jackson. McGary was standing near.

"Whar's thet gawdam chicken o' yourn, young Jackson? I'm a-goin' to wring his neck."

Twin fires sprang instantly up in Jackson's eyes, but his voice when he spoke was level and cool. "Oh, air ye?" said he. "That's int'restin'. Only ye better know right now that his neck an' mine go together."

Bean had looked into the blaze of Jackson's eyes several times before —at the Salisbury race-track with amusement, at the cock-fight with surprise, and beside the Holston, after the young man and he had left the Parson to his morning meditations, with extreme discomfort. But now he saw something different there. It was not rage or anger but a perfectly self-confident manhood. At the same moment he became aware that Jackson had on his side, and knew that he had, all the by-standers. Bean was daunted. His self-assurance was all at once weakened. In a flash it came to him that perhaps he was no longer the cock of the walk he had thought himself, and that another man, much younger, far less experienced and accomplished, a man who did not know how to dress or run or make love or cut the lands of a rifle-barrel, was taking that place as of right.

Nevertheless, Bean was able to reply without hesitation and in suitably truculent tones: "Wal, then, I got one hand for each neck o' yeh."

"An' my neck too," McGary cut in, thrusting forward a craggy un-

273

shaven jaw. "Then mebbe, Russ Bean, that 'll fill one more hand 'n ye got."

"Seemin'ly I got a foot or two left. I dunno but that 'll be 'nough."

"That's on'y a part o' what ye dunno," McGary went on, speaking with almost excessive calm. "Fust off, ye dunno yer own job. Ye give aout ye're a-goin' to watch both sides o' the trace an' then spend the next ten days off som'ers with yer fancy Injun gals. What's more, ye don't know a good man when ye see one, nor yet a good chicken. Las' night we'd all lost our ha'r 'thouten thisheer Li'l David ye wants to wring the head offen."

Bean stared at McGary and then at Jackson. He glanced at Perthy, now at Holdfast's side and violently nodding his head up and down. He looked swiftly about the circle of faces, and found no admiration, no sympathy, in any one of them.

"Anythin' more?" he asked, striving to force some overtones of sarcasm into the words.

"Hell!" sneered McGary, and spat. "We-uns cain't stand raound hyar goin' through the hull list o' yer igner'nce. We wanter git to Nashville tonight." And he turned away.

"Wal, I'll be damned!" said Bean, as though merely making an observation of fact. What this event would mean to him, as the tale of it was bruited among the hills and along the creeks of Western Waters, he was beginning to foresee.

With his head held high, however, and his rifle firmly gripped in his two hands, he walked up the creek-bottom, slowly, pretending to look for a squirrel. What he really wanted was to be alone, but Wash was following close at his heels. A long way up the creek he sat down on a log and stared at the water. After a while he covered his face with his hands, trying to think, to decide what he ought to do.

Many long and painful minutes passed. They brought no plan, no hope, except the thought of ignominious retreat and escape from all who knew him, all who had ever heard his name. Then he heard the voice of Holdfast, who had come up quietly behind him. "I've found out one thing, Russ," the voice said, "that helps a little. You and I know that it doesn't let us out, but all of McGary's people are here, safe and sound. Andrew Jackson and his game-cock saw to that. Those four men we found butchered at the camping place must have come in and gone to sleep there after McGary's company had left.—We might have saved the lives of those four men."

Bean looked round with a sigh of relief. Then for nearly an hour he

274

and his friend sat together on the log by the water's edge, quietly talking. The dog Wash sat at their feet, his mouth hanging open and his tongue dripping, with his tail steadily and softly thumping the ground.

Parson Blandison, resting his horse at the top of the last long hill above Nashville, turned away from the glories of the sunset and looked back at the straggling groups of his fellow-travelers still toiling upward. He watched them closely, in a mood of compassionate admiration, as one by one or by twos and threes they reached the crest and looked down for the first time upon the little town's huddle of cabins and the few windows showing the flicker of hearth-fires. This was their goal. Here, or close at hand, would be the fields of grain won from the wilderness by their labor. Here would be their homes, their schools and churches, their graves. It was no wonder that a quietness came upon them as they stood there, momentarily ennobled by the red light flooding from the west, or that a new expression, hard to define but profoundly touching, awoke in their weary faces. These people, the Parson felt, were pathetic and heroic at once. He saw the pathos of all human life in their simple bravery as they paused on the hill-top, a little shelterless company of people obscure, bitterly poor, for the most part ignorant, who had left behind them all the safeties and restraints of government, tradition, and law. How undismayed they were as they gazed into the western mystery! How elate! How beautiful!

Yet these were the same people, he reminded himself, who only three weeks ago had seemed merely vulgar and squalid. Had they changed, or had he? How much should be allowed for the fact that many of those who had then been strangers were now his friends? How much to the fact that those who had once been so diverse, so quarrelsome and bickering, had been welded together by a common toil and danger?

Gosse, the Virginian planter and graduate of Oxford, had hitched his mettled hunter to the traces of a wagon in the place of an ox that had died. At this moment the wagon was creaking up the steepest pitch of the hill with Gosse himself tugging at the spokes of one hind wheel and the one-eyed jail-bird at the other. Next came that young Boanerges of Crockett's, now appropriately christened "Little David," on the back of Bean's leading mule. Bean was walking beside the child to see that he did not fall off. Behind the pack-train and the Crockett family labored one of the Wives of Bath, puffing hard as she propelled her ample bosom up the hill and leaning on the arm of a second jail-bird.

275

Another Wife of Bath was trying to lull a restless infant, not her own, to the tune of "Barbara Allen."

Parson Blandison was fumbling here and there in his not inconsiderable word-hoard. He wanted some quotation adequate to the moment, so strangely compounded. He was seeking a line or phrase that would express his grateful wonder at finding Beauty even here—and not so much in the sunset or the lustrous coils of Cumberland River as in the kindness of human hearts, in the bed-rock goodness of quite ordinary human beings, in their occasional up-soaring to the levels of nobility and splendor.

But no; he could think of nothing in Horace, Virgil, Chaucer, Shakespeare, or even the Bible, that quite served his turn. The poets had not been out here. Poets, he felt, would have a great deal to learn if ever they should really discover America.—In the meanwhile he might have to see, think, and feel for himself, and make his own phrases.

But what could Holdfast have found to say to Russell Bean up there in the creek-bottom? Certainly he had gone there with him, and he must have said something highly effective, to judge from the thoughtful demeanor of Bean all the afternoon. And yet it seemed hardly credible that any words, even Holdfast's, could assuage the wound of such a public defeat and ignominy.

Bean paused, as the others were doing, at the crest of the hill. He turned over to Perthy the care of the child and the pack-train. Then he walked back a little way, clearly waiting for some one.—For Jackson?

When the three young lawyers came up Bean walked over and laid his hand on the mane of Jackson's horse.

This was an exciting, perhaps a serious, event. Holdfast was there, to be sure; but it was not certain that he could do much, now that matters had gone so far. The Parson reined his horse closer. Others crowded round.

"Mr. Andrew Jackson," Bean was saying in a voice strangely quiet and composed, "thar's a thing I'd take it damn kindly iffen ye'd let me do."

"What's that, Mr. Russell Bean?"

"I'd like it an' take it kindly iffen ye'd let me tote Li'l David down into Nashville."

"Why, hell, ye got 'im a'ready, ain't ye?" asked Jackson, jerking his head toward the child on Bean's leading mule.

"I mean the *rale* Li'l David, the fust one, the game-chicken, whut all these hyar folks owes their lives to."

This was the same request—though couched, to be sure, in quite different language—that Bean had made a few hours before. No wonder, then, that Jackson should lean forward over the saddle and peer into Bean's upturned face.

"What ye want with that chicken, Russ Bean?"

"Jest want to tote 'im down on my fist, a-crowin', so's the hull damn town 'll know they ain't nothin' c'n stop a town whar even the chickens got hearts like hisn.—I won't harm a feather."

Jackson's eyes, drawn to slits, glittered in the lurid light as he scanned Bean's face for second after slow tense second. He seemed to be listening, waiting for some inward voice. But then, as suddenly and surprisingly as a beam of the sun struggles free from a low western cloud and strikes eastward over the sullen land, his face brightened into a boyish, friendly, confident smile. He dismounted, opened the sliding door of the wicker cage on the crupper, drew forth the fluttering bird, and said: "Hyar, Mr. Bean, is yer Li'l David. An' he *is* yourn too, from now on. Ye c'n make soup of 'im fer supper tonight iffen ye want, an' I'll come an' holp yeh eat it."

"Aw, hell, Andy, I didn't mean . . . "

"I know ye didn't, Russ. But I won't hev 'im back. I druther hev a friend any day stiddier 'n the best damn game-chicken on arth.—He's yourn, fer keeps."

Bean grasped Little David with his left hand by the frantically kicking legs. With his right he caught the right hand of Jackson. "An' I," he said in a voice that strove for calm, "an' I, Andy, am sincerely yourn, forever!"

The two men bowed, as though on a ball-room floor. The light of the after-glow shed a splendor upon them. The crowd gazed in silence, moved by the beauty of the time, the place, the strange event.

But now the fifty dogs of the village below were sending up a huge vociferation, answered by the dogs on the hill. More windows were dimly lighted down there. Voices of men were heard, shouting a welcome. Russell Bean started down with the game-cock, fluttering and struggling and pecking, held high above his head. His bared right arm was soon streaming with blood.

"Li'l David comin'!" he shouted over and over as though in an ecstasy, perhaps not knowing clearly what he meant but voicing the joy of those behind him at their conquest of toils and dangers past, and their confidence too in confronting all that was yet to come. "Hurrah! Li'l David!" rang out the cry again and again from a hundred throats, until all the hollows of the darkening hills were crowded with echoes and every branch and bend of the blood-red river had heard that challenging name.

"Li'l David an' Andy Jackson!"

"Andy Jackson an' Li'l David" came rolling back from many voices of men unseen below.

CRY OF THE WOLF

"An' I s'pose time 'll come," said Robertson, "some Gawd-fersaken writin' feller 'll set an' bite his quill an' try ter figger aout haow 't war, long ago, to trace two hunnerd parlous miles to Nashville."

"Huh! Writin' fellers!" Bean exclaimed disgustedly.

"Bet yeh he won't git in 'baout the painter-cats an' wolves, Russ Bean, nor yet the cane-brake twenty foot high whar the caows is allus gittin' lost an' et up."

"Nor the lice an' fleas," McNairy added, "that feed on a man's very soul.—Please to pass the tangle-foot."

"And again," said the Parson, "how will he ever imagine the smells?"

"Eh? Anan?"—from Robertson.

"He means the stinks," Bean prompted. "Allus carryin' on 'bout stinks, The Cloth is."

"Oh, them. Wal, trace-stinks cain't shake a stick at the stinks ye git when a hunnerd folk ben forted up fer a month in a fort 'bout one acre squar."

"Never taking a bath, I suppose," said the Parson.

"Bath! Not iffen I know it, they don't. They's better ways o' usin' the water—when we got some."

"An' then the beastes," said Bean, "brung in every night, whut stay thar all day when a raid's on. An' don't fergit the dryin' buck an' b'ar skins, the privies thet ain't raley, an' all whut the hawgs won't eat. Them stinks, The Cloth, they raley do smell bad. They're 'nough to make a man climb the stockade an' run fer a week jes' to smell one clean sweet skunk."

"An' thet 'ar writin' feller," Robertson went on, "he'll cal'late aout

278

hyar folk must 'a' kep' better watch o' nights, or built their stockades afore hearin' the war-whoop. Or he'll mebbe say they didn't bite one tother so bad in the back 'caount o' them bein' mos'ly backs o' dead men purty damn soon.—But he'll be wrong."

The Parson sighed, lifted one leg over the other and held out a hand toward the fire. "I see," he said, "that I've reached Western Waters too late. Human nature is out here before me."

But none of his companions smiled at this sally. He would have liked to know what they were all so gloomy about, and especially this dark-haired, heavy-browed Robertson, founder and head-man of Nashville, who had taken them in for the night. He looked a man of sense, well-seasoned by toil, danger, and the habit of command. The tiny town he had planted here some years ago had not, at any rate, been blotted out. It boasted two taverns, two stores, four rows of ramshackle cabins, certain bark-tents and wagon-camps, a log court-house eighteen feet square, and even a distillery. Without the last item there would not have been this keg of corn-whisky—crude and raw, no doubt, but yet a remarkably authoritative drink, which was even now warming Robertson's frontier eloquence and making a low music in the Parson's veins. In addition Nashville had a kind of fence to keep the buffalo from the corn so that there might be more whisky next year. Robertson had a roof overhead, four walls about him, a puncheon floor underneath, and a blazing hearth. After his three weeks in the wilderness the Parson considered these things very substantial blessings.

"Oh, human nater!" Robertson groaned, gulping from the noggin of whisky on the mantel. Dark and sad his face looked, with wrinkles like furrows at sun-down. "I seen my share o' human nater an'—wal, I dunno."

For a while he was silent, brooding.

" 'T ain't the killin's so much," he went on in a deep inward tone. " 'T ain't thet every week, an' times every day, somebody's brung in daid, or not brung in but jes' left thar. An' 't ain't wholly the way them bodies look. I c'n thole thet. Yeah, Tony Bledsoe, my friend fer twenty year, he wa'n't a purty sight when we laid 'im away, but I never guv a shudder."

The news of Bledsoe's death, so casually conveyed, was shocking to more than one man in the room, but no one cared to ask questions about it of Bledsoe's old comrade.

"I c'd jes' stand it," Robertson continued, "when they murthered my brother Mark last winter."

279

"What's that?" McNairy cried. "Mark Robertson?—My friend I was goin' huntin' with soon 's I got out here?"

"Thet's so, Jedge. Ye'll never hunt with Mark agin. An' I c'd—God damn it, I say I c'd *try* to stand it even when they kilt my boy Peyton come termorra seven months back."

"Oh, not Peyton, Colonel!" Bean groaned. "Ye don't mean Peyton's gone!"

"I said so, didn't I? Haow many times ye want a man to say so? His throat was slit when we faound 'im, Russ, but ev'y other way jes' same Peyton we all useter . . . On'y he—wa'n't alive."

Robertson suddenly turned his back upon the room.

A human heart fighting its battle, the Parson reminded himself, makes no sound.

At length, facing round again, Robertson said almost fiercely: "Can any man tell me what fiend o' hell is a-settin' 'em on? What the Creeks got agin us—or the Chickasaws, Cherokees? We've allus treated 'em fair—or tried to?"

"I'm sure that's so, Colonel," answered Holdfast Gaines, gently, "but there are those, there are many, who have not even tried."

"Sech ez?"

"Well, last year, for example, General Sevier asked for a conference with the Indians living near the upper Tennessee, and twenty chiefs gathered at Hanging Maw's to meet him."

"Yeah, I know."

"While they were waiting there in the council house, unarmed, forty white men under Captain John Beard broke in and killed fifteen of them. Then they went into the village and killed Hanging Maw's wife. They killed a guest of his from the Chickasaw towns, and the daughter of another guest who was a Creek chieftain."

"Yes, that was bad, Mr. Gaines. I do not justfy them ways, nor foller 'em."

"But you may suffer for the wickedness of those who do. The news of such a deed travels fast and far. It is not soon forgotten."

"No. I see you unnerstand these things."

"Not entirely; but I've been thinking about them and learning all I could. Among other things, I've learned that you yourself broke the Treaty of Hopewell, two years ago, a few weeks after you had signed it, by your Cold Water expedition against the Indian villages near Muscle Shoals."

When the silence had lasted more than long enough, Bean said:

"Fiddle-footed, Colonel, thet's whut our Holdfast is. Traipsin'est man on 'arth. Runs all day, thinks all night, an' etarnally keeps his trap shet. Nachally, he larns a lot."

"Yeah. Course naow I reelize his real name is Sleepin' B'ar . . ."

"Last night," Holdfast interrupted, "I talked for hours with a Shawnee chieftain called Tecumseh—a young man, but worth watching. He asked me by what right Nashville was here at all. I couldn't tell him."

"Why, sir, we bought this land, fair an' squar, from the Injuns."

"For how much?"

"Aw, I fergit. Few ole muskits an' some fire-water, prob'ly."

"And you know, of course, that this land has never belonged to any tribe. That was one reason why you and Anthony Bledsoe came here. No Indians have ever had the right to sell the Big Salt Lick. The place has been a common hunting ground for ages, a gift of the Great Breath to all men."

"Wal, yeah, mebbe."

"Therefore your purchase, Colonel Robertson, was not legal. Your Indian neighbors believe that you stole this land. What they held in common you have taken for a few. They resent that. And they loathe the way you destroy the forest, kill off the game for the love of killing, drive white men's wagon-roads ten feet wide through the buffalo-grass, and break your oaths and your treaties."

"I told young Avery thet trace 'd be makin' trouble," said Robertson.

"You hear what I say," Holdfast went on with growing earnestness, leaning forward in his chair, "but do you understand what it means, how it feels?—For ten thousand years the red men, my people, born of this earth and loving it as a man loves his mother, have dwelt here in these forests and beside these rivers, doing not the least harm. In all that while they have not cut a single road in their mother's body or plowed one furrow across her sacred breast. In ten thousand years they have not set up one fence. They have been childish, I know, often violent and cruel, often foolish, but they have not been greedy. They have not befouled their own nest. They have slain for food, not for the sake of slaughter. They have fought one another for glory, not for gain. With all their many faults, they have at least shown a manly pride, a dignity, and a sense of honor."

"In a word, Colonel Robertson," said the Parson as Holdfast paused, "they have been nature's gentlemen, not shop-keepers."

281

Robertson was shifting uneasily from one foot to the other, avoiding Holdfast's earnest gaze. It was fairly evident that he felt the need of another noggin of whisky.

"But now comes the white man," said Holdfast, "with his roads and fences and bridges, his churches and shops and stores. He brings with him his laws and religion to back his greed and make it look holy. No one asked him to come here. As an uninvited guest he might be expected to follow the custom of the country. He does not. He tries to overturn and uproot that ancient custom. Any Indian guest in an Indian village who behaved himself as the white man behaves throughout this broad land would certainly be burned at the stake."

"I see what ye mean, Mr. Gaines," Robertson muttered.

"I hope you do. I try to make each side see how the other feels.—Do you know that Indians call the white man a hog because he never knows when he is full?"

"No."

"Do you know that they call him a dog because he defiles holy things without even knowing that they are holy?"

"Ahem! No."

"Have you heard that they call him a snake because he slides on his belly and slimes his trail and talks with a double tongue?"

"Not egzackly. Fack is, I'm s'prised, Mr. Gaines."

"Have you ever tried to guess, Colonel Robertson, how a white man smells to an Indian?"

"Wal, no. Never thunk much 'baouten thet. Ye got me thar, Mr. Gaines. Course I do know whites stink suthin' tar'ble, times.—But then, so does Injuns."

"They do, at times." And Holdfast smiled. "I'm not trying to make out that all the right is on one side and all the wrong on the other. If I ever thought so, I've learned better. But I do say that a good deal of what the Indians are blamed for is not done by them. For example, the four corpses that we found this morning at last night's camp had not been scalped. Neither, you say, had—well, at least one body of those you have mentioned. Now I think you know enough about Indians to agree that they would rather take a scalp than kill a man. The proof of that is that there are hundreds of persons, white and red, who have been scalped but are still alive. From scalps an Indian gains honor, but from dead bodies, nothing. And so I suggest that white men have had something to do with these killings. If there is someone setting the Indians against you, he may be a white man.—Have you ever heard of The Knife?"

Colonel Robertson was obviously startled. "Why," he stammered, "ye—ye've jest come aout hyar!"

Holdfast looked at him closely for several seconds before he replied, somewhat dryly: "Your answer, sir, is neither direct nor clear, but I think I see what you have in mind. A man so fair as you are will not go on trying to lay the whole blame upon Cherokees, Creeks, and Chickasaws for something in which he knows or suspects that white men have played a large part.—You may be relieved to hear that about The Knife I don't yet know much myself—aside from the name, which I first heard last night from Tecumseh. It was your mention of 'a fiend from hell' that brought it to my mind."

"Oh.—Wal, fer my part, I don't know nothin' 't all."

And it was clear, too, that Colonel Robertson did not care to pursue the topic, or his conversation with Holdfast. He walked unsteadily to a far corner, refilled his noggin of corn-whisky, tossed it off, and filled it again.

"But whut we was talkin' 'baout," said he, returning. "Last August 't was a year, me an' Bledsoe writ a scribin' to the head-man o' the Creeks—thet's Alec McGillivray—an' axed 'im whut they meant by 't. Alec writ back arter while sayin' course his braves allus did love the whites but kinder larned the habit in the ole war o' killin' on England's side. Said mebbe they hedn't all heered yit ez haow thet 'ar war was over. Haowsomever, he'd look to 't.—Arter which fust off his people come an' kilt Tony Bledsoe."

"Same man 't wrote that letter with you?" Jackson asked, astonished.

"Same."

"What ye do then?"

"Whut could I do? 'T war a-gittin' on to harvest-hum. Best crap o' corn we'd ever hed. Needed ev'y man, caountin' them to guard the harvesters."

"An' so?" persisted Jackson.

"Injuns may come or not, young man, but hunger 'll come sartin sure.—We couldn't fergit aour fust crap o' corn aout hyar hed failed, an' a bushel brought a hunnerd an' sixty dollars."

"Wal?"

"Wal, jes' try ter unnerstan' it, Mr. Jackson. I set me daown an' writ thet damn liar to come live in Nashville. Offered 'im a good six-forty to live on, I did."

Jackson's face was flaming. "That is," said he, "ye axed the murderer o' yer friend Bledsoe to be yer guest?"

"Yeah, ye c'n put it thet-away. Fack is, I went furder. These hyar be the very words, an' I 'member 'em cause o' takin' so long to think aout: 'In all prob'il'ty,' I says, 'we cannot long remain in our present state, an' if the British or any other commercial nation who possess the mouth o' the Miss'ippi River would furnish us with trade, the people west of App'lachian Maountings will open their eyes to their true int'rusts,' I says. 'We shall be happy to receive your sentiments of this matter.'"

Jackson rose to his feet. "Then, sir," he shrilled, "what that means is, you offered to turn your back on your own country if either Spain or England would make it wuth your dirty while!"

"Think so, young man?" Robertson's voice was weary, and his face sad.

Jackson answered in a tone of partially controlled rage: "I can't rightly tell you what I think whilst I'm a guest in your cabin. I wish you a very good evenin', sir."

With that he turned sharply and strode toward the door. But he hardly reached it. He was raising his hand to the wooden latch when he felt himself lifted and borne irresistibly back to his stool by the fire.— And the strangest thing was that when he saw Holdfast beside him he seemed to be no longer angry. Instead, he looked somewhat ashamed.

Robertson was still standing with one arm on the mantel-piece and his large head, shaggily maned and bearded, resting on his hand. There was a care-worn look in his eyes as he went on quietly speaking, now and then fumbling for a word.

"Mr. Jackson," he said, "you an' me don't know one tother yit so good ez I hope we're a-gwineter. When we do, ye won't never take me fer a man to be afeared o' McGillivray, nor yit the hull o' his haowlin' Creek nation. Leastways, not fer myself I ain't. On'y aout hyar I hev to think an' do for all Western Waters—all the men, wimming, childern—an' not on'y jes' fer James Robertson. Time 'll come, mebbe, ye'll larn fer yerself haow that 'ar makes a differ. An' when ye ben aout hyar more 'n jes a two-three haours, Mr. Jackson, why then mebbe thar 'll be things ye don't unnerstan' so good ez ye think ye do naow."

McNairy chimed in: "That might happen, Andy.—Please pass the pop-skull."

"An ez fer turnin' ag'in' my own kentry, don't say 't, Mr. Jackson.— Ye mought be s'prised iffen I war to tell yeh who guv me thet idear 'baout offerin' McGillivray a six-forty."

"Who?"

284

"Man by name o' Gin'ral George Wash'n'ton."

"H'm."

"Yeah."

"Thet so?"

"Yeah—a man ye cain't say *he* ever turned his back on his kentry. But same time he knows ye cain't do much thet's rale useful jes' by slam-bang an' rucktions an' stompin' aout the haouse."

"Ye mean by ketchin' yer tail on fire, Colonel?" Bean innocently inquired.

"Ye c'n put it thet-away. The Gin'ral, he c'n wait, he c'n larn, an' arter he's larned he c'n set an' think 'baouten whut he's faoun' aout. Takes time, takes patience, thet do. Arter he's thunk some mebbe he'll git a plan, an' then, b' God, he'll do suthin' quicker 'n greased lightnin'.— On'y not afore, Mr. Jackson. Not afore. Iffen he did, we wouldn't hev *hev* a kentry right naow."

"H'm."

"That's right, Andy.—Kindly pass the wring-jaw."

"Gin'ral Wash'n'ton, 'course he knows Alec McGillivray's a damn Tory, allus hez ben an' allus will. Knows, too, Alec's playin' off Spain agin England an' England agin Spain an' both on 'em agin Western Waters. Knows Alec hez mebbe two thaousan' warriors honin' fer the war-path, an' we got mebbe a hunnerd wi' plenny else to do. He sees we cain't git up a hull 'Merican army to go smash Alec, but same time we cain't let him trade off the maouth o' the River fer whatever 't is he's a-gittin' from England an' Spain. So the hull thing gits—wal, whut I heered a feller say oncet, 'compelcated.' Anyhaow, the Gin'ral he sets an' thinks, an' fin'ly writes me a scribin' to say we gotter play fer time. We gotter watch this man, he says, an' try to git 'im thinkin' we mought be on his side. Arter which I sets daown an' writes to Alec, like I tole yeh."

"And how 'd it work?" asked Jackson.

"Alec didn't come, o' course. Smelled suthin', prob'ly. 'Sides thet, whut's a six-forty to him—richest man west o' the maountings?—Hear tell Gin'ral Wash'n'ton oncet guv Alec a hunnerd thaousan' dollars jes' to keep quiet, an' 't wa'n't 'nough."

"Did the killings stop, after Bledsoe?" asked Jackson.

"Not by no means. Aout at Asher's, tother side o' river, they shot Jesse Maxey an' stuck a knife through 'im. Daown ter Drake's Crick they kilt the three sons o' Bill Montgom'ry, hunnerd yards offen his cabin. John Johnson, frien' o' my boy Peyton, they run off with, nobuddy knows

285

whar to. Bob Jones they kilt at Wilson's Station, an' Ben Williams at Station-Camp-Crick. Wednesday was a week they kilt Widder Neeley at Neeley's Bend. Not nice to look at, she wa'n't, when I come thar. This mornin' I heered 'baout my friends Dunham an' Astill, both good men an' both daid naow an' mammicked to shreds fer ten days 'thout my knowin' hit."

"I'd say General Washin'ton must 'a' set an' thunk too long," said Jackson. "Give a man like McGillivray time, and he only does more killin's."

Colonel Robertson was filling his corn-cob pipe. The cry of a timber-wolf came from the valley below. At first it was like the frenzied bark of a dog, and there followed a swift series of howls in crescendo.

"Know whut thet 'ar wolf's a-lookin' fer?" asked Robertson.

No one answered.

"Daid bodies, thet's whut. An' wolves keeps fat raound hyar."

He lighted his pipe with a brand from the fire. "Course we do whut we kin. Colonel Rains is a good man on the trace. So's Major Evans an' Major Winchester. 'Lijah Robertson ain't bad, iffen he *is* my cousin. But haow 'n hell they goner watch a thaousan' squar mile an' a red-painted Injun behint ev'y cane-stalk? A Creek c'n lay in the cane fer a week, watchin' a door, an' not even the dogs 'll smell 'im aout. Then he does whatsomever 't is an' dodges back inter cane-brake, arter which God-a'mighty don't see 'im no more."

"Taking a white scalp with him," the Parson mused, "back to the pools and swamps and the dark woods—a scalp that covered a brain once, and thoughts of a sort, and hopes."

"Yeah," said Bean encouragingly. "Ye're a-gittin' it, The Cloth. We knowed ye would."

Robertson drained the noggin of whisky at his elbow. "Thar's times," he said, "I think mebbe all this 'll go on forever. Mebbe allus two men 'll hev to stand an' watch when one hoes, an' three when one bends daown fer a drink at a spring. An' aour wimming, I say, will they allus hev to wonder, startin' aout, will their babes be rightly borned?—'Cause I seed a babe oncet thet—wal, hit wa'n't."

"Don't ye think 'baouten thet, Colonel," called Bean.

"All I know is," Robertson went on, dropping his hand now and facing round, "I feel like I've swum nine year up a river o' blood, an' thet river keeps comin' daown.—Of all the men thet hev died since we fust come aout, only one has died in his bed, an' thet was Bob Gilkey."

"Well, then, Colonel, who's behind it?" asked McNairy. "And how 'bout this 'Knife' of Holdfast's?"

"Oh, thet. Wal—hit's an onhealthy subjick."

"I see," said Holdfast, "that you don't want to talk about it, even among friends. But perhaps you will tell us who *has* The Knife—supposing that it's a real one. Is it McGillivray?"

"H'm—ah—wal, naow, Mr. Gaines, he mought know who 't is, but 't ain't him."

"What makes you think not?"

"Alec never bought all the paowder an' lead these Creeks hev naow'days—spesh'ly, all the lead. Not aouten his own pocket."

"You think he might be working for someone else whom he calls The Knife?"

"Mought."

"And The Knife is wealthy?"

"He don't hev to skimp."

"Ole England an' Spain," said Bean, "they ain't pore."

"It's mostly England," McNairy opined, "takin' over the old French plan to run the Mississippi. She knows the nation controllin' that river owns America."

"An' she's right, so far," agreed Jackson. "But what Old England don't know is when she's licked. We'll have to take an' larn her agin."

"Wal," said Robertson, tacking toward the whisky-keg, "who's 'we'?"

"Jever hear o' 'Nited States o' 'Meriky?"

Robertson paused with his hand on the spile, looking back. "Naw," said he. "Not hardly."

"Ye will, though, mebbe. Back at Jonesboro news came through that N' York hed jined up. That makes 'leven."

"Ah, but North Car'liny, she ain't one on 'em."

" 'Leven's 'nough to make a Union. North Car'liny c'n go shake her shins."

"But whut's 'Nited States to us, iffen thar be sech?" Robertson inquired, coming back to the fire. "A good month's journey off, them States 'll be."

"They mought larn England to keep hands offen the River."

"Don't b'lieve 'Nited States ever hearn tell o' no sech River, no more 'n River ever hearn tell o' them."

"But Colonel," put in McNairy, "mebbe we could *tell* 'em.—Where's the rot-gut?"

287

"By thet time they won't none on us be left, the way things a-goin'. Quickest an' cheapest way o' keepin' the River away from us is to kill us all off, an' thet's whut Alec McGillivray an' his Creeks are up to!"

"With the help of The Knife?" Holdfast suggested.

"Wal, mebbe."

"If so, someone might go down and ask McGillivray a few questions."

"Yeah. Mought ask 'im who kilt John Donelson."

"Whut's thet?" Bean cried. "But Donelson, he ain't daid!"

"Do ye go take a good look at 'im, Russ, an' see whut ye think. Ye'll find 'im sixty mile north—an' six foot deep."

"But my God, Colonel! John Donelson, Cap'n of my boat? Rachel Donelson's dad?"

"Same. An' dad o' this hyar town, next to Bledsoe an' me."

"How 'd he die?" asked Bean, staring.

"Filled full o' lead aout 'n bresh. Lead 'nough to kill a b'ar."

"Was he scalped?" asked Holdfast.

"No; but cut up some."

"By who, d'ye reckon?" Bean asked again.

"I reckon one o' you young men mought go an' find aout."

Once again they heard a long-drawn cry from the bank of Cumberland River.

GO AND FIND OUT

Holdfast Gaines had come back perplexed and baffled from his two-day visit with Alexander McGillivray. That opulent and ostentatious Scotch-French-Creek gentleman and savage had treated him with the politeness to be expected by one Indian chieftain of another. Down there on his comfortable plantation at Little Tallassee beside Coosa River he had offered his guest women and wines of various colors and provenience, had narrated a sufficient number of lascivious stories recently imported from New York City, had taken him to a game of ball-play in which several young Creeks were seriously injured, and had offered him a share of his own profits in the fur trade with Spain

288

and England—but with regard to really important matters, had told him nothing whatever.

To Hippo Ilk Miko, the Little Child King of the Creeks, the prices of peltries at Mobile and Pensacola seemed to be of more interest than the fate of the Creek nation. He had much more to say about his prosperous father, a merchant of Edinburgh, than about the half-Creek princess to whom he owed his chieftainship. He was prouder by far of his hundred Negro slaves than of the thousands of Creek warriors who, by their blind fidelity, maintained him in his affluence and power. He had striven to bedazzle Holdfast Gaines, a man poor by deliberate and determined preference, with the childish gauds and fripperies earned for him by the toil of others. Therefore, in spite of his plausible talk and silken manners, Holdfast had seen him as a strutting homunculus bedaubed with the grease of wealth and its attendant vulgarity.

And yet the man was clever, astute, and a master of evasions. One had to listen chiefly to what he left unsaid.

Did The Knife exist?—Was he The Knife?—Had he The Knife?—Did he know who had it or was it?—Such were the questions, naïve and all but absurd, that Holdfast had asked him. To each of them he had replied with a patient and tolerant smile, just a shade on the safer side of condescension. Freely admitting that he had heard some idle talk on the topic, he said that hitherto he had been inclined to leave such superstitious chatter to his elder medicine men and to the old women. Of course if Mr. Gaines really thought such things worth the attention of enlightened persons, why then . . .

And precisely what was it that Mr. Gaines actually *knew* about The Knife?

Oh, well then, if nothing . . .

At this point McGillivray had returned to a discussion of the considerable profits to be gained from traffic with the Spanish and English in furs brought down to tide-water by the Creeks. Did he understand correctly that Mr. Gaines did not care to have a share in those profits? —And was Mr. Gaines acquainted, by any chance, with an interesting young Shawnee by the name of Tecumseh?—Ah. M'm . . .

But the Creek chieftain's skill in evasion had not been quite sufficient to conceal itself. His mannner had been a bit too casual and off-hand. Therefore Holdfast had carried away a few convictions which, though formless, were sufficient to justify his round-trip journey of two hundred and sixty miles. He saw that The Knife—whether a tangible object, a person, or only a deliberately concocted myth—was a real and important fact. Also he felt quite sure that Alexander McGillivray knew as much about this fact as there was to be known, and meant to use his knowledge. Finally, he realized that, by his own exhibition of curiosity and his firm refusal to become McGillivray's partner, he had won for himself a powerful and dangerous enemy.

At Donelson's station, ten miles from Nashville, where he had left Perthy in charge of Jackson and the women of the family, Holdfast found that Russell Bean had been no more successful in his investigations to the north of the Cumberland. The body of John Donelson, "sixty miles north and six feet deep," had yielded no evidence other than seven leaden bullets, any one of them large enough to kill a bear, shot from a smooth-bore, and the fact that the body had not been scalped. Daniel Boone, with whom Bean had sat and talked by a camp-fire in Kentucky, had averred that the murder of Donelson was certainly "not Injun work." Boone had heard of The Knife, and believed in it, but evidently felt, like Robertson, that it was an "onhealthy subjick."

After a day and a night near Nashville, spent in talking with Bean, Jackson, the Donelson clan, and, last of all, with James Robertson himself, Holdfast set out once more, leaving Perthy behind, on a vague and wandering quest of The Knife.

Often it seemed to be a real knife. He met a Shawnee who had talked with a boy who knew a man who had seen The Knife itself.—Or so, at any rate, the man had certainly told the boy.

Yet sometimes The Knife was said to be a man, terribly and inexorably powerful, who was to be obeyed, whatever his orders were. And sometimes, too, it was a woman, green, with a beauty that drove men mad.

The Cherokees believed one thing and the Chickasaws another. Creeks and Choctaws had their different opinions. The only conviction upon which all agreed was that The Knife was extremely dangerous, mysterious, and important. All of them, round their camp-fires, and the whites as well by the firesides of a hundred scattered cabins, were conjecturing, dreaming, lying, and gradually shaping an enormous incredible myth about The Knife.

One could hear anything and believe what one would or could—as, for example, that She walked naked and green in the night when the camp-fires dwindled, stabbing at random here and there like moonlight down through the wind-blown leaves. One heard that He sent whom he

290

liked on his frightful errands, and that his messengers never returned to the homes and the paths of men. It was said that the wavy blade was as long as the River itself, and that the haft was begemmed like the midnight sky. One was told that the haft was a nude green woman, the blade a man, and that their children were corpses. Some said, by the flickering fires, that a man who had once seen that haft and its strange green beauty would live as chaste as a stone for love of her. Moreover, it was whispered from camp to camp that The Knife was carried by two huge brothers, white, and probably gods. Others held it to be a god in its own right, whoever might carry and wield it.

Not in a few days, or even weeks, did Holdfast gather this information, such as it was. The quest drew him on from the winter's howl of the wolf to the gurgling of red-wings and reed-birds. It led from the Cherokee country to the lands of the Choctaws, from the shining loops of the Cumberland to the headlong Tennessee. For if The Knife was an actual and single weapon, then it traversed wonderful distances at miraculous speed. At dusk of one day it might kill on the beveled banks of the Ohio and at dawn of the next on the heights, laurel-crowned, of the French Broad. It seemed to strike at random, like lightning, the veritable dagger of the gods. Like the lightning, it flashed and vanished, leaving only a corpse for trace. Wherever it struck it slew, and where it had not yet struck it was feared.

The fear, the horror, ran before it with even swifter foot. In all Western Waters there was not a man who did not glance about him into the brush before every third or fourth stroke of the axe. In Washington County there was no wife who did not more than once hurry to the cabin-door and look anxiously out for her returning man between the frying of bear-bacon and sending the children up the loft-ladder to bed. No knowledgeable child dropped asleep between Blue Ridge and the River without some shuddering thought of The Knife that was creeping from tree to tree in the darkness.

Holdfast, brooding far into the nights by many a lonely camp-fire, thought often and long about the children. Why should they, at any rate, have been caught in this blast from hell? He thought of young Perthy, the beloved burden that had in some degree taken the place of Rebecca Chester, and wished that all the children of Western Waters might be as safe as that boy in the Donelson stockade. The widow Donelson and her handsome black-haired daughter Rachel would take good care of him. Besides, there was Andrew Jackson, who rode out

291

to the stockade every night and usually spent the night there in a separate cabin of his own. Ah, yes; Perthy, at least, was safe.

Now and then, however, a faint question rose in Holdfast's mind about the safety of Andrew Jackson himself. That young man, he believed, was falling in love with Rachel Donelson Robards, a married woman. Her husband, whom Bean had described as "a jealous skunk of a man," was not living with his wife but was evidently keeping some watch upon her. On the whole, therefore, whatever might be one's faith in Jackson's integrity and courage, the situation was somewhat disturbing.

Holdfast had set forth on his present vague errand with the hope of proving that by no means all, or even most, of the crimes attributed to Indians were really committed by them. Of that much he soon became certain. It grew clear, also, that no one man, and indeed no single band of outlaws white or red, could be perpetrating so many crimes in places so widely sundered. Thus his previous suspicion was confirmed that The Knife, if indeed it existed, was hardly more than an emblem, and that the power it represented was wielded by one man who kept himself hidden and worked through many agents.

But no such conclusion as this could live long in the weather of Holdfast's mind without undergoing a gradual enlargement and transmutation. Profoundly mystical by nature, he tended at first to see the terror of Western Waters as only another skirmish in the everlasting conflict between Kiehtan and Hobbomok. Even the most powerful of men, he felt, were blameless agents merely, and Hobbomok was the wielder of power who hid himself most completely away.—Thus he made his own myth of The Knife. For him it became the symbol of transcendent Evil working out its purposes not there in the bosky wilderness of Western Waters alone but in all times and lands.

Ever more and more, by night and day, that image possessed and poisoned his thoughts. Often in clear sunlight, while walking the trail or thrusting through a thicket of cane, he saw before him the phantom, at least, of a blood-dripping knife, wavy-bladed, green-handled, pointing the way. And often at night, staring into his solitary fire, he saw a ghostly dagger grow burningly clear as though in a vision.

Why should visions not come from Hobbomok also? Those Puritans of the old time picking their path through the dark up to Pequot Fort with faggots, King Uncas cleaving Miantonomoh's skull from behind with a hatchet and eating his shoulder, the red-coats at Fort Griswold

292

slaughtering surrendered farm-boys and young Mohegans—had they not one and all been the agents of some divine setting-on?

But divinity was of two kinds—and why should Hobbomok alone use The Knife and Kiehtan never? Why assume that this prompting came from the King of Wrong? Must the votary of Right sit forever paralyzed, locked, muscle-bound, struggling with one arm against the other, suffering life-long the inward roil of a quieted outside? . . . Did St. Christopher the Giant carry no weapon? If not, how could he have defended the Child?

By footprints in the snows of February, by distant calls of jays and movements of April leaves not moved by the wind, he knew that he was being followed, watched.

With that discovery something spoke to his savage blood. A cynically smiling face came before him, prosperous, suave, smug, and the little round paunch of a human spider fed on the blood of children. Blotched the face was from too much drink, and feeble the body from too many women. The hands were weak, white, and unskilled in the use of tool or weapon. The eyes were small and shifty. Tight little bargain-thoughts filled the busy brain—of how to use a tincture of Indian blood to buy more Negroes, more wines, more women. In order that this bloated vulgarian might feed his lusts the Creek nation was being debauched, white women were being disemboweled, and children like Perthy were living in fear.

But one blow could change all this. That pointing knife—and he knew which way it was pointing—could do the work. Oh, to break loose from the chains of thought and to grip it once and to plunge it!

Meanwhile the terror grew along the trace, the buffalo trails, the rivers, and the little plunging brooks. One morning in May he saw three corpses floating down the Tennessee, rocking a little in the swift water, lingering a while at the willow-islands where the white-throats sang, and then floating on with no haste. The next day he came upon a child's body sprawled across the trace, with flies there, crows wheeling, and a crude picture scratched on the flesh with the point of a knife.

After burying the body of the murdered child Holdfast started and ran for Donelson fort. He ran all day, and most of the night. At every mile he ran faster, but whether to escape from some pursuing temptation or on account of a deep anxiety he hardly knew. It was only after he had been admitted to the stockade and had learned that Perthy was gone, had been lost for three days, and that earnest and steady search of all the region had discovered no trace of the lad, that he understood.

293

Mother Donelson, her four sons, Rachel Robards her daughter, John Overton, Andrew Jackson even, could give him no help, no clue. They could only say that three nights before Perthy had gone out into the cane with his playmate George Davidson after the cows. The two boys had been separated. Long after dark George had come home, crying, only two cows with him. Russell Bean had started at once in pursuit, and had not returned. He had said only that he would leave signs behind him so that Holdfast could follow his trail.

By dawn of the next day Holdfast was standing beside the heap of slaughtered cattle. By noon he had overtaken Bean, who had with him four of the best scouts of the region. These men had spent most of their time beating back and forth in the neighborhood of the stockade, looking for a foot-print, a hoof-print, a broken twig, a bent cane, a bruised blade of grass. They had found nothing. They were weary, bedraggled, and discouraged. Holdfast could see by their averted eyes that they had lost hope.

He took command, sent Bean back to Nashville to get more scouts, indicated a separate route for each of the remaining hunters, and named a rendezvous, ten miles southward, for sunset.—Southward why? It was in the direction of McGillivray's country. In the absence of all other guides, he would move toward the center of the web. He would follow the general course, moreover, of the ancient trail, one hundred miles long, running from Great Salt Lick to the crossing of the Tennessee.

These and many other decisions he made instinctively, without a moment's pause for the labor of thought. Gone completely for the nonce was that old trouble of the mind to see both sides of every question and so to stop always short of action. Though his heart was breaking, his mind was clear and his body set free of its gyves. The other men, by his direction, were covering strips a hundred paces wide. He covered three hundred, including the Creek trail itself. He grew more and more certain, without tangible evidence, that Perthy was living. On the third day out he found a willow whistle, lying clearly in sight beside the trail, which he himself had made for the boy.

Now and then the hunters paused for a moment of breathless talk beside a cabin-door. They heard less of The Knife as they ranged southward, and more about "The Sharpes." Was it that these mysterious people were carrying The Knife now, or doing its bidding? Or had they been given that symbolic name because of the terror they spread?

But sometimes the name was "Tharpe"—and Holdfast, whenever he heard it so spoken, went straying back in memory to the hunts of long ago in far-off Gungywamp, with John Ledyard, Bill Pertwee, the Avery brothers, and 'Bijah and Riley Tharpe. It was a cool delight, in the midst of this present horror, to recall those wild suppers of squirrel, turkey, rabbit, and partridge over there among the Pequot council-stones. What extravagant boyish tales they had told one another! What a furious fight that day with the old she-bear when she had rushed and slashed Bill Pertwee!

"Tharpe"—a strange name, and a dear one. It lay in his little treasury of the names of old companions, all lost now but never forgotten.

Bean, on the fourth day, brought down half a dozen fresh men. Others were coming in, each with his own tale of terror.

On a lonely path near the Swananoa these Sharpes or Tharpes had cut a small boy to shreds, apparently for the sack of beans he was carrying. The boy's father joined the hunt.

Down by Nick-a-Jack Cave at Look-Out Mountain a young man, returning at twilight to his cabin, had found his bride of two weeks impaled upon trees by the door. After burying her, he rode north and found the company of hunters under Holdfast.

Old Man Cassell, beloved throughout Western Waters, had been dragged from his horse on Natchez Trace and hacked to death. His two sons, riding up an hour later, found the body. That same afternoon they were overtaken by two horsemen who said they were out after "the Tharpes." For some time the four had ridden along together, talking. Suddenly the larger of the newcomers had set his horse across the path, whipped up his smooth-bore, and yelled "By God, I bet ye're the Tharpes yerself now!" When the younger of the Cassell boys got back to the place with four or five helpers he had found his brother's head grinning from a tree-crotch.—He too joined the gang of hunters.

A certain Jack Nolan of Kentucky joined them, bringing with him frightful stories of the horrors perpetrated by the Tharpes at Cave-in-Rock on the Ohio and round about.

Toward noon of the seventh day, near Elk River, they saw a man lying on the ground beside the trail, apparently resting. Coming closer, they found that his belly had been ripped open and that his right leg was protruding from the cavity as though someone within were trying to climb out. He had not been scalped. His flesh was still warm.—And then, while they were digging, a hideous laughter sounded from the brush.

After half an hour of fruitless beating up and down in the thicket the men returned to their task.

"'T war thet same laughin' ez I heered arter they kilt my brother Jake," said Dick Cassell.

"I know," Holdfast answered. "But Dick, you saw them that day. Can't you tell us something that might help?"

"Wal, ez I tole yeh afore, one on 'em was a big feller, built very damn staout, wi' curly h'ar comin' low daown in front. Hed a smooth-bore with a red stock to 't, he did. An' tother was 'baout half ez big an' hed a li'l sad squinched-up face on 'im like he'd jest et suthin' saour."

"Is that all you remember?"

Dick Cassell scratched his head for a moment.—"Oh yeah," he said, "an' I rec'leck haow dretful scairt he was on 's brother, an' haow he jumped when the big un yelled aout 'Hold the path thar, Riley!'"

"What's that you say? Riley? Riley Tharpe?"

"Yeah. Thet's 'zackly whut he called 'im. Riley."

"You didn't . . . you didn't hear the little one call his brother any-thing, did you?"

"No.—But whut 'n hell's matter, Holdfast? Y' ain't hurt, be ye?"

"Oh no. No, Dick. I'm . . . I'll be all right."

But what could have changed those two gay-hearted lads with not a spark of evil in them?

Was it possible that . . . ? But no; the "little sad squinched-up face" of Dick Cassell's description was certainly Riley's.

Moreover it was clear why the trail had been so hard to follow. Hold-fast suddenly recalled a remark made by the elder brother one day in Gungywamp after a wounded bob-cat had escaped them. "The bob," 'Bijah had said, "is a smart critter. When she's hurted she takes to the bresh an' thrashes round in thar till ye go in arter. An' then, when ye're well stuck an' can't see much, she jumps back an' runs straight down the path ye were on."

The members of the posse were looking at Holdfast with concern as he stood before them motionless, his hands closing and unclosing con-vulsively on the muzzle of his long rifle. They waited, wondering what lonely pain it could be that had made his face so tragic.

At length he looked up and said: "We'll find the Tharpe brothers a few miles down the trace. They'll be going fast."

When Big Tharpe heard them behind him he turned in the saddle and sent a ball from his smooth-bore, flying wild. The father from

296

Swananoa, who was riding ahead, returned the fire with his rifle, but also missed. Then, as they pounded together round a bend of the trace, Dick Cassell's horse, furiously lashed, rushed forward. At twenty paces Dick jerked his mount to a stand, drew a long steady bead, and pulled the trigger.

The big man's arms thrashed. His tomahawk, swung in a great arc, flew from his hand. They could see before they came up that his back was broken, yet somehow he kept his saddle while his maddened horse dashed off into the brush.

A shot from behind, where Holdfast was running, was instantly followed by a scream from Little Tharpe's horse and a long scrambling fall. The rider was up and into the woods before they could reach him.

They found Big Tharpe rolling helpless, dazed, in his saddle. His horse had slowed to a walk. Three or four of them dragged him to the ground and crouched on either side, panting. Jack Nolan of Kentucky was there, watching narrowly. The bridegroom from Nick-a-Jack jabbed a knife into the wounded man's cheek, afraid that he might die without returning to full consciousness. "I'm a-goin' to cut yer heart aout wi' this!" he screamed. But the others forced him back.

Holdfast came up and looked for a moment.—Yes. It was 'Bijah.

One of the watchers, seeing a slight movement in the brush, suddenly threw up his rifle and fired. There followed a sharp cry and a crashing in the bushes.

"Hello, Holdfast," sighed a tired low voice from the ground when they had crossed the clearing fanwise, moving cautiously with rifles cocked, and found the spot.

"Hello, Riley."

He was pressing both hands against his right side. Dark blood oozed between his fingers.

"Takes New London to . . . to ketch New London. Eh, Holefas'?"

"Yes, but Riley . . ."

"Oh, my side, Holdfast!" The little man writhed. He made one think of a small helpless animal pitifully caught in a trap.

"Riley Tharpe, did you . . . ?"

"No, Holdfast!—Oh, my side!—But no! I ain't never . . ."

"But Riley!" Holdfast knelt beside the tormented body, gazing deeply into the brown, affectionate eyes.

"I say, no! But 'Bijah, he's ben blood-crazy ever sence that day—at Griswold. *You* know."

"Yes."

"It crazed 'im. An' then . . . Oh, my God, Holdfast, cain't ye do suthin'?"

"Your side will soon be better now, Riley," said Holdfast, laying a hand on the young man's brow.

"Thanks, Holdfast!"

"Where's Perthy?"

"Ye mean—that boy?"

"Yes. What have you done with him?"

"We didn't . . . He's all right. Soon's he said yer name . . ."

"Where is he?"

"Down Nick-a-Jack. The Breath has 'im, safe."

"Oh!"

"Soon's he said yer name . . ."

The men of the posse came crowding round. Jack Nolan came, his long rifle tilting downward. "The big un 's daid," said he.

"Oh, my side! I wish to God ye'd shoot me, Holdfast!"

"But about 'Bijah?"

"Eeah. 'Bijah. An' rec'leck thet day ye tuk us over to see Old Occum?"

"I do, Riley."

"That was good day. Then 'nother time . . . Mr. Hale. Becky she went 'long too . . . He's dead now."

"Yes, Nathan Hale is dead. But about 'Bijah, now."

"The battle . . . An' then . . . an' then they rolled us down hill."

"Yes."

" 'Bijah was shuk out an' tried to crawl off. A Tory lammed 'im hard on the head with a musket-butt."

"Ah!"

" 'T would 'a' kilt most men, I reckon."

"I see."

"It's gittin' dark, ain't it? Le' 's hev fire like . . . in Gungy."

"Yes. We'll build a fire soon."

"Seems like I'm gettin' lost . . . these dark woods."

"What about 'Bijah after the Groton fight?"

A spasm convulsed the dying man's face.

"Oh! Jersey prison-ship an' . . . an' The Knife, Holdfast!"

"Let's put an end to this nonsense!" growled Nolan, stepping closer.

"The Knife!" Holdfast exclaimed, bending lower. "What about it? Is it a man?"

"Yeah. An' when he saw how 't was wi' 'Bijah then ev'y time they

298

done suthin' to the pris'ners he hed it done whar me an' 'Bijah was chained.—Hold my hand hard, Holdfast!"

"I'll stay with you.—And so, 'Bijah . . . ?"

"Got so 'Bijah hed to see blood ev'y day. Crazed, he was. He wa'n't a bad boy, 'Bijah!"

"No. And then next?"

"Oh!"—and for a while the little man's thoughts went staggering toward a strange dim country.

But Holdfast called him back. "Who's The Knife, Riley?" he called in a commanding voice.

Jack Nolan took another step forward.

"Ye call me, Hol'fas?"

"Who is The Knife?"

"Brung us out hyar. Made 'Bijah do 's killin's fer 'im."

"Did 'Bijah kill Donelson for The Knife?"

"Yeah."

"Why?"

"Knife does . . . McGillivray's killin' fer 'im."

"Riley! Who *is* The Knife?"

"Ye know 'im. Back home we . . . Out hyar they call . . . call 'im . . . call 'im Tra—"

A rifle spoke from close at hand. Looking up, Holdfast saw Jack Nolan lower his smoking barrel.

For several seconds Nolan strove to tear himself free from the glaring eyes that held him as though impaled. When at length Holdfast glanced down at Riley Tharpe, Nolan broke and ran toward his horse. At a sign from their leader four of the scouts ran after him. Four scattered shots rang out a few seconds later from the clearing. The scouts returned.

Little Tharpe, they saw, was lying limp in Holdfast's arms.

"Le's light fire, Ho'fas', like . . . like Gungy . . ."

Holdfast bent over and spoke to the passing spirit: "Yes," said he. "We'll build it across the River by the great oak. You go get a big pile of sticks ready, and I'll come soon to light them. We'll be there together always—Mr. Hale, Colonel Ledyard, you and 'Bijah and I.—Yes we will, Riley. I tell you so."

Then, as though he had reached the goal of all his hopes, Riley Tharpe jerked once in Holdfast's arms, and was gone.

MORE BEGINNERS

Landlord McKniff scratched the back of his head so that his coon-skin cap fell forward over his eyes. "Hain't I seed thet 'ar game-chicken somers afore?" he inquired.

"Cain't say," replied Jake McNab after deliberate expectoration, "but whut I do know fer sartin, I seed his spittin' image some years back on Catawba Trace."

"Whut doin'?"

"Lookin' fer suthin' to kill, seemin'ly, jes' like his mahsteh."

"Which was who?"

"Young red-head with his tail on fire jes' like the chicken."

"Yeah; but whut war 's *name*?"

"Li'l David he called 'im, nigh's I rec'leck."

McKniff swung his portly stomach so as to block the narrow path for McNab and his long-drawn-out family. "Whut I'm axin' yeh," said he, "is 'baouten the name o' thet 'ar red-head whut owned the chicken."

"Oh, him? Wal, le's see naow.—Young feller name o' Johnson.—But naw; thet ain't right. Jackson, 't war. Yeah, naow I got it; Andy Jackson."

At this point McNab spat again, with vigor, by way of rhetorical climax.

McKniff's tone of voice was unmistakably respectful as he exclaimed: "Mr. Andrew Jackson he come inter yer cabin daown Catawba Trace?"

"Why *not* inter my cabin? Best cabin they war them parts them days. Fack is, 't war the one an' on'y."

"Yeah, but . . . but Mr. Andrew Jackson!—Come alone, did he?"

"Wal, 'course he hed thet 'ar Li'l David along on 's fist, an' Mr. Russ Bean the rifle-man, an' a slew o' lawyers I disremember. Come an' slep' over-night they did, the hull kit an' bilin'. Likewise an ole white-poll called 'The Cloth' they hed with 'em, an' a boy name o'—wal, I fergit—an' a faust-dog called Wash, *and Mr. Holdfast Gaines!*"

McKniff's little eyes, creased with fat, opened wide as they were able. "Mr. Hol . . . !" he said, and stopped there.

"Yeah. Maw an' me we won't never fergit thet night. We-uns all got splashed to the years—thet is all 'cep'n' Mr. Gaines an' the dog an' cock an' boy, which o' course they didn't drink much.—An' whut a tell! Ye never did see sech a tellsome time. Candles we hed—white

300

fotched-on candles offen Bill Gomme! An' brandy! Maw, she got aout her vascinater!'"

McKniff, moving onward, felt impelled to say something which might tend to restore his relative importance. "I seed Mr. Andrew Jackson oncet win a pot o' money wi' thet 'ar chicken," he observed.

"Wal, I dunno's thisheer's jes' the very same; but Li'l David warn't never a one to let hisself run aout, so to say, an' this un mought be his gram'boy or so. Anyhaow 'pears like we're a-ketchin' up wi' Andy Jackson an' Mr. Holdfast Gaines, like I allus did hone teh."

The small red cock was pecking gravel among his hens outside a large stockade on the Cumberland Road, ten miles from Nashville. He looked up and crew a cheerful welcome as McKniff and McNab went in at the gate, followed by the former's three stalwart daughters and McNab's numerous descendants, their horses and dogs, their wagons, and dangling pots and pans.

Pausing to look about them while the dogs of the place made their official investigations, the new-comers saw that the high surrounding wall of sharpened logs set on end enclosed at least an acre of land, roughly square, dominated by a top-heavy block-house of generous size standing in the middle by itself. Each corner of the enclosure was defended by a smaller block-house. Rows of stout lean-tos, their roofs sloping inward, filled all but the spaces left for gateways on the four sides. The place had a friendly and prosperous look in the warm red rays of the descending sun. It swarmed and bristled with life. Cows were lowing to be milked, horses munching, sheep bleating, pigs sucking, hens scratching, and dogs barking all over the open area. Negro slaves were laughing, singing, or, here and there, at work among the out-houses, and pickaninnies by the dozen played at the doors of the white-washed slave-quarters. The place was neither slovenly nor yet anxiously clean. It was comfortable, like an old coat stained and bleached by many weathers. It was like a coat of slightly antiquated style, and one which its owner had nearly out-grown.

Landlord McKniff looked appraisingly about the enclosure, with eyes not unlike those of a sagacious and well-conditioned hog. It was clear to him at a glance that Fort Donelson, built fifteen years before as a defense against savages, now required nothing more than vigorous masculine management to become a thriving hostelry that would fatten upon a trade moving both ways along what was already a main-traveled road. He believed, moreover, that the place had connubial possibilities which, as a widower, he ought not to neglect. Turning to McNab he

301

softly asked: "Hain't I hearn tell ez this yar Mrs. Donelson is a widder ooman?"

"Ye mought—an' then agin ez haow she likes it thet-away, an' hain't figgerin' on no change."

McKniff made a few swift adjustments in his attire and then abstractedly remarked, "Ah. Jes' so," in a tone which did not suggest despair of his own chances. "But jes' same," he went on, "hit don't look right, somehaow. She oughter hev a man 'raound to kinder give an eye naow an' then. Widder oomanfolkses is tar'ble easy tuk in an' put upon, times."

"Yeah," McNab agreed, and spat. "So they be, times.—But this un . . . Wal, hev a try, McKniff. Hev a try."

"An' ye won't say nothin' 'baout . . . ? *Ye* know."

"Hell, no! Aout hyar in these western parts every man gits a new start."

A youth in a leathern apron came out of the nearest shed carrying a horse-shoe, crimson and smoking, in tongs. When half-way to the horse-trough he looked up for a moment at the strangers and shouted back: "Hey, Perthy! Here's some more beginners!"

A well-grown, handsome youth looked out the doorway. He held an unfinished rifle-barrel in one hand while the other shaded his eyes from the glare of the setting sun. "Why, Russ," he called out after a moment's hesitation, it's . . . I think it must be Mr. McNab!"

"Wal, danged iffen 't ain't!" boomed a voice from within. "Hit's the hull McNab nation, an' thet ole bumblins-adulterer McKniff 'long with 'em.—Welcome in, folks! D'ye hev a good trace? Anyhaow, ye got hyar jes' on time. I c'n smell supper."

Russell Bean's bright hair in the sunlight, his aquiline face and bared chest, had a discernible effect upon the McKniff sisters. The daughters of Clan McNab, at the sight of him, looked suddenly more alert and made little twitches and pats here and there at their travel-stained raiment. Bean, however, seemed not to observe these familiar symptoms. "Perthy," said he to his apprentice after a few hand-shakes and perfunctory bows, "kindly run tell Rachel hyar's 'bout half a hunderd new beginners perishin' fer a bait. Tell her she better kill the y'arlin' male-brute.—An' on the way back ye mought fotch us a big crock o' strike-me-blind outen loft. Thet's how McNab done fer us back on Catawba, an,' 'sides thet, I wanter show this raskilly ole McKniff some bumblins whut raley do bumble."

McKniff, somewhat red in the face, began "Naow, Mr. Bean . . ."

but the younger man cut him short, taking him and McNab by the arms and walking them into the smithy. "I hain't much of a hand fer the gals," he briefly explained, "'thouten I'm dressed fer it special."

The place smelt of leather, oil, and burnt horse-hooves. A handful of live coals on the forge gave most of the light. Hammer-heads, scythe-blades, anvil-horns, and at least a dozen rifle-barrels, shone dully. One could see that Western Waters no longer suffered from any dearth of iron.

"Set yeh down," said Bean. "Save yer moccasins."

Looking through the open doorway the new-comers saw their families standing, awkwardly, at a little distance. Indeed the whole situation, brought about by Bean's absurd pride in his appearance, was slightly awkward. The sunlight was lifting from the enclosure now and gilding the tops of a few distant trees where cardinal birds and thrashers were singing, as McNab put it to himself, "fit to bust." The scent of lilac blossom drifted in and mingled with the odors of the smithy. There came sounds of a bucket bumping down a well, of someone grinding corn in a quern, and the comfortable grunting of hogs. McKniff sighed as his senses drank in the beauty of the spring-time evening. He thought of his lonely state. At the very least, he resolved, he would discourage Russell Bean from making any more allusions to things past and best forgotten.

Young Perthy appeared in the dog-trot of a cabin not far from the block-house. Under one arm he had a large earthenware jug. A handsome raven-haired young woman came with him, striding like a man, her full bosom held high. Even from a distance one could see her black eyes flash in the after-glow.

"Drat thet Russ Bean!" she called. "He's a shame to Fort Donelson, leavin' y'-all a-loaferin' aout hyar this-away. I'll pull his yaller curls fer 'im so's nex' time he goes callin' he won't look so purty."

She welcomed the company as a group and then one by one, heartily. "An' naow," said she, "do ye march yerselves up to block-haouse an' make to hum whilst we git yer supper victuals. Hit won't be long. George Davidson, hyar, an' the black boys 'll see to yer critters. Perthy 'll show yeh whar to bed daown.—Come 'long naow!"

Maw McNab looked up at her with a wistful smile. "Be ye Mrs. Donelson?" said she, somehow managing to express in those few words a longing for feminine companionship which no number of daughters could ever quite satisfy.

"No. That's Mother. I'm Rachel.—Thet is I mean, I'm Mrs. Andrew Jackson."

"Oh! I . . . I didn't know!"

Rachel suddenly put an arm round the elder woman's waist and the two walked away together, leading the procession toward the block-house.

"Mrs. Andrew Jackson!" McNab exclaimed.—"Ye don't mean, Mr. Bean, he's gone an' got married!"

"Jedge fer yerself. That 'ar Rachel, *she* thinks so anyhow. Carries her head higher 'n ever now-days, an' won't look at no other man no more 'n iffen he warn't thar—'cause she's ben married afore, an' most any ole husband 'd be better 'n that pizen-pot name o' Robards she useter hev."

"Ah—widder-ooman, war she?" inquired McKniff. "An' rich, I s'pose?"

"No, she warn't rich; an' Robards—I dunno why—he's still alive."

"Then—haow come?"

"Wal, her hevin' a husband a'ready, thet did kinder slow things up fust off, but ye know how Andy is—when he wants suthin' bad he jes' nach'ly takes an' runs off with hit."

At this point, Perthy having brought in the crock of "strike-me-blind" and departed, there was a brief interruption in the talk while the two visitors refreshed themselves.

"But naow, Mr. Bean," said McKniff, helping himself to a third noggin, " 'baouten them two words ez ye war pleased to mention when we-all come in."

"Whut two ye mean, Mr. McKniff?"

"Wal, they was suthin' 'baout a 'bumblins-marchant,' iffen I don't disremember, the which no man don't like to be called. An' then too, whut's mebbe wuss, they was 'adulterer.'—Naow them two words, Mr. Bean, they jes' nach'ly ain't good fer business."

"Aw, haow ye know they ain't? Jever hear 'em afore?"

McKniff treasured his pendulous stomach while he considered this question. He felt it to be unfortunate that Bean was not drinking, and in order to reduce his disadvantage he poured himself a fourth noggin of whisky and tossed it off.

"Wal, fack is," he admitted at length, "I *hev* heered 'em, not only in Morganton but then agin to Jonesboro. Fack is I come aout hyar to Western Waters hopin' never to hear 'em no more; an' then fust off ez I come inter this yar gate thar is them two words spoke by you, Mr. Bean, which ye reely hedn't oughter."

304

"How ye mean I hedn't oughter?"

McKniff leaned forward, elbows on knees, and gazed earnestly at his host through the dusk. "Mean this yar," said he in a tone emboldened by half a pint of potent liquor. "Back to Jonesboro I heered a tale 'baouten Mr. Russ Bean whut wouldn't be good fer the rifle business iffen 't war to git noised raound in these hyar western parts."

"Which tale was thet?" Bean asked, looking up with a pleasant smile through the smoke of the pipe he was lighting. " 'Cause arter all, they's so many on 'em, an' I lose track."

"Oh, jes' li'l tale 'baouten Mr. Bean gittin' cuckled by a linen-draper an' bitin' off the years of a by-blow an' then tryin' to burn daown the hull damn taown."

"Oh, yeah. That un. Naow I rec'leck."

"I thunk ye mought could. An' whut I say is, Mr. Bean, thet 'ar tale would be bad fer the rifle-buildin' iffen hit war to git brooded abaout in Western Waters."

Bean's laughter was comfortable and friendly. "I see whut ye mean," he answered, "but hit don't work aout thet-away. Folks tell thet tale f'm Charleston in South Car'liny clar out to Miss'ipp' an' down to Nawlins. 'Course they tells it in hunderds o' differ'nt ways—but whut ye eggspeck? P'int is, more they tells it the more they all hez to rush out an' git 'em a Russ Bean rifle or bust, so's me an Perthy is nigh-'bout daid tryin' to ketch up with orders."

"Whut ye mean is," put in McNab, finding that McKniff was temporarily silenced, "thet 'ar noration made yeh a famious man."

"Hit holpt," Bean modestly agreed. "Course good rifles, they holpt too. I don't adulter my rifles. When I say my sights are made o' Car'liny gold, why gold they be, from Car'liny, an' not brass from somers else. Yeah, an' when a man finds my bar'ls be rifled true he don't give a damn iffen I *hev* ben cuckled—no more 'n I do."

"Whut's thet?" exclaimed McNab in a tone of moral reprobation. "Ye mean ye don't give a damn?"

"Why, suhtinly not. Never felt none the wuss fer it. Felt better, in fack. Hit tuk her offen my hands."

"Wal, but, looky hyar . . ."

"Naow, gen'lemen, thet 'ar tale mought jes' well be tole right fer oncet, an' so hyar 'tis. A while gone by a gal by name o' Robison, darter of ole Colonel Robison o' King's Maounting, she up an' got me married to her wi' preacher an' ring an' all them she-male fixin's. To this day I dunno how she done it, but one mornin' I woke up an' looked an'—b' God, thar she war!"

"H'm! Awk'erd!" McNab commented.

"Yeah. But 'bout thet time—an' mebbe 't war thet same mornin'—I rec'leck how my friend Holdfast Gaines was allus pesterin' me to go look how things was a-goin' on up in C'neckticut, an' mebbe git me some more good iron fer my locks. So I packs my train an' off I starts, an' whut wi' this an' thet I'm gone fifteen months. I say, pertickler, fifteen months, gen'lemen, hopin' to be unnerstood as man to man. Wal, an' so comin' back an' gittin' close to Jonesboro I kep' a-thinkin' 'bout thet 'ar empty cabin with no babe a-comin' this year, or not anyhow o' my doin', an' so I crope up to cabin door kinder queerious-like, the way a man would comin' back thet-away, an' be damned iffen they warn't a babe in thar a-yellin' like a wild-cat. My wife—or her 't called herself Mrs. Russ Bean anyhow, an' hed a ring to prove it—she'd sky-hooted, ye see, mebbe thinkin' I wouldn't like it or suthin'. But p'int is, I *did* like it, even arter I'd done a li'l sum in my haid an' figgered some kind neighbor must 'a' ben helpin' me out—kinder spellin' me, iffen ye take my meanin'. So in I goes an' takes a squint at 'im layin' thar, an' I knows suthin' 'bout babes red an' white, an' I c'd see this war a good un an' nigh-'bout two month ole."

"An' ye ben away fifteen months," said McNab, spitting across the room and into the forge so as to extinguish the last of the red embers. "See whut ye mean."

"Wal, two month ole is when I begin to like 'em bestmost, so I picks up thet 'ar brat an' lays his head on my shoulder, pats the wind outen his pore li'l holler belly, an' he stints his yowlin' to-oncet an' smiles up at me an' tries to swaller his thumb."

"H'm. Fambly-like."

"But right thar, whilst we war gittin' 'quainted, thet devil's squaw of a Mrs. McCracken, spyin' fer my wife, she hez to stick her long filthy nose i' the crack o' the door an' seed me a-kissin' 'im on the cheek an' runs yammerin' daown the street. 'He's a-bitin' the babby's years off!' she yells, an' raises the town."

"An' didn't ye?" asked McKniff, looking up for the first time in several minutes.

"Didn't I *whut*?"

"Bite his years off."

"Huh! Mr. McKniff! . . . but no; ye're a guest o' mine. Whut I *will* say is, ye c'n go look at 'im this minute. Ye'll find 'im asleep in the crib betwix' my bed an' Perthy's, up over the dog-trot. An' ye'll

306

find he's got his years *on*—jes' ez many an' jes' ez good ez ever a boy begot an' brung up in wedlock."

"Ye raised 'im, then?" asked McNab in a hushed voice.

"Raised 'im! Why not? His maw didn't want 'im, nor yet his mis'rable bug-tit of a dad, name of Allen. I guv 'im a dacent name, Roy Bean, an' raised 'im on a suckin' bottle, easy ez a pig. Why, Perthy an' me, we *love* thet 'ar li'l bastard."

There was a pause, until McKniff asked: "But whut 'baout tryin' to burn up Jonesboro?"

"Oh, so thet's how they tole it to yeh?—Wal, God he knows I done more 'n any other ten men to keep thet flea-bit town from burnin'. Later on, 'course, I seen my mistake. But 't war like this hyar. Arter Mrs. McCracken let out her yawp 'bout a hunderd of 'em come an' clapped me in jail, mebbe thinkin' I'd try to kill Allen. Fack is, I *war* a-lookin' fer 'im, but on'y to thank 'im kindly an' wish 'im joy. Anyhow, thar I war when the fire bust out in the barn next door at midnight. Andy Jackson's race-hoss war in thet barn, 'Injun Queen,' wuth two thousan' dollars at least. Wal, an' so I bruk out o' jail, hove them barn doors offen hinges, tuk out the hosses, clum' the roof an' spread wet blankets and saved the town, till Andy Jackson come an' yelled 'Come down f'm thar, Russ Bean!' an' he put me back in jail agin.—So thar's the God-begot truth, Mr. Bumblins-Marchant, an' I got Andy Jackson to prove it."

"Ye see haow 't is, McKniff," said McNab in the brief silence. "Tales will git twisted, times."

"Aw, hell," said Bean, rising. "No hard feelin's, I hope. But this I will say as a friend, Mr. McKniff: iffen ye wanter git rich out hyar, don't go in fer a good repitation like Pore Richard back in ole Philadelphy. Go in fer a bad un, so folks 'll say: 'Why, hell, he's jes' like us!'—Why do'ncher paint yeh a sign with yer famous name on it an' tell 'em ye sell pure pizen? Tell 'em ra'lesnakes blush wi' shame when they smell yer drink, an' cotton-mouths turn up their tails an' drown. Thet 'll git 'em. They 'll love yeh fer thet, like they do me fer thinkin' I bit off the years of a by-blow. Tell 'em ye're the masterest adulterer west o' Blue Ridge, an' arter killin' off all the grog-bruisers in Morganton an' Jonesboro now ye're startin' in on Western Waters.—Folks 'll buy yer rot-gut by the bar'l."

"Suthin' to 't," opined McNab. "Suthin' to 't."

"Wal, anyhow," Bean concluded, "le's go git us a bait o' supper."

* * *

McKniff and McNab were amazed, twenty minutes later, as they sat down with some twenty others at the long trestle in the block-house, to see what a transformation Bean had made in his appearance. The stains and habiliments of his trade had disappeared, and he shone now, as the firelight played upon him, resplendent in cream-colored buck-skins heavily fringed and beaded, all the long labor of some Indian squaw. Broad silver bracelets with turquoise eyes glinted at his wrists, and his necklace of wolves' teeth was glowing with garnets.

"Humph!" said Rachel, wrinkling her nose as she walked by him with a huge wooden bowl of fried chicken, and "Thank yeh, my dear," he replied.

Twilight was deepening at the windows, but the flourishing fire on the hearth gave a ruddy glow to the large, oblong, low-raftered room. It was a room old in use if not in years, worn and stained and scarred by human occupancy, and comfortable as a veteran cow-hide boot. Work and play, joy and sorrow, safety and disaster, death and child-birth, had soaked and seasoned it in the essence of humanity. Though made by the simplest tools out of materials drawn directly from the wilderness, though it was pinned together by tree-nails of locust and its doors hung on hinges of buffalo-hide, it was the product of old tra-dition and deep experience in the building and keeping and cherishing of homes. It bore evidence of a quiet prosperity, a sober and unostenta-tious wealth, solidly based upon the largess of the deep black soil and the immemorial forest. The food and drink that made the trestles sag had grown in the fields hard by or been drawn from the udders of the cows that were lowing at the pasture bars. The golden honey in the pot beside the wooden salt-cellar had been taken from a hollow bee-tree before the bears had found it.

Landlord McKniff looked about him with keen appreciation, partly professional but also partly personal, of every creature comfort. Seeing, however, that the Widow Donelson was sitting at the head of the table with her numerous sons and daughters about her as a body-guard, he realized at once that all blandishments must be postponed until after his first meal in her house.

For a while there was only the rattle of horn spoons against wooden trenchers to be heard, but then rose the voice of Russell Bean answer-ing some question from McNab. "Oh, yeah," said he, "folks do keep their ha'r on better these days, now they got their Russ Bean rifles."

"Ye mean, Russ," called Rachel, "naow they got their Andrew Jackson."

"Well, mem, he hez holpt, sartin shore," Bean agreed. "But even Andy he couldn't 'a' done much 'thout my rifles."

"What good yer rifles do thet night he woke y'-all up daown 'long Avery Trace?"

"Aw, wal, 'course ye cain't caount that, Mrs. Jackson. Even a Russ Bean rifle cain't do much iffen a man's daid asleep.—Dretful sleepish I war that night. An Injun c'd 'a' crope up on me an' tuk off my own scalp an' I wouldn't 'a' missed it none till I woke up in the mawnin'."

"Then haow come ye got away alive, iffen ye slep' right spang through the night?"

"H'm," said Bean, temporarily non-plussed and all but acknowledging a palpable hit; but then, after a moment's pause, he replied, severely: "Thet 'ar ain't the kinder question a respectable young gal oughter ax."

Rachel's friendly laughter rang through the room.

"Hear tell," McNab remarked with his mouth full, "ez Mr. Andrew Jackson begun ter be a great man right then an' thar."

"Yeah. Fack. Sence then they ain't ben nothin' c'd stop 'im—not even gittin' married. Andy takes over all the law practice o' Western Waters, c'lecks all the ole bad debts, wins all the cock-fights, fights all the dools, kills most o' the Injuns, an' in betwix' times makes Jack Sevier stan' round an' pay 'tention. Like right now he's off a-layin' down the law all the way from Jonesboro to Nashville. Now we got the McNabs out hyar, Andy 'll prob'ly say we got 'nough people to make a State an' hev a standin' army so's he c'n be Gov'ner an' Gin'ral."

"A State!" exclaimed McNab.

"Sartinly. Andy's ben a-talkin' it up fer years. He's got a name fer it."

"Whut name?"

"Tennessee."

"Huh! Injun. Why couldn't he 'a' called it 'State o' Sevier'?"

"Wal, him an' Jack they don't git 'long good. Tried ter shoot each other up a two-three times, but hell, they's both too tough!—Rachel over thar, course she thinks it oughter be 'State o' Jackson,' but iffen ye ax me I'd say jes' call it 'Sleepin' B'ar' an' be done with hit."

"Is thisheer whut-ye-call-it State a-goin' ter charge taxes?"

"Betcher back teeth. What the hell else is a State good fer?"

"Wal, then, I'm movin' aout."

"Not 'thout Andy's say-so, y' ain't. Andy's the law 'round hyar—or the law is Andy."

309

"Jes' same, I'm a-movin' aout iffen they's a-goin' to be taxes. I give yeh fair warnin'."

"But hell, y' ain't on'y jes' got hyar, Jake McNab."

"Don't give a cont'nental iffen I hain't got hyar *yit;* I'm a-movin' aout afore the tax-c'lectors moves in.—Young feller back thar at the gate he called me a 'beginner,' an' by godly thet's jes' whut I be. Maw an' me's ben an' gone an' begun more 'n ten times a'ready—or purty nigh, anyhaow—an' we c'n keep it up till we comes to the end o' the sky. I betcha we git thar, too, ahead o' the lawyers an' taxes."

"Y' got a fine scelp thar, McNab," said Bean. "Injuns 'll shore hone fer it out thar beyond Western Waters."

"Hain't nary an Injun pushed me back faster 'n taxes pushed me forards!"

"Same time," remarked McKniff, whose preoccupation with plans for the future had kept him from following this conversation closely, "'t ain't the law alone ez c'n keep scelps on an' growin'. By whut I hear they's some new big med'cine aout in the Choctaws."

"Oh, yeah," Bean replied with his mouth full. "Ye mean The Cloth."

"Anan? The whut?"

"Course they call 'im 'The Ha'r' now-days, but he's the same man."

"The Ha'r?" said McNab, and laid down his spoon, completely mystified.

"Yeah. *Ye* 'member 'im, thet night in yer cabin.—Long black coat he hed on, collar buttoned behind, white dew-dabbers under 's chin, cloth leggin's, an allus squintin' inter a li'l green book whut don't mean nothin'."

"Oh yeah.—An' guv me a nip o' brandy."

"Thet's the feller."

"I 'member him naow," said McKniff. "He bet agin Mr. Andrew Jackson at Morganton, an' lost."

"Wal, losin' to Andy don't make 'im no differ'nt f'm nobody else," Bean answered. "But whut I'm a-sayin', The Cloth he went Injun a while back. Said he couldn't stand white smells no longer."

"White smells?" inquired McNab, once more bewildered.

"Yeah—places like Jonesboro, Morganton, Nashville, an' raoundabaouts. He says they smells tar'ble. When The Cloth says 'smells' he means stinks, an' by stinks he mos'ly means us.—Wal, fin'ly Holdfast tuk 'im out to visit the Choctaws, which seemin'ly they must 'a' smelled better, 'cause anyhow he didn't cor.e back. He's stuck thar."

"Do get on with your supper, Russ Bean, afore it's cold," said Mother Donelson.

"Thankee, mem; but I c'n chaw my victuals an' talk same time."

"Iffen he couldn't," laughed Rachel, "he 'd 'a' starved hisself long ago."

Bean cocked his eye at her. "I'm a say-nothin' man by nater, like Holdfast," he replied; "but beaucheous young gals allus do make me blab. Cain't help m'self."

"Go 'long with yeh!"

"Wal, an' so nex' time I war tradin' out thar I walks me up to Chief Pushmataha's biggest town, on the bank o' Miss'ssip', an' axes fer the Reverent Blandison. They jes' look at me. I ax fer the Parson, then. Same answer. Wal, then, how 'bout The Cloth? They begin to laugh. All right, thinks I, they've gone an' knocked the ole feller over, an' mebbe a good job too. So I druv my train on 'bout a mile an' come to the Big Chief's house—an' whut do I see thar?"

"The Cloth," guessed McNab.

"Nope."

"Chief Pushmataha smokin' his pipe an' watchin' his women work," ventured Mrs. Donelson.

"No, mem."

"A beaucheous young squaw," called Rachel.

"Right ye be fer oncet. She *war* young. Nigh-about fifteen I cal'late, like a gal I useter whirl offen her feet on the flat-boat *Adventure*. An' then too, like thet same gal, she war beaucheous ez day-bust in the mountings in the time o' thin greenery, with the turkeys in the tree-tops all a-gobble."

"Do *tell!*" said Rachel.—"But otherways 'n thet . . . ?"

"Oh, otherways, o' course, she war differ'nt ez day f'm dark. Not lippy, she warn't, nor come-onish, nor yet so tore-down outdacious. Give a man some peace an' comfort, thet 'ar gal would, arter the hard day's work, stiddier 'n tryin' to make 'im feel like a worm when he gits hisself dressed up a li'l fer comp'ny."

Rachel's laugh, though perhaps a bit tom-boyish and rollicking, was good to hear, and one could see that Bean enjoyed it as much as anyone. At length she asked: "Haow big war she?—an' course I mean haow big 'raound, like most squaws."

Bean thought for a moment, with a rapt look. "Whut I'd say," he then answered, sighing, "she war big in the right places, iffen ye take my meanin'. Yeah—an' small whar she hed a right to be. She hed a shape to her, light an' strong, like a rifle-gun whut a man hez gone an' made as good ez he knows how. Takin' her up an' down, thar war a-plenty to her. She warn't a sawed-off, but tall, like a seven-foot rifle our Holdfast mought carry, or mebbe one o' these hyar heathen she-gods by name o' Venice 't The Cloth useter tell us 'bout wi' no clothes on."

"Ye meanter say thisheer Chocter gal . . . " began McKniff.

"Naw; ye don't git me. I know thet kind, an' she warn't it. Look ye: 't war jes' corn-tasselin' time, an' a wind come offen the River through the popples, ye all know how. Git it? See her thar? Oh me, oh my! I see her standin' thar now in the flicker o' them popple leaves with her ha'r blowin' black an' long an' the wind snugglin' up agin her white doe-skins. Iffen I went blind this minute I'd never lose the look o' thet B'loved Woman fust time these eyes war blest by her."

There was a short and somewhat uncomfortable silence before McNab inquired: "B'loved Woman, eh? Thet's a she-male chieftain or suthin', ain't she?"

"Yeah. An' not jest fer Choctaws, but Creeks, Chickasaws, Cherokees, even the wild Chickamaugas. 'Cause thar's 'nother thing"—and here Bean shot another humorously severe glance at Rachel—"*thet* gal's got a head-piece on her, an' all the Injuns o' Western Waters they know it. They do like she tells 'em. So thet's mebbe one more reason, 'sides Bean rifles, why we keeps our ha'r on now-days."

Supper was over now. Negro women dragged the trestles back, cleared the board, and took the trenchers through the dog-trot for washing. Young Perthy and George Davidson mended the fire. Candlewood spluttered in the sconces. Mother Donelson, Rachel, and then Maw McNab, lighted their corn-cob pipes. So did Bean, McKniff, and the numerous male and female scions of Clan McNab. The head of that clan, preferring to "spit amber" and wishing on such a ceremonial occasion to take no chances, sat close to the hearth. Benches skreaked across the floor of hewn puncheons. The rafters and cross-beams were soon blue with smoke.

"But afore ye got lost on thet beaucheous young gal," said McNab, "ye war tellin' 'baout Mr. The Cloth whut they calls The Ha'r."

"Oh, yeah.—Wal, when I come up she war a-brushin' out with a brush o' hog-bristles the longest an' whitest scelp ever growed. Course I seed hit b'longed to The Cloth.—Ye know, Maw Donelson, thet scelp he c'd doff an' don so's to make an Injun scelper feel dizzy."

312

"His wig."

"Thet's the word. We-uns useter laugh at it back on the trace, but the Choctaws they don't. They say it brings rain an' keeps off the pox, an' when The Ha'r puts on them long locks he's all same as the gods an' cain't go wrong, they say. So thar's 'nother thing, thet wig o' his'n, why we-uns keeps our ha'r on."

"Haow ye mean?" asked McKniff.

"Mean this-away.—S'pose in comes a passel o' young red-sticks wi' their tails on fire an' says 'Le's go take ha'r!' Wal, the Ole Man, the Big Med'cine, he puts on thet 'ar wig an' shuts his eyes like he's listenin' hard an' arter while he says 'Better not. The gods say No,' he says. So all them red-sticks they wash off their war-paint an' start in hoein' corn."

"Saves trouble," said McNab.

"It do. An' ha'r. An' iffen thet won't work . . . Wal, I tell yeh. Oncet I was over to see him, thar come in a band o' young Creeks, blood-thirsty, an' says they cain't stand it no longer. Hedn't tuk more 'n a two-three scelp in three long year, they says, an' them mos'ly wimming. Said The Ha'r's white scelp war all wore out, an' thar hed to be some new med'cine. 'Okeh,' says The Ha'r, an' 'Mebbe so,' sezee. Then he gits out his li'l green book called 'Horatius Flaccus,' which don't mean nothin' in English nor yet in Choctaw. He says it's the language o' the gods, an' reads it out to 'em. Then he says it means 'No.' But still them young Creeks they don't like it. They say it raley do sound like god-talk but mebbe he ain't a good linkister, an' they wanter go take ha'r. An' so 'Okeh,' sezee, 'kill a dog.' "

"Whut the hell is thet 'Okeh,' ye're a-sayin'?" asked McKniff.

"Hit's Choctaw fer 'thet is so.' But anyhow, they split a dog open from nose to tail an' The Ha'r he pokes at the innards a while with a li'l black stick an' then he ups an' tells 'em plain an' final the innards say *No!*—Wal, they c'n go agin the wig, they c'n go agin the book, but the innards of a daid dog is too much. Purty soon I looks outen teepee flap an' all them blood-thirsty Creek red-sticks is a-squattin' round a fire with the Choctaws an' Chickasaws an' mebbe a few Cherokees playin' the dices, the which is a mis'rable game The Ha'r went an' taught 'em jes' to keep 'em from broodin' on white man's ha'r."

"Huh!" said McKniff. "Never heerd tell afore o' thet 'ar kind o' med'cine."

"No; but p'int is, it works. Ha'r says he larnt the daid-dog part offen

313

the ole Romans. Called hisself an 'auger,' he did; but o' course I know whut an auger is better 'n he do."

"Ye don't s'pose, naow, do ye," inquired McNab, "ez Mr. Holdfast Gaines put 'im up to any o' thet med'cine?"

"I don't s'pose it, naw. I'm damn shore he did. Fack is, iffen ye bolt it to the bran, Holdfast is behint all this hyar new-fangled business o' lettin' ha'r grow. Him an' the B'loved Woman they works at it night an' day, the hull year round.—But o' course it holpt some when Alec McGillivray up an' died."

"Daid is he?" asked McKniff. "Ye shore o' thet?"

"Tol'able shore.—Anyhow, ye don't see 'im round these days."

"Heered tell," said McNab with a hint of innuendo, "ez McGillivray died in his bed—which is an oncommon way, an' too good fer 'im."

Russell Bean shut one eye. "I heered same thing," said he, "but I didn't pay hit no mind.—Main p'int is, they come a time when he warn't thar no more, not long arter we brung Perthy back f'm Nick-a-Jack."

"Whut ye doin' thar, boy?" asked McNab. "Thet Nick-a-Jack Cave, ez they tell it to me, is a dangersome place."

"Stole, he war," Bean replied, answering for Perthy. "Tuk an' runned off with by the Tharpes right spang away f'm thisheer fort. Holdfast an' me had to go git 'im."

"Hev any trouble?"

"Naw—or not much. An ole med'cine man, name o' The Breath an' friend o' Holdfast, kep' 'im fed an' hid in the Cave, so's tothers couldn't git at 'im."

"Who's 'tothers'?"

"Why, hell, McGillivray, o' course, an' his howlin' Creeks, come to git Perthy an' the rest o' them white childern the Chickamaugas hed captered an' sell 'em to the Spaniards."

"Fer slaves?"

"Yeah. Slaves an' sech."

"Whut's Chickamaugas?" inquired McKniff.

"You fellers f'm way back thar in Blue Ridge don't seem to know nothin' much, do ye? But anyhow, the Chickamaugas they got started back in the ole war when Draggin' Canoe—an' he war a young man them days—brung a passel o' young red-stick Cherokees down the Tennessee to Lookout Mounting or thar'bouts to live on the loot o' the river. They hed a town on the mounting called Nick-a-Jack, danged iffen I know why, an' likewise a cave same name down in under the

314

mounting close by the river. Fack is, a canoe c'n float spang outen the face o' the mounting an' inter the Tennessee 'thout a bump, on a crick they hed thar runnin' outen thet thar cave. Anyhow, 't war the best place fer a nest o' river-pirates ye ever sot eyes on."

"I ain't never seed no sech a place m'self," said McNab, expectorating into the fire in his most refined and cultivated manner. "Whut's more, I don't wanter."

"Anyhow, thar 't war, an' all the nachal-borned river-pirates f'm Blue Ridge to Miss'sip' they come a-runnin' an' squat thar an' look out f'm top o' Lookout Mounting till they see a boat comin' down an' then run down into cave an' inter canoes an' out an' slam-bang inter the boat an' kill some an' capter the rest an' run off with 'em an' all their goods up the mounting an' start in all over agin."

"Russ Bean," said Rachel, "ye're talkin' yerself blue in the face. Why cain't ye let Perthy tell some o' this tale? He was thar, an' ye wa'n't."

"Wal," Bean continued, "ez I was a-sayin'—an' do ye try to run on'y one man at a time, Mrs. Andrew Jackson—the pirates drapped into Nick-a-Jack Town f'm all the four winds. 'Sides the Cherokees under Draggin' Canoe thar come runaway no-count Chickasaws an' Creeks hed ben druv out o' their own tribes, an' mebbe a few Choctaws. Thar come Spanish an' French an' wild Irish, but not Scotch-Irish, o' course, 'count o' pirate life bein' too tame an' not payin' good 'nough fer thet 'ar breed. Anyhow, jes' like Holdfast useter say, they was a mort o' white men in Nick-a-Jack, an' most on 'em Tories. In cahoots with McGillivray they war, the damn traitors, an' livin' offen the river-loot like rats. An' then they was the Tharpes f'm Conneckticut, that's 'Bijah an' Riley. They come thar times, but their rale hang-out was up to Cave-in-Rock on the Hiah.—'T was the Tharpes whut tuk young Perthy."

"Now, Perthy, it's your turn," said Mrs. Donelson with quiet authority. "I'm sure Russell Bean needs a rest."

Though blushing slightly at first, the lad plunged at once into his story. "After they heard me say Uncle Holdfast's name," said he, "the Tharpes were good to me and let me ride on their horses. They let me take Wash along. They wanted to talk about Holdfast and Connecticut all the time. It took us three days to get to the Chickamauga towns. When we got there The Breath took me into his wigwam. He was an old Creek. The Indians said he was more than a hundred years old. He was good to me, because he and Uncle Holdfast had been friends for a long time. I liked him too. Of course I knew some Creek language,

315

so he and I could talk. He tried to get word to Uncle Holdfast about where I was and to come and get me, but the runner couldn't find Holdfast. I stayed there in the village and played with the Indian boys and the other white children, and had a good time until one day The Breath heard that Alec McGillivray was coming after us white boys to sell us to the Spaniards. Then The Breath got together about twenty other old Creeks that didn't like Alec McGillivray, and they took us up into Nick-a-Jack Cave, where it was pitch dark. At first we had a little fire, but when Alec came and camped just at the mouth of the cave with his braves we had to put it out and be quiet. There were bats in the cave. Sometimes they crawled on us, and got in our hair. We were sitting by the side of the stream. The water didn't taste good. We didn't have much to eat—only a little corn. We had a canoe up there, and I had our dog Wash. He helped to keep me warm, and never made a sound."

"Ye mean thet same faust-dog name o' Wash ye hed with yeh daown Catawba Trace, boy?" inquired McNab.

"Yes. He was getting old then, and he's dead now, but we have his son and call him Wash too. He's just like his father."

"Lookee hyar, boy, ye talk different, somehaow, f'm whut ye useter daown thar. Ez I rec'leck thet night ye couldn't say 'soup-soap-sugar' to save yer life."

Once again Perthy flushed a little. "Oh, I can talk that way now if I want to," said he, "but when I'm with friends I try to talk like Uncle Holdfast."

"H'm. Int'restin'. A white boy larnin' to talk good f'm an Injun, eh?—But go on with yer tale, lad."

"Well, we waited there in the dark a long while. The Breath said it was three days and nights, but of course he couldn't tell because it was pitch dark, and I thought it must be a month. I began to get hungry, and so did the other boys. The old Creeks didn't eat much of anything. They saved the corn for us. The Breath thought that Alec was trying to starve us out, and that was the reason he didn't come in. He had fifty young braves at the mouth of the cave, and the Creeks inside with us were all old. If we went out, they'd take us and sell us. If they came in, they'd kill us. If they didn't come in but we just waited there, we'd starve."

"H'm. Awk'erd!" murmured McNab. "Whut ye do 'baouten hit?"

"The Breath remembered a little hole on the side of the mountain that he'd seen many years before when he was hunting. He thought we

316

might as well die looking for that hole as die where we were. He and Wash and I got into the canoe and paddled up-stream. We took some pine torches with us and some corn and a little meat for the dog. We paddled a long time. Sometimes we could touch the rocks on both banks at the same time, and then next we would be paddling across a lake. Sometimes we had to bend our heads to keep from hitting the rocks above us, and then the ceiling would go up so high that we couldn't see it. The Breath sat in front with a torch to watch out for rocks in the water. I did all the paddling. Sometimes I had to drag the canoe up and over a water-fall. I could see that The Breath was getting weaker. He didn't eat anything. He talked about Holdfast when he talked at all. He knew he was going to die, but he said I must go on. He kept me from being afraid. He kept saying he knew we'd find Holdfast. When we saw the light shining through the hole in the mountain he wasn't surprised. He just said 'There it is. You get out now, and leave me here.' I said I wouldn't leave him. He said 'You must.' Then I said 'I won't.'"

"Good fer you, lad!" said McNab.

"That was the first time I'd ever said 'I won't' to The Breath, and it was the last time, too. I said 'I'll send Wash through the hole, but I'll stay here.' So I sent Wash out, and told him to go find Holdfast. I went back to the old man, but I couldn't do much. I was hungry and weak myself. I couldn't stand up. I didn't care if I died, but first I wanted to see Holdfast. A long time went by, and I lost track of everything. When I came to, there was Holdfast standing beside me with a pine-torch. Wash was with him. Wash looked all worn out. His hair was full of burrs. The Breath was dead."

"No tellin' how long the boy laid thar," said Bean. "Mebbe only a few hours, but mebbe a week. Anyhow, Wash found us on the ole Nick-a-Jack trail jest arter we'd killt the Tharpes. By that time we had thutty men. Andy Jackson, he come along, but he tuk his orders f'm Holdfast like we all did. Fer oncet in his life Holdfast clum' out on top, whar he allus b'longs, an' run things, stiddier 'n hangin' back an' etarnally puzzlin' whut to do. Suthin' 'd ben bruk loose inside 'im whut mos'ly he keeps tied down. I seen 'im laugh like never afore sence back in Connecticut. He grabbed a-holt of us thutty by the throats an' rushed us down the trail like a storm o' wind, b' God. All the way down 'long River Sequatchie we seemin'ly rid on his shoulders, an' fust we knowed we was swimmin' the Tennessee arter dark from Moccasin Bend with McGillivray's camp-fires ahead. We could 'a' bruk in on 'em

327

an' killt every man, but Holdfast he guv us our orders an' tuk the dog Wash an' clum' up alone on the mounting, Wash leadin' the way. At dawn us thutty guv the whoo-whoop an' rushed the fires an' killt some an' druv the heft on 'em inter the cave. They had 'bout a hunderd to start with, 'count o' some o' the pirates hevin' come down to help McGillivray's braves. Anyhow, we druv 'em in, them 't c'd stagger. They tuk burnin' brands along, the damn fools, so's to make good marks fer our rifle-guns. I seen Alec McGillivray go in at the mouth, but he didn't hev no brand. I seen 'im go in thar, I say, but no man ever seen 'im come out, dead or alive."

"Et up, mebbe," suggested McKniff.

"Whut ye mean? Et by who?" asked Bean.

"Mr. Holdfast Gaines, prob'ly.—Hain't I heered tell he et an Injun oncet back whar he come from?—Et his shoulder, anyhow."

"Naw, thet war his granfer, by name of Uncas."

"He et his granfer, ye mean?"

"Naw! Git this right, McKniff. His granfer et Miantonomoh."

"Yer aunt who?—I heered 't war an Injun man he et."

"Oh, my Gawd!—But . . . wal—they ain't no tellin' whut ye mought hear tell, but I'm tellin' yeh Holdfast Gaines never would of et Alec McGillivray. Pure pizen thet 'ar feller was, an' not fitten fer rat-bait. 'Sides all which, Holdfast thet day was too damn busy to think 'bout eatin' nothin'. When I dodged round the corner o' thet 'ar cave-mouth an' got in thar 'mongst them lights an' shadders I seen spang off they wa'n't no more use in us thutty killin' no more Creeks an' Irish an' Tories an' sech. Whut I mean is, I heered it, 'count o' thar bein' no lights up-stream in the dark whar the thing war a-goin' on."

"Whut thing, Mr. Bean?"

"Yells, mos'ly, an' screams, an' then splashes o' daid bodies inter the water. Ye c'd tell them daid bodies was daid by the way they splashed. Arter while they come floatin' down-stream—or parts on 'em —an' we c'd see fer ourselves they was daid fer good. Half on 'em was bodies o' white men gone bad, which is same thing ez Tories."

"But whut the hell war a-causin' all thet 'ar ruckus up thar, Mr. Bean? A wild animile?"

"Yeah. By name o' Sleepin' B'ar. On'y fer oncet thet B'ar hed wucken-up, I reckon!"

"But I thunk ye said he war up by thet 'ar hole i' the maounting, with Wash, savin' Perthy."

"He and Wash found me an hour after dark," Perthy explained.

318

"Then Uncle Holdfast laid me in the canoe and we dropped down the stream during the night. By dawn of next day we were back where The Breath and I started. I didn't see the fight because it was dark, but I heard the screams and splashes."

"Jever find out whut happened to Alec McGillivray?" McNab inquired.

"Uncle Holdfast never talks about such things."

"Iffen ye ax 'bout whut come of Alec he jes' looks sad," Bean remarked.

"An' haow 'bout thet 'ar dead body o' him ye call The Breath?" asked McKniff.

"When I got strong again," Perthy answered, "Uncle Holdfast and I went back there, through the hole, and found the body. We made it sit up straight, with its arms folded and its eyes still open. Uncle Holdfast said goodbye to The Breath in Choctaw and told him he hoped to see him again before long. He said to the dead body that he had been a brave man, and wise and good, and that the Great Breath would be glad to see him. He said the Great Breath was only drawing back into himself the breath He had sent out, and that this was the way it was with everything that has life in the world.—We left a little corn and hickory milk there by the body, and The Breath's bow and arrows. Then we came away."

"Arter which," Bean added, "all the Injuns round 'bout they figger ez Holdfast must hev The Breath's sperrit in 'im—the which I don't deny he prob'ly hez. An' they figger likewise ez Holdfast must 'a' tuk over fightin' The Knife whar The Breath left off."

"Thar's thet 'ar Knife agin," McKniff complained. "Ev'body noratin' all time 'baouten The Knife, an' nobody sayin' whut the hell 't is!"

Russell Bean's right eye slowly closed. "More they knows 'bout hit," he drily remarked, "the more they don't tell yeh."

"Wal, but caincher tell a feller *suthin'*?"

Bean considered for a moment, and then "Naw," said he. "Or anyhow on'y this much: sence Alec McGillivray went an'—wal, an' wa'n't hangin' 'round no more, thet 'ar Knife hit's ben a-layin' low, mebbe gettin' a mite rusty f'm the ole blood on the blade. But hit's thar yit, do ye betcher back teeth. Hit's thar, an' thet's all I'll tell yeh. Holdfast, he ain't never guv up a-s'archin' fer The Knife."

No one spoke for some minutes. The bountiful supper, the warmth of the fire, and the sheer solid safety of the room filled with flicker of shadow and shine, made danger seem distant, historic, legendary. There was a shivering kind of joy in remembering the time, far back, when the terror of The Knife had walked every night in the forests of Western Waters. Bean's warning could not damp that joy. It was only Russell Bean's exaggerated way of talking.

"I had a knife once," Perthy said at length in a dreamy tone, "that was a beauty. My father brought it to me 'round the Horn on his last voyage to China. It had a long wavy blade, and a green stone woman for a handle. I'd give anything to find that knife again."

"H'm. Int'restin'," said McNab.—But 'bouten thet 'ar Mr. Holdfast Gaines. Times, I cain't sleep o' nights f'm studyin' 'bout thet man. Course I ain't never seed 'im only oncet, but a thousan' times I've said to Maw: 'Whut ye cal'late thet 'ar Mr. Gaines is up to naow?' An' then Maw she says: 'S'pose we-uns 'll ever set eyes on him agin?' "

"Wal, thet's a question," Bean answered. "Ye mought, an' agin ye moughtn't. Disappearin'est man of his size thet ever was, Holdfast is—an' the ontalkin'est."

"Yeah. Daown on Catawba he didn't open his face, fur's I rec'leck; but arter he was gone 'peared to me an' Maw he must 'a' said a bookful."

"I know. Oh, my God, don't I know! Holdfast c'n say more in a minute with his mouth shet than a ridin' preacher c'n wedge into three turns o' the hour-glass. Jes' by lookin' at yeh—or, whut's mebbe wuss, *not* lookin'—he c'n make yeh wish to God ye never hed ben borned. An' then agin . . . Wal, I tell yeh. I knowed a feller oncet was ready to die, he war so tore-down 'shamed o' suthin' he'd gone an' done, or mebbe hadn't done which he'd oughter of. Wal, an' so thisheer feller war a-settin' on a log by a li'l crick somers out 'long Avery Trace, say, with his head in his hands an' a-figgerin' how he c'd git away somers whar nobody 'd ever knowed 'im, which war hard to figger on account he war a purty damn famous man. Anyhow, arter while he looked up an' be damn iffen thar warn't Holdfast Gaines a-settin' on the log right 'long-side 'im an' not sayin' nuthin' but jes' a-settin' thar. Wal, the feller he didn't say nothin' much nuther, but he tuk one look at Holdfast an' —an' then he went an' done whut he hed to do to make things squar, an'—wal, I won't swar my bottom oath he's ben a li'l tin Jesus ever sence, but anyhow he c'n hold his head up an' call his name his own."

"An' jes' whut," asked McKniff, "war thisheer feller so tore-down 'shamed on?"

"Thet 'ar ain't in the story; an' 't ain't no man's business but his'n.—Howsomever, he ain't the only one. Not by a damn sight. Iffen ye war

320

to name all the fellers whut Holdfast keeps a-talkin' to 'thout sayin' a word, or mebbe when he's a hunderd mile off, why then ye'd hev to git in most o' Western Waters, not fergittin' The H'ar nor yet Andy Jackson.—No sir; not by no means fergittin' them two."

"An' yet I s'pose he c'n talk when he wants to," said McNab.

"Talk! Say, y' oughter hear 'im go it in an Injun council-house, now, 'mongst his own people!"

"His own people?" said Mrs. Donelson, evidently intending not so much a question as a statement.

"Holdfast hasn't any people of his own," Rachel agreed. "An' yet I s'pose he has more friends than even Andrew."

Russell Bean rose and knocked the ashes out of his pipe against a burning log. "Friends?" he said. "Yes; he has 'em. Red and black and white he has 'em, by the kentryful, all up an' down the land. But the thing whut's wrong wi' Holdfast, hit's deeper down than any friend c'n go. I useter think 't war a gal, like wi' most men; but now I know his heart's bruk the way no gal on 'arth c'd ever break it."

"What is it, then?" said Rachel.

"Mebbe hit mought come o' studyin' too much on how things oughter be in thisheer world but seemin'ly ain't. I've watched 'im studyin' thet-away, many 's the time, by camp-fires at night in the wilderness; an' whilst he'd be settin' thar still as a stun, a-listenin' to no sound an' a-watchin' whut warn't thar 't all, he'd go 'way so fur ye'd think he was daid, an' I couldn't call 'im back.—Oh, I tell yeh, folks, when ye think whut a man our Holdfast is, an' all ye'd like to do fer 'im, an' ye cain't do a gawdam thing . . . Oh!"

Bean's voice shook on a low note. He turned and gazed into the fire. At length he said: "They must 'a' ben a time, somewhars, way back, when Holdfast went an' drunk 'im a long deep dram o' lonesome water. I dunno whar he found it, but mebbe in some black pool o' the forest springin' up from the lakes o' hell. Anyhow, hit changed 'im. Lonesome as a whip-poor-will he is nowadays: an' times I think only thet 'ar Beaucheous an' B'loved Woman o' the Choctaws will ever make 'im smile agin."

BOOK THREE

THE BLACK DRINK

*But his word was in mine heart as a burning
fire shut up in my bones, and I was weary
with forbearing, and I could not stay.*

JEREMIAH XX, 9

THE FATHER OF WATERS

(April, 1809)

"Thar's suthin' 'baout this hyar Miss'sip' thet stills a man daown," drawled Russell Bean, lolling on deck one day. "Hit picks 'im up an' totes 'im like a cat her kitties, an' thar ain't nary a thing he c'n do 'baout hit iffen he wants ter—the which he don't."

Holdfast considered this, swaying slightly from side to side with elbows on knees as he sat on the deck-house. Then he lifted his head and looked down along the wide sun-lighted water. "I don't see it quite that way, Russ," he said. "A man can go up or down or across, as he decides."

"Wal, mebbe; but anyhow the River keeps a-pushin' an' pullin' at 'im all the time, whatsomever way he wants to go. He better larn to lean on the River, not fight it."

"That's true.—Yes, that's true, Russ. A good river-man learns to let the River help him."

"M'm," said Bean, apparently half asleep. But then, as though rousing himself: "They's a mort o' things c'n help a man iffen on'y he'll larn not to try an' do it all.—Now, ye take a man's friends, f'rinstance."

"Ah," said Holdfast softly, and stopped there.

Realizing that he had gone too far, Bean began again: "Whut I mean say is, they's a thread in things, like the thread o' the River—an' a grain, like the grain in wood."

The answer was only a deep inward glow in Holdfast's eyes.

"Hell, ye know how 't is, better 'n I do. Take mowin', like back at Four Winds Farm. I 'member ye useter say: 'Ye don't hev to push, Russ. Let the pull o' the yarth help yeh.' Or then agin, take out in them western maountings wi' Lewis an' Clark. 'Member how them fellers whut never seed a maounting afore threshed 'emselves to death, nigh-

325

abouts, gittin' through the bresh? But you an' me, we-uns went through thet 'ar bresh like wild ducks flyin' back hum. We let the bresh help us."

Holdfast sat still for a while. Then "Yes," he said, "underneath are the everlasting arms."

"Hey? Anan?"

"Oh, something I read in a book once."

"In a book, eh? I see."

Bean rose, stretched, and said: "Wal, somebody's gotter do some work 'round hyar." And he walked back to the small rifle-shop he had rigged up in the deck-house of the keel-boat.

The red-wings, just returned, were gurgling "O-ka-lee" among the willow catkins. The song-sparrow's volley of notes rang out from bank to bank. Blue-birds and robins were crowding northward in undulating companies. Higher up flew the long wavering arrows of the geese. Now and then Holdfast heard the bump of an ice-cake against the side of *Pride o' the West,* though the planking was hot to the touch in the April sun. Odors of fresh-sawn wood brought drowsy recollections of three winter months at Nashville with Russell Bean, hammering and chopping and sawing there to make this boat. Three months of steady toil had earned them the right to lie for a while in the drench of the sunshine and drift with the thread of the River.

Not for years had Holdfast been so nearly content. It did him good to think of Perthy, happily married now to a Nashville girl, and of Russell Bean growing more thoughtful year by year, with a business that prospered mightily. To be sure, that idea of selling fire-water on the *Pride o' the West* . . . But then, of course, some one would sell it on the River, and, at any rate, Bean would give honest measure. And it was a good thing that Russ had young Roy Bean, his adopted son, along to instruct in the craft of rifle-building. Russ behaved himself better with women—indeed, perfectly—when he had boys like Perthy or Roy in charge. That was one of the many fine things about Russ. He was good with boys.

At this moment Bean's voice came across the deck: "Yeah, boy, hit's b'ar-ile makes the world go round. When things gits to skreakin', put b'ar-ile on the axle. When skeeters makes yer life mis'rable, slap on plenny o' b'ar-ile. Iffen day don't come inter yer cabin, grease the winder-paper wi' b'ar-ile, Roy. An' when day goes down, why jes' light the wick in yer b'ar-ile lamp an' thar ye be."

There came sounds of respectful amusement from young Roy.

326

"Ye laugh, do ye? But I'm tellin' yeh, lad, ez the b'ar is man's best friend. When awake, he shows yeh whar to find honey. When sleepin', he shows yeh how to wait an' bide yer time. An' when daid—wal, his bacon fills yer belly, his hide warms yeh, an' his ile helps yeh make yer rifle an' grease yer patches so's ye c'n go an' kill more b'ar."

This time Roy really did laugh.

"An' so thar's some o' the reasons why I'm a-goin' to put a pitcher of a b'ar on this hyar rifle.—But now whut I war a-sayin'; one thing ye gotter be partic'ler shore is to draw a bead through yer head-blocks agin yer bar'l. Thet's how ye make sartin yer saws won't gouge inter one side an' leave tother smooth."

Holdfast could see little drops and curly shavings of bright metal fall from the barrel every time the saws returned to the muzzle. "Easy does this job," said Bean, "like ary other whut gits done proper. Ye cain't hurry it no more 'n ye kin the River."

"Thet iron's purty soft, by the sound, Russ."

"Yeah. Soft an' heavy 't is, so's ye don't hear nothin' now but a hum like bees in a bee-tree holler. An' she'll soak up the noise o' powder same way like they war some Injun god way down in her sayin' 'hush.' This hyar banger, she'll pitch a ball four times ez fur ez ye c'n hear it—an' thet's a handy thing when ye're workin' through en'my kentry."

"What are you going to name it, Russ?" asked Holdfast.

"Hain't thunk yet," Bean answered, turning his back.

From far up-stream, so faint at first that it scarcely rose above the blue-bird's warble, there came a waft of song. Holdfast listened. Russell Bean and Roy looked up from their rifling-jig and listened also. The drowsing men on the deck-house lifted their heads. Clearer and nearer the sound came from round a bend half a mile up-stream. The man at the steering-oar of the *Pride* slewed his craft out of the current and waited in a back-water. Many voices up there were roaring a song in chorus to a rhythm of stamping feet. At length the square bows of four flat-boats, floating abreast and probably lashed together, swam into view, and the song rolled down the water as though a door had been opened:

> We're a-floatin' daown to the Promised Land,
> A happy band, hand in hand;
> We're baound fer the strand whar the angels stand
> An' wave to you an' me.

Caincher hear them angels singin'?
  Oh brothers, 't won't be long!
Pull on the beech oar, lean on the steerin' oar,
  An' sing 'em back this song.

Come aboard an' float on the Salvation Boat!
Salvation's free! Halleloo! Ya-ee!
Oh woncher come jine us on the shinin' sand
Whar the River meets the Sea?

Caincher hear them big bells ringin'?
  Oh brothers, 't won't be long!
Lean on the steerin' oar, pull on the beech oar,
  An' sing ten thaousan' strong!

"Wal, boys," Bean called to the deck-hands when the last echoes had died away, "whut ye goin' to do 'baout hit? Ye got anythin' to sing back at 'em?"

There was a brief consultation among the men, after which, raggedly at first, but with steadily increasing vigor, they sent back a song they had made for themselves during recent evenings round the deck-house fire:

We're a-floatin' daown teh Nawlins.
  Sing sin, boys! Sin!
An' Nawlins knows we're comin'.
  Sing sin!

All the girlies gittin' painted—
  Sing sin, boys! Sin!
All the whisky gittin' pizened—
  Sing sin!

Caincher smell thet brimstun burnin'?
  Sing sin, boys! Sin!
Caincher hear the ole Devil laughin'?
  Sing sin!

Then come along, boys! Chune her up, boys,
  Sing sin, boys! Sin!
We're a-floatin' daown ter Nawlins.
  Sing sin!

Boat after boat was now seen coming after the first four. Some had washing hung out like signal-flags on the deck-houses. A lowing of cattle was heard, a neighing of horses, and now and then the crow of a cock. Moreover, they had babies up there. Plenty of them.

"Hillo thar, ye fellers baound fer hell!" called a man in a red shirt from one of the foremost vessels.

"Hillo thar, ye holier 'n usses!" Bean yelled back.

"C'm on over hyar an' git religion."

"I got mine aboard," said Bean, pointing to a crude picture on the side of the deck-house in which a whisky-keg was shown with flames rising from the top.

The red-shirted spokesman paused for a moment before he replied: "Wal, let's jes' kinder mix 'em up a li'l. We'll unnertake to save yer hull boat-load o' pore damned souls fer—ah—say fer three gallon o' snake-bite."

"Our souls ain't wuth it. But come aboard, neighbor, an' mebbe we c'n fix up a dicker."

The *Pride o' the West* was soon a recognized member of a rapidly growing fleet. Her regular sailing position was between the flat-boat which came to be called *The Barge o' Venice* and the one nicknamed *Hallelujah*.

"Ain't ye feared yer lad Roy'll be gittin' idees or suthin' f'm the gals over thar?" asked an old trapper who had come on board for a "nip an' a tell."

"Figger he mought," said Bean, "but the younger he larns them sort o' wimming is mos'ly varmints the quicker he'll git shet of 'em.— 'Sides thet, best time fer 'im to larn is naow, with all them Methodies tother side."

"Saounds like sense," agreed the trapper, spitting over the rail. "How 's traps?"

"Pore."

"Prices?"

"Wuss."

"Yer furs git down river good?"

"Naw. Injuns."

"I don't think so," said Holdfast with quiet assurance.

"Haow ye figger, then?"

"River-pirates and trace-bandits—painted like Indians. If the pirates don't get your furs going down, .hen the bandits get your money on

329

the way back. The whites take the money or the furs and lay all the blame on the Indians."

"H'm. Suthin' teh chaw on thar.—But course, iffen ye're right, then thet looks like they war a plan to 't—an' a planner."

"Yes, so it does."

"Wal, course I dunno nothin' 'baout hit, but oncet, years back, I met up with a feller ben tuk by a river-pirate he called 'Black Bill,' 'cause he hed a beard, whut's oncommon fer Injuns. An' this yar feller he figgered ez Bill got orders from aoutside. Some Injun runner 'd come in with a letter fer 'im an' Bill he 'd set readin' it close up agin the fire, so 's it 'd look like he 'd burn the paper. An' arter readin' it thetaway, why then he'd know whut boats fer to lay fer."

"Mebbe Bill war short-sighted," said Bean; "but pirates mos'ly ain't.—An' whar ye cal'late a planner the likes o' thet would hold out, now?"

The old trapper rose and spat again over the rail. "Wal," said he, "'course they's allus Natchez-under-the-Bluff. Reg'lar den o' sarpints, thet 'ar."

As it moved down the River the fleet grew and grew. At New Madrid the people of two boats stayed to settle on the land, but three broadhorns came in at the Hatchie, loaded with hemp and flour. Little by little a floating town was formed. A tinsmith from Pittsburgh sold everything that could be made of tin. A blacksmith, also from Pittsburgh, sold axes, scythes, and iron tools. He shod horses at every riverside town. A kitchen-boat cooked meals for the single men of the fleet. Swine were butchered, cows milked, calves born, and game of many kinds was brought aboard by the hunters ranging the banks. Fresh vegetables taken in exchange for goods from the east were piled in heaps on the decks.

Early in the evenings, when the boats had been nosed in and tied along the bank, people went paying calls. The broad-horns and keelers lay so close together that an active man could sometimes go from end to end of the line by stepping or leaping from craft to craft. Such a man would be able in such a journey to find representatives of almost every class, race, dialect, stripe of opinion, or trait of character that America contained. He could hear yarns and legends from the Penobscot mingling with tales brought down by fur-traders from the upper Yellowstone. Indian myths of lost and forgotten gods were exchanged for Saints' Lives drawn up from the Christian and Oriental past. Crime and vice were huddled together with virtue, even with holiness. Filthy songs interrupted hymns, and curses were heard in the midst of prayers.

Many motives, plans, and purposes had brought these many people to their fortuitous association. For the most part they had never met before, and would never see one another again. Yet now for a few days of drifting together and during these few nights of dance, song, prayer, and story-telling, they had so much in common that their differences seemed of little account. Fame or obscurity, poverty or wealth, learning or ignorance, refinement or vulgarity—such merely eastern or foreign discriminations meant little to them while they shared the vast largess of the plains and the steady downward impulse of the River.

Under the songs they sang and the cry of the fiddles and flutes there was always the drone of the River. To the lover, the whore, the gambler, the trapper, the priest, and the merchant it said over and over the same not quite comprehensible thing. Late at night, when the fires on the deck-house roofs had dwindled and the fiddles were put away, the mysterious whisper of waves and low gurglings along the bank were more distinctly heard. At such times those who listened intently could almost understand. Lying so close to the heart of the continent and borne on the pulse of its midmost artery, they came by their different ways to the firm realization that the River was indefeasibly their own, to have and to hold.

Almost anywhere beside the fires in the evening one might learn that the Father of Waters was a messenger carrying news. He took tidings of the mountains to the sea. He told in Natchez and New Orleans what had been done and said and surmised in Pittsburgh and among the Sioux and Blackfeet. Or those who floated on his bosom at any rate did so at night, under the stars, often speaking with a wild grandeur of utterance and a splendor of fancy befitting the time and the place. Tales of long-hunters, old winterers, keelers and broad-horn men, sharp-shooters and Indian fighters, having begun with a few bare facts, soon ballooned and soared away into myth like the ancient tales of Woden and Heracles. Hero-worshippers one and all, these people meant to mar no man's tale in the telling. On other occasions and with regard to men of their own stature they were as subject to spite and envy as human nature allows; but concerning their champions, the demi-gods of their western world, they spoke the truth as they felt it, adorned with all the embellishments of a generous and undisciplined imagination.

Here the greater engrossed the lesser fame, transforming its very nature. In his nightly visits from boat to boat Russell Bean heard the story of the Jonesboro fire in several equally incorrect versions, all of which made him the villain and Jackson the hero of the piece. Popular legend was now asserting that Andrew Jackson had led the Nick-a-Jack expedition, slain the Tharpes, saved Perthy, routed the river-pirates, and conducted the obsequies of The Breath. The only important deed generally attributed to Sleeping Bear in that series of events was the eating, whole and raw, of Alec McGillivray's dead body. Moreover, it was widely believed that Jackson knew where or what or who The Knife was, and that he would soon cleanse Western Waters of his or her or its evil presence.

Yet the events in which Andrew Jackson had really played some part were not neglected in the rapid growth of his saga. The River was rife with tales of his truculence in the court-room, his browbeatings of witnesses, council, and judges. It was said that he had never lost a case, although he was often quite ignorant of the points of law involved. His summary snatching of his wife away from her former husband, his several brushes with Jack Sevier in which the Governor always came out second-best, his caning of young Thomas Swan, and his fatal duel with the crack-shot Charles Dickinson, provided matter for endless narration and debate. Already he was a central theme of eloquence, of creative imagination, of patriotic prophecy, and even of a strange new kind of frontier scholarship in which a lordly contempt for the actual facts went together with the power of penetration to essences. Andrew Jackson was already the eponymous hero of a huge, inchoate coarse-grained epic, never to be written down, which grew and shifted and changed every night by the fires on the deck-house tops while the stars that remembered Samson and Odysseus gazed tolerantly down and the ancient River went chuckling by.

The one event, however, which had done most of all to make Jackson a popular hero, setting him above all rivals as a master of fate and fortune, was the famous race at Clover Bottom between his tall bay Truxtun and Captain Edwin's horse Plowboy. "I was daown thar in Truxtun's stable m'self," Bean and Holdfast heard a river-man say one night, "jest afore the race. I went to look Truxtun over, an' thet 'ar off hind leg o' his'n did look consumed bad. Hit looked bad to Andy too, I reckon, when he come in. Never seed 'im so daown in the dumps. But d' ye know whut thet man did? He tuk one long sad squint at thet 'ar laig an' then he gits up an' looks Truxtun squar in the eye an' sezee: 'Naow lookee hyar, Truxtun! All o' my friends an' backers are a-sayin' we hain't got a chancet. They say we oughteh pull aout an' pay the forfeit. Wal, naow, thet's six hunnerd dollars, an' fack is I hain't got it. Iffen we win today, thar's three thousan' fer us from the wager an' mebbe twicet ez much more from the side bets. Iffen we lose, I go to jail fer all the debts I owe. Git it? Unnerstan' me? I go to jail, Truxtun.

" 'Naow I ben an' looked thet Plowboy over,' says Andy, talkin' straight hoss-talk to thet 'ar stallion an' lookin' 'im squar in the eye. 'He's a good hoss, but not so good ez you be. No sir, even with yer bad laig he ain't so good by a damn sight. He's two year older 'n you, an' he'll be carryin' six paound more weight. Don't fergit that. Them paounds an' them years is a-goin' to caount 'long toward the end o' the second mile,' sezee. 'An' 'nother thing don't ye go an' fergit is this-heer: 't war Diomed got yeh aouten Nancy Coleman, an' they ain't a hoss better sired an' dammed in the hull cussed world. Naow course we-uns both on us know ye're a-goin' to win, but I jest thunk I'd drap raound an' tell yeh 'baouten hit so's they won't be no mistake. Fack is, we gotter win, Truxtun. We *gotter*!'

"Then Andy he didn't say nothin' more but jest looked squar into Truxtun's eyes a two-three seconds so's a chile onborned c'd 'a' seen he was puttin' a spell on 'im.—An' shore 'nough, be damned iffen thet 'ar hoss with the swole-up laig an' a shoe he went an' twisted in the middle o' the heat didn't come a-prancin' home sixty good yards aout in front o' Plowboy!—I do b'lieve th' ain't nothin' c'n stop thet Andy when he wants suthin' bad 'nough, even when 't ain't poss'ble."

The spire of a church, washed in moonlight, pointed up from Natchez-on-the-Bluff. Utterly pure, withdrawn, and other-worldly it looked, as though the religion it represented were not for common and sinful men. Gazing up at it from the deck-house of the *Pride*, Holdfast recalled the graceful mansions of the upper town, their lordly white pillars and trellised verandahs. He remembered the fragrance of southern blossoms that wandered all day and night through the quiet streets.

Some ghost of that redolence strayed or sank, now and then, into the lower town, to mingle with the stench of things decaying and foul, but the moonlight held aloof. Few lights of any kind were showing in the hovels and huts dimly huddled on the mud between the bluff and the water, and those that could be seen were mostly red. From the

333

twisting alleys and lanes came a wild confusion of noises—bawdy songs in three languages, shrill female laughter and shrieks, shouts of drunken men, and the squeal of fiddles.

Nearly all the men of the fleet had gone into the lower town for a night's carouse. The other boats of the fleet, more than sixty in number, lay unseen and silent on either side of the deck-house where Holdfast lay, wrapped in his blanket. Except for young Roy, asleep below, he was alone on the keeler.

Only two hundred feet of precipitous bluff separated the beauty and peace of the upper town from the lust, squalor, and darkness below. Inevitably, in such a place, confronted by so perfect a symbol of good and evil in their everlasting juxtaposition, Holdfast's thoughts slipped back into their old accustomed paths. But those paths, he had long since learned, led only to a torment of the mind. He was striving to think of other things—of Four Winds Farm, now so far away not only in miles but also in the years, and of the happy strenuous months he had spent with Meriwether Lewis, Captain Clark, Russell Bean, and many other good companions on an expedition up the Missouri, down the wild Columbia, and on to the stormy tides of the Pacific.

"Hullo! Boat!" called a thick, drunken voice from forty feet off toward the town.

Holdfast sat up and stared into the dark. He could just make out a figure lurching about in the mud near the landing. He thought it might be some deck-hand trying to find his way back.

"Well?" said he.

"Got fire-water?"

"You've had enough."

"Huh! Whar Knife?"

"What's that you say?" said Holdfast, on his feet now and leaning over the side.

"Want fire-water."

"Come aboard, and we'll talk it over."

"No want talk. Want . . . want fire-water."

Holdfast helped the drunken man up the plank, saying *"To yits kist Muskogee?"*

"Annee Muskogee, ngkah. Creek, yes. I run strong."

"Ngkah, annee hee-tse-ta," Holdfast replied with an ironic smile, seeing that his guest could hardly stand upright.

"I damn big runner. Got letter for Knife. Whar Knife?"

So here it was again. For years The Knife had been lying still, with

334

the blood on it slowly corroding; but now . . . Holdfast's heart was pounding. Somehow he must get a look at whatever message the fellow carried.

"*Chee-mee lit-ke-ta awo-lee fo-tso, ngkah*—you run a race with a duck, yes!" said he with a derisive laugh.

Greatly insulted, the Creek plunged his hand into his pouch and brought out something dimly white. This he waved in Holdfast's face. "*Slof-ka!* For The Knife!" he shouted. "I damn big runner."

"You are a drunken, lying old woman, and you make too much noise. I'll not believe you until I read the letter myself."

The runner hesitated—and yet he did want another drink. At length he said, in a tone of crafty interrogation, "Fire-water?"

"Well, yes, I suppose so. Come along."

A minute later, in the keeler's kitchen, Holdfast held a brimming cup of corn-whisky toward the Creek. "Now," said he, "let's see that letter."

The runner pulled it from his pouch with one hand and took the cup with the other. He gulped down the contents. "Huh! Good!" he grunted, and rubbed his stomach with satisfaction.

There was no envelope, and no address. Lifting the kitchen-lantern to read, Holdfast found only a list of indigo-prices in New Orleans, apparently written by some merchant to an unknown planter in Natchez.

"You come far?" he asked, looking sharply up.

"Nawlins."

"How long?"

"T'ree day an' night. Damn big runner."

But why should a man run so fast and so far with such a message? Did it seem likely that The Knife had settled down as a peaceful planter of indigo? Of course this message might be written in a secret cipher, importing something quite different. And then again . . .

Holdfast set the lantern down and stood for a few moments thinking. He was trying to recall just what a certain old trapper had said, somewhere up the River, about a river-pirate to whom Indian runners used to bring messages. He would read those messages . . . he would read them . . . yes, he would read them "right close up agin the fire."—And that would mean, of course, that they had been written in an invisible ink.

The runner had slumped into the only chair the kitchen held, and was now drowsing off. Holdfast looked at him closely. Would another cup of whisky . . . ? Well, no. It was not needed. Then he said, going over and laying his hand on the man's shoulder: "You must be tired, my friend. Come! I'll show you a bed where you can sleep all night."

In a few minutes Holdfast was holding the letter above the fire in the kitchen-stove. Between the lines of black ink new words, unseen before but now slowly emerging in some pale brown fluid, came pushing forth. It was addressed to "Sir John Sherbrook, Governor of Canada," and its only signature was a crude drawing of a knife with a long wavy blade.

Written by The Knife! And yet the Creek runner, too drunk to lie with any plausibility, had said that he had brought it from New Orleans, and he had wanted to deliver it to The Knife, personally, in Natchez.

Completely mystified, but with his heart pounding again, Holdfast began on the message itself as it stood forth more clearly, moment by moment, in the heat of the fire. "New Orleans and Louisiana," he read, "are now fruit ripe for the picking . . ."

"Boat, there!" called a voice from the river-bank.

After a momentary hesitation Holdfast blew out the lantern, stuffed the letter inside his hunting-shirt, and stepped out on deck.

A thin segment of silver was showing, he saw, at the edge of the bluff above. In another minute he would be standing in the light of the moon. Yet he could see nothing of the man who had called him.

"What do you want?"

"I came down to ask," said a clear but quiet voice from some distance, "whether you have happened to see an Injun prowling about down here."

Holdfast vaguely felt that he had heard that voice before. But where? When?

"Indians are numerous in these parts, stranger."

"Well, say a drunken Injun."

"Even that description is not very distinguishing, I'm sorry to say."

"You don't seem to want to answer my question."

"I speak more freely when I can see the person I'm talking to."

"I can't find the way to you through the mud."

"But at least you can tell me why you came here."

"Why, the fact is, the people at the tavern close by have sent up to my house on the bluff to say that an Injun, rather intoxicated, was

336

looking for—ah—an acquaintance of mine. That acquaintance is now out of town, and I thought I might do him a service by coming down to see what is wanted."

Yes, that voice had once, long ago, been familiar.

Holdfast strode forward, leapt upon the deck-house, and peered into the dark. The light of the full moon shone upon his head and shoulders. Holdfast could faintly discern a figure, a darker spot of darkness against the dark, standing some forty feet away.

"There *has* been a drunken Indian down here tonight," he said, "and he has been making inquiries.—Won't you come nearer?"

No answer.

"There's a landing here, you know, by which you can come right up to the boat.—I have something to tell you which might interest your acquaintance.—It is something about The Knife."

But the figure was moving swiftly away. There would be no use in trying to follow it through those slimy and intricate runways of the night.

"I have a letter for your friend, The Knife. You can read it here on the boat."

The only answer was a distant sound of boots squelching in mud.

After a moment's hesitation, Holdfast returned to the stove in the kitchen, still wondering where and when he had heard that voice before. Once more he held the letter brought from New Orleans in such a press of haste, and this time he read it to the end:

To Sir John Sherbrook, Governor of Canada:

New Orleans and Louisiana are now fruit ripe for the picking. There is a rumor here of a British attack coming from the sea, but this does us no harm as they have never dreamed of a second attack at the same time from the British in Canada so taking us both in the front and rear at the same time. It has caused all available men to be enlisted for the defense of the city and I command these men. I can promise you, sir, that His Majesty's forces will have no trouble with what some people call my army. I have encamped them in a fever-ridden swamp called Terre aux Bœufs. My contractor supplies them, sparingly, with rancid pork, weeviled bread, and kill-devil whisky. Their only water is from the river which they drink below New Orleans. They have no uniforms but rags, no bedding but full of vermin, no medicine but bad whisky, and no shelter but holes in the ground. After a month here one third of my command is now either dead or shortly expecting that

337

mercy. Our gracious King could not desire a better preparation for the advent of His Majesty's troops and for the capture of the city, the river, the whole country. All is in readiness and I advise send troops and ships at once by river and sea.

Yours to command,

Mid-morning sunshine had changed the water, immensely widened now, into a dazzling metal. Far and far away the low banks were. The fleet, though actually augmented by many recent additions, looked tiny and negligible as it floated round the final bends of the River's magnificent course.

Russell Bean, busy in the rifle-shop at the forward end of the *Pride*, was singing to himself:

> How wonderful, how glorious, how marvelous I am!
> How wonderful it is to be me!
> I think I am the finest man in all this wondrous land,
> Why sartinly I'm positive I be!

He was putting the last touches to the great rifle at which he had been working, between his many other jobs, ever since the *Pride* had left Nashville. To the brass lids of the tallow-box and the flint-box in the butt he gave a final polish. Once more he rubbed the front-sight, or bead, made of Carolina gold, as though he had not rubbed it a hundred times before. He examined the lock of Connecticut iron with care, adding a drop or two more of bear-oil with a blue-jay's feather. He lifted the curved butt to his shoulder and squinted along the barrel as though aiming at some distant mark. Two or three times he leaned the rifle in a corner and walked away from it, but only to return and oil or rub it again. He was acting like a meticulous writer of prose or verse who tries over and over upon the ear some single sentence of his own creation, delighting in subtleties of rhythm and tone which no one else, he feels sure, will ever recognize, and yet thinking that one more hour of toil might perhaps make it still better. And also he was acting very like a man who puts off a painful task by pretending to himself that he has other and more pressing duties.

At last, however, he set his jaw firmly, grasped the weapon as though he feared it might try to escape, and climbed to the roof of the deck-

338

house where Holdfast was sitting, plunged in thought.

"Wal, thar," Bean said with unaccustomed gruffness. "Cal'late ye're the biggest an' best damn shot in Western Waters, an' so thar's a rifle-gun to match yeh. Take it, an'—an'—an'—*receive* it."

Holdfast got to his feet. "But . . . But Russ!" was all he found to say.

"Yeah. Weighs forty paound. Too gawdam heavy fer any other man in 'Meriky. Yes, an' too gawdam good, iffen I do say so. An' so she's yourn. See 'f ye like her. Iffen ye don't—wal, chuck her overboard."

Holdfast saw at once that here was no accidental gift. It was clear that Bean had made this rifle for him alone, planning it for him ever since he had beaten out the first scab of iron for the octagon barrel back there on the Cumberland. The lid of the tallow-box was a strip of shining brass roughly carved to the shape of a bear, asleep, with head on paws. An inlaid thread of gold on the flattened top of the barrel spelled the name *"Nusi-Nita"*—Choctaw for "Sleeping Bear." And then too, let into the stock of curly maple, and also done in gold, there was the rifle's name, the name of his old smooth-bored "murtherer," the name of that Other One, the Mischief-Maker, "Hobbomok."

Holdfast turned the rifle over and over in his hands. He glanced into Bean's eyes and then, swiftly, away. Here was the best of Russell Bean himself, together with a finished skill got by many years of learning and practice. Here was a gift that one man could make to another, made out of the giver's hand, head, heart, and marrow. Therefore it was right that the rifle was signed, as a poem or a picture might be, with the maker's name—"R. Bean."

About six feet and a half long it would be, this new companion. A rifle would keep a man from starving and protect him from his enemies. It would go with him through the wilderness many a darksome night and dreary day. Other friends might grow cold or die; women had to be left behind; dogs got lost or were killed; but a rifle never tired of a man's company, never quarreled with either his words or his silences, and it could be buried with him at the end of the trace.

"Thanks, Russ!" said Holdfast, grasping his friend's hand.

"Aw hell! 'T ain't nothin' to whut . . ."

And then, to the huge relief of them both, they heard sudden cries from the boats on either side: "Hallelujah!" . . . "Fire an' brimstun!" . . . "Hit's the City o' Sin, boys!" . . . "Hit's Nawlins!"

A filmy cluster of domes and towers, lying so low that they seemed to

339

be floating on the dazzle, and dim with distance as though they had just emerged out of dream, could be discerned far off to the south and east.

All the voyagers in the fleet, numbering now well over a thousand persons, crowded forward and stood gazing. Thus an hour passed, while the city grew and grew.

Built lower than the water-level and protected by its embankments, New Orleans began to look as though it were hiding behind a delicate tracery of masts and spars. The shipping of all the world, it seemed, must be tied up at those many finger-like wharves. Nearest at hand was the "American Section," where hundreds of broad-horns and keelers were already wedged in together to form a floating city of their own.

Another hour went by, filled with the bustle of preparation for landing.

"Hillo, the fleet!" yelled a man, still tiny in the distance, from the roof of a flat-boat. He appeared to be waving his shirt. His call spread out like oil over miles of water.

"Hillo thar, Nawlins!" went back from a score of throats.

Several minutes of silent floating passed before he was heard again: "Whut ye got?"

The answer was returned in stentorian tones from boat after boat. "Beef, pork," said one. "Indigo an' pervisions," another replied. And then came a medley of offerings: "Snake" . . . "rifle-guns" . . . "fancy ladies" . . . "babies" . . . "salvation" . . . "kebbidge an' pertaties" . . . "clean salt" . . .

For some time he seemed to be thinking this over, but his final decision was emphatic: "Ye won't sell none of 'em hyar."

"Why not? Wha's matter? Yaller fever?"

"Naw. Embargo. Market's deader 'n I wish my mother-in-law."

"Embargo? What's it feel like, Mister?"

The reply could be distinctly heard. "Feels like starvation, thet's whut. —No ships comin' in or goin' aout. Consekence, no trade. Pris'dent Jeff'son's idee."

"Haow 'd he think up an idee like thet un?"

"Says England's ben stealin' our sailors an' France our ships. This-heer embargo 'll punish 'em both, he says."

"Wal," said a voice from another tied-up flat-boat, "I hain't heered 'em yelp none."

"Ye won't, nuther," asserted a third. "Gives their own trade a boost."

"Whut Jeff wants," a fourth voice contributed, "is to smash the Fed-

340

erals back east. Federals owns all the ships, so the Jeffs are aout to make them ships rot in harbor."

"An' whut 'baouten *us*?" called out an energetic, bald-headed little man in the bow of the foremost flat-boat now approaching the bank. There was a tone of unmistakable indignation in his squeaky voice.

"Hell, Mister, nobody ain't never heered nothin' 'baout *us,* way aout hyar. We-uns don't b'long to 'Meriky."

"Is thet *so*! Then whut *is* 'Meriky iffen we hain't hit?"

"Hain't ye heered yit? Why, 'Meriky's jes' a lot o' rich ole ship-owners back east, lot o' rich ole slave-owners daown saouth, an' 'nother lot o' bankers an' Jeffersons clawin' each other's eyes aout—an' success to 'em both—up to Washin'ton."

"Then whut ye call *us,* Mister?"

"Say, li'l feller, we hain't got no more time to waste on a feller ez igner'nt ez ye be. Same time, I'll jes' take an' tell yeh.—*Us* is jes' *folks.*"

"Yeah. Reckon ye're right thar, pardner. But whut we gotter do aout hyar is to git us a Pris'dent whut's jes' folks too; an' then, by the 'Tarnal, ez Andy Jackson says, we'll let the Beni'ted States o' 'Meriky know ez we're *on arth,* an meanter *stay* hyar!"

"Hooray! Thet's a-sayin' hit! Good fer you, li'l feller," went up in chorus from the boats already tied up along the landing and also from the incoming fleet.

PLEASURE PARTY

"Ye don't reely eggspeck a Gin'ral to meet us in a low-down groggery likes o' this un, do ye, Holdfast?"

"He said he would."

"But he's a damn liar."

"Yes, I know. On the other hand, he does want to get that letter back."

"Whut he say 'baout the letter?"

"He said some enemy of his must have forged it. Said he'd never heard of The Knife."

"Nachally.—Tell 'im how ye got it?"

"Yes; and about some one coming down to find the Creek messenger."

"Tell 'im Meriwether Lewis was a-goin' to take it back east to Jefferson?"

"Certainly not.—And besides, Russ, I don't feel easy even yet about letting Governor Lewis carry it on such a journey. It's too dangerous."

"No more fer him 'n fer you."

"Oh, well, but . . ."

"Main thing is to make Jefferson see this hyar Gin'ral's a stinkin' traitor."

"On that matter the letter speaks for itself, whoever carries it."

" 'T ain't signed, 'cep'n' by thet 'ar mark."

"Well, then, I know as much about The Knife as Meriwether Lewis—and more."

"Mebbe. But Lewis is an ole friend o' Jefferson's."

"So am I."

"He useter be Jefferson's sec'tary or suthin'. He's an officer in the army, an' this hyar's army business. He's Gov'ner o' North Louisiana Terr'tory. Ye're jes'—wal—Sleepin' B'ar."

"Oh, well . . . But I don't like it."

"Thet don't sinnify. Ye gotter larn to think 'baout suthin' but jes' savin' other folkses' hides."

"What are *you* thinking about, Russ?"

"Don't change the subjick."

As Bean's glance swept round the half-lighted filthy room in which the presence of evil amounted to a stench, Holdfast saw a swift change in his friend's eyes, face, and jaw. "Not but whut," Bean said, leaning forward and speaking softly—"not but whut thet 'ar varmint would give a lot to git his letter back."

"No. That's why he will come here—or send someone."

"Yeah. Naow ye're a-gittin' at it. Ye cain't see 'em wi' yer back turned, but he *hez* sent a passel o' rats leakin' in through the back door—by the looks all friends o' his'n."

"Well, don't stare at them."

"Why not? They're a-starin' at us, I c'n tell yeh—all thutty of 'em givin' us the very sad eye. The wimming's skyhootin', nobuddy's drinkin', an' pistols an' knives is loosenin' up all over the place."

"If there's going to be trouble," said Holdfast, puffing slowly and thoughtfully at his pipe, "let them start it."

"Wal, but iffen we wait we'll be dead afore we begin. We're trapped! They prob'ly got both doors guarded! An' not one damn keeler in the room!"

Holdfast went on puffing for a while. At last he said: "I saw a dozen keelers, as we came along, in that grog-shop across the alley.—And the Snag came in last night. He's with them."

"Whut say? The Snag!—Then whut in hell we waitin' fer?"

"Hold on to yourself, Russ."

"Now lookee hyar, Holdfast, thet's jest whar ye're allus wrong—allus holdin' on to yerself so damn tight ye cain't never git a good grip on snakes like Wilkinson an' choke 'em. Ye wanter set an' think things out whilst hell's a-bustin' loose all 'round yeh. But this time ye cain't do it. They ain't time fer it. Whut's more, I won't let yeh."

"Someone's bound to be badly hurt if we fight in here."

"Criminently!" Bean's voice rang out so that all the listening room could hear him. "They's 'baout thutty slant-eyed rats in hyar whut's a-goin' to hev their lights ripped aout an' splashed 'crost their greasy faces."

"Do you want to force a fight?"

"Sartin shore. Hit's aour only chancet."

"We have a right to risk our own lives, but—there's the letter."

"Only way o' savin' the letter is to fight fer it, now, an' hyar.—I know ye wanter fight ez much ez I do, but ye're afeared o' hurtin' somebody. Wal, I ain't!"

Holdfast continued to puff at his pipe of red stone.

"When I think o' them thousan's o' pore bastards a-dyin' down thar at Terre aux Bœufs," Bean went on, his voice steadily rising, "I *wanter* hurt somebody, bad. Yeah, an' iffen thet misbegotten belly-goin' bastard of a Wilkinson comes 'round hyar this arternoon, I'm goneter flay 'im alive an' peg his greasy hide out to dry!"

Bean raised his rifle from the corner and handed "Hobbomok" to Holdfast. "But by the looks," he said in a ringing voice, "we're a-goin' to hev a li'l pleasure party even afore he comes. Jes' take a look, will ye, Holdfast, at whut's crawled in hyar aouten the privies an' dumps an' sewers o' Nawlins.—My Gawd, whut friends thet Gin'ral Wilkinson hez got!"

Holdfast threw his left arm over the back of his chair, turned half way round, with "Hobbomok" snuggled inside the crook of his right arm, and surveyed the room. "Click . . . click!" went the pistol-cocks under the table-tops. Every eye was on him, and clearly no one wished him any good. He smiled, as though thinking of matters far-off and delightful. "Make for the door behind you when I give the word," he said to Bean in a low tone. "If they start shooting, throw up the table to take the bullets.—Now!"

The two men sprang to their feet at the same instant. Thirty pistols

343

were whipped out and up. Holdfast, as he came round, pulled the table over, and he and Bean dodged behind it. They held their fire while the pistols barked and blazed, but then, as the crowd rushed toward them both rifles spoke and the long heavy barrels went lunging out over the table's edge. They had the corner behind them and were near the door leading into the alley. Bean, his face streaming red from the slash of a thrown knife, rushed to the door for a second. "Kaintucks!" he yelled. "Hi! Keelers! Ya-e-e-e-e-e!"

An Italian in a red night-cap who seemed to be leading the band of ruffians gave the order now for another charge, but before it could form Holdfast and Bean hurled themselves into the mass. Bean was stopped and surrounded. Holdfast flailed his way back to the swinging door and called: "Kaintucks! Snag! Ya-e-e-e!"

Turning back, he saw that Bean was wielding a chair for a weapon, and also that several of the enemy were reloading. Using his long rifle to mow the way, he fought back to Bean's side and then, together with him, slowly retreated across the room toward the long high bar. He felt his left arm go numb. Bean too, he could see, had taken a pistol-shot or a knife-thrust in the shoulder. Matters were growing serious. Suddenly remembering an old trick, he tossed "Hobbomok" over the bar, caught up two men from the crowd, dashed the weapons from their hands, and held them up as screens. "Jump over!" he yelled to Bean, and Bean did manage to scramble over the bar without more hurt while the pistol-balls crashed among the bottles.

Holdfast felt the man in his left hand suddenly jerk. "Take this fellow," he called out, and tossed the body up on the bar.—That left arm could not be so badly hurt after all.—And then, steadily holding the other man between himself and the enemy, he sidled down the front of the bar to its farther end. Standing there, he caught his breath, summoned all his force, lifted the squirming captive above his head, and hurled him back into the crowd. The living missile swept a six-foot swath as it thudded down.

Behind the bar the floor was littered with glass from the shattered mirror, and slippery with rum, whisky, gin, and imported wines. The pistol-balls were making havoc in the shining array of bottles. Bean, reaching up from below, was snatching those that were left and hurling them out over the corpse.

"Slow down, there," Holdfast called to him in a gleeful voice. "We're running short of ammunition."

"Wal, we cain't load, an' they're shootin'!" Bean seized by the handle a bottle of Chianti encased in straw, and sent it hurtling out over the dead man. They could hear it explode.

"I like them Eyetalian wines," said he. "They do 'em up proper fer throwin'."

"Yes. I always have wondered what they were good for." And Holdfast threw three at once.

Bean glanced up along the ravished shelves. "But thet's 'bout all of 'em," he said, "an' so now question is . . ."

Holdfast snatched up "Hobbomok" from the floor. "Keep your hair on, Russ," he called. "I'm going out there."

"Like hell . . ."

But at that moment they heard through the swinging door a sudden trample and thud as of charging buffalo. The door banged open and in burst a fury of yells and bodies and milling fists. A huge harsh voice cut the clamor: "Scatter an' skyhoot an' skedaddle, fer this hyar is the Jedgement Day!"

"Ya-e-e-e-e! Kaintucks!" Bean shouted, standing up now.

Eight, ten, perhaps a dozen of them there were, stampeding across the room toward the twenty men huddling against the farther wall. A short man built like a bullet led them, yelling as he ran and still yelling as he splashed with feet and fists together into the foe. "Whoo-oop!" he called. "Hold me daown! I'm the eldest son o' Hurricane an' Earthquake! Don't let me evil passions rise!"

"Ya-e-e-e-e! Go it, Snag!" Bean shouted, vaulting the bar into the mellay. Holdfast was already there.

"I'm twin brother o' Sudden Death, an' Slaughter's my fav'rite sister!"

"Le's take their stinkin' taown apart an' hang it aout to air!" yelled someone from up the River.

"Lift their ha'r!"

"Gouge 'em!"

"No gouging, boys!" called the voice of Holdfast.

It was man against man now. There was no time for loading of pistols. Even knives and tomahawks were at a disadvantage. Holdfast and Bean, after a few shrewd strokes with their rifle-barrels, went to work with bare hands.

"Whoo-oop! Gin'ral massacree is my trade. When I drink, herds die of draought. Whar I've et, famine stalks behind me through the land!"

"Thet's the talk, Snag. Talk to 'em, Snag. Tell 'em who ye be!"

"Naw. They'd drop daid. I wanter fight 'em."

"Sail in then, dead-body-eater!"

345

For a few moments the Snag and Holdfast were fighting back to back. "Hear tell ye et McGillivray?"

"No!" said Holdfast.

"Spat 'im aout, eh? Don' blame yeh. Helluva taste them half-breeds got!" And the Snag, having quieted his antagonist, moved on, yelling his battle-cry: "Don't git me het up! *Don't* let me come to the bile!"

But those of the aggressors who were still on their feet soon made signs of surrender, leaving only one major combat still in progress. Bill Pillows, a raw-boned keeler from Tennessee, had the night-capped Italian under him on the floor and was doing something violent to his face. Several other keelers gathered round as soon as they were disengaged and looked on with interest.

At length the Italian gave one agonized scream and covered his face with his hands. Pillows straightened up from his work, looked about him for approval, and then spat a mouthful of bloody gristle on the floor.

"Hit don't seem wuth all thet 'ar trouble, come to reely look at hit," drawled a voice.

"Hit don't, hey?" said Pillows. "Wal, I hain't a-praisin' it up none m'self, but thar 't is fer any feller whut wants hit." And with that he brought his outspread thumbs down upon the Italian's eyes as though to begin fresh operations.

"Santa Maria! Not my eyes!--I tell! I tell Wilkinson! I tell The Knife!"

"What's that?" said Holdfast sternly, pulling Pillows off. "Do you admit that Wilkinson set you fellows on to attack us here today?—Tell the truth, and we'll spare your eyes."

"*Si, si! Veramente!*"

"For how much?"

"One-a hunnerd dollar for each heads of you."

Holdfast turned away in disgust.

"Ye've told the truth fer oncet, an' so ye c'n keep yer eyes of a rat," said Bean. "An hyar," he added, kicking the bit of gristle across the floor. "This nose o' yourn 'll stay aout of other folkses' business from naow on, I reckon. Take it back to Gin'ral Wilkinson an' make 'im a *present* of it, *with* the complements o' Bill Pillows an' Russell Bean an' Mr. Holdfast Gaines."

346

BROTHERHOOD OF THE GULF

The three guests from up-river were feeling ill at ease as they sat, some days later, on the wide breeze-swept verandah of a rambling house near the mouth of the Mississippi. Even Russell Bean was finding his natural loquacity somewhat restrained by the strangeness of the place and the occasion. Holdfast Gaines and the Snag were saying almost nothing as they ate their way through an interminable dinner of viands they could not even name. Their long voyage down from New Orleans, in a dug-out canoe paddled by men who called themselves "shrimpers," had been more and more surprising as it took them through a maze of bayous and estuaries alive with alligators, turtles, and long-legged waders. Strange, too, was this glistering island of Grand Terre, mostly composed of crumbled white sea-shells. The aquamarine of the Gulf, like a vast misted jewel as they gazed out upon it from the shadowy porch, looked strange to the point of incredibility. The palmetto leaves sibilantly brushing their fingers together in the breeze from the Gulf were utterly unlike the clumped or pendulous foliage of their northern forests. Never before had they seen such a house as this, such a glitter of table-ware, such a repast. The sumptuous quadroon woman, with lingering liquid-amber eyes, whom they saw for a glimpse now and then through the doors that were also windows, added a new theme of speculation, especially for Russell Bean. So did the waiting-man in dark red plush and the cook, in white, speaking French, who came out to talk about the dinner with the host in a tone of easy and cooperative familiarity.

But strangest of all was the host himself, who had invited them down here ostensibly out of gratitude for the sound thrashing they had administered a few days before to a band of local ruffians. No one of the trio felt that he deserved any thanks whatever for his part in a scuffle which he had so thoroughly enjoyed for its own sake. Was not this suave and picturesque foreigner—known to his friends as a smuggling slave-trader, and suspected by his foes of piracy—somewhat too effusive, even lavish, in his acknowledgement?

Where this man came from no one pretended to know. Half lands-man and half a sailor, obviously rich but with no visible means of support, wild and lawless in a remarkably cultivated way, brutal perhaps and yet certainly refined, his very frankness and friendliness of demeanor bred a question in the minds of his three guests: what was he holding back? Wide and various as their social experience had been, here, they saw, was a man who did not fit into any of the familiar categories. Strongly disposed as they all were to respect the secrets of every man's past, and to grant him the full swing of his idiosyncrasy, here was a man to think about, to be cautious with, and to watch. The deepening mystery of The Knife, its nature and identity and hidden working, was uppermost in the thoughts of all three guests as they watched and listened to Jean Lafitte.

Even if they had been able to ignore his garish attire—his shirt of green silk, his ruby ring, his black velvet breeches, his tall boots of supple bleached leather—there would still have been his foreign look, his long and wavy black hair, his mustache, and his eyes that somehow managed to be at once cautious and bold. Tall, lithe, with long sinewy hands, he looked, at thirty, in the prime of his physical strength. One guessed that he would be an admirable swordsman, and also one felt sure that his sultry good looks would do considerable execution among the Creole and quadroon women of the region.

As though he also were uneasy, Lafitte talked too much—or so it seemed to the men from the River and the forest—in an English by no means easy to follow and liberally interlarded with a barely comprehensible French. His trick of closing his left eye, slowly, in the middle of a sentence which apparently contained no confidential hint or innuendo, was at least disconcerting. His courtesy seemed excessive, and his humor too elaborate. Was he laughing at his guests, perhaps?—The doubt kept them quiet and on their guard.

"Messieurs, you mek to me ze grettest honneur de ma vie," Lafitte was saying. "Men famous, conquerors, champions, you entair my poor house, you eat my humble food, you . . . "

"Food's good 'nough fer's I see," said the Snag with his mouth full, scooping up his fourth helping of gumbo.

"Ah, you excite wiz joy, Monsieur le Snag, at zese kind words. Mais, Messieurs, je vous—I owe you truly for a lesson sorely needed to a crew on Barataria violent, stupeed, foul as ze peeg. It iss ze lesson zey weel forget not ver' damn queek. For when le Capitaine shall sink up somesing hereaftair men weel say, 'Aha, but zere iss lacking to heem ze nose,' and men weel laugh. Because a man may be grett capitaine, Messieurs, wizout ze brain, wizout ze heart, but—wizout ze nose? Mais non!"

Jean Lafitte's smile was becoming to his darkly handsome face. One did not so much distrust him for his little black mustache, waxed at the ends, when one saw him smile.

"And already," he went on, "ze Capitaine iss called 'Le Nez Mangé,' or what you say 'Ze Eaten Nose.' Already he iss lying his nose has been lost by ze saber-cut honorable; but, Messieurs, it is now one week and ze mark of ze teeth are yet veeseeble. Oh, Messieurs, je vous —I owe you truly!"

"Y' oughter hed Bill Pillows daown hyar," the Snag suggested. "*He* chawed the nose."

"Oui. You haf ze problem indicated exactement. For when zere come report of your combat I return to my cook and tell: 'Here iss one who eats ze nose. Can we haf heem to dine?'

" 'Le nez humain?' say my cook to me.

" 'Oui.'

" 'Exclusivement?'

" 'En apparence.'

" 'Pas des légumes?'

" 'Je pense que non. No vegetables.'

" 'Un goût extraordinaire!' say my cook. 'Très recherché!'

" 'A rare taste, indeed—mais, can we haf heem?'

" 'Une semaine, vous dites, Monsieur?'

" 'One week from today,' I tell to him.

" 'Non, décidément! Eet ees too short,' say my cook, who has not well ze Engleesh. 'Geef me one month,' he say, 'for mek research pour les nez humains en quantité. Mais une semaine?—Non!' "

Jean Lafitte shrugged his shoulders and held out his hands. "And so," he concluded, "it is desolate in my heart today for ze company of Monsieur Bill Pillows, for whose appetite for ze nose I owe so truly."

He sipped his Madeira as though he were thoughtfully comparing it with some twenty other vintages, gazing out at the dazzling beach and the blue Gulf. He seemed to be expecting someone.

"Thisheer feller got his nose chawed off—ye call 'm Nay Manjey?" Bean asked at length.

"The same," said Lafitte, his luminous dark-brown eyes turning slowly toward the speaker.

"Give us to unnerstan' he ben hired to kill us by Gin'ral Wilkinson."

"Ah!" Lafitte exclaimed, suddenly alert, "You say so?"

"*He* say so—this Cap'n Manjey. Hunnerd dollars a head."

"From le Général Wilkinson?"

"The same," said Bean, who admired the phrase.

349

Lafitte sprang from his chair and paced to the end of the verandah and back. He pulled a long slender cheroot from his pocket and bit off the end with a jerk. "Ah," said he as though to himself, "il se trouve ici? Je me demande s'il m'appose le Gambi et le Nez Mangé. Peut-être que ces gens-là lui conviendront mieux que moi."—Then he returned to the table and looked down at Holdfast and Bean.

"Why iss it?" he asked.

"Dunno yet," Bean answered. "Mought a-thunk we knew too much 'bout how he's starvin' his army down 't Terre aux Bœufs."

"And ze rizzon why?"

"Ye got the idee, I reckon."

"Your beeg frien' does not mek remarks," said Lafitte, glancing respectfully at Holdfast.

"No; he don't talk much 'thout he's got summat to say."

"Eh, bien! Un trait honorable. Le silence is mark of grett man. Mais le Général Wilkinson he iss one to look at ver' damn close. Comprenez-vous?"

"I understand you," said Holdfast. "And have you ever heard of The Knife?"

Jean Lafitte hesitated, his eyes turning back to the Gulf. "Le silence," said he, "voilà une grande vertu!"

"And yet, like any other, it may be overdone. There is a time for silence and a time for speech."

There was a slight motion of the Frenchman's eye-lids. "I haf heard," said he, "it iss not for ze health to spik of Le Poignard."

He took his place again at the table.

"An' how 'bout all them other thutty we fit back in Nawlins?" Bean asked. "Were they Manjey's men, an' all hired by Wilkinson?"

"Probablement, Monsieur. Zey geef to us ze bad name. Damn queek zey geef to us ze name 'Pirates,' and zat weel be too much."

"Why d'ye let 'em in?" asked the Snag, hoisting a small fish to his mouth with a dextrous sweep of his knife.

Lafitte shrugged his shoulders. "Zey come," said he, "—ten crews of zem."

"From whar?" Bean asked.

"Seven seas, Monsieur. Pirates French, Spaneesh, Italian, Engleesh, Toork, Lascair, Américain—ze Briteesh haf drove zem out it iss one year from ze Indies of ze West, since when it iss tous les jours murder and war civeel in Barataria Bay."

As he spoke he swept a dark hand toward the water, and all four

350

men looked out for a moment at the cluster of little islands with their cottages and flowering gardens, at the schooners riding at anchor and the gigs and dinghies and long-boats pulling lazily back and forth. They heard the laughter of women and the cries of children at play.

"Purty!" the Snag ventured.

"Oui, Monsieur—en apparence. It iss ze home of simple fishermen for ze shrimp. Sometime when shrimp iss not good my men zey tek mebbe un bateau Spaneesh weeth slaves. What would you? To liff it is necessaire. In addition it is duty patriotique for all good honest privateers of Cartagena, which iss revolting to Spain. We haf what you say 'commissions' to privateer, which iss ver' damn different to ze work piratical."

Lafitte's three guests nodded polite agreement.

"But now come ze last efening zis damn pirate wiz ze eaten nose an ze ozzer pirate Gambi, who yet kip ze nose, wiz ze cutters of ze sroat of many names, and we talk a council—mon frère and Monsieur Dominique You and Monsieur Beluche and I wiz zem. We mek clear zose pirates kip hand off les vaisseaux Américains or get ze hell out. Some mek good promise, but ze Capitaines Gambi and Nez Mangé zey call us ze hypocreets and ze liars of many bad kinds, which iss intolerable. Zey employ to us ze very worst of ze language. Zen zey go home, but mek promise mek return zis day at noon wiz reply final.— Et maintenant, Messieurs, it is later zan one by ze clock."

"Mais ils arrivent, Jean! Zey come by ze plage ce moment!"

It was a short, powerful, broad-shouldered man, coming up the stairs toward the table. His light-colored hair, falling thick over a sun-tanned brow, gave him an outlandish look. His eyes were blue, frank, and fearless.

"Capitaine Dominique You," said Lafitte, rising, "we haf here mes amis les grands hommes Monsieur Gaines, Monsieur Bean, et Monsieur le Snag. Tous les trois, comme vous savez, sont hommes de la gloire."

The four men bowed.

"And haf zese pirates wiz zem brung zeir goddam crews?" Lafitte inquired.

"Oui, mon Capitaine. T'ree, four hunner'."

"Très bien! Our men—are zey ready?"

"Oui. Ils sont ici."

"Say to zem remain en arrière. Zis affair I weel to manage alone, seul, par moi-même, eef posseeble. Comprenez-vous?"

"Parfaitement."

351

But as the three guests looked out now at the crowd of revolters swaggering up the beach, they began to think that their host might have his hands more than full. From a distance, at any rate, those three hundred men looked dangerous. Their cutlasses, sabers, swords, knives, and hatchets flashed in the sun as they rolled along, keeping no order and most of them straddling as they walked. Many had three or four pistols in their belts. The shapes and hues of their garments, of their head-gear, and also the heavy sea-boots that some of them wore, made them look more formidable.

"Iffen thisheer Lafitte licks all them pirates alone," muttered the Snag, "it'll knock the spots offen thet li'l job we done las' week in Nawlins."

"Criminently," Bean agreed.

Holdfast reached for "Hobbomok."

It became evident, however, as the gangrel mob drew nearer, that a good half of their number were drunk. They had not the strength of disciplined, united, or even stoutly determined men. Apparently they had no leader. The red night-cap of Nez Mangé was wobbling from side to side at the rear. Nez Mangé was very drunk. A red rag covered most of his face.

—Yes, and it would help that a few of these men had been given a thorough trouncing within a week. The news of what had happened to those few must by this time have spread throughout the islands.

They were straggling to a halt now, some thirty feet from the verandah. A low mutter of voices, much of it obscenely abusive, showed that they were undecided and already half-cowed. They seemed to be trying to find a leader, or at least a spokesman.

Pierre Lafitte, a tall, heavy Frenchman, older than Jean, came out of the house and stood beside his brother on the verandah. Behind him came Captain Beluche and several others—all perfectly calm and heavily armed.

"See thet Eyetalian wi' the bandage an' silver ear-rings?" Bean whispered to Holdfast. "He's the knife-thrower that got me in the face back thar. They call 'im Gambi."

"Oh?"

"Yeah. Thet feller oughter hed a bellyful. I got him with a bottle, side o' the head."

Jean Lafitte, his back to the crowd, was talking quietly with Pierre and Beluche, examining his pistols in the meanwhile. When satisfied that they were ready for use he stuck them loosely into his belt, both on the right side, and turned round toward the uneasy crowd.

Standing on the topmost stair, he looked them over one by one until every member of the mob had felt the force of his eyes. Then he took his cheroot from his mouth, glanced at the end of it, and said, without turning round, "I want a light."

Pierre Lafitte covered with his hand a proud and affectionate smile. A black slave came from the kitchen with a glowing coal. Jean Lafitte puffed three or four times at his cheroot, took it in his left hand, and sauntered down the stairs. He moved slowly, deliberately, but with the supple and silken ease of a prowling panther. The stillness was intense.

"But my Gawd," Bean heard the Snag whispering, "thet ain't no way! Why 'n hell don't he *talk* to 'em? Ye kain't lick three hunner' jest smokin' a seegar."

At ten feet from the verandah and twenty from the front row of the crowd Lafitte stopped walking. He flicked an imaginary ash from his cheroot, and waited.

"Well?" said he, in a tone of mild surprise. And, although his back was to them, the men on the verandah were sure that his daunting eyes were once more ranging swiftly, as though stabbing, from face to face.

The only reply was a low sullen murmur.

They saw him return the cheroot to his mouth and then, with his left hand, pull a thick gold watch from its fob. His right hand, meanwhile, was fondling a pistol-butt.

"I like it," he said in a carrying voice, "to haf my guests arrive on ze time. You are now late, Messieurs, by one hour and minutes sree and twenty. By gar, zat iss late too much!" He paused while he put the watch back. "And eefen now," he thundered out with a sudden astonishing force, "you sons of ze feelthy beech haf not sought up one leetle word to say!"

Some of the faces were going foolish out there, and a few of them submissive—perhaps even admiring. The men were shifting from foot to foot. Most of them were still trying to look contemptuous, but they could not meet Lafitte's steady gaze. Voices of children at play were heard from a distance. A white gull swooped over the crowd with a plaintive cry. Seconds lagged by.

"My Gawd!" whispered the Snag. And then, "Mebbe *not* talkin' to 'em is a good way too."

A young giant lurched forward from beside the man with the silver ear-rings. He might be Gambi's lieutenant. In each hand he clutched a cocked pistol. One of them went off wild as he staggered up, the ball raising a shower of golden grains from the sand. Then he stood and swayed, trying to aim with the other pistol, belching foul words in French, English, and Italian.

Lafitte's pistol-hand moved like a lunging snake and the stream of obscenity ceased. The drunken giant leaned slowly forward, threw up both hands, and fell. His body twitched violently two or three times, as though to throw off a weight, and then lay still.

From the verandah a rifle-shot rang. The pistol that Gambi, back in the crowd, had aimed at Lafitte flew twirling from Gambi's reddening hand.

Once again the white gull swooped, screaming.

Pierre Lafitte, Dominique You, Beluche, the Snag, Russell Bean, and Holdfast Gaines walked down the stairs and stood on either side of Jean Lafitte. Holdfast was reloading "Hobbomok." Close behind the group, on both sides of the house, three or four hundred "simple fishermen for the shrimp" fingered their knives and waited.

The mob stood and stared, especially at the three Americans whom several of them had encountered, a week ago, in the tavern at New Orleans.

A white goat came round the corner of the house and looked at the crowd, its long narrow head cocked on one side in an attitude of tense interrogation.

Then all at once the crowd lost all semblance of cohesion and purpose. It melted down into a congeries of beaten individuals, most of whom had quite obviously found, and would henceforth follow, their master. The men went straggling and slouching away in different directions, many of them eventually coming to mingle with the fishermen beside the house, laughing and offering drinks around to indicate that nothing really serious had happened that should prevent good-fellowship among friends.

Only four of Gambi's crew shuffled forward and picked up the dead body by the arms and legs. They turned back. The head sagged. They shuffled back from the soft shelly sand to the hard. They went along the hard sand slowly, staggering, bowed by the weight of the dead giant, with knives and swords and sabers flashing fiercely in the sun.

"Mais when you do spik, Monsieur Gaines—aha! how ze pipple listen!"

Holdfast was polishing with his thumb the brazen image of a bear on his rifle-butt.

"We shall ineetiate Monsieur Holdfast Gaines—c'est a dire, 'l'Ours

354

Dormant'—into ze Brozzerhood of ze Gulf! Capitaine You, lift ze Barrel of Blood. Our champion weel tek his oath upon it!"

"On one condition, sir."

"And zat iss?"

"That you tell me all you know about The Knife."

"H'm.—Okeh."—And Lafitte drew Holdfast to one side.

"Probablement, je vous—Monsieur, I owe to you, I sink, ze life. Zerefore I say to you zat I haf conjectured it ees long time. Ziss Knife, ees he a man, ees it un vrai poignard, je ne le connais pas du tout. Mais ziss I say to you: it ees one—what you call?—symbole de la pouvoir et l'autorité mauvaise. Ziss man who iss ze Knife, ou peut-être qui l'a pour le temps en son possession—zat iss, who has it—he moves himself fréquemment from here to zere. Les Indiens zey obey zat man à la mort, Monsieur—to the death. Ils croient que le Poignard est le grande médicine. Zey carry what you call ze lettaires to ze Knife, and ze Knife advances zose lettaires by ze hand of ozzer messagers. When he say 'Keel zat man,' zat man ees so good as one cadavre. A se mêler des affaires du Poignard, c'est dangereux, Monsieur, extrêmement. L'en mention, même, n'est pas pour la santé. Eet ees not, you say, good for ze healt' to spick of heem.—En voilà assez, n'est ce pas?"

"You have told me little, Mr. Lafitte, beyond what I already knew. You have not yet spoken like a true brother. I want you to tell me how to find The Knife."

Lafitte pulled at the ends of his neat black mustache, and twirled them. For a moment he glanced up into the eyes of the great dark man beside him, finding that they were extremely earnest, determined, and by no means to be hoodwinked or deceived. A slight change in his expression showed that he was making a swift, perhaps an important decision. And then "En un mot, Monsieur l'Ours Dormant," he said, looking straight and steadily now into the eyes of his guest, "seek ze man—he hass many names and places—who bears a deep scar, long and white, sur le bras droit." Suiting the action to the words, he drew the fingers of his left hand from the crease of his right thumb up to the elbow.

"I thank you. I shall."

"Fort bien.—Et maintenant pour le baril de sang!"

THE BUSK AT COOSA

(July—1813)

Over in the cook-room of House of the Bear the women chattered all
night long. A man could not sleep for their chatter, even though he had
run and walked a hundred miles in the day and the night before. Let
him toss and turn as he might on his corn-husk bed, their voices—or
was it what they were saying?—held sleep away.

But no one, apparently, was sleeping tonight in the "old beloved
town" of Coosa. Perhaps everyone was too much excited at the prospect
of holding one more busk, after an interval of at least two generations,
in the half-ruined public square which many regarded as the sanctuary
of the Creek nation. Perhaps they were kept awake by the news that
Tecumseh, the Meteor, was coming—or, more probably, by their knowledge that the Beloved Woman of the Choctaws, daughter of Pushmataha, was here already. And then, too, the fact that Sleeping Bear
had arrived this morning was not a thing which the Upper and Lower
Creeks, or indeed any other Indians between the Blue Ridge and the
Father of Waters, would be likely to ignore.

Through all the hours of darkness, at any rate, huge fires of hickory
leapt and roared in the square, flapping and clutching upward almost
to the height of the gigantic popple and tulip trees. Looking out through
the loop-hole windows of House of the Bear one saw the whole town,
aflicker with red dancing light. It was a dreadful omen, that war-dance
of the flames in the midst of a town always sacred to peace. They
changed to red the white front of the Miko's council-cabin itself, on the
square's western side. Even the white eagle-tails that hung there, those
holy emblems of peace, they turned blood-red. They picked out in red
the conical top of the great round-house to the south. They ruddied
the faces and arms and chests of the hundreds who shouted and danced
and sang round the old year's fire that was dying.

Yet the women brewing tomorrow's black drink in the cook-house
of Clan of the Bear ignored the crimson fury. What had set their
tongues a-clatter was the sudden advent among them of the wisest,
loveliest, and most universally beloved woman in their Indian world.
Few of them had ever seen her before, and she had been at Coosa only
three days, yet by this time they had all made up an opinion of her or

356

else were busily doing so.—"Is her hair long?" . . . "Is her bosom deep?" . . . "Has she ever borne a child, or can she?" . . . "Can she sing?" . . . "Can she cook?" . . . "Can she sew?" . . . "Can she dance?" Thus the old and the young women spouted their questions and seldom waited for answers over there in the cook-room, boiling the black drink for tomorrow's busk.

"And how old is she, then, Old Crone?" said a girl's shrill voice, distinctly heard from ten feet off through the flimsy walls of the guest-cabin.

The answer went back in a strident scream: "At thirty a woman is just growing up, you'll find if the gods are good to you."

"But then she's as tall as a man," said another girlish voice.

"I know a man who wouldn't find her tall."

"But she's Choctaw, and he . . . God knows what tribe he is of."

"As you say, God knows; and that is enough."

"She's Clan of the Wind, but he's Clan of the Bear. And so . . . ?"

"If that Sleeping Bear had ever once opened his eyes he would not be sleeping alone this night."

"He has known her for years, Old Crone. Since she was a child he has known her, they say."

"Ah—but has he known himself?"

"I think he has sworn not to look into any woman's face. There is some one thing he must do first, or someone he must forget. That is what I think."

"Who speaks of a woman's face? A woman has more than that, you ignorant child. Yes; and even though he be but a *sleeping* bear he has seen what more this one has."

"What do you know of that, Old Crone?"

"A maiden has told me—one who was there. If you had been there you would have said so. But you missed your bath this morning, you foul thing!"

"It is true. I am sorry. But tell us! What did the maiden say?"

"Will you cease your clack and get on with your work if I tell you?"

"Yes, good Crone. But tell us! What did he see?"

"She told me he came to Coosa at dawn today, tired out from a day-and-night's running—for you should know that he has come to the busk all the way from the Father of Waters. And she told how, because he did not well know the old beloved town, he came by mistake past the bathing-place that the maidens use before sunrise."

"Yes, yes! Do go on, good Crone! Did he see her there?"

357

"I will take my time. In good time I may tell you."

"Good Crone!"

"Well, then, yes; he saw her standing naked there among the other maidens in the dawn by the cold gray water."

"Naked, did you say?"

"You heard me well enough."

"Did she see him?"

"Her face was turned from him; but the others have told her."

"Ah! It is wonderful! And what did he do then?"

"What would he do, you wicked girl? He looked for as long as the beat of a humming-bird's wing, and turned away."

"But do you praise him for that?"

"He does not need my praise; but it is forbidden that a brave should see the maidens bathing. It is against what the gods have ordained."

"Yes; but to one who has seen all that this one has, a maiden's bare body is surely no secret."

"I tell you, child, that a maiden's bare body is always a secret to every man. He never learns it. He cannot remember."

"Tell us! Tell us!"

"Humph! Tell you what? It is not what words are good for."

"Tell us more!"

"I will tell you only this—that if he cannot remember, still less can he ever forget. Something burns in him, and will not let him sleep. I tell you so. That is what the gods have ordained."

Then once again the songs, the shouts, the laughter, the thud of drums from the square, and roaring of alligators from the banks of Coosa River. Red light from the fires in the square streamed all night long through the cracks and flickered along the flimsy walls of the guest-room of House of the Bear. And yet it was not so much that portent of war as a vision of beauty, pearl-pale, unapproachably dim and distant, that held sleep away.

In one sense it was true that he had known her for years; yet even now he knew her scarcely at all. She had seldom been at home in the Choctaw villages when he had gone there to visit her father and old Parson Blandison. Her work, like his, had enforced a roving life. Whenever and wherever there rose a threat to the peace of the civilized tribes —Cherokee, Chickasaw, Choctaw, or Creek—the Beloved Woman was soon at hand. That, no doubt, would explain her presence in Coosa at this time. No doubt her father, Chief Pushmataha, the most influential of all white-sticks, had sent her. He too must have heard that Tecumseh was planning to make one more of his incendiary talks at Coosa busk.

For long hours he tossed and turned; but when the red flicker from the fires began to pale he rose from the corn-husk mattress and spread his long narrow blanket on the floor. He lay down on the blanket, pulled half of it over him, and placed near his heart a shaggy bag which held something warm and hard. And then, as though the familiar warmth of the past had drawn him away from the plots of Tecumseh, had blurred even the vivid image of a woman standing pale beside cold gray water, he slept peacefully while the first day of Coosa busk came on.

In the morning it was easier to think about other things. One could walk about the square and talk with young men and old from fifty towns. One could go with Tukabahchee Miko into the public buildings that fronted the square—his own council-cabin on the west with its guarded sanctum for holy vessels, the house of the warriors on the north, the shed for young men on the east, and the bed of the "beloved men" on the southern side.

Not without reason, the old man was proud of his work in restoring Coosa. He had brought to bear not merely a complete command of labor but a large fund of antiquarian knowledge and no little architectural skill. His effort had been, he said, to bring back the Coosa of times long past when the gods had particularly loved this town, so safe and beautiful on the bluffs above the green rushing river. He wanted his old friend Sleeping Bear to observe that in all the haste of reconstruction there had been no neglect of symbolic ornament. Round every pillar of his council-cabin writhed white carven snakes, for the snake was his totem. Pictures in white of men and animals, all grotesque and many obscene, adorned the walls of the cabin. White eagle-tails and snowy plumage of the trumpeter-swan hung from the eaves and the rafters within.—Considering, he said, that there were so many wild young red-sticks about, and also in view of the fact that Tecumseh himself was coming, it had seemed wise to display great plenty of the color of peace.

But Tukabahchee Miko was proudest in showing the great round-house standing to the south of the square on an artificial mound. Inside, it was sixty feet across, and from the ground to the smoke-vent overhead it was thirty feet high. It had no window, and the single entrance admitted the least possible light and air. Broad benches in concentric rings ran round the interior, and inside the innermost ring twelve stout pillars held up the roof. A quantity of split cane, well dried and ready for burning, had been carefully laid in a spiral round the great central bole of a tulip-tree which projected through the smoke-vent.

The planning of this round-house, the Miko told Sleeping Bear, had taken him six days and nights of sleepless and solitary thought. During that time he had, to be sure, taken certain medicines to assist the labor of the mind, but not a mouthful of food or drink. At the end of it he had a hundred sticks cut in miniature showing every log that the finished structure would require. These sticks he had distributed among the fifty Creek towns with strict injunctions that the corresponding logs were to be delivered at Coosa on such a day. They had been so delivered, and all had fitted exactly together without the slightest change. He himself had overseen the cutting, carrying, and setting of the great central pillar, so as to make quite sure that it should not for one instant touch the ground.

"Tecumseh," he said in conclusion, "is coming to make a talk. And Tecumseh will be answered by Sleeping Bear.—This round-house will hold a thousand men."

The square was a dazzling rectangle of sunshine when they looked down upon it from the mound after coming out of the gloom. It was a constantly changing pattern of many colors. Men, women, and children all gaily bedizened for the chief feast of the year were darting and weaving in and out. A tall man in pure white buck-skins moved slowly up and down and across in the crowd on a large gray horse.

All round the square, crowding up to the very eaves of the cabins, stood the lofty whispering forest. From the square itself, however, because its soil had been packed so hard during generations of human use, the hickories and tulips and moss-hung oaks stood back. They seemed to be patiently looking on, biding their time.

Over the brilliant square and the green of the forest thin mile-long streamers of cloud were floating high, and among them two eagles went spiraling up and up. A steady draft of cool air from the river-gulch kept the leaves in gentle motion. Under the rumble of human voices the trees kept up a soft multitudinous lisping speech.

It took a long time for the two friends to make their way through the crowd. The Miko knew every Creek by name, and every Creek seemed to know Sleeping Bear at least by reputation. Certainly William Weatherford, the tall horseman in white buck-skins, knew him. That was why he rode away, without a greeting, to the farther edge of the crowd.

Quite unnecessarily, the Miko confided to Sleeping Bear that Weatherford was a man to watch. Son of a white trader and a fierce dark Seminole woman, he had recently gained as complete a sway over the Creek nation as ever his uncle, Alexander McGillivray, had exerted at the height of his power. And this influence he seemed to be using in just his uncle's treacherous way. He was suspected of intrigues with the British, with Tecumseh, and even, perhaps, with that highly dubious American General, James Wilkinson. During the last year or two he had built up about himself a dangerous half-secret society of young Creeks, all clamoring for war against the white settlers and all as devoted to Tecumseh as they had been to McGillivray.

Inside the chunky-yard at the north of the square they came to an excited crowd watching nine young dancers vivid in war-paint from crest to toe. These young men were miserably gaunt, as though from prolonged fasting. Their dance was a convulsive frenzy which began with a trembling and jerking of every limb. It went on with violent symbolic gestures of chopping, rending, disemboweling, and ended with a tearing of actual human scalps between their teeth.

Tukabahchee Miko said that this was "Dance of the Lakes." "It was taught to these young men last year," he said, "by Tenkswatawa the Prophet, Tecumseh's twin brother. All winter they have lived in the forest and starved themselves and danced that terrible dance. They all say that they have seen visions and know what the gods ordain. But their visions, if they are real, are sent by the God of Evil. They are driving our people mad."

By noon the two were sitting in the sunshine on the front bench of the council-cabin, watching the crowd in the central square. It was a festive and a happy throng—hundreds of men and women in holiday garb, troops of naked children with roguish faces, and not a few Negro slaves who entered completely into the spirit of the occasion. Shriveled hags were chatting here with damsels resplendent in bear-grease and vermilion. And here were wizened veterans of a hundred winters tottering about among tattooed young gallants, stiff-crested, with huge copper rings in their ears and little bells at their knees. Of such ambitious youngsters, no doubt, the strength of the red-sticks was chiefly composed. Real warriors held apart from them, talking among themselves or proudly sauntering, lounging alone.

It was the old men and women who best remembered and obeyed

what the gods had ordained for the ritual of the busk. Since the first red of dawn they had been bringing their last year's clothing, utensils, bedding, feathers, and furniture to last year's fire. Considering that most of them had somehow transported their property from towns far away, this burnt-offering had entailed much labor. Harder still it must have been to bring from distant hearths their old ashes and yet-living coals. But this too they had done. Some were still dumping old embers into the old flames even while the sassafras drill was begetting new fire in the womb of a poplar log.

Sleeping Bear watched the burning of last year's goods with close attention. There, he felt, was the very heart of the ritual, profoundly symbolic, deeply true, ancient beyond calculation, and Indian entirely.— Ah, if the white man's world could but learn such wisdom!

But the making of new fire was another thing. No doubt it had been derived, through the ages, from a savage notion that the sun grows weary in heaven, or else that fire wears out its virtue. He did not like that notion. With his hand resting upon the warm woodchuck-skin at his belt he said to himself that it was not true.

Dances and songs innumerable filled the afternoon and evening of the first day. On the second morning the men smeared themselves with old ashes, plunged into the river, and, upon their return, fell to eating the roasted ears of the young maize. At dawn of the third day the women took flaming brands of the new fire and, singing and dancing, bore them into the houses.

And still Tecumseh did not come. Tukabahchee Miko suspected that he was trying to show his importance by making them wait. That would be like him.

The fourth morning was sultry. Great clouds lumbered up from the south-west, and the alligators in the pools of the river were roaring for rain. A sense of uneasiness was spreading among the people. Little heed was paid to the turkey-dance and the tadpole-dance of the women. The Young Prophets—one of whom had dropped dead, yesterday, of exhaustion—were drawing a great throng in the chunky-yard.

It was with a sense of prophetic compassion that Sleeping Bear saw the warriors rub their bodies with ashes of pine-cone and watched the aged Miko as he walked slowly about the central fire to make his offering of old man's tobacco. Ages had come and gone in the shaping of this symbolic ceremonial, and now it was being performed at Coosa for perhaps the last time.

At noon a warrior of Clan of the Wind ran out of the crowd with a wand in his hand—a wand with two white eagle-feathers floating from the tip. This he stuck upright in the ground before the council-cabin, and darted back. A warrior of Clan of the Fishes snatched it up and went bounding down the steep incline to the river, yelling the death-whoop. Every able-bodied man in the square dashed after him, and stood waiting on the bank for him to reappear.—To Sleeping Bear, looking down from the bluff, there was a tone of unfeigned sorrow in the howlings with which they mourned for the year that was dead.

After a minute under water the diver came out and stuck the wand, still feathered at the tip, into the bank. Seeing this sign of the year new-born the others plunged into the stream and washed themselves.

The busk at Coosa was ended.

DANCE OF THE LAKES

The sound of a finger-drum was throbbing faintly from among the trees, mingled with a far-off grumble of thunder.

Sleeping Bear on the bluff saw the climbing tribesmen glance at one another in surprise. "Who could be up there?" they seemed to be asking. The finger-drum was for warriors.

At first hardly more than a whisper of leaves and then like the beat of a quickening heart, the sound came from the entrance between the council-cabin and the bed of the henihas. Though distant and faint, its boding persistence was so intermixed with the far-off drumming of the gods that it raised the hair on a listener's nape.

Sleeping Bear said to himself "This is Tecumseh," and returned to his seat beside the Miko.

Tecumseh came first in the single file, proudly erect, walking slowly and yet with a springing and powerful tread. On his left arm lay a long broad belt of wampum, every bead jet-black. Except for his loin-flap he was naked. So was the warrior behind him, the next, and the next. Each man, however, wore a buffalo-tail, as though he had come from a ball-play. Their faces and bodies were black, the plumes in their crests were vermilion, and their tomahawks were stained in the hue of blood.

363

Thirty there were in all—Shawnees. Last came the one-eyed Tenk-swatawa, twin-brother of Tecumseh, known as "The Prophet." Hideous, tall, gaunt, with his one little eye glittering like a snake's, painted black and green, he was fingering the drum softly, persistently, drawing from the taut skin a rhythm that shook the blood.

Round and round the new fire they marched, while the old men and women and children stared. The men coming up from the river stood and stared at the top of the bluff. Sleeping Bear watched them with narrowed eyes. He looked again and again from Tecumseh to the Prophet and back as though trying to make it seem a credible thing that the noble chieftain who led the thirty had once lain and grown side by side in the same woman's body with that incarnation of evil who fingered the drum at the rear.

Tukabahchee Miko's thin old hands were trembling a little—not with fear, certainly, but with restrained indignation. The masters of ceremonies drove the people back. Every voice was still. Even that distant mutter of the gods died down and left only the tiny human thunder of the finger-drum.

When the Shawnees had marched thirty times around the central fire they came to a stand, facing inward and raising their right hands in salutation. Then Tecumseh turned about and came toward the cabin of the councillors. In his right hand he held a long-stemmed pipe, superbly wrought, with a bowl of roseate pipe-stone. In his left was a brand from the new fire.

At ten feet from the front bench he paused and lighted his pipe. He offered it to the sky, to the earth, to the four quarters, and then to the Miko. Two crimson feathers dangled from the stem as he held it out.

But Tukabahchee Miko shook his head slowly from side to side, keeping his arms folded.

Tecumseh appeared to be astonished at this refusal. He recoiled a step or two, the stem of the pipe trembling. Then, as though he thought there had been some mistake, he made the offer a second time, and was again refused. A third time he made it; but when he saw that same determined shaking of the head his brow cleared and he turned to the man sitting next to the Miko.

And now there could be no doubt that he was genuinely surprised. It was clear that he had expected at Coosa no such antagonist. He drew back and folded his arms. The muscles of his throat and jaw were visibly working. The end of the pipe-stem trembled still.

After a few tense seconds Tecumseh bowed slightly to Sleeping Bear and turned again to the Miko. "I come," said he, "to make a talk."

The Miko rose and replied with the tremulous voice of an old man: "I know you, Tecumseh the Meteor. Since your childhood I have known you. I know you have come into this old beloved town to set the hearts of our young men on fire. I think that the talk you will make may lead to the death of us all, but I cannot keep you from making that talk. I see that my warriors are taking your broken tobacco. It is poisoned, I know, and I think it may put them to sleep forever, but I cannot keep it from them. Your brother the Prophet has taught our young men the dreadful Dance of the Lakes. It should have been called the Dance of Death; but you and he will do, and we shall suffer, what the gods ordain."

Tecumseh said in a great voice: "I will make my talk tonight."

"And you will be answered," the Miko replied, "by Sleeping Bear."

Well before midnight all the chief men in Coosa were assembled in the great round-house on the mound. Already the fire of split canes was burning about the central pillar, sending up along it a volume of smoke that hung and hovered among the rafters. The room was intensely hot. From his seat at the Miko's right Sleeping Bear looked out upon hundreds of sweat-streaked faces. Every mat was filled, from the edge of the fire to the circular outer wall. Peace and war parties, old councillors and young warriors—the main power of the Creek Confederacy was gathered in the torrid, reeking room. At the Miko's left sat the Beloved Woman, especially invited as a testimony to her wisdom and power. She was the only woman present. Directly across the circle, consciously handsome in his fringed and beaded buck-skins, William Weatherford sat and laughed amid a boisterous company of young redsticks.

For the most part the men were seated by clans—the Bears at the Miko's right in honor of Sleeping Bear, then the Wind people, the Birds, the Beavers, the Alligators, the Fishes, and so on round the circle. Many were wrapped to the ears in their blankets, but more sat bare to the waist.

Two young men with white feathers in their crests made their way through the crowd to the mat of the Miko. With the help of Sleeping Bear on his right hand and that of the Beloved Woman on the left, the old man rose to his feet and acknowledged their obeisance. Then he took from one of the youths a large gourd filled with a dark, steam-

365

ing liquid. For a moment he held the gourd above his head, while the entire gathering murmured with him a brief formula of praise, thanksgiving, and supplication. On the instant when he set the vessel to his mouth one of the attendants, standing with folded arms and half-closed eyes, began a musical intonation of the syllable "O." He drew out the note for a full minute, during which the Miko did not once take the gourd from his lips. Then, catching his breath, the chanter intoned the syllable "He" on a higher note for another minute. Again the Miko drank, or pretended to, until the young man's breath gave out. The vessel was then passed on to Sleeping Bear, who took only a sip and then gave it to Tecumseh.

Many other gourds were passing from hand to hand, and wherever they went the eyes of the drinkers brightened. Here and there pipes were lighted, and the odor of kinnikinnick began to mingle with that of the burning cane and of bear-grease.

And now the Miko had risen again in his place. He was courteously introducing a man who, he said, was well known to them all, a chieftain partly Creek in blood who had come among them, not for the first time, to speak the words of his heart. Let him be heard fairly, with the respect due to every guest. And let each man who heard him weigh the words that he spoke with full knowledge that life and death were at stake.

Into the brief stillness that followed the Miko's dignified introduction there stole a muttering from far away of the storm which the town had escaped in the afternoon.

Tecumseh rose from his place on the bench to the left of the Beloved Woman. A single red eagle's feather fastened upright in his long flowing hair made him look even taller than he was. He let his blanket fall from his shoulders. He folded his arms across his chest. A broad silver bracelet on his left wrist gleamed in the firelight, and the two green stones it held were shining like the eyes of a cat. From his right arm hung several belts of black wampum. The light striking up from below deepened every line of his noble aquiline face as his gaze swept slowly round the three-banked circle. The power of the man began to speak before he opened his mouth.

Sleeping Bear's heart sank. Against such an opponent, so majestic in mien, with such dignity and depth of mind written clear on his face for all to see, he felt helpless, a weed by the wall. Every thought of rivalry was swallowed up, for the moment, in admiration. He saw before him a man greatly wronged, righteously angered, who had devoted his en-

366

tire life to one huge dangerous task. He saw—and for the moment he envied—a man who had never known doubt, a man undivided, who had always pulled with his total strength on one side in life's tug-of-war. And here, moreover, was a deliberate and veteran artist in speech, a lord of language, who played upon men's nerves and hearts as others on flutes and drums. Not for the first time by hundreds was he standing now before a critical audience, summoning all his skill. Every gesture of his, every glance, every dramatic pause, would be studied, calculated, and right. Every word and intonation would be the choice of a master perfectly aware that he had reached a crisis in a great career.

"I come," said Tecumseh, proudly, "to make a talk of seven belts."

"Seven belts!" And Sleeping Bear had brought no wampum at all.

Tecumseh went on, in a lower tone, "This ancient and holy land of the Creeks has always been dear to me. It is my mother's country. As a boy I took part in your ball-play. As a youth I hunted in these forests. As a man I have sat by your council-fires in talk with your foremost chieftains. I need not tell you whether my council has been wise, whether I have brought back my share of meat from the hunt, or whether the towns for which I have played have been victors at ball. But one thing, brothers of the Creek Nation, I will tell you: I am no stranger."

During the burst of applause he turned slowly round and looked gravely, inquiringly, into the eyes of Sleeping Bear. He laid at the Miko's feet a wampum belt. The black beads glistened as they moved in the firelight like the scales of a sliding snake.

Then again his deep, mournful voice: "When I first came among you I came as the wandering wind. Even in youth I was alone. I had known sorrow even then. But, brothers, there has come a change, as seed-time changes into harvest. Once I grieved for myself, but now I grieve for my people.

"You will think that I mean the Shawnees; and, indeed, if I spoke of them only there alone would be the fuel of a mighty sorrow. But I am thinking also of Creeks, Choctaws, Chickasaws, Cherokees—aye, and of Delawares, Hurons, Catawbas, Sioux, Winnebagoes, and many another tribe whose name you may never have heard."

There was a stir in the room and a murmur as though of dissent as he spread before the Miko a second belt, with a graceful and courteous gesture.

"When I say that I grieve for my people," he continued in a steadily mounting voice, "I mean all of those who once owned this land entire, from the deep seawater to the mountain-tops, and from the mountains again to the sea where the sun goes down. I grieve for all of those who have been wickedly defrauded. My people are those, of whatever name, who have been cheated of their birth-right, basely deceived, driven from home, despised and derided. broken, spat upon, poisoned, and butchered!"

That murmur of dissent had died away. From the ranks of the Younger Creeks sitting with Weatherford there came a scattering cheer.

"Brothers, I know that this is hard for you to understand. Not for many winters have we known ourselves to be one people. For ages we have dwelt apart in many lodges. Our songs, our prayers, our dances, even our words, have been different. If we were sitting in a lofty cloud tonight we should see numberless little camp-fires twinkling here and there in the forests and beside the rivers, but no one great camp-fire anywhere among them.—I come to tell you only this: we must draw those fires together.

"For it can be done, my brothers. Here in your own Creek Confederacy you have shown the way. In my home on the Tippecanoe the Shawnees, Delawares, Ojibways, Ottawas, and Pottawattomies once dwelt in peace side by side.

"I say that we did once dwell there, but now we do so no longer. The white man who has driven us from so many other hunting-grounds desired this one also—this little covert where broken and wandering tribes had come together for refuge. We pleaded with him, we prayed, we reminded him of his promises and treaties. At last we fought him. A hundred of our young men were killed and we lost our home.

"But the loss of Tippecanoe adds only a single tear to the sea of our sorrow. I do not mention it because the grief is mine but because it should be yours also. And I speak of it because I learned there, at last, whence the strength must come for drawing our fires together. Brothers, it must be the strength of hatred!"

A strong cheer went up from the young men near Weatherford as Tecumseh violently flung down a third belt before the Miko.

"You know," he shouted, "whom we hate; and well do you know why. You have seen him furrow a winding way through our forests and over our prairies. He has crawled like a snake into our houses, our councils, our very beds. He has grown deadly because we have warmed him. With the swift forked tongue of a snake he says two things at once. With the glittering eye of a snake and with head swinging from side to side he is making ready to strike for the last time. Already our veins are foul with his poison. Our young men drink it and fall asleep forever. The slime of his trail befouls our hearths.—How, then, can we fail to hate him?"

"But we do not hate him enough. By far too many, even here on your holy ground, have listened to his black-coated preachers of a weak and womanish religion. Some of you have learned to use his witchcraft of paper and ink, and that is a shameful thing. Some have taken his filthy coin for lands that were given us all. Some fight with his weapons, drink his liquor, sleep with his wicked women, and give their daughters to him. Shame! Oh, shame! Some of you have learned to tear the breast of our Mother the Earth with the knife of his murderous plow.

"Ah, woe! Woe to Coosa! Her days will be few and evil unless we face down this creeping horror with scorn and contempt and hatred. We must say to the white men: 'Keep far off; pollute not our sacred places; and let us not see you, hear you, or smell the stench of your presence. We loathe the ways of your pale-faced kind as those of the slavering wolf, the rooting hog, and the snake that slides on his belly!' "

Here Tecumseh dashed a fourth belt to the ground. Among the yells of applause a death-whoop was heard here and there. The Miko laid his trembling right hand for a moment on Sleeping Bear's left.

Then, with a dignity that increased with the excitement he aroused, Tecumseh went on: "Oh, Councilors and warriors of the Creek Nation, I am not an untried man. While I was yet a child my father was brought home dead from a battle with white men. While I was yet a youth my two elder brothers were killed at Fallen Timbers. Many dear companions of the hunter's trail and the warrior's path have gone before me into the shadows. I too have felt Death's frosty breath. I have stood many times where bullets have rattled like sleet in the branches of winter. But the going-hence of friends, and one's own going, any heart can learn to bear. It is the death of a nation, a people, a race, oh Councilors, that bows and breaks the bravest."

He paused and looked again round the room. With a solemn and mournful motion he spread a fifth belt at the feet of the Miko. He held his hearers with eyes that gloomed and smoldered. No one stirred. The tobacco-pipes were growing cold.

It was in a hushed and tender tone, as of a lover's flute played far off among trees in the dusk, that he continued now, speaking as though to himself: "I have heard the voice of the hidden thrush in the twilight, talking there with the Giver of Breath—and the Giver himself there listening, surely.

369

"I have heard the passenger pigeons fill the night sky with a winnow of numberless wings.

"I have seen the violets come in the spring-time, and vast tossing armies of daisies.

"I have seen, and you too, the wavering wing of the blue-bird, and the quail's low nest by the thistle.

"And, brothers, this beauty of small and helpless things was given to us to love. It is ours to save from the greedy despoiler, to keep from the snout of the rooting hog and from the dog's defilement. This land is ours from Him who giveth and taketh breath. This motherly Earth is our own—to defend, or else to return to, at once, and forever.

"But now we are losing it day by day. From the coasts of the Gulf, from the Blue Ridge, from the banks of the Tennessee, and at last from the Father of Waters, the white man creeps and crawls each day a little farther into your ancient home. Already your tall trees are crashing down to let in the plow and the hoe. Already the elk and the buck and the doe smell the taint of white blood on the wind. Ah, woe! Woe to Coosa, unless now at once and once for all you break the back of the white snake and grind his head under heel."

A sixth belt was flung down, and once again Tecumseh's eyes burned round the circle of rapt and eager faces. Then he stooped and took from the fire a two-foot stick of split cane, burning at one end. He held it high over his head.

"Do you ask," he said, "how one man, one tribe, one confederation of tribes can stand against those that swarm like lice? I will ask you another question: What can be done by one little burning stick? For a breath or a breeze may put it out. A man with one stamp of his foot can kill its flame. Ah, yes, but when you put many burning sticks together—a hundred, a thousand, a million—and when you draw many such fires into one and stack them against one great central pillar, then you can bring the wind, bring the rain, bring a million stamping feet, and the wind will but fan that flame, the rain will feed the fire, and every white stamping foot will be burned to a little cinder."

In the uproar following these shouted words Tecumseh stood quietly looking at the flame that burned on the end of the cane in his hand.

"This is Coosa!" he suddenly called in a voice that rang over the clamor, and again he thrust the flame high over his head. "Shall I add it to the fire?"

A great roar of assent went up from the younger warriors.

He stooped again and laid the burning stick in the midst of the cen-

370

tral flame. With one sweep of his arm he spread a great crimson war-belt, a full fathom long and two feet across, on the ground.—And then a moment later he was seated at the Beloved Woman's left hand, filling his sharp-elbowed pipe with kinnikinnick from a pouch made of the skin of a wildcat.

Sleeping Bear, in trying to recall that frantic scene, could never quite understand how he had gained so much as a hearing from the ecstatic crowd to which Tecumseh turned him over. Certainly nothing had been gained by the Miko's introduction, for it was not heard. In fact the old man had said little more than that Sleeping Bear would speak for the white-sticks, for the Miko himself, and for the Beloved Woman. No; it was only that he had risen to his feet when the Miko sat down, and had looked quietly about the room. And then, for no reason that one could name, the shouting had swiftly died away until there was nothing to be heard but the soft crunch of the fire eating into the split cane close to the central pillar.

Not all the faces he saw about him were hostile. By no means all of the young warriors, even, were red-sticks—or had been, at any rate, before Tecumseh began to speak. Perhaps, then, there might even yet be hope.

"I bring you no belts of wampum," he said. "My purpose is only to save you."

He watched that thrust go home, and continued: "A most beautiful song has been sung us by Tecumseh the Meteor. He has shaken our hearts with fear and with love, like the finger-drummer who drums in the twilight. He has brought before us our Mother the Earth and shown us her beautiful breasts. He has uncovered the things we have known and loved, the things we pray to and die for. Moreover, the pith of the pine, and the mountain, the sea, have strengthened the voice of Tecumseh. There is in him the power of pain and of loss, the might of sorrow and exile. Therefore it is that he sings so well and moves our hearts so strangely. Thence come the thrill and throb of that voice which has lured our thoughts down the dark paths leading to ruin.

"And now, what clear simple words can I speak to draw you back from that music? What wisdom, now, will the gods send down to save you while there is time? For my help must come from above, not from any human trick or wile. I must be a smooth pipe for the breath of the gods, speaking their simple truth, and not a delicately fingered flute to filch men's hearts away. Our brother has chanted a beautiful tune, but his words have been awry. The words have come from his fevered heart and not from his wise, cool brain. He has spoken in tones of thunder, but I would speak like the lightning. His words have been like a wind-blown fire, but mine must be as the light of the stars which no earthly wind will ever blow out."

A breathless quiet filled the room. Even the thunder held for a while aloof. Every eye was fixed upon the speaker, and among the most violent of the red-sticks there was spreading a slow sense of awe. For here was a speaker whose words reached beyond art. The speech of Tecumseh seemed now no more than a work of crafty calculation as compared with this quiet simplicity, this patient waiting for whatever the gods might send. In the red light of the fire flickering up along his body, with bare unpainted shoulders and chest showing the hue of darkened alligator tooth, Sleeping Bear was looking steadily upward. His face was deeply furrowed, yet calm.

"The power of Tecumseh," he said at length, "is what we all have; for we too have known pain and loss. But if he has been orphaned, driven from home, and a wanderer, then that should have made him all the more a compassionate brother of all sorrowing and lonely men. If he loves the Earth, our Mother, should he not love every child, black or red or white, of her womb?"

Even yet the thunder-bird poised over Coosa with outspread wings held its breath, as though listening. The speaker paused and listened, looking upward. Moment by moment the stillness grew more intense. It could not last. It must soon burst in storm.

Up to this point the voice of Sleeping Bear had moved easily out through the hushed assembly like ripples on still water; but now, as he suddenly wheeled about and faced Tecumseh, his tones rang sharp and clear. Yet he spoke not in thunder but, as he had promised, in lightning. And whether it was by chance or by some uncanny calculation, he and the gods did verily seem to be speaking at the same instant, with the same terrific voice and gesture.

"Tecumseh," he shouted, lunging forward and pointing with outstretched finger and arm, "you have told us to hate the white man, but you have *not* told us that you are fighting now on the side of the English whites in this new war."

An instantaneous illumination from overhead filled the room. Tecumseh's face was like that of a dead man, and if he made any reply it was not heard above the following bellow of thunder.

Sleeping Bear turned back to his audience.

372

"You have heard and seen," said he, "that the gods are angry. It angers them that one who pretends to love Coosa should strive to sow in the holy ground of the Creeks that same hatred which has brought the Shawnees to ruin. They remember that the wise Pushmataha, Chief of the Choctaws and father of the Beloved Woman, would not smoke Tecumseh's pipe, would not take his broken tobacco, but called him a wicked man and told him to go away. The gods wonder that this Tecumseh, calling himself your friend, should offer you no part of the price that is paid by white men for the scalps of white women and children. Does he, like his old friend Alexander McGillivray, wish you to be his butchers for no pay? Is it thus that he would save you from the corruption of the white man's filthy coin? The gods are astonished that he said nothing of McGillivray, who was three-quarters white, and nothing of William Weatherford, McGillivray's nephew and successor, who is the son of a white man. But most of all the gods are amazed that he made no mention of his understanding with General James Wilkinson, friend of Benedict Arnold, or of his pact with the infamous Knife. Therefore the gods will not fail to ask Tecumseh, when he stands very soon before them, by what right he spoke with a sneer tonight of the snake with a double tongue."

The long-lashed sentence swished and sang through the smoke-laden air like a muleman's whip that is tipped with a tough bull's-pizzle. And now it was not the white-sticks alone that yelled and stamped and pounded. Young men and old, red-sticks and white, councilors, henihas, warriors, banged feet and hands and shouted acclaim of the most tremendous heart-stopping rhetorical climax they had ever heard or heard tell of. All round the three-banked circle the shaven and stiff-crested heads of old critics were nodding approval. The names of "Wilkinson," "McGillivray," and "The Knife" were whispered and hissed here and there in surprise, but everywhere the incongruous name of the speaker himself was roared and chanted: "Yah! Sleeping Bear!" Henceforth men would say that Tecumseh had spoken as a crafty, sly, experienced man, but Sleeping Bear like a god.

"Brothers and Councilors," the speaker continued when quiet came, "Tecumseh has added one stick to your council-fire and called it 'Coosa.' He would not have you remember that it is the way of fire to consume and destroy. He would have you forget that the stick of cane he laid on this fire is now a small pinch of ashes. And just so, if you follow his council, will Coosa soon be. Tukabahchee, Talladega, and Atasi will be but ashes. Chiaha, Coweta, and Alabama will turn to

373

blowing brown dust. Tallapoosa, Wetumkey, Old Tallassee, Puckentalla will go back to the wolf and the fox and the hooting owl. I know it. I I see it. I tell you so. It is so that the gods have ordained.

"Tecumseh comes bringing a war-talk. Tecumseh comes preaching hatred. Is that how he would draw our fires together? Have we not tried it long? Has it worked well? Has it been by war and hatred, oh Councilors, and by ever more hatred and war, that this Creek Confederacy has been made and kept? Nay, it is these that have scattered our fires asunder. The thing that Tecumseh offers will stamp them out forever. I tell you so. That is what I say.

"Tecumseh is a great and good man gone mad. He is a noble man crazed by sorrow. If he were not crazed he would have told you that it was the English, with whom he is now at league, who killed his father in Lord Dunmore's war. If he were not mad he would know and acknowledge that the traitor Wilkinson, whose scalp-money he does not disdain, is a greater danger to red men than all the settlers in Western Waters. Let us be glad of our brother's nobility and grieve that his sorrows have crazed him.

"I also urge, Tukabahchee Miko urges, and our Beloved Woman who is here with us tonight as well, that we draw our many fires into one, though not by hatred. We plead for escape from the poisonous greed of the white man, but not by slaughter. We too would call you back to the love of our Mother the Earth, but for that we shall need no help from Wilkinson and his treacherous Knife. What we do need, and greatly, is Tecumseh, the Meteor, himself.

"For I will not end my talk with words of wrath. Tecumseh, whatever he may think, is not my foe. I would that he were my friend. Together we might do a work for our people which neither he nor I can do alone. My own task of drawing our tribes together for peace has been like twisting a rope of sand while he has worked to unite them for hatred and war. Many thousands of warriors are waiting and watching now for his signal-smokes. I know it. Since Pontiac there has been no such mighty man among the council-fires that burn from the Sea to the River. Oh, may he not use his power with Pontiac's dreadful purpose! Oh, may he not rush headlong upon Pontiac's dreadful end!

"Brothers of mine, Councilors, warriors of the Shawnee, Tenkswatawa the Prophet, and you first of all, Tecumseh, I tell you now, speaking as I would if these were my last words upon earth, that if you hang the red club of war in the chunky-yard of Coosa then this round-

374

house will soon be fiery ashes, every ripple of Coosa River will be horribly stained with blood, and throughout these forests and meadows, so long the home of your fathers, there will be nothing left of the Creeks but the clean-picked bones of the dead. I see it. I know it. I have never lied to this people. On the faith of Sleeping Bear I tell you so."

A rattle of thunder and a patter of rain on the roof filled the pause during which the speaker stood with folded arms and head down-bent. Gigantic he looked in the glimmer, and his voice when he spoke came as though from outside and above the darkening room.

"But all this," he said, "need not be. In a moment, now, when I offer the right hand of brotherhood to Tecumseh, he will decide whether to die or to live. If he chooses to live then we shall live also. We shall live far away from the white man, forgetting his greed and filth, until the time when he too shall put away his childishness and learn the ways of peace.

"Beyond the Father of Waters there is a country made by the gods for our home. From that country the Creeks first came. I have been there. It is vast, it is rich, it is beautiful beyond any prophet's dream of the Happy Hunting-Grounds. There is room there and game and fish for a thousand Creek Nations. The gods of that land will remember your songs and dances, for they knew them of old. They will understand your medicine. They will breathe divine truth through the mouths of your prophets and poets and dreamers. They will touch your women with fruitfulness and bless your fields with much corn.

"Oh, brothers, let us arise now and go, while yet there is time, from this place that is foul with the stench of on-rushing death. I say, let us go! Let us leave the pale-faces to build their pitiful fences and say 'This is mine!' Let us find a clean place where each man, though he keeps his own dance and song and obeys his own vision, may say 'This is ours!' Let us eat like brothers again of one dish while the white man snatches at many. Let us drain the black drink from one huge gourd till the breath of the gods is exhausted. Let us build a huge round-house for all the tribes whose brows are reddened by sunset. Let us draw all our fires round a pillar reaching the stars, and there let us sit and be ruled by the noble beloved king of us all—Tecumseh!"

Here he turned, reaching out his right hand, and said: "Tecumseh, which shall it be?"

The two men gazed into each other's eyes, deeply and long. And then—was it only some trick of the dancing shadows, or did Tecumseh's right hand slightly move as it lay on his bare left arm? Did not his head move forward, as though he were about to rise, strike hands, and accept this startling proposal?

But suddenly the Prophet leapt from his place at the left of Tecumseh and rushed with a yell to the central pillar. He struck his tomahawk with great force into the pillar and left it there, the head embedded and the red-painted handle hanging. One after one his followers leapt and rushed and yelled and struck. One by one they pranced behind him in single file round and round the pillar, kicking up live embers and sparks, screaming the war-whoop, brandishing a huge club painted red from end to end, tearing at human scalps with their teeth, until there were twenty-eight whirling with him in a frantic orgiastic dance.

Sleeping Bear, knowing that this was the Dance of the Lakes and that all was lost and over, quietly sat down beside Tukabahchee Miko and began to fill his stone pipe from a pouch of mole-skin.

Except for the swiftly intermittent flashes from the sky there was little light in which to see the whirling figures. They soon stamped out most of the embers, and the rest were quenched by the rain rolling down the central pillar. As darkness deepened the dance grew more frenzied. The Creeks were joining it now. The war-whoop was ringing from every part of the room. Now and then a dancer fell into the coals and was trampled upon, and then he either crawled or else he was furiously kicked to one side.

All at once, cresting the tumult, there went up a cry in Shawnee of "The Prophet! The Prophet! The Prophet will make a talk!"

"There has been talk enough," screamed a voice from out of the half-dark. "We have heard the talk of a squaw, the snore of an old she-bear. I will tell you the vision of a man, of a prophet, who knows what the gods ordain."

"Ai-ee! The Prophet! Hear him! Whoo-oo whoop!"

"I fasted forty days and forty nights. I drank strong medicines. I went naked in the cold. I watched and waited and listened and prayed. I offered tobacco. I played the finger-drum as the gods love to hear it. I crawled close to the door of death. I heard what the dead were saying. —And then, on the fortieth night, it came!"

"What came?"

"My vision."

"What was it?"

"The gods may slay me for saying, but I saw the bloody hand and arm of a god stabbing downward. In the hand was a knife with a long

376

wavy blade. It was bloody. It had been plucked from the heart of a white man. And the handle of the knife was shown me also."

"What was it? Tell!"

"The handle was a woman, of stone, naked, beautiful, and green as the locust that sings in the tree-tops of August."

"Ai-ee. The Knife. Whoo-oo whoop! The Knife!"

"That was my vision. I tell you so. It showed the will of the gods that we kill and kill and kill. The gods command that we hang the red war-club in the chunky-yard of Coosa and kill and kill and kill. Let the will of the gods be done!"

During the hours of darkness that remained Sleeping Bear sat quietly on the bench of the round-house listening to the shouts and yells from the square, hearkening to the rain, the wind, and far-away thunder. Again and again he filled his stone pipe, lighted it with a bit of smoldering punk from his clam-shell, smoked it through, and emptied the dead ashes on the ground.

When the first glimmer of dawn came down the tall central pillar he saw that he had eight or ten companions. A little more light showed that all but one of them were old men, and that of these three or four were sleeping. The Miko himself was asleep. At the Miko's left hand sat the Beloved Woman, her dark compassionate eyes faintly shining in the half light. When Sleeping Bear rose from the bench she rose also and, in defiance of all custom, walked beside him to the entrance. At the door she put her hand in his and they two walked out together into the new day.

VIEW FROM A TREE-TOP

(August—1813)

All day long and for day after day the sun poured down heat as though through a funnel. In the late afternoon torrential rains blew up from the Gulf and turned the ground inside the pickets, daily trodden by scores of cattle and five hundred human beings, into a viscid mud. At night everyone crowded as close as possible to the open fires—not, certainly, in order to keep warm, for the heat abated little until after

377

midnight, but to escape the myriads of mosquitoes that came warping up on the evening breeze from Lake Tensaw.

Day following monotonous day brought no change in the heat, wet, noise, dirt, or danger. If any change there was, it could be discerned chiefly in the rapid increase and diversification of the stench. Many took sick, with precisely what disease no one seemed to know. The medicine chest which Dr. Holmes had thought to bring with him was soon exhausted, and Dr. Osborne, the surgeon to the militia, had not thought to bring any medicines whatever. Concerning the five persons who had died since coming to the fort, and had been buried hugger-mugger in the night, a rumor was rife that they had been carried off by yellow fever after passing it on to a dozen others.

Under such circumstances it was necessary to find someone to blame, and the choice soon fell upon the host of the whole miserable company. Twenty times a day it was pointed out to Samuel Mims that he had selected for his contemptible fort the worst spot in all the world. People told him candidly that he must have been inspired by the devil when he planned to fortify this low and level potato field with its amazing variety of strategic disadvantages. Why could he not have considered, they asked, that there was an almost impenetrable cane-brake just to the north along the Alabama River, that a dense thicket hid Lake Tensaw from view, and that less than a rifle-shot off to the eastward there lay a ravine in which a thousand red-skins could lurk unseen for days and nights and watch them? They wished to be told why it was, if he was bent upon building a fort at all in such a pestilential hole, that he could not have built one large enough for a fair number of people? Why were his log-pickets only eight feet high, and many of them left unsharpened at the tops? Why could he not have braced them inside with something more substantial than fence-rails? And why, above all, could he not have finished the fort when once he had begun it?

The suspicion and rumor grew that Mims was in league with the red-sticks, that he had an understanding with Weatherford, and that this miserable mud-flat which he had the effrontery to call a fort was in reality meant for a trap. But Samuel Mims himself heard all this with an affable smile. He did not pretend that his fort was a good one or that its location was particularly fortunate. Nevertheless, he pointed out, it did seem to be popular. He had planned the place only for his own family, cattle, and slaves; but then, before it was completed, here were five hundred and more of his neighbors—Indians, Negroes, half-breeds, and whites—anxious to visit him. If any of his guests felt that

378

they could endure the place no longer, there was plenty of room out-side. In fact, there was Fort Pierce, only three miles away.

No one left, partly because it was known that Fort Pierce was at least as crowded and certainly no stronger. Five hundred and fifty-three persons crowded into the fifteen ramshackle cabins and sheds and stables scattered in the larger of the two enclosures round the house of the owner. They had water enough, and for fuel in case of need they could use the buildings, but in the matter of food they could not stand a siege of a week—at any rate unless their cattle chanced to be inside the stockade when the siege began.

Yet the fact that these people were caught in a common danger did nothing to deepen or extend their Christian charity. Hatreds and animosities grew up in three days which, under normal conditions, would have taken as many years to mature. They led to frequent scuffles and a few bloody encounters. The Negroes quarrelled with the Indians, the whites stormed at them both, the women screamed and scratched, and everyone united in detesting Major Beasley, Captain Jack, Captain Middleton, and the hundred so-called soldiers under their command.

The language used in the original square stockade concerning the soldiery could be matched in vituperative vigor only by that employed by the soldiers to characterize the civilians. A main contention of the civilian party was that Beasley's militiamen had been sent by Governor Claiborne mainly to finish the fortifications. The militiamen insisted, however, that their duty was to fight and not to do "nigger-work." As for the Negroes, they apparently took the view that so long as there were no red-sticks actually swarming over the pickets it was too soon, as certainly it was too hot, for them to exert themselves.

Major Beasley did, in fact, complete a new stockade for his men on the eastern side of the old one, thus making two separate compartments with a common wall—a wall interrupted by the old gate-way. His new eastern gate, however, was hard to close on account of a small quantity of sand and gravel left by the workmen. Captain Bailey complained about this to Major Beasley more than once, and on each occasion the Major promised with profane emphasis that he would have the gravel and sand removed. Yet it remained there, the gate was left open at night, and Captain Bailey decided not to annoy his superior officer again.

Sleeping Bear was one of the few who were quite sure that the red-sticks were coming, and soon. The Beloved Woman had told him so.

379

Tukabahchee Miko had said the same thing. The only reason, he said, why they had not struck at Fort Mims immediately after the Prophet's triumph at Coosa was that Weatherford had taken them down to Pensacola to get arms from the British.

On the other hand, Major Beasley was almost as sure that they would not come. He wished that they would—but just when and where, he inquired in truculent tones, had a gang of red-skins ever dared to attack a body of well-armed and diciplined American troops? What they had always tried for was a swift descent upon some lonely plantation, a few easy scalps, and then—disappearance. As for Bill Weatherford, he might be a good breeder of horses but he had no more idea of soldiering than a goose pecking grass by moonlight.

The Major was unimpressed by the rumors leaking into the fort of an Indian victory at Burnt Corn Creek over the hundred and eighty troops of Colonel Caller. Such things, he said, did not happen. Lies too, in his belief, were the thick-coming tales about war-painted Indians in the region of Fort Mims itself. Possibly a few such might have been seen now and then, peering out from the cane-brake, but the assertion that any considerable number had come close without being discovered was a thing he resented as an imputation against his excellent scouts.

It was the "niggers," Major Beasley said, who made the most trouble. They believed the damnedest things, and got even some of the whites to believe them. They kept the whole place in turmoil. If a single cow should show some hesitation when the cattle were driven out in the morning, then that, the "niggers" put it about, was because she smelt Injuns! And then they were coming in nearly every day with hair-raising yarns about the things they thought—or, at any rate, said—they had seen in the cane-brake, in the thicket, on the lake, or across Alabama River. Beasley's scouts had run themselves ragged to investigate these reports, and not a red-skin had they anywhere seen. It was getting to be a question in his mind whether the "niggers" weren't telling these lies just to keep his scouts on the run. Maybe they wanted him to send out his whole force some day against an enemy who wasn't there, and then . . . Anyhow, he let it be known that his patience was nearly exhausted.

The heat increased as the days of late August burned interminably by and were consumed at sunset in terrific thunder and lightning. The stenches increased, and the sickness. Some of the animosities that had sprung up inside the fort were approaching the point of murder.

At noon of the twenty-ninth the soldiers idling in the shadow of the eastern gate, waiting there for the dinner-bell, saw two Negroes running at top speed across the open field. Peter Randon recognized one of them as his own 'Lijah. The faces of both runners, when they got inside the gate and dropped there, panting, were ashen. They gasped out a story of having seen "a passel of Injuns"—some twenty-five of them according to 'Lijah, but forty at least in the estimate of Mr. Charles Fletcher's Brown Boy—"a-layin' back thar in the gulch." They agreed that a few of these lurking Indians had chased them a little way but had dropped down behind the bushes when they came in sight of the fort.

Major Beasley, bustling out of his cabin near the gate to see what was going on, heard the last few sentences of the Negroes' report. Knock-kneed and pot-bellied, he did not look much of a soldier, but he meant at least to speak like one in his prompt assertion that the Negroes were lying.

"N-n-no, suh!" stammered 'Lijah, the more intelligent of the two. "We-uns tellin' de Gawd's trufe, cross mah h'aht hopes ter die. Dat gulch am cram full ob Injuns all black an' raid, Majah. Ah done seed 'em wid mah two eyes."

"Don't you contradict me, you black trash! When I say you're lyin', then you *are* lyin'. Savvy?"

"Oh, yassuh. Dat's so. On'y Ah jes' done seed 'em wid mah two eyes, all black an' raid an' covehed wid feathahs, suh. Mos'ly raid feathahs."

There was a tone of honesty in the slave's voice, and the gleam of recent fear in his eyes was unmistakable.

"Very well, then," said the Major harshly, "we'll see about this. Ensign Randon, take fifty men, fully armed, and go over thar to that gulch on the double-quick. Let this boy o' yourn show you jest whar he thinks them Injuns are a-layin'. If you find any, kill 'em. If you don't, bring your nigger straight back to camp an' we'll damn near kill *him*."

Randon saluted and turned on his heel. In three minutes he and his fifty went through the gate at a brisk trot, with 'Lijah leading the way. —Looking after them from his door-way the Major was both shocked and angered to see that Sleeping Bear was going with them. He ran to the gate and yelled out a stern command, but with no effect.

Major Beasley was making it as clear as possible that he was in no way intimidated, or, for that matter, particularly impressed, by the presence in his cabin of a rather famous visitor. He did not rise from the little table at which he had eaten his dinner alone.

"Didn't you hear me tell you to come back?" he asked in a rasping voice, gazing hard at the end of his cigar.

"I'm not under your command, Major Beasley," said Sleeping Bear, smiling down at the little man.

"Oh, you ain't, eh? Wal, I c'n tell yuh . . ."

"And it was not about that matter that I came to speak to you," the quiet voice went on. "I'm here to say that the Negro 'Lijah was entirely right in his report that there were Indians in that nearest ravine when he and Brown Boy came through there."

"Right? Nonsense! Weren't ye thar yerself when Randon's men tromped from end to end of the ravine, and didn't find hide nor hair of a red-skin? That nigger's lyin', jest like I said, an' I'm a-goin' to hev 'im lashed half to death."

"I was there with Peter Randon's men, watching them tramp up and down, and after they had left I found proof that at least twenty Indians had been hiding in the ravine since night before last."

There was a sneer on the Major's face as he looked up, for the first time, at his visitor. It soon disappeared. "What kind of proof?" he asked. "Haow c'n you be so sure how long they was there, and haow many, when Randon didn't find nothin'?"

"What kind of proof? Oh, the ashes of two fires, one of them still warm, and broken twigs, many footprints which any Indian child would have seen, and this."—Sleeping Bear held out a tomahawk. The iron blade and hickory handle were vividly red.

Major Beasley stared at the weapon, but did not take it in hand.

"And so 'Lijah told the truth. I thought you would want to know it at once so as to change your order to have him whipped."

"Change it I will *not*," snapped the Major, leaping so suddenly to his feet that his chair fell over backward. "What kind o' 'fect you think that 'd hev on dis'pline, choppin' an' changin' that a-way?"

"In the long run it might have a worse effect to punish an innocent man."

"I don't admit he's innocent. I called 'im a liar an' I'll stand to 't."

Sleeping Bear again held out the red tomahawk.

"Huh!" Beasley grunted. "How do I know whar ye got that thing? You *say* you picked it up in the ravine, but how do I know? May be yourn fer anythin' I know. Why, damn it, you may be a red-stick yer-self."

382

Major Beasley felt his jaw suddenly gripped as though in a trap of steel. His head was bent slowly backward. His puffy and pock-marked face grew almost as red as the tomahawk. What hair he had left was red also. His nose was a small sharp-pointed wedge, red at the tip. He had not shaved that morning, or for several mornings. In the little piggish eyes that stared almost vertically upward there was not a sign of fear.

"Wal?" he gurgled at length.

"I told you that I found this tomahawk today in the ravine. Do you believe that now, or would you care to call me a liar also?"

"I—wal, I kinder b'lieve yeh, naow."

"Then you must believe what 'Lijah said too."

"Mebbe. But I'm a-goin' to hev 'im lashed jest same."

"Why?"

"Sake o' dis'pline. But I'll tell 'em not to hurt 'im much—let 'im off easy, like."

"Have I your word for that?"

"Word of a sojer."

"How about Brown Boy?"

"Same."

Sleeping Bear let the little man go. Rather a brave little man he was—or as brave as a man can be who has not intelligence enough to know that he is in danger. And yet Sleeping Bear found himself vigorously rubbing against his hunting-shirt the hand that had clutched that unshaven jaw.

"Major," said he, "I think the red-sticks under Weatherford are coming down on us soon."

"I don't. But what of it?"—Major Beasley had moved back to his little table, and he spoke now, from behind it, in a tone somewhat more belligerent than that which he had used a moment before.

"We ought to be more ready for them. We should finish the blockhouse, strengthen the pickets in a dozen places, and see to it that the new gate here in front of your house can be closed."

"That's *my* business."

"True."

"An' I'll tend to it."

"I'm glad to hear you say so, although you have said it more than once before. I think you should set your men at work on it today, now."

"An' *I* think, Mr. Sleepin' B'ar, that ye're takin' too damn much *on* yerself. I'll let you know I'm a-runnin' thisheer fort, an' I ain't to be dictated to by an Injun no more 'n I would by a nigger, by God."

"I'm not trying to dictate, Major, but only to help you save about five hundred and fifty human lives, including your own."

"Huh! Say, lookee hyar, iffen ye don't like haow I'm a-runnin' thisheer fort, s'posin' ye traipse yerself over to Maount Vernon—'t ain't more 'n twenty mile—an' jest tell Gov'nor Claiborne 't Dan Beasley don't know the sojer business. See 'f he don't send yeh back a-haowlin' with a burr in yer breeches."

"I'm sure you know it, Major," was the smiling reply. "You've been acting like a soldier for the last week. Now I suggest that you begin to act like a man of sense."

"Naow lookee hyar . . . "

"I shall leave the fort at once and try to find out what Weatherford's men are doing. Some of them are certainly near by, and all of them may be here before I return."

"Naow . . . "

"When they do come you will want to have the block-house finished, the pickets strengthened, and the sand and gravel out from under the eastern gate.—Goodbye, Major."

"Naow, lookee hyar, Mr. Sleepin' B'ar, I don't give a Cont'nental damn haow big ye be nor yet haow all-fired famous. Iffen other fellers raound these parts wanter think ye're Gawd A'mighty, let 'em; but I'm a-tellin' yeh agin 't Dan Beasley's a-runnin' thisheer fort, an' he don't request no advice from no raoust-abaout red-skin whatsomever! Savvy?"

The effectivness of these remarks was diminished by the fact that the little Major had to stand at his door and yell them in crescendo. Before he had finished Sleeping Bear had disappeared through the old gate-way and into the main stockade.—Several militiamen, however, had heard the vigorous peroration. They would spread it abroad through the camp, and that would be good for "dis'pline."

Ah, it was good to be here among the leaves, three hundred yards at least from the squalid acre of filth, smells, quarrels, and monotonous misery called Fort Mims. Sleeping Bear could hear the barking of dogs, the lowing of cattle, but only at long intervals did a human voice interrupt the peace of the noon.

The leaves of the great live-oak were perfectly still, as though painted on the hot blue sky. Gray-green, burnished, bristling with tiny spikes, they seemed to be listening, waiting. Twenty feet below, the delicate tops of the cane-brake stood erect and expectant. No bird called. In

Lake Tensaw, near at hand, and over in Pine Log Creek, the alligators were quiet. The day was holding its breath.

Many miles of wide flat country, all tremulous under the heat-waves, lay spread out below him. Gazing down the shadowy valley of the Perdido he thought he could catch even the shimmer of Pensacola Bay, where the British were now handing out arms to Bill Weatherford. Nearer at hand was Mobile Bay, whither he had gone only last night to reconnoiter. British boats were lying there also, handing out arms to the red-sticks.—Well, it was a strange situation. He could survey hundreds of square miles; he could see that Mrs. Bynum over there in the fort had donned her scarlet calico again to defy Mrs. McGirth who had said it made her look like a whore; but the things he could not see were those that might be going on among the long glaucous shafts of the cane-brake within a hundred feet.

Of course there had not been time, since yesterday, to finish the block-house. Worse than that, the western gate lay wide open. So, for that matter, did the eastern gate—no doubt still clogged with gravel and sand. Probably the Major had been too busy maintaining "dis'pline" during the last twenty-four hours and showing that he was not to be dictated to by any red-skin. Probably by this time the two Negro boys had been publicly flogged.

Yet—no! Looking through into the oblong enclosure of the militia-men, Sleeping Bear saw a dozen soldiers dragging a stripped Negro to the whipping-post. They were hurrying, as though they wanted to get this bit of duty done before the dinner-bell sounded. It would sound very soon. The shadows on the ground were pointing almost due north.

They tied the Negro to the post and left him there, sagging on the rope that held his arms above his head.—That would be Brown Boy, to judge from the color of his skin. He seemed to be sobbing as he waited for the whip.

The civilians in the larger enclosure were beginning to gather about the pots slung over the fires. That much they could do, at least, in order to go on living. Why, then, could they not take the little more trouble of closing the gates? Why was there no armed watch at the corners of the picketing?

Now a soldier was sauntering up toward Brown Boy, swinging a long bull-whip. Other soldiers gathered about him, laughing. The whip was thrown back, raised, and snapped forward.—Had Major Beasley kept his word?—When they heard the scream of the suffering slave

385

many of those round the fires dropped their dishes and hastened toward the whipping-post. Apparently the spectacle of pain was dearer to them than food.

A second and a third stroke fell, laid on with all the power of the soldier's two arms. Beasley had *not* kept his word. Angered as he had been by yesterday's interview, he had probably given orders that Brown Boy should be cut to death.—Ah, what to do?

There came the roll of a drum from the mess-tent in the eastern stockade. Some of the men about Brown Boy turned away. He was still screaming. Others, who had not risen from their games of cards on the grass, now got up, stretched, yawned, and rambled toward their dinner. The tall and soldierly form of Captain Dixon Bailey strode through the old eastern gate-way. His sword-hilt flashed in the sunlight.

And then, suddenly, Sleeping Bear gripped the great rough branch before him in both his hands. His face went pale. Across the open field on the other side of the fort, running at top speed toward that unclosable eastern gate, there came a horde of Indians—six hundred, eight hundred, perhaps a thousand! They were coming from that same ravine in which Brown Boy and 'Lijah had seen, yesterday morning, their reconnoitering party. And well out in front of them, war-painted and yelling the war-whoop, Bill Weatherford rode in gala white buck-skins on his huge gray horse.

Heart-shaking it was to see the level field, a moment ago still and empty, all at once come alive with fierce colors, grotesque forms, and headlong speed. The great horse came first, bearing Weatherford; then a group of five Young Prophets, all black and running together; and last the throng of the warriors, hideous in black and red, leaping with huge strides across the four hundred yards of open land while they screamed and howled and yelled.

Captain Bailey ran out of the mess-tent and dashed through the inner gateway shouting orders, herding the women and children toward Samuel Mims's central cabin. Captain Middleton and Captain Jack tumbled after him, together with a dozen soldiers, all scrambling for their arms. There was no time to draw the men up in line. One and all they were making for the inner gateway and crowding through without a shot, many leaving their muskets on the ground. They were getting ready to close the inner gate when Major Beasley exploded from the front door of his cabin, looked for a moment at the on-rushing horde not fifty yards off, and ran directly toward it. He reached the outer gate, set one foot against the gate-jamb and jerked for a second with all his might and tugged. The gate would not budge. Bill Weatherford dashing through on horseback struck down at his head with a war-club and felled him. Beasley struggled to his hands and knees and crawled a little way. His arms crumpled and he fell prone on his face and lay, jerking. The first warrior through the gate leapt upon him, made a few deft slashes with a knife round the skull, set one foot on a shoulder, jerked hard at the hair, and then with a yell held aloft the first scalp of the day. At the same moment he caught sight of Brown Boy, writhing and straining against the whipping-post. In a bound he stood behind the slave and sank a tomahawk into his skull. A few seconds later he was waving the red hair and the kinky black together, and yelling, racing on.

The soldiers had crowded into the civilians' enclosure. They were dragging to and barring its ponderous gate. Thus Sleeping Bear's view of the military stockade beyond was in part shut off. He could just make out that as the main body of the red-sticks came rushing in from the eastward they were pausing there to watch the Young Prophets do the Dance of the Lakes.

Here, if they only knew it, was the chance of the soldiers. And indeed they did shoot down the Young Prophets almost at once, but their fire through the loop-holes upon the crowd of warriors on the other side of the wall was badly organized and scattering.

Nevertheless the prompt slaughter of the five Prophets was unmistakably a shock to the attacking party. The bodies were being carried through the outer gateway and to a distance of a hundred yards. Some kind of parley was going on over there among the chief men, with Weatherford among them. No doubt they were discussing the promise of Tenkswatawa that bullets would split and fall harmless when they touched the sacred persons of the Prophets. A good deal had to be reconsidered now that the Prophets were unquestionably dead.

Thus far there had been no carnage inside the larger stockade, but the crowding and confusion augured ill for what might follow. Captain Bailey, taking the place of Major Beasley, was trying to be everywhere at once—sending the soldiers to their respective cabins in the corners, assigning loop-holes to the civilian men and boys, and arranging with a few of the bolder-hearted women to load the muskets passed back to them. He had all the buckets filled with water and placed near the several buildings. He set Surgeon Osborne and half a dozen girls to tearing linen for bandages. Sleeping Bear heard him call out above the

387

din beseeching every man to be sure that his musket and ammunition were ready.

But these last-minute preparations looked pitifully inadequate when the red-sticks, having finished their parley, dashed back through the eastern gate and began firing through the party-wall. Captain Middleton, in charge of that wall, was killed at once, and many of his men ran away and hid behind the buildings. Captain Jack's rifle-men on the south side held the enemy off for a while. Ensign Randon, although invisible from the live-oak, was evidently holding his own on the west. It was from the undefended loop-holes of the eastern wall, and also from those on the north, that the greatest execution was being done. Clearly, there were not enough men inside the fort to hold it against the swarm of their foes. At the end of every minute there were fewer.

In spite of Captain Bailey's frantic exertions, the red-sticks soon commanded all the hundred or more loop-holes on the northern wall as well as the hundred on the east which had been theirs from the start. They were drawing away from the west and south walls, which were better defended, and gave a wide berth to the unfinished block-house on the south-west corner from which some single rifle-man had cut down several of their number. For ten minutes or more they crouched on the north and east, taking turns, firing rapidly, reducing the defenders by at least a hundred men. To approach any of those loop-holes from the inside meant certain death; and yet to avoid them could only mean death for a little while postponed. Soldiers and civilians, young men and old men and boys of ten or twelve, could be seen to stop all at once and stagger a few steps or else fall like lumps where they stood.

A bullet well aimed brought a clean, quick death. Fire and torture did not. And these who were falling now had weapons in their hands. Not a few of them were in some degree responsible. But the unseen women and children packed in the central house, able only to watch and wait, peering out through the shattered windows and the cracks of the splintered door, seeing their fathers and brothers and lovers and sons stand up for a while in the deadly sleet and then stand up no longer . . . ah, the white-faced children who could not cry and the women praying for death to come swiftly and cleanly and soon!

Meanwhile Hobbomok lay still and cool in the crook of Sleeping Bear's arm. Nowhere among those yelling hundreds could he find the tall, gaunt, black-painted form of the one man he had to kill. These maniacs had not used holy things for deceit and destruction. They were that man's dupes and tools. There was no way of preventing them from doing his evil work. There was nothing now to do but to wait, to watch, and to see what he had foreseen. He could only wait and watch through the shattered windows of the mind, the splintered door of the heart, this spectacle of his own utter ruin, defeat, and over-throw.

The western gate toppled inward, apparently crushing a number of those who had been striving to support it from within. Twenty, fifty, a hundred, two hundred warriors rushed over it, yelling, brandishing muskets, tomahawks, fire-brands. The defenders were cowering back into Patrick's loom-house near the southern wall. From the doors and windows they began a withering fire. Others, having climbed to the attic of Mims's house, were knocking out shingles and shooting down from there. The women must be helping to load. It must have been the women who carried up the attic ladder those few buckets of water that extinguished the first fire-arrows.

But there was no water left for the fire-arrows that followed. The roof caught fire. Mrs. Bynum in her scarlet calico—whore or not, a heroine—dashed out from the broken door with a bucket toward the well. A huge Creek brained her, stripped her, began pulling the gown over his own head. A shot from the loom-house dropped him. A second Creek, snatching up the garment, fell dead before he got it on. It lay sopping in a pool of blood beside the corpses.

Mims's house was crackling. The flames rose straight and pale into the quiet sky. The doorway began to belch women and children. They ran for the loom-house, but that poor refuge was already crammed. Standing on either side of the door, some twenty red-sticks clove the skulls of the women as they came on. They took the younger children by the legs and swung their heads against the log-ends. Mims's roof fell in with a fountain and shower of sparks. The other buildings were catching fire—even the loom-house. The hundred or more who had crowded in there were dispatched as they came out. The things being done to the pregnant women could not be watched. Someone—Dr. Holmes, apparently—was chopping mightily at the log pickets in the northern wall. Ten men stood round him in a circle, facing outward, firing. Peter Randon was there, and Charles Fletcher, owner of Brown Boy. Some of them might escape, although before they could reach the swamp on the south they would have to pass a strong fence where a score of red-sticks were lying in wait. Captain Bailey, unable to wait, was trying to climb the stockade. His friends were pulling him back.

Sleeping Bear slid to the ground and set out along the soggy trail leading to Fort Pierce. Although it was now too late for help to do any good, he would run to Fort Pierce, if necessary to every other fort and blockhouse in the region, seeking help. As the crackling of the fires and the screams and shots died away behind him he ran faster and faster. Less and less, as he ran, could he understand why he had not started twenty minutes earlier, when the attack began. The best that he could say was that he had been looking for the Prophet—and also that he had been, as it were, frozen by horror.

It was eight hours later when he climbed again to his place in the live-oak. He had returned alone, after seeking vainly for help through half the day. As he had feared, every other strong-hold in the neighborhood, including even Mount Vernon, twenty miles away, was either fully occupied on its own account or expecting soon to be so.

The sun was burning down in a tumultuous splendor. Every stiff little green-gray leaf was flurried like a plucked bow-string in a wind from off the Gulf. The tops of the canes were sighing and faintly clashing together.

Inside Fort Mims all was still except for the dance of flames here and there among the embers.

Far away on the edge of the forest the Creeks had built a dozen large fires. Some were dancing round the fires, and others were preparing their evening meal.

Sleeping Bear descended, walked across to the western gate and stood looking in. The ground was heaped with smoldering ruins and hundreds of huddled bodies. A shaft of level light from the setting sun struck in through the gate before him. It laid an almost life-like flush upon the faces of the slain. And he saw that his own shadow reached across the acre of death clear to the eastern wall.

Was it because he could not save them? Was it because through all his life the sight of this field would smolder in his brain? Was it because he would gladly have died in their stead?

Throwing his head far back and his arms abroad, he stood for a moment in the Indian attitude of salutation and farewell.

390

THE PROPHET

One thing he had left to do.—As he groped and fumbled his way among the swamp-rooted canes on the first night of his journey, one thought possessed him and pushed him on. In the morning and all the next day it drove him up the snake-infested trails of the Tombigbee. During the nights and days that followed it pursued him through the Chickasaw towns, across Colbert's Ferry, and over the Natchez Trace to Nashville. Along hundreds of miles of trace and trail it kept him free from harm. He felt that he could not die until he had killed the Prophet.

All else—places, faces, events, weariness, the ache of his own failure, even the recollection of the Beloved Woman—seemed now a trivial dream. All else was circumstance, to be wrenched to the service of his will. And there came a strange kind of joy, even of peace, from having his duty so clarified, so focussed upon a single deed. Moreover he felt that a man was not yet completely defeated while it still lay in him to rid the world of one father of lies and to cleanse one spot of corruption.

In any other mood he might have found it hard to report the Fort Mims massacre to General Jackson, propped up in bed there at the Hermitage, yellow-faced, hollow-eyed, his grizzled bristling hair all awry, with a shattered shoulder to make him curse all the more volubly and with two bullets from Jesse Benton's pistol in his body. But Jackson did not waste a minute in pointing out how this news confirmed the opinion he had always held of Indians, that they were a treacherous, lying, thieving and blood-thirsty lot whom the whites must simply obliterate. All of that now he took for granted, and got to work. The news did him good. Later news that the Creeks under Weatherford were rioting in arson and plunder worked upon him, his doctor said, almost a cure.

He read to Sleeping Bear parts of a letter from a certain Major Kennedy who had gone to Fort Mims with a detachment of troops to bury the bodies there. This Major had seen the air dark with buzzards when he arrived, and there had been hundreds of wild dogs within the enclosures gnawing the bones. "Indians, Negroes, white men, women and children," he wrote, "lay in one promiscuous ruin. All were scalped, and the females of every age were butchered in a manner which

391

neither decency nor language permits me to describe. The main build-ing was burned to ashes, which were filled with bones. The plains and woods around were covered with dead bodies. All the houses were con-sumed by fire, except the block-house and part of the pickets. The sol-diers and officers with one voice called on divine Providence to revenge the deaths of our murdered friends."

But Jackson did not wait for Providence—or perhaps he felt himself to be its chosen angel. Within a week after the arrival of Major Ken-nedy's letter he was lifted into the saddle, his left arm strapped to his side, and rode out of Nashville at the head of several hundreds of volun-teers. He was going to find William Weatherford. Sleeping Bear went with him, determined to find and to kill Tenkswatawa, the Prophet, twin-brother of Tecumseh.

Then for month after month the dream went on of forced marches, starvation and mutiny, of battles and routs and slaughter. The dream moved across Tennessee River, over the Raccoon Mountains, and down into the Holy Ground of the Creeks on the Coosa. Young Davy Crockett was in that dream, and so was young Sam Houston. The gigantic John Coffee, Jackson's partner in war as well as in business, was in it too. At Tallasahatchee Coffee's thousand killed two hundred red-sticks. In the chunky-yard of Coosa Jackson's men killed three hun-dred warriors and burned the old Miko's round-house to the ground. At Emuckfaw and Enotochopco they killed three hundred more. But the Prophet was not seen in any of these battles, nor was his body among the slain.

Yet the poisonous working of the Prophet's lies was everywhere apparent. Every Creek town and every party of red-sticks encountered in the woods and swamps included some fanatical imitation or echo of him. At Tallasahatchee, when the attack was hottest, a Young Prophet, painted black, sprang suddenly to the roof of the council-house and harangued the contending warriors. "The Great Spirit," he cried, "is on the side of the Creeks and the British and The Knife. For every bullet that these Americans fire he sends a ghost to catch it and stop it in air. Look at me, on the roof of the council-house. I stand in full view of the foe, but their bullets cannot reach me!"—A boy from Tennessee who understood Creek a little heard this boaster, took quick aim, and brought him tumbling headlong to the ground.

In another part of the dream there was Andrew Jackson at Fort Strother facing down a starving and mutinous army. He had a rifle

392

across his saddle-bow as he sat his horse barring their homeward way. His face was twisted with wrath, his eyes like live coals, his left arm was in a sling, and "By the Immaculate God," he was shouting, "the first cowardly villain that takes a step toward home I'll blow to Kingdom Come!" The rifle was not loaded, but the men did not know that. What they saw was that Jackson's arm and trigger finger were shaking with fever. They grumbled, but returned to their duty. At that time Jackson was living on such acorns and hickory nuts as could be found in the wintry woods. His men had begun to call him "Old Hickory."

In the midst of the dream there came news that Tecumseh had been slain while fighting far to the north on the British side. His American foes had flayed him and were using his skin for razor-strops. But there came no word of the Prophet.

Thus the winter passed, with misery and wounds and sudden death for many men under Jackson and Coffee, for more of those who were serving with Governor Claiborne nearer the Gulf, but above all for the Creeks both red-stick and white-stick. Many a round-house was burned, many a chunky-pole thrown down. It was the most painful phase of the dream in which Sleeping Bear was living that he had to see the once proud and powerful Creek Nation violently done to death. He had to see what he had foretold. In every burned village and heap of corpses he saw the inevitable outworking of the Prophet's lies—one more result of the way he had profaned holy things to do the work of hell.

It was at Horseshoe Bend, half-way up the shadowy windings of the Tallapoosa, that certain white-stick scouts finally found the Prophet. He had been lurking there, they said, ever since the great busk at Coosa, hidden among the darkest fastnesses of the Indian country and surrounded by forests and swamps and cane-brakes through which only the wildest beasts and men had ever hitherto found a path. There, they said, he had been constructing a stronghold, designed by Weatherford, as the last resort of the red-sticks in case of extreme disaster. Every day and far into the night he and the younger Prophets gathered about him danced, sang their incantations, and carried on their black magic to assist in building the fort. The scouts said that this fort had a huge breastwork of logs, ten feet high, ten feet thick, and four hundred yards in length. In their opinion the Prophet's medicine had been very strong, and they doubted whether even General Jackson's two cannon

—one of them throwing three-pound and the other six-pound balls—would be able to blow that breastwork down.

Questioned further, the scouts reported that this great crooked line of logs lay across a neck of land at the bottom of a deep loop made by the river. Inside it were heaps of brush among the ravines and thickets, and on the high bank of the river itself was a cluster of huts with a place for fires and dancing. A hundred canoes, they said, lay below the bank in the water.—Thus, even if the General's cannon should destroy the breastwork, there would still be the thicket and brush to fight through, and, after that, the village. Supposing that the great General should take even the village itself, the red-sticks would escape by way of the river. In short, they felt obliged to advise the General not to go to Horseshoe Bend. It was more than fifty miles off from Fort Strother, through a terrible country, and if he ever got there he would find the place protected by a very strong medicine indeed. They also advised Sleeping Bear to leave the Prophet alone. Certain friendly Choctaws who had gone with the Creek white-sticks on this scouting party expressed a firm belief that the Prophet must have The Knife.

And so the dream went on through ten days and nights of furious toil—ten nights and days of road-making, bridge-laying, pulling cannon up precipitous slopes, and dragging provision wagons out of swamp-holes in the cane. During that struggle not a man among Jackson's little army was for a moment warm or dry or fed or rested. Toward the end of it the General took his arm out of the sling. On the same day Sleeping Bear stripped off his buck-skins, blackened his body, laid his rifle aside, and kept only his long hunting-knife for a weapon.

"You look like a prophet yourself," said Jackson.

"So I am," was the grim-faced reply. "But I have two eyes."

In the middle of the morning of the eleventh day—March 27th, 1814—the two cannon began to pound at the breastwork. They made little impression. The iron balls plumped into the logs of popple with a dull softened thud, raising no splinters. From their double row of loop-holes in the logs the red-sticks replied with bullets and screams of derision. Over the ping of the rifles and the bellow of cannon could be heard the Dance of the Lakes.

At noon, with General Coffee and his cavalry, a white-stick scout crossed the river two miles below the Bend and came back on the other side. From there he swam the stream, for the most part under water, and set the canoes adrift. Then, finding the public square and the huts on the upper bank deserted, he gave the signal for Coffee's men to cross. The red-sticks were soon fighting between two fires.

They fought with desperation, asking no quarter, from behind trees and brush and in the gullies running down to the river—with rifles and muskets at first, then with bows and arrows, and finally with toma-hawks, war-clubs, knives, and stones. They fought from behind the heaped bodies of their own dead. And all the afternoon, while their numbers dwindled and the circle of fighting men grew smaller, the cries of the Prophets dancing in the center of the circle were ever more loud and clear.

At sundown, however, that frenzied shouting ceased; and then it was that Sleeping Bear caught his first glimpse of the Prophet. Standing just inside of the breastwork and near the river-bank, he was looking back over the corpse-strewn field of the battle with an expression on his face of agonized despair. Evil though he was, his grief lent him a transient nobility. All at once he threw wide his arms in a gesture of farewell to those hundreds of dead comrades—and plunged down the bank toward the river.

Sleeping Bear ran to the bank. There was no sign of anyone there swimming. With utmost caution he moved up toward the breastwork, holding his long knife ready. No one. But between him and the shat-tered line of logs, and reaching down to the water's edge, there was a great pile of brush-wood obviously placed there to serve for conceal-ment.

Young Sam Houston must have seen the Prophet also, for now he came running along the breastwork sword in hand, with the blood streaming from an arrow-wound in his thigh. He seemed about to leap down into the tumbled brush when three muskets flashed at almost the same instant from below him in the tangle. Houston fell, clutching at his shoulder. Then at once, leaving not a second for the warriors in the brush to reload, Sleeping Bear sprang down the bank at the spot where the Prophet had disappeared.—His dream was at an end.

"Are you The Knife?"
"No."
"Who is?"
"I have never been told."
"Have you it?"
"I have never seen it, except in my vision."

"Look into my eyes, and remember that it will not be well for you to go before the Great Spirit with a lie on your lips."

"Kill me now, Sleeping Bear, before my heart is soft, before I say anything unworthy of my vision."

"Did you see The Knife in your vision?"

"I did."

"How was it?"

"With a long and wavy blade. The handle was a woman, naked, cut in some green stone. She was very beautiful."

"Have you been true to her?"

"I have gone wherever she has pointed. I have done her will only. Since my vision I have loved her alone."

"From whence do you think your vision came?"

"From Him who giveth and taketh breath.—Kill me now!"

Sleeping Bear relaxed his pressure on the Prophet's throat. For ten seconds, no more, though it seemed an age, he stared down into the one little eye less than two feet below his own face with the fascination of loathing. It was an evil eye, unspeakably, and yet not the eye of a liar. It stared back in defiant hatred, with no flinching or fear, and behind the hatred there was a kind of perverted devotion.

Not for an instant could Sleeping Bear doubt that the Prophet had told the truth about his vision and his fidelity. The man had been true and faithful to the light—or should one say darkness?—that had been sent him. Could more than that fidelity be required by a fellow mortal who knew himself to be utterly lost and benighted? Could even the gods themselves who so twisted and braided the strands of good and evil expect more than that? To hold fast to the best one knew—was not that the sum of life's duty?

Thus the doubts and conjectures of many years were concentrated in the agony of a few moments. In that one little eye, utterly faithful unto death to its own evil vision, Sleeping Bear saw life's central mystery brought to a focus. The old question that had tormented him during his days and nights in the Cave of Hobbomok was forced in upon him again—and almost intolerably now because he must act, or refrain from action, as though he knew the answer. His brain reeled under the burden of a dreadful uncertainty. On the one hand he was all but overwhelmed by the headlong savage passion to rend and throttle and destroy which had been gathering momentum ever since his tragic defeat in the round-house at Coosa and the consequent horror at Fort Mims. He held between his two hands, he firmly believed, the very incarnation of that Power of Darkness which he had pursued through ten thousand shadowy forms and disguises. Why should not those hands do their work now, and clutch, and stifle? What checked and held him immobile as the mere stone statue of a man caught forever in a moment of agonized effort? Was it the recollection that the wickedness represented by Alec McGillivray had not been destroyed when his body was broken and strewn on the sable stream? Was it the thought of what his own life might have been if, instead of Occum, Nathan Hale, and the Chester household, he had known from childhood nothing but savagery? Did he ask himself how he would have lived if, instead of Saint Christopher, the gods had sent him a vision of a blood-dripping knife? Or did he perhaps try to imagine the situation of one who, never hearing of Mount Machimoodus, had spent all his days and nights in the Cave of Hobbomok, seeing only the images of evil depicted on its slimy wall?

Sleeping Bear rose to his feet. He helped the Prophet to rise. Then, with his hunting-knife, he cut a slender cane growing near the water, and began forcing out the pith.

"Your brother Tecumseh," said he, "is dead."

"Oh!"

"You killed your brother. You killed these hundreds of Creeks who here lie dead, and those who fell at Tallasahatchee and Emuckfaw and Enotochopco. You burned the old Miko's round-house at Coosa and broke his heart. You have broken the power of the Creeks forever. You have given their Holy Ground to the pale-faced thief. You have utterly failed in your life and in all your purposes."

"Kill me now!"

"Therefore I cannot kill you. It is the will of Him who giveth and taketh breath that we both live on, knowing that we have been faithful to our visions and yet have failed."

There was no answer.

"Take this hollow cane to breathe through. Swim under water, deep, to dodge their bullets. Ten miles down-stream you will find the Creek canoes. In one of them is food."

Tenkswatawa took the cane without a word.

"Now go, brother of my soul, and let me never see your evil face again!"

The two men saluted with uplifted hands. The Prophet slipped into the water so quietly that he raised barely a ripple. A minute later

Sleeping Bear saw the end of a green cane-stalk moving smoothly out into the main current of the Tallapoosa where the water ran gold and gules in the sunset light.

A LETTER FROM FOUR WINDS FARM

Deer Holdfast—I send these fewe lines by a pedlar comes from town of Berlin over Hertford way & sez he will git to New Orleans this hear winter or bust and was thare 2 years ago & sez has heerd tell abowt you & a man cald Andy Jackson owt theer who ye helle is this Andy Jackson allso a riffle makere cald Russ Beane. How aire ye Russ Bean & this hear pedlair selz Tin Pans from Berlin and Clocks from Bristow whch donot runne 2 days and seegars from Winsor wch same you can taike it frm me aynte wuth a dam so donte bye anny Holdfast offn him but his nuse is fresh and good ez his segars are not. These lynes leve me wel as evare egcep for this dam knea I gott at Bunkarr Hill witch does nott limber upp mutch alltho it was sum time ago ass no dowt ye arre awaire and yure Mother Chester she is verry well ownly short of breth witch is a gude thing and Rebecca she kepes wel two altho she ownly had 2 boys whitch is a pitty and 1 of theme dyed yung grettly to owr sorough ye otherr 1 is a saylor like his father John Reid whom no dowt you rekoleck but is dead now drownded att sea years back but had a paper mill up Norwitch way and a store down in Chelsea whar the shepe walk was an so gott preety dam ritch whitch is moore than most foulkes thes parrts thes tymes. Samson Occum is ded two & the reverent Lord both gode menne. Holdfast I was up to Hartford nott long ago sence and in the Stayte House thar ye cd look downe Stayt Strete and cownt most a hunnerd skuners and ketches & pinks & briggs lyin at the wharf in ye River Holdfast and theyre timbres rottin with nothin to do accownt this heer embargo & warre with England Jeffairson & Madison hev gotte up & putte down on us. New England and Connecticut haytes them two for we kno they made this war jest to ruynate us uppe North hyar whut do you think out West theire. Annyhow Connecticutt and Mass & R.I. and sech heer in New England be fixin to hold a convention up to Hartford and see yffen may bee we better brake off frm the Union Holdfast they ast mee to go but I sed to hell I gotte a bulet in my nee I said witch sayme bullet has sarved

398

me well manny is the time yer Mother has tryed to dragge me out hither an yon but jest same I wisht I knu whut they be a fixin to cook upp over thair becuz I fit old England onct and will agin sune as evairr I can bend my nea and sum of the things my grandson Sam Chester Reid tels me abowt British conduck at see Holdfast it wd sartingly maike yer blud bile. But whut I tuk my penne in hande fur to say a weak aggo it taikes me a longe tyme to writ a lettair lik it allus did Old Putt who is gone now is this yer Mother Chester sais she wd lik to hav you cum hom and see us we aynte gettin yunger year by yere she says but wee love our bigg sone much ez everr that is what yer Mother Chester said Holdfast and I dunnot kno az I hev mutch to add nor yett subtrack. Rebekka she sais much the saime and she says that is Rebekka tell Holdfast iff he come home agin I will runne down Hill with Him like we useter to Smith Cove and does he rekleck that time we gott lost over bye Cotchegan Rock and he said the spierit of Uncas the Moheegan wd taike care of us whitch apperingly she said he has done. And more speechully she said iffen evarre youe shd see or heer abt her sone Sam Chester Reid who is a saylor now out of New York will you taike keer of him ye sone lyke you allus done of ye motherr says Rebekka wch is all verry wel butt I tell her hell my dere that Holdfast has otherr fysshe to frye but romin all overr Meriky taikin keer of the Chester fambly wich I hope yuw aynt becas that boy Sam is quyte a boy iff he is my grandson and so I say the sayme. He is maried to Mary Jennings of Willington whose father was in my regmint at Bunkare Hill and yung Sam he do git into fytes pritty frekint sence he was mayd captiff by the Frenssh and was on the *Constellation* whin she tuk thet Frensch frigat an' he got tuk by Tripoli pirats an' was Master's Mate of the *Constitution* when Isaac Hull tuk the *Gerrair* but he's Sailing Master now & commands a lytle 7 gun pryvateer out of New York. Holdfast wee ownly kep 4 or 5 cowes theis days caus of nott 2 manny hands and we solde ye olde bulle long sense and the barns neid shingles and so sum plaices on ye hous ruf whar ye rayne comes thro on yer bedde ownly donnot git the idear we hav gotte olde nor pore by cause we anyt not by a dam site ownly jest restin uppe a whyle ontell our boy coms home. Nowe here it is 2 wekes past Holdfast sence I tuk this heere penne in hand and so far I aynte sed whut I started owt for like a man settin sayle for Montauk Pint and endin up somers offen Grande Bank but whut I meen is it neverr ben sayme heer on Quaiker Hill sence that nite of thanksgivin ye started owt in snow with ye little dog I cann see ye now and so can all of uss ekksep

399

John Reid has gone down at see pore boy we often tawk abt that night and some times it do seem long aggo and then again it do nott. And all ways when yer Mother or Me shutts kitching doore for the nite Holdfast we hates to locke itt and so we do not locke itt and so iffen ye was to com home toonite and we was in bed aslepe why helle Holdfast ye cd wawk rite inn and therr wd be ye old fyre waytin upp fer ye and mebbe suthn to eate on shelf evven iffen the times be harde the Lorde hath ben good to us Holdfast and we still have enof left over for the neabors and for oure boy wharevver he be wheneevver he comes Gode buy Holdfast ye pedlar is goin now hee is at the dore in fack but dunnot by anny seegars offn him thare is not grait chaynges heer you will find speshully in our love for our boye yowre Motherr sends mutch lov and allso Rebecca she does tew who is a widder woman now & long hez ben pore gal.

Yrs to commande in gt hayste
John Chester.

THE FIRE OF HOME

(May—1814)

Perfectly still and dark it was in the kitchen when, long after midnight, Mother Chester opened her eyes. She could not guess what had awakened her. Perhaps an ember had fallen into the ash on the hearth, or her husband had slightly stirred in his sleep. Some bird of the night, perhaps, had been calling high up in the sky.

She lay awake for an hour, listening to a silence that seemed to be filled with music, thinking back to her girlhood and the days of her courtship, thinking of the good man beside her who for more than sixty years had been her trying, troublesome, and utterly dear companion. She thought of Rebecca and Holdfast and of her dead son, John Reid. Then, after whispering a prayer of thanksgiving for the love that had blest and sheltered all her nights and days, she fell asleep.

When next she awoke there was a pearly light in the room, and soon after a thin golden bar of sunshine began to quiver on a beam overhead. Cautiously, then, so as not to arouse the Colonel, the little white-haired woman slipped from the bed, donned her gray linsey-woolsey, stepped into her moccasins, and began to move about the room as softly as a moth.

First of all there was the fire to be fed, and then came the question what kind of day it would be. Going to the south window she saw the Thames a-gleam all the way to the shimmering Sound. A breeze was stirring in the lilac-bloom at the window. Robins were awake in the old apple tree, clearing the dark from their voices. There was not one fleck of cloud in the sky.

Turning then to the kitchen table, thinking of breakfast, she saw lying on it a long dark object, apparently a huge fire-arm of some kind, which had not been there the night before when she blew out the candle. It was cold and hard to the touch.—Yes, certainly it was a fire-arm, although the barrel of it was not round but eight-sided. It was much too heavy for her to lift.

She fumbled for her spectacles and put them on.—H'm. A strange fire-arm indeed! It must be more than six feet long. On one side was a piece of shining metal cut into the shape of a bear. She spelled out the queer word "Nusi-Nita" on the barrel, and on the stock, in gold, there was the word "Hobbomok." She thought she might have heard that second word before, but not the first one. But then her face brightened, and she smiled. On the lock, and in very small letters, she had found the name "R. Bean."

So, that young scalawag had come back to visit them again.—Still, perhaps he had settled down a bit. Certainly he must be more thoughtful than in the old days, considering how quietly he had come in during the night. He might bring news from Holdfast. At any rate, he would help to entertain the Colonel, and Rebecca would be glad to see him. She might even invite him to meet some of her fine friends up in Norwich, if only he would promise to dress himself less like a heathen and not be too bold with the young ladies.

But there, beside the fire-arm—what was that large rough object, made of the skin of some animal and sewn with deer sinews? It was warm to the touch. It held a large clam-shell, still warmer. Would Russell Bean carry a thing so crude and worn, so bare of all decoration? And besides . . . ! Yes, she suddenly knew that she had seen this pouch before. She remembered when, and by whom, it had been made.

With one hand pressed against her heart, she went quickly back across the room toward the door opening upon the attic stairway. When half-way to it she paused and looked down at the sleeping Colonel. Ought she to call him? Should she make quite sure that he had not brought in that queer leathern pouch and the great fire-arm while she slept?— But no; for that might make him hope for something—for something too wonderful to happen.

And so she moved on to the door; but just as her hand was lifted to the latch she stopped again. On the floor at her feet were two moccasins, very large, old, muddied, and nearly worn out.—They were *his!* Oh, unmistakably, certainly *his!*

While she was bending over to touch them the door beside her swung slowly outward. She well knew why it was swinging. Her heart was too large and loud for her small body. It was he!—although she could not see him yet because the stairway was still dark and the sight of those soggy moccasins had flooded her eyes with tears. She saw and heard almost nothing, but felt herself lifted from the floor as lightly and gently as though she were going to heaven.

"Hey! What the hell's a-goin' on over thar? Why cain't ye let a tired man git a wink o' sleep?—Stint that blubb'rin', Mother."

"Oh, John! It's Holdfast!"

"Holdfast, nothin'! Mother, ye ben dreamin' agin. Allus dreamin' 'bout that dratted boy! Ketch yer death, ye will, roamin' round the cold house dreamin' 'bout boys!"

"But John, I *ain't* dreamin'—not 'lessen we all be. I say it's our boy Holdfast come home, John."

"Stuff an' nonsense! Climb back inter bed hyar, an' let me sleep."

"Well, Father," said a quiet, deep, perfectly remembered voice, "you go on sleeping. Mother and I'll see you at breakfast."

"Hey? Whut say?—Doncher try to fool *me,* now! I'm wide awake, an' not b'lievin' no nonsense."

"All right, Father. You go right on dreaming that you're awake."

"Mother, d'ye hear thet 'ar voice too?"

"Why sartinly, John. It's Holdfast!"

"Whar's my specs? Mother, git me my specs, cain't ye? I won't b'lieve it 'thout I see 'im through my own specs, an' mebbe not then."

Holdfast brought them from the highboy, and the old man, sitting upright in bed, adjusted them with shaking hands. And then, as he looked up and up along the gaunt frame clad in worn buck-skins, they could see him bite his lower lip hard, almost viciously.

"H'm! Wal! I swan!—How be ye, boy?" he gasped out. His hand still had a vigorous grip, for all its trembling.

402

"I am not sick," Holdfast replied, and gravely smiled at himself for using that western phrase.

"That's good. Me nuther. Feel a damn sight better 'n us'l, in fack.—Wal! An' so ye come home, eh?"

"So it seems."

"Yeah.—Wal, 'pears like we're a-goin' to hev a fine day."

"'Pears like we'll hev the grandest day 't ever dawned," said his wife. "But now, John, do ye git some clothes on yeh an' make yerself look decent whiles I flax round an' git suthin' to eat. I never did see our boy look so gaunted an' holler."

An hour later, sitting before the fire, with the Colonel to the left of her and Holdfast on her right, each smoking his pipe, Mother Chester asserted that no queen upon a throne could be happier than she was in her own kitchen.

"Aw, kings an' queens an' all that trash, they don't git a chancet at nothin' so good as this," the Colonel declared.

"An' yet I will say that Holdfast has changed," said his wife. "Don't ye think so, John?"

"Wal, mebbe. Looks like he hadn't laughed sence he went away, no more 'n Cochegan Rock."

Holdfast stirred in his chair. "Things haven't been going well with me out there," he said. "I came home with the notion that I might be able to help someone. In the West, I've failed."

"H'm," said Mother Chester, laying her hand for a moment on Holdfast's sleeve, "I don't see how a man like you c'n reely fail anywhars.—Same time, o' course a man like you allus *thinks* he's a-failin', wharsomever he be."

"Yeah," the Colonel added. "An' a man like you c'n sartinly help round hyar iffen he's a mind to. Ye'll obsarve we don't hev the sarvints we useter."

"No, Father. I've seen that."

"Wal, hell, why should we?—jest two old church-yard bodies. Yer mother, she tuk the notion 't was sinful to keep what she called 'slaves.' All I know is, it don't pay. So when old Jon'than Trumbull an' the rest died off, we didn't git no more.—Ez fer young Pompey, I guv 'im his freedom an' a small farm an' some cows."

"I see."

"An' then come this hyar Embargo o' Jefferson's, an' New London lost all her trade, an' Sam Avery went off to God knows whar in the

403

Rebecca, an'—wal, Mother an' me says 'Hell, we c'n stick it out,' we says. 'We got our land an' our old house. We'll keep a cow or two an' a few hens an' a sarse-patch; an' so let Mr. Madison *hev* his damn war an' we 'll hev Four Winds Farm,' we says."

"You've had enough to eat and wear and the best of places to live in, but not much money. Is that it?"

"Aw, money! I've hed it, an' then agin I hain't, an' I don't see much differ. Nobody has money now-a-days.—Nobbut what the farm meanwhiles ain't a-goin' back'ards. She be. I cain't seem to mow like I useteh, Holdfast, an' the bresh gits thicker year by year. Over by Bolles Wood whar we useteh ha'nt twenty cows they ain't 'nough grass to keep a rabbit fat. Down Hempstead medder way the elders an' ivy are gittin' twenty feet high. An' ez fer the stun walls an' barns an' shingles— wal, ye c'n help, my boy. Ye c'n help."

"We don't ask yeh to do any work 'lessen ye wanteh, course," said Mother Chester, creaking back and forth in her chair. "All we ask is for our boy to be happy, ez 'pearingly he hain't ben o' late."

The Colonel stumped to the mantel-piece to get himself a fresh pipe. "An' 'nother thing we ask of 'im is," said he, "to tell us whar he's ben all these years, an' what doin'."

Holdfast sat for a while in thought. There were so many things that he must not say, and so many more that would not be understood. At last he rose from his chair, walked to the mantel, and rested one arm upon it, looking down. "My story," he said, "won't take long. Mostly I've wandered about, living with many tribes, learning their languages and how they live and think and feel. Most people would say that I've wasted my life, and perhaps I have. At any rate, the thing I've lived for is lost, ruined."

"Why don't ye jest start at the beginnin', Holdfast?" suggested Mother Chester. "That way we'll git it all ez it happens 'long."

"Well then, I will.—After I left home on that Thanksgiving night I lived until Christmas in a cave over near Connecticut River."

"What the hell fer?" the Colonel exclaimed.

"I may tell you about that some other time, Father.—From there I went back to Mohegan Village, got Perthy and the dog, and we three went out to the Oneida country, across the Hudson, where a number of Mohegans that I knew were living. Samson Occum had taken them there, years before, to get them away from the whites, but already the whites were crowding in and taking their lands away. They were falling into bad white-man habits. After we'd been there a while about fifty

404

of them agreed to go farther west, and a long way farther, if Perthy and I would take them. We did take them, to a place on the other side of Lake Michigan called Green Bay. There they got some land from the Winnebagoes and started a town called Brotherton. I suppose they are there still."

"Right smart of a march, wa'n't it?" the Colonel asked.

"Yes. It took us quite a while, and we had some troubles on the way; but the thing I wanted most at the time was hard work. After that we went into trading for furs and such things with the Indians along the Mississippi. We did so well at it that I had to stop, or Perthy might have come to think that money is important."

"Who is this hyar Perthy ye're talkin' 'bout?"

"Why, John, ye 'member that little orphant Holdfast brung in one night, an' laid 'im down in our bed."

"That's so. Now I do. Liked maple sugar, an' ye fell in love with 'im, o' course, an' wanted to keep 'im, but I wouldn't hear to 't."

"An' I would of kep' 'im too, iffen Holdfast hadn't needed 'im more."

"Ah, hum.—Wal, git on, lad."

"I can't tell you all of it now, but after a while we met Russell Bean."

"Ye did? That young scallywag?"

"Yes, and another one called Andrew Jackson."

"That so? Heered tell o' him a'ready. Injun fighter."

"Well, with these two and some others Perthy and I went over Blue Ridge to Western Waters. We lived there for a while, near Nashville, and then out in the buffalo country."

"What's 'buffalo'?" asked Mother Chester.

"Wal, o' course anybody oughter know what they be. But what's the Blue Ridge an' Western Waters?"

"I'll tell you later. But while I'm thinking of it, Father, I met your old friend Waightstill Avery down there."

"Wal, wal! Old Waightstill, eh? Allus wondered whar he got to. One o' yer Groton cousins, Mother. Met him on the Blue Ridge, did ye?"

"At a cock-fight, yes. He asked me to stay there with him."

"What's a cock-fight?" Mother Chester inquired.

"Aw, now, Mother, we cain't stop to eddicate you now!"

"But as I was saying, we stayed near Nashville for a while, and there we had something to do with Colonel Robertson, one of the founders of that town, and with Daniel Boone."

"Heered tell o' him too. Must be the Old Put o' them western parts."

"But mostly we tried to keep the whites from stealing Indian lands, and the Indians from taking white scalps."

"Didn't ye never hev any life o' yer own?" asked Mother Chester.

"In the winters, when the Indian attacks died down, Perthy and I would go out, sometimes across the Mississippi, after skins and furs. We went a good many times, and got to know the tribes west of the river fairly well. It was peaceful and clean out there. People used to call us 'Long-Hunters' at first, and then 'Old Winterers' or 'Wilderness Men.'"

"Seems a queer way to live," said Mother Chester. "Kind o' makes me shiver, them lonesome names.—An' how did young Perthy take to 't?"

"I don't think Perthy's been unhappy, and he's grown up to be a fine man, and a good rifle-builder. He's married now, to a Nashville girl, and has two sons."

"Wal, wal! That little boy! An' how 'bout the dog?—I forget his name."

"Wash, his name was. Well, he got old and died, but now there's a great-grandson of Wash living with Perthy. He has the same good heart, and is always hanging round when you need him most. His father it was that went with us on the Lewis and Clark Expedition."

"What! Ye went that journey, boy?" said the Colonel, strongly excited. "Why, that's one o' the grandest things ever done!—Way out to the Pacific Ocean?"

"Yes. Perthy and Wash and Russell Bean and I went along as scouts. We knew part of the country, this side of the mountains, already. And then, the Indians out there knew something about us."

"Clar out to Pacific Ocean an' back!—Ye 'member, boy, how John Ledyard useter carry on 'bout goin' that journey, an' most folks hyar in Connecticut useter think he warn't too strong in the head?"

"Yes, Father, I remember it well.—What's become of John?"

"He's dead, so his folks 'cross the river tell me."

"Is that so? How did he die? Where?"

"In Egypt, they say, years ago. An' they do say, too, that he was 'way over thar jest a-tryin' to reach the west coast o' 'Meriky by sea, so's he c'd walk 'cross kentry to Connecticut."

"You gave him that idea, Father."

"I did?"

"Certainly. And to me, too, when I was a boy. I've often thought that you've had as much to do with my wanderings up and down the land—after Samson Occum—as any man."

"Wal, wal! An' hyar I've gone an' forgot all 'bout it!"

"At any rate, Ledyard talked a good deal to Thomas Jefferson about the west country, and Jefferson finally asked his friend Meriwether Lewis to go out there. I went along."

"Huh! Cain't say I like that 'bout Jefferson. We hate that man in these parts. The damn . . . ! But what's the matter, lad?"

Holdfast had returned to his chair and was staring moodily into the fire.

"Why don't ye go on?"

"I was thinking about Meriwether Lewis. He was my friend too. He could lead forty men for three years through those dangers and lose only one, but he himself was killed, not long after, in a tavern near the Mississippi."

"Who killt 'im?"

"I wish I knew. That's one of the things I've failed in. He was carrying a letter to President Jefferson at the time. I gave him that letter. I should have carried it myself."

Again Mother Chester laid her hand upon his arm.

"Well, Mother, I suppose you mean that I must have done my best; but it hasn't been good enough.—You asked me to tell you what I've been doing. All this time I've been trying—yes, certainly trying—to save the Indians of the West from destruction. That's what I have lived for, and would have died for. But I've failed—terribly!"

"Now Holdfast, I reckon mebbe ye've told us 'nough fer one day. Ye're tired, I know—dretful tired. Why don't ye jest set an' smoke yer pipe an' rest yerself a spell?"

"Oh, I can't rest!"

"Wal, then, course yer father an' me don't want to let yeh outen our sight now we got yeh agin, but ye mought like to take a look round. Thar's Gungywamp an' Cochegan an' Larrabee Oak an' the Village an' hunderds o' places an' folks ye'll want to see."

Holdfast rose from his chair, pulling at his belt.

"An' ye mought like to go clean up to Norwich an' see Becky," the Colonel suggested.

"How's Becky?"

"She's well," Mother Chester replied with some hesitation. "We don't . . . O' course ye know John Reid was drownded at sea."

"Father told me that in his letter, yes. Has she married again?"

"No. An' that's a queer thing, too. She's had a plenty o' chances."

"Becky," the Colonel added, "is a purty damn rich woman, what with the mill John built up an' left her. Ye 'll find it's changed her some. She lives in a big house John built for her jest thar by the Mohegan buryin'-ground above the Yantic—d' ye rec'leck that place? —with a lot o' sarvints to wait on her hand an' foot. She goes round with all them old Tory fork-users up thar—or with their childern anyhow. Mother an' me don't go thar much—but she'll be glad to see yeh jest same."

"Does she come down here much to see you?"

"Wal . . . some. But ye see how 't is, lad—we don't use forks."

"Now, John, don't go givin' Holdfast wrong idears. Becky's a good gal iffen she is rich, an' not a mite proud. An' I will say that fer all her white hair an' the trouble she's hed she's the best-lookin' widder woman I ever set eyes on."

Holdfast moved again to the mantel and stood there with his left arm resting upon it. He looked about the room with a lingering gaze, pausing for several seconds upon each familiar object: the clock, the queen's-arm, the table, the turn-up bed, and the chairs. His own oaken chair, by far too large for any other member of the family or any probable guest, stood precisely where he had left it one stormy midnight long ago. Then he walked to the south window and stood gazing for several minutes down the long glitter of the Thames. His face was happier when he came back to the fireplace.

"There's one thing," he said, "that I haven't failed in."

His hand closed, as he spoke, upon the rough leather bag which Mother Chester had found upon the table at dawn. He took out the clam-shell and undid the thongs that bound it. A blue wisp of smoke curled up.

"What ye got thar, lad?" asked the Colonel, limping over to Holdfast's side.

"The fire I took from this hearth on the night of the day Becky was married."

Mother Chester also came close. "Ye don't mean—" said she, "ye cain't mean it's never gone out!"

"Yes, I do mean that."

"God!" said the Colonel.

All three stood and gazed at the curling smoke and the tiny seed of fire.

"D' ye reelize, Mother, that our old fire—the one we lighted the day I carried yeh over this hyar threshold, has ben to the Pacific Ocean an' back?"

408

"Yes, John. It's wonderful."

"Think o' the fires it's kindled in the wet woods at night! Jest think o' the faces it's lighted, the beasts it has kep' off, an' all the folks, black an' white an' red, it must 'a' warmed! Eh? An' yet this hyar blessed boy calls hisself a failure.—My good God!"

"We did give 'im the right name, John, when we called 'im 'Holdfast.' "

Then the two old people were silent, feeling that their familiar kitchen had all at once become something like a church. They watched their foster son, now in some ways almost a stranger, kneel before the fire of home as though at an altar. For a few moments he bowed his head. At last, leaning forward, he emptied the clam-shell over the midmost dancing flame.

NO MORE BEARS

It was true, as Mother Chester had said, that Holdfast wanted to see hundreds of places. During the first days after his return he ranged far and wide among the scenes that had long been shining clear in the country of his mind. He revisited them now at the high tide of the year with the lilac and apple-tree in flourish, every glade and meadow set a-tremble by the ecstasy of bobolinks, bluebirds, thrushes, and wrens. Never before, whatever his heart might say, had Connecticut been more beautiful to his eyes and ears.

Yet the zest for such ramblings did not last long. Too many places had changed, or reminded him only of lost companions. From others the indefinable spirit which had once made them dear, all but holy, had vanished away. One and all, they seemed to have shrunk. Often for minutes at a time he stared down at the Thames, hardly able to believe that it had not dwindled. Its wildness was gone, and its glamor. He could no longer call it the holy stream of his fathers. It had been polluted and poisoned by greed.

Fort Griswold, over in Groton, he kept away from. When Father Chester told him how lush the grass grew over there, and how the sheep loved it, he made no reply. He tried not to glance at the long steep slope, toothed with granite, down which long ago a wagon-load of wounded farm-boys had crazily rolled and bumped. He walked swiftly by the weather-worn old homestead on Poquonock Plain which people were now calling "The Hive of the Averys." That seemed to him a sadly unsuitable name, considering that bees bring home their honey—or, if they have found none, come back at least laden with news of travel and with gold-dusted thighs through the sunset.

Farm after farm was deserted, abandoned to scrub-oak, sheep-laurel, and hard-hack. Holdfast leaned over pasture bars and stared at eyeless windows of houses he had helped to raise, at broken-backed roofs of barns in which he had danced as a youth to the tunes of a left-handed fiddler. The lads who had danced there were dead, or tossing at sea, or had wandered away into Wyoming on the Susquehanna, into the Northwest Territory, or Kentucky's Dark and Bloody Ground. The land lay widowed, leached, drained of its manhood.—Had ever any other country so blotted out and forgotten the marks of man's toil?

Not the land only but the towns, the still lingering people, made his heart ache. Often harder to bear than the thought of those who would never return was the sight of those who had never been away—of the wizened, shallow-eyed, frozen-faced men and women whom he could remember as children, once his play-mates. They remembered him also, he saw, but with fear, and an instinct for avoidance. He could see their glance veer away from the strange, the distant, the unknown. He read their timorous town-bound thoughts: to stop in a public place and chat with a huge dark man in worn buck-skins, a Mohegan, wearing his hair in a most outlandish fashion, probably a poor man, possibly a drunkard, perhaps about to "go on the town" and become a public charge—would that be good for their standing at the bank, the store, the shop, the church? In short, would that be "good for business"?

Sitting alone by the river-side, near the moldering Chester store, Holdfast listened for the faintest whisper or tread of the past. He heard only the call of a gull high up, the scream of a hawk, and the rustle of reeds in the thrust and pull of the tides. Though he sat in the place he had longed for, never in rain-soaked woods at night had he felt so sick for home. He had to learn that home is not only a place but a time, and that though a man might return through the miles from Western Waters, or even from the trebly distant Pacific, he could not walk back through the years. The treasure of home, during his long absence, had been filched away with every clang from the old church tower, each tick of the clock on the kitchen shelf.

Yes, and with every beat of his heart, each out-and-in of his breath.

In him too, he was vaguely aware, there had been a change, a darkening, a deepening. Borne down by the sense of failure, lost in life's mystery, he could not recapture the mood of the youth who had once borne his own name—a youth exulting in untried strength, confidently trusting that right would triumph, quite sure that truth lay always and clearly on one side. To the number of those who would never return, therefore, he must add that young Holdfast Gaines who had stepped out long ago with a marching song into the dark and the storm.

Mother Chester guessed something of this. It was often pitiful to see her groping back for the boy and youth she had loved. How could one tell her just when and where he had died? How make her understand what it meant that even while gazing into the beloved old fire on the kitchen hearth one often saw the corpses huddled among the licking flames at Fort Mims and the charred ruins of Coosa?

He did what he could for her and the Colonel. Every night, after the candles had been set in the window for John and Rebecca, he sat in his great oaken chair by the hearth, sometimes tinkering with "Hobbomok" or mending a bow-string, and listened to their cheerful talk about people long dead, old times and events, and Mrs. Hempstead's rheumatism. He could see that it warmed them to the heart to have him there, sometimes talking a little, then covering the old fire with the day's ashes, and creaking up the attic stair to his long hard bed between the queen-posts. His presence helped them to make believe that the many years had brought no change to Four Winds Farm.

Now and then he tried to tell them something about the western wonder. He spoke of the Mississippi, of multitudes of horse-riding Indians, the grandeur of the prairies, the flowers there and the grass like a blowing sea, the mysterious distances, the herds of slowly moving buffalo that darkened a hundred square miles, the grizzly bears, elk, moose, caribou, trumpeter swans, and mountains covered with snow at midsummer.—They listened with mild interest, and then returned to some Thames Valley matter.

According to Colonel Chester, the new war against England was "Mr. Madison's war; let Mr. Madison fight it." In his belief it had been brought on "by the damn Demmycrats jest to spite New England and spile Connecticut trade." Although he had finally decided not to attend the Hartford Convention, he was clearly in sympathy with its main purposes: to thwart and embarrass the President while the country was at grips with a mighty foe, to overthrow the party in power if the war had to be lost in so doing, and, failing all else, to secede from the

411

Union. It was a grievous thing to Holdfast to see the old Colonel, once a true patriot and always a man of the people, thus hoodwinked by a group of "Tories" and treacherous plotters whose main concern was for their own money-bags.

Because Captain Isaac Hull was a Connecticut man commanding a New England ship, and still more for the reason that his own grandson, Samuel Chester Reid, had served under Hull in the battle, the Colonel rather enjoyed talking about the victory of the frigate *Constitution* over the British *Guerrière*. On the other hand, he seldom mentioned the frigate *United States,* captained by no less a man than Stephen Decatur, then lying with her splendid prize the *Macedonian* within sight of his own front windows. Twenty or more British vessels at the river-mouth were blockading Decatur there—"but what the hell!" said the Colonel. "It's a habit they got inter way back, an' iffen they was to go away I'd think mebbe they didn't like us no more." He had not been much moved by the British burning of American ships at Essex on the Connecticut River, and even when Sir Thomas Hardy bombarded the town of Stonington, close at hand, he thought it enough to point out that only one townsman had been wounded, while twenty-one British were killed.

Holdfast wondered if the Colonel would have felt quite the same about these things if he had talked with young Jeremiah Holmes of Mystic. Holmes it was who had aimed the two eighteen-pounders and the little four-pounder cannon with which Stonington had beaten off the three-days' bombardment from Hardy's great seventy-four-gun ship of the line, a frigate, brig of war, and bomb-ship. Jeremiah Holmes felt rather strongly about the British attacks, and he never let any one forget that he had learned his gunnery while serving several years' impressment in the British Navy.

Holdfast himself was more and more concerned, as the summer passed, with the gradual southward sweep of a great British flotilla under Sir Alexander Cochrane. Realizing that the spasmodic attacks it was making here and there along the coast could serve no immediate naval or military end, he began to wonder whether they were not meant to divert attention from something more important—say a major move in Canada or one against New Orleans. Now that the British were free from Napoleon, he thought, they might be reviving the old French scheme to take the Mississippi at both ends and so eventually dominate the whole vast country it watered.

Colonel Chester roundly declared that it was nothing to him who

412

owned New Orleans. Some Spanish town, he thought it was. And the good old man grew red with wrath when told that the city and a vast stretch of country roundabout it had been purchased from France, years ago, by Thomas Jefferson. By what constitutional right, he demanded, had Jefferson spent the money of American tax-payers for any such nonsensical purpose?

And so there were a good many things that could not be discussed with the Colonel. One could not tell him about those days and nights at Monticello talking over the Louisiana Purchase, the Indian problem, and the plans that led up to the expedition of Lewis and Clark. To point out that Jefferson had converted into deed and solid possession the Colonel's own idea about the westward extension of Connecticut . . . Ah, what would be the use?

The talk of the old folks, resembling a dry chirp of crickets warmed by a winter fire, often made Holdfast feel that he too was growing old. Or rather, he was like his old gun "Long Tom," flawed from the start, and now, the Colonel said, completely lost and forgotten. It had seen some action in the undeclared war with France; young Isaac Hull had at least talked of taking it with him on an expedition against the Barbary Pirates; and it probably had been lent to the Negro Toussaint L'Ouverture during his revolt in Haiti. After that, nothing. Probably, the Colonel thought, it was rusting away in some West Indian jungle. He did hope, though, that the Negroes down there had had the sense to keep the muzzle pointed downward so that moisture would not collect in the barrel.

Yes, Holdfast felt a good deal like that old gun; yet he found that he could still be of some use. The stone walls, the barns, the roof of the house, were in real need of repair. The two old elms, injured by a recent hurricane, needed saw and chisel. The chores of the farm were a comfort. Three cows were calving. When grass-harvest came on he got down his six-foot scythe from the attic and swung slowly back into the well-remembered rhythms of mowing. It was a motion he loved, for some deep dark reason. Although he had to work without human companionship, it was good to feel once more a partner of the sun, the rain, and the south-wind. During the week it took him to cut and ted and cart the grass of the Great Meadows the burden of his heart was lightened.

Aunt Lucy Tantaquidgeon, though now well over eighty and quite blind, remembered him well. So did Henry Quaquaquid and Robert

413

Ashbow. But most of the other Mohegans he had known were either dead or else so far-wandered in successive migrations that they no longer counted as members of the tribe. Bitter poverty, disease, and strong drink were rapidly reducing the few that were left. They were like the withered leaves that hang for a while at the top of a dying tree. They had lost the use of the bow, and the Mohegan language was dying out. King Uncas was hardly a known name to them. The name of Samson Occum was growing dim. Holdfast found, with a sense of shock and shame, that the chief bond of union in the tribe was the legend of his own youthful prowess as an athlete and a wild myth of his imaginary exploits as a slayer of white men in the West.

At Mohegan Village, therefore, Holdfast took the full measure of his defeat. Habitually unfair to himself, forgetting the charge of Occum and all other circumstances of his departure long ago, he bitterly blamed his turning aside from a near and dear duty, a task he might have performed, to spend his strength among strangers in an effort hopeless for any man.

But unmistakably one way of life—though comparatively weak yet manly, simple, dignified, sometimes noble—was dying out into another. And so a number of questions arose about that other way, the white man's. Just what and how good was it, really? Was it triumphing because of a true superiority or for some other reason?

Holdfast pondered these questions as he went about his chores at the farm, during his long silences in the kitchen, and while sitting by a little fire he often built for himself under the great Larrabee Oak or among the Pequot Council Stones in Gungywamp. He tried to think of them dispassionately, letting the facts speak.

Characteristically, he began with religion, convinced that a people's real wisdom and worth were best shown by what they thought of their gods. What those gods might be called, or the tales that were told of their doings, no longer seemed of much moment. After all, he had heard so many tales, beginning with those about Jehovah first told him by Uncle Occum, going on through Indian myths innumerable, and ending with Parson Blandison's accounts of amours on Mount Olympus. In a way they were all false; and yet they all pointed to the central truth that man's life, engulfed in mystery, woven of dream and defeat, surrounded and admonished by symbols on every hand, is, in essence, a life of the Spirit.

This fact had always and everywhere been recognized by the American Indians. It was implied in their legends, their dances, their songs,

414

their hunting and planting and reaping, even their customs of war. Every moment of an Indian's life was lived in the conviction that the eyes of the gods were upon him. An Indian tribe without a medicine-man—that is, without at least one mind reaching upward to catch the messages of the gods and draw them down to man's spiritual need— would feel more helpless by far than one that had no corn-roots, bean-roots, squash-roots groping into earth for the body's food.—And could the same thing be said of these Christians? Holdfast remembered that for a full decade of his own boyhood and youth there had not been one settled minister in New London.

He was more or less intimately acquainted with hundreds of Indian tribes scattered all the way from one ocean to the other, and among them all he had never known an instance of persecution on grounds of religious belief or unbelief. No Indian ever asked another what he should think about the gods. He waited for the gods to tell him. No Indian ever absurdly supposed that he had the right to tell others what they must believe, on pain of damnation.—And for contrast he needed only to think again of New London where, in his boyhood, there had occurred the last of many outbreaks of legalized violence, condoned if not fomented by the local clergy, against the Rogerene Quakers.

To an Indian all times and places were holy. Christians, on the other hand, had set aside one day in the week as the "Lord's Day," and one building in town as "the Lord's House"—or, as Venture Smith had called it, "the god-box." From their point of view this had the advantage that in all other places and on six days of the week they could go about their "business" with no uncomfortable sense of divine supervision.

That would explain a good deal. It helped one to understand how the clergy of Norwich and New London could for a hundred and fifty years watch without one word of reproof the iniquities visited by white men upon their Mohegan neighbors. In all that time, apparently, no Connecticut minister, searching the Gospel and his own conscience for a text, had ever tried to defend the Mohegans by quoting the words: "Inasmuch as ye have done it unto one of the least of these my brethren, ye have done it unto me."

Yet Holdfast could remember a time when many Connecticut ministers had been true leaders of their people, afraid of no man, boldly outspoken against the Mammon of Unrighteousness wherever its ugly head was shown. Dominions, principalities, and powers had been trifles to them as compared with their holy errand. They had bidden the great

415

ones of this world to bow before an authority sent from above, and they had been obeyed.

Going farther back, Holdfast recognized that in Puritan days the pulpits of New England must have been served by men of really heroic stature, by tragic men who had snuffed the brimstone of the Pit, faced the Giant Despair, and come up through the Slough of Despond. Bigots they might have been, but at least while such men as the Mathers and Jonathan Edwards lived the Spirit had still its spokesmen and the Mind its citadels. In a country scornful of poets, prophets, and dreamers, amid a people all too sordidly inclined, they had beaten it home that man cannot live by bread alone. They had been the salt of this American earth. A few of them, like Thomas Hooker of Hartford, had seen a vision of what their country might become—had seen and shown that she might be, nay, must be, an answer at last to the cry of the human heart, the substance of things long hoped for. In their time the central object if every Connecticut town had been the long white finger of the church-spire pointing right away from the shop, the law-court, and the jail.

But now that the salt had lost its savor, wherewith could it be salted? What hope for Connecticut, New England, America, now that the places of those staunch and stern old champions were almost everywhere usurped by a glib little black-coated gentry, eunuchs of the mind, poltroons of the spirit, ducking, obsequious, mainly busy to twist the teachings of Jesus the poor man so as to flatter and soothe those who paid the highest rents for their pews? Could a nation be better than its medicine-men? A lie about the gods—could it fail to corrode and corrupt the very heart?

Yet perhaps it was not a deliberate lie. In comparing the Christian clergy with Indian medicine-men one should remember that they had never experienced or imagined real tragedy. That was why their faces were often so bland and blank, their manners so oily, their voices so shallow, their words so void of meaning. Simply, they had not been tried. Never having dwelt for even an hour in the Cave of Hobbomok, what could they know about Machimoodus? Leaving out of account all the darker strands, how could they guess at God's way of weaving his blanket?

In his bitterness against the Christian clergy, Holdfast turned back with a warm sense of companionship to him whose name they habitually took, as he thought, in vain. And partly because they spoke of him as a god—hoping thereby, no doubt, to escape the rebuke of his

416

example—Holdfast was the more content to regard him as a man. Indeed it helped the ache of his loneliness not a little to think of Jesus as another wanderer and ne'er-do-well like himself, a man deeply perplexed by life's riddle, a ruler without a realm, a lover of friends who was always lonely, a virgin holding aloof from all women for the sound Indian reason that he had a long hard trail to run.

In so many ways Jesus would have made a good Indian! He too had belonged to a race outcast, despised, and grossly maltreated. He had kept his vigil, fasting, in the wilderness, and had seen his vision. To that vision he had been sternly true. Like an Indian, he had taken little thought for the morrow, what he should eat or put on. He had considered the lilies of the field. He had borne torture with no outcry. Moreover, though the preachers tried to make out that he too was a preacher, the fact shone clear that he had spent most of his time in solitude and silence, listening. His words came loaded with silence, and his deeds with the dignity of one who lived much alone.—Yes, there was a man whom one would like to meet on a lonely trail, and to sit with hour after hour by a fire in the forest, saying nothing.

What would Jesus have said or done in the council-house at Coosa? By what eloquence of speech or silence, what majesty of mien, what force or gentleness, what heaven-sent wisdom, would he have tried to avert that disaster? And would he have succeeded?

Would he too have allowed the Prophet to swim away unharmed?

And then came the further question, a hard one: Had not the life of Jesus also been a failure? Even his teaching and example, had they not failed?

At any rate it was amazing how the words of the Galilean peasant came crackling across the centuries when one thought of them closely, like the message Ben Franklin had brought down from the clouds on a kite-string. Holdfast pondered them more and more as the summer went by—on the milking-stool at dawn, in the hay-field, and again at dusk in Gungywamp while the hermit-thrush was singing. Marvelously pregnant, packed, and explosive they seemed to him, like so many kegs of gun-powder.

Partly because latter-day Christians tried to ignore it, he gave due weight to the sheer masculine force which had once earned the admiration of twelve tough-palmed men of the open air. To begin with, at least, those twelve must have taken Jesus as a man, a companion. Seeing him so, they had no reason to shuffle out of sight his occasional outbursts of wrath, his blasting of the barren fig-tree, his cursing of the corrupters

417

of childhood, and his lashing of the money-changers out of the temple. These modern Christians, on the other hand, being utterly unheroic themselves and at bottom disbelieving in heroism, seemed never to guess that Jesus had been, if anything, a hero.—Or perhaps it was, rather, that they did guess just that, and were afraid. Perhaps they were vaguely aware that the kernel of fire in this man, if once let loose, would burn down their smug little lady-like world and make room for one more manly.

Yes; that would be the reason for their eagerness to change Jesus over into their own effeminate likeness. Instinctively they understood how much depended upon keeping him heavily swathed in a theological winding-sheet. At any rate, they must never let him walk abroad in Connecticut. They must never hint what he would say about the slave-trade, child-labor, whore-houses, or the treatment of Mohegans. Otherwise their more prosperous parishioners might be offended and look elsewhere for spiritual comfort.

On the whole, then, the white man's religion was not religious enough. Christianity was not sufficiently Christian. Founded in the blood of martyrs and established by millions of brave men and women, it was being used as a blind by weaklings who wanted above all to be comfortable, to look respectable, and to evade all stress and strain of the spirit. White men were beginning to lie about holy things, and that seemed to Holdfast a bad omen.

The town of Norwich had prospered through the years by virtue of New London's adversity. She was getting to be called "Swallow-All." Her rich people were much richer now, and her poor were poorer. The rich and the poor were no longer neighbors. The power of returning favors for benefits received, which had gratified the sturdy pride of the poorer neighbors in the old days, had now been taken from them; and those who once held up their heads in town-meeting now slunk about the taverns as despised paupers dependent on the town. Acts of kindness, though by no means rare, were now performed by organized "charities" which left the recipients no means of making a return. Moreover, it seemed to be agreed in Norwich that poverty was a perennial thing. How, in fact, could there be riches if there were no poor to produce them? Hadn't Jesus himself said that the poor would always be with us?

Here, then, Holdfast saw, was a widening rift in a community which had once been a small triumph in the art of living together. Another

418

such he found in the gradual disappearance of those domestic indus-
tries in which groups of neighbors had formerly gathered to work in
one another's barns and sheds and houses, each individual sharing in
the total proceeds. That too had been a warmly human relationship. It
was in that way that men had worked on the ketch *Rebecca,* every
carpenter, blacksmith, rope-walker, calker, sail-maker, and member
of the crew owning one or more "lays." Now that kindly old custom
was giving way to "manufactures" carried on in "factories." The children of people who had once been neighbors were becoming either
"bosses" or "hands." To Holdfast's ears, neither word had an American
sound.

There was no more talk in Norwich about the problems raised by
Jonathan Edwards in his "Freedom of the Will," and none about those
discussed by Tom Paine in his "Rights of Man." Theological dogma
and revolutionary enthusiasm were now considered somewhat ridiculous. Substantial citizens had a new philosophy: "every man for himself and the Devil take the hind-most." Both "rights" and "freedom"
were apparently now dependent upon money, and money was most
readily made by machines of metal and wood and human flesh.

The Connecticut that Holdfast remembered had been a home of
farmers, handicraftsmen, and sea-farers, but he felt that the place he
saw about him was more like a lodging-house for mechanics and mill-
hands and peddlers. Or, as he sometimes put it to himself, Connecticut
was a field of battle in which the opponents were men and machines;
and it seemed to him clear that men would inevitably lose the fight
against these children of their own wits and skill. Such freedoms and
rights as men might enjoy in future would be only those that machines
provided and allowed. The old leisurely rhythms of life, timed by suns
and seasons, had been shattered now by the scream of the factory
whistle.

He talked with a Mohegan youth who had worked for a year or two
in Eli Whitney's fire-arms factory near New Haven. It appeared that
this Whitney, already famous for a labor-saving device called the cotton-
gin, had secured a "goverment contract" for a large number of arms to
be made and delivered post-haste. Seeing that he could not fill the order
by the old method of setting each workman to produce a whole pistol,
he had taken over an English system in which every "hand" made only
one part, and made it by mechanical methods so exactly that it could be
fitted into any of the thousands of weapons turned out in his shop.
So far as the weapons were concerned, the system was working ad-

mirably, but it was not so good for the "hands." What with the long hours of monotonous labor, the bad air, the confinement, but most of all a sense of utter futility in what he was doing, the young Mohegan had come down with quick consumption and had only a few weeks to live.

It was of some concern to Holdfast that fire-arms were being "standardized," but that men should be so, that workmen were being robbed of their delight in free creative labor, that human beings were sinking into mechanical automata driving machines to make more machines—that to him was a horror.

He thought of Russell Bean, who had always built his rifles as another man might compose poems. He thought of Perthy, now Bean's partner. And he fondled his beloved rifle, "Hobbomok," a thing of beauty such as no factory hand would ever have the knowledge, patience, love, or time to make.

And where could this thing be stopped? Would it not range on through every phase of the white man's civilization, like the pox through an Indian town? Beginning with the manufacture of fire-arms, how could it be prevented from going on to the fabrication, also in "standardized and interchangeable parts," of human beings? Pistols and muskets were made for killing, but surely, given a hundred years in a field burned clear of all intellectual and spiritual opposition, this idea would be more destructive than all the fire-arms in the world.

He went to see Rebecca's paper-mill at the Falls of the Yantic, standing on the spot where thirty Narragansetts, pursued by King Uncas and his Mohegans, had taken, long ago, the death-leap. It was a ramshackle building, ugly with greed, a fire-trap, and under its rotting floor-boards the imprisoned water went roaring down with a sound of loud indignation. John Reid must have seen when he first came across here how serviceable that water would be for mill-power and the making of money.—Just when would it be that John first saw the place?

The "hands" in the mill were working from dawn to dark on every week-day of the year. The arrangement of wages, house-rentals, and prices at the company store were such as to keep most of them permanently in debt to the owner. Children of men and women with whom Holdfast and Rebecca had grown up, including several Mohegans, were employed in the mill. Their faces looked as blank as the paper they produced.

Of course it would be absurd to blame Rebecca. Her foreman attended to all details, and he, if one should point out that he was running a

420

slave-pen, would instantly grow voluble about the "competition" he had to meet. Under that magic word he might include the fact that in other mills roundabout little children were chained to their benches. It appeared that the "bosses" of Connecticut were growing extremely fond of children, whose services they could often secure at fifty cents a week. Like Jesus of old, the Christian employer was saying "Suffer the little children to come unto me."

Rebecca herself was helpless. Something impersonal, fatal, not of her choice or making, he saw, had changed the laughing girl he had known, free as the wind, clean as the dew, by whose side he had often climbed this very ravine where her factory now polluted the air and the once wild water. She too was a victim of the hurrying, rattling belts and wheels.

But if the canny Scotchman, John Reid, was the man who built this monster here on this holy ground so close by the grave of Uncas, then who was it that had spared the life of that same Scotchman and brought him home to marry Rebecca?

Could anyone be blamed? Could the gods themselves say to anyone "Thou art the man"?

Sitting alone among the Council Stones, smoking his stone pipe and thinking, Holdfast came one evening to a strange answer. So strange and startling it was that he suddenly rose to his feet and paced up and down.

The Embargo! Jefferson's prohibition of all sea-borne trade!—And, after that, what choice for Connecticut farmers, craftsmen, and men of the sea? They could starve, they could go west, or they could sell themselves to the machine. Therefore if the gods accused anyone, their fingers must be leveled at the man who had brought New England's sea-borne trade to a stop, and he was the very man whom Holdfast had long regarded as America's main champion of human rights and liberties. Thomas Jefferson's effort to defend the simplicities of American life was bringing about their ruin. His love of the land had depopulated Connecticut's countryside. His hatred of machines had nourished this young but rapidly growing monster of mechanism.

Knowing well that the time for real help to his tribe had gone by, Holdfast nevertheless set himself to draw up a petition addressed to the Connecticut Legislature. He recited once more the long list of grievances which the tribesmen held against their white neighbors, including the devious history of the "Mason Claims" and the legalistic devices by which England's just award had been set aside. He challenged Connecticut to show evidence that anything more than token payments had ever been made for the great stretch of territory once owned by Mohegans. He reviewed the shameful history of the "Sequestered Lands," including Mount Machimoodus, and declared that the so-called "bequests" of King Uncas and his son Attawanhood had no validity because neither those Mohegan chieftains nor any others had ever held the right to alienate any tribal lands whatsoever.

The petition urged that there was a gross injustice in requiring the Mohegans, on pain of starvation, to conform to ways of living that were foreign to their own convictions and customs. To an Indian, Holdfast wrote, it seemed both wicked and absurd for any man to build a fence around a plot of land, great or small, and to call it his own. To an Indian it seemed wrong that human beings, and especially little children, should be herded together in factories from dawn to dark as slaves of machines. If the whites liked that sort of thing it was their affair, but Mohegans hated and despised it. All Mohegans had for ages shared the bounty of the woods and fields with one another, so that no one had either too much or too little. They preferred that way of theirs to the white man's way of fiercely self-assertive private ownership. They wished to return to it. Having learned something about the Christian religion from a native preacher of theirs called Samson Occum, and being besides, many of them, quite able to read the record for themselves, they believed that Jesus of Nazareth and his twelve companions had practised and taught a way of life much closer to the old Mohegan custom than to that of the whites. Would the Connecticut Legislature kindly make inquiries of Connecticut clergymen in this matter and find out what they thought Jesus, in the circumstances, would have advised?

Meanwhile the subscribing petitioners requested the prompt return to the tribe of one full tenth of the lands, lakes, and rivers which at various times and in sundry devious ways had been stolen from them and their fathers. They asked that the lands thus returned should not be, like their present small holdings, unfit for the support of human life. They wished it to contain valley-land good for corn and tobacco, forest-land good for fuel and game, shore-land where they might once more gather shell-fish, and streams of wild water good for salmon and trout. In particular they asked that Mohegan River, now sometimes called the Thames, be kept permanently free of mill-filth and sewage so that the fish upon which their livelihood partly depended should not

422

be poisoned. They asked also that the waters so returned should include their sacred Lake Chargoggagoggmanchaugagoggchaubunagungamaugg, now sometimes called Lake Thomson, at which from time immemorial the Indian tribes of the New England region had gathered to ratify and renew treaties of peace. And lastly they asked that there should be given back to them the great womb-shaped cave in the town of East Haddam which they called the "Cave of Hobbomok," and the rocky mount at the head of Salmon Cove called "Machimoodus" where the gods sometimes appeared in visions and spoke to their young men.

These requests they could not back up by any show of force. That, indeed, had never been their way. In five wars the Mohegans had fought on the side of their white neighbors, and they had never fought against them. Rather, they based their claim upon legal rights which had been fairly and repeatedly established, upon the sense of justice which they took to be in no way affected by questions of race or color, and, finally, upon the Golden Rule, "Do unto others as ye would that they should do unto you."

The sudden apparition of an American Indian in buck-skins, bare-headed, and treading straight-toed in moccasins, caused a considerable stir in Hartford as Holdfast strode up from the ferry toward the Connecticut State House. Pedestrians at a distance nudged one another and made ready for amusement when they first caught sight of his head and shoulders moving above the crowd. Shop-keepers came to their doors and stared. Two or three ladies daintily lifted their skirts and crossed the muddy street to be out of the strange man's way. A group of young louts idling at a corner made a few awkward and tentative noises of derision. But their ridicule faded rapidly away, as its object drew nearer, into an oafish awe. The butcher stopped wiping his hands on his gingham apron and stared, open-mouthed. The pedestrians gathered in little groups as though for mutual support. The ladies, having crossed the street, seemed to wish they had not. They paused and looked back, lingering.

Holdfast, meanwhile, was gazing at the gilded female figure of "Justice," blindfolded and holding a pair of scales in her pudgy left hand, which topped the dome of the small but dignified State House. A faint smile brightened his face as he asked himself whether she too would not have lifted her voluminous skirts and crossed the street if her eyes had not been covered.

Inside the handsome red-brick State House, on the stairs and in quiet corners, Holdfast saw while he waited that there was a good deal of guarded talk going on among small groups of gentlemen who did not look as though they had come from Connecticut farms. Prosperous looking gentlemen they mostly were, of the sort that the Colonel called "fork-users," and yet they looked somehow uneasy. An attendant, speaking behind his hand, informed Holdfast that they had come from Boston and other remote parts of New England. Most of them, he said, were "marchants" who cared more for their trade than they did for their country. He thought they were planning to denounce the war and the President, possibly even the Union.

Ah, yes, this was the beginning of the Hartford Convention, which the Colonel had written about. In the midst of his own struggle to preserve the remnants of the Mohegan tribe from the greed of their white neighbors, Holdfast saw in this convention of secretive black-coated merchants and factory-owners a rock upon which the American Ship of State might well strike, split, and founder. With the government paralyzed in Washington, the West ready as it long had been for rebellion, and now the East quite openly talking secession, what hope was there for the Nation which Washington, Israel Putnam, and John Chester had striven to establish?

That same white man's greed which had all but destroyed the Mohegans was now driving these merchants to propose breaking off from the Union in order to make a separate peace with England—a peace which would lift the blockade and send the golden dollars rolling into their pockets while their country went down to defeat.

Lieutenant Governor Goodrich, a paunchy little man in spectacles, had heard of Mr. Holdfast Gaines. A "leap-dancer," wasn't he?—a wrestler, a runner, a strong-man? Ah, yes; Mr. Holdfast Gaines, to be sure. It was an honor.

He read the petition with becoming gravity and something of a scholar's patience. Here and there, as he read, he said to himself "tht! tht!" and then "too bad!" Regarding the merits of the case he begged to be excused from expressing an opinion, but he promised that the document would be submitted at once to the suitable senatorial committee. Mr. Gaines, he added, was no doubt aware that the matter of the Mohegan claims, in its—ah—legal aspects, was extremely—ah— intricate. The best lawyers would hesitate to—ah . . . In short, had Mr.

424

Gaines ever actually examined and carefully considered the pertinent documents in the case?—He had not done so? Ah, well, then perhaps the present opportunity had better be improved.

Within a few minutes a clerk brought in from the office of the Secretary of State a neatly written manuscript dated September 28, 1640, and signed with the mark of a sheathed knife. Holdfast studied that mark for a moment with the vague premonition that once more a knife was pointed at his own heart. Then he began to read:

This writing witnesseth that I, Uncas, alias Poquaiom, sachem of the Mohegans, have given and freely granted unto the governor and magistrates of the English upon Connecticut River all the land that doth belong, or ought of right to belong, to me, by whatsoever name it be called . . . and this I do upon mature consideration and good advice, freely and without constraint, in witness whereof I hereunto put my hand.

The mark of POQUAIOM alias UNCAS
In the presence of THOMAS STANTON /

The said English did also freely give to the said Uncas five and a half yards of trucking cloth, with stockings and other things, as a gratuity.
A true copy of Record.
Examined by GEORGE WYLLYS, Secretary.

Holdfast laid the manuscript on the table and sat thinking.

"Have you ever seen that paper before?" asked the Lieutenant Governor.

"No. I have never even heard of it."

"And what—ah . . . ?"

"In the first place, I don't believe that Uncas ever drew this mark of the sheathed knife. I have seen his true mark many times, and he was not so clever with the quill as the man who made this imitation —or, as one might say, this forgery."

"Its authenticity has, I know, been doubted," replied the Lieutenant Governor in a tone of voice suggesting real respect for his visitor. "Quite possibly, however, it was from the first recognized as a mere copy. The document you have in hand does not purport to be the original."

"Furthermore, in the year 1640 Uncas could not have known enough English to be sure what he was signing, or signing away, in this paper."

"Yes, that is one of the points made by the English Commissioners who reviewed the whole case in the time of George Third. And—ah— perhaps I should say that the Commissioners found in favor of the Mohegans."

"Did the Colony, and later the State, of Connecticut accept their decision?"

"No. It has been set aside."

"On what grounds—and how?"

"I fear, Mr. Gaines, that it was done by—ah—by deceit, bribery, and corruption."

"I see.—And, in any case, neither King Uncas nor any other Mohegan has ever had the right to give away or to sell any part of the tribal lands. Those lands are owned by us all, in common."

"On that matter you speak, of course, with authority."

"Moreover, the white men who drew up this paper must have known that they were not acquiring title to the land in question."

"Why do you think so?"

"Because even they, if they had thought that they were really purchasing one-third of Connecticut, would never have offered in exchange, even to an Indian ignorant of their language, so contemptible a price as 'five and a half yards of trucking cloth, with stockings and other things.'"

"You argue acutely, Mr. Gaines. May I say that I think you would have done well in the law?"

Holdfast's grim smile did not suggest that he felt flattered.

"But now, granting all the points you have made," the Lieutenant Governor went on, "I think we shall have to admit that this paper represents—ah—a real transaction of some sort in which Uncas did take part."

"It would seem so. Yes."

"No doubt there was ignorance on both sides, but on both, too, there was probably a good deal of—ah—shall I say human nature?"

"Do you mean 'deceit, bribery, and corruption'?"

"I fear they would be included, on both sides. Yes."

"Do you charge such things against King Uncas?"

426

"Well, now—ah—it seems to me that you implied something of the sort regarding the English settlers of 1640, and I did not defend them."

"But King Uncas . . . !"

"Please believe me, Mr. Gaines, that I should be sorry to wound your pride of ancestry in any way. On the other hand, are you really unaware that such charges have been made—and, I fear, substantiated—against him?"

"Governor, I have never known, or tried to know, anything about King Uncas except the legend of him kept alive in his own tribe."

"Ah, I see. That is entirely natural. I suppose that we all prefer the legend, when it favors our side—and that can always be managed—to the facts. Yet you would no doubt agree that in matters of—ah—property in land, facts have—ah—shall we say a certain bearing?"

Holdfast looked almost fiercely into the little man's glittering spectacles. "What are these 'facts' about Uncas that you speak of?" said he.

Lieutenant Governor Goodrich spoke for a moment to his clerk, who again left the room, and then replied: "With some of them, Mr. Gaines, you are undoubtedly acquainted.—The man you call King Uncas was, to begin with, a Pequot. Is that correct?"

"Yes, and a sagamore of the Pequots under Sassacus, their chief sachem. The Mohegans at that time were only a Pequot clan."

"Precisely. And he was related to Sassacus both by descent and by marriage?"

"That is so."

"Against that kinsman, then, and against the chieftain to whom he had sworn fealty, this Uncas, before the English came here, revolted, plotted, and stirred up strife.—Does your Mohegan legend include these facts?"

"We believe that Uncas had a better claim than Sassacus to the sachemship."

"That may be. I am only concerned to show that he broke faith with the Pequots, his own people, and that he did not need to wait for the white man's example in order to learn the ways of treachery.— You see, I am not completely ignorant of these old affairs. Both as a lawyer and as an amateur of Connecticut history I have made some study of them. From both points of view I have found them fascinating."

The clerk returned. He laid three or four manuscripts on the table.

"I'm sorry, Mr. Gaines, but—well, to make a long story short, Uncas was beaten in his first armed attack upon Sassacus. He fled to the Narragansetts in Rhode Island, who were the deadliest foes of the Pequots. Whatever further treachery he plotted while there was unsuccessful. Twice, upon his sworn promise of good behavior, he was taken back by the Pequots and twice expelled when new plots of his were discovered. Then came the whites into the Connecticut Valley, and Uncas saw his chance of doing by their help what he could not have done—and I mean against his own people and kin—alone."

"Sir," said Holdfast, staring thunder-browed at the little man, "I shall need strong proofs of that statement before I believe it."

"Proofs, Mr. Gaines, of events that happened so long ago, are not easy to come by. The archives of Connecticut are in a sadly fragmentary condition. But here, for example, is the chief account of the Pequot War, written by Captain John Mason, who led the expedition.—Have you read it?"

"I have not."

"Well, then"—and the slim white fingers worked rapidly among the written leaves—"Mason makes it clear that Uncas not only went along with the Connecticut white men in their attack upon the Pequots but actually guided them to the fort on the hill near Mystic River where several hundreds of his people were burned to death."

Holdfast reached out with one hand to the table.

"See here. Read this."

And Holdfast read: "I thenne enqwired of Onkos what hee thot the Indeans wd doe? who said the Narragansetts wd all leve uss but as for himselfe hee wd nevver leve uss and soe it prooved, for wch expressione & som other speaches of his I shal nevver forgete him he was a good friend & didd uss grate sarvis."

"Can you think of any reason, Mr. Gaines, why John Mason should have lied about that matter?"

"None," said Holdfast after a long pause, speaking hardly above a whisper, and the Lieutenant Governor saw that the grandly shaped earth-colored hand on the table top was twitched as by a sudden spasm of pain.

"Neither can I.—But besides that, I think we can now make a reasonable—ah—guess at the motive of Uncas. I think he hoped that the overthrow of Sassacus and the Pequots would greatly increase his own power. That hope, as you know, was not—ah—disappointed. During the remainder of his long life the whites left him in at least nominal control of the entire Pequot country. Is that true?"

"Yes."

428

"And I suggest that in exchange for the white man's support he made out the original of that first paper I showed you, pretending that the land was his to do with as he chose. In so doing he tried to deceive the white settlers, as they, in turn, have repeatedly deceived his people. The whole story, on both sides, is shameful to a degree. One can only say that both sides got what they wanted. It is only the Mohegans of later generations who have—ah—suffered."

"Have you other proofs of this man's treachery?"

"Here is Lion Gardiner's 'Relation of the Pequot Wars.' You will remember that Gardiner was the man who built the fort down at Saybrook Point in 1636—not much of a writer but an able and honest man. The whites and the eighty Mohegans under Uncas stopped at the fort, of course, on their way down river. Well now, here—yes, here it is. This is how the whites, at Lion Gardiner's suggestion, tested the good faith, so to speak, of King Uncas."

Holdfast took the manuscript and read: "Then I asked them how they durst trust the Mohegin Indeans who had but yt yeare come from the Pequits, they said they would trust them for they could not well goe without them for want of guids, yea said I, but I will try them before a man of ours shall goe with you or them, & I cald for Uncas & said unto him you say you will help Maior Mason but I will first see it, therefore send you now 20 men to ye bass riuer, for there went yestrnight 6 Indeans in a Canoe hithr, fetch them now dead or aliue and then you shall goe with Maior Mason els not. So he sent his men who kild 4 brought one a traytor to vs aliue whos name was kiswas and one ran away and I gaue him 15 yards of trading Cloath on my own charge to giue vnto his men according to thr desert."

Seeing Holdfast look up from the manuscript with anguish in his eyes, the Lieutenant Governor laid his hand on the buck-skin sleeve and said, "Believe me, sir, I am deeply sorry. But of course you know, we all know, that facts cannot always accord with our—ah—dreams."

"Is there anything more I ought to know about Uncas?"

"Perhaps one thing—and I mention it not as another charge against him but rather as a symbol or emblem, if you understand me, of what life means to all thoughtful and sensitive men."

"Yes?"

"You remember Lion Gardiner's mention of Kiswas, the Pequot whom Uncas brought back alive?—Well, Uncas demanded the right to torture that prisoner. It was granted—I hope reluctantly. Uncas tied one of the man's legs to a stake. Call that stake the 'facts,' if you like.

To the other leg he tied a rope. Call it one's dream—yours and mine—of what the world ought to be but is not. Then he and twenty other strong men tugged and pulled at that rope until . . . Do you see what I mean? Isn't that what life feels like to you and me?"

"Goodbye, Governor. I wish we had met years ago."

"Goodbye, Mr. Gaines. And—ah—believe me, sir . . ."

Holdfast stumbled out of the room and down the State House stairs. He had meant to spend the night under the Charter Oak, feeling that there, at any rate, he would not be trespassing upon the white man's domain. When he came to himself, however, he found that he had crossed the Connecticut River and was already walking back on the sixty-mile highway from Hartford to New London which had once been an Indian trail. He walked all night, much of the time in the rain, with blank horror in his heart and a corroding sense of the evil that lived in his very blood.

Below this present suffering and degradation there could be, he felt, no deeper hell. Whatever demon or deity it was that hated him had now driven home the barbed spear with the poisoned point. To this moment all his other agonies had merely led the way. In the massacre at Fort Griswold he had lost only his happiness, his youth, and his friends. At Coosa he had seen the destruction only of that influence which it had taken him half a lifetime to build. At Fort Mims he had witnessed no more than the utter rout and ruin of his hopes for his people. All these had been outward defeats and failures which had seemed to leave his innermost self untouched. But now he felt that the very shrine of his soul had been from the start defiled, that the blood he had meant to keep pure had always been foul. King Uncas, the ancestor of whom he had striven to be worthy, had himself been a liar, a thief, a traitor, and a blood-smeared savage. Holdfast Gaines knew at last that in his own heart was the true Cave of Hobbomok, with dreadful images indelibly drawn on its walls.

Somewhere high up in Gungywamp, among the tumbled rocks where the bears had haunted, there had been a pool in the old days, very small, clear, cold, with sand-grains deep down in it, always dancing. The picture of that pool came vividly to Holdfast's mind when he found that he could no longer sit by the Pequot Council Stones where King Uncas had once lied and plotted. He remembered how often, in boyhood, he had lain among the ferns gazing down into its cup of tremulous crystal, seeing dimly there, or believing that he saw, things past and things yet to come. Its water, though fresh as the dawn, had seemed to him older than white men, more ancient than red men, and co-eval with the earliest gods. It had seemed to spring from a country older than time which had never known the strife of Hobbomok and Kiehtan.

The pool had been his secret, shared only with beasts and birds who would never tell—or if it was known to the small brown people, the Muckowheese, who dance under ferns by moonlight and make their moccasins of lady-slippers, they too would keep their council. No drunken Mohegan or Pequot, stumbling by chance up there among the sharp-edged rocks guarded by rattle-snakes, could have seen it with his bleared eyes. No blundering white man, thinking only of "water-power" and "mill-rights," would have given it a second glance.

Surely, then, it must still be there, undefiled by greed, unstained by slaughter, forgotten by time. For three long evenings, after his work at the farm was done, Holdfast searched for it, beating up through the blurred paths he had once known like the lines in his own hand. They were blocked by brambles now. Fallen oaks, rotting and green with decay, and great hemlocks long dead which he had known in their majestic prime, held him back. Old land-marks, unless he was grossly mistaken, had shifted their place. Often he could have sworn that the very shape of the hills he had wandered among had altered.

At night-fall, on the third evening, when he had come to fear that the pool had dried away, he found it, safely hidden under a cluster of maiden-hair ferns. He had only to brush one frond aside with his staff and there it lay, with the image of a star on its bosom, delicately shaken.

After that rediscovery Holdfast paddled every evening across the Thames to sit for an hour by the dancing spring. It was smaller than he had thought. A cricket could leap across it. A fawn could drink it dry. It made a bath just large enough to cool a scarlet tanager's feathers. And yet it was large enough also to wash the poison and pain from a human heart. Sitting beside it and gazing down, Holdfast felt him-self grow younger. He ceased to mourn over the corpse of the past. He forgot that there were no more bears in Gungywamp, and the ever-increasing multitude of rats in Norwich and New London. The hor-rors of Fort Griswold, Coosa, Fort Mims, the Horseshoe, and Pequot Fort sank down and were drowned.

Then up rose the faces of far-away friends. He saw forests unbroken, unlimited prairies, and rivers running free, unstained. Beside one of those visionary streams there stood once or twice, very distant, but tall, beautiful, naked as a beech tree, a woman's form in the dawn.

And not the past only but some dim shadow of the future floated up to him as he sat in the twilight and gazed. Cochrane's flotilla moved steadily southward with flames about it. Long Tom was there, the rickety old *Rebecca,* and some huge final battle gathering up like heat-lightning and distant thunder far in the west.

Though these might be phantoms or fancies, the dance at the bottom of the pool was certainly real. The golden grains rose, fell, and rose again as though to a music which only they could hear. They never tired of their dancing, nor so much as changed its figure. They thrilled to a rhythmic pulse of power which had never known defeat, weariness, age, or shadow of turning. Holdfast gazed at their mystical dance until he could hardly have said whether it was going on in the pool or in the depth of his glad and confident heart.

Not far off rose the Larrabee Oak, ancient of days, with the many generations of his offspring round him. He had heard the howl of the wolf-pack and had sheltered the bear and the moose. The catamount had crouched among his branches above the browsing deer. He held the white man's world at bay as a sole and proud survivor of the pristine wilderness. Even the ship-builders of Mystic and Noank had left him untouched, though not on account of his majestic beauty but merely because his twenty-foot girth had defied their saws and axes.

And yet, for all the tree's hoary age ranging back far beyond the time of Columbus, he was flourishing still, springing and expanding, drinking up every April a deep fresh draught of sap from the dark, pushing forth every May a million new waxen leaves, dropping every autumn ten thousand acorns, and wrapping about him every winter against the cold another growth-ring. The twigs of his present season were as young and tender as those of a sapling.

The life of the tree, both old and young, rose and fell like the fountain of sand-grains in the bubbling pool. Like them it throbbed to a rhythmic pulse and danced to an unheard music. The rock-like strength of the oak's main trunk, the deposit of all the years since its infancy, enabled it to stand against the hurricane, and also to provide a chantry for the hermit thrush.

From sundown to cockshut of many a summer evening, while the thrush sang unseen above him, Holdfast lay at the foot of the Larrabee Oak, smoking his stone pipe and meditating things past and things to come. Once more, as often in his boyhood, he had a vague sense that the spirit of the huge old tree was passing into him, or he into it, until he

432

could almost have said that his very thoughts were oaken and that his hopes were fluttering aloft on the highest bough. He no longer felt that his fifty years were a burden. They had become a reservoir of wisdom and power. And often, as he left the great tree and started back through Gungywamp on the edge of the dark, he went rejoicing as one who sees before him his real life at last, his true work, and his love.

COCHEGAN'S CHILDREN

". . . and, do you know, I haven't been here to Cochegan Rock in all these years. Not once, Holdfast. Isn't that strange?"

"It doesn't seem strange to me."

"But I mean, when you think how often we used to come up here from the farm, walking all those miles up and back and never thinking it was far at all.—Or if it did seem far then we were glad, because it made us feel more independent or something."

"Yes."

"But the last time we came you really were very stern. You said 'Don't toe out like a white woman!' and 'Stop that!' and 'Carry this haversack!'—Do you remember that day?"

"Oh, yes."

"Somehow you were always more severe with me here than in other places. You almost frightened me, as the rock did too."

"See if it doesn't frighten you still more today."

"I'm sure it will. There's a ghost in Cochegan . . . I suppose it's the ghost of King Uncas."

"Not his alone; but there are spirits here, certainly."

"Oh, I meant to tell you that we have a sewing-circle of ladies in Norwich who are doing all they can for the poor Mohegans. We meet once a month—sometimes at Sarah Huntington's, sometimes at Lydia Sigourney's, or else at my house. Every Thanksgiving we send them down baskets of food and clothing. We are hoping that some day we can build them a little church. Lydia Sigourney has written a beautiful poem about them."

"H'm."

"Well, what else can we do?"

433

"Nothing.—And will you tell me, Rebecca, why your servant, the man who drove you down here in your gig, is following us a hundred yards or so behind, keeping us all the time in sight?"

"Oh, Holdfast! I didn't think . . . I mean, I didn't suppose . . . And I . . ."

"You didn't think I'd *see* him?" For a moment the man from the western wilds looked as though he would break into derisive laughter; but then his grave and saturnine expression returned. "Send that man back to the gig," said he, "and tell him to stay there."

When Rebecca came back from this errand, her face aflame, he went on, quietly: "As for the poor Mohegans, it is most kind of you to remember them. No doubt they are properly grateful. And please thank Mrs. Sigourney for her poem—but don't ask me to read it."

"Please, Holdfast, don't make things too difficult."

"Do I, Rebecca?"

"I think you are a little hard. You are 'dern' today, like the rock. You seem to have something against me."

"No! Great god o' the mountain, no!—Not against *you*, Becky."

"Well, then, against what?"

"I don't blame you for being what people call 'a rich widow' and a 'pillar of society.' You can't help that. Your big house and the mill, all those servants, even Lydia Sigourney and her poems—they're just a misfortune."

"Well, then?"

"It's only that I can't find in Mrs. John Reid of Norwich the girl I used to know."

"Girls don't last forever, Holdfast. But what's the matter with—well, with a woman?"

"With *what* woman?"

"Oh! If you were anybody else . . . !—But there's the rock standing up all blue and bald above the trees. It frightens me, I tell you; and if you can't be a little more pleasant I shall run away."

Holdfast built and kindled the fire in the shelter of the great boulder. Then, because it was clear that Rebecca's hands and clothes must not be soiled, he also got out the dishes from their hidden crevice and broiled the two rabbits he had shot that morning, with bow and arrow, at Quaker Hill. In the ashes he cooked the corn-meal he had brought from Winthrop's Mill in New London, moistening it with water from Stony Brook. Then, having completed these preparations with a skill and speed that came of long practice, he called Rebecca.

434

"Why," said she, stepping carefully in her delicate slippers among the rocks, 'you've done all the work, Holdfast!"

"I didn't get the Others."

"Oh, let's not have them. They'll only make me cry, and . . ."

"Get them, Rebecca."

She moved toward the back of the shelter and there stood as though lost, looking vaguely here and there into the shadows. At last, when she turned slowly round, her look was contrite. "I don't think," she said, "that I can find them. I've forgotten where we put them.—Oh, Holdfast, forgive me! It is so long ago, and so much has happened since then."

"Yes, Becky; but I can see them now as they were when we left them here. I could find them on the darkest night."

He drew a flat stone from the earthen bank at the back of the shelter and took from the hollow behind it a box wrapped in cow-hide. She watched, wide-eyed, as he unwound the wrapping and opened the box.

"Oh! Oh!" was all she could say when she saw what lay there. She covered her face with her hands and turned away.

But Holdfast gazed down at the two wooden images for so long that he seemed to have forgotten her presence. To them the years had brought not the slightest change. They were as fresh and young as on that day when he, then twelve years old, had finished carving and painting them in the wigwam of old Quaquaquid the medicine-man.

"Here," he said at last, looking up as though from a trance, "you set them at the table. It is the woman's part."

After she had done so, and when Holdfast had made a burnt offering for all four, they ate in silence. No breeze visited the leaves of the chestnut tree overhead; there was no voice of any bird; but from the brook below there came up a patient murmur.

Rebecca felt the silence growing uncomfortable, so that she was glad when Holdfast, having finished his meal, rose abruptly and strode out of the shelter. No longer, as in the old days, could she guess at his thoughts with no word spoken. He looked to her huge, wild, and almost a stranger as he moved on the rock-strewn hill-side, scanning the ground.

He came back with a club in his hand, six feet long, four or five inches through, evidently part of a broken chestnut bough. One end of it he was hacking with his tomahawk, to bring it to a point.

"What are you going to do?" she asked.

435

"I am going to dig a grave."

Then he thrust the end of the club into the fire and began twirling it there, precisely as hundreds of his barbarous ancestors must have done in this very place for centuries past. His long straight hair, blue-black in the sunlight, his dark moving hands, the bone-hard lines of his face, but most of all the glow in his eyes, brought to mind the tales she had heard from her childhood about King Uncas.

How much did she know about this man? A boy and youth called Holdfast Gaines she had once known, to be sure, by heart; but this man's name, he had told her, was "Sleeping Bear." And during these many years where had this man been? What sights had his burning eyes looked upon? What had his hands been doing?

The great dark hands that were now twirling the club could do whatever they would. They could be grandly gentle and, just as easily, they could destroy. His eyes, so intent now, with gleams breaking through as though from an inward fire—what were they really seeing?

Yes, there was a spirit in him—and why not a spirit of evil? Why should not the foul and treacherous Hobbomok, of whom he had told her, have overcome in his heart the beneficent strength of Kiehtan? More and more he looked the human counterpart of Cochegan Rock. In this wild hidden place, the last pitiful refuge of a people who had once ruled one-third of Connecticut, what might a deeply wronged man such as he, the hereditary king of that broken people, be feeling, thinking, and planning to do?

Thus, little by little, a fear grew in her of the companion whom, in her girlhood, she had learned to trust completely. There was so much about this man, after all, that was strange, unknown.

Her thoughts raced backward to what he had been as a boy. She remembered that Nathan Hale had called Holdfast a burning-glass. She remembered the concentrated intensity with which he had gripped and held an idea, a mood, a fancy even, and made all else revolve about it. His very games, like playing house at Cochegan, had been more serious to him than most boys made their work. There was always the feeling, also, that he lived on two different levels. These two wooden images, for example, had never been toys to him. They were symbols.

Yes, there was the clue to Holdfast. That was the chief mark of the Indian in him. Every act and relationship of life was to him religious, and every object symbolic. There had been, for example, the dreadful vigil in the cave near Machimoodus in which he had gone so near, and

436

no doubt with perfect indifference, to the verge of death.—And so, what did this great club stand for? What sacrificial deed was he planning? Whose grave—for he had never told her a lie—did he mean to dig?

Her fear was mounting into a panic. She was shivering, although she sat within two feet of the fire. Cold sweat trickled down her back and between her breasts. She clamped her jaws to keep her teeth from chattering. Why would he not speak one word, or look at her? She lifted her hand to her mouth and bit it hard, to keep from screaming.

He glanced up for a moment and held her gaze with precisely that look of quiet command which had so often, in the old days, controlled her tendency to hysterics. From that look she got enough courage to speak.

"You know, Holdfast," the words came faintly at first, and breathless, "one reason for my forgetting about the—the Others?"

"Well, Becky?"

"Well, one reason was, I've had two boys of my own."

"Of course I know that," he answered, with a warm, deep gaze upon her.

"And do you think that is a—a good reason?"

"As good as any. With the same reason, I might have forgotten them too."

He was still looking at her, and not in anger. Not even in scorn.

"Father and Mother have told me about your two boys," he went on. "One of them died, I know, when he was a child."

"Yes, Holdfast. He was the elder one. John."

"And the other is Samuel Chester Reid, a sailor."

"Sam went to sea when he was eleven, just before his father was— was drowned. He's been away from me ever since, or nearly. He's all I have, and I think of him most of the time."

"Of course. Tell me about him, Becky."

"Oh, I'd like to. I do wish you could know him.—At first his father wanted to keep him at home, and of course I did too; but then Cousin Sam took him on a voyage to the West Indies, and after that there was no holding him. He went another voyage and was captured by a French privateer. They kept him for six months in a prison under the ground, in Guadeloupe. He was hardly more than a boy then, but he dug and fought his way out and got home, bringing Cousin Sam and his crew and the ketch back with him."

"Yes, Father has told me, and about his fighting the French and the

Tripoli pirates and serving on board the *Constitution*. I'd like to meet that boy."

"You'd like him, Holdfast, and—well, maybe feel proud of him too. In some ways he is like you."

Holdfast's gaze returned to the end of the twirling stick.

"He isn't afraid of anything."

"Of course he takes that from his mother," said Holdfast with a slight smile. "But after that?"

"Well, at twenty he was captain of his own brig, the *Merchant*, of New York. When this war came on he joined the Navy again on the *Constitution*, but after the battle, when his friend Isaac Hull was relieved of command, Sam left with him. With so many of our ships blockaded he was unemployed for a while, even though he had been promoted to Sailing Master in the Navy—but finally he signed with Jenkins and Havens to take out their new brig, the *General Armstrong*. He has gone four cruises in her already. Sam has changed her into a brigantine since the last cruise, so that now she is probably faster than ever."

"Four cruises as a privateer."

"Yes. And before long he's going out again. I had a letter from him three days ago. He said the only thing holding them back is the trouble he's had in mounting a big gun, a forty-two pounder, on a pivot amidships."

"A forty-two pounder! I should think he *might* have trouble."

"The owners say the gun is too heavy for a vessel only about seventy-eight feet long. They think it will make her crank and hard to sail. And then too, they say there's something wrong with the gun. It has a chip out of the muzzle, a deep one, made long ago by a cannon-ball."

The club dropped from Holdfast's hand. He leaned forward, much excited. "A forty-two pounder," said he, "with a chip out of the muzzle on the left-hand side?"

"That's what Sam said.—But how did you know it's on the left-hand side? And the owners seem to think it might break or explode if it got too hot. Besides that, they say, where can they get a man to handle such a gun?"

"But Becky, that's—that gun is my Long Tom!"

"No!"

"It certainly is."

"The gun you fired that night so long ago at Fort Trumbull, and that meant so much to us all?"

438

"I mean that very gun. It can't be any other. Where it's been all these years and how your boy got hold of it I don't know, but it's mine."

"Oh, he came across it in a foundry in Duane Street, New York, where they were just going to melt it down for the metal. Before then it had been used as a hitching post in South Street. I—I guess Sam had known the gun all his life, but he'd lost track of it after it was taken off that Haytian privateer he commanded during the Embargo. He bought it for two hundred and fifty dollars.—You see, I know his letters by heart."

Holdfast picked up the club and thrust it again into the embers. "Long Tom!" he murmured. "A thousand times I've wondered where that gun might be."

"I think it must be swung on a pivot-carriage aboard the *General Armstrong* by this time. Sam generally gets his way."

"You say his brigantine is about seventy-eight feet long. That would mean, at most, twenty-one feet in the beam and not more than eight feet from deck to keelson. And on top of that he swings a gun too big and heavy—or so the British thought—for a full-rigged ship. Your boy Sam takes long chances, Becky."

"Yes, he does. He always has. He—he has red hair, Holdfast." And Rebecca darted a glance at her companion not wholly in keeping with the fact that her own hair was nearly white.

"I see.—Like a girl I knew once."

"Oh, you are the most . . . You are the hardest man to . . ."

"And you say they can't find a gunner to manage Long Tom? I don't wonder."

For a while, then, he sat silent and mused. Studying his face intently, she saw its hard lines relaxing. The look she had always loved, the look of a youth at once dreamy and dauntless, was coming back into his eyes. How young, how amazingly young, he still was! Aside from a thin streak or two of gray in his hair, the years had not touched him! Somehow he had kept his body's perfection, and the wild flower of his spirit was still uncrumpled, unsullied.

All at once, for the first time in her life, Rebecca felt old and lonely. With almost a physical pang at her heart she saw herself growing every day older, alone. Ah, what was the use, the good, of being safe, sheltered, prosperous, respected, or even in living on equal terms with the Huntingtons of Norwich and Mrs. Lydia Sigourney, if youth was gone with all its dreams, its hopes and fears, its devotions?—But was it gone, completely and forever? Was it not, rather, near at hand—so near that she could still reach out and touch, perhaps even grasp it?

And then another thought that was half feeling, gentler and more womanly, swept through her. This oldest friend and best companion had given her years of his life at a time when he might easily have found other occupations. Without knowing how, she felt perfectly sure that he had always, even in that western wilderness, been true to her. And did such devotion call for no return? Could she do nothing for him? Was there not one thing she might do that would make them both happier for the rest of their lives?

But he looked up now and spoke, breaking the thread of her meditations: "Did you know, Becky, that the British burned Washington five days ago?"

"Why, no, Holdfast! Why, that's a terrible thing!"

"Yes. The news came in last night. It will be all over Norwich when you get home. I thought I wouldn't tell you until the day was over."

"But—our capital!"

"No worse than New London and Danbury and Buffalo. It's a habit they've fallen into. And I have a feeling that they won't stop there—that this is only part of a larger plan."

"Well, you always could tell what was coming."

"I can't do that; but sometimes it's as though I saw smoke-signals—saw two puffs that say 'Come! We need you!' Well, I understand it now. After all—your boy and my gun! The gods don't often signal more clearly than that."

He rose to his feet and helped her to rise. Then he reached down for the club.

"What are you going to do?" she asked.

"As I said before, I am going to dig a grave."

"And what are you going to bury there?"

"Something, Becky, that we won't need any more."

"What's that?"

"The Others."

"But why?"

"I started out with one reason, but now I have a better. You said that you had forgotten the children, as we used to call them, because you had borne real children of your own. Now I've been thinking that you might share with me the boy you still have. Then I too could forget these wooden people."

440

Although she was not quite sure what he meant, her heart leapt at the words. She clasped his arm impulsively in both hands and looked up into his face. "Holdfast," she cried, with that same mingling of laughter and tears at which he had always wondered, "I'll trade you half of my boy for one thing that won't cost you a penny."

He stood steady as Larrabee Oak on a windless midnight as he looked down at her and replied: "That's good, because pennies are just what I haven't.—But what is it?"

"I think you ought to know."

"I don't."

"It's something a girl doesn't usually have to ask for—and what you call a 'rich widow' still less."

"Still I don't know."

"You are very stupid. But—we've known each other for how long?"

"From the time we began to know anything."

"Yes. And yet you have never—you've never kissed me, Holdfast. Not once. Ever."

He searched her face and eyes, feeling her tremble against his arm like a slender birch in a breeze.

"It is not," said he, gravely, "an Indian way."

She laughed, almost like a girl. "No," she said, "but I think it's a good one, when two people have loved each other for all their lives. At least, it's a better thing to remember than just wooden dolls."

For her only answer, at first, there came up through the listening woods the voice of the brook which had been talking to Cochegan Rock for a million years.

Holdfast moved slightly away, disengaging his arm. "The sun," he said, "will soon be down, and we have to dig that grave."

Her hands fell at her side. Her gaze dropped from his eyes to the ground. Her face was pale, blank, and pitiful.

"Wrap the Others well, Becky, and lay them back in the box."

She began to do as he bade, her hands moving slowly and awkwardly like those of a very old woman. Again and again as she worked she looked up and watched him as he struck and thrust and pried with his great chestnut club at the earth just under the shelving rock. He had pulled off his hunting-shirt. The muscles along his spine and shoulders were moving like bronze snakes. The soft earth and gravel poured from the hole and still he struck and struck again. He was digging a grave, but not only for two wooden images. Already the hole was six feet deep, and wide. A little more, and would he not

441

loosen the foundations of Cochegan itself, bringing down upon them both that unimaginable bulk and weight?

She stood and watched, spell-bound, longing to hold him close, and overwhelmed by a sense of desolation. A chill breeze, fore-runner of the dusk, came up from the brook-bottom, crept under the edge of rock, and made her shiver. She lifted her cloak from the ground and drew it about her shoulders.

Holdfast did not glance at her, but went on striking into the hillside with the full power of his body. He seemed to care not at all whether a man and a woman were to lie there or only two carved and colored pieces of wood. He was merely digging a grave, and leaving the rest to Cochegan.

And all at once Rebecca realized that she cared no more than he did. Death might come at any moment, but it would be a death with him and therefore noble. In many ways it would be better than old age and its loneliness. Let the gods, then, decide. She walked forward into the shadows and stood quietly beside him, holding the box in hands that did not tremble.

"That's a brave girl, Becky," said he, flashing at her a friendly smile. And as he fell to striking again she saw that his hands had been torn and bloodied by the jagged butt of the club.

When at last he could reach no farther inward he paused, threw back his hair from his face, reached up with his right hand and pushed with all his power against the rock.

He waited a moment, listening. "Well, then," said he, "it's the Others that Cochegan wants. Let's have them."

She watched him shove the box to the farthest side of the hole, so that it lay just beneath the newly exposed under-surface of the great boulder. Pathetically small and dim it looked back there in the dark of the earth. Then for minute after minute she watched as he scooped the earth by double handfuls back over their childhood and youth, and rammed it tight with the butt of the club. Before he had finished, the level rays of the sun were reaching under the rock.

At last he fitted a few flat stones across the grave and pounded them deep into the soft earth.

"Come," he said. "You and I have something left to do.—As for those two, they are Cochegan's children now, forever."

442

BOOK FOUR

ECHOING GUNS

Behold, how great a matter a little fire kindleth!
THE EPISTLE OF JAMES, III, 5

THE INSOLENCE OF IT

(September 26, 1814)

A fog, like wool, had blanketed the *General Armstrong* since early morning. The brigantine was fumbling along under easy sail.

Captain Samuel Chester Reid had seen no reason for remaining on deck. Let Lieutenant Worth manage. It was good for the men to have their captain stay below except when he was needed. It was very good for them to see him suddenly appear on deck, after hours of absence, with full and exact knowledge of his vessel's situation.

Sitting comfortably in his green-and-white cabin, Captain Reid was noting down certain details of his cruise to be included in the letter he would send, as soon as he touched Fayal, to Jenkins and Havens of New York.

"We sailed fm Sandy Hook," he wrote, "on the eve of 9th Sept., 1814, & abt midnight fell in close abord of a razee & Ship of the Line. They pursued us til next day noon when thot proper give over chase. On 11th after 9 hrs chase borded private armed skuner *Perry*, John Colman, master, 6 days fm Philad; had thrown over all his guns. Foll day fell in with enemy gun brig; exchanged few shots & left him. On 24th borded Spanish brig & skuner & a Portugee all fm Havana. On 26th . . ."

"Land ho!" the lookout's voice thrilled through the deck timbers, sounding distant and airy.—Captain Reid dropped his quill and looked up at the chart tacked on the cabin wall. His blue eyes sparkled and his strong white teeth glistened for a moment in a smile of almost boyish pride. New York to the Azores in seventeen days! What would Jenkins and Havens think of that!

Lieutenant Worth stuck his bushy head through the companion door-way and reported: "Land sighted on the lee bow, sir. The fog's lifted. I think it's Fayal."

"Very well, Mr. Worth," said the captain. He took up his quill and continued the line he had been writing: "On 26th following came into Fayal Roads for ppose of filling water."

A captain must preserve his dignity at all times—must never allow himself to look surprised or happy about anything. All the same, it had been a remarkable run. The *General Armstrong,* with this new brigantine rig, must be one of the swiftest privateers afloat. Not even that tremendous "Long Tom" had slowed her down much. Jenkins and Havens were going to be greatly astonished.

Of course the mounting of that huge old gun had been a chancy thing, for all the advantage it would give him in combat. No one had been sure what would be the effect of its three tons of metal upon the sailing of a vessel that registered only a hundred and forty-six tons herself. Another thing the owners had feared, and rightly, was that no one might be found to work such a monster.—But then, on the very last day in New York harbor, to pick up the one man in the world who knew Long Tom and could manage him! That had been pure luck.

Well, no prizes thus far, to be sure, after all that chasing and boarding. Still, the cruise was yet young.

Captain Reid rose from his chair. He took off the second-best coat in which he always worked in his cabin, brushed his best one, and put it on. Then he arranged his vividly red hair by the little mirror that hung in his wardrobe closet. Once again, as always on such occasions, he recalled a casual remark made long years ago by his dead father, that a ship's officer could never be too careful about his personal appearance. And to that remark his mother had added, years later: "Dress like a gentleman, Sam. Talk like a gentleman, always. And don't just imitate a gentleman, but *be* one. Then all the rest will be easy."

She had a way of saying things, his mother. She could use the simplest words in ways that sang—or stung. Her phrases stuck and clung, like burrs. Well, her hair had been red too, once.

"Mount Pico to port, sir," said Worth as he came on deck.—Just a bit too voluble, perhaps, that Lieutenant Worth. He had a slight tendency to announce the obvious. Only a blind man could have missed the huge craggy mass of Pico rising nearly a mile and a half into the eastern sky and standing straight up from the sea.

"Yes—and Fayal to starboard, of course," Reid answered, looking slightly bored. "There's Horta, with Guia Head at the end of the harbor.

446

We'll make for it, Mr. Worth, and come to anchor as quickly as possible."

And yet it was not easy for the young captain to conceal his delight as he stood at the rail and gazed across the dancing waves, turquoise blue, at the tiny chalk-white houses half hidden amid the glister of orange-groves. Readily stirred as he was by beauty of any sort, he felt a strange elation growing in him, as though at the approach of some exciting event.

"That's good water, Captain Reid. Not more than two days in cask."
The American consul, John Dabney, had returned with the captain to inspect the privateer, and the two were standing now on the quarter-deck watching the men hoist the casks on board and into the hold, under the supervision of Starks, the sailing-master.

"Lucky for us, Mr. Dabney. I hope to be gone by sunrise tomorrow."
"I'm sorry for that. It's seldom we hear a Yankee voice with this war on, and we're famished for news."
"The chief news I heard just before sailing was that the British have burned Washington to the ground."
"What! Washington burned?"
"They burned it, I say, as they did New London before we were born."
"But, Captain Reid! Burning our capital—that looks like the end!"
"I don't think so. We New Englanders never thought much of Washington anyway. If they should try to burn Hartford, say, why then we might get excited."
"But surely, we're losing the war."
"I can't agree.—Not so fast with that cask, Mr. Starks. Easy does it.— At sea and on the Lakes we have done far better than hold our own. By land, one has to admit, they have beaten us, thus far—but what good has it done them? We can lead the British all up and down the country until they're worn out, as we did in the Revolution. We can retreat clear down to New Orleans if we have to. And they 'll never drive us out of the West. It's too big."
"You think so?"
"I'm sure of it. You ought to hear what my grandfather says. He's been out there. Better still, have a talk with Mr. Holdfast Gaines, now a member of my crew. He's an Indian, and . . . Well, he knows the West as I do the *General Armstrong*. He *is* the West, although he was born

447

and reared in Connecticut. He knows New Orleans and the Mississippi and what's beyond. He says old England can never take that country."

"Oh, yes," the consul exclaimed. "That reminds me."

He drew a yellowing newspaper from his pocket as he spoke, and opened it. "Mrs. Dabney," he continued, "brought this to my attention the other day. It's a year old, and may not mean a thing, but when I heard you were here I thought I might just bring it along."

"Will you read it to me, Mr. Dabney? Then I can go on watching these fellows load in the casks."

"Yes, certainly. Well, it's in the *London Courier* for June the seventeenth of last year, 1813, and at the top it says 'Policy of Taking New Orleans.'"

"Ah. Interesting title."

"I thought so. And here's what it says: 'There are arguments in our colonial journals tending to prove that there exists a necessity for our government's taking possession of the Province of New Orleans. We extract the following observations on that subject: If Great Britain will only take New Orleans she will divide the States. By shutting that outlet to the fruits of Western industry, she will make herself known and respected by those States, in spite of the power of the rest of the Union. If, in the war of 1755, France had been as superior at sea as Britain then was, we should never have heard of the United States of America. The back country would have been as well settled before this with Frenchmen as it now is with the descendants of Britons. We ought at present to take the benefit of former lessons, and make these people our friends, when so much is in our power. Take New Orleans, which is at the threshold of our West India Islands, and which could furnish them with provisions at half the price they have been accustomed to pay. By such conduct firm allies would be created on the Continent of Europe, our West India planters would be gratified, and the integrity of the Spanish dominions in America would be guaranteed from traitorous insults.'"

"But the *insolence* of it!" Reid exploded.

"That's what I thought, Captain. As though whatever they might want they had only to reach out for and—and grab!"

"Precisely. And I spoke a while back as though, because I was born in Connecticut, I didn't care what might happen elsewhere in America. Well, that isn't quite so. Now that you've read that article I find that I care a good deal."

"But I've wondered, Captain Reid, whether one can really believe this article. There's something so—well, I think I will say so *brutal*

448

about it. And then too, if you mean business about a thing like this you don't publish your plans in a newspaper."

"I don't know about that. Depends how cock-sure you are that the earth and sea are yours, and the fullness thereof."

"Well, it makes me feel helpless, lost and forgotten as I am out here in the Atlantic."

"Me too, Consul. As I came into harbor I was congratulating myself upon having made a fairly good cruise, thus far, in my little brigantine, but now I'm reminded that the British Navy has two hundred and twenty ships-of-the-line. We haven't one. They have three hundred war frigates. We have three, and they're 'most always blockaded.—Only fast little privateers like mine can get out, but no one expects us to do anything."

"Well, if they don't expect you to, then . . ."

"By the way, have any British vessels called here lately?"

"Not for several days. No sir."—And Dabney put the yellowing newspaper back into his pocket.

Dusk was falling on the harbor now, though the little waves were still delicately tipped with western light. The town of Horta, built in a half-moon round the curve of the harbor, was washed and soaked in the violet hues of evening. To Reid, looking up from the deck of the brigantine, the houses of the town in their steeply terraced gardens seemed to be jostling for position, and peering over one another's shoulders as though in the hope that something might happen, at last, in the harbor below. But nothing ever had, apparently, or would. The castle of Vera Cruz, black, grim, antique, jutted bluntly up from the volcanic crags as a bulwark against all change. Rocky Guia Head guarded the southern tip of the harbor's crescent, and over to eastward on its separate island Mount Pico, an enormous sentinel, towered up into the lingering sunset glow.

Little lug-sails of the fishing-fleet were wafting home from the outer sea like colored moths of the twilight.

The blue-and-white flag of Portugal fluttered down from the staff on the castle battlements to a few scattered notes from a bugle.

Gulls by the hundred, lilac-winged, were sliding down to the deep-hued water with dwindling cries.

Candles glimmered in the windows of the town. Whale-oil lamps went jiggling up and then held steady on mast after mast in the harbor.

But what was that taller pile of canvas, dim and distant, moving

449

round the north-east headland? Reid thought at first that she might be only a larger fishing-vessel nosing down the channel between Pico and Fayal for a night of quiet sleep away from the plunge of the sea. But no—at least a merchantman or whaler. She was being smartly handled, too, in the light breeze. More and more closely he watched her ghostly approach, straining his eyes through the murk. He could hear voices now, apparently speaking English, from her deck. She had three masts, square-rigged. Nine gun-ports, if he could count them correctly, were faintly discernible in the single white streak along her side.—And so, a sloop-o'-war, almost certainly British!

The three lieutenants, Worth, Williams and Johnson, came to the quarter-deck. Came Starks, the sailing-master, and Allen, the captain of marines. They crowded round, staring first through the dusk at the sloop and then at their captain.

"Shall we cut cable, sir?" asked Worth. "We could be under way in two minutes."

Reid moistened his forefinger and held it up for a few seconds.

"There's hardly enough wind, Mr. Worth; and what there is, they have. We could hardly hope to scrape by without an action."

"But we can handle a sloop-o'-war, sir. We've done it afore!" said young Johnson, pushing forward with out-thrust jaw.

"Not in a neutral port, Mr. Johnson. We must respect neutrality."

"But what if they begin it?"

"Ah—that would be a different thing."

More and more candles and lamps were showing up there in the windows of Horta. The child that had begun to cry somewhere in the little rock-built town fell asleep in the middle of a wail. They heard the comfortable rustle and cluck of small waves under the bow. A full moon, or the half of one, was peering round the shoulder of Pico. By its light they could see a pilot's boat nuzzling up alongside the sloop-o'-war like a week-old calf with its mother.—The sails of the Englishman, which had been hauled aback to let the pilot come aboard, filled again almost at once, and the sloop stood up into harbor.

"So," said Reid under his breath, "the pilot has told 'em who we are."

Yes, there could be no doubt about it. She was heading directly for the *Armstrong*, whatever that might mean.

Perhaps it had been just as well, after all, that he had taken no prizes

450

on the present cruise, and so had still his full complement of ninety men aboard, most of whom would normally have dribbled away in prize-crews. Ninety men on a deck only seventy-eight feet long could stand off twice that number of assailants if the British should try boarding. With the boarding-nettings triced up, they might hope to keep out three or even four times their own numbers, if they had plenty of loaded pistols and were well commanded by officers they liked.—Reid smiled at the recollection of his grandfather Chester's remark, about the fight on the little *Rebecca,* that after Holdfast Gaines climbed on deck there was no room left for any British boarders.

"Clear for action if you please, Mr. Worth," Reid said over his shoulder, exactly as he would say at table "Mr. Worth, will you please pass the salt?"

The sloop-o'-war was within musket-shot now, and still she was coming with all sails set. Would they try to run alongside and board without warning or palaver? That would not be unlike them. Watching her come head-on, Reid fought a temptation to rake her deck from stem to stern. He imagined the havoc one charge of grape from Long Tom would do among those crowded men and officers on her forecastle. The other guns would join in laying a broad swath of death and wreckage from her bowsprit to the wheel. Then there would be not the slightest danger of boarders, and the *Armstrong* could continue her cruise undisturbed. Reid knew plenty of privateer captains who, with such a chance, would not have hesitated for a moment. Indeed, was it not his duty to Jenkins and Havens?

But no, Sam C. Reid was still listed as a Sailing Master in the United States Navy, and this was a neutral port.—"I'll pull in so close to shore," he muttered to Williams, "that all Horta will see them breaking neutrality. I'll set the whole town sneezing with their powder-smoke."

She was within pistol-shot. The sing-song of the leadsman in her fore-chains sounded clearly across the narrowing water: "By the deep, six."

"Take her clothes off," some officer ordered. "All but fore-tops'l. Hand and stow! Smartly, now!"

With the shrill of a bosun's pipe, squeal of blocks, cries of midshipmen and bosun's mates, the main and mizzen masts came clean of canvas.

"And a half, five!"

"Bit your cable. Lee your helm. Fore-tops'l clew up! Set your spanker
451

an' mizzen-stays'l."—It was an arrogant voice, a hateful voice, a voice pronouncing its English out of the dark in a hateful alien way. It was a voice that one would give much to quiet.—But, nevertheless, hold still now; clamp your teeth; remember that easy does it. Remember how softly the Thames flows down between the slumbering meadows.

"By the mark, five!"

Twisted round by her stern-canvas, the sloop-o'-war began to come up with her head to the wind.

"Le' go anchor!—Strike mizzen-stays'l an' spanker!"

The anchor plunged. The cable ran out with a rumble.

"Nothin' wrong yet," said Worth, close to Reid's shoulder.—Well, where did he come from? One thought he had gone away.

"P'r'aps they on'y want to be near the town for water, like us," suggested Johnson.

"Frigate coming into harbor, sir," said Williams on the other side.

He was right. Round the north-east headland a second vessel came walking. She was clear-cut in the light of the moon now shining full like a shield on the shoulder of Pico. Twice the size of the sloop-o'-war, she came in stately and tall as though she owned this place and had made it. Who else, she seemed to ask, has any right to ride here?

Next, close behind her, came floating a third, a castle of canvas, majestic and beautiful, huge, overpowering.—Reid clutched the rail of the quarter-deck and bit his lips hard and stared. Her massive black bulwarks grew and grew, pierced for two banks of great guns, as she trod through the dancing glimmer, a seventy-four-gun ship-of-the-line!

And oh, the maddening deliberation with which these omnipotent queens of the sea stalked up the harbor and dropped anchor! They took their own time. They had no need to hasten. They asked permission of no power on earth. It was enough to make a helpless man grind powder off the tops of his teeth.

Steady, though! As yet the frigate and the ship, whatever might be said of the sloop-o'-war, had shown no signs of hostility. Their draft did not permit them to approach so close as the sloop had done. It was only that they blocked the channel, perhaps by intention, and easily commanded all the shallows through which the little *Armstrong* might try to escape.

"What do you think of it, Mr. Gaines?"

"As you know, Captain, I'm no sailor."

"No; but what do you think of the odds?"

"I have seen victory won against odds almost as great as these."

"For example?"

"At the moment I was thinking of an attack by sixty British sailors and marines upon a Yankee ketch with ten men and boys on board."

"You were with those ten, I believe."

"Toward the end, yes."

"And that night you slept beside my father, and he did not—ah—kill you."

"I didn't suppose he had ever told that story."

"He told it, I think, to me alone. My mother doesn't know it."

"No.—And there's another thing which even he never knew."

"What's that?"

"I came very close to killing him that night."

"While you and he were lying side by side in the cabin of the *Rebecca*?"

"Oh, no. Not then. I mean while his launch was sliding past Fort Trumbull. I had Long Tom, here, trained on his boat, and could have destroyed him by lifting my arm. I didn't do so, for reasons that have grown clearer with the years."

"I've never known that."

"No one has. Not even Beck . . . your mother."

"And could you tell me any of those reasons?"

"If I had lifted my arm, Captain, you would never have lived.— And so what you do here tonight may be one of the things that held down my arm."

"You are a very strange man, Mr. Gaines.—Of course, I've always known that. Since I was a child Father and Mother have told me about the best friend either of them ever had. But now that we meet, I don't feel that I know you at all."

"I'm not an officer, Captain. I'm only one of the crew."

"Yes, but—but you seem to know, in some way, what I shall do tonight. I don't. I wish you would tell me."

"You will be their son."

"Can't you say anything more definite than that?"

For several seconds Holdfast seemed to hesitate. Then he said "No, Captain," and turned away.

"The sloop's signaling, sir," said Worth.—Why couldn't the man assume that a captain had eyes in his own head?

A line of vari-colored lanterns was going up to the sloop's mizzen-peak. On the seventy-four, other lanterns rose in answer.

"Hoist out the long-boat, the pinnace, the launch, the cutter," barked that same hateful voice from the sloop's deck. "Get your pistols and cutlasses from the arms-chests, men."

There was a sound of scrambling, scraping, shuffling, banging, and then the voice: "Now into the boats with you! Marines, in your places. Stand ready to push off!"

It was strange that just before action, when every other man in the ship was straining like a race-horse on the home-stretch, the captain should have almost nothing to do. Later on, of course . . . But now he could only hand the keys of the magazine to the master-gunner and pace the length of the deck.

Stripped to the waist the men were, with gaudy handkerchers over their heads and ears to stop the sweat and noise. They were yanking their belt-buckles tighter. John Harrison, captain of the aftermost gun on the port side, was pulling the tompion from "Bouncing Betsey" as Reid walked by. It came out of the muzzle with a hollow "plop," like the cork of a wine-bottle. At the next port Jim Davis was worming the old cartridge out of "John Bull's Belly-Ache." Moonlight gleamed on the copper loading-ladle as Eli Sheffield thrust a fresh bag of powder down the throat of "Hell an' Destruction." The captain stopped to speak with Eli, who came from Chesterfield near Quaker Hill.

On the starboard side Pete Tyson was ramming a round shot and a bag of musket-balls down "Orders in Council." At the next place John Piner and his crew were hauling "Lord Nelson" back into its port with the side-tackles. Reid remembered that Piner had been impressed into the British Navy and had served under Nelson at Trafalgar. The last nine-pounder, "Free Trade and Sailor's Rights," was in fighting position. Her crew were laying out her rammer, worm, sponge, and crow-bar beside the netfuls of round-shot and wads. Her captain, Tom Parsons, went down to the gunner's store-room, along with the other gun-captains, to get his horn of fine-mealed priming-powder for the vent. Finally Holdfast was testing the firmness of the flint in the gun-lock screwed to Long Tom's massive breech while the gun-crew was greasing the circular tracks under the pivot-carriage.

"We are ready for action, sir," Worth reported. His voice was gay.

"Very well, Mr. Worth. Cut your cable, please, and then get the sweeps through the ports and man them."

The twenty-foot oars of pine were thrust through the small ports

454

between the guns, five to a side. Crews of six men, three pulling and three pushing at each sweep, began edging the *Armstrong* in toward the castle.

There was a sudden splash from the sloop.—"She's cut her cable, sir!" called Worth. And the sloop was, indeed, making after them. Four boats, bristling with men, emerged from her side into the glitter of moonlight on the water.

"Drop your spare anchor, please, Mr. Worth. Get a spring on the cable and haul her round till the guns bear."—And again it was only as though he had said at table: "I will thank you, Mr. Worth, for the bread."

The anchor plunged. A hawser was bent to it and brought in at the stern port. Then the cable was slackened, the hawser was hauled in, and her broadside swung toward the sloop and the oncoming boats.— How easily they could be raked!

"Sweeps in, Mr. Worth, and prepare to repel boarders. Don't let the great guns fire until the sloop fires at us. Don't fire at the boats until they touch our sides. But then, if they do . . . ! You understand me?"

"Yes, Captain."

A sensible man, he thought, would have raked those boats before they came near. Any one could see what they meant to do as soon as they came alongside, and then they would be too low for his great guns.—Still, this was a neutral port, and the British had not yet committed one act of violence which would exonerate him in a navy court-martial.

"Boats ahoy!" he called from the taffrail.

No answer.

"Boats ahoy, there! This is the United States privateer *General Armstrong,* from New York. We are in a neutral port. Keep your distance or we fire."

They came steadily, silently, on. The foremost was now within ten strokes.

Eight bells went on the *Armstrong,* and then from the sloop. Eight o'clock of the evening.

"I now hail you for the last time. Keep off."

A gruff, stupid voice in the leading boat asked "What's matter?"

"Make no answer," barked the same voice that had been issuing orders from the sloop. "Give way! Give way, all!"

"Are you ready, Mr. Allen?" asked Reid.

455

"All ready, sir. Take aim with your small arms, men. Each cover your man in the first boat, but don't fire until the Captain gives the word."

The water was like a vast dark mirror. Looking down, Reid saw the serpent of moonshine suddenly broken in two. A tiny wave edged with light ran before the bows of a boat sliding forward. Its prow bumped the port-quarter right below him.

"Fire, and board her, my lads!" yelled that hateful voice.

"Fire!" shouted Reid.

The two bursts of musketry mingled, and Reid saw Burton Lloyd, one of the best men on the forecastle, leap three feet from the deck and fall back lifeless. When he glanced down a moment later the red glare of the musket-flashes lit the large white face of the boat's lieutenant, not eight feet away. That would be the officer with the hateful voice. In his right hand he had a double-barreled pistol, leveled at Reid's head, and his left was reaching for the rail. He had thick black eyebrows and a flat broken nose. He was yelling "No quarter!" as he climbed, and Reid could see that two of his upper teeth were missing.—Then all at once the left side of the white face crumpled. Blank astonishment and a kind of wild appeal were in the eyes that stared up over the rail. The mouth, still open, now gaped across the left side of the face right to the ear. The thick flesh of the torn cheek hung down over the jaw. And then, as the blood slowly came, the lieutenant twisted half-way round, threw up both his arms, and splashed back into the sea.

Holdfast Gaines, standing ten feet away and beside the rail, was swiftly reloading his rifle.

The marines in the forward boat, a moment before, had been standing in line down the middle between the rowers, each with his bayonet fixed. The seamen also, rising from the thwarts, had waited only for their lieutenant to say the word. But then they collapsed together like a house of cards. A marine's top-hat of black felt, with gold lace round the brim and a cockade, went skimming away in the moonlight. When the noise of the muskets died down there were a few screams from the boat, now slowly drifting off. "Quarter! Quarter!" wailed a voice, growing weaker, fainter.

The voice was drowned out by the yells and cheers from the three boats coming up at the bow and along the starboard side: "Up and board 'em, lads!" "Give 'em cold steel!" "No quarter to the damned rebel bastards!"

456

They came on with perfect confidence, as though every vessel in the seven seas was theirs for the taking—as though it was theirs already and had been temporarily usurped by ignorant, inferior persons. Yet they seemed to be firing rather in the spirit of a lark than with intent to hurt anyone. Certainly they could not be aiming much as they came. But just as they were making ready to climb aboard there fell a silence, and into it rang Worth's full deep voice like a bell—"Fire!"

Eighty muskets and pistols answered in one long crackle and roar that beat against the terraces and walls of the town and then out into the bay. Reid could see his men by the flashes all along the deck, some kneeling to rest their muskets in the sweep-ports, some aiming over the gunwales, and some with their legs crooking into the shrouds to fire straight down.

In the midst of this, and while Reid was walking toward him, Worth clapped both hands to his side, spun round, and fell heavily on his face.

Reid turned him over, gently, and felt for his heart. The beat was steady. Inside his shirt there was a long red furrow, not deep, across the right side. Ah, good! Worth had only been stunned by the blow of a heavy ball.

"Here, Scalsan! Harrison! Please carry Mr. Worth down to Dr. Brosnahan in my cabin."

Those cries for quarter coming up from the three boats were absurdly different from the confident yells of two minutes ago. "Rebels," eh? And "bastards"! So let one of them limp away into the shimmer, with only two oars pulling on a side. Leave enough of them alive to tell the news. Not for some while would they do much harm to New Orleans.

"Man the sweeps again, please, Mr. Williams, and up anchor. Pull in as close as you can to the castle."—He hoped that his voice still sounded calm to the men, in spite of its slight tremor of exaltation.

With a thump of bare feet around the capstan they marched her up to the anchor and hauled it in. The monotonous creak of the sweeps in the ungreased ports began once more. A man in the fore-chains was heaving the lead with regular splashes.—"By the deep, four!" Thud . . . thud . . . thud . . .

They'll come back. We've only winged them. Now their blood is up they 'll crowd in every man their boats will hold. They must have more than a thousand men in those three ships, against our eighty-five. Well, say ten to one—odds that ought to satisfy even Holdfast Gaines.

457

"Up with the boarding-nettings, please, Mr. Johnson. Hoist them all round, and lash them to the shrouds and back-stays."

"Yes, Captain"—and in a few seconds Johnson had gathered a score of the crew about him and disappeared down the hatch.

"And a half, three!" Thud . . . thud . . .

All the western flank of Pico was silvered by the moon. The sails of the sloop-o'-war were pearly white as she glided away to get help from the two great ships. Between the slaughter past and the slaughter to come a Spirit of Beauty was walking the sea. From a tower in the town there fell a chime, and the *Armstrong's* bell answered once. It was half-past eight.

That chant of the leadsman forward made one think of feeling in through the fog across Fisher's Island Shoal and then up the River Thames. The windows of Groton and New London would be bright by half-past eight, like those of Horta, with lamps and candles. Cow-milking would be over at Four Winds Farm, and the beasts bedded down for the night. At the fireside there the sweet-faced grandmother would be sitting with her husband beside her, his once powerful hands now trembling like a leaf.

"How goes it, Mr. Gaines?"

"Nothing from Long Tom yet, Captain."

"But you've kept your long rifle busy."

"Yes. Hobbomok has made a few remarks."

"He has a soft voice, but . . ."

Ah, but they can crowd five hundred men into their boats. We've held them off once, but now they'll come from all sides together, giving us no time . . .

"By the mark, twain!"

"In with the sweeps, please, Mr. Williams. And drop anchor."

Already Johnson and his helpers were furiously at work among the shrouds, lashing the heavy tarred nets to a height of ten feet above the bulwarks all round.

"They didn't hoist their boarding-nettings on the *Rebecca* that night, I think, Mr. Gaines."

"No, Captain; and if they had, Leftenant John Reid would never have got aboard."

Reid's strong white teeth glistened for a moment in the moonlight. "Well then," said he, "leave an opening, please, Mr. Johnson, six feet wide, along the after rail."

"Aye, aye, sir!"

458

The castle gloomed huge, half a pistol-shot off. There was a stench of whale-oil, of dead fish, and of sewage from the town.

"Moor by the stern too, if you please, Mr. Williams."

The men came aft, at the call, with muskets and pikes in their hands, pistols and cutlasses in their belts, and iron-strapped boarding-helmets on their heads. Their faces, though begrimed with powder and streaked with sweat, shone pale in the moonlight. Their bare feet made a soft padding sound as they ranged themselves before him.

"Men," said Reid, "the force against us is overwhelming. In our situation any privateer would be justified in surrendering without another shot.

"Each of you has done well on this cruise and in this fight. I will give an honorable discharge and a draft for pay upon Jenkins and Havens to any man who wishes to leave the vessel now. I shall not blame him for leaving, and neither should any of his ship-mates.

"As some of you may know, I hold the rank of Sailing Master in the United States Navy. I was a master's mate on board the *Constitution* when we took the *Guerrière* at the beginning of this war. If my friend Captain Isaac Hull had a ship today I would be with him. But with our small navy almost entirely blockaded in harbor many of my brother officers are now serving in privateers, which is the only way in which we can hope to strike the enemy. Therefore, as a navy officer, my duty is clear.

"I shall remain here because I think those three vessels may be part of a large squadron now moving against some part of our country. It may be that they intend to attack New York. My wife and child are there. Mr. Dabney has suggested that the British may be going against New Orleans, which is the key to the Mississippi and the country lying beyond. At any rate, I feel sure that they plan some kind of attack upon America, now that they are free from the danger of Buonaparte. Otherwise, why should they be here, eight hundred miles west of Europe? Otherwise, why should they violate the neutrality of this port? Otherwise, what could they want of the *Armstrong*, that they should pay down so many lives to take her?

"Men, during the last war soldiers fighting for the King of England massacred scores of Connecticut farmers after they had laid down their arms. On the same day they burned the town of New London, near my birth-place. Last month, as you know, British soldiers burned Washington, the capital of our country. For my part, I feel that this sort of thing must stop. Therefore I shall remain. I cannot hope, of course, to destroy this squadron, but with the help of some of you I may perhaps detain it for a while in these waters."

"Three cheers on that!" shouted Parsons. "Hip-hip . . ."

"No! Stop, Tom! The British always cheer *before* a fight. If we are to cheer at all, let it be *after* this one."

"Can't we cheer for you, Cap?" asked a voice from the back row.

"Certainly not! Save your wind.—But now, men, I've told you how matters stand. All those who intend to leave will take one step forward."

No one stirred.

"What?" Reid exclaimed, looking from face to face. "I tell you again that it's the reasonable thing to do.—But also I say, as the time is short, that this is your last chance."

The men glanced at each other with uneasy smiles. No one stepped forward from the uneven ranks.

"Well, then," said Captain Reid in a somewhat heartier tone, "I'm glad you're all standing by. We're probably the only American vessel within hundreds of miles, and we must fight for all those ships and men that would be here if they could."

"Aye, aye, sir!" sang out a cheerful voice.

"Stations, men!" Reid ordered, crisply.

"Carpenter, I want two new gun-ports cut through the starboard bulwarks, one for'rd and one aft of the four ports we've got now. Fasten breeching and tackle-bolts as fast as you can. The gun-crews will help you.—Davis, get your gun over into the spare port now. Harrison and Sheffield, help the carpenter, and get your guns over to starboard as soon as the new ports are ready.—We'll be using all six great guns now that we know what they're after."

In twenty minutes the new ports were cut and the three gun-crews from the port side had cast loose the breechings and tackles, had rumbled their guns across the deck, and secured them in their new positions. The *Armstrong* heeled over slightly to starboard under the total weight of her guns.

"Now, gun-captains, you'll have time for only one discharge after they come in sight. Settle among yourselves which boat each of you will make sure of. The moment you've fired, run the guns back into place and lash 'em fast so the enemy can't come through the ports."

"Aye, aye, sir!"

"Load every musket and pistol we have. Lay the muskets on the hatches and the pistols in baskets beside the bulwarks. When they come up, keep low. Wait until they've begun to climb the nettings. Hold your fire until you can burn their hair off."

LONG TOM AWAKES

Four hours they had been waiting. At ten the sloop-o'-war had towed up a long fleet of boats from the larger vessels at the mouth of the harbor. Then these boats had left the sloop and taken cover behind a reef of rocks within musket-shot to the south-west of the *Armstrong*. And there they had lurked ever since, while the sloop stood back and forth across the harbor to prevent escape.

Four weary hours. The moon was giving less light.

Probably that was what they were waiting for. With the dimming of the moonlight they would have a better chance.

The moonlight made a silver path across the end of the rocky reef. Captain Reid saw something move from behind the reef, cutting the strip of lighted water. Again and again it was cut. He found himself counting: "—eight—nine—ten—eleven—twelve—thirteen—fourteen."— And that, apparently, was all.

"Now's the time, I think, Mr. Williams. Pass the word, please—and tell them to lie low until I give the order."

Williams went round the deck, speaking quietly to the men.

"All wide awake and ready, sir," he said, returning.

"Good. You will command the fo'c'sle, Mr. Johnson the waist, and I'll take the stern. Of course we shall help each other all we can if one gets more than his share. Remember to lash the guns back in their ports after the first fire. After that, don't let the men use their small-arms till the British are hacking at the nets and biting our pistol-ends."

Fourteen boats. Now, would the men stand firm? Strangely quiet they were in the half-darkness along the bulwarks. From where the captain was standing, at the forward end of the cabin-trunk, the only group he could clearly see was that of Harrison and his crew about the aftermost gun. Harrison was making a final test of his firing-lock. His gun was laid to rake any boat coming up at the stern quarter.

"Canister, Harrison?"

"And grape; yes, sir."

461

Harrison answered without looking up from his work. His voice was quiet and absorbed. It seemed of a piece with the moonlight, the glassy water, and the solemnly beautiful night. Decidedly different this Harrison was from the man who had turned handsprings all round the deck when he hit the floating barrel a week ago in gunnery practice.

Fourteen boats, tight-packed, might possibly hold five hundred fighters.—Well, if all the men were as cool and studious and bitterly determined as Harrison, then fourteen boat-loads of town-burners would be a lot for the British squadron to lose. It had to be considered, too, that boat-crews were usually chosen from the best men in a ship. Many of those boats, moreover, would be damaged or sunk. Many would have to be repaired before the squadron could get the water for which it had come to Fayal.—Yes, if these six nine-pounders and Long Tom were coolly laid and accurately fired, if the pikes and small-arms were well handled afterward, then the squadron might be held up for a full week on whatever deadly errand it might be going. And that week might make an everlasting difference in the way the future would be woven.

Oh, it would be a petty little fight, no doubt, thought Captain Reid to himself as he paced up and down. That is, it would be so if any fight in which a group of honest and determined men give their utmost can be petty. No one, probably, would ever hear of it. The queer slack-wristed pucker-browed people who wrote official histories would ignore it. Fame, Honor, and Reward, those mercenary strumpets, would bestow their favors elsewhere. And yet if a man should go on from thirty to eighty years of age he would scarcely find a fitter time or a better place to die in than this, with such comrades about him, such a cause, and such a foe to face.

The boats were in point-blank range now, and moving in single file. Thanks to his withholding the guns during the first attack they might think they had only some petty one-gun pilot-boat to deal with. Perhaps that was why they came on so carelessly. A shot that missed the first boat might hull the next behind.

Fifty feet off they were. The other gun-captains would fire after Harrison.

"Ready, Harrison?"

"Ready, sir."

"Boats there! This is the United States private-armed brigantine *General Armstrong*. Back water and keep off, or we shall fire into you!"

The line came on with a steady thud and splash of many oars.

"You may fire, Mr. Harrison."

462

It was astonishing that a sentence so quietly spoken could transform the silent and silvery night into such an instantaneous hell of noise and flame. The flash of Harrison's gun seemed to explode all the other nine-pounders. A second later, the yell of Long Tom shook the timbers and violently canted the deck.

Out there over the rail the men in the boats were beginning to bend and fall like trees bitten through by steel. Their mouths were open to yell, but no sound came. Their faces were dreadfully pale. All round them planks, oars, and splintered wood were flung up as though from a fountain. Reid was certain that the leading boat, at least, must have been sunk.

Again the harbor was lighted up as the remaining men in the boats began firing their carronades and muskets in answer. They gave three feeble cheers, trying thus to drown out the screams of the wounded. Then their oars splashed in the water, a little raggedly, and they came on with a rush.

"Shall we cheer 'em back, sir?" yelled Parsons.

"No! Lash the guns into their ports!"

"Up and at 'em, lads! Up boarders and away! No quarter!" shouted a voice from below.

While firing at the first man that rose, Reid heard the bark of pistols all down the deck. Nearly all those thirteen boats must have come into action at the same time, on all sides of the *Armstrong*. He was glad he had hung the boarding-nets.

And now it was hand-to-hand. Once again a captain was worth little more than a common seaman unless he had steadier nerves, a better aim or a stronger wrist. He found that he had a cutlass in each hand. Just out of reach a pistol glinted in the moonlight with a man's eyes through the nets out of a dull white face. His jowls were wide and fat. Then the face splashed open under the butt of a musket.

And here was a fresh boat coming up under the stern, where the opening was in the nets. She was filled with men—forty at least. The midshipman in the stern-sheets was leveling a musket at Harrison. At the next moment a cutlass was sticking into the lapel of that mid-shipman's coat. The midshipman was staggering backward.—How had that happened? Now he had only one cutlass, in his right hand.

Three or four hands appeared, gripping the top of the taffrail. With the cutlass he still held he slashed at the fingers. The hands disappeared.

How many of his men were hurt or dead? Was Williams holding the

463

forecastle, or were the British cutting the nets and swarming over the rail up there? Was Johnson, in the waist, still beating them off? Was he himself doing all he could? It was maddening not to have an instant in which to look about the deck and direct his men.

How hard it was to think after the day's sail, that first attack, the long hours of waiting, and with this maddening noise of pistols and muskets, the rasping snarl of steel against steel, the screams, cheers, yells, and groans of friends and enemies on all sides! His sweated shirt was clinging to his body. He was gasping for breath, and all he drew in was the fumes of burnt powder. His voice was hoarse from the effort to make himself heard above the din, and his mouth felt as though it were filled with sand.

Someone was yelling in his ear: "Mr. Williams is dead, sir. They're breaking in on the fo'c'sle!"—It was Sheffield, captain of the foremost gun. He had a cutlass slash on his left cheek.

At that instant a young lieutenant vaulted the taffrail and leaped on deck, sword in hand. More men were climbing up behind him.

"Hold 'em back long as you can!" Reid yelled to Sheffield—and then it was hack, parry, dodge, lunge, and thrust. The two steels struck a spray of sparks. The lieutenant had a strong wrist and was not winded. They fought across the tiller and round the cabin-trunk. Reid let the lieutenant take the offensive while he got his wind. A terrific horizontal slash missed his head by inches, and he heard a backstay snap behind him. "This fellow knows his steel," thought Reid, "but I have an advantage in being left-handed. He isn't used to that. And I know my deck."

Retreat forward now, to see how things are going there. Watch the flash of that white cuff! Here we are by the capstan, and round it, slashing over it. We're passing the pumps, the after hatch, the mainmast . . .

"I'm done, sir. Give it to 'im sir!"—Young Johnson staggered and fell on deck, blood flowing from his left leg. With his hands he dragged himself toward a pistol lying on deck and fired it at the lieutenant—but missed.

Circling the mainmast, Reid began retreating aft again, taking the lieutenant with him. Past the pumps, the capstan, and the after hatchway they fought, and again up on the cabin-trunk. Near the stern Reid dropped his guard, as though exhausted, and at the same instant stepped backward to the deck three feet below. The lieutenant brought down a terrific blow and his foot slipped over the edge of the cabin-trunk.

Reid's cutlass slid as though greased through the toppling body. The lieutenant gasped once, and lay still.

For the effect it would have on the men below, Reid lifted the body and heaved it over the taffrail. He heard it thud into the boat below, and then voices: "The Leftenant!—God! He's dead!"

Now for the forecastle.—"Forward, men! Make 'em eat fish!"

The after-guard pounded down the deck behind him, past the main-mast, Long Tom, the main hatch, the galley-stack, the bitts. With boarding-pikes low, cutlasses slashing and clubbed muskets swinging they sliced and thrust at the British packed on the forecastle. Some ran round the top of the bulwarks to catch them in the nettings behind. They were all but fighting in the boats!

"Heave cold shot!" Reid heard himself yell, recalling the tale of a battle of long ago.—Strange brittle crunches the round shot made as they crashed through the wooden bottoms. There were cries of "Quarter!" and "Don't murder us, for God's sake!" from the dark water, and gurgled yells as a boat sank along-side. There were boats making off in the light of a sinking moon. Four boats were moving away of fourteen, feebly rowed, with few oarsmen left, a boat pulling five oars taking two others in tow.

"Quick! Long Tom! Load him, Holdfast, while I see to the priming!"

"He is loaded, Captain, and laid."

The sea was still. The deck made a steady platform as Reid jerked the lanyard. The sky seemed to crack. The great gun leapt from his carriage and smashed the deck where he fell.

"He doesn't like you, Captain!"

But Reid was peering out over the water into which the nearest boat had entirely disappeared. The next was drifting, lifeless. Two others, two of fourteen, were limping away zig-zaggedly, drunkenly, blindly, into the dark.

LAST WORDS OF LONG TOM

"Mr. Alexander Williams, Second Lieutenant," said the tired voice. "Musket-ball in the forehead. Died instantly. And Burton Lloyd, seaman. Musket-ball throught the heart. Died instantly."

They were standing round the lantern on the main-mast, some eighty men with bared heads, while Mr. Starks, the sailing-master, read off the list of their losses.

"And is that all our dead, Mr. Starks?"

"That is all, sir."

"Thank God!"

But then the voice went on: "Mr. Frederick Worth, First Lieutenant. Two ribs broken in right side. Will recover.—Robert Johnson, Third Lieutenant. Cutlass slash above left knee. Doing well.—Bazillah Hammond, Quarter-Master. Splinter in left shoulder, but says he is ready for action.—And John Piner, Gun-Captain. Pistol bullet in right knee. Amputated."

Mr. Starks folded the paper carefully and put it back in his pocket.

"Amputated!"—The word had been spoken with no emphasis whatever, yet now it rang and echoed in Captain Reid's weary brain as though it summed up the whole issue of the conflict. A sailor with only one leg! And Lloyd had a wife and three children. What would become of them now? The navy itself gave little enough to those left destitute by war's destruction, but the owners of a privateer would give nothing. For there would be no prize-money. Nothing whatever.

In the reaction from the excitement of battle he blamed himself bitterly. By what right had he given the order which had doomed those innocent people to misery? And to what end? What had been accomplished? There stood the seventy-four, the frigate, and the sloop-o'-war, unharmed. They would be ready to sail on the morrow.

To be sure, they would not sail with quite their former complement of men. Three dead English marines lay near the tiller and seven on the forecastle. There was a launch filled with dead men bumping idly against either side, and two more launches with the same grisly load lay under the stern with no one left to row them away. In addition, there must have been at least a hundred men killed in the boats that had escaped, and perhaps half as many more had been drowned. But, by the latest vote of Parliament, the British Navy had one hundred and forty thousand seamen and marines. These three ships were probably only a fraction of a huge armada bound against New York or New Orleans.

And yet perhaps they might attack again, give him another chance to weaken or maim them seriously, to slow them down. In spite of weariness, he must make ready. The deck must be cleared of dead, and swabbed. In at least a dozen places the cut rigging ought to be renewed. The two nine-pounder carriages that had been shattered in the battle should be turned over at once to the ship's carpenter. Moreover, the men ought to have some rest before they had to fight again.

Holdfast Gaines, with eight or ten helpers, was already getting a sling round Long Tom with a purchase from the head of the mainmast. Good! Although he said he was no sailor, that man always knew what had to be done without being told.—And that was fortunate, because one would not feel quite comfortable in issuing orders to Holdfast Gaines.

Six bells sounded faintly from the sloop. Three in the morning. The enemy might be expected to attack, if at all, at the first streak of dawn.

"Mr. Starks, we must get our wounded ashore at once.—But first, bring up Mr. Williams and Burton Lloyd."

Standing there in the light of the lantern beside the two bodies wrapped in their canvas hammocks, it was pitiful enough. There could be no ceremony. There was no time to honor in any way these two who had died so far from home—and under his orders. Yet he had the men called together, and when they were all there in a circle about the two bodies he took off his hat and bowed his head. The others followed his example, and stood for a silent moment about their dead shipmates.

—Burton Lloyd, a strong, square-built, good-natured fellow of thirty, rather handsome, with a pig-tail. He had been a skillful and fearless reefer. Only yesterday noon his firm bass voice had rung out from among the upper sails:

> Oh Shanneydore, I love your daughter—
> Away-y, my rolling beauty!—
> I'll take her 'cross the wide blue water—
> Across the Western Ocean!

—And Alec Williams, Lieutenant, his long bright hair blowing wildly in the wind as he took the sun's elevation at noon. He had been a blithe, courageous spirit, not over twenty-three, a good sailor, a good officer, firm and kind with the men, mannerly, well-spoken, thoughtful. One day before they sailed he had brought a girl with him to see the smart black brigantine where she lay off the Battery. For some time they had stood together, laughing, and admiring the bright-painted figure-head of General Armstrong in a Roman toga. Williams had hoped to marry that girl on the money made from the cruise.

Well—and so this was the end.

467

Parsons took the two bodies ashore in the gig, and then returned for the wounded. He brought back with him the seventeen-year-old son of Consul Dabney, bearing a letter:

Dear Captain Reid,

You have performed a most brilliant action in beating off fourteen boats of the British Navy in this road. We have just heard from Commodore Lloyd, however, that they are determined to carry the *Armstrong,* cost what it may, and that their sloop will haul in close to the castle to attack you. My dear Captain, do not uselessly expose yourself now that you see victory to be quite impossible. Let me urge that you abandon the brigantine at once and come on shore with your brave crew. We can care for you and them here.

Yours to command,

J. B. DABNEY

"That was a marvelous fight, sir!" young Dabney burst out as soon as Reid had finished the letter. "We could hardly believe our eyes and ears. The whole town's going wild! But—and oh yes! There's an old merchant captain here who seems to know you. He kept shouting 'Bang it to 'em, Sam!' all during the fight. He'd yell 'make 'em eat fish, boy!' and 'There's one for New London!' "

"What's his name, Charles? What's his name?"

"Avery.—He's been round here a long time."

"Not Sam Avery!"

"Yes. That's right. That's his name!"

"Well, I'll be . . . ! Why, I was named after that man, Charles. He taught me to sail.—And has he got the old *Rebecca* with him?"

"Yes, she's here too—hidden somewhere in a little bay on the other side of the island."

"Well, come on; I've got to see him! Mr. Starks, fire three muskets if there's anything suspicious, and I'll be back before the smoke's out of the barrels. Now; down with you, Charles."

Half a minute later, when he had leapt ashore, Reid was surrounded by a crowd of highly excited islanders, jostling, gesticulating, brandishing flambeaux, and shouting in several languages. A tall dark man was shouldering toward him through the crowd, and he felt himself gathered in by two powerful arms. In the half-dark he could scarcely have recognized the man who held him, but there was in the air a familiar reek of Connecticut tobacco.

"Sam, boy!"

"Hello, Sam Avery!"

468

"Sugar my buttons, it's good to see yeh! Y' all right, boy?"

"Absolutely. And how 're you?"

"How's yer mother an' the old folks an' . . . ?"

"Is that you, Captain Reid?" called a voice from the sea-wall.

"Yes, Mr. Dabney. Good morning."

"And a good morning to you, sir. You and your men have fought like—well, like Americans, Captain. But I fear I have bad news for you."

"Yes?"

"The Portuguese Governor here has sent two messages to the British Commodore, a brute by the name of Lloyd, begging him to respect the neutrality of this port. He has received in reply nothing but insults and abuse. Your stubborn defense, where he expected an easy capture, seems to have angered him."

"I don't wonder."

"Nor I. But he actually demands that the Governor hand you and your vessel over as prisoners of war."

"What?"

"I'm telling you the cold facts, sir. For some reason he seems particularly anxious to get hold of the *Armstrong*."

"So it seems.—Perhaps because she has such a shallow draft."

"That may be; but he told the Governor that if any help was given you from the island then he would consider Horta an enemy port and act accordingly.—And Portugal is the oldest ally England has in the world. The man's insane, sir."

"Evidently. But that won't help us much. He'll attack again."

"He'll go on attacking until he gets you, and he won't mind battering the town to dust while doing it."

"I see. Interesting situation."

"D' ye hear anythin' from Holdfast, Sam, afore ye sailed?"

A signal of three musket-shots in rapid succession rang out from the *Armstrong*.

"I must go," said Reid, turning toward the boat. And then he added, over his shoulder: "Oh, yes, Holdfast Gaines—he's on board."

"What! What's that?"

"Yes. Manning Long Tom."

"Hey! Take me with you!"

"See you after the fight, Sam."—The words came mixed with the splash of oars.

"Like hell ye will, ye didy-wettin' youngster! I'm comin' aboard!"

469

"They're coming in, Captain," called Holdfast from the main shrouds.

How could the man see that far through the dark?

Two bells went on the forecastle. On the majestic summit of Pico budded the faintest tinge of pink. A few gulls were rising here and there from the water, heavily flapping at first, calling sleepily. The faces of the seven dead English marines, still lying on the forecastle, were like old ivory.

This time it would be the sloop, not the boats. If the sloop should fail, then the frigate and the seventy-four, standing off and pounding steadily all day long as though at gunnery practice. Besides, they would be able to lay their guns by daylight now.

"Please call all hands on deck, Mr. Starks. Then double-shot the guns with round. Reload every musket and pistol. Lay the cutlasses ready."

How tired and worn his voice sounded, even to himself! All at once he felt overwhelmed, engulfed in a vast wave of weariness.

One of Harrison's gun-crew was leaning against the rail, pretending to watch the harbor but resting his head on his arms.

The men ought to eat before they were called upon to fight again. But no time for that. Coffee, then? The galley fire was out. As for rum?—No. It was a British custom, and did not make for accuracy of aim.

"All right, men. Tie lanyards on your match-buckets, drop 'em overside, and wash the sleep out of your eyes."

They began to move like live men.

"Oh, Harrison," the captain called, stripping off his shirt as the first bucket came slopping up, "please come over here and drown me."

The cold sea-water, splashing, trickling, salt on the lips and smarting the eyes as in those late September plunges into Smith Cove under Quaker Hill . . . ! The men liked it too. All over the deck they were splashing each other, laughing. This was better than breakfast, coffee, rum even.

Holdfast, dripping, stripped to the waist, a sight worth going a voyage to see, was pushing powder and balls down the ravenous throat of Long Tom. Sam Avery, also dripping sea-water after his swim from shore, was clambering over the rail and rushing toward Holdfast.— Well, one could hardly send him back!

The bud of pink on Pico's top had blossomed into a rose. The sloop-o'-war was beating up into harbor, still smartly handled in spite of the loss of her lieutenant. Someone else was barking the orders, unheard

470

as yet, this morning. The lieutenant's face would be looking like pale old ivory now, laid aside somewhere on her decks this morning. Old ivory, yellow and pale as an acient unicorn's horn or the handle of that keen damascened dress-dagger which the Bey of Algiers had given to Stephen Decatur in token of homage.

But oh, he was tired. His wits seemed to be wandering. He must pull himself together!

Nine gun-ports punctured her side, so that last night's count in the dimmer dusk had been exactly right. Not counting probably two long sixes in her bow, that would make nine thirty-two-pounder carronades against his own six nine-pounders and Long Tom. Let's see, now. Let's try to work this out. Nine thirty-twos is—ah—is two hundred eighty-eight pounds as against ninety-six, as near as a tired brain can figure it. That's more than twice. Yes, a good deal more. Why, they're exactly three times as heavy as we are! It works out neatly as a school-book problem for ten-year-olds.—Interesting situation!

Captain Reid took ten paces along the deck, his hands behind him.

H'm. Long guns against carronades. I'd have the better of him in open sea. With sea-room I could pound him to a froth, but here where I can't move he'll come in and smother me, batter me, crush me to little splinters. Dear God! Two hundred and eighty-eight pounds against ninety-six!

And yet, don't forget that carronades, though terribly destructive at short range, are treacherous things. Don't forget that they recoil much harder than longs, and yank their breeching-bolts right out of the bul-warks occasionally. They smash their carriages and turn over some-times, and never are much good for accurate shooting. Perhaps then, after all . . .

Behind the sloop-o'-war came rowing a string of boats, probably all they had left after last night. Their job would be to lie safely behind the sloop until the guns of the *Armstrong* were silenced, and then to rush out and board.—Yes, on the whole, a very interesting situation indeed!

Dawn-light was flooding fast round the shoulders of Pico. The waves, awakened by the morning breeze, were saying "cluck-a-clock." All the harbor was coming alive with the cries and the wings of gulls. Horta was waking up—at least that part which had not been watching the battle all night. Cocks crew. A cow lowed. A child began to cry. There rose a wisp of smoke from here and there among the twisted chimneys of the town.—Oh, beautiful unbroken peace going back to the time of

471

Walter Raleigh, beyond that to the Carthaginian quinqueremes that had left their coins on Corvo, perhaps even to the fat Phoenician cargo-ships making their audacious voyage to the far-off tin-bearing Cassiterides!

Oh, beautiful ancient peace, so rudely broken! And old peaceful mornings, too, on Quaker Hill, feeding the pigs at the farm! On Groton Hill also, inside the earth-works where the massacre was long ago and the grass grew so long and green and the river went sliding by under the calling of crows winging over from Gungywamp and gulls beating up against a wind from the Sound!

"Don't fire until I give the word, remember. Then one at a time. Harrison first."

Like statues they stood about their guns all down the deck, staring out. So still they were that they might be dead men already, standing.

William Castle has Piner's gun now.

Sam Avery and Holdfast haven't found much to say to each other. They've simply gone to work on Long Tom, and now have him ready.

This will be the gun's last chance, probably.

"Sure the guns are all double-shotted, Mr. Starks?"

"Yes, Captain."

What a queer time to be killing men when the sky and the land and the sea are just coming alive!

At the moment when the first rays of the sun grazed past the shoulder of Pico the British sloop-o'-war, very close at hand, having slewed her broadside round, fired. A fierce whistle and scream tore the morning calm. Two back-stays and some of the shrouds snapped near the main-mast. Behind the nine puffs of white smoke the sloop's masts and hull rolled heavily back. A flaming wad or two fell, hissing, into the water.

And that was all, apparently—except for the sounds of crashing in the town behind and the cries of numberless gulls. All their shots had been too high.

"Whenever you please, now, Mr. Harrison."

Like coordinated parts of an intricate machine the seven right arms of the gun-captains—Harrison, Parsons, Castle, Gaines, Davis, Tyson, and Sheffield—jerked suddenly upward one after the other, each holding a lanyard. Ninety-six pounds of metal answered two hundred and eighty-eight with a long continuous bellow.—Not one of the men had been hurt by the sloop's first fire, and now from her deck came cries and screams. Came curses and cries also in Portuguese from the town

472

behind. Looking round, Reid saw that many windows had been shattered. The glass was still falling from a high gable. A chimney was toppling. It crashed through a roof. An old house, built over the water, was slowly sagging.

"Load and fire as fast as you can!" Reid yelled.

Holdfast was aiming high. He stepped back and to one side now, and jerked the lanyard of the gun-lock. Once again that incredible voice—and then, slowly, like a tall candle that has been set too near a hot stove, the sloop's fore-topmast began to bend and buckle. Backward, downward it went in a thrashing tangle of rigging, and crashed to deck with a thunder heard over the roar of the guns.

"That's stoppin' his jaw!" yelled Sam Avery, instantly beginning to reload.

"And now," Reid answered, "let's hand him something on the water-line. He won't have shot-plugs big enough to stop the hole."

Once more he felt the deck leap and swing under his feet with the huge concussion and recoil.—By comparison with Long Tom the other six guns seemed silent and inactive. Whether a person, a beast, or a striking snake, Long Tom was alive. He was uttering now, with dreadful finality, certain thoughts he had brooded upon all the years since that day at New London.

"All guns load with grape and aim for his deck!" Reid shouted.

The sloop-o'-war had been loading and firing her short carronades at great speed, but nearly all her shot had gone high overhead into the town beyond. The British gunners could not seem to understand how small and low in the water the privateer lay. But now Reid saw there was confusion and much apparently aimless rushing up and down over there. What was it all about? Had Long Tom really got them between wind and water? Because if he had . . . Their guns were firing more slowly, and wildly.—Yet a thirty-two-pound shot passed clean through the main-mast of the privateer, ten feet above the deck. The shrouds, back-stays, and running rigging were badly cut here and there. Castle, serving at Piner's unlucky gun, had been wounded in the arm and carried below. Many others had splinter-wounds and bullet-scratches, but stood to their stations. Bloody handkerchiefs were knotted around heads and arms and legs.

But what was the sloop doing? It was hard to see through the smoke! —Three, four boats and launches, suddenly appearing from her opposite side and rowing with all their might, were pulling her round by a cable passed from the bows.

Reid leaned far over the rail and stared. Could it be?—Yes; it was true! They were towing her out of action. An eighteen-gun sloop-o'-war was running from a seven-gun privateer!

And then he found himself racing along the deck behind his guns. "Now's your chance, boys!" he was shouting. "Rake her! Rake her!"

But only Long Tom was ready when her stern came round, exposing to fire the whole length of her crowded and cluttered deck. In that moment, choked as he was with round-shot and grape, the great gun spoke for the last time with all his gathered power. Then, staggering backward off his carriage, he crashed down upon the broken boards below.

Swiftly glancing from the gun to the sloop, Reid saw a dark shower of splinters falling into the sea. There were yawning holes in the transom. The rigging was like a wind-torn spider's web. Forty men at least must be prostrate on her deck. Dark dribbles of blood were trickling down the bulwarks from her waist-scuppers.—And beyond her, a mile away, the seventy-four and the frigate were coming round into the wind. They were making sail. Undoubtedly they meant to enter the fight and finish the task which the sloop was giving over.

Harrison now jerked his lanyard. A blinding burst of flame shot up from the breech and there followed a scream of flying metal through the air. Harrison and Scalsan, his loader, were hurled across the deck by the exploding gun.

"Mr. Parsons, please ask Dr. Brosnahan to step up here."

The doctor came and bent over the wounded men. He made preparations for taking them on shore.

Captain Reid paused before Long Tom. "What do you think we should do now, Sam?" he asked.

"Wal, it depends. Iffen ye've figgered to do all possible harm to the enemy, ye mought's well call it a day. But iffen it's dyin' ye want, them two comin' on will prob'ly 'commodate us all in 'bout—say twenty minutes."

"And you, Mr. Gaines?"

"I think your mother would say 'That's enough.'"

"And my father?"

"He too."

"So, I think, would Jenkins and Havens."

Three of the men had sawed the painted figure-head of General Armstrong off the bow and were waiting to carry it ashore. "They shan't get the old General, sir," said one.

474

"Good.—Or anything else, if I can help it."

"We can help it, Captain," said Holdfast. He had got a sling once more round Long Tom, and now, with the help of a dozen men, was hoisting the gun out of the hole it had made in the deck.

"How do you mean, Mr. Gaines?"

"By dropping these three tons through the bottom."

"Ah, yes, I see. It seems a pity but—yes, that'll take care of everything. I didn't want to blow her up and endanger the town. I leave it to you."

Reid went down to his cabin and rummaged about in the debris there. He found his log-book and privateering-certificate, his pistols, his sword, his unfinished letter—blood-spattered—to Jenkins and Havens, a miniature of Mary, his wife, a horn of fine powder, and some pistol-balls.

"Mr. Starks!" he called, standing by the empty arms-chest.

In a few seconds Starks answered down the cabin ladder: "Yes, Captain."

"Please collect all the arms on deck and put them into the boat. We'll need balls to fit, of course, and a keg of powder."

"Yes, Captain."

Two bottles of Madeira—but then, of course, there would be plenty of Fayal wine, grown on Pico, to be had of Mr. Dabney—his razors, a shaving mug, the walking-stick of Gungywamp oak given him by Grandfather Chester, all the letters from his wife, a well-cut goose-quill or two, some ink, a mirror . . .

The face he saw in the mirror . . . ! There was a long deep scratch on the forehead and dried blood on the left cheek. The lips were black, perhaps from the biting of pistol-cartridges. The eyes were staring, blood-shot. The right cheek was black and burned where a pistol had flashed in his face. The mouth and chin were trembling, not much but uncontrollably. A stubble of beard . . . Yes, even in battle, beards grew.

The table of his cabin was bare and covered with blood-stains. Dr. Brosnahan had been there, operating. A shot had come in and smashed the swinging lantern. There was broken glass on the floor, on the chairs, the bunk.

He stared about for a moment, trying to recall the by-gone time when he had sat here congratulating himself on the speed of his eastward cruise. Very swiftly indeed the *Armstrong* had rushed upon death.

Well, there seemed to be nothing much left to do, and certainly there would not be much time before the frigate and seventy-four opened

475

fire. Things looked rather dismal, true. With better luck, he might have sailed home in his comfortable green-trimmed cabin with prize-money to look forward to and something for the men, for the owners. Instead, there would be a dead loss to the owners, to himself, to Piner and Harrison and Scalsan and Castle and Worth, and to the wife and children of Burton Lloyd and the girl Aleck Williams had loved. And in this cabin where he had worked and thought and dreamed the fishes would swim henceforth and the sewage of Horta would settle.

He pulled himself up the cabin ladder, feeling old. The frigate and seventy-four were very near.—What of it?

"All ready, Mr. Starks?"

"Ready, sir."

"Then you and the rest go ahead. Mr. Gaines and I will follow."

The cutlass sawed back and forth at the thick tarred rope. Holdfast had tipped the great gun in the sling so that it would drop through right beside the keel, with the pommelion breaking way.

"Stand clear, Captain."

Reid stepped aside, and watched the single strands of the rope curl upward. Suddenly the last of them cracked, and the gun crashed down through the open hatch and on through the planking of the hull as a bullet would pierce an egg-shell.

"I won't look at her again," said Reid to Holdfast as they stumbled into the waiting boat, and again he felt a vast wave of weariness sweep over and bury him.

Ten seconds later, "She's settled to the bottom," said Holdfast. "She's done what she could do. And so have we all."

SAILORS ALL

The bed was soft, the sheets smelled of lavender, and warm sunshine was streaming into the room. A cock crowed, far away, and then a jingle of little bells—perhaps of a donkey-cart—came up the hill, passed by underneath the windows, and died away again.

Captain Reid's watch told him that it was nearly ten o'clock.—Well, but had he been sleeping steadily for twenty-four hours?

He lay and considered this question, drowsily. The morning air, with no powder-smoke in it, was wonderfully sweet. The light of the morning, not made by the flash of guns, did him good. The quiet was musical.

After a while he heard a gentle knock at the door.

"Come in."

"Good morning, Captain," said Consul Dabney, entering. "You look well rested."

"Thanks to your kindness, I am. But can you tell me about my men?"

"By your orders, they are all quartered in a monastery close at hand. Your friend, Captain Avery, is looking out for them, and I don't think that even the British will try to attack them there. The wounded men are in the monastic hospital, under good care."

"It's impossible to express my gratitude to you, Mr. Dabney."

"Oh, in a way it's my duty—and certainly it has been a pleasure. I've been proud to play even a very small part in one of the gallantest fights I've ever heard of.—You've fought as brave a delaying action as Sir Richard Grenville did in the *Revenge,* two hundred and odd years ago, over there at Flores."

"Well, we all did what we could; but I'm afraid it wasn't enough. My vessel's gone, and . . ."

"But Captain, the most extraordinary thing has happened. There's a young British officer in the street who wants to invite you to some banquet or other."

"He's in the street, you say?"

"Yes. I'm sorry if I was wrong, but I didn't care to invite into my house one of the fellows who attacked you the other night in this neutral port."

"Well, perhaps this particular officer didn't have much to do with that. I think I'd better speak to him."

After throwing on a few clothes, Reid went to the open window. A bright-faced young midshipman smiled up at him.

"Are you Captain Reid?"

"Yes. What can I do for you?"

"Captain Reid, the junior officers of His Majesty's squadron now lying at Fayal request the honor . . . Oh, rot!—Captain Reid, we're giving a feast tonight at the British consulate, and we'd most particularly like to have you with us. You're quite the lion of the day with all us juniors, I can tell you. Will you come?"

"Don't go, Captain." whispered Dabney at Reid's elbow. "It might be a trick."

477

"Why, thank you, sir," Reid called back. "At what time, please?"

"At eight, if it meets your convenience."

"It does—and my pleasure. I shall hope to see you at the British consulate tonight at eight o'clock."

The midshipman waved his hand. "Till tonight, then, Captain!"

A dozen men, mostly young, were standing at the door-way as Reid walked up. The candle-light revealed several bandaged heads, arms in slings, and sticking-plaster on cut faces.

"Here he is, boys!"

"Three cheers, boys!"

"See, the conquering hero comes!"

The cheers were given heartily, and Reid was introduced all round. He could not help feeling slightly awkward. Two or three of them had to shake with their left hands.

"Why, damme, he's flesh an' blood! He's mortal, after all!"

"What a battle, sir!"

"By Gad, sir!"

"Captain Reid, sir, I b'lieve we may be considered unbiassed judges with some professional knowledge in such matters, and our opinion is that you have made the most masterly defense of a small vessel in all naval history."

"Yes, sir! There's no Frenchman, Spaniard, Dutchman, Turk or Dane could have done it. We've fought 'em all, and we know!"

"Oh, you are too kind, gentlemen."

"Not at all! Not at all!"

"Three hundred men at least placed *hors de combat* by one small vessel!—And what were your own losses, if I may inquire?"

"Two men killed and six wounded, I deeply regret to say."

"Well, but . . . Of course I believe you, but England must never know!"

"My name's Reid, too," said a tall and blond young man in military undress. "I'm in the army, of course, but they let me in tonight on account of my name."

"Ah, indeed.—And your first name is . . . ?"

"William. I'm secretary to General Keane. I had an uncle who went over to the Yankees in the last war. Leftenant John Reid of the King's Navy he was."

"Leftenant John Reid!"

"Yes. He would have been Laird Reid of Glasgow if he hadn't stayed over there and married an American girl. He lived, I believe, in a place called—do you say 'Conneck-ti-cut'? But I suppose you've never heard of him."

"Heard of him! He was my father."

"Your father! Why, sir, what a chance! Then we're cousins!"

The two men—both of them tall, slender, blue-eyed, with light curly hair—clasped hands warmly. "Can you sit with me tonight?" asked the captain. "Then we can talk."

"I'll arrange it, Cousin Samuel.—But first, please meet my friend Jack Stockbridge. Leftenant Stockbridge. He's in the army too, but they let him in because he is my friend."

The captain passed on to meet his other hosts. A strange company, this! They were mostly midshipmen, young and old. The oldsters looked rather pathetic.

A gray-haired man came up to him. "My dear Captain," said he, "nearly every one of us here tonight is beholden to you for a sudden promotion. I've been a mid for almost thirty years. You've made me first of the *Rota* in place of Bill Matterface, and Dickie Keeble over there has stepped into Charlie Norman's shoes as third."

"Well, it's good that you can look at it in that way," said Reid.

"Course we miss 'em—but we're all going to get a canvas suit some day.—Glad they're not us, that's all. And thank you."

When they were seated at dinner someone called out: "We have desired the pleasure of your company, Captain Reid, partly in order to settle a question among ourselves. Did you and your crew, or did you not, wear shirts of mail during the battle?"

Captain Reid laughed. "Why, gentlemen," said he, "we were all in our shirt-sleeves. That's the way we Americans go to work when, as we put it, we 'mean business.'"

And then they were all laughing and drinking together. The hosts had forgotten, apparently, that their guest was a Yankee. To them he was another sailor—one who had stood many a hard watch in rain, snow, and sleet, who had dodged the water-spout, ridden out the hurricane, and often clawed off a lee-shore, trying thus to snatch a livelihood from greedy merchants and heartless governments.

"Do you happen to know Nathaniel Bowditch, Captain Reid?"

"He's a friend of mine, yes. The last man in the world you'd take for a ship-master, and yet a good one. He looks as though the first puff would blow him off the deck. Nat didn't have much to eat when he was a boy, and he got his education mostly in a dame school."

"What kind of school?"

"A dame school—kept by a dame, a widow lady, up in Salem, Massachusetts. He learned to read, write, and figure from her. Then he taught himself Latin so that he could read Newton's *Principia*. Before he was twenty-three he had worked his way through a large mathematical and scientific library."

"A scientific library! But Captain, will you please tell us how such a thing found its way into a place with such a barbaric name as 'Massachusetts'?"

"Why, yes, sir, I can do that easily. That library, belonging to Dr. Maskelyn, the Astronomer Royal, was on its way to England, but it never arrived there. It was captured in the Irish Channel by one of our privateers—perhaps John Paul Jones, the Scotchman, of whom you have probably heard—during the War of Independence. From there it was brought to Massachusetts, where the barbarians have used it to rather good purpose."

"Certainly young Bowditch did," said one of the elders. "I hear he made over eight thousand corrections in the tables of old Moore, the standard English navigator. We're using his corrections now ourselves."

Someone proposed a toast: "Nathaniel Bowditch! His Yankee genius helps Britannia rule the waves!"

When that was down there was a cry of "Captain Samuel Chester Reid, greatest benefactor of British midshipmen since Lord Nelson!" It was honored standing.

"And now," shouted the young officer who had brought Reid his invitation in the morning, "here's to England and America! If they can fight so well against each other, what couldn't they do side by side!"

The party was growing noisier by the minute, and, in particular, Lieutenant Jack Stockbridge of the army. Captain Reid, however, was keeping his wits about him, drinking as little as possible. So, he saw, was his cousin William at his right hand. When the shouting was at its loudest he leaned over and said: "Considering that we're cousins and you are in the army, I wonder whether you'd care to tell me why those ship-captains were so determined to take my small vessel?"

"Well, they're English, aren't they? Isn't that enough to say? They make their living by taking things away from people."

"I see you speak as a Scotchman, Cousin. But seriously, now. Here's this flotilla of war-ships, heavily armed, packed with soldiers, and evidently going on an important mission. Why should they try to take my brigantine? What good could it have done them?"

"Keep it in mind," William Reid answered, "that they expected to take you easily, at little cost. But in reply to your question I can only suggest that they wanted, and wanted badly, a vessel of shallow draught."

"You wouldn't care, I suppose, to suggest the reason why they wanted such a vessel."

"As your cousin, Captain Samuel, I should be delighted to tell you all the little I know about that; but as private secretary to General Keane I am in honor bound not to do so."

"Ah, of course. I should have seen that. Pray excuse me."

A loud voice made itself heard from across the table. "There 'll be plenty more p'motions through Davy Jones's locker 'fore this campaign's over. O' course we don't know where we're goin' or what the plans are, but ev'body knows the army can bungle the best plans ever made."

Lieutenant Jack Stockbridge rose unsteadily to his feet and stood swaying, hair-touseled and red-faced, glaring down at the speaker. For a few moments his indignation prevented all speech, but then he burst out with "D' *you* say 'bungle,' sir? Good God, wha' ri' navy man say 'bungle' after Fayal!"

"Sit down, Jack. You're drunk."

"Won't sit down. Army man drunk talks better 'n navy man sober, an' fights better too. Hear that? Wan' ev'body hear that. Fights better. Army just now licked Boney. Wha' hell navy ever lick? Huh! Bungle!"

"Sit down!"

"Won't sit down. Why, navy—navy don't even know—don't know where it's goin'. Army knows."

"Where is it, Jack? Where *are* we goin' to?"

"So. You don't know that! Said so. Army has tell you."

"But do you know, Jack? You don't act like it."

"Cer'ly do. But won't tell you."

"You'd better not, Jack," called William Reid. "Sit down."

"Who says 'better not'? Do as I please. It's N'orl—N'awl—"

"Do you mean New Orleans?"

"Well, wha' 'f I do?"

"Who told you so?"

"Nev' min' who tol' me, but army tol' *you*. 'Member that."

"You're making this up, Jack, out of your own head."

481

"Is tha' so! Want to call me a liar, do you? Look here, I heard it from Gen'ral Keane, this mornin'."

"Oh, so he called you into his cabin, did he, and told you all about the campaign! Kind of him, to encourage the young man that way."

"Jack! Be quiet!" called William Reid from across the table.

"Don't int'rup'." Stockbridge was still on his feet, his red face stubbornly set. "Goin' by Keane's cabin 's mornin', door open, Keane in there yellin' at Com'dore Lloyd o' the navy. Hear 'im all over ship. Good listen to. Enjoyed it. 'Lloyd,' heard 'im say, 'Lloyd, you blund'rin' jackass, you bleary-eyed idjit, you *navy man*, I'm goin' report you Adm'ralty soon's ever we get home for a nincompoop,' Keane said. 'Just for tryin' take one bawblin' brigantine we didn't need, an' then *not* takin' her,' Keane said, 'you'll make us two weeks late at N'orlins!'"

The eyes of the diners brightened at these words, not quite all of which could be attributed to the fiery wine grown on Mount Pico's volcanic flanks. Captain Reid, glancing at his cousin, saw that William Reid was looking at him with a grave, slow smile. All round the table the others were nodding their heads. "So it's New Orleans, just as I thought," said the gray-haired midshipman.

Someone called out to Stockbridge, whose lucid moment had obviously passed: "Any more, Jack? Did you hear Keane say any more?"

"Plenny more. Heard 'im tell whole plan o' campaign. We go up the Miss—the Mississ—I mean that big river, with hunner' thousan' men. Provost comes down same river same number an' burn Wash'n'ton, easy. Ver' easy. Take ev'thin' an' run it. The Knife says easy. Ev'body throw arms round us. Capture P'cific Ocean. 'Nited States fly Union Jack f'rever. Perfeck plan.—Don't wan' ever again hear navy man say 'bungle.'"

Suddenly overcome by his emotions, Lieutenant Stockbridge slumped into his chair and rested his head upon his arms. "Bungle!" said he, half in tears, half in wrath. "Bungle!"

"You cannot say I told you, Cousin Samuel," said William Reid.

"No. But I wish you 'd tell me how I can use this information, now I have it, with my vessel sunk two fathom deep."

"Ah. As a cousin and a Scot I almost wish I could. All that talk about burning Washington and taking over the States to run them makes my northern blood boil. Just listen to these fellows!"

They listened. A voice cried: "Hurrah for New Orleans! I hear there's three million pounds there, just for the taking."

482

"Pounds!" cried another. "But think o' the girls, man! Haven't you heard o' those golden girls?"

And then boomed a third voice: "Gentlemen, I give you the booty and beauty of America!"

WHILE SHE WESTED

The *Rebecca* was homeward-bound. With tangled weed and barnacles fouling her bottom, with rotten rigging and filmsy sails, she was slumping and bumping back, dejectedly, to her native shore.

Most Yankee craft depended upon speed for safety, but the *Rebecca* upon her manifest decrepitude. Three years of lurking among the Azores had left her, at least in outward appearance, a slattern, a dawdler, hardly to be distinguished from a filthy Portuguese fisherman. Most of her crew, moreover, could now jabber enough Mediterranean languages to deceive an Englishman bent upon the impressment of American sailors. No stranger could have guessed that all the ragged and dirty men on her had been born beside the Thames in Connecticut. In dress, in their listless attitudes and gait, even in their complexions, they seemed to belong to the countries of the southern sun.

Holdfast Gaines was deeply glad to be once more among the friends of his boyhood. Here, at least, was one small part of that earlier, simpler Connecticut. And yet, how old they were—some of them white-haired! Even Bill Small was now middle-aged. Holdfast and Sam Avery sat for hours every day on the main hatch recalling events of their youth, but they made slow progress toward the present. Though happy to be together again, they were strangers really, sundered not only by time but by all the miles between Western Waters and the eastern sea.

Yet there was only one thing that the twelve men wallowing westward could steadily think about. Speed! They must make speed! Hardly more than a week would it take the British behind them to bury their dead, ship home their wounded, make repairs, and then . . . Oh, speed!

Beyond a doubt, Young Captain Sam had told them, the three British vessels at Fayal belonged to a huge flotilla now on its way to attack New Orleans. Packed with soldiers seasoned under Wellington, these vessels were part of a far larger British force converging upon the Mouth of the Mississippi. That much he had learned from a drunken officer at a banquet given him by the British shortly after the battle. What Holdfast knew, or guessed, confirmed it.—And so, hurry on, old girl! Don't limp and stagger so! We too are old, but we must find Jackson! Oh, speed!

Day-long and night-through she staggered and limped. They had to be cautious in heaving the shrouds and back-stays even a little tighter. When a real wind came on they had to strike all sail, but for the most part the winds were weak and fickle. The sun beat hatefully down. In the dead calms they got out their sweeps and pulled her as though she were an ancient Mediterranean galley, making her crawl like a slug on a huge flat leaf.

What were the British doing? How much had Young Sam hurt them? Did they know that the *Rebecca* had slipped away? Had they guessed her errand?—Fearfully, anxiously, all day long, a watchman scanned the eastern horizon.

To be sure, there was a wonderful possibility, not to be counted on, of which they had learned just while they were weighing anchor. Captain Lloyd of the *Plantagenet* had demanded the surrender of all the *General Armstrong's* crew, threatening that if it was refused he would go ashore and take them, dead or alive. But this was almost too good to be true. Surely not even an English naval officer would attempt a thing so arrogant, so contemptuous of neutral rights.—Yet Young Sam, hoping for the best, had withdrawn his eighty men, well armed and provisioned, to a ruined convent safe from the British guns. He had destroyed the convent's draw-bridge and made ready for what he hoped would be a long and determined siege.

But that was not to be counted upon.—Oh, speed!

On quiet days, when the water was clear, they could see the weeds splaying and fluttering out from the vessel's hull as though striving to clutch, hold, and pull her back. Sam Avery groaned as he gazed at them, cursing himself for having neglected to career and clean her while she lay hidden round the head-land near Horta. More than once Holdfast proposed to go over-side with a knife and scrape the hull, but this Sam Avery, speaking as captain, forbade. He backed up his prohibition by pointing out two or three of the sharks that followed them night and day. Then Holdfast would return to his seat on the main hatch and smoke his stone pipe in short explosive puffs.

More and more he hated the sea, its meaningless heavings, its languors and sudden furies, its dreadful blank waste and monotony. Oh, to be able to go once more on one's own legs, using one's strength and skill, and no longer meanly to wait on the whims of the sky!

The details of the deck, the rigging, the masts, ground themselves into his brain. He studied the coehorns and swivel-guns mounted on the bulwarks, and the four little three-pounders, one of which had gone crashing, long ago, through the bottom of a British long-boat. Ridiculously, pitifully inadequate this armament looked to him.

And there was that little stub of a windlass at the heel of the bowsprit, battered and scarred by many cables in many gales. Numberless seas breaking over the forecastle had washed all its paint away. Sundry dints, gashes, and scars it bore as the honorable wounds of a long stanch life. Holdfast gazed at them idly, imagining a history for each one. There seemed to be nothing else for him to do, though the liberty of a nation might be in peril.

Into one of the mortises of the windlass Captain Sam Avery stepped a crutch and spindle for making spun-yarn. Then for hour after hour in the calms he trudged back and forth, bare-footed, twisting yarns from the twirling spindle and rubbing them together with old pieces of canvas. And Holdfast recalled, as he watched, the night of many years gone by when two young men had fought for their lives round this same windlass, with swords. To be sure there was nothing else for Sam to do now, yet his present dull toil was pathetically different from that swift bicker of blades in the glint of the battle-lanterns.

And the difference—what was it? What had caused it? Should one be content to say, merely, that the captain, his crew, and the ketch were growing old? Ah, but Connecticut also, and New England, America herself, were fading from the vivid to the dun, slipping from the bold to the cautious! The delight in danger was giving way to a quest of mere safety, dull and spiritless.—Or so it seemed to Holdfast as he lay on the deck in the night-watches, tossing uneasily, listening endlessly to the rhythmical creak of block and tackle and the drone of the breeze among the shrouds. Why should one care, he asked himself, whether such a land kept a freedom of which it felt no need, which it did not know how to use? Why should one even try to save the Father of Waters for a people who would merely despoil and degrade it with that same vulgarity, greed, and mill-filth which had already smeared the Thames?

Thus the *Rebecca* merged in his thoughts and dreams with the American Ship of State. His fears for the one were transferred to the other.

Often he scarcely knew whether he was thinking about the time-worn ketch or his endangered country.

He remembered that this beloved vessel had been shaped by young and unskilled men, by youths really, with no experience in the ancient and intricate art of ship-building. Certainly they had done their best, but had they done well? They had followed the models of older builders, but had they understood them? Had their unquestionable devotion atoned for their lack of knowledge and skill?

How eager they had been, how boyishly happy, back there in the tiny ship-yard by the Chester store! What a joy to see their own handiwork rising day by day and week by week, from keel to frames and from planking to taffrail! Odors of freshly cut oak and pine, of tar and oakum and paint, were borne to Holdfast on the winds of memory. Once more he heard the steady dulled rap of mauls driving trunnels, and the musically metallic "ping-ping" of the calking-mallets knocking looped oakum into the seams. "Hot stick! Hot stick!" he could hear Sam Avery calling as a sheer-stringer came from the steam-box. "Hot stick! Hot stick! Man wants his boat! Look alive thar, boys!"

There was good crooked Gungywamp oak, at any rate, in the *Rebecca's* timbers. That Holdfast knew. He could even recall where some of those gnarled old trees had stood, in their pride, among the strewn rocks of Massapeag, Konomoc, Poquetannock, and Manetock Hill. Two or three of them had borne the blaze of the King's broad arrow, so that if it had not been for the War of the Revolution they might now be triumphantly riding the waves, pursuing instead of pursued, hearts of oak in the ribs of the mighty *Plantagenet*.

And the *Rebecca* had been a lucky craft. In that also she resembled the Ship of State. She had taken prizes many times her cost, and in time of peace had carried many a cargo from the Connecticut Thames to the West Indies or, in later years, to the Mediterranean. Though forced to hide in this present war, she had never been captured—a record attributable to the skill of her captain and to the fact, hardly believable now, that she had been built for speed.

But now she was aged, barnacled, weed-grown, wormy, wracked and warped in the masts, open-seamed in the hull, water-logged, sodden. At every roll she grumbled and groaned through all her timbers. Her standard-knees worked visibly back and forth against the bulwarks. Her trunnels of Mamecoke locust were rotting out of the frames. The first bold blast would sink her. Waves she would once have gone over with a dancing foot came creaming in round her worn bitts. What her open foes could not do the stealthy years had triumphantly done; and now, leagued with the years, the masters of the seven seas were racing to stem, smash, and roll her under. The crew was old also, drained of laughter and dream, forgetting the blithe manly mood of that night long ago in Shaw's Cove. "Wal, whut the hell!" the men were murmuring here and there about the deck in the dog-watch. "Whut hell we care? It's Madison's war. Let 'im fight it. An', s'posin' we do beat the biggest power on 'arth, d' ye wanter turn the kentry over to Tom Jefferson an' his rag-tag an' bob-tail? —An' 'sides thet, who the hell is this Andy Jackson, anyhow?"

And yet, in spite of these anxieties, or partly because of them, Holdfast's love for the *Rebecca* deepened day by day. A quiet pride in her, different entirely from what he had felt when she first slipped into Thames water, grew and grew in his heart as she lumbered onward. He came to see a kind of heroism in the steady persistence with which, in spite of weakness and age, she held fast to her westward way.

Day after day she crept, toiled, and bored her way westward, heavily breasting the tall crests, deep-sunk in the troughs. Blasts from the north found her, struck, and tormented her, making her scarf-joints groan. Great billows caught sight of her and gathered and charged with tossing banners and streamers of torn spume. Still she labored and creaked her way westward into the mystery.

Gulls circled round her, screaming. Porpoises rose and plunged. Far off or near the whale spouted his spray. Sharks, slicing the brine, looked up with expectant side-long eyes. The lordly albatross, king of the air, kept her in sight for day after day, winging steadily westward like a guardian spirit.

Then calms glassed the water. Fogs rose and walked the sea, closing her in from the stars, moon, and sun. She was a lost thing. She was the loneliest creature the sea held, groping into the west wraith-like as though in search of a grave, gliding alone on the edge of the world.

"Sail ho!"

"Where away, Simon?"

"Nor'-nor'east.—Two of 'em, I think, Cap."

The men crowded to the rail, peering, wondering.

Ten minutes passed, and then Holdfast said "Yes. I see them. Two schooners."

An hour went by, during which the captain made every possible preparation for battle. The *Rebecca* seemed to be standing still as the

487

two long and low black vessels came down the wind, knifing through the short seas under clouds of canvas. They carried no flag. They looked too swift, too low in the water for British, and yet it seemed more clear every minute that they had no peaceful intent. Captain Avery, using his glass, reported that they were getting their pivot-guns ready.

"Run up the flag," he ordered. "Iffen they're friends they won't fire at it."

Before the Stars and Stripes had fluttered quite to the mast-head they saw a puff of smoke amidships of the leading schooner and then a long slash of foam in the sea a cable's length ahead of the *Rebecca*.

"They're a-goin' to stop us," said the captain, looking round at his men, perplexed. "But iffen they're British, what they wanter give us warnin' fer?"

"Pirates, mebbe," suggested Bill Small.

"Let me use that glass a minute, will you, Sam?" said Holdfast.

He peered for more than a minute while the strangers came on. Even without a glass the figures of men moving rapidly about the decks were now clearly visible.

Another ball, this time from the pivot-gun, plowed a white furrow close to the *Rebecca's* laboring fore-foot.

"Next one we'll take in the belly," said one of the crew.

"Sam," said Holdfast, lowering the glass, "I have a notion. Will you let me try it?"

The captain shrugged his consent.

"Now this water-barrel we emptied last night," Holdfast went on, speaking rapidly. "Get out your buckets of red paint, Bill, and all the brushes on board. Then slap it on, four or five of you, fast as you can."

"Wal, but whut . . . ?"

"Get at it, boys. I'll tell you why later."

A minute later, while hard at work, they heard a wail, then a scream, and a sudden gaping hole showed in the bulge of the mainsail.

"Looks like a pleasant game, Holdfast," said the captain, "but salt water's bad for my gouty toe."

"Now, Sam, we'll want a purchase-block to hoist this barrel."

"Oh, Simon! Drop us a line from the top-block, will ye?—But Holdfast, what . . . ?

Banging against the mast as it rose, the barrel, dripping red, was hoisted to the mast-head. But the crew, open-mouthed, were now watching the little man on the nearer schooner, a man in a red hat, just about to touch his long lighted match to the vent of his pivot-gun. They saw him pause as the crimson barrel rose against the clear blue sky. Then, running to the bulwark, he dashed the match into the sea and began to yell, to dance, and to wave his arms, wildly.

"Wal!" said Captain Sam, and spat over the rail.

"Oh, it was only a chance, Sam; but I'm glad we took it. Let's have your glass again."

"Yes," Holdfast went on after a moment, "that fellow in the red hat is one of my Baratarian brothers. He's not Dominique You, as I thought, but Beluche."

"Don't talk nonsense, Holdfast!—Your Bara . . . Your what?"

"I happen to belong, Sam, as an honorary member, to the Brother-hood of the Gulf. Most of the brothers live at Barataria Bay, near the mouth of the Mississippi, when they're at home. Our sign is a barrel of blood—meaning that we're all blood-brothers together, united as though in one body."

"Wal, I be damned. Iffen we'd 'a' knowed ye was a pirate, Holdfast, we wouldn't 'a' tuk yeh aboard."

"No; and then by this time the sharks would have had their break-fast."

Many other figures, in vividly chromatic garments, were crowding along the bulwarks of the oncoming schooner. A storm of affectionate profanity grew upon the breeze: "Sacré . . . ! Diable!" "Nom du chien!" "Holà, mes frères!" "Mon gros Kaintuck!"

"Hello, Beluche!"

"Holà, Monsieur L'Ours Dormant!" yelled the little man through a speaking-trumpet.

"We thought you were British!"

"Breeteesh? I pray you! But eet iss so we did sink you waire. Eet iss ze treek favoreet of zeirs à faire parade de votre beau drapeau. May ze saint de mon nom grant to me ze plaisir to spank for zem ze pan-talons!"

"You'll soon have a chance, Beluche. They're after us. They're on the way to attack New Orleans. We must find Jackson. He may be a thou-sand miles off."

"Non, non! Le Général Jackson, he ees to Mobile.—Time presses you, I see eet, mon grande frère. You haf preety damn pauvre li'l ole bateau zere. La Belle Josephine, she tek ten hop your one.—Viens ici avec nous, et tu navigueras plus vite!"

As Holdfast leapt from the Rebecca to the deck of the schooner,

Beluche burst into a storm of orders, threats, and oaths that speedily turned his vessel round upon her heel and sent her driving toward the Gulf of Mexico.

BARATARIAN BREAKFAST

The leaves of the palmettos faintly clashed and rasped together when the dawn breeze reached them. The ripples fingered and lisped more briskly along the bright sands. Gulls rose from the gray-blue water and tilted and swung and sailed, with raucous cries. A pure-white goat trotted out from the shadow of the banana trees and stood, waiting to be milked.

From the black side of a brig riding not far off-shore there came a puff of smoke, and then the report of a gun rolled over the level lands. It startled the herons and pelicans among the reeds into low, lumbering flight.

No answering gun was fired from the little brick fort at the point, but in a few minutes a group of men, outlandishly garbed for the most part, were to be seen straggling down the tangled paths that led from the main house to the water. They did not hasten.

Soon a boat put off from the point, with two men at the oars and one in the stern-sheets. Half-way to the brig it was met by another boat bearing two officers.

"I am Captain Lockyer of His Britannic Majesty's Navy," said one of these, a heavy-jowled and low-browed officer sitting up very straight and tight-laced on the after-thwart. Then he added, "And this is Captain McWilliams of the Royal Colonial Marines."

The tall dark man in the stern-sheets of the out-coming boat bowed, silently.

"We have—ah—important messages for a certain—ah—Mr. Lafitte. Is he among the islands?"

"Vous le recontr . . . you weel meet heem sur le plage, Monsieur."

Having led his guests up the steps of the large low house farthest from the water, the dark man turned and said: "You seek Jean Lafitte, Messieurs? It iss my nem."

490

"Then why couldn't you . . . ?" Lockyer began—but after looking more closely into the large brown eyes of the man before him, he changed his mind. "Oh . . . ah. Oh, very well," said he. "I didn't know."

He fumbled for a moment with large thick hands in one of his pockets, and brought out a packet of papers wrapped in sail-cloth.— "Here," he went on, awkwardly offering the packet to Lafitte. "His Majesty's business. Very urgent."

But Lafitte only held up his hand. "Bissness?" said he. "At zis hour of ze matin?"

"But the King's . . ." Lockyer began again, still holding out the bundle.

"And if ze King of England come at zis hour and say 'Monsieur Lafitte, let us talk ze bissness,' I mek answer 'Most happy, Votre Majesté, aftair you haf share wiz me my humble brek of ze fast.'"

Lafitte opened a French door as he spoke. It gave access from the long verandah to a dining-room large, cool, shadowy, and richly furnished. A mahogany table standing near the door glistened in the early sunshine. It was set for three with platters, dishes, cups, knives and forks, all of heavy silver and gold.

"But how is this?" McWilliams exclaimed: "How could you know we were coming?"

"Ah, my cook," Lafitte replied with a shrug, "he iss ze wonnerful man!"

And soon there began to arrive upon the table such a breakfast, gradually and subtly merging into a dinner, as the two Englishmen, who had spent much of their lives knocking weevils out of ship's biscuits, had never imagined. When McWilliams expressed his amazement that a man could live so well in so remote a place, Jean Lafitte smiled and slowly closed his left eye. "Zese sings, Monsieur," said he, "you do not comprehend. Zey are for ze Breeteesh to mek marvel."

One could put up with a good deal of such nonsense, Captain Lockyer was thinking, in order to drink, while listening to it, such wines of France, Spain, Portugal, Italy, and the Indies. And it was a main article in the captain's working philosophy that it did not much matter what opinions a man might pretend to hold, or what absurd things he might say, if only he lived expensively and was obviously prosperous.

But Captain McWilliams was troubled in his mind about this pirate —so subtle, reticent, and smooth-spoken. Unless he was greatly mistaken, Lafitte was not thinking respectfully about his two guests. He was treating them, to be sure, with utmost courtesy; but there was an ironical over-tone in some of his remarks that left one uneasy.

Not until the morning was well advanced, when the Cuban cigars were lighted, did Lafitte open the packet wrapped in sail-cloth. Three letters and a large broadside fell out.

He read them all, carefully. He set them down, puffed at his cigar, sipped his brandy—and then read them through again.

In the keen dark face before him Captain McWilliams could discern nothing but a kind of intellectual interest. So far as its expression went, this pirate might have been considering the subtler arguments of a theological treatise.

They were rather hard terms, McWilliams remembered, that Sir William Percy had offered. In substance these letters told the pirate that he was to hand over his ships and men immediately, and that if he did so he might be recompensed by a grant of American lands at the end of the war. It was also suggested that he might be considered for the rank of captain in the British Navy. He was directed to cease all hostilities against Spain and surrender—to Great Britain—whatever Spanish property he might now be seized of. Should he be so insane as to refuse, the British Navy would immediately confiscate his ships, imprison him and his men, and carry fire and destruction over the whole of Barataria.

Yes, on the whole, they were rather stiff terms—and, if McWilliams remembered correctly, they were not expressed in quite the most ingratiating language.

Lands? But land was no good to a seaman. And besides, Lafitte already had land enough.—A captain's rank? But this fellow must be well aware that no Frenchman could ever command a vessel in the British Navy. Even if his name were listed, he would never get a ship.—Stop fighting Spain, and give back all Spanish property? Why, Lafitte and his men were living off Spain, as England herself had done for centuries, before she needed Spain's help against France. Look at the silver and gold on the table here. Where did that come from? And whence all these wines and this brandy?—And then as for the threat of destroying Barataria, Lafitte must know that the English had their hands full already. Otherwise they would be offering him nothing but a rope's end.

McWilliams shook himself in his chair, hoping to clear his head. He decided, not for the first time, that his habit of seeing things through the eyes of an enemy simply must be overcome. This French-born Yankee must somehow be fooled, hoodwinked, or browbeaten into sub-mission—that is to say, if New Orleans was to be captured, if Louisiana was really to be joined to Canada, and if the vast country along the Mississippi was ever to be brought under the British flag.

When Lafitte had read the papers a second time he sat back in his chair and gazed out through the open door at the waters of the Gulf.

"Ahem!" began Lockyer. "You are a Frenchman, Mr. Lafitte."

There was no denial of the accusation.

"You must know that His Majesty King George is now at peace with France and has an alliance with Spain."

Again no answer.

"You are aware that New Orleans and the whole of Louisiana have been built up by French and Spanish people. But now you see it over-run by stupid and tyrannical Yankees."

"It was sold to ze Americains, it iss ten years, by Napoleon Buona-parte," Lafitte remarked, flicking the ash from his cigar.

"I know there was some nonsense of that sort; but Boney never had the right to sell it. This continent, all of it, belongs by rights to His Majesty. Always has, and always will."

Lafitte's eyebrows were perceptibly raised.

"And now King George sends an army over here—the same men that have just licked Boney, sir—to liberate you Frenchmen from the Yankees."

"Ah, zat is too kind! How can we hope enough to zank him!"

But Lockyer went plunging on—"And conseqently, sir, we think it your moral duty to place your ships and men at His Britannic Majesty's disposal."

Lafitte indulged himself for a moment in a faintly ironic smile. "It iss perhaps," he said, "zat I haf not enough considaired ze 'moral duty,' as it iss well known ze Breeteesh ever do. It iss a sing well known zat Jean Lafitte iss but a man mondain, hard of ze head and ze heart. Zere-fore it occurs to esk it, why Sa Majesté Britannique who send ze grett army of best fighters on earth must need my poor fishermen of ze shrimp."

"Aha, sailor! Answer that one!" McWilliams silently exulted.

But Captain Lockyer, now crimson, had little taste for this rapier-play. Suddenly abandoning all effort at diplomacy, even at politeness, he delivered what he thought his really cogent arguments like blows of a bludgeon. "We know, sir," he said, "that you are a damned pirate, whatever fine names you may call yourself. We officers of His Majesty's Navy are not fond of pirates, sir. We are not accustomed to treat with them. We do not ordinarily bring them honorable terms like these that Sir William Percy offers you. Usually the only choice they get is between hanging from the yard-arm and hanging at tide-water."

Lafitte's smile was now blithe and frank. He was almost laughing as he said: "But iss it ze usual and accustomed, Monsieur, for ze off'cers of zis navy so majestique to abandon ze temper, to redden ze face, and to spik so loud like—shall we say?—ze damn pirate?"

McWilliams, to the temporary neglect of all patriotic loyalties, was feeling extremely happy.

"Why, damn your eyes . . . !"

"Yes; it iss ze known phrase wiz pirates, but not ze accustomed and usual wiz—wiz gentilhommes."

For a few moments it seemed to McWilliams that fire must flash between the keen dark eyes and the angry blue ones. But then Captain Lockyer suddenly drank his glass of brandy, and then at once another. One could see that he was resolved not to lose his temper. "Mr. Lafitte," said Lockyer, jerking his chair forward and squaring his elbows on the table, "now let's come to business. In a few weeks ten thousand British troops will be going up the River to take over the government of New Orleans and all that country beyond. Our only trouble is that we haven't any shallow-draft transports to take the troops up stream, nor have we any pilots acquainted with the shoals and sand-bars in the River. Now those small schooners and sloops there in the bay would do very well, and your men doubtless know these waters by heart. In return for this service—which, to be sure, we might easily command—we are authorized, sir, to offer you the sum of thirty thousand dollars. Please let me know, sir, without further nonsense, what you say to that?"

"I plead, Messieurs, do not neglect ze brandy. It iss, à mon gout, excellent. It was in a ship Spaneesh bound for England. She did not arrive zere."

"Is that so!" growled Lockyer, with all the truculence consistent with the fact that he was helping himself to another glassful.

"Oui, Monsieur. Many sings England esk for and eggspeck, zey do not arrive."

"But there you go, talking again! What I want ish ansher!"

"Do you think zere weel be ze opposition conseederable?"

494

"Shertainly not. We shall meet no resist—no resistance whatever from the Spanish and French pop'lation. They see that Hish Britannic Mashty was forshed limits o' human patience before this war with the Yankees. For 'leven years the noble Creoles have shuffered under the cruel tyranny of a Yankee governor. You know how they laugh at him, and . . ."

"Ah! Pardon! While ze pipple can laugh at ze governeurs, zey do not suffer ze *cruel* tyranny. Considaire, Monsieur, how zey laugh in England at Sa Majesté Britannique!"

But Lockyer was not to be deflected. After gulping down another glass of brandy he went on: "The Creoles will join us with shouts of joy—I shay *s'outs,* shir. The French and Spanish, rich merchants, plantation owners, 'Cajians, shturdy farmers of the German coast, even the rude hunters of Kentucky who have been plotting for years to break free from the eashtern shtates, the noble red men, the enshlaved blacks—all will be shet free and armed against their mashters!"

Captain Lockyer glanced at McWilliams for approval of this eloquent outburst, but he was not satisfied. It was all right, of course, for a mere captain of marines to be sitting there without saying much, but some sign of appreciation would be welcome.

"You say 'free ze enslaved blacks'?" said Lafitte, returning to his chair after giving some brief direction to his cook. "But Monsieur, do you considaire what you spik? You haf seen ze insurrection of blacks, it iss sree years? You haf known zey starfed in ze marshes?"

"We shall releash an' arm all shlaves," Lockyer affirmed with moral fervor. "—That ish, after they have carried the merchandise of New Orleans from the warehouses into our ships."

"Ah! I see it! Aftaire you haf lined ze pockets you do what you say 'moral duty.' Eet iss so Breeteesh!"

"Why, shir, you re'lize fifteen million dollars' worth of merchandise ish in those warehouses this moment? All the wealth of the Wesht comes down River, and sinch war they haven't been able to ship it out. Think of it! Fifteen million dollars! Wouldn't you like to have your share? And then think of the girls, shir—choicest beauties of France, Spain, and—if they have any—America! Aha! Think of *them!*"

McWilliams could see an expression of strong disgust sweep over Lafitte's face.

"It would mek to you ze grett surprise," said he, fiercely, "to know how I sink of ze gels."

495

"Oh?"

"Oui. I haf heard of ze soldiers of Sa Majesté Britannique in ze city of Badajoz when zey haf it captured, it iss two years. And I haf heard of ze gels zere aftaire ze 'moral duty' was done."

Captain Lockyer could not blink the fact that this was a definitely unpleasant speech. He was obliged to admit, whatever McWilliams might think, that matters were not going well. This pirate was not jumping at the chance to join the conquerors and share the loot.

For half a minute Lockyer sat in surly silence—improving the time, however, by two returns to the carafe of brandy. But then a new idea appeared to strike him, and his face brightened. There came into his piggish blue eyes a look of crafty calculation. He rose unsteadily from his chair and, after two or three experimental tacks, found and brought to the table a canvas sack which he had left, upon entering, in a corner of the room. "Now I'm goin' read you," said he, rummaging among the sack's contents, "a letter—very import' letter. Shecret letter. Don' wancher tell anybody. Hear that, McWilliams? Very shecret. F'm one of our friends in 'Merica. While I read it you gemmen look at thish map. Shpread it out there on table."

While McWilliams rose and spread out a map of the Mississippi Valley, Lockyer, after a vigorous clearing of his throat, began: "'An 'normoush opp'tun'ty lies open any Power wish will an' force to sheeze it,' he says here. 'Durin' lash' twenty years have made it my foremosh bus'ness look into defenshes weshtern portion this country. For thish tashk my pos . . . my position as mil'tary commandant of Shou'west Ter'tory afforded me amp . . . hash afford me amplesht opp'tun'ties. More rechen'ly have been p'moted Northwest Ter'tory where am able aid any forshes comin' through Lakes into Oh-hi-o and Miss . . . Miss .·. . Mish'ippi Valleys.'—Don' sheem to read 's well 's us'l today, McWilliams. Don' know whash matter."

A swift glance of mutual intelligence and amusement flashed between McWilliams and Lafitte. "Ah, Monsieur," said the second of these listeners, "nous vous comprenons parfaitement."

"Thash good. Well, our friend goes on: 'Thish opp'tun'ty I refer ish easy capture of thish great valley, an' also vash country to wesh of it, by comin' up Miss . . . Mish'—well, you know, gemmen—'to meet an army comin' down the Ohi-o.'—Get that, McWilliams? Thash the old French plan, but now we take it over an' make it work. But then he shays: 'No 'fective reshist . . . resistance need be feared N'orlins. 'Mediately British standard raised whole pop'lation come flocking to

496

its protecting folds.'—H'm. Fine language, McWilliams. Shprisin' what language these Yankees can use. Reg'lar Shashpeare! An' then he says: 'The Creoles are tired incom'tent Gov'ner Claiborne who does not unner-stan' shiv'lized people.'—How could he, the mis'rable igner'nt barb'rian? —'All Negro shlaves will welcome anyone releash from shackles. In-dian tribes will rush to help againsht op . . . oppresshers. Lasht but not leasht, the cut-throats of'—ah, ahem! Well, ye might 's well know what he shays here—'the cut-throats of Barataria who live but for shlaughter will jine you wish s'outsh o' joy.'—This is good, doncher think so, McWilliamsh?"

"Excellent, Captain!"

"But haf anozzer glass of ze brandy, Capitaine," Lafitte suggested, "before ze sroat iss cut."

The suggestion was at once adopted, and Lockyer continued: "Lesh shee, now. 'Shlaughter . . . S'outsh o' joy' . . . Oh, yes: 'Shuch allies would be shufficient destroy any troopsh thish region. They are not sholdiers but on'y farmers an' hunters led by igner'nt young lawyer no mil't'ry trainin' whatever. They have shev'ral times threat'ed she-shede from Wash'n'ton unlesh it gives them free navigation o' the Mish . . . the Mish'—well, thersh that River again! 'They are not farmersh but on'y sholdiers'—Oh, I read that.—'Moment they shee you command mouth of Mi'—that river—'they will eagerly jine you hoist Union Jack on White Housh.—What think o' that McWilliamsh? Hope ye're followin' thish."

"Oh, yes, with keen interest."

"Well, an' sho he goes on: 'Ash for myself, the battle of Chrysler's Farm should be shuff . . . sufficient show my power an' good will. On that day I commanded two thousan' five hunnerd men opposed by eight hunner' British. My loshes were about five hunnerd. His Mashty, I am shorry say, losht some fifty. This battle hash had mosh shtrikin' effec' on 'Merican forshes. The door ish now open to river. Therefore advise Hish Mashty's troopsh crosh from Canada an' jine brozzers marchin' up from N'orlins. No trouble whatever.'—See it, McWilliamsh? Unner-stan' it? Thash how we're goin' work plan. Canada army comes down river, we go up."

"Yes, Captain. It's quite clear to me."

"An' how 'bout you, Mr.—ah—Mr. Lafitte?"

"Et moi aussi."

"Ah . . . Good . . . 'No trouble'—an' then he shays: 'An ecshellent shystem o' c'munication hash been arrange'. My partner hash carrier pigeons will inform me when you are ready attack. I also have pigeonsh ready. By these meansh we can ensure our unity in action an' ever-lashtin' glory.'"

At this point Captain Lockyer folded the letter with something of a flourish, returned it to the canvas sack, and then, turning sharply to Lafitte, remarked: "Now. Shee what kind o' friends we have?"

"Mais, oui, Monsieur! An' zey do not geef me ze grett surprise."

"Who is this man?" McWilliams asked.

"Don't plan tell yeh. Letter ain't shigned—or not by name anyhow."

"Eet ees not necessaire," said Lafitte. "La signature est l'emblème du Poignard—c'est à dire, The Knife!"—And then, suddenly, Lafitte was bending forward in his chair, his eyes drilling into Lockyer. His teeth were clamped and his face was cruel as a hawk's as he hissed: "How much is Weelkinson getting out of zis?"

"He will be Governor of—" began Lockyer, without fully comprehending. "Oh, 'Wilk' . . . 'Wilkinson,' did you say? Why, ah, nothing. Nothing whatever, I assure you, shir!—Never heard o' him, i' fack!" And to cover his confusion Lockyer helped himself to a brimming glass of brandy, much of which he spilled.

"Faugh, Nicholas Lockyer, you lie like a sailor, for all the practice you've had," thought McWilliams.

"It iss grett pity you do not hear of le Général James Weelkinson," said Lafitte, lying back in his chair with a look of complete satisfaction. "He iss one you would look at what you say 'eye-to-eye,' as ze two sneks zat meet in ze grass."

"You mean to say . . . !"

"Ah, no! For ze snek iss a clean and loving-peace creature. He sting not for pleasure, he sting not for gain, he sting not even for ze 'duty morale,' but only zat he may live. I mek ze humble apology—to ze *snek*!"

While Captain Lockyer was struggling to express his feelings after this remark, Lafitte rose and strode swiftly to the door and looked out. He appeared to be somewhat apprehensive. McWilliams and Lockyer, also rising from the table, could see that a large number of the islanders were gathering out there. They were gesticulating, and their voices were rising.

"My poor feeshermen of ze shrimp," Lafitte remarked, still looking out, "haf not ze grett love for soldiers and sailors of Sa Majesté Britannique. Zey spik of zeir ancestors maternal as of ze dog. I mourn it."

"But you mustn't let 'em talk that way! We can't have it! What do they mean by it?"

Lafitte shrugged. "Eet iss perhaps zey do not comprehend ze Breeteesh 'moral duty.' Zey are simple of ze mind, but violent extrêmement."

"H'm.—Well, you got us in here, and . . ."

"Let us depart promptement, by way of ze cuisine," said Lafitte hastily, laying a compulsive hand on the shoulder of each of his guests. "So we shall deceive ze feeshermen for ze shrimp, and all zat ze Breeteesh weel lie about the violence deplorable done by me to my guests, eet weel not be so."

By the time Captain Lockyer had stepped aboard His Majesty's Ship *Sophie* and ordered her course set for Pensacola, Jean Lafitte's quill was scratching the first words of a letter "À Son Excellence Monsieur Wm. C. C. Claiborne, Gouverneur de l'État de la Louisiane . . ."

YOU MAY GO

"From Mobile to Pensacola and up to Fort Toulouse," Jackson murmured, moving a long, blunt, hairy finger across the map, "and then to Fort Strother on the Coosa . . ."

"No," said Holdfast quietly, "I'm not going that way."

"Why not? It's the shortest."

"I don't think so. Besides, I don't care to run through the old Creek country."

"Y' ain't afeared o' dead men, are you?"

There was no reply.

"Well, then, let's say from Mobile up the Tombigbee to Yowanni. Is that right?"

"Yes. That way, I'll be running up the valleys instead of across them."

"Okeh. And so you go up from Yowanni to—ah—to Old Pontotoc.— Just stop an' see Jake McNab on the way, will you? Find out if he can bring us down 'bout a hunderd Choctaw braves.—An' so from Pontotoc to Colbert's Ferry—an' for God's sake don't let his old squaw guess what you're up to. She'd blab. An' then from Colbert's over Natchez Trace to Nashville. H'm . . . Let's see now."

Jackson was silent for a minute, pursing his lips and frowning as he measured off the distances with a bit of cord.—What a thing, thought Holdfast, looking down at him, to order men about in this way, to call men and they came flocking, to tell a man to go and he leapt like an arrow from the string! And there was little in the mere look of the General, now that his daunting eyes were lowered, to explain or justify this strange power of command. Yellowed by jaundice, pitifully lean, his hands shaking with fever and ague, he sat slumped in his camp-chair before a flimsy table, obviously tired to the bone. Nothing in his dress suggested military uniform. His thread-bare blue coat with bullet buttons, his high dragoon boots, mud-spattered, even the little leather cap on the back of his head, were the same that Holdfast had seen him wearing for years at cock-fights, horse-races, and in his general store at Clover Bottom. The thread-bare coat of faded blue huddled over his narrow shoulders was the very one that had deceived the eye of Charles Dickinson when he aimed at Jackson's heart and missed it by three inches.

Jackson was still bearing in his body the ounce of lead that had so nearly killed him in that famous duel of eight years ago. No doubt he still carried the slugs and bullets fired into him by the Benton brothers in the tavern fight at Nashville. His shattered shoulder had never prop-erly healed, and perhaps never would. Such things aged a man—and just after the Benton fight had come the winter campaign against the Creeks, mutinies and desertions, the effort to work with a timorous government six weeks off through forest and swamp, the bombardment of Fort Boyer, the swift stroke against the Spaniards at Pensacola, and then these weeks of anxious waiting at Mobile, wondering what the British would do. And so it was no wonder that the body of Andrew Jackson, though never his heart or mind, was showing wear. The un-trimmed hair bristling up from his brow had the color of iron slightly rusted. His long narrow face with the chin like a plow-share looked to be of iron also, but iron gouged by the chisels of pain, wrath, and fierce determination.

"Mought be four hunderd mile in a straight line," he said, looking up from under close-knit brows, "but it'll be over six hunderd the way you have to go. And the trails this time o' year . . ."

"The trails will be bad, yes."

"But just same, you got to git thar, Holdfast. Unnerstand that?"

500

"Perfectly."

"Wal—an' so, watch out! An arrow in your back, a tomahawk in your skull, a broken leg, a sprained ankle, and then all that you tell me about Fayal and the *Rebecca's* voyage might as well not have happened."

Holdfast stared for a moment at the map lying before him upside down on the table. Then he strode across the tent and stood 'Hobbomok' in a corner.

"What? Y' ain't takin' your rifle-gun?"

"He weighs forty pounds."

"H'm. I see.—Well, here's your letter to Bill Carroll. Course he's been tryin' for weeks to get the m'litia together, but now he *will* get 'em."

"Yes, General, now that you've made up your own mind."

"Well, but, good God, Holdfast, Mobile was the nateral place for 'em to strike! Any fool could see that. Only thing to show they mought come straight to N'Orleans was those papers from Lafitte. How could a sensible man trust a lyin' pirate like him?—that is, until you came in with this news about what Reid heard at Fayal."

"Ah, but General, don't try to pretend that you're only a 'sensible man.' You're more than that. A sensible man in your place would run away. You won't. A sensible man wouldn't win the battle at New Orleans. You will."

"That's so! By the 'Tarnal, that's so!"—and Jackson banged the flimsy table with his clenched fist.

He sat still then for a while with a dreamy look in his eyes, as though listening. Then he said: "D' ye know, Holdfast—hyar's a thing I wouldn't tell to most men, but fack is I never set eyes on a real army in all my born days. No, sir. Not 'lessen ye count Tarleton's lobster-backs in the Waxhaws when I was a boy. An' what's more, I ain't a sojer. I'm jest a Western Waters lawyer, a man that can c'leck other men's debts but not pay his own. O' course, as ye know, I hev fit a few Injuns hyar an' thar, but this 'll be differ'nt. Them British want the River bad. They'll come agin us this time with all they can bring. They'll bring the men that have jest licked Napoleon, the best troops on 'arth, an' the best commanders. They ben plannin' this thing fer years.—Wal, we ain't got troops, nor gin'rals, nor plans, nor forts, nor guns. Iffen we did have troops thar wouldn't be uniforms fer 'em, nor arms, nor food. Most o' the men we do bring down never fired at anythin' bigger 'n a squirrel—an' missed him. They never set eyes on anybody 't wanted to kill 'em, an' they never met afore the day o' the battle.—So, thar 't is, Holdfast. Thar 't is."

501

The two men smiled at each other with a look in which a kind of desperation mingled with perfect confidence.

"But now," said Jackson, "returning to the map, "let's say six hunderd mile. I can give you ten days, Holdfast. I'd like to make it more, but ten days up and five weeks for Carroll to gather his men and get them down here—that brings us to Christmas. And the British advanceguard is here already."

"Ten days for six hundred miles.—What if I do it in less?"

"It would help, o' course; but you can't. No livin' man could, on those trails. I say ten days for you and five weeks for Carroll. And remember this: if the British lick us below New Orleans we'll fight 'em through the town. If they lick us out o' thar, we'll fight 'em up-river s' long as we can stagger an' shoot. So you tell Bill Carroll to be lookin' out fer what's left of us all along the River an' up the Trace. There 'll come a time, you tell him, when we'll turn round on 'em an' drive 'em down River an' back through N'Orleans an' out o' 'Merica to *stay*. —Now, git along thar, an' may the Lord God o' Hosts bless your legs!"

Holdfast saluted, and left the tent.

"Oh—and Mr. Gaines!" rang out the high-pitched voice.

Lifting the flap again, Holdfast found that Jackson had risen to his feet.

"Yes, General."

"Mr. Gaines, a good many years have passed . . . But what I mean say is thisheer: hit's a right smart spell sence you an' me run that race back in Sal'sb'ry.—'Member thet 'ar race, Holdfast?"

"Yes, General; and how you beat me there."

"With the help of a dog, ez Russ Bean said at the time."

" 'God works in a mysterious way his wonders to perform.' "

"Ha! Ha!—Does me good to hear yeh make a joke now an' then. But I s'pose ye know hit's a dangersome trace ye're a-goin'."

"Aren't we all of us?"

"Right . . . o' course. Nothin' so dangersome ez bein' alive—an' the more alive we be the more we got to lose.—Wal, I got Rachel, I got the boy, an' I got you. Times, I think I got all 'Merica."

"And you won't lose it, General.

"God damn it, don't call me 'Gin'ral'! What kind o' way's that to address an old friend? People say 'Gin'ral Wilkinson,' don't they? Wal, then . . . "

"I'm sorry, Andy."

502

"But what I called yeh back fer, takin' yer precious time . . . I jest wanted to—wal—say 'Good-bye'!"

"Good-bye, Andy. But we're going to meet at New Orleans. *Below* New Orleans, I think."

"Mebbe so. But I guv yeh a letter to Bill Carroll, didn't I?"

"Yes. I have it here."

"An' don't ye know that's only half o' what I got to say to the folks up thar?"

"Less than half, Andy."

"All right, then. Hyar's the rest." And Jackson strode brusquely forward, laid his hands on the shoulders of Holdfast, pulled him downward, and kissed him, awkwardly, on both cheeks. Then he walked back to his chair.

"If you should have the opportunity to communicate that there military salute to Mrs. Andrew Jackson," he said, coldly, with his back turned, "and if she will kindly pass it on to him we call 'Little Andy,' why then, Mr. Gaines, I shall be greatly obleeged."

"Yes, General," said Holdfast, respectfully saluting.

"You may go, sir."

You may go at eight miles an hour for as long as you can stagger, distributing those hours among as few days and nights as possible. You may ignore the agony in your lungs, your heart, your legs. You may try to forget that these pounding feet learned to run in Mohegan Village a long, long while ago. You may try to remember how young men run, light-hearted, with no burden of dubious thought upon them—young men who have never felt the cureless ache of the years in their mid-most bones. You may run as you never have run before, having reached the time of life at which most men chiefly sit by the fire and smoke their pipes and remember.

The swollen streams and the many swamps made slow going on the way north from Mobile. The broom-pine, pawpaws, and swamp-oaks hung with moss were gray, weird, ghostly. The long swinging vines held him back. Twisting, bending, and writhing back upon themselves, the trails he followed were like the paths of a snake through tall grass. Always they took the easiest way, and the longest, unlike the wide roads by which white men scored their will and their haste upon the subjected land. Twelve to eighteen inches wide and in the softer places often a foot deep, they made an intricate net-work which no map could possibly represent, a maze which had to be carried in memory or else worked through by the instinct that brings a lost animal home through strange country. They were centuries old. The feet that had beaten them out were part of the dark-brown earth itself; and soon the trails too would be over-grown, lost, and forgotten.

As the chill of night came on, the ground grew firmer. Holdfast could feel his way in the dark with his feet, and could guess something of what lay about him by the gravel or grass or mud on which he trod. Odors and sounds told him something, and the pitch of the path up or down. Yet running on trails such as these in the dark was out of the question. Moreover, his strength was beginning to wane before the end of the first half-day of his journey. Even swift walking became a matter of sheer will, of telling his legs that they had to go and then trying to forget them.—Ah, those weeks on the *General Armstrong* and the *Rebecca*! He was heavy from that long sloth.

At last, some forty miles above Mobile, he built himself a tiny fire on an Indian mound beside the trail, ate a handful of parched corn, and lay down with his back to a log.

It was colder in the morning, and that would mean better trails. Then too, he could strike a little westward now, toward the higher lands and the friendly Choctaws. By noon he was running straight north beside the Chickasawhay, toward McNab's. Ah, now, if he could only reach that hospitable hearth before he slept again, there would be a day's run of which even a young man would have no reason to feel ashamed.

His first wind, that morning, lasted him for five miles perhaps, and his second for a good ten. By noon he began to feel as though he could run forever. Evidently those lazy weeks at sea had not harmed him much after all. The years had scarcely diminished his power of lung and limb. If ever he had run more strongly as a youth along the Thames, with legs more like tempered steel and a heart that pounded more steadily like a drum to his stride, then he had forgotten.

While exulting thus in his strength and bounding down the bank of Chunkey Creek, he slipped on a rotten log just as he came to the water, and fell, heavily.—His first thought, when he dragged himself out, was for the fire in his clam-shell. Yes, thank heaven, that was still burning! And then he found that his right shoulder had been wrenched and badly bruised in his fall.

That would bring down his pride. That would teach him caution.—If it had been a leg, now, or an ankle! He went on more carefully, admonished by the grind of pain in his shoulder that this was not a race of a youth for some paltry prize but a run for future millions.

Perhaps he was going light in the head, for he had eaten little since leaving Mobile. It might be that his fierce concentration of will was leaving his mind a prey to wild fancies. But no matter for that, if those fancies served his purpose and drove him, drew him, ran with him along the trail. All afternoon and into the night, at any rate, he felt that he had a companion beside him. But it was not the grown woman, the wife, the mother and widow who went with him step by step as he ran and leaped and climbed and waded, burning his way through the miles. Rather it was the child and play-mate, his all but sister, of long ago. Her vivid hair was blown back by their speed as it used to be when they ran down-hill through the autumn leaves. "Can't I run fast!" she called out now in that same exultant treble. He caught at the words and forgot his body's anguish. "Can't I run fast!" his mind sang over and over, in time with his long low stride.

It was long after dark when he came to the top of the hill above Mc-Nab's clearing and heard the dogs below. There was a dim light in the cabin window. The door opened, and a man came out. He yelled at the dogs in the unmistakable tones and language of Jake McNab himself. Maw stood at the open door with a flaring pine-knot in her hand.

"You people," Holdfast said before he came up to the light, "would make a good target for anyone who didn't like you."

"Huh!" replied McNab, after only a momentary hesitation, "ev'y man, red or white, in a thaousan' mile knows ez me an' Maw is friends o' Sleepin' B'ar."

Hours of talk by the fireside, more hours of tossing on a corn-husk mattress, and the heavy breakfast given him by Maw McNab in the morning, were not the best preparation for a good day's run. Still, Maw's decoction of red-oak bark for his bruised shoulder made up for some loss of time and distance. McNab, moreover, gladly agreed to see Parson Blandison and get him to collect at least a hundred braves for Jackson. He thought it likely that some arrangement could be made, by means either of the "little green book" or else the innards of a dog, to make it seem right for the peaceful Choctaws, on this special occasion, to dig up the tomahawk. "An' iffen they won't go fer The Ha'r," said he, "then they will 'cause Sleepin' B'ar asts 'em. So 'll Jake McNab an' his rifle-gun 'Honeybee.' We hain't tuk a British scelp fer Godfrey knows haow long, an' we're spilin' fer slaughter."

It was a darker and colder day, this third one, with a wind. Gloomy clouds were lumbering out of the north, with a threat of snow. That would be bad for running, and good for tracking a runner down.

Until the snow came, however, it was easy going up there on the ancient trail to Old Pontotoc. The ground was firm. There were few trees. In some places a runner could have been seen from a mile away.

What Andrew Jackson had suggested about an arrow in the back or a tomahawk in the skull had been, of course, rather absurd. Probably there were no Indians anywhere who wanted to kill Sleeping Bear. The real danger lay in the fact that many of them, and perhaps the Chickasaws especially, would be glad to adopt him, even by friendly force. The Chickasaws had never been reconciled to his apparent preference for the Choctaw people. And this was Chickasaw country.

Holdfast felt that he was gathering strength as the morning of this third day wore on. The cold air did him good. It made him think of Connecticut Octobers. To be afoot, free, alone, dependent only upon himself, exerting his full strength, and charged with an important errand, filled him with sheer delight.

He was going now at nine miles an hour, against the wind. That was too fast, perhaps. It was a white man's way. A good white runner could draw ahead of most Indians in the first mile or two, but any good Indian runner would overtake him at twenty miles and still be going strong at fifty. Chief Red Shoes of the Choctaws had run down and killed a French trader who had started out mounted on a good fast horse. The horse had died of exhaustion. And Red Shoes, more than sixty years old at the time, had done that by not being in a hurry.

He slowed down to eight miles an hour, twice as fast as a walk, and held it all morning. At noon he lighted a fire, cooked and ate a little of the food he had brought from the McNab cabin, and rested. Then he ran on through the afternoon and for an hour or two in the darkness. It was beginning to snow when he waded the Oktibbeha, a few miles west of the shrunken Tombigbee, and knocked at the cabin door of the half-breed Jack Pitchlyn.

On the fourth day he made an early start, but the light fall of snow on the ground slowed him sadly. His moccasins had been wet all the way from Mobile. In itself that was no great matter, but the serious thing was that Jack Pitchlyn had hung them last night too near the fire, so that now a great hole was wearing in the sole of the left one. A pure Indian would have known exactly how close to hang them, and of course he would have known, too, that no man's running can be better than his foot-gear allows.—As for Andy Jackson, who had no Indian blood whatever, he could think about arrows and tomahawks, but it had not occurred to him that the fate of New Orleans and the River might depend upon a few square inches of elk-skin.

When he topped the rise that looked down upon Cowpen Creek and the Colbert settlement, Holdfast paused to consider this matter. He lay flat on his back among the brittle canes, thinking and resting.

His feet were in bad condition—as why should they not be? Even the feet of a young man, after such a pounding through wet and dry, rough and smooth, up and down . . . A few more miles of running on snow with the sole of his left foot almost bare would lame him for good and all.

To be sure, he might limp to Old Pontotoc, ten miles off, and try to find new moccasins there, but one sharp stick, pebble, or broken bit of cane, trodden upon in those ten miles, would cripple him. And after all, wasn't old Colbert, the sly Chickasaw, the paid spy and agent of the British, just as powerful in Old Pontotoc as here at Cowpen Creek? Moreover, here it was mid-morning of the fourth day, and there might be three hundred miles yet to go.

Having decided what he would do, Holdfast came out of the cane-brake and walked down-hill toward the straggling settlement.

Half a dozen Chickasaw boys saw him coming, and, after a moment in which excitement struggled with decorum, they started on the run for the village to spread their wonderful news.

Three minutes later Holdfast lifted the flap of Chief Colbert's bark-sided cabin and strode in.

"Ishla cho?" said a voice thick with fire-water.

"Alali-o!" replied Holdfast, seating himself on the buffalo robe nearest the entrance.

"So it seems. Howdy?" said the old man dim in the shadows, rubbing his stomach.

Holdfast rubbed his, and said "Good."

"All good?—Aliha achukma?"

"Aliha achukma, amba shulush sipokni."

"Huh! All good, but moccasins bad. Huh!" Colbert seemed to be much interested. And then with a sly look in his watery old eyes, he inquired—"Damn bad?"

"Yau. Sipokni okpulo." And Holdfast held up his left foot in the firelight.

507

Colbert smiled as he leaned forward to examine the worn sole.

"Sleeping Bear come want new moccasin," said Holdfast, realizing that nothing would be gained by a less direct approach.

There was a quizzical expression in the old drunkard's eyes as he leaned back and said "Shulush sipokni maletit kania keyushke—bad moccasin do not run away." Then he laughed, vigorously rubbing his stomach meanwhile as a sign of hospitable intentions.

But Holdfast looked at him with indignant amazement. "Shulush himmona kia?" he asked.

"Hatoshke, kia," Colbert firmly replied. "Chickasaw keep Sleeping Bear now they have him."

Holdfast took the proffered tobacco-pipe, rested his elbows on his knees, and puffed for a while, as though considering the situation in all its aspects. "Okeh," he said at length.

"Good. My son Sleeping Bear very damn wise man. He stay here Chickasaw all time."

"Fo," said Holdfast, puffing. "Okeh."

"I give him my son tanshi pushi. I give him nita nipi. I give him mebbe if good plenty wishki. I give him two three ohoyo haui very damn pretty. But moccasin? No. Good moccasin run away."

The old man gave himself up to drunken and senile laughter, rocking back and forth. At last he fell off his stool and lay on his back, his legs feebly waving—a dismal and disgusting object.

Holdfast laid down the pipe he was smoking, rose, and courteously helped his host to a sitting posture. Then he said, moving toward the entrance, "I go now."

Colbert, momentarily sobered and somewhat ashamed, found his pipe and took three long puffs. "But you had no black drink," said he.

"It is for friends to drink together."

"You had no food."

"I asked for moccasins."

"You had no council fire."

"They are old men who sit there. They take money from the British for white scalps. They get drunk and fall off their stools. I go now."

"So it seems," said Colbert with a sidelong glance. "But my young men will look for you."

"Good! They will have a good run." And Holdfast dropped the flap of the cabin-door behind him.

The youth of the village drew suddenly back when Holdfast came out of the door, already on the run. Round the corner of the cabin he ran and at once found the southward trail reaching out for Natchez. Good! How should they guess which way he was going, those thirty boys and twelve or fifteen young braves? Let them follow. One of them was a giant. Huge feet he must have. Let him, especially, follow. Come along now, young Chickasaws, and let's all run for a while like white men!

The boys were streaming out along the path behind with their mouths full of high-pitched yells. Nice boys they were, and could run well. Fortunately, this was a clean hard path for running. The light was good. There was little danger of wounding that bare left sole.— All right, then, boys, come along! Yell your lungs out, run your legs limp, and live to tell your grandsons that you once chased Sleeping Bear. Tell them he was three times your age and he ran you to a stand-still. Tell them he had already done four hundred miles in four days and nights but he ran like a man starting out. Tell them his feet were sore, his shoulder ached, his heart was heavy, and he had almost forgotten why he was running, but he went away like the wind.

Pausing to look back for a moment at the end of the second mile, Holdfast saw that the boys were trailing off, discouraged, tuckered. The young warriors were moving ahead now, with a short, bow-legged, stiff-crested fellow out in front. He carried no weapon, and neither, apparently, did any of the others. They merely wanted to capture their hero, lead him home, adopt him, keep him, make him their brother, so that they could say in triumph to visiting Cherokees, Creeks, and Choctaws: "Look what *we* have!"

He gave them four stiff miles of white man's running before he looked round again—four miles that would have to be done all over if he was ever to reach Nashville. They made the black spots dance before his eyes. When he did look back the stubby, bow-legged warrior had disappeared. Only three or four young men were following now, but among them, thank Heaven, the big fellow.—What was that fellow's name?—And then he let them have two miles more, at top speed. That left only the giant in the race, and he was far behind.

Holdfast threw himself down beside the trail and rested, trying to recall the big fellow's name.

Very big indeed he looked as he came loping up. His moccasins must be enormous. The stiffened crest of his hair was flopping at every

509

stride. But he was coming cautiously, and wondering. He was slowing down.

Holdfast suddenly sprang to his feet and advanced with outstretched arms. "How, Eats 'em Alive!" he called.

The big man came to a stand, twenty feet off. His coppery skin glistened with sweat. His chest rose and fell like a blacksmith's bellows. His moccasins *were* enormous, and they were new. "I am not sick," he gasped. "How?"

"Good.—That was a great race we ran at Old Pontotoc three years ago. But you run better now. You look bigger."

The warrior's smile was boyish and friendly. "Every year grow, run faster," said he, coming close. "Hunnerd year mebbe grow big like Sleeping Bear. Mebbe beat him then."

Holdfast laughed, and slapped the giant's brawny shoulder. "Come," said he. "Sit. Rest."

For several minutes they sat, panting, side by side, until the warrior burst out, almost plaintively: "You come back, Sleeping Bear! Big runner! Big story-teller! Very damn big man!"

Holdfast hesitated for a moment before he replied, laying a hand on the young man's knees: "I wish I could, Eats 'em Alive. But not now. Too busy."

"You come sometime?"

"Yes. Sometime. I will."

"Oh! Good!"

That seemed to settle the matter, and for another minute there was a friendly silence. Then Holdfast raised himself on one elbow and looked down at his companion's foot-gear. "Eats 'em Alive," said he, "will you give me those fine big moccasins of yours, or shall we fight for them?"

The giant grinned with pride and pleasure. "Fight Sleeping Bear?" said he. "Not now. Too busy. Mebbe sometime."

He laughed at his own joke, and Holdfast with him, heartily. Then he stripped off his new elk-skin moccasins and handed them over.

"Good!" said Holdfast. "Many thanks! And here are mine."

Eats 'em Alive took the worn, wet, bedraggled things with a look of reverence. "What!" he exclaimed. "You give me him?"

"Yes. You have them. And many thanks!"

"Huh! Good! Many thanks!"

"These are the best moccasins I have ever worn," said Holdfast, rising. "They fit me. Thanks again."

"Thanks again," said Eats 'em Alive, also rising to his feet. "Wish better. My best squaw make him. Take long time. Whole moon mebbe."

"Ah. They have a long trail to go.—I think a red man's trail, from now on."

The two men stood silent, looking into each other's eyes.

"I go now," said Holdfast.

"So it seems.—Come back sometime, big brother. We wait for you."

"I will. I tell you so."

Then they shook arms, and parted.

When he had gone a hundred yards, Holdfast turned and looked back. Eats 'em Alive had strung the two old moccasins over his shoulder like a necklace. He was trudging homeward along the snowy trace bare-footed, proud, and humble. He too turned, and, with a noble gesture of farewell, lifted his right hand high above his head.

But then there was still the problem, how to make the Chickasaws go on thinking that he was bound for Natchez rather than Nashville. It involved a search for places blown bare of snow, much wading in creeks, and loss of time. Yet he managed to make good progress northward against the wind and to cross the divide between the Tombigbee head-waters and the brooks pouring into the Tennessee. That night he slept with his back to a log near the source of Big Bear Creek, forty miles from Colbert's ferry.

"My old man," said Saletia Colbert, having listened with apparent indignation to Holdfast's account of events at Cowpen Creek—"My old man is a son of a bitch."

"So it seems," Holdfast politely agreed.

"And he is a disgrace to his mother."

"You have said it."

"He gave you no black drink?"

"No black drink."

"No food?"

"I asked for moccasins."

"No moccasins?"

"I have said so."

"Was he drunk?"

"He fell off his stool."

"Oh!" And the ugly old woman with the slinking eyes covered her face with her filthy wrinkled hands. "Major Levi Colbert, Chief of the Chickasaws, fell off his stool while Sleeping Bear was his guest!"

"That is so."

"And all that," she said, looking out between her fingers, "is because of the fat young squaw he has got him."

Deeply sympathetic she seemed, and yet Holdfast felt uneasy. Saletia Colbert had not been running this infamous tavern and ferry for thirty years—associating with trace-bandits, river-pirates, Spanish spies, French spies, British spies, and all the come-and-go of Natchez Trace—without sharpening her wits considerably. It was not impossible that her outcries might really be due to an old woman's jealousy of a younger wife, but also they might have some connection with the smoke signals he had seen this morning far to the southward.

Holdfast rose, wearily, from the bench beside the fire. "I go now," he said.

"What! I thought you would sleep here tonight."

"Then where should I sleep tomorrow night, Saletia? Do you know that?"

Her eyes like a snake's slid away.

"Tell the young men of the Chickasaws when they come for me," he said with a pleasant smile, "that I was sorry I could not wait."

Seeing that his suspicions had some warrant, he moved at once to the door.

But the door was opened, slowly, from outside; and there, standing close together, were some thirty braves—by their crests, Chickasaws.

"Ah! Okalona!" said Holdfast cordially after a moment's pause, recognizing the tall warrior who stood nearest. "How?"

"Good. How, Sleeping Bear?"

"I am not sick."

"We come take Sleeping Bear back home."

"Ah," said Holdfast with a friendly smile. "It's kind.—Come far?"

Some of the younger men in the back of the group put their hands over their mouths at this.—As if Sleeping Bear did not know that they had come a long, hard, grueling day's journey!

"Pontotoc," replied Okalona.

"Huh! Very far. Very kind.—Come fast?"

t only the younger braves but a dozen seasoned seniors were
 ⁀ this dry witticism. "Come fast?"—Oh, what a man! They
 ⁀other in the ribs.

fast," Okalona admitted, looking modest and

friendly. "But Sleeping Bear he got here first. We come take Sleeping Bear back home."

"Many thanks," said Holdfast, throwing the door open. "He is always looking for a home.—But now come in, brothers. Have a good big drink whisky and then go home."

Would it work, this worst of the white man's medicines?

"Achukma!" said an elder brave, striding straight-toed through the door-way. Two or three followed gazing expectantly at Maw Colbert and the kegs in the corner.

"Have many drinks whisky, brothers," Holdfast called out in a hearty tone, feeling deeply ashamed. "Maybe drink all night and go home tomorrow."

"See," said Okalona, laying a hand on Holdfast's arm. "I know this trick."

"Of course, Bench Chief. But help me to play it."

"Why?"

"It is necessary."

"You come back sometime, like you say Eats 'em Alive?"

"I will. I tell you so."

"Okeh."—And Okalona, the most redoubtable warrior in the Chickasaw towns, elbowed in toward the corner.

"Who pays for drink?" Maw Colbert called from the keg.

"Sleeping Bear," said Holdfast. "Later."

"Okeh."

There was a growing hubbub as the crude spirits began their work: "Ah, wishki! Achukma!"—"Sleeping Bear very damn big man!"— "Run fast?"—"Run far?"—And then there was good-natured laughter.

"Brothers," called Holdfast, speaking in fluent Choctaw, "let me tell you a story about a friend of mine."

Every one in the room paused to listen. Whisky-cups stopped half way to mouths, and liquor dribbled out of the keg to the floor through the half-opened tap.

"He was just a little fellow, about so high"—and Holdfast held his hand some four feet from the floor. "His forehead was flat, he had never been married, he had never been on the war-path, and had not taken one scalp."

There were expressions of contempt on the faces of the younger men, and sage noddings of the head among the elders.

"But when he was very young this friend of mine had killed a raccoon —by accident, I think."

513

"Aw!" exclaimed a warrior. "A raccoon!"

"Yes. And he had a picture of that raccoon-killing pricked on his chest. He was very proud of the picture. He went round among all the Choctaw villages, showing it to everybody."

The men were beginning to laugh.

"For every Choctaw, you know, has to have a picture of every brave thing he does pricked on him in colors, so that people won't forget."

"Aw! Choctaw! More wishki!"

"And then when he began to get famous people would come to him and say: 'Little Raccoon Killer, why not get married? Why not take a squaw?' But my friend would say that he was afraid of squaws. He said they made him sick."

"Haw! Haw! Choctaw!"

"Well, one day," Holdfast continued, "the Chickasaws came over the hills into Choctaw country with a big war-party."

All eyes were fixed upon him, eagerly expectant. For a moment the braves forgot to drink. "What next, Sleeping Bear?" said one.

"Little Raccoon Killer got very angry. He danced the war-dance and yelled the war-whoop and had himself painted black and red. Then he took his tomahawk and chased those Chickasaws back home. He brought back three Chickasaw scalps."

No one laughed at this. Some of the faces were definitely grim.

"Then Little Raccoon Killer went to the medicine-man and had a picture of the Chickasaw killing pricked on him. It covered him all over—every inch."

Well, yes; clearly this was a joke. A warrior here and there permitted himself to smile.

"Next year the Chickasaws came over the hills with a bigger war-party, hoping to take my friend's scalp. After he had chased them home again Little Raccoon Killer went to the medicine-man with six Chickasaw scalps and he said 'What shall I do?'

" 'Take a squaw,' said the medicine man.

"Little Raccoon Killer said 'But I'm afraid of squaws!'

"Then he went to all his brothers and cousins to see whether they had any room left on them, but they and their squaws were all filled up with their own Chickasaw pictures. So my friend was obliged to take a squaw for himself, and the story of those six scalps covered her all over from head to foot. Every inch of her."

The room was ringing with mirth. "Every inch! Oh! Haw! Haw! What next, Sleeping Bear?—More wishki!"

"Well then, next, the Chickasaws came down once more after my friend, and that time he brought back nine scalps to the medicine-man. He said: 'What shall I do? My squaw is all used up with the last pictures.'

" 'Take two more squaws,' said the medicine-man. And that is what my friend had to do, although he was very much afraid. He took two more squaws and had the story of those nine scalps pricked on them. It used them all up, every inch."

Oh, what a story! "More wishki!"

"And the last time I saw Little Raccoon Killer he said to me: 'Sleeping Bear, this is getting too much. I'm only a little man,' he said, 'and I'm almost a hundred years old, but I have nine squaws all covered with pictures of Chickasaw scalpings—every inch of them. My squaws are very rough with me, Sleeping Bear, and I don't think I can stand any more.—Please ask the Chickasaws to stop sending down war-parties!' "

The warriors stamped and howled and beat one another with their fists. They coughed and sputtered and wept and sneezed into their whisky. They demanded more and more whisky. It made them blissful to think that such a superb story-teller as Sleeping Bear would always hereafter be sitting among them telling such glorious big-man jokes, such marvelous side-splitting stories.

When the gale of laughter was at its loudest Holdfast nodded to Okalona, walked out at the door, strode down to the ferry, loosed the boat there, and began rowing across the Tennessee River.

And yet as he lay by his lonely fire that night, and again on the Natchez Trace next morning, he took little pride or pleasure in his evasion of the Chickasaws. Those stalwart simple fellows had offered him companionship, fidelity, affectionate admiration, and here he was racing northward away from them, running his heart out, reaching for the final ounce of his strength—with what purpose, to what end? He, a pure-blooded Indian, was running to bring down the badly mixed folk of Western Waters so that they might help a Scotch-Irishman beat the British Army out of the French-Spanish city of New Orleans!— The thought of that absurdity almost stopped him in his tracks.

Did it really matter at all, to what was deepest in him, whether the English or the Americans might "own" or "control" the Mississippi? From neither could his own people expect anything but contempt, poison, disease, treachery, and destruction. The pale-faces of both sides, and equally, were marauders, thieves, interlopers. Their roots were not

515

here—or, for that matter, anywhere. What did they know or care about the beauty of this western land, hallowed by ages of Indian toil and dream and worship? What to them was the sheer loveliness of the woman-breasted prairie, so chaste and holy now in the waiting winter, so passionate in spring-time with blood-root, blue-bell, fire-pink, violet, buttercup, and infinite wind-blown grasses? They came not to love but to rape. Crude, coarse-grained, and greedy to the core, they came to seize and trample.

British? Americans?—What choice between them? The British would try to burn New Orleans if they could not keep it for themselves, and the western settlers wanted to keep it merely for purposes of trade. At any time in the last thirty years most of them would gladly have abandoned their country's flag and gone over to any nation that could assure them a market at the River's mouth and free access to the sea.— Faugh! They smelt bad, these clutching whites. Tecumseh's only mistake about them had been that he preferred one group to the other.

For that mistake Tecumseh had paid with his life—but how of Sleeping Bear? His error had been much the same, and so had his punishment. His life also had been lost, or had never been fully his own. His inveterate clinging to the past, his feeling that the debt of gratitude could never be fully paid, had kept him from putting forth his whole power in any self-chosen direction. Even this present run had begun, really, far back there at Cochegan Rock when, realizing that he could do nothing more for Rebecca, he had set out to help her son. Even his tragic failure at Coosa had been due to his divided mind, his double loyalty. The Prophet had won that conflict because, though dreadfully wrong, he had struck with his total force.

And Sleeping Bear, by opposing the Prophet so powerfully, had forced his hand. In order to overcome the peace-talk at Coosa, the Prophet had been compelled to excite the Creeks to such a pitch of blood-lust that immediate war had been inevitable. The massacre at Fort Mims must have occurred long before Tecumseh and his British allies had intended—well over a year before the British could hope to act in support of the Creek uprising. If Sleeping Bear had not spoken at Coosa—if Tecumseh had simply won the sympathy and support of the Creeks, and had held that nation of warriors in check until the British were ready, until Jackson was far away and the militia of Western Waters was drained out of the whole territory—what a chance for Tecumseh!

And so Holdfast, thinking only as an Indian, saw that he himself had been the destroyer of the Creeks, and of the last hope of his people east of the River.

This was what had come of a mind divided against itself.

Ah, Samson Occum, that good old man, acting with great love and all the wisdom he had—it was he who had laid this doom of bewilderment and division upon the life he had cherished above all others. "Henceforth, I know," he had said—and the words rang as clearly now under the western stars as in Occum's little study with the open window looking out among scarlet maple leaves—"Henceforth, I know, there will be two natures struggling within you, two loves at strife, and your heart will be like a whirl where two winds meet."

Yes, and the ways he had followed, the intricate devious paths of his feet, had been like the trails in the swamps above Mobile, like the track of a snake in long grass. Oh, for a straight path, now, though narrow and lonely, going his way!

Thus again, as in the Cave of Hobbomok and on Mount Machimoodus, the exhaustion of the man's bodily strength cleared his mind. Out of Weariness Well he dipped up a deeper wisdom than the buckets of common and comfortable living could have reached. He was breaking free from old trammels. This run would pay his debt in full to the white man's world. Take it then, Nathan Hale, dead at twenty-one, you who thought that you had only one life to give for your country. Father and Mother Chester, Rebecca, take it, although you do not need it now and will never know that it was given. As for "carrying weight," there is a people who do need it, and know they do, very much.

"Come back sometime, Sleeping Bear! Big runner, big story-teller—very damn big man!"

The fog hung thick about him when he awoke on that last morning. His strength was all but gone. Again and again, starting out, he stumbled and came near to falling head-long. His thoughts were wild and fantastic. There were voices calling in which he could not believe. They called to him in English. There were moving forms with white frozen faces, their gaze averted, that could not be real. From far behind him shrilled a girl's voice: "Can't I run fast?"—Well, apparently not fast or far enough. That voice died away.

Other visions came, more vivid and earthy. There came the whirl of smoke on November mornings out of Mohegan wigwam-tops into

517

bare oak-branches. He saw the soaked half-sunken crimson of cranberries down in the bog by Mamecoke, and goose-arrows cronking over.
Cochegan, Gungywamp, Manetock Hill rose before him, with the
tiny dance of sand-grains under the maiden-hair fern, ancient Larrabee
Oak, and King Uncas sitting lordly by the Pequot Council Stones considering how to meet and beat white guile with red.

The fog shrank away as the sun climbed, uncovering a land of
dreamy horizons arched by a sky of majestic breadth and height. Ever
larger and more exalted the day grew as he ran on, catching his second
wind and settling into his Indian pace. More luring and lovely at every
mile was the look of the deep-bosomed swales and the sweeps of up-
land stripping bare of the raveled fog like a woman who waits in the
dawn by a cold dim water.

At noon he stopped and built him a fire on the summit of an Indian
mound. Into it he emptied all the contents of his clam-shell. Then, after
loading the farther end of his blanket with stones, he faced eastward
and sent three clouds of smoke into the blue. When the last cloud had
disappeared he called in a great voice: "Go—and God bless you!"

New strength poured along his veins as he raced northward. "Can't
we run fast!" the Beloved Woman seemed to say on the hard thirty
miles beyond Duck River. King Uncas joined them at Harpeth River,
and then came his stalwart sons, Owaneco and Attawanhood. Tecumseh
the Meteor and Tenkswatawa the Prophet lived again like a glory in
his blood. As though he were riding the breath of those strong brothers,
he felt himself blown like a feather along the trace. Their cries of exultation were in the wind that sang past his ears. Their joy in the hunt
and the war-path, their gladness at home-coming, their passion for
freedom, was beaten out, as he ran, on the finger-drum of his heart.
He was a people united, a people of one mind and will, running now
one way, toward home.

The rocky height of Cedar Knob came into view, with Napier's two-
story house among the trees, Judge McNairy's mansion, and the path to
Sulphur Springs. The Cumberland River was slowly unloosening into
the western woods its coils of sunset gold.

As the sun dipped down he rounded the curve near Tate's mansion.
Candles shone already in young Robertson's windows and in McKane's.
There was a stench in the air of gun-smithies and mills. The clat-
ter of George Poyzer's machine-shop jarred the evening calm. Hogs

wallowed in the mud of the road. A paunchy store-keeper driving down Market Street nudged his fat wife so that she too might stare at the great gaunt man racing by. A drunkard lay prone on the court-house steps. Along the porch of Talbot's tavern a dozen loafers were draped in as many attitudes of extreme boredom. Two or three of them called out to him as he ran by.

General Carroll would be at supper now in Parker's Nashville Tavern across the square. Past the jail he ran, the stocks, the whipping-post. He took the tavern steps at a bound, burst through the door into the dark hall, and went on, groping as though blind.

Carroll looked up, surprised, and then with an expression of concern, "What is it, Holdfast?" said he, rising so abruptly that his chair fell on its back. He was dressed, as always, in the latest Philadelphia fashion, and wiped his mouth as he came forward with a dainty handkerchief. His lieutenants rose also and crowded round him to read Jackson's letter over his shoulder.

"But, good God," said one of them, "how can we start at once? How can he expect us to be in N' Orleans in five weeks?"

"Andy must think sojers grow on trees!" exclaimed another. "Or mebbe he thinks they got wings!"

Holdfast suddenly felt very tired. The room seemed to be going black. He leaned forward against the table, supporting himself by his out-spread fingers. Even with that support he tottered a little.

"He ought to know it's a thousand miles by the Trace, and Coffee's taken all the good hosses."

There was a fire burning on the hearth, and a huge buffalo-robe was spread before it. That much Holdfast could still see. He began to edge his way round the table, leaning heavily as he went.

"If we try to march 'em down when we do get 'em, we'll meet the British half-way, comin' up."

The buffalo-robe was soft and warm. His long narrow blanket made a good pillow.

"Until right now, how 'n hell 'd we know if he wanted 'em at Pensacola, at Mobile, or N' Orleans?"

"Yeah. Or *when* he wanted 'em?"

The words came as though from a huge distance. What were those things: hosses, British, N' Orleans, the River, the Trace?—Well, no matter now.

"But, great Heaven!" Carroll suddenly burst out, "General Jackson wrote this letter on the seventh, and here we are on the night o' the twelfth. D' you see what that means, gentlemen? Holdfast Gaines must have made it from Mobile—and that's a good six hundred miles for a runner—in . . . in five days!"

"Six days and . . . and some nights," murmured Holdfast on the verge of sleep, drawing half of the buffalo-robe across him. "I tried to do it in five but I . . . we . . . we couldn't.—You may go."

SHOULDER ARMS!

"Dunno whut Andy's a-gwineter say when he sees us a-comin' daown afloat thisaway," said Corporal McCuskey. "'T ain't 'cordin' ter army rules an' reg'lations. Not by no means, 'tain't."

"If I know Andy Jackson," Holdfast assured the little man, "he'll be more interested in our arrival than in how we get there."

"I shore hope ye're right, Mr. Gaines, 'cause when Andy gits a tantrum he do cuss like a hoss a-kickin'. He c'n chune 'er up consid'able when he's ashy."

"Aw," said Sergeant Mansker, "course Andy *is* a rale ole tore-daown name-caller, times, but ye don' heve no call ter be 'feared on 'im, Jake. 'T ain't li'l shoats the likes o' you he cusses much. Prob'ly he wouldn't take no notice iffen ye war a-settin' right spang o' the bump of 's nose."

"Wal, mebbe so; an' hit's a comfortin' thought.—I s'pose Andy's cussed you quite a lot, hain't he, Sergeant?"

"Oh, more 'r less, naow an' then. But a man cain't raly call it sw'arin'. He don't never take the name o' the Lord *in vain,* as the preacher says. Not by no means. He jest—wal, he jest kinder explains to the Lord whut Andy thinks the Lord oughter take an' do 'baouten whutever 'tis."

"H'm. Yeah. Ketch the differ.—An' 'baout floatin' daown . . . "

"Wal, hell, iffen 'Nited States don't pervide no hosses then 'Nited States M'litia cain't ride on 'em. Stands ter reason."

"So it do. You tell 'im that, Sergeant.—An', by gum, I druther walk the hull way on my own hind feet 'n try to straddle a hoss."

"Then I s'pose ye war purty damn glad when ole Snag faound these hyar fifty flat-boats fer us."

"Axin' yer pardon, 'twarn't the Snag faound 'em. 'Twar Divine

520

Providence pervided 'em, so's naow we-uns gwineter be jes' like to hum all the way daown."

"Yeah—takin' aour own haousen 'long with us like a slew-full o' gawdam mud-turkles!—Wal, keep yer ha'r on naow, li'l Corp'ral."

Whether Jackson liked the method of conveyance or not, General William Carroll had performed something like a miracle, Holdfast knew, during the five days and nights of furious toil in which he had gathered up these thousands from the hills, the prairie, the rivers, the creeks, the forest, and had herded them down to the Cumberland. To be sure they were mostly raw and boyish, with no uniforms, no military discipline, and little knowledge of how to care for themselves away from home. People had taken to calling them "squirrel-hunters" back in Nashville, but hardly one in three would have been able to bring down a squirrel even if he had something to shoot with. Knowing Natchez Trace as he did, Holdfast shivered to think what would have happened to them along those miles of winter, camping out in the cold, wet all day and night, half-starved, foot-sore, chill-blained, tattered, and unarmed. On the flat-boats they could at least be drilled a little. There was a possibility that they might be fed. If another miracle should occur, even weapons of some sort might be found.

It was a problem over which Holdfast pondered long that the young militiamen of Kentucky and Tennessee should have come in with hardly more than one fire-arm to three of them. This puzzled him because he knew how short a time had passed since every land-looker venturing into Western Waters had considered, correctly, that a rifle was more necessary than breeches. And he found, too, that most of the weapons they brought in were thirty or more years old. Deckards, Drippards, Allbrights, Gresheims, and Gougers of the seventeen-eighties they were, chiefly, brought from Pennsylvania down the Ohio or over Blue Ridge by the fathers and grandfathers of the present owners. He came across two or three rifles that Russell Bean had made back in Jonesboro when that town had been no more than a straggle of cabins and huts. Queer old contraptions they were, and no kin to the sleek long-shooters that Bean and Perthy were making now.

But little by little, moving among the men and talking here and there, Holdfast began to see that there was no reason why they should be so concerned with the latest tools of slaughter as their fathers had necessarily been. Few of them had ever heard a war-whoop or the howl of the timber-wolf. It was no longer possible for them to live on the

521

turkey, the deer, the bear, and the buffalo. They were farmers, really, and came nearest to hunting when they went out with bags and baskets to knock a few bushels of passenger-pigeons out of the poplar trees. What they wanted of fire-arms, chiefly, was to keep the hawks from the hen-runs, the crows from the corn-field, and rats from the barn.

These young sowers of seed, then, were taking the place of the old winterers, the long-hunters and trappers, the bearded and bedraggled wilderness men who had lived with danger for wife, the horizon for lure, and freedom for daily wage. The Manskers, Robertsons, Donelsons, Girtys, and Adairs had finished their stint and were gone, with their rifle-guns. Daniel Boone had long since crossed the River, taking "Tick-Licker" with him, and soon the rifle-builders like Russell Bean who knew how to make such rifles would follow. Masters of a craft that was half an art, exact and incorruptible, refusing to hasten, doing the whole honest job with their own hands and signing it when done with sober pride, never turning out two weapons alike, striving always to transcend themselves—Holdfast saw with a pang that such men would get little honor and less worldly reward round that sharp corner of American time which lay just ahead.

How would this change affect Perthy, once Bean's apprentice and now a master rifle-builder with his own shop and trade?

In the sheer happiness of being with Perthy again Holdfast found a sufficient reason, apart from his promise to Jackson, for accompanying the expedition to New Orleans. And here would be a chance of answering, one way or the other, the doubts he had often felt about the method—to call it that!—of Perthy's up-bringing. How had they worked out in character and attainment, those years of wandering with a lonely and homeless man?

Perthy was now happily married, a father, and a respected citizen of Nashville. He had grown up into a self-reliant, utterly fearless manhood. He had seen his America through and through, and had associated on terms of respectful equality with the barbarians of forest and plain and also with persons of high cultivation. He stood on his own legs, thought his own thoughts, and spoke—without stammering when he wished to—for himself. He put first things first, and held them there.—Did it seem probable that even he would have grown so straight and clean in the atmosphere of New England's money-minded respectability? Could he have escaped the coarsening and shallowing influences that had worked so sad a change even in Rebecca? Had the young men at Yale College, placidly lapping up their social and political prejudices from the Reverend Timothy Dwight, learned so much as he about what it meant to be an American?

Perthy was good to the core, and he was also strong. Though quiet in demeanor until thoroughly aroused, he was by no means the sort of person with whom sensible people took liberties. His ability as a rifle-builder and his expert marksmanship commanded respect wherever he went, and he was famous throughout Western Waters for his phenomenal skill at throwing a knife. If Perthy had a serious fault it was the boyish notion, deeply ingrained in his childhood and never outgrown, that he must, and would, some day find and kill a certain man. His whole life, indeed, had been slightly warped from its natural bent by that persistent idea. Holdfast had done what he could, in the old days, to change it, but now it had to be accepted.

Many times a day, as the little chance-gathered army floated down the Cumberland and into the Ohio, Holdfast gazed at Perthy with a fond paternal pride. This, he knew, might well be his last chance of seeing the man who had been, and still was, as dear to him as a son of his own body. For hours at a time he sat in the sun and watched Perthy throwing his knife from twenty feet away into a three-inch circle he had drawn on the wall of the deck-house. He watched as though fascinated by the power and the beauty, the taut, alert, position, the single short forward sweep of the right arm from behind the right shoulder, the glitter of the steel through the sunny air—and something vaguely symbolic, too, in the figure of a man armed and ready and perfectly trained to send back an instantaneous answer into the eye of evil.

At this one beloved task, Holdfast decided, he had not failed. In one respect he really had "carried weight." Like the Saint Christopher of his vision on Mount Machimoodus, he had borne a child on his shoulders across the torrent of the world's danger and wickedness.

The fleet grew day by day. Shortly after reaching the Ohio it overtook and absorbed a number of farm-boats laden with provisions and commanded by the popular and highly pugnacious keeler whom everyone knew, at least by reputation, as "the Snag." Boredom and low spirits could not live in this man's company. Although they were often wet, cold, and weary, the men began to see that with such abundant food and drink as the farm-boats had brought and with the store of entertainment which the Snag always carried under his flopping hat, they were in for a good time.

Moreover, they were learning the elements of military discipline. Looking back over the long line of boats at any time of day one saw that on most of them half the men were pulling at the sweeps while the others were going through ludicrously cramped maneuvers. Their intentions, one could not fail to see, were good, and they were intelligent enough to realize that a few days of preparation, before they went up against the troops that had recently beaten Napoleon, would not be amiss. Perhaps the main trouble was that the "arms" they so vigorously shouldered and presented were, for the most part, hickory sticks and wands of willow.

Rifles! From where in hell or heaven were they to rise or fall? There might be a few at Natchez, but not enough. Even smooth-bores such as the Regulars carried would be something. They would go off. They made a noise and frightened people. Smooth-bores would be better in several ways than willow wands.

"Main part o' thisheer war's a-gwineter be," said one of the older men to Holdfast, "we gotter grab their muskits away from the British afore we begin ter fight 'em."

"Hillo, the fleet!"

It was a thin, far hail from a keel-boat moored at the end of a willow-island.

Holdfast, looking up, recognized the long rifle and keg of fire-water painted on the side of her deck-house. He rose and called through his cupped hands: "Hillo! *Pride o' the West!*"

This was good luck. He had hoped and expected to find Russell Bean somewhere on the River, but not so soon.

At length, after a minute of silent floating, the voice came again, more clearly: "Hillo, ye gloomy ol' med'cine-man! Whut ye doin' on thet 'ar mud-scaow? Jump acrost hyar an' set daown whar ye belongst."

"Hillo, Russ Bean," yelled the Snag. "Haow many rifle-guns ye got over thar?"

"Two three, mebbe. How many ye want?"

"Wal, say three thaousan', fer a starter."

"Right smart of a turkey-shoot ye fellers a-fixin' fer.—An' who's a-payin' fer them shootin'-irons?"

524

"Feller by name o' Andy Jackson. He's got a mad on, Andy hez!"

"Who with this time?"

"British army an' navy. He's a-goin' ter lick 'em aout o' N'orlins."

"You fellers goin' daown to help 'im?"

"Help 'im! Hell, we'll do it all, iffen we git suthin' ter shoot with."

"Roy!" Bean shouted through the door-way of the deck-house. "Fire up the forge an' call the boys!"

" 'Ten-SHUN! . . . Shoulder ARMS! . . . MARCH! . . . HALT!
—Damn it, fellers, don't tromp so nigh the aidge! Ye won't be no good fer Andy iffen ye all comes in draownded!"

From the *Pride* came the day-long clink-a-clank of a dozen hammers beating out rifle-barrels and locks, occasionally interrupted by Bean's powerful voice singing:

> How wonderful, how glorious, how marvelous I am!
> How wonderful it is to be me!

Bean, Perthy, and the men might make fifteen or twenty rifles on the way down if they all kept sober, and that would be a great help. Meanwhile the militiamen, when they were not drilling or at the sweeps, whittled rifle-stocks from bird's-eye maple, ash, curly cherry, and black walnut.

Some reaches of the River, the Snag told them, were safe enough for night travel; and when they came to one of these all hands would be at the sweeps or watching out for sand-banks, planters, and sawyers. But mostly they tied up for the night, sang their songs round the fires built in sand-heaps on the deck-house roofs, told their stories, and whittled rifle-stocks.

They were three thousand men bound together by a common purpose—or, rather, a good many more, when the crews of the boats that had joined them were added. In all there were more than eighty boats by the time they were half-way down. Looking back from the deck of the *Pride* at night, Holdfast could see a long winding procession of fires. They made a ruddy five-mile-long serpent of light. And the songs that rose from the fires had the pathos of all human speech confronting the unknown. Something there was in the rollicking words and dauntless tunes that snatched at the heart-strings and twanged them.

The men had little enough to say about patriotism or saving the country. It was not clear that they felt any special hatred for the British. The main thing seemed to be that they were having a good time.

Coming mostly from lonely farms and woodland cabins, they were keenly enjoying the songs, the tales, the banter, and the comradeship of the hugest gathering they had ever seen. Most of them would probably have agreed that this expedition was better than a camp-meeting— partly in the respect that there were no women about, partly that it was larger and longer in duration and somewhat more uproarious, with more drink going round, but perhaps chiefly because there was good prospect of a glorious scuffle and killing-bee at the end.

Holdfast, Perthy, and Bean, as privileged scouts, often went ashore in the evenings, or visited from boat to boat. Once again they listened to fragments of old ballads at the different fires, and tales handed down in ever-changing versions from the earliest camp-fires of wandering men.

On the second boat up-river from the *Pride,* one evening, they heard a drawling voice: "—So thar wuz Zeke up the tree, thar wuz me in thet big hole daown 'side hit, an' thar wuz thet 'ar fee-rocious bellerin' devil of a bull a-prancin' an' a-tearin' all raound us. Ev'y oncet in a spell the bull 'd lose int'rust an' go 'way, an' then Zeke he'd start ter climb daown an' I'd come up outen my hole an' the bull 'd come a-tearin back, tossin' sile.—Wal, bime-by, Zeke he's gittin' kinder oneasy, an' he yells aout ter me: 'Damn yer ogly picter, Ezry,' sezee, 'why 'n hell,' he says, 'kaincher stop in thet hole a spell so's I kin git daown outen this consarned tree? They's *wasps* in this tree!' he says. 'Me stay in thisheer hole nothin', I says back to 'im. 'They's a *b'ar* in this hole!' "

And then, moving on a little, they heard at another fire the end of another equally ancient tale: "—Sure, an' 't were a foine-lookin' hoss as a man c'd wish to see. 'They's on'y jes' the wan thing ye hev ter look out afther, Mr. McJunkin,' says the farmer to 'im, 'an I wudden't wish to chate ye. Niver let 'm git near eggs, fer he do set on eggs fer wakes at a toime when he gits the chancet. Eggs is his wan wake pint. He must be discinded from a hin.'—Wal, an' so Mr. McJunkin don't think thet's too damn ser'ous an' so he buys 'm the hoss an' rides away on 'm. But afther a shpell back he comes agin ter the farmer, dhrippin' wet an' tearin' mad. 'Here, you,' he yells out, 'does hins lay eggs in brrooks?' he says. 'Becase thet devil-begotten hoss is a-coolin' his bum in the brrook down thar, an' ter budge 'm away I cinnot.'—'Och! Howly Mary!' the farmer says, 'I clane fergetted ter tell ye. He sets on fish too!' "

Very late one night, when the fire on *The Pride of the West* had

526

sunk to a few embers, there came on board an old trapper in black and draggled buck-skins. He had been an Indian fighter also, and said that he had been out with Andy Jackson on some unspecified campaign. About that hero he told a simple tale in which a few elements of fact were woven together by a fond creative fancy.

"—Wal," said he, "an' so one evenin' 'long 'baout bat-time I war prospectin' 'raoun' arter 'gater-tail an' I seed thisheer li'l light 'way off through the canes, an' I crep' up an' thar was a hut o' bark, an' I went scroochin' daown like an Injun ontwell I come right up whar the light war shinin' through a crack so's I c'd see through, an' by the great horn spoon thar set Old Hick'ry hisself, scribblin' away at a kinder bench the boys 'd stuck up fer 'im out o' logs. His left arm war in a dirty sling so's he hed ter put a chunk o' wood on the paper ter hold it daown, an' he hadn't slep' fer a month or washed fer a year by the looks an' his long red hairs war scragglin' inter 's eyes an' the wrinkles in 's face war like ole 'gater-tracks in the mud an' he looked ter be 'baout five hunnerd year ole at the least an' ogly ez everlastin' hell."

The trapper, evidently a sensitive and well-mannered person, walked to the side of the keeler and spat, incisively, into the water.

"An' so," said he, returning, "thar he sot, wi' the candlewood sputterin' yaller an' the flitter-moths an' skeeters aouten the swamp a-flickerin' raound 'im, an' he hed in thar with 'im thet 'ar li'l faoust-dog ez some folks calls 'Source o' the Miss'sip' an' likewise 'Father o' Waters,' but course thet ain't right an' his real name is 'Wash the Fourth.' Annyhaow, thar war thet faoust-dog a-lookin' up at 'im wi' glory-be in his eyes like he war prob'ly the Lord God A'mighty at the very least, an' Ole Hick'ry screws up his face whilst he's a-writin' so 's a blind man c'd see he druther march a thaousan' mile 'n write one letter, an' from time ter time he'd mutter suthin' like 'Ye gawd-fersaken by-blow of a she-male dog without no morals!' or tarms to thet effeck, by which words I c'd make aout he must be writin' ter some pol'tician or mebbe a banker back East, but arter while he throws daown the ink-feather an' stretches up his one good arm an' right thar he sees the faoust-dog. An' so Ole Hick'ry he scrooches daown an' looks at thet 'ar dog a long time, sad an' solemn, an' fin'ly he says: 'Wash,' he says with a sigh, 'why in the 'tarnal don't ye hev the dog-sense fer ter go draound yerself?' he says.

"An' then o' course whilst Ole Hick'ry's a-talkin' to 'im thet dog jest thumps the graound with his pore ole chawed-off tail an' pricks

527

up his years—whut thar is lef' of 'em—an' smiles back at Ole Hick'ry like he war 'baout ter enter the Kindom o' Heaven."

Once again the trapper walked to the side and spat.

"But Ole Hick'ry he goes on: 'Doncher unnerstan', Wash,' he says, 'thet ye ain't nothin' but jest a col'ny o' lice an' fleas an' scabs an' diseases whut's trapesin' 'raoun' with a no-'caount failure of a lonesome man? Why the hell doncher end it all, Wash, afore a water-moccasin gits yeh, or mebbe a pack o' wolves tears yeh inter li'l bits some night when I ain't 'raound?'"

Here the narrator paused to contemplate the picture in the mind which he had himself created.—"Wal," he then continued, "Wash the Fourth he don't say much, 'cep'n' with his tail; an' fack is mebbe he didn't git the hull idear, seein' ez he ain't so strong in the intellecks ez he be in the heart. Annyhaow, Ole Hick'ry he snatches up thet 'ar ole hoss-pistol whut allus lays on table when he's a-writin' letters—same one he kilt Chuck Dickinson with—an' p'ints it inter the li'l faoust-dog's year. 'Hyar,' he says, 'haow 'd thet do yeh?' sezee. 'Don't ye corn-sider, Wash, ez thet 'd be the ack of a friend whut's ben up an' daown an' knows whut the world is made of?—Whut say, Wash?'

"Wal, an' then I looks daown at the dog, an' I wish ter remark thet with all o' his scabs an' scratches an' whar he 'd tore the ha'r off hopin' mebbe ter ketch an' kill jes' one o' his nation o' fleas, he war the mos' beautifulles' objick these ole eyes ever see. Fust he lookd at thet 'ar hoss-pistol an' then at Andy so's ter say 'Jes' whut ye think best, Master'—an' be damned iffen they warn't a light o' love in 's eyes like he war one o' God's blessed angels.

"But right thar war the most s'prisin' thing. Ole Hick'ry put the pistol back on table, an' I wish ter drap daid iffen they warn't thet same light in his eyes too, an' he says, like he war in church: 'So,' he says, 'it's love is it, Wash? So thet's whut keeps yeh a-staggerin' on through the swamps an' briars an' all the piz'nous varmints o' thisheer so-called world!'

"An' then Wash, he thumps the graound some more with the stump of 's tail, the which I tuk ter be his way o' sayin': 'But hell, I cain't see nothin' much wrong with a world whut's got Ole Hick'ry in it.'—An' 'baout thet time I crope away an' lef' 'em thar, 'cause I didn't seem ter b'long."

Hardly had the old trapper returned, for the third time, from the rail when one of Bean's workmen began to pluck, on a five-string banjo, the chords of a ballad-tune. "I'll give yeh," the player said, "the

528

ole ballet of 'Andy an' Charlie,' an' y' all c'n come in on the chorus."
Then, resting the neck of his instrument against his left shoulder and
looking up at the stars, he sang:

Come listen to my story
  O' the Dark an' Bloody Land
Whar Andy Jackson rode one day
  An' thar did take his stand.
"Walk aout hyar, Charlie Dickinson,
  An' load an' fire," he said.
"Fer slander'n' my wife I'll take yer life
  If ye shoot me through the head."

O tum tee dee I day-dee,
  O tum tee dee I day,
Upon thet Dark an' Bloody Graound
  Thet's whut I heerd 'im say.

So Charlie come an' stood thar,
  An' a crack dead-shot was he,
Could bring daown with one bullet
  A high an' hustlin' bee.
"Git ye ready, Andy Jackson,
  From this world to depart.
I don't waste lead on no man's head;
  I shoot 'im through the heart."

They measured off eight paces
  An' Charlie he fired fust,
When up from Andy's blue frock-coat
  Thar come a puff o' dust;
But Andy stood thar grinnin'
  Like 's if he felt no pain.
"Ye cain't hurt me with lead," sezee,
  "If ye shoot me through the brain."

"Oh, my God! Hev I missed 'im?"
  "Git back thar whar ye b'long
An' take yer turn at dyin' naow!"
  Says Andy high an' strong.
"Make ready, Charlie Dickinson,
  To spend this night in hell."
He cocked an' aimed. His pistol flamed.
  Pore Charlie reeled, an' fell.

529

"But Andy! Andy Jackson!
    Yer boots is full o' blood!"
"Why, so they be!—but I c'n git
    Some others jest ez good.
My blood is cheaper 'n the honor
    O' my wife's name," he said,
"An I'd a-killt thet man o' guilt
    If he'd shot me through the head."

O tum tee dee I day-dee,
    O tum tee dee I day,
Upon thet Dark an' Bloody Graound
    Thet's whut I heerd 'im say.

A dozen or more canoes were pulled up on the bank below the Choctaw town in which Parson Blandison was spending his declining years. As the *Pride* floated closer Holdfast could make out that they were laden with Indian goods—piles of furs, war-bonnets, garments of white buck-skin, beaded moccasins, richly ornamented pipes, and scalps by the score stretched on twiggen hoops and gaudily painted. The canoes were guarded by white men, heavily armed, in English clothes.

"Ever see those fellows before?" Holdfast asked the Snag. He spoke softly, for the ripple of the *Pride* was now washing among the canoes themselves, and the guards were staring.

"Naw.—An' I hain't lost much, nuther."

"Them goods ain't Choctaw," said Bean. "They're Creek, Cherokee, Chickasaw, Seminole—they're the loot of all the Injun nations!"

"I see a pipe in that third canoe that I've smoked somewhere myself," said Holdfast. "Why—it's New River's!—Well, we have to stop here anyhow. Let's tie up at the next willow and leave a strong guard on board."

They found the village strangely quiet. The fire in the central square was burning low, the bark houses were empty, and there was not even a squaw to be seen. But then, just as he was about to call out, Holdfast caught a glimpse through the trees of a crowd of Indians gathered up there to the northward where the Parson lived beside a little stream. They were huddled together—men, women, and even young children —all very still, absorbed in whatever was going on at the center of the ring they made.

Was the Parson dying?—for Holdfast could think of nothing else that would draw such a congregation of his friends and admirers. But this crowd was much larger than the town by itself could turn out. Besides the Choctaws there were Cherokees, Creeks and Seminoles, even Chickasaws! In all his years among the tribes Holdfast had never seen such a gathering of old and traditional enemies. This was the very kind of thing that he had hoped and striven for, vainly.

And the Parson was not dying. Far from it! Resplendent in his best white buck-skins—a gift of the Beloved Woman—and with his neatly curled and powdered bob-wig on his head, he was sitting cross-legged on an Indian blanket from the far western plains and playing cards with a handsome young man dressed in the height of the London fashion. He was so absorbed in his game that when Holdfast sat down near the blanket he made no sign of recognition.

Heaps of Indian wealth and finery lay beside the two gamblers; and some of these things, unlike those in the canoe, were Choctaw.

Rather disconsolate the two or three hundred Indians from distant tribes were looking. They hardly glanced at the in-coming white men, and only a few appeared to realize that this was Sleeping Bear, no less. Their dark eyes were fixed upon the two Englishmen and the colored cards with strange pictures.

One could see at a glance what was happening, and had happened. The Englishman, coming up the River and the Trace, had plundered the tribes, near and far, on his way. He had done extremely well by himself. The loot in the canoes and here on the ground would be worth many thousands of dollars at Detroit, not to mention the poisonous rumors and incitements to strife which he had probably spread as he came. It was clear, also, that the Indians from a distance had followed their lost property in the hope that somewhere, somehow, the gambler would meet his match. And now the whole crowd was held breathless by the hope that this exceedingly ancient man whom the Choctaws revered—he with the miraculous white scalp which he could don and doff at will, the scalp that brought rain and averted the lightning—might have an even stronger medicine than that of the young gambler for controlling the little pictured cards.

The young Englishman did not look happy. He was not quite sober, and his hands trembled somewhat.

"No," the Parson was saying, "Lord Byron writes well—remarkably well for so young a man—but he will never reach the level of Pope.—You know him?"

531

"Three cards, if you please. I have seen him, only. We do not frequent the same clubs. He is a handsome man, and highly successful with women, though lame."

"Ah, a pity! I knew his grandfather, the vice-admiral. I raise you three. 'Foul-weather Jack,' we used to call him. The fact is that the Honorable John Byron and I went around the Horn together."

"Round the Horn!"

"Yes. Under Anson. I raise you back seven pebbles."

"But, sir . . ."

"Do you wish to see my cards?"

"Very well, I'll see them. I have two pair."

"Three of a kind."

"But, sir, with Commodore Anson! That was a long time ago."

"Quite. My deal."

"You are not, by any chance, the chaplain who wrote a very eloquent account of that voyage!"

"That account—which I am glad to hear you call 'eloquent'—has been attributed, rightly or wrongly, to a man by the name of Walter.— Still, as Shakespeare's Jacques somewhere remarks, 'One man in his time plays many parts.'"

"I trust you will pardon a personal remark, Mr.—ah—shall I say Reverend Walter?"

"You may call me 'The Hair,' if you please."

"Well, sir, I will if I can. Mr. The Hair, I was merely going to say that I greatly admire your wig."

"You show your good taste, sir. But allow me to add, to discourage unwarranted expectations, that I never wager my wig. Men may cheat me of my raiment, my horse, and my teeth, but this wig and my copy of Horace are to be buried with me.—Two pair."

"A pair of deuces.—I should think that wig might have considerable value as—well, as a curiosity, as an example of what is called 'the antique.'"

"Conservative speakers in my day used to say 'the antic.' In fact, I think I have heard that pronunciation even from Dr. Johnson."

"You knew him, Mr. . . . ?"

"Oh, yes. I've drunk tea with the Doctor many's the time, both in Gough Square and when he came up to Oxford in his old age for his degree.—However, I raise you ten pebbles, sir."

"I'll see you.—Well, your hand again, Mr. The Hair. You seem to

532

be doing remarkably well at a game which, you tell me, you have never played before."

"Ah, sir, it is such a simple, not to say a barbarian game! One learns it in a moment. I am glad that I did not devote the best years of my manhood to considerations so—ah—so elementary. Poker would have stunted my intellectual development. I'll draw one card if you please."

"It is an American game, Mr. The Hair, and America is a crude young country, wholly given over to elementary considerations. My hand, for once."

"My deal. Yes, I recall that I once held some such opinion; but let us not forget that *caelum, non animum mutant, qui trans mare currunt*."

"You mean . . . ?"

"Surely, in speaking to a gentleman, I need not translate one of the most familiar of Latin tags. I allowed myself to quote it merely to remind you that when we English discern this or that fault in America we ought to know where it comes from."

"From England?"

"Nine times out of ten.—And, of course, in our judging of others we are always most severe with those defects which we secretly know to be our own."

"Would you say that we English are elementary?"

"To a childish degree.—Consider, sir, how easily we are deceived, hoodwinked, and led by the nose when we sit down to games of chance —even simple ones, such as poker!"

"Ah, some of us, perhaps," replied the young Englishman in an unsteady voice. "But about your wig, sir. Of course one sees a few wigs in London nowadays, but none like yours.—Your hand."

"No, sir, I should think not. Like all the other habiliments of the gentleman, such as knee-breeches, wigs died of the French Revolution. We live in an age of sans-culottes and slatterns. *Damnosa quid non imminuit dies?*"

"Am I to understand that your wig antedates the French Revolution?"

"I won this wig, sir, from Lord Throckmorton in a game of chance at White's Coffee House in 1765. He had won it from Beau Nash, then an old man, at the Cocoa Tree, I think in '56. Nash had it from Nick the Wringer at the Old Cock Tavern, Temple Bar, in '31. Nick, in turn, got it from Jack Sheppard, the most renowned of England's highwaymen, at Tyburn Tree in 1724, now ninety years ago.—And so there you have the total history of my wig, so far as it has come to my knowledge. Three of a kind."

The younger man did not quite suppress an audible sigh. "Well, your hand again, Mr. The Hair," said he. "I think I have never before seen such marvelous—shall I say 'luck?'"

"Only say that the Goddess Fortuna, whom I have faithfully worshipped for thrice your years, is smiling over my shoulder."

"I see.—But why do you not say from whom Jack Sheppard stole the wig?"

"'Stole,' do you say? Why, sir, Jack never *stole* anything. He was a highwayman, a bandit—or, as Jack Falstaff so precisely put it, a 'gentleman of the shade,' a 'minion of the moon.' Besides that, Jack grew this hair himself. Probably it was the only valuable thing of his own production that he possessed at the time of his sudden and painful departure.—Well, just before the final ceremony, Nick the Wringer cut it off and took it as his perquisite, solemnly assuring Jack that it would be treated with due respect. Nick had it done into a wig by the best perruquier in London—an artist whose name I would give you if it lived in my memory. I raise you back three.—By the way, how is White's nowadays?"

"Bad, sir. These damned wars have taken the money out of gentlemen's pockets and put it into factories. Play is no longer what it must have been in your time. I raise you back five."

"I feared not. More and more abandoned by gentlemen I hear it is, and taken up by the sort of persons whom I believe you now call 'business men.' Ichabod! Ichabod! I raise you back ten pebbles."

"I raise you ten, Mr. The Hair."

"And I, discerning a sudden effulgence of the Goddess Fortuna's smile, shall raise you—allow me to consider . . . I raise you one hundred pebbles."

"A hundred!" exclaimed the young man, going pale about the mouth. "One hundred, did you say?"

"I said one hundred rather than a thousand only because I suddenly recalled a remark made, or perhaps written, by my friend the Reverend Laurence Sterne. It was something about tempering the wind unto the shorn lamb."

"But that means one hundred pounds!"

"Exactly.—Pounds sterling, of course. Would you care to raise me?"

"I'll see you!" said the young man, counting out his pebbles and

534

casting them into the earthen pot with hands that trembled violently. "Four kings!"

"A royal flush," responded the Parson, and he displayed his cards with a slight flourish.

"By Gad, sir! But . . . but I have never seen two such hands meet at poker before!"

"No? Well, live and learn. Gamaliel, three, six."

"But, sir, this seems to involve the presence of a fifth king in the pack!"

"Ah, you have observed that, have you? And so, as it happens, have I. It is the sort of consideration which I have referred to as—ah—elementary."

"Yes. Quite."

"But would you care to suggest how this phenomenon may have occurred?"

"I hesitate to . . ."

"Your hesitation is natural, sir, considering that you are yourself so *integer vitae, scelerisque purus.*"

The old man paused a moment, letting this sink in, before he continued: "On the whole, then, perhaps we had better recall that poker is a game of chance in which anything may happen.—Shall we—ah—leave it at that?"

The young man discovered, upon an instantaneous examination, that Mr. The Hair's eyes were boring into him like two gimlets. There was no hint of hesitation in those old eyes, no confession of weakness or of guile, nothing but pure inquiry. For another second or two the young man's glance took in the circle of Indians, all of them profoundly interested although somewhat mystified. He had seen before that most of them were armed with knives and tomahawks. What he had not previously observed was the astonishing face and figure of the newcomer sitting perfectly still a few feet from the blanket and regarding him steadily with eyes that glowed and burned.

The young Englishman's own eyes fell. "Your hand," said he.—"It is a hand I shall long remember. And I shall never cease to—ah—to admire the way you played it."

"Many thanks! My deal.—And so you have come over here to escape the business man and to see whether there are any gentlemen left. You have done well. The American Indians are the last gentlemen surviving in the western world. That, indeed, is why you find me here, for I also may say 'odi profanum volgus, et arceo.' "

535

Such a speech, an hour or two earlier, would have amused the young Englishman. At first he had taken his antagonist to be just another white derelict living among the tribes because he could not make an easy livelihood elsewhere, but now for some time he had been reconsidering that opinion. His respect had grown with almost every hand. He had been amazed at the cards this octogenarian somehow managed to get hold of, and yet had been unable to catch him in any demonstrable trickery. Names of famous and all but fabulous old gamesters kept coming to his mind: Jack Greene, who had died by his own hand; Sir Horace Blaine, who died in a mad-house, and even that legendary Parson Blandison who had disappeared from the gaming tables, no one knew whither or precisely why, many years before the young man was born.

Gradually, as the brief winter afternoon wore by, his pile of pebbles dwindled. If he won eight or ten by one hand it was only to lose perhaps twice as many by the next two or three. He grew bewildered, and lost his sense of what a given set of cards should be worth. Mr. The Hair's enigmatic old face, so subtly wrinkled, so deeply acquainted with the ways of a wicked world, told him nothing—or, at any rate, nothing that turned out to be true. His heaviest losses were likely to occur just when his opponent was talking most volubly, quoting Horace and Homer and the Bible and Shakespeare most profusely, and bringing to life the sporting history of eighteenth-century England with a memory inexhaustible and prodigious.

At one point, however, Mr. The Hair laid his cards face-down on the blanket and looked, with a smile not easy to interpret, into the eyes of the huge newcomer. "I recall," he said, musingly, "a certain Indian, a Mohegan of the clerical profession, whom I once knew, and knew well, in the Old Country. He was one of the few men I have known who have also known me. But just now I am thinking of his strong, even stern, opposition to what he called 'gambling'—in which category he would probably have included even this quite childish game of poker. All games of chance, he used to tell me, were positively sinful—and, strangely enough, my own efforts to reduce the element of chance to a minimum seemed, if anything, only to increase his opposition. Yet now I wonder what Samson Occum, that doughty gatherer of ill-gotten pelf for a worthy cause, would say about the game we are playing here this afternoon—this game in which nothing but pure chance, of course, is involved. Perhaps he might agree that the end, for once, is justifying the means.

536

"And yet I am not sure: for Samson Occum, though a pure-blooded Indian and a deeply thoughtful man, never plumbed the depths of the philosophy of gambling. He failed to recognize, I think, its celestial origin. It may be, Sleeping Bear, that he never knew that profound Indian myth about the twin gods, children of the sun, who have been sitting from creation's dawn until now at one endless game of chance. The names of those two vary, of course, from tribe to tribe, but another Indian friend of mine used to call them Hobbomok and Kiehtan. Each of them strives with all his wit to win, using every wile he knows. Now the one and now the other will have on his side the blanket nearly all the pebbles; but the game goes on forever. Some say that it is not a game at all, but a battle to the death. I think it is a game. Some say that the two players are deadly foes, but I, an old man, believe that they are twins, loving and inseparable. And I believe, too, that the game they play is really, at least in large degree, a game of chance. Of that infinite and eternal contest our own paltry pastimes with cards and dice are but the temporal imitations. That fact and that realization, however, should not prevent us from playing the games of time with all the determination that is shown by the celestial twins in eternity.— I raise you fifty pebbles, sir."

Mr. The Hair won that pot, holding two deuces against the Englishman's four queens, by making a final wager so huge that his antagonist refused to meet it. He went on winning. A messenger came up from the *Pride,* reporting that the fleet had gone on ahead and was now out of sight. He was sent back to say that the keel-boat must wait. For this game, as Holdfast at any rate could clearly see, was a thing of first-rate importance. If the Parson could give back their goods to all the civilized tribes, what would become of their old and meaningless enmities?

At last, when the sun was smoldering like a great garnet on the breast of the River, the young Englishman rose from the blanket and held out his hand. "Well, sir," said he, "I am stripped to the bone, as perhaps I deserve to be; but I've caught up with a legend of White's and Bath and Birdcage Walk. I have met a hero of myth, sir.—You must be Parson Blandison!"

"H'm! Hah! Oh!" groaned the other, rising painfully and slowly, with Holdfast's help, to his feet. "Parson Blandison—where have I heard that name before? But . . . yes! A notorious gambler, was he not? Surely I have heard of him as a renegade, a disgrace to his noble family, a hard drinker, a doubter, a sneerer, a profaner of holy things.—To be

537

frank with you, sir, I knew him. I remember the man. But he is dead, I can confidently assure you. Yes—dead, long ago."

And yet, as Mr. The Hair sat alone by his fire in the deepening dusk, smoking his pipe of red stone and drinking a little now and then from the jug of corn-whisky that Russell Bean had left him, he kept on thinking about Parson Blandison, the mocker and blasphemer, the notorious gambler of old days, who had died and gone away into the mystery. The Hair had spoken the superficial truth in saying that he had known that man. The effort to recollect him now brought only a drift of fleet and fading images: great houses and parks and gardens, clustered towers of schools and colleges, the *Centurion's* voyage round the world through storms and glassy calms, the horrors of scurvy, ten or a dozen bodies washing about the decks for want of hands to bury them in the sea, the capture of the rich Manila galleon, home again with prize-money, sudden wealth and the swift loss of it, clubs and coffee-houses and gambling-hells of London, then Paris, the Alps, the spectacle of half-buried Rome, a glimpse of the Parthenon, Dr. Johnson, Thomas Gray, the Earl of Dartmouth, Samson Occum, the laughter of the cynical fops of London, retreat to Virginia and North Carolina, and then Holdfast Gaines.—Had it not been at about the time when he met Holdfast that Parson Blandison, the mocker and blasphemer, had died?

What had ailed that man? What weakness or ignorance or pride, what shallow vanity, had kept him blind to the simple things that even a child could see? Had it been his learning, his reputation as a "wit," his birth and breeding, the wealth that had come and gone, or perhaps an ingrained stupidity, that held him away from joy? Such friends the man had been given!—the wise and the gay, the stanch and true, the strong, the beautiful, the tragic—and yet he had learned little from them all, unless it were from Samson Occum, born in a wigwam, who had moved so guileless and unbesmirched among the iniquities of London.

Mr. The Hair felt a little lonely tonight, as he had done in his very long lifetime but seldom. Ordinarily on such evenings as this, sitting alone by his fire while the Choctaw boy who was supposed to take care of him was asleep in the tent behind, there had been enough entertainment in merely whispering through to himself a dozen Horatian odes, savoring their packed felicities of expression as one would a generous old wine. Ten thousand times he had congratulated himself, now that he could no longer read, that he knew the odes from end to end without book. So exactly suited in mood and thought they were to his present situation here in the wilderness, living as a friend with a people who had kept the wisdom of simplicity, and cheerfully waiting for what would soon come on the very bank of the dark River. And yet tonight better even than Horace, that almost inexhaustible companion, would have been the bodily presence of Holdfast Gaines, sitting there once more on the other side of the little fire and saying nothing, with the Beloved Woman beside him. Holdfast, after so long an absence, had remained in the village today not more than two hours, and then had gone away toward the gathering battle.—Would he ever return? Would the quiet fidelity of the Beloved Woman ever have its earthly reward?

As he sat thinking for a long while about those two, The Hair heard now and then the faint beat of an Indian drum and the quaver of a flute from the village where Pushmataha and his daughter were entertaining guests from several once hostile tribes. There was rejoicing tonight in the village, and a new amity among the tribes of which a great deal might be made if Holdfast should ever come back. There was no telling what things might grow from this afternoon's game of poker, this tiny imitation of the universal game of chance at which the Eternal Twins had always been sitting.

A faint smile puckered the mouth of the victor in the afternoon's contest as he recalled how crest-fallen the young Englishman had looked when paddling away in his empty canoe, leaving all his Indian finery behind him. It had been ridiculously, almost pitifully, easy to confuse, outwit, deceive, and browbeat that brash young man. "It seems to involve the presence of a fifth king in the pack!" he had exclaimed, and at the recollection the victor smiled again. Not for a moment did he regret or blame himself for any of the quite simple and long-familiar sleights of hand by which, during the game, he had endeavored, not unsuccessfully, to "reduce the element of chance." He had played and won not at all on his own account, as Parson Blandison the notorious gambler had nearly always done, but on behalf of the two persons to whom he owed most and whom he loved best in all the world. It was a main article in his simplified creed that love makes all things pure.

Moreover, the young Englishman could well afford to lose. Though in an empty canoe, he had paddled away up-stream with his life before him, and tonight The Hair was feeling, after the excitement of the day, very old and weary. His Indian friends had for a long while been boasting that he had passed his hundredth year, and now he felt inclined to agree with them. His hands in the firelight—those very hands of which Parson Blandison had been so careful and proud—looked wizened and parched with age.

The fire was almost out now, and the night was growing chill. Ghostly fingers of fog were reaching up the bank from the unseen River. Now and then, as they groped and fumbled there on the edge of the dark, he thought they must be beckoning. He was cold to the bone, even under his gorgeous blanket brought from the western plains. There were no more sounds from the village. He heard the splash of a sturgeon in the darkness and the roar of a bull-buffalo rousing up among his cows across the water.

The old man shivered. With effort and pain he got to his feet and stamped out the embers of his fire. Then, very slowly, as though reluctantly, he hobbled into his tent and dropped the flap.

THE KNIFE

"I trust, gen'lemen," said Mr. Trask, "that you'll convey to Gen'ral Carroll my sense o' deep regret.—Although, o' course," he went on with a sidelong half-bow to Holdfast on his right and then toward Perthy and Bean across the table, "o' course, to have *three* guests tonight when I had allowed myself to hope for only one—it is an ample compensation."

He smiled, unpleasantly, but with an obvious effort at hospitable ease. With his left hand he was pulling at the pointed gray beard that hid his mouth, chin, and cheeks. His eyes, restlessly darting here and there, seldom glanced from under their bushy brows into the eyes of his guests.

There was no audible answer from Perthy, Bean, or Holdfast, who may have been listening to the chuckle of the River, just below them, among the old worn piles. Accustomed as they were to the long silences of the wilderness, they found it easy to be still. Mr. Trask, on the contrary, was growing at every moment more embarrassed. He began to draw lines with a fork on the table-cloth.

At length he burst out: "I hope Gen'ral Carroll's army is in good health. Has he had good weather on the way down from Nashville?"

"Yeah," Bean admitted.

540

"An odd way to transport an army, isn't it?"

"Yeah," said Perthy.

"Could you tell me how many men he has on those flat-boats?"

"No," said Holdfast.

"Well armed, are they?"

"With the best rifle-guns in the world," Bean answered, speaking with more emphasis than the words seemed to require.

"H'm. I see. And I suppose the Gen'ral has told you about the destination o' this large and well equipped army."

"He don't have to tell uth," Perthy replied. *"We told him."*

Mr. Trask opened his mouth in a silent but evidently ironical "Oh!" Then he went on toying with his heavy silver fork. Back and forth in the crease of the table-cloth went the fork's tine, digging into the fabric and cutting the threads.

Evidently Mr. Trask did not much concern himself with the cost of things in terms of human labor. For many years, as the owner of this unsavory tavern at Natchez-under-the-Bluff, he had prospered easily and basely by pandering to the appetites of others. His long white hand, stealthy and repulsive, had not done much of the world's hard work. It was a soft hand, yet by no means a weak one. On the ring-finger a splendid diamond blazed in the light of the six candles. From the crotch of the thumb a deep livid scar ran up to the wrist and disappeared under the cuff.

Trying to deflect his thoughts, Holdfast went ranging back in memory to his early days of swimming, canoeing, and fishing along the Thames with a dozen comrades, and to other days of hunting with them in the woods of Chesterfield or among the rocky hills of Gungywamp.

There was a rumble of voices from the thirty or more villainous-looking river-men in red shirts at the tables scattered throughout the large low room. The five backwoodsmen in buck-skins, sitting at a separate table in a far corner, were making no noise. They had come in shortly after the arrival of Holdfast, Perthy, and Bean, bringing their long rifles with them. They were not drinking at all—and, for that matter, the river-men were not living up to their opportunities. The main consumption of alcohol was going on among the twelve or fifteen women, all of them obviously prostitutes, whose screams and squeals and curses rose from time to time above the bass of the men.

"That Jacques o' mine is certainly takin' his time," said Mr. Trask angrily. "We must have been waitin' here for ten minutes."

There was another silence while the white hand went back and forth.

541

"Your Jack?" Bean asked at length.

"Yes; my cook, you know," the host replied with almost a sigh of gratitude.

"Oh, I see. Your cook."

"A truly marvelous fellow," Mr. Trask confided, making the most of the conversational opening. "I bring him down from my house on the bluff for special occasions like this one."

"I should think it would be easier," Holdfast suggested, "for you to invite your guests to your own home, instead of bringing your cook down here."

"Oh, well, yes—but, well, in fact, no. You see, we have the girls here. They make it more—more sociable."

"Wal, ez fer gals," Bean answered, after a brief and disgusted glance about the room, "I kinder like to use my own jedgment, an' ketch 'em wild. I don't ast no man to c'leck gals fer me."

"Ah, just so. But as to my cook, Jacques is a Frenchman, o' course. Only a Frenchman could work such wonders with the crude materials we get here—sturgeon, cat-fish, buffalo-hump, and frogs."

"What can he do with a frog?" Perthy asked in frank surprise.

"Wonders," said Mr. Trask. "Simply wonders.—It was my friend Lafitte who sent him up-river to me."

"You know the Lafitte brothers, then?" said Holdfast.

Mr. Trask darted a swift glance at the speaker, whose eyes he had seemed, thus far, to avoid. "Oh," said he, continuing his attack upon the table-cloth, "not intimately. Only, as one might say, by correspondence. Only as they are known by every one along the lower Mississippi who likes good food and drink and can pay well for them.—And are you acquainted with these interesting brothers, Mr.—ah—Mr. Sleeping Bear?"

"Very well. In fact it is partly the strong recommendation of your tavern by my close friend Mr. Jean Lafitte that has brought us here tonight."

The long white hand on the table-cloth paused for a second or two—and then moved on again. Mr. Trask's uneasy breathing was distinctly audible.

"Ah," he said, obviously forcing himself to speak, "It is excellent wine that those brothers somehow manage to secure—why ask how? And occasionally they share a little of it with others who know its worth.—But I see, gen'lemen, that you are not drinking. Do let me urge you again to have some whisky."

All three guests refused the offer, and another silence seemed to be threatened.

"There's one thing they lack at Barataria, though," Mr. Trask went on, "and that is oysters. Well now, without oysters no dinner can get well started. Perhaps that is what is wrong with this one. Where *is* that Jacques?"

"We have good oythterth at New London," said Perthy.

Mr. Trask suddenly raised his wine-glass to his lips, spilling several drops upon the table-cloth. They left a dark red stain.

"Is that so?" he drily remarked, and set the glass down again with an unsteady hand. "—Oh, but here is Jacques, at last, with our soup! Where in hell have you been, rascal?"

"Mais, but eef le monsieur weel but considaire! Zee ordaire ees pour *deux* messieurs, et maintenant, soudainement, ils sont *quatre!*"

"Well, what of it? Is that any reason for keeping my guests waiting for half an hour?"

"C'est difficile extrêmement, monsieur, à . . ."

"Scoundrelly pirate," Trask yelled, "get back to your pots and pans! If that roast isn't in here, properly done, in ten minutes, you go down-river tomorrow—probably not in a boat."

Jacques slipped quickly out of the room.

"Ah!" Trask exclaimed, taking up his spoon. "Bouillabaisse! There's nothing in Jacques' repertoire better than his bouillabaisse. Oh that Gen'ral Carroll were here!"

"He'll be gittin' hisself suthin' to eat, I reckon," said Bean.

"But what? That is the question."

"He'll be havin' what his men have, like always."

"Why, but that is dreadful—for a gentlemen, a sportsman, let alone a man of wealth! Besides, it must be bad for discipline."

"We'd call thith thoup a fith-thowder back in New London," observed Perthy. "On'y what'th he done to thpoil it? Put a frog in?"

The stare with which Mr. Trask greeted this sally was unmistakably hostile.

"Aw, I dunno," said Bean. "Gin'ral Bill Carroll has other ways o' keepin' disciplyne 'sides starvin' his men to death. 'T ain't the same with us as it was with Wilkinson's army down 't Terre aux Bœufs. Carroll tries to keep his men *alive*."

Mr. Trask poured himself another glass of wine. "Wilkinson?" said he, his voice quavering upward.

"Brigadier-General James Wilkinson, sir," said Holdfast. "Com-

543

mander-in-Chief of the western army. You have perhaps heard the name?"

"Oh . . . oh, yes; certainly."

"By correspondence?"

"Yes—ah, in fact, just so."

"General Wilkinson," said Holdfast, "seems to write a great many letters; but some parts of them—I mean the really important parts—are often hard to read."

Trask rose so suddenly from the table that his chair fell with a clatter behind him. "Damn that Jacques!" he shouted. "I'll disembowel him!"

As Trask was disappearing through the kitchen door Bean rose and walked casually across to the five frontiersmen in the corner. He spoke a few words to them in a low tone. While he was returning to his chair the five rifles leaning against the wall were taken down.

"Perthy," said Holdfast in a low tone, "I think we're going to have a pleasant evening. Keep up that New London talk, but remember that this man is no fool. The place is his, and full of his people. His men aren't drinking. They're under orders. We must be careful."

Perthy could only reply with a wink as the kitchen door swung open and Trask reappeared with a wine-bottle under each arm. He was closely followed by Jacques, bearing the roast.

"Now then," said the host, pulling up his chair and preparing to uncork the first bottle, "perhaps we can proceed. I have just given this rascally cook quite definite instructions."

The cork popped, and Trask refilled his glass.

"I do not fully agree," he said after taking a sip, "with your Gen'ral's new-fangled notions. For my part, I've always found it better to keep the lower classes, like this Jacques here, in their place.—It's better for what you, Mr. Bean, call 'disciplyne.'"

"We thay 'dithiplyne' back in New London too," Perthy confided with an affable smile. "That ith, if we want to. We don't athk nobody, not even the upper clatheth, to tell uth how to pernounth our wordth."

"Evidently not," said Trask. "And how will you have your roast, Mr. —ah—Sleeping Bear?"

"As it comes."

"And you, Mr. Bean? Rare or well done?"

"Rare."

"Rare it is, and there you are. And now, ah—pardon me, I fear I have forgotten your name."

544

"Aw, jetht call me 'Perthy o' New London.' My fambly name, iffen I ever had one, don't thignify, theein' all my folkth wath wiped out by the New London mathacree an' fire.—But I'll take it jetht like Hold-fatht—like it comth."

Then once more there was silence at the table of the four men, a rumble of male voices from the room behind, and now and then a stupid half-drunken squeal from the women. Best of all to listen to was that endless chuckling of the River among the tall worn piles on which the tavern stood. The River was high tonight. It was moving with a strong determined current, as though it had a plan and a purpose.

"When I was down hyar last time at Trask Tavern," Bean remarked, "they didn't have a meal like thisheer. They had some kind o' rat, seemin'ly, what they'd caught up the alley-ways. Didn't taste good to me."

"Ah, but Jacques didn't cook it, you see," Trask replied. "Jacques can make rat taste like buffalo-hump."

Holdfast laid down his knife and fork. "What is this that we're eating now?" said he. "Rat or buffalo?"

"Why should you care? It's good, isn't it?"

"That's what I'm trying to find out. The buffalo is a noble beast; but the rat—no art can change him."

"It can hide him, anyhow."

"I doubt even that."

"Art, you'll find, is more than nature."

"I don't think so. Suppose we take for an example of 'nature' the dead body of my friend Meriwether Lewis lying over there in your ball-room behind that door."

Trask was raising a loaded fork to his mouth, but he set it down again.

"Is the example a good one?" Holdfast inquired after a few seconds.

"Very well," said Trask in a faint voice. "Suppose it."

"Aw, hell," Bean cut in, "don't only s'pose it! Good Gawd, ye saw thet dead body, didn't ye?"

"All right then," answered Trask, his voice rising sharply. "Yes; I saw it. Why shouldn't I? Dozens o' people saw it. Scores. And they all saw that Meriwether Lewis killed himself. Everyone knows that. The coroner said so."

"Yes, yes, Mr. Trask," Holdfast continued in a soothing tone, "we remember what the coroner said, but we haven't come to that yet. You go on too fast."

"Well, naturally—to have a famous man like that killed—that is, die, right here . . ."

"Quite so. Many tavern-keepers would have feared that such an event would be bad for their business. However, I mentioned that dead body only as an example of what we have agreed to call 'nature.'"

"Well?" said Trask, obviously striving to breath less explosively.

"And yet there were a few touches of art upon that body to which the coroner—who was, I believe, a friend of yours—did not seem to pay much attention."

"Such as?"

"We three lived with Meriwether Lewis for many months, on his journey to the Pacific and back. We all knew him to be a left-handed man."

"What of it?"

"And so it seemed strange to me that the bullet-hole in his head should be on the right side, and that the pistol found on him was in his right hand."

"Oh. That seemed strange, did it?"

"And another thing: the pistol found in Lewis's hand did not belong to him. He was a rifle-man. He hated and despised pistols."

"That may be so; but when a man wants to kill himself . . ."

"But the main thing that your friend the coroner did not mention was a letter from General Wilkinson to the Governor of Canada. I saw and read that letter. It was written in invisible ink. Lewis was carrying it to Washington. If he had ever reached there with it, Wilkinson would have been a ruined man. But Lewis never got beyond this tavern. Neither, I think, did the letter."

The dark shifty eyes under their grizzled brows were darting again about the room. For a moment Trask seemed about to cry out—but then his glance fell upon the five men in buck-skins sitting quietly, yet alert, at the far table. Each of them had a long rifle in hand, the muzzle resting on the table-top.

"And so you see, Mr. Trask, why we came in here tonight. It wasn't for your dinner of doctored rat, and it wasn't for the pleasure we expected to take in your company and conversation. It wasn't only that we couldn't let General Carroll run the same risk that Lewis did. We didn't know much against you—that we could prove, but we did hope that you would help us to decide how our friend Lewis came to die. His dead body was nothing but nature; but in the way he died, and in what happened just after his death, there was a good deal of what you call 'art.'"

546

Trask suddenly turned, for the first time, full upon Holdfast. His face was flaming. "Are you trying to insinuate," he shouted, "that I know who killed Meriwether Lewis?"

"You save me the trouble, sir. Everyone can see that you do."

"Why, damn your insolent red . . . I don't know why I don't have you thrown out of my tavern!"

His right hand was slowly moving while he spoke toward some inner pocket of his coat, which, in his excitement, had been partly thrown open.—And now the eyes of Holdfast, following that stealthy movement of the hand, suddenly brightened. He leaned forward a little, his breath coming faster. His face, sternly hard, looked strange to Perthy and Bean. Yet when he spoke his voice was even more quiet than it had been before. It was almost as though he were talking to some familiar friend.

"One of the reasons why you will not even try to have me thrown out," he said, "is that you are going to be so deeply interested in a thing I have to tell you."

Trask's hand moved a little farther, the diamond viciously sparkling. His blood-shot eyes still roved the room but always returned to the five quiet and intently watchful men in the corner. His face, purple with wrath a moment before, was now putty-colored. He was breathing heavily, with half-open mouth.

"You are nearing the end of your trace, Mr. Trask. We have followed you on it a long, long way. Dan'l Boone set us on it when we were trying to find out who killed John Donelson. Riley Tharpe of New London helped a little when he told us how someone drove his brother 'Bijah blood-crazy in a British prison-ship. We saw that Donelson was killed because he knew too much about General Wilkinson. So did Meriwether Lewis know too much about that same subject. But even then—yes, and even after what Lafitte and the Indians could tell us, and the letters in secret ink from Wilkinson to you—there was one thing we needed to know."

"One thing!" snarled Trask. "Why, man, you know nothing. And, curse your insolence, why are you saying all this to *me*?"

"Because," answered Holdfast, leaning forward still farther and speaking softly but with increasing rapidity, "I have seen the head of a woman carved in green stone just there at the opening of your coat where your hand is moving now. You are *The Knife*!"

Before the last word was spoken Trask was on his feet and plunging down a long wavy glitter of steel.

For a flash this frantic attack upon a seated and unarmed man looked

547

to mean nothing but certain and sudden death. But Holdfast's left hand shot upward and stopped Trask's down-sweeping right. The dark hand held the white one gripped at the wrist now. The diamond blazed. The blade, a foot long and waved at the edges, hung like an icicle in mid-air. For a full five seconds of silence the linked bodies of the two men were as still as though they also were carved in stone. Only the blade, smeared at the tip with some dark ointment, trembled a little.

Then came a crash of falling chairs, a scrambling of feet, a tumult of voices, and Trask's yell slicing the din: "Now's the time, boys! With knives!" But already Russell Bean was half-way across the room shouting "Hands up!" and "Shoot the first man that moves!" On the instant there bristled up from the far table five Kentucky rifles, cocked. Bean's own rifle made a sixth. And again he shouted: "Leave Trask to Holdfast!" Trask yelled again some frenzied order. It was not obeyed. The river-men stood irresolute, and the women left off screaming. Russell Bean leapt upon a table near the ball-room door, kicked the glasses and dishes away, and stood there with the roomful before him, his rifle in the crook of his arm, finger on trigger. The muzzle kept moving from side to side incessant as a snake's head ready to strike.

"Hands up, thar, I tell yeh!" Bean called again, and up went a thicket of hands.

"You Jack Jones, c'm out hyar an' c'leck every damn weepon ye c'n find.—An' whilst he's at it any man ez lets down s' much ez one leetle finger gits his lights blowed out, suddent an' permanent.—Thet goes fer ladies' lights, too."

Jack Jones came from behind the far table and went swiftly to work.

"Don't ye fool with 'em boys," Bean concluded. "Don't give 'em no benefit o' no doubts. They wouldn't of to us, 'member."

Tense as their own danger was, most of those in the room turned slowly round, still carefully holding up their hands, to watch the silent struggle of the two hands above the six candles.

The blade was lower now, although evidently Holdfast was not trying to draw it down. Its point was trembling more. Holdfast's knuckles were whiter and Trask's fingers were going blue. The great diamond was burning a thousand tiny camp-fires, red, blue, green, and gold, all huddled together. It seemed to drip crimson flame.

Perthy, still seated at the table, was leaning eagerly forward, his gaze fixed in fascination upon the knife-blade.

A woman screamed suddenly, and then, as though about to faint, dropped her hands for a moment; but when the muzzle of Bean's long rifle rounded at her bare bosom and she saw the merciless glint of his eyes she cursed and put them up again. Evidently there had been some mistake. This Russell Bean, widely famous for his amours, did not really love women.

The crowded, foul-smelling room grew still.

Suddenly, shattering the quiet, the great knife dropped with a clatter among the candle-sticks, glasses, dishes, and silver-ware on the table-cloth.

Perthy leaned over and stared at it. He picked it up and held it by the long wavy blade, gazing at the figure of a woman carved in jade on the handle. His eyes were soft and dreamy, as though he were remembering times and places far back.

"Wipe the poison off the point," said Holdfast.

"Now you degen'rate sons an' darters o' second-rate bitches," shouted Russell Bean, striking as well as he could a clerical attitude on the table-top, "I wanter thank y' all hearty fer thisheer off'rin' o' hardware. Hit's a-goin' to do a power o' good down-River thar with Andy. Hit 'll holp to save the kentry ye don't desarve to live in.

"Same time, ladizangents, 't ain't 'nough. I know y' all come to thisheer meetin' tonight with yer best weepons on yeh, an' I feel sartin shore ye c'n do better 'n this. We cain't leave them pore boys to go floatin' down jest to claw an' bite the British. Whut they want is weepons, an' they got a better right to 'em 'n ye got.

" 'Course I dunno all you ladizangents like a man raly oughter iffen he's a-goin' to keep alive in these parts. I know Jack Nolan over thar, him 't shot a dyin' man jest to keep 'im from sayin' the name o' Trask. Ev'body knows Jack Nolan fer a misbegotten hoss-thief an' wishes to God he war daid.—An' he will be, too, iffen he lets down that bloody right hand o' his'n half an inch jest one time more.—But 'bouten the rest o' yeh, the on'y good thing I c'n say is I know ye come hyar tonight prepared to con-tri-bute hardware."

At the mention of Jack Nolan's name Perthy had risen from the table. He stood now with his long-lost knife in his right hand, the blade pointing backward over his shoulder. He was looking keenly, expectantly, from face to face in the crowd.

Bean glanced down for a moment at the weapons of many sorts that lay on the table at his feet. "Hyar's four rifles," he said. "Course they're not much good, bein' made by Dutchmen back in Pennsylvany, but I never look a gift-rifle in the muzzle. An' hyar's a smooth-bore— prob'ly from London Tower an' s'plied by Gen'ral Wilkinson to his *dear* ole friend Mr. Trask. That's the kind that killed John Donelson. I'll give it to one o' my seventeen three-year-olds to show 'em what good guns *ain't*.—An', lessee now, hyar's tommyhawks, six, seven, eight. Git s'more, Jack Jones, git s'more. I'm tol'able shore they must be a two-three gents in thisheer congregation will con-tri-bute one more tommy-hawk apiece.—Wal, then, say knives. An' hyar I see seven, eight, nine knives. Mebbe ten, but don't ast me ter count too acc'rate 'cause we all ree'lize whilst I was a-countin' some red-shirted mother's mistake mought suddenly con-tri-bute one more. Anyhow, say nine knives. Now raley, ladizangents! Nine knives? Right hyar whar The Knife hisself holds out? Seems like he oughter of begot a bigger fambly 'n on'y nine in all these years. Brother Jones, will ye kindly cir-cu-late oncet more an' git more knives? Even four-inch knives—git 'em from the gals fer the pore boys floatin' down on flat-boats. Git some on 'em, mebbe, in places whar ye wouldn't like to look—say in garters, Deacon Jones. (I blush ter say it!) Or, wal, in buzzums, Deacon. (This is turr'ble!)"

Bean pretended to hide his imaginary blushes for a second with his left hand, but he was peering out between his fingers and his rifle-muzzle was still swinging like a rattler's neck and head from side to side, commanding all the room. So were the four muzzles left in the far corner swinging. Everyone saw that. The whole room seemed to swing and sway with those muzzles. It was an unjoyous dance.

While Jones was going the rounds a second time, securing here and there a remarkably short weapon which had escaped his first and rather hasty search, Perthy's right arm was seen to snap suddenly forward and there was a momentary glitter through the air of hurtling steel. The thing had happened so without warning that few at first could guess its cause, or connect it with the instantly following "pong" of a thrown dagger into the wall three feet above Holdfast's head. But then, while the handle was still vibrating, everyone heard the thud of a body falling to the floor. Perthy glanced round, saw that Holdfast was unharmed, was not even in fact looking up, and then walked across the room and plucked his knife with the wavy blade from the socket of a dead man's eye.

"So much fer Jack Nolan," said Bean, drily. "I tried to tell 'im whut mought happen, but he couldn't quite b'lieve me. The rest o' you ladizangents better take notice."

Having drawn Trask down again into his chair, Holdfast was gazing at the hand, still firmly grasped by the wrist, which lay before him on

the table. There was something, one would have said, that he was trying to remember.—All at once, with a sweep of his own right hand, he
pushed the coat-sleeve half-way up the arm. The livid scar ran clear
from the crease between the thumb and fore-finger right to the elbow.

As though they were two close friends, or a patient and his physician,
Trask and Holdfast gazed at the scar. Something there, one could see,
bound them together, and not with the bonds of hate. Trask was not
struggling now. For a moment he looked almost thoughtful.

"That was a fine day we had back in Gungywamp," said Holdfast
at length, musingly. "There were the Avery boys, the Tharpes, John
Ledyard, Nathan Hale, and you and I—ten in all, and all young. Most
of them are dead now.—Do you remember the hickory leaves, yellow
as the gold of this ring, twirling down?"

Trask made no audible answer.

"I had known for years that there was an old she-bear living up
there near the top of Gungywamp, and I had persuaded the other boys
to leave her alone. You I never told, because we all knew that you
weren't to be trusted.—Well, you saw her that day, with her cubs, as
we went up through the beech-mast. You shot her. But you didn't know
how to shoot a bear, and she didn't drop. You didn't even know how to
run away from a wounded bear. She rushed you up-hill and got you
cornered among the rocks. I can see it now, and so can you—how her
claw slashed along your arm and the blood spurted. You remember
how the two Tharpes and I pulled her off you by the hind legs, and
then we all ran off down the hill. When we'd got clean away I sucked
the dirt and poison out of the slash and tore up my shirt to bind it and
took a twist in the bandage with a stick. If I hadn't done that you
would have bled to death, or died of lock-jaw. Isn't that so?"

Trask sat very still.

"It is so, and you know it. Ten thousand times, looking at this old
scar, you've remembered that you owed your life to the Tharpe boys
and to me. That's one reason why you've hated us."

The voice of the River, during the pause that followed, seemed to call
more clearly from below.

"I can see now," Holdfast went on, "that you have tried again and
again—perhaps under Wilkinson's orders—to have me killed as you
did Meriwether Lewis. If you had thought that you could do it safely
you would have tried to kill me yourself, that night when I stood on
deck in the moonlight and you were down in the shadow. When I came
here tonight you knew me. That's why you went to stabbing at the

table-cloth and wouldn't look into my eyes. That's why you tried to keep your coat-sleeve down over your wrist. You were badly frightened, but you had some hope of killing me here. That hope may not be quite gone even now."

"Boys!" Trask yelled, leaping suddenly to his feet and striving desperately to wrench his captured hand away.

"But you had better give up that hope," said Holdfast, pulling Trask slowly back into his chair.

"Hands up, thar, leetle lady!" called Russell Bean. "I know they're tired, but they 'll be a damn sight tireder afore ye c'n let 'em down an' keep alive same time."

"You brute, you!"

"Right, my dear—but hold 'em up all the same. Th' ain't a one o' you fancy gals whut wouldn't look purtier ez a corp, with some o' the paint washed offen yeh an' a few decent grave-clothes put on."

"An' Mr. Bean," sang out one of the backwoodsmen from the corner, "will ye kindly tell thisheer fancy gal to pull her skirt daown? She's a-winkin' her laigs at me, sir."

"Wal, Jake Robbins, be they any good?"

"Hell no! That's jes' the pint, sir. I know a gal back home with two laigs ez 'd make thesen look like chitterlings. Fack is, she's—she's my wife, too."

"Git this, gals," Bean thundered. "Hands *up* an' skirts *down* is the abs'lute orders! No more winkin' o' laigs. My boys ain't thet kind, an' don't like it."

"But it will take more thinking than you have time for," Holdfast was saying, "to understand how the best things get tangled with the worst. The Tharpe boys helped to pull that bear off you, and so you lived on to drive one of them blood-crazy. You set him loose to kill innocent men and women, even children, while you sat here drawing blood-money. This diamond ring came out of that."

"You can have it, Sleeping . . . I . . . I mean Holdfast, if . . . it cost seven thou' . . ."

"And because I sucked the poison from your arm you have been able to poison many lives, Bill Pertwee."

Trask flinched at the sound of that name, and his fingers writhed again. His face looked white as the table-cloth when Perthy wheeled suddenly round and cried: "What? 'Pertwee'? Why, Holdfast, that's

552

the name of *my* man!—Oh, what a day! The man and the knife together!"

"Yes, Bill," said Holdfast, bowing his head, "we must add that to the rest."

"But it was long ago," Trask pleaded. "It was far off, Holdfast! It's forgotten, and nobody ever . . ."

"That foul deed of yours, long ago, back there in New London, left a child alone in the world—his companion a homeless and wandering man."

Before Perthy could speak Trask was stammering out: "But I've changed, Holdfast. I made a new start. I'm a different man. And besides—I deny it!"

"You deny it?" said Perthy, leaning forward over the table and speaking in a voice of merciless glee that surprised those who knew him best. "Then where did you get this knife? How have you used it? Why did you bring it here tonight?"

"And so," said Holdfast after a long pause, speaking slowly and with his head still bowed, "because I saved your life long ago in Gungywamp I have to kill you now."

"Oh no you don't, Holdfast," said Perthy. "I know you don't like to kill things, but I've been waiting to kill this one a long, long while."

"So you have, Perthy. Your life has been poisoned too. But . . ."

"And now I won't wait any longer. I have a plan. I'll kill him where he killed Lewis—and hoped to kill General Carroll tonight."

"Murder!" Trask yelled. "Oh boys, do something! You're five to one. Ain't I always been good to you?"

From somewhere in the room there came back a sound of mocking laughter.

"Murder, nothing!" said Perthy. "I'm going to give you a fairer chance than you've ever given any man."

"How can you? I'm twice your age."

"I've been thinking about that, and about how you've always liked to work with a knife. All right, then. I'll use this one, and you can borrow the one that Jack Nolan threw at Holdfast. It's sticking there in the wall."

"But a fight with knives between a man of my age and one of yours, between a gentleman and a . . . well, is that your notion of a fair chance?"

"Don't interrupt, Bill Pertwee. I'm telling you what's going to happen. You've always liked to do your work in the dark, and so we'll

553

fight in your ball-room with all the lights out. You know the room well. I don't. Is that fair enough?"

"No!"

"What's wrong with it?"

"If I should kill you . . ."

Perthy laughed aloud.

"I say if I should kill you, still your gang of cut-throats controls the room. What chance would I have then?"

"Far better than you deserve," Holdfast answered. "We should turn you over to the law, and then you would have all the help of your friends General Wilkinson and Judge Innes."

"I can't trust you," said Trask, leaning back and drumming on the table with the fingers of his free hand.

"Can you stretch a rope, then?" called Russell Bean from the table-top.

Trask struggled to rise again, yelling out "Oh, boys! Will you let them murder me?"

"We'd *help* 'em to iffen we could, y' old bastard!" a voice shouted in answer.

"Too much talk," said Perthy. He stuck the great knife into the belt of his buck-skin coat and strode across the room toward the ball-room door. "Just bring him in, will you, Holdfast?" he added, speaking over his shoulder.

DUEL IN THE DARK

"Where are you, then, you filthy coward?"

(No answer. No sound of a breath or a footfall. No glimpse of a figure moving against the faintly discernible oblongs of the windows. No shape of a foot in the faint line of light drawn under the door. Only the endless and dreadful drone of the River, and darkness all but complete.)

There were moments when Bill Pertwee could have sworn that he was alone, that Perthy had somehow managed to slip away, and that this whole fantastic plan for a duel in the dark was a hoax meant only to try his nerve.—Well then, why not laugh aloud, walk to the door, and tell Holdfast Gaines that half an hour of bare-footed padding

554

round and round a dark room was all that he would endure? For, clearly, the whole thing was absurd. If they had really meant to kill him they could have done it back there at the table while his wrist was clamped down.

But yet Holdfast Gaines did not have the look of a practical joker. Indeed, he had never been one. Besides that, he really did know a good deal—not a tenth of the truth, to be sure, but more than enough.

(Was that a footfall just behind? Turn, and stab!—Nothing. Nothing. Move on again. Keep moving every moment. Keep stabbing back and forth, left and right, up and down; and every stab to kill.)

What power of malicious evil had sent Holdfast Gaines into Western Waters?—the one man left alive in the world, perhaps, who could recognize and trace back that old scar? Ah, why that one man—incorruptible, indifferent to money and power, inaccessible to fear, and apparently, as the Indians asserted, immortal? At the least, he must bear a charmed life. In the cane-brakes and along the trails and traces he had escaped a score of trusty men sent out one after the other with instructions, on pain of their own deaths, to kill him. Several of those men had later become his friends and supporters. He had destroyed the Tharpes, evaded and perhaps killed McGillivray, and soundly thrashed the gang of cut-throats sent against him at New Orleans. Even the Prophet had failed to kill him at Coosa, Fort Mims, and the Horseshoe. Less than an hour ago he had escaped a thrown dagger merely because the man who threw it was struck in the eye by a knife at the moment it left his hand. Was one expected to provide against things such as that? Bill Pertwee felt that his conscience was clear, that he had done his uttermost—except, perhaps, in the moment of weakness down at the water's edge when Holdfast's head and shoulders had risen suddenly, terrifyingly, into the moonlight. He had done his best, and if it had not been enough then fate, ill-fortune, or some power of malicious evil must have been working against him.

The giant Mohegan had nearly ruined a once-flourishing business. The fur trade with the Spanish, based upon promises of help to them in their effort to take over Western Waters, was rapidly declining. The trade in human scalps and white slaves was no longer what it had been. The whole carefully thought-out plan of setting Indians against whites and whites against Indians—Creeks against Choctaws, Chickasaws against Cherokees, Spanish, British, French, and Americans against each other—was showing less profit every year. And all this, Bill Pertwee said to himself as he moved swiftly and silently along the wall, stabbing into the dark as he went, was due to the sly, insinuating, persistent work of Holdfast Gaines. What the man's motives might have been he did not try to guess, but the results had long been vividly clear.

The man knew much, and had done much. Bill Pertwee was amazed to discover how often his own designs had been crossed and thwarted by one whom he had seen for only a few seconds in more than thirty years. Holdfast Gaines had almost certainly been implicated in the death of Alexander McGillivray, an event which had reduced the triumvirate known as The Knife to only two members. He had somehow intercepted the most important letter ever signed with the mark of The Knife, and in so doing had broken for the first time the excellent system, invented by McGillivray, of changing runners in such a way that he who first got a letter never knew to whom it went and he who delivered it could not guess whence it came. Backed and enforced by the talisman of the actual knife itself—a thing exactly designed to inspire awe and implicit obedience among the Indians—this system had worked decidedly well. But then a meddler, an interloper—one who had refused McGillivray's highly advantageous offers, and who apparently had no interest or even belief in business—had discovered the secret of the invisible ink, and the system had to be abandoned!

Holdfast Gaines had somehow discovered other things, even more important. Just the other day there had come news from Saletia Colbert that Sleeping Bear had run from the Gulf to Nashville to bring Carroll's men down to New Orleans. But how had he, or anyone, found out where the British were to strike? Or when? Only The Knife knew that. The last Jackson knew of the British, they were burning Washington. That had been part of the plan—Wilkinson's plan, and a good one—that the British should conceal their real purpose by drawing all attention to the East.

Nevertheless, all might yet be well. A British defeat at New Orleans was unthinkable, even now that they were expected there. The only possible danger for them lay in the postponement of action, giving Jackson time to bring down plenty of defenders and dig in below the city. In delay, Pertwee decided, there might be some danger. Benedict Arnold might have been defeated at New London if he had been dilatory, but certain information from one of his Tory friends had led him to strike promptly and so to carry the town without trouble. Benedict Arnold had not forgotten the source of that useful information, and neither had General James Wilkinson, once Arnold's secretary.

But Wilkinson was now out of it. Only last week a letter had come from him stating that he expected soon to be relieved of his command. He might have to face a court-martial and try to clear himself of a charge of treason for his conduct in the Battle of Chrysler's Farm. That would leave only one man who knew and could assist the British plans, only one man to receive and enjoy the emoluments of British gratitude. —Oh, now, to get out of here, to send off the two pigeons to Canada and New Orleans which he had been holding back only for further information about Carroll's army, and then, what a future!

(Keep stabbing, though. Keep along the wall. Jump that sliver of light under the door without making a sound. Crawl below the sills of the six windows. Keep moving.)

But why couldn't the fool say something—anything! Was he afraid? Was he hiding?—Ah, there was something to work on!

"Where are you, I say again, you filthy coward. I came here to fight and kill you, not to hide; but you, after suggesting this nonsense, daren't go through with it. And now it's too late. Unless you make a bolt for the door and cry for help I'll catch and kill you yet."

(A bold effort, that!—Ah, but keep stabbing, keep moving, keep close to the wall!)

No answer, except for the water washing below against the rotted piles.

"Look here! I see what you want—what you've been waiting for. Well, you can have it. This ring—it really did cost me seven thousand, and it's worth more—is yours. Take it. Put it in your pocket until this is over, where it won't be seen. We'll say—we'll make up some yarn. Down in New Orleans it 'll make you a rich man. Think of the fine clothes it 'll buy you, the wines, the women!"

No answer.

(But had he gone deaf, then, or dumb? Had he been frightened out of his wits?—Keep stabbing.)

"If that isn't enough, I know where there's a lot more. Plenty. We'll slip out o' the window, wade in to the bank, go up to my house, and get it. That way you can give your friends the slip, and keep it all."

Again no answer, except for the soft contented chuckling of the water just below.

"Well then—but I'm not a rich man, and you mustn't think so—say fifty thousand. Yes, let's make it an even fifty. That'll leave me just enough for my old age.—And if you think you can't trust me, I'll agree

557

to leave this knife here in the room when we slip out, and you can keep the one you took away."

Oh, the dreadful, the intolerable silence, with the drone of the River under it to make it more dreadful still! It was this that Meriwether Lewis must have heard all that first night as he lay here in the dark with the bullet-hole in his right temple.—But then Meriwether Lewis was a dead man. Don't imagine things! Keep your head, now! Great God, how terrible it would be to die here!

"I'm sorry if I have said anything tonight that may have sounded harsh or unfair. Perhaps I have not shown all the courtesy that is to be expected from a host. But I have many anxieties, many cares, and I admit that they sometimes try my temper. Yet I think I have never injured you in any way. Other men, I confess, I have injured, and I hope to make restitution; but you and I—why may we not be friends? More than that . . . for I have not told you that I have no children, or none that are legitimate . . . Well now—do you see what I mean? Don't make it too hard for me!"

How strange that as the silence deepened the voice of the River seemed to grow louder, as though it were calling! How terrifying this darkness, blotting out every hue and shape! Out of the manifold world of the senses, nothing left but that summoning voice!

"Pray excuse me, sir! I do most sincerely beg your pardon. I admit that I have done you the gross discourtesy of under-estimating your judgment, your wisdom, your character—in a word, your knowledge of business. While I have been offering you such trifling considerations as this diamond ring, fifty thousand dollars, and adoption as my son, you have known, of course, that I hold almost within my grasp a really enormous wealth and power. You were entirely justified, therefore, in making no reply. In your place I should have treated those offers with the same contempt. But now that I see what you are, we can come to a business understanding. McGillivray is dead and Wilkinson is under such suspicion that we can ignore him. Therefore I am able to offer you, sir, full partnership with me in the power and prestige of The Knife. With the inevitable success of British arms at New Orleans that power and prestige will be vastly increased. Even now the British are greatly indebted to The Knife. We can deepen their sense of obligation by going up to my house and despatching two letters—one for the British forces in Canada and one for those now approaching New Orleans. In those letters we shall tell them what we know about the American plans and forces. We shall advise them to set forth at once from the two ends of the River. We shall send off our letters tonight, by carrier pigeons. Within two days the British can be on the march. Within a month they can meet. When once they meet they will command the Valley of the Mississippi River. The power commanding that River will soon command the continent. And, finally, it stands to reason that the two men who have done most to make that conquest possible will not be forgotten.—Do I make myself clear? And what do you say?"

The silence was all but incredible.

"Don't you realize that I should be putting myself in your power— that if I failed to divide with you fairly, then you might betray me?"

No answer. Even that supreme temptation had failed. Dear God, he might have to die here, like Lewis—and die on the verge of an unimaginably huge success!

(Keep moving, though. Keep close to the wall. Keep stabbing.)

There was nothing more to offer. There was nothing left but to beg, to plead for one's bare life. But plead to whom? Not, certainly, to this man who for an hour had been unheard, unseen, to this bodiless will which nothing could change or move. What hope, then? Where to look for strength, for protection, for the calm and controlled authority which tempers justice with mercy? Where, indeed, unless to the man, near at hand, within hearing, who once before, long ago, had saved one's life?

"Holdfast! Help, Holdfast! Don't let him kill me!"

"Ah, now, that's better, Bill Pertwee. I see you're beginning to learn."

"Where are you?"

"Sitting here in the middle of the floor, where I've been since we came in. Won't you come over and join me? I think you must need a rest."

"No."

"I'm sorry; but I suppose you can listen just as well if you go on traveling round the wall."

"Why don't you lisp any more?"

"Now that I've found you I'm through with lisping."

"Where did you learn to speak English like a gentleman?"

"That's part of what I mean to tell you."

"You may die before you finish."

"And remember, while I'm speaking, that this Knife can see in the dark. It waits until its prey comes, and then it kills when it likes. It

559

is like the sting of a spider that sits in the middle of the web and waits."

(Ah—so he would be sitting still! A thing to know.)

"But about my learning to speak good English: I owe that partly to you."

"What's that?"

"I've spent most of my life with a man who can speak like a prince in a dozen languages—and best of all in the English of Connecticut. I owe that partly to you."

"How?"

"I think you know, but I'll tell you while The Knife is waiting."

(Now to creep up from behind and . . . !)

"Suppose your father and mother were dead and your grandparents were taking their place. Suppose they did it as well as they could, and you loved them. Can you understand that, Bill Pertwee? A boy can, when he's five years old. He can love the old house he lives in, and every-thing in it. He can love the queer green-handled knife that his dead father brought back for him from over the sea. Suppose there is a green woman carved on the handle. A five-year-old boy can fall in love with her, thinking of the mother he has lost."

(Out from the wall, now. He must be very near. But which way facing?)

"And suppose that one fine September morning, early, you are out under the elms with your grandfather. He is raking leaves, and your granny is back in the kitchen making apple-pie. It's a clear blue Con-necticut morning with a wind from the north.—Do you remember, Bill Pertwee, how the wind tosses the tops of those New London elm-trees? Do you remember how the north wind blowing down the Thames in September used to smell? You ought to remember those things because you too—think of it!—were once a five-year-old boy in New London."

(Make no answer. Make him think you're remembering all that nonsense.)

"But after a while you hear musketry and shouts far off toward the center of town, and you ask your grand-dad what the noise is about. The old man listens, and then says: 'It must be the sea-fencibles having some practice. They need it.'

"So you go on playing a few minutes longer and your grandfather goes on raking. But the noise is growing, and coming nearer. The old man doesn't hear it, because he's a little deaf and because of the rasping sound that the leaves make. He doesn't seem to notice even that sharp

sour smell in the air, so different from the smell of the north wind.—
Oh, well, you say to yourself, if he doesn't think those things are important then they can't be.

"But even he hears the fife and drum when they turn the corner, and
the sound of twenty men marching. He drops his rake and hobbles to
the fence. I run toward the fence to look through the cracks, and while
I am running I hear the old man call out, surprised: 'Well! What are
you doing there, Bill Pertwee?'—And a second later I hear a musket-
shot from the street."

(Keep low. Creep nearer. Let him talk right on.)

"By that time I was at the fence, looking through—and there, sure
enough, was Bill Pertwee, just lowering his musket. It was smoking
at the muzzle. He looked to me very big and grand as he stood there,
beginning to reload. I couldn't understand what that other man meant
when he shouted out: 'Now, damn it, Bill, what you want to do that
for? That old man wa'n't doing any hurt—and besides, he was a neighbor of ours!'"

(Yes; but all that happened long ago, far away. It was unfair to bring
that up. How could one have known there was a child there, hidden
behind the fence? So easily one might have killed that child! No; it
was all unfair. Kill him now!)

"Of course I wondered what old man he was talking about, and I
turned round to see. My grand-dad was lying, face-down, on the pile
of leaves he had been raking. I couldn't make him speak to me. There
was a little hole in his head.

"You don't make any answers, Bill Pertwee, but I hope you are paying attention. Don't use all the time you have left in trying to kill me
—crouching down there about six feet off and making ready to spring.
Save a little time for trying to understand what kind of life you have
lived. And don't try to hasten matters. When The Knife is ready, you
will come.

"Why don't you sit down and rest, Bill Pertwee? Is it because you
know that you are going to begin a very long rest very soon? Or perhaps it is that you don't know just where I am, whether sitting or
standing, and whether to the right or the left. You can't see me as well
as you did that old man whom you shot through the head long ago—
not even so well as you did Meriwether Lewis. And I suppose it will
seem unfair to you that I can see every motion you make. I haven't
lived all these years in the woods without growing the eyes of a cat.
You sent me into the woods. I owe you that, too."

(Damn his eyes! But where is he? One has to know!)

"Well, then, the next thing I remember is that granny gave me what there was of the apple-pie and told me to go and get lost. I did. Some might say that I've been lost ever since."

(Ah, stop that childish babble! Kill him now!)

"When next I saw her my granny was dead—of fright, I suppose. You didn't shoot her, but you did burn her house to the ground, and she died after that. This green-handled Knife—I looked for it for days among the ashes—was gone. You had it."

(Yes; and may have it again in less than a minute.)

"But before that I got lost in the woods. I was five years old. I was afraid of everything. A world that had seemed safe and warm and friendly had suddenly turned terrible. I heard shots everywhere, and screams. I saw many dead men. The town was afire. I heard cannon from the river, and from across the river there was a noise of muskets.

"In the afternoon I came to a crowded road, going up-hill. At the top of the hill I met a man who was kind to me, and while I was talking to him I began to lisp—I don't know why, but it seemed easier. When I got older I went on lisping with a reason. I thought it would always remind me of things I might otherwise forget. When fools sneered at me for it, as you did tonight, they put me in mind of what I had to do. I've been sneered at by fools all the way from Connecticut to Florida, and from the Atlantic to the Mississippi. All that way and all these years they have kept me looking for you, thinking of you, and feeling sure that God would not let you die until I found you.— And now, to have you die not by my hand really—for Holdfast has always told me that that would be wicked—but by The Knife! That is better than anything I have hoped for!

"But I want you to know before you die that you've held my life together and given it a purpose, a meaning. Excepting Holdfast, I owe you more than any other man in the world. When you're gone I don't know that I shall ever find a job so important as cleansing the world of Bill Pertwee.

"However, The Knife is waiting, and I've said what I had to say. The River is calling you, too.—Listen! Do you hear him?

"You remember how dead men go down the River. Their arms are limp and they twirl in the thread of the River. And if there's a seven-thousand-dollar diamond on the hand of a dead man, he twirls and floats just the same. Whatever it is in the River that eats dead men, it does not eat that ring. Maybe only that ring and a bone or two will ever get to the Gulf. God knows. It may be that God is collecting

562

diamond rings, down there in the Gulf, to make a hell for rich men."

(May God damn him now and shut that mouth and bring that voice to silence! Oh, may this knife pierce through his mouth and nail his tongue to the jaw-bone!)

"And now that you have said your last prayer, Bill Pertwee, your time has come. I am sitting six feet away, directly in front of you, holding The Knife. It stands up here in my hands like something alive. It has done long enough the will of the dark and the devil. Now let it act like the lightning."

For half a minute, then, there was nothing to be heard in the room except the voice of the River and the laboring breath of a man.

"Well, Bill Pertwee, what are you waiting for?"

"Yes," said Perthy, looking down, "that is how I thought it would be."

The dead man was lying on his back. His face was calm and still in the candle-light, as though he were listening to a solemn music. Just above the right eye-socket there stood up the figure of a nude woman, superbly carved in jade. On the right hand was that old livid scar of a bear's claw. The clustered camp-fires on the diamond ring were still vividly twinkling.

"Great God o' the Mountain," Holdfast murmured to himself, "I do not understand how things are tangled."

Half a minute passed while they looked and listened before Perthy answered: "Well, then, if you don't, of course neither do I."

With a jerk he plucked the knife out of the cooling clay and wiped the blade on the dead man's hair. "Take a hold, there, will you, Holdfast?" said he. "We'll dump it down through the trap-door and let it twirl."

After the splash they heard only the confident voice of the River softly chuckling among the old worn piles.

CREOLE PLANTATION

(December 23, 1814)

The morning sun was hot on the wide verandah. Young Major Gabriel Villeré was enjoying a Spanish cigar given him by his friend and business associate Jean Lafitte, and was gazing dreamily down at the grassy river. His free hand caressed the head of his favorite setter bitch. He was half asleep.

"Gabriel, leesten to me," said his younger brother, Célestin, who was cleaning a fowling-piece beside him.

"Eh? Whad ees id?"

"Do yo' t'ing de Breeteesh har comin'?"

"Oh, dey won' iv dey're sonseeb'.—An' iv dey do, de reever 'll jus warsh—warsh—warsh dem bag 'g'in. Dey cain' teg dis cundry. Id ees too beeg, an' too hod."

"Bud Ah steel sez, Gabriel, iv Ah 'd been ordered to blog up our Bayou Villeré wid logs ligue all de odder bayous har blogged—wal, A 'd 've done id."

"Don' fret, li'l brudder. De Breeteesh har ad Cad Islan' in de Gulf. Mah pigged weel tell me iv dey do come."

"Bud yo' pigged may be s'prise' befo' dey can tell uz!"

"No. Doze stoopeed Breeteesh always shoud t'ree beeg cheers befo' dey kin staht annyt'in'."

"Bud de Général Jacksone ordered . . ."

"De Général Jacksone ees juz a Kaintuck, an' he don' unnerstan'."

"Yo' know de Mayricains har sayin' uz Creoles won' fide."

"Mais, id ees fo' dad riz'n Ah lef' open de Bayou Villeré!"

"Wad?"

"Iv hall de odder bayous har blogged egcep' dis wan, de Breeteesh muz come hyeh. An' den Ah shell hev opp'tun'ty to show de Mayricains."

"Bud yo' cain' fide de 'ole Breeteesh army!"

"Ah kin han'l dem all ri'!—Be quied. Ah'm ti'ed."

The sun beat down. Everything would be all right. Everything always *had* been all right at Villeré Plantation. While it remained so, why worry? It was hard to imagine invaders coming into this region of peace. And even if they should come, when once they had felt the heat of noon-day they would have the sense to go away again. Or, if they were stupid enough to camp in this marsh-land over-night, they would find a quarter of an inch of ice about their ankles in the morning. In a week most of them would be down with sun-stroke, frost-bite, fever-and-ague, and cholera. The River would drive them away.

The setter bitch awoke with a moan, yawned, and then began sniffing the air.

"Lie down," said Gabriel.

But, for once, she did not obey. After glancing adoringly up at him

564

she walked to the edge of the stairs and stood looking out, her nose nervously twitching. She began to whimper.

Gabriel Villeré opened his eyes half-way, so as not to waken himself entirely. For a minute or two he sat gazing drowsily out into the sun-soaked clearing. Everything seemed to be all right. But then, just as his eyes were closing again, he saw something vividly red dart out from the shadows of the distant trees and down toward the River. Another moving splash of red followed, and another. Célestin was on his feet. The bitch was barking. Gabriel lunged forward in his chair and rose. They were men in red coats, running. There were five, seven, ten, thirteen . . . !

"Dey s'prise' yo' pigged, Gabriel!"

As Célestin dashed down the steps and ran for the woods his elder brother turned into the dark cool hall of the house and made for the rear door. There he found a dozen British regulars—and an officer, who called upon him to surrender.

"I am Colonel Thorton. And you, sir?"

"Major René Philippe Gabriel de Villeré."

"Of the militia, I presume."

"An' dis ees mah brudder Célestin," said Gabriel as the youngster was brought in by another party.

"Have the goodness to step into this room, gentlemen."

Their hands were not tied. Evidently the British were quite sure of their prisoners. By this time, probably, the house had been surrounded.

There was a rumble of voices in the passage, and then another prisoner was brought in—Joseph Ducros, a member of the picket that had been stationed at the bayou. Half a dozen Spanish and Portuguese fishermen came in with him. A portly officer and a red-faced white-haired man in worn naval uniform entered last and took seats to examine the prisoners. Colonel Thorton began: "General Keane and Admiral Cochrane, these gentlemen are Monsieur Gabriel . . ."

"That's enough, Colonel," Cochrane cut in. "We don't care about their unpronounceable names.—Now, you Ducros, you're lyin' in your throat. Jackson can't have anything like twelve thousand men."

"Twelf to fifdeen dousan', oui, ad Noo Orleans, an' four dousan' in reserve," Ducros stoutly answered. "An' hall of dem well ahmed."

Gabriel was amazed that Ducros should say such a thing. Surely he must know that Jackson had scarcely more than five thousand, and that half of those he had were not armed at all.

"Fiva . . . fiva tousan'! Notta manna mo'!" exploded one of the

Portuguese fishermen, making wrathful gestures at Ducros. And the other fishermen nodded their heads in vigorous agreement.

The situation was becoming clearer. Gabriel guessed that these Portuguese had received some British gold already for leading the troops up the bayou, and that they were working for more from the same source by telling Cochrane what he wanted to hear. But Gabriel saw that Ducros was telling the only story that might hold the British back for a while and give Jackson a chance.

"Pedro! Sebastian!" he said, stepping suddenly forward and speaking sternly, "zee good Breeteesh hev come to sev uz from zee Mayricains. Yo' wand lead our frien's into a trep? Yo' meeserab', bleck-ha'ted, shemless villains! Fo' money yo' sell yo' souls! Fo' money yo' sell yo' chile into Mayricain slav'ry fo' evvah! Ah-ah! Yo' mek me seek!"

Finding that the fishermen were recoiling into a corner before the sheer violence of his attack, Gabriel turned to the officers. "Messieurs," said he, "evva sense de proclamation of de Cunnel Nicholls hev ridged uz, we Creoles hev hanxiously egspected yo' comin'. We har ti'ed of de Mayricain inz'lence an' stoopeed'ty. De Général Jacksone, dat dirty Kaintuck, hez ordaired de bayous blogged; bud, ez yo' see, Ah 'ranged fo' dis one be hopen an' de pigged fas' 'sleep w'en yo' do come."

"Dat one dem lie!" cried a fisherman from the corner.

Gabriel shrugged his shoulders and smiled at the British officers. "Teg yo' choize, gen'lemen," he went on, "bitwin de trude an' doze reptiles. Dey weel teg yo' money of coze, an' stab yo' een de bagg fo' wan picayune mo'. Jacksone kin geev dem hall de money een Noo Orleans fo' leadin' yo' in dis trep, bud Ah don' esk fo' nodding fo' tell yo' true."

"How many men do you say Jackson has?" asked Keane, looking up sharply from the table.

"Fifdeen dousan', well ahmed, entrench', an' proveeshion' fo' six mont'."

"Pah! Nonsense!" Cochrane exclaimed.

General Keane turned to Cochrane, and Thorton joined them. There was a brief council of war, with frequent explosions from the white-haired admiral: "The bastards are lying!"—"I'll lay my last pound on the fishermen!"—"You'll be an everlasting fool, General Keane, if you don't attack at once."

Colonel Thorton was equally urgent for immediate action. "Jackson thinks we're still at Cat Island," said he. "If the fishermen are right we can be in New Orleans in two hours and overwhelm him."

566

"That's possible, *if* they are right," Keane answered. "But the fishermen have at least as much motive for lying as these others. Moreover, we're in enemy country with scarce two thousand men. At midnight we shall have three thousand more. We can surprise Jackson as well tomorrow as we can today if nobody tells him we're here. Therefore, gentlemen, I intend to show ordinary caution.—Colonel Thorton, please issue orders that all deserters and escaping prisoners are to be shot at sight. Post strong pickets, and have the men pitch camp here for the night."

Gabriel found himself alone with Célestin and the guard when the three officers, followed by the fishermen, had left the room.

For the time being, his ruse had succeeded. To be sure, it would not do the Americans much good because no one had got away to tell Jackson about the British landing.—Oh, well, since it couldn't be the tri-color of France, he didn't much care what flag waved over Louisiana. First there had been the French, then the Spanish, and now it was the American; and if it was next to be the British flag—what difference? He had exerted himself in this matter chiefly on account of his young brother. After seeing General Jackson riding a splendid horse in New Orleans the other day, the boy had come home with some childish notion about being a patriotic American, and had even gone about the house whistling a nauseating tune called "Yankee Doodle"! But now, of course, Célestin would realize that his big brother had done all a man could to fool the British.

Gabriel looked down at the youngster, expecting approval; but instead he saw a blush of shame on the boy's face. "Ah s'pose," said Célestin, "de Mayricains har ride 'boud uz Creoles. We won' fide."

Ah, that put a different face upon the matter. It was not so much a new-fangled patriotism that was troubling Célestin as a fear that the honor of his own people would be sullied. No matter who owned this country, Célestin was remembering that the Creoles had founded Louisiana. He hated to think that anyone would ever be able to say: "It was a Creole, and a Villeré, who left the bayou open for the enemy."

With a trick of his foot which he had learned from Jean Lafitte, Gabriel suddenly tripped the nearest guard into the arms of the next and dashed for the long French door giving on the verandah. He took the low verandah railing at a leap and ducked and ran under the

567

floor-level to dodge the bullets. He was around the corner and over the fence before the British had found their muskets.

"Bring him back dead or alive!" he heard the voice of 'Thorton shouting.

The cane-brake opened on a plowed field, and that into a cypress swamp. Twice he nearly turned his ankle in the furrows, and imagined himself being carried back to the house a helpless prisoner. Then Jackson would be surprised and outnumbered . . . then New Orleans . . . Louisiana . . . and all the gossips saying "It was a Creole, a Villeré, the son of the old General . . . !"

Before he was half-way across the field he heard them crashing through the cane behind him. There were a few wild shots. He dodged back and forth, bent double. He heard a dog bark sharply. Were they running him like a fox, with dogs?—But no; the lifting note at the end of the cry came from his own setter bitch. That was bad. Nothing but a bullet could keep her from following, and she would show them the way.

He knew that he was in prime form, after years of hunting and racing in the open, but that had been with horses, not on foot. Still, glancing back for an instant, he saw that he was gaining. He plunged thankfully into the cypress shadows.

The woods soon dipped to a swamp, and he was bogged to the knees. While he floundered there the soldiers came in among the cypresses behind, spreading out and calling to each other. They were hardly more than a hundred yards behind, but they had not seen him yet among the hanging mosses. Soon they too would begin to flounder. He came to a large live-oak tree, with thick foliage and heavy festoons of moss. That would hide him until they grew tired of the pursuit. They would think that he had either found a way through the swamp or else had drowned there.

As he swung himself up into the lower branches Gabriel heard a low whine behind him. It was his setter, dripping with water and mud. He could not take her with him into the tree, and he knew that she would not leave the spot alive unless with him.

Taking every precaution to hide himself from the floundering redcoats, he got back again to the ground and there found a heavy club. "Here, Nancy," he called in a low voice. "Come here, girl."

For a moment he fondled her, looking deep into her faithful dark eyes, before he said "Lie down now, Nancy. And goodbye."

Her skull cracked at the first blow. She died without a whimper.

568

He had just time to sink her body in the swamp and to reach the leafy top of the oak before the soldiers came in sight. It was evident that they had no liking for this sort of thing, and no experience in it. They had not found the tracks that he must have left in the oozy earth. At no time did they come within fifty feet of the live-oak.—"Plucky devil," he heard one of them say when they were closest. "He must 've drowned in the bog. You can never tell about these Parley-voos!"

Half an hour later Gabriel came out of the woods at the plantation of his nearest neighbor, Colonel de la Ronde, who was hurrying with his family and slaves to New Orleans. In five minutes two swift little Creole ponies were hammering up the road along the levee.

"Seven thousand rifle-flints, you say, Mr. Lafitte?"

"Seven t'ousan' five hunner', mon Général, an' feefty kaigs of powdaire à votre service. Also, two t'ousan' of my fishermen weesh not'ing bettaire but join wiz your army."

"Mr. Lafitte, I need that powder and those flints, but your men are pirates, sir."

"Non! Mais non! Privateers against Spain, but nevaire pirates!"

For several seconds Jackson gazed steadily into Lafitte's remarkably large and clear brown eyes.

"Privateers, eh? And can they handle cannon?"

"Zey are ze bombardiers foremost of ze world, mon Général."

"I see," said Jackson, drily. "Well then, I suppose they wouldn't be afraid to stand up against the gunners of the British army and navy."

"Afraid! Monsieur!—Zey haf stand so before, bien des fois."

"Bring 'em in.—But just because I'm letting you help defend New Orleans, don't think I'm pardoning your offenses against the law. That's for the President of the United States to do—perhaps—though much depends upon your conduct in this battle. Is that clearly understood?"

"Parfaitement, mon Général!"

"Good. And how soon can you get that powder and the flints here?"

Lafitte looked at his large gold watch. "At five zis après-midi," he said.

There was a sound of running feet and a hammering at the door. De la Ronde and Gabriel Villeré burst into the room, followed by the guard.

"What news, gentlemen?"

"Importan'!" gasped De la Ronde. "De Breeteesh hev arriv' ad

Villeré plantation an' camp dere tonide. Hyeh ees Major Villeré who hez escep'."

Gabriel told his story. He reported that the British had about two thousand men already on land, and that they were expecting large reinforcements at midnight. He said that they thought Jackson had at least fifteen thousand.

Weakened by fever-and-ague and holding hard with one hand to the edge of the table, Andrew Jackson swung round to face his lieutenants.

"Gentlemen," he called in a high-pitched voice, "the British are below. We must fight them tonight."

BLACK MAGIC

"Ah-oo-oo-oo! Ah-oo-oo-oo!"

Tum-tum, t'tum-tum-tum, t'tum-tum-TUM-tum!

"Bo aba-ntu babi babota tu-ba-tia!—Bo aba-ntu babi babota tu-ba-tia!"

"We fear, we fear dem!" answered the chorus, swaying from left to right together round the fire. "We fear dem. Dey bad men. Dey kill. We fear dem!"

It was six o' clock in the evening, and already the dark had fallen. In the yard of the slave quarters at Villeré plantation a great fire lighted a circle of ebony faces. There must be a hundred blacks here, McWilliams thought, counting the young and the old, the men and women and children. Half of them were so savage in appearance that they must have been born in the heart of Africa. The intricate and endlessly repeated rhythms of their drum-beat, subtly answered by the chant and swaying of the chorus, were savage too. They spoke to something far older, deeper down, and darker than white man's music. They made McWilliams wonder, not for the first time, whether the thing called civilization were not a huge mistake, a recent one, soon to be corrected.

Inside the circle of slaves was a circle of fire, surrounding a powerful young Negro who stood, naked, with his arms reaching up toward the stars. Mysteriously beautiful that black body looked to McWilliams. He had never seen a naked Negro before, but now, all at once, black seemed to him the right color for a man's body to be. It was the color of fertile earth, out of which men come and back into which they go. His own body, he felt, was pallid, bloodless, bleached.

"Bo aba-ntu babi babota tu-ba-tia!" chanted the young coryphaeus for at least the thirtieth time.

"What's that black babble he's sayin', Mac?" asked Captain Woodbine, suddenly appearing out of the shadow. "D' you know the language?"

"The crowd is translating it. I think it means they're afraid we're going to kill them."

"Stupid fools! We mustn't let 'em think that. Why don't you go in there and say we're goin' to set 'em free?"

McWilliams did not answer at once. His eyes were roving about the circle of honest, intensely earnest black faces. At last he said: "You tell 'em, George. I won't."

"Why not? They're slaves, aren't they? Old England is against slavery. Why don't you tell 'em?"

"Because sometimes I get tired of lies and lying—yes, and even, occasionally, of liars. Because I know a little about how we English have treated the people of India, and our part in the African slave-trade. Because I've been up north in our own Black Country. Because I've seen the debtor's side of Fleet Prison. Because I've been in Ireland.— Do you want any more reasons?"

Captain Woodbine looked somewhat overwhelmed. "Ah, you need a drink, Mac," he muttered, moving away.

Tum-tum, t'tum-tum-tum-tum, tum-tum, t'tum-tum-TUM-tum, TUM-tum!

"Ah-oo-oo-oo! Ah-oo-oo-oo!"

"Bo aba-ntu babi babota tu-ba-tia!"

"What's that infernal howling over there in the slave-quarters?" shouted Admiral Cochrane, emptying his second bottle of Gabriel Villeré's port.

Colonel Thornton, looking up from the map he was studying, admitted that he didn't know.

"Don't know, eh?" the admiral snorted. "I thought not. And when that young Creole escaped this morning you *didn't know* how to stop him. If he hadn't died in the swamp Jackson would know all our plans by this time.—That is, if we *had* any plans."

The army officers in the room shifted uneasily in their chairs and glowered at one another under knitted brows.

The admiral was filling his wine-glass from a third bottle when he burst out again: "If any o' those niggers escapes, General Keane, or if there are any riots, Lord Castlereagh will hear of it. My advice is that you shoot them down at the slightest sign of anything suspicious."

"You do well to call that your advice, sir," the general answered, "and not to issue it as an order."

"I don't know about that. Someone ought to be issuing orders in this campaign, and if the army has forgotten how, then it's time for the navy to save the honor of England."

General Keane leaned forward in his chair. "Do you mean, Admiral," said he, "in the way it did at Fayal?"

Two or three of the younger officers discreetly hid their smiles of satisfaction at this home thrust.

"No, sir!" exploded Cochrane, now purple in the face, "I do not refer to any third-rate engagement in which His Majesty's ships were loaded down and cluttered and held back by a crowd of land-lubbers calling themselves soldiers. I have in mind, sir, a long series of actions under my orders in which a large part of northern Massachusetts has been captured and annexed to the British Empire, the town of Eastport has been burned, Nantucket has been taken, Cape Cod has been sacked, Long Island invaded, Stonington bombarded, Block Island captured, Alexandria plundered, Baltimore shelled, and the President's House at Washington leveled with the ground.—That's the sort of thing that happens, sir, when the *navy* issues orders; and if I had been running this campaign Jackson's Dirty Shirts would be on the scamper before now. But, as it is, that whole series of victories in which the navy terrorized the Atlantic seaboard is being brought to nothing—to less than nothing, sir—by a pack of dunderheads that can't even keep a crowd of niggers quiet. What do you think we came down the coast for, burning and sacking and capturing as we came so that the banks buried their coin and New York and Philadelphia started to build fortifications? Why, of course, just to give the army a chance at New Orleans. You know that. And how have you used that chance? You were twenty-six days late at Jamaica. And now that you're here in front of New Orleans, what are you doing? You sit round a table studying maps while those niggers out there are making ready to scalp us. My God!"

To this torrent of words General Keane attempted no direct reply. Turning to his secretary, a tall and strikingly handsome young man with reddish yellow hair, he quietly said: "Have the goodness, Captain Reid, to step outside and see what is going on among the Negroes. I shan't be needing you for some time."

William Reid found Captain Woodbine on the verandah, rather obviously trying to overhear what was being said within.

"What's the old walrus bellowing about now?" Woodbine inquired.

"The Negroes. He thinks we're going to let them scalp us, or else tell Jackson we're here."

"Drunken old sea-cow!"

"He keeps blowing Keane up for being late at Jamaica. Says if we'd reached the rendezvous on time we could have taken New Orleans before Jackson heard of us."

"Huh!—When in fact it was one of his own precious commodores, an idiot called Lloyd, who delayed you at Fayal by attacking a pitiful Yankee privateer—yes, and getting pretty damn well trounced by her, too. That right?"

"That's about right, if you call being twenty-six days late a delay."

"Must 've been a grand fight that privateer put up, to stand off three British ships."

"So grand a fight that I'm proud to say the captain of that privateer was a cousin of mine."

"You don't say!"

"Yes. A man by the name of Samuel Chester Reid."

"How 'd you find that out?"

"Oh, we younger officers gave him a banquet after the battle, and he talked a little about himself. He might be Laird of Glasgow if his father hadn't turned Yankee in the last war."

"That so!"

"But let's walk over and take a look at the Negroes, Captain."

As they went through the grove of orange-trees near the house, Reid and Woodbine could see the glimmering camp-fires of the troops in the plowed field to the north. The men were preparing their evening meal of salt pork, beef, and ship's biscuit moistened with rum. At least a hundred fires there must be over there, and from all of them at once— or so it seemed—there came rolling up and out the strains of the old song:

> Some talk of Alexa-ander
> And some of Her-cu-les!
> Of Hector and Lysa-ander
> And such great names as these!
> But of all the world's great he-e-roes
> There's none that can compare,
> Singing tow-row-row-row-ROW-row
> To the BRI-tish Gre-e-e-na-diers!

From the slave-quarters nearer at hand there was throbbing a savage drum beneath the half-wailed and half-chanted words: "Ku-ngu-mbona! Ku-ngu-mbona! Ku-dabo ku-anza ku-juba! Ku-ngu-mbona!"

"What in the world can that gibberish mean?" asked Reid.—But then at once came the chorus: "Yo' moon, you' ribber, yo' sky! Yo' see dis. Yo' see our fear!"

The night sky, the moon and stars, the fire, the chanting circle of black faces and bodies, began to work a charm, to fix a spell, upon the two young officers. They looked on and listened beside McWilliams, wondering. Inside the circle of the fire the leader was still standing like a black burnished statue, his arms uplifted to the stars and the little week-old moon.

To McWilliams the dull thud of the tom-tom had become as the beat of his own heart, and the chant like a music fiddled out on his spinal chord. These savage faces in the firelight, these rhythms born of the jungle, were immeasurably old, like the mysterious River out there. They were strange and yet somehow familiar, like a wordless memory handed down from the first fathers.

"Ku-ngu-mbona! Ku-ngu-mbona!"

Tum-tum, t'tum-tum-tum-tum, t'tum-tum-TUM-tum, t'tum, t'tum, t'tum-tum-tum-tum-TUM-tum, t'tum!

"I must go get a drink," said McWilliams, turning back toward the plantation house.

The "British Grenadiers" had died away. Something deeper and more elemental had silenced that boastful song. Many privates had left the camp in the furrowed field and were crowding about the circle of Negroes. Plowboys from sleepy English villages along the upper Thames were gathering on the bank of the Mississippi to listen, fascinated, to a chant brought from the Congo.

"Ah-oo-oo-oo!" yelled McWilliams, suddenly reappearing from the direction of the house and making toward the great fire. "Ah-oo-oo-oo!"

Captain Woodbine caught at him as he reeled past and tried to stop him, but McWilliams turned and yelled in his face "Ah-oo-oo-oo!" Woodbine let him go.

The others were feeling the effects of the wild scene in different ways. Some of them pretended to scorn the whole affair, but more were frankly enjoying it as a welcome change from soldierly routine and sentry-go. More still were silently approaching McWilliams's sense of elation, freedom, and sudden release from a weight. Captain Reid was

conscious of a steadily strengthening throb somewhere within him—
not of his muscles, not of his heart, but of something more primal, vital,
visceral. His diaphragm seemed to be throbbing like a drum-head.

There was a change in the chant. At last the chorus-leader had
received the message which he had for hours been seeking, and now
he was telling it to the people:

"Ya-anza ya-juba ya-bi-eru-bantu-dia! Ya-bi-eru-bantu-ta!"

Tum-tum, t'tum-tum-TUM-tum!

"Ya-bi-eru-bantu-ta! Ba-bi-eru-bantu babota!"

"He god ob de ribber eat bad whide men!" chanted the chorus. "He
god ob de ribber strike bad whide men dead!"

"Ah-oo-oo-oo!"

Tum-tum-tum, t'TUM-tum!

"Ya-anza ya-ba-dia! Ya-anza ya-ba-ta!"

"He de ribber swaller dem up! He de ribber strike dem dead!"

Tum-tum, t'tum-tum, t'TUM!

The voices, the swaying dance, the drum-beats swinging up into a
frenzy of intricately concerted black rhythms, made every heart beat
faster in expectation of some dire event. The British soldiers, marines,
and sailors crowding now in hundreds about the outer circle stood
speechless. From time to time they glanced at one another, furtively.
The faces of their fellows looked to them strangely pale. They looked
like the faces of dead men. In the clutch of the furiously climbing and
clashing rhythms they forgot why they had come to this place and
what they were to do here. They remembered the darkness out of
which all men come and back to which all men go. They were gripped
by the fear of empty darkness. It made their bowels quake.

NIGHT BATTLE

"It's ghostly, Captain."

"What is?" said Woodbine, pretending that he didn't know.

William Reid paused a moment and swept with his right arm a broad
gesture which included the barely visible Mississippi to the west and
also the farthest camp-fires twinkling on the edge of Villeré's cypress
woods.

Woodbine shivered slightly, and turned up the collar of his coat.

Then the two men moved on together along the top of the levee. They had been together continually, except for the minute or two in which Reid had made his report to General Keane, ever since that savage chant had died away in the slave-quarters. And yet it was not, apparently, that they had much to say to each other. Their acquaintance had begun at noon of this very day.

To their right, in the plowed fields of the plantation, many fires were still burning brightly, with soldiers moving here and there about them and others wrapped in their blankets. On the other side a fog was thickening up from the River, growing denser and deeper from minute to minute. In the fleeting light of the moon they could see how that fog was woven, as though with some secret purpose, out of the raveled threads and yarns of vapor exhaled by the huge dark stream. Already it lay like a vast woolen blanket, vaguely gray, drawn from edge to edge of the River's bed and reaching across the wide batture to the outer slope of the levee. Little by little, yet irresistibly, it was climbing the levee's bank. At the rate it was rising now, they saw, it would soon overflow that bank and pour shapelessly down among the clustered fires to blur and blot them out.

Just that, although they would not have said so, was the reason why neither Woodbine nor Reid cared to walk alone. Rather as a dim premonition than as a clearly formulated thought, it came to them that the fog was repeating what the black chorus-leader had chanted. He had drawn his confidence down from the stars, and this fog was the River's corroborative answer. They began to feel that they were intruders, that the River had plans of his own.

On and on they walked, staring northward into the silvered dusk that hid New Orleans, nine miles away, and whatever preparations the enemy might be making. Now and then they caught a glint of steel from the nearest line of pickets that Keane had posted up-stream. There were six or seven of those lines—some on the levee, some in the fields below, and others on the batture or exposed bed of the River.—Well, that ought to be enough, even though discipline had been relaxed throughout the camp and the two officers themselves hardly knew what their own men were doing. Neither Reid nor Woodbine could have given a valid reason for his mounting anxiety.

Half a mile above the plantation house they came to a place where the levee turned to run nearer the stream, and within the angle they saw a conical hut improvised out of fence-rails, rotted posts, and driftwood. It was illumined, evidently by candles, and at its door-way burned a flourishing fire. Three or four private soldiers, blood-red in the leaping light of the fire, lounged beside the door. From inside came the convivial voices of two men singing the songs of home.

"Let's go down there and try to get warm," said Woodbine.

An old white horse, startled by the noise they made as they blundered down, lumbered off stiff-legged into the dark.

The singing ceased when they came to the entrance, and two young subalterns, Gleig and Gray by name, crawled out to bid them welcome. Being superior officers, Reid and Woodbine took the seats of honor in the hut, the subalterns sat outside, and the privates were shoved still farther away from the fire. The six tall wax candles which had been purloined an hour before from the Villeré stock-room illuminated the pile of cleanly picked chicken-bones, together with eight or ten small bottles of claret from the Villeré cellar, most of them empty.

Reid and Woodbine enjoyed the claret and the candle-light and the fire, but they were not so well pleased with the opinions of young Gleig. Apparently he had not heard the chant in the slave-quarters, nor was he aware that a stealthy fog was slowly reaching and creeping up the other side of the levee within fifty feet of where he sat and chattered and jested. He expected, he said, to eat his Christmas dinner in New Orleans—and this for no better reason, so far as could be seen, than that he held just at present a skinful of Creole chicken and claret. The suggestion that Andrew Jackson might do something on his own account—might even take advantage of the steadily darkening night to pounce upon the British camp—filled his brash young mouth with jibes of derision. He wished to be told when and where the "Yankees" had ever voluntarily attacked His Majesty's troops. Furthermore he wished to assert, with profane emphasis, that the only trouble Englishmen had ever found in licking "these rebels" had been the difficulty of catching up with them.—Reid and Woodbine, overwhelmed by the subaltern's spate of violent language, climbed back up the bank with their anxiety unrelieved.

The fog, they saw, had climbed higher in those ten minutes. It lay now scarcely a foot below the levee-top. When the moon brightened out from behind the rapidly gathering clouds they saw that it had thickened. Its upper surface was like a sea of quieted billows, weirdly gray. It hid the River completely.

Hardly had they set foot again on the upper road when they heard the voice of someone coming along it from the direction of the Villeré plantation-house, and singing as he came.

"Who's there?" called Woodbine.

"A friend to this ground, but liegeman to the King."

"Is that you, McWilliams?"

"A piece of him."

"Oh, hello, Mac! Glad to see—that is, to hear you. And this is Captain William Reid that I have with me."

"Good. Have you had quiet watch?"

"Quiet enough, but cold."

"It *is* a nipping and an eager air."

"Talk English, will you, Mac?"

"I'm talking Shakespeare.—Isn't that good enough?"

"Shakespeare, eh? I thought it was all those drinks you've had.—Any news from the army and navy?"

"Only that they haven't cut each other's throats yet. But they're still trying to. 'Waw! Waw!' says old Keane, and 'Waw! Waw! Waw!' says the old walrus back at him. They take to each other like cats and dogs. —I agree with both of 'em."

Even Captain Reid permitted himself a short and nervous laugh. He was finding Captain McWilliams, for all the oddity of his notions and behavior, an agreeable companion.

"But, gentlemen," said the new-comer, taking each of the others by the arm and starting forward, lurching slightly, "we waste moonlight. Let's march up and down here and try to . . . 'Angels and ministers of grace defend us!' "

"Why, what's wrong, Mac?" and "What is it, Captain?" asked Woodbine and Reid at the same moment, feeling McWilliams pull back at their arms.

After a second or two of wild-eyed staring into the fog he turned first to the one and then to the other. "Didn't you see it?" said he.

"See what, Mac?"

"Why there, just now, ten paces ahead and to the left, standing up out of the fog . . . Mean to say you didn't see it at all?"

"Go *on*, Mac!"

"Well, it was the head and shoulders of a man—I *think* of a man— with straight black hair down to his shoulders and a dark face, Indian-looking. Only his head and shoulders I saw—but huge, enormous, they were, Olympian! He knew we were here, but he was looking out over the camp. In a second he took it all in—how many fires, and where. Then he dropped back into the fog."

Woodbine laughed uneasily. "Anyhow, Mac," he said, "that wasn't a ghost you saw."

"Not a ghost? Well then, who . . . what . . . ?"

"No man wears his hair that way except the Mohegan called Sleeping Bear. I saw the man once myself for a second, down at Mobile—and, as you say . . . I s'pose he's out scouting for Jackson."

"Who is this Sleeping Bear?" asked Reid.

"Oh, that's so, Captain," Woodbine replied, "you wouldn't know. Well, it's hard to say, because most of what you hear about him is what his friends, red and white, make up."

"And his enemies?"

"He hasn't any.—But if you believed all the tales they tell, you'd say he's a living myth, or an Injun god in the making."

"He looked like all America to me," said McWilliams.

"Yes, Mac; but then of course you've had quite a few drinks."

"Not enough, though, if any more Indian gods are going to revisit the glimpses of the moon."

"Let's go back and get him one more," Reid suggested. "I ought to report to General Keane, and you and McWilliams might like to find out where your men are."

Jackson's teeth were chattering as he sat his horse on the levee-top in front of de la Ronde's "Versailles." Partly it was the chill of the fog that made them chatter, partly it was his persistent fever-and-ague, but mostly it was impatience. Almost an hour ago he had sent the *Carolina* down through the fog. It was half an hour at least since Coffee and his mounted six hundred had stolen away behind the live-oaks with Pierre Lafitte for guide. Holdfast had been gone for half an hour. The Seventh and the Forty-fourth Infantry were drawn up in line, together with the battalions headed by Daquin and Plauché, all the way from the levee to the Versailles gardens. The two six-pounders were on the levee itself, well manned by a group of marines.—What was left to do?

It was a task for which he had no talent, this standing in the dark and merely waiting for Patterson, Coffee, Holdfast, Hinds, Denis de la Ronde, Plauché, Daquin, Lafitte, and Beale, to carry out orders.—And yet he should have learned how to wait. In a sense, deeply true, he had been waiting more than forty years for just the chance tonight had given him. With the fingers of his left hand he felt along the old scar of a saber-cut running across his brow and into the rusted iron bristle of his hair.

He did not know how many troops might be gathered about and behind the flicker of the enemy's fires a quarter of a mile away. One prisoner had said twenty-five hundred, and another ten thousand. Young Villeré had reported that Keane was expecting strong reinforcements by midnight. Therefore Jackson felt obliged to strike as soon as he could with his total force, bringing in from their outposts Plauché's Creole militiamen, Daquin's free men of color, the Choctaws under Sleeping Bear, and even Jean Lafitte's Baratarians, many of them recently taken from jail. He would have to take the chance that the fresh British troops now probably marching up from Lake Borgne might pass around him to the eastward and move directly against New Orleans.

He would have to take the chance of leaving New Orleans for tonight unprotected, on the side away from the River, from perhaps the very men who had recently, and horribly, raped the Spanish city of Badajoz. But then, had not his whole life been a matter of taking chances?—hitherto on his own account for the most part, to be sure, but seldom unsuccessfully. Swift and vivid images flickered through his mind of cock-fights, horse-races, moments of danger in the cane-brake and on the trace, and of the morning in Kentucky when he had taken Charles Dickinson's bullet in his breast in order to make sure of killing Charles Dickinson. Desperate chances some of them had been. All his friends had urged him to withdraw the badly lamed stallion, Truxtun, from the race at Clover Bottom. Yet Truxtun had won that race by sixty yards, in spite of his swollen thigh and a twisted shoe. And as for tonight, what was there that an ignorant, inexperienced, and wretchedly equipped commander could do, except to take chances? And besides, over there behind the British fires there might be some commander—Lord Wellington himself, perhaps—so magnificently equipped for victory, so perfectly trained in the art of war, such a veteran of many campaigns, that he would take no chances whatever.—In that case, of course, one could smash him.

Jackson groaned aloud, nevertheless, as he reviewed his own situation. Where was John Adair with his two thousand Kentuckians, unheard from for weeks? Had Adair been such a fool as to obey orders by marching down, instead of breaking them as Bill Carroll had so boldly and successfully done? Carroll had brought in his three thousand men from Tennessee five days ago, arriving even before the runners sent out from Nashville to say they were coming. Carroll, moreover, had picked up eleven hundred muskets on the way, in addition to the few rifles that Russell Bean and his men had been able to make and some fifty thousand cartridges manufactured on the *Pride o' the West*. That was something; but the thought of what Carroll had done merely led on to the irate recollection that a certain flat-boat loaded with muskets from Pittsburgh, promised for weeks ago, had not yet arrived or been heard from. Andrew Jackson confided to the darkness a series of definite and strongly expressed opinions about the captain of that flat-boat, specifically referring to his parentage, his character, his eternal destiny, his physical appearance, and certain respects in which Jackson thought that appearance should be violently altered.

He called down the slope of the levee to his secretary and chief aide: "Please ride out, Major Reid, and tell every company to bring back all the British muskets and cartridge-boxes they can find."

The moon, which had given little light when it first appeared, was more and more obscured by slow-moving clouds. A thick fog was rising. It had reached almost to the top of the levee. Darker and darker the night grew.

In a way, of course, this darkness and fog would be an advantage. It would hide his pitiful weakness in numbers, training, and equipment. It would give full play to whatever skill his men might have in rough-and-tumble fighting. It would wipe out the advantage of the British in the mere appearance of their marching columns. That was what old General Jacques Villeré had meant, half an hour ago, in saying: "Mais, id ees darg, mon Général, et votres soldats zey weel nod run away joost from ze uniforms."

Coffee's men had slipped into the night like the veteran Indian-fighters they were, making no sound. They had blackened their faces with river-mud, and also every bit of metal about them that light could cling to.—And now it seemed as though some of them had dismounted out there in the darkness, for horses by the dozen and score were straying loose toward the enemy's fires, nibbling and browsing.

Well, Coffee would know best. But even if he and all the others should do the wrong, the ruinous thing, it was now too late to stop them. Jackson dismounted and began pacing up and down behind the marines and the brass six-pounders. His nails dug into the palms of his hands. He was shivering. His shirt was wet with perspiration.

When would Holdfast come back and report? When would Patter-

581

son open fire from the *Carolina*? Why couldn't Coffee send a scout to say where he was, and what doing?

Jackson strode faster and faster along the top of the levee, muttering and cursing. A little yellow dog, very muddy and ill-conditioned, trotted beside him, taking turn for turn.

Coming back from Keane's headquarters, arm-in-arm, Reid and Woodbine and McWilliams could see from a distance that the fog had spilled over the levee-top and was wallowing down among the fires in the field. They also saw that the men left awake about the fires were staring, walking, or running toward the levee and the River. The two subalterns and the private soldiers with them had climbed the bank. Twenty or more others had joined them there.

"It's a ship in the River," exclaimed Woodbine, starting to run.

"A schooner, you mean," said Reid.

And they heard one of the subalterns call: "Hello, there! Are you the *Sophie*? Is that you, Captain Lockyer?"

But there came no reply from under the two ghostly sails not a hundred yards off. Some sounds there were from out there—hollow rumblings of heavy round objects, it seemed, across a deck—but nothing to show what this vessel might be, or its errand.

Many more men, by this time, had scrambled up from the field. They stood in a dark huddling crowd, peering out.

"Keep down, men!" Reid shouted. "She may be Yankee, and ready to fire."

"Hell," answered the drunken voice of young Gleig, "Yankees 'd never come so close."

An uneasy laughter was spreading through the crowd when they heard someone quietly speaking out there: "Give 'em this one, boys, for the honor of America."

A great flame-colored flower of battle bloomed for an instant in the fog, and before it faded the night was crammed with a rolling roar and the screams of stricken men. Seven other guns stabbed the dark in swift succession, firing grape, double-loaded. The air was peopled with flying ghosts that whistled and wailed and moaned. Beneath the two sails serenely dreaming in the moonlight the mysterious deck was bristling with fierce stiff quills of fire.

"Christ!" Gleig yelled, and turned to plunge down the bank. He stumbled at starting against a prone body and fell and rolled over

582

and over to the bottom. Every man of the crowd who could run, walk, stagger, or drag himself disappeared from the top of the levee. The three captains, unhurt, ran down at top speed and huddled up with a hundred crouching others in a gully of mud and slime.

There for several minutes they all cowered, gasping, and heard the roar of the second and third broadside as though from far away. A few of their number were dying, but the rest hardly knew it. When their first fear was past they looked back at the field where a thousand or more of their comrades were scrambling among the scattered fires, some yelling frantic orders, some seeking their arms, some reeling and falling, while others were staggering up from sleep. It was a shocking sight for well-trained men with the habit of victory to look upon.

But little by little, as they began to realize that they themselves were at least temporarily safe, consternation and shame gave way to a strong sense of grievance. They began to curse, not themselves but others, and the opinion gradually prevailed that they had been grossly deceived and insulted. At first their rancor was directed against the enemy, who, as everyone was aware, was not supposed to attack at all but, whenever possible, to run away. They seemed to feel it had been an act of insolence, deserving of the severest rebuke, for a Yankee schooner to fire without warning into a crowd of the Duke of Wellington's soldiers.— And yet they were men who had all their lives been taught to respect sheer force, and as they lay there listening to the sternly authoritative remarks that continued to boom and bang from over the levee-top they decided that these Yankees were not, after all, contemptible. Having got thus far, they soon reached the conclusion that they had been led into a trap by their own officers. They wished to know why the navy had not protected them on the side of the water. They particularly asked to be told where that paunchy old blow-hard of an admiral was hiding himself now.

"You stop that talk!" said Woodbine, edging closer to a Devon private whom he had seen half an hour before at the subaltern's fire. "That's enough of it."

The yokel glanced sullenly about for a moment and saw that there were no officers in the gully except these three young captains, no one of whom had any immediate authority over him.

"Do thee putt thee pan on vire, Cap'n, an' vry thee own bakkon," he snarled. "Us common volk wull zay oor zay withoot no 'elp vrum quarlity."

583

"Shut up, I tell you, man! We're in danger here."

"Zo us be—an' who brung us, doost knaaw? 'T were hold Cochrane, the girt fat squallopin' to-ad. An' whilst us be a-liggin' 'ere i' the muck her's be zettin' yonder by vire a-warmin' his vittle-place an' zuckin' oop wines an' arl. Ees fai! It's the wines for the navy but bullets an' muck for we."

"You're bloody well right," said another private, lying prone on the slope of the bank. "It's the loot o' N'orleans the navy's arter. They gits the gold an' the girls. We gits the lead."

Woodbine could not reach the second speaker, but the socking thud of his fist against the jaw of the man from Devon was clearly heard by them all in a momentary lull of the schooner's guns. "Now, the next man," said he, "who opens his filthy face in that way, I'll see him flogged, if I have to do it myself."

Subdued muttering followed, and curses that made up for what they lacked in volume by their blasphemous intensity. The chance-gathered herd of men, weaponless, resentful, and still badly frightened, was approaching the verge of mutiny. And the three young officers themselves were finding it hard to maintain the prestige of command while groveling in the mud.

Five minutes had passed since they had dived and stumbled down here, and still the guns of the schooner yelled and the deadly hail came hurtling over.

McWilliams recognized two or three marines of his own command among the men cowering round him. He rose on one elbow and looked back over the bullet-beaten camp-ground, now all a whirried blur of reaching, raveling fog and bewildered men. The fires had been knocked about into random scatters of sparks. The men were running, crouching, crawling, yelling unheard. They were seeking their companies, their captains, their muskets. The cartridge-box of a private was kicked into one of the fires while McWilliams watched. It went off like a Chinese fire-work, spattering death in a dozen directions. Many riderless horses, saddled and with stirrups wildly a-swing, were running loose among the troops and the embers. Some of them were laced with blood, and the cry of one white stallion cut through the din as the very voice of the moment's horror and havoc.

"What's that?" whined a corpulent private near by, striving to burrow deeper into the mud.

"It's a hurt horse, shrieking," said McWilliams.

"Oh, God!"

584

"And that rattle you hear up above is our first picket-line firing down from the bank at the schooner."

"Firin' into the bloody fog, ye mean. We're like rats in a barn, with dogs at us."

Then the sparse straggling fire from the bank was drowned by an Indian scalp-whoop and a crackle of rifle-fire from the north and east of the camp.—Yes, and from the south too, from the out-houses of the Villeré plantation itself, was ringing the thin "ping-ping" of Kentucky rifles.

"Oh, God, we're s'rounded!" the fat private yelled. "We're cut off from the ships! Oh, God!"

McWilliams got the frantically kicking hulk by the collar, up-ended him, and slapped him hard on one side of the face and then on the other. "Now then, you blubbering girl-baby's doll, toddle out there! Find a musket! Get to fighting! Run!"

With the point of his sword McWilliams gave the reluctant bundle of grease an initial impulse in the right direction.—And then, suddenly, he saw himself as the central and ludicrously romantic figure in a painting of battle-glory. He was brandishing his blade over-head, he saw, like all the standard heroes of painting and poetry who had gone down scornful before many foes. That picture in the mind was laughable, he knew, and there might be a time to laugh at it, but just now he was too much surprised to hear himself calling, with lungs that seemed to be blown by the bellows of Wayland the Smith: "Woodbine! Reid! What are you digging for? Can't we go on a little farther to find our graves?"

Yes; that was the right accent for martial scenes in the grand manner, and if King Henry the Fifth had said much the same words in Shakespeare's play of that name . . . Anyhow, they had brought the two captains to their feet.

"Come on, now! Once more to the field, good friends! Let's spread it level with our English dead! Let's make a mound of English flesh and bone that will show the mettle of our pasture! Come, I say! We'll leave a copy to these western men that will teach them how to make war. We'll show ourselves the masters of our fates, and look down on our own deaths like some great rock that's swilled with the wild and wasteful ocean."

McWilliams was amazed, and keenly delighted, to find his own spirit soaring free on the lift of those windy words. Still more astonishing it was to see, as he strode up and down before the men, gesticulating, how

585

they too were moved, enthralled, and taken. They were rising to their feet. Their eyes were shining. Their mouths were hanging open and their breath came fast.

But then McWilliams suddenly realized, with a sick sense of overwhelming responsibility, that although the bodies, hearts, and minds of these men were in his control he did not know what to do with them. He had not even yet made up his mind whether old Horace was right in saying that it is a sweet and honorable thing for a man to die for his country—especially if that country were trying to steal some other man's country away. No, the poison of Shakespeare's half-remembered phrases had worked too swiftly, out-running his own convictions. He had taken too many drinks, or else too few.

But there was no time left for thought. In a moment the men would begin to wonder whether he really was their heaven-sent leader, their man with his mind made up. Therefore he thrust his sword high over his head, flourished it, and shouted in a huge voice: "For there is none of you so mean and base that hath not noble luster in your eyes. I see you stand like greyhounds in the slips, straining upon the start. The game's afoot! Follow your spirit!"

With that he turned sharply about and ran at full speed toward the middle of the field. A hundred men went streaming after him through the dark with cheers and hoarse indistinguishable cries.

"Is that you, General Coffee?" asked a boyish voice from among the out-houses.

"No. Hinds's Dragoons. Who are you?"

"John Donelson's Company. We've lost the Gin'ral. Ye seen 'im?"

"Not sence we lef' that grove of oaks in front o' the de la Ronde place. But I heard he'd cut 'way over east, toward the swamp."

"Yeah. We lost 'im thar, jest arter we'd got offen our hosses. An' naow he ain't to be faound in the hull damn camp."

"Wal, he'll turn up. Haow ye makin' aout?"

"Cain't say. Tuk a few an' lost some more. Cain't do much, 'caount o' half the time yer firin' inter yer own people."

"I know. Damnedest killin'-bee I ever see. Tuk a Britisher back thar was so consarned turned 'raound the only way he knew which way to fight was to look see how he'd p'inted his little brass three-paounder afore sunset. 'Yeah, sure I'll s'render,' sezee when we tuk 'im up, 'but fer Gawd's sakes gimme a compass an' a lantern!'"

"Shut up, thar!" commanded Donelson in a low voice as his men

586

started to laugh. "Colonel Hinds, thar's a party comin' up on our rear. —Hillo! Who be ye?"

"General Coffee's men," came the answer.

"Like hell!" said Donelson softly. "Thet feller never larned ter talk in Tennessee. He dunno the language. Watch aout, boys! Git yer rifle-guns ready!"

A few seconds later some thirty dim forms emerged into view at a distance of ten paces, and the same voice spoke again: "Now, you Yankee rebels, throw down your arms!"

"Go chase yerself!—Blow 'em ter hell, boys!"

For the moment, Captain McWilliams was a completely happy man. He had always delighted in physical conflict, and the more violent and confused it was the better he liked it. The queer thoughts and guesses and doubts that so often crept out of the caves of his mind and leered at him were driven back by the shock of battle. In a stiff struggle against the bodies of other men, when life and limb were at stake, he found a kind of peace even better, while it lasted, than that which drink could bring.

And tonight's battle was one of the best, for in this all but total darkness it was impossible to tell friend from foe. Here, at last, he was not obliged to take sides. Here was pure conflict, uncontaminated by a cause. Here was war for its own sweet sake, trimmed to the quick, laid bare of all specious and trumped-up motives. He loved it. His heart went out to this whole broad brotherhood of embattled men drawn together in the fog and the dark by one deep fascination. He gloried in the huge hoarse music they made of discordant yells, thunderous guns, gnashing steel, as they rushed to embrace one another and drink together one long dram of death.

More than once, he felt sure, the muddy and miscellaneous hundred who followed him—for no reason except that he had spouted at them a bombastic speech out of Shakespeare—had fired, without knowing it, into other British troops, and even at one another. The Americans must be doing the same thing. It was being done, of necessity, all over the fog-bound midnight field. Indeed, it had always been so, ever since that darkling clash of arms round the walls of ancient Epipolae described by Thucydides. All armies marched and fought and died in great darkness, not knowing why. Every blow that they struck was an ignorant blow at an unknown companion, a friend, a brother, half-seen through the fog.

587

How touching, human, and right that was! How good to be here, taking part in this beautiful dance of death! For once the gods had imagined, and in this battle they were creating, a perfect symbol of man's life in its total strangeness. There were no answers here, no trivial solutions. The gods were not preaching. But ah, how they were loading the heart tonight with the burden of the mystery!

Thus McWilliams made his way to the peaceful heart of the storm. His happiness deepened and soared into the serene mood of high tragedy which he had touched once or twice before while witnessing, on the London stage, the death of Lord Hamlet, Prince of Denmark.

Meanwhile, in some quite different country of the mind, he was vividly aware of what went on about him. As nearly as he could make out, the British forces were now arranged in the shape of a huge irregular letter V, the base of which rested upon the Villeré plantation-house. Sounds of rifle-fire from that direction told him that the Americans must be swarming among the out-houses and slave-cabins. Perhaps by this time they had captured the general and the admiral, thus bringing their debate to an abrupt close. The British left flank was still being hammered by the guns of the schooner, and also by two small but extremely spiteful guns on the levee-top some distance up-river. The right flank was now retreating, stubbornly, before a strong body of Americans who had got round to the cypress woods and were striking inward.

Apparently, then, the British forces were surrounded—a sweet situation for a body of His Majesty's troops who had recently "covered themselves" with what was called "glory" in the overthrow of Napoleon!

"Captain McWilliams!" a voice shouted at his side. It was Colonel Thornton, who had come up with a hundred reserves to brace the wavering lines. He pointed through the reek with a shaking sword.

"Yes, Colonel."

"We must take those two guns on the levee-top. They are beating our lines to flinders."

Half a dozen of the muddy hundred that McWilliams had aroused from the gully were bowled over in their charge across the field. A dozen more fell in climbing the bank. When the rest reached the top they were greeted by bursts of grape. Still they staggered on, with McWilliams out ahead of them, yelling. Thornton's company, which had cut round behind the little battery, came driving forward now so that the American marines who manned the guns were caught before and behind. The horses hitched to the gun-carriages were going frantic. . . . "Save the guns, boys, at any cost," screamed a high harsh voice through the clamor.

"Hasta mas no poder," someone answered.

A tall gaunt man on a black horse, a man with bristling hair, was crossing swords back there with Thornton. An instant later these two were driven apart by a horde of Indians in war-paint who tore into the fray with a huge man at their head—a man with black hair falling to his shoulders. "Illichi! Illichi!" yelled the Indians.

"Push on the bayonet! Charge! Charge, my lads!"

"Fatevi avanti, voi figli di cagne!"

"Illichi! Whoo-oo whoop!"

"À la bayonette! Marchons vite, mes enfants!"

"Give 'em hell!"

"De 'possum meat am good to eat . . . Carf 'im to de heart!"

"How wonderful, how glorious . . . !"

A crowd rushed in from the other side of the guns, and Thornton and McWilliams were swept down the bank as by a wave of the sea.

"Frenchmen! Spaniards!" gasped Thornton when the two came again together.

"Yes, and Negroes, Indians, Italians!" panted McWilliams.

"What kind of a country is this? We can't fight the whole world! . . . Here they come again!"

To McWilliams it felt then as though he were picked up and violently hurled. Unseen bodies slammed against him. Someone yelled in his ear "We'll pitch them British sons o' bitches back into the Gulf!" His own men—he was almost sure they were—twisted him round, butted him, and hauled him hither and yon. A white horse with no rider went plunging by on the dead run. Not knowing where to strike, McWilliams struck in all directions. There were fewer musket-flashes now. Both sides had burnt their powder. It was mostly a play of bayonet, knife, and tomahawk. The Yankees would be better at this, and the Indians best of all. They kept up their savage howl of "Illichi! Illichi!" That yell made the hair on McWilliams's head bristle, ready for the knife.—Ah, this was better by far than drink!

"To the ditch!" yelled Thornton. "Make for the ditch behind! There's a fence there. Back to the ditch, men!"

589

Then came a wild scramble back to the ditch and over the zig-zag fence. As McWilliams was climbing over he felt a terrific blow on his chest below the breast-bone. It knocked the breath from his body. For a moment he clung to the topmost rail, half-dazed, struggling to breathe, striving to think what had happened. He felt no pain. He merely clung there, vaguely wondering whether this that was now at his lips might not be the last, best drink of all. Then, pulling himself forward a little, he fell, heavily, to the ground on the other side.

"Hey! Why in hell can't you look where you're jumpin'? That's my leg you dropped on, you blunderin' fool!"

But the men were too exhausted, too terrified, to laugh. They were panting, peering anxiously out into the dark and the fog between the rails.

"I say!" called the same voice again. "It's a captain o' marines!—It's *the* captain! I don't know his name, but it's *our* captain—the one that talked us up out o' the mud!"

"That's so. But he's shot. He's shot clean through.—Hell, man, he's dying!"

"Here! Captain. Can't you hear me? You'll be all right. Can't you speak? Can't you say something?"

For half a minute the men behind the fence waited, listening. Then they heard their comrade say: "He's gone, boys. He's dead."

"Did he say anything?" someone asked.

"Nothing with any sense to it. Something about 'rest.'"

"Well, what was it?"

"He only said 'the rest . . . the rest is silence.'"

CHRISTMAS DAY—1814

Muddy wateh,
Lazy wateh,
Caincher heah me call yo' name?
Yo' tuk mah cabin an' yo' tuk mah gal—
Naow whut mo' does yo' claim?
Roll 'er aout!
Oh, heave dat cotton!
Ah hain't got long ter stay heah!

590

Muddy wateh,
Waitin' wateh,
Whut's a-bitin' on yo' min'?
Yo' big mud-cat an' yo' gater-maouf,
Whut yo' waitin' deah to fin'?
    Roll 'er aout!
    Oh, heave dat cotton!
    Ah hain't got long ter stay heah!

Muddy wateh,
Bloody wateh,
Is yo' wukkin' on some plan?
Is yo' got a dream, is yo' got a hope
Whut calls fo' de blood of a man?
    Roll 'er aout!
    Oh, heave dat cotton!
    Ah hain't got long ter stay heah!

"Song-builder," called a friendly voice, "iffen I couldn't make no better noise 'n thet, I'd shet my maouf."

"Whut de matteh wid dat 'ar song?"

"Cain't say; but hit do make my belly ache."

The disappointed poet strolled down the bank of the levee with his banjo under his arm. There was something in the natural grace of his gait by which one could tell, without the evidence of his features or his hair, that at least three races—white, black, and red—had gone to his making. Everyone knew and liked him. He spoke and sang for everyone in a language that everyone understood—and this at a moment's notice, on any topic, in any mood.

"Ah's sah'y," said he, with a smile by no means sorrowful, when he came to the ditch the men were digging, "'case Ah allus laks mah las' song bes'.—But co'se Ah'll mek yo' boys any kinder song yo'-all want."

The offer seemed not unreasonable, considering how hard the men were at work. Since before the blink of dawn they had been laboring by the hundred in the abandoned mill-race, five miles below the city, called the Rodriguez Canal. General Jackson had ordered that the ditch be deepened and water let into it by making a cut in the levee. General Jackson's word was law, not only among the soldiers and militia but even in the city of New Orleans. Therefore it was that these Choctaws, Free Negroes, Kaintucks, keelers, broad-horners, Frenchmen, Spaniards, Cajuns, Baratarians, jail-birds and lawyers, planters and beggars, merchants and clerks and thieves and clergymen, were toiling all day in the slime, tossing out mud to be used in building the parapet thirty feet behind. The delicate white hands of city gentlemen were being for the first time blistered. The home-spun and buckskin of Tennessee rubbed elbows with fine linen and broadcloth.

The rampart, parallel with the ditch, was being made of sharpened cypress logs driven into the mud, together with planks from adjacent barns and slave-quarters, sugar-kegs, cotton-bales, and broken-down farm-wagons. Even a ruinous flat-boat found near at hand was broken up and put to use. This roughly improvised fence was supported behind by a wall of mud and turf, in some places twenty feet through. Upon the wall the men were mounting their eight batteries of cannon, one group of which commanded the road along the levee, another the central plain, and the third the cypress woods. The whole line of the wall, stretching from the levee to the woods, was nearly a mile in length.

The men raced one another, company by company, with cries of friendly derision. In driving stakes for the rampart they struck water three feet down.

"By Jeremy," one digger grunted, "we gotter swim like a nalligater an' work like a hoss same time."

"Half hoss an' half 'gater, thet's us," laughed another. "Hey, Songbuilder. Toss us up a chune to go on with—an' this time make it a good un."

"D' ye think good songs grow on trees, boys?"

"Aw, hell, we don't want no good songs raound hyar. This ain't no gawdam camp-meetin'. Jes' give us suthin' to 'member the gals by, an' help swing this blasted spade!"

"Okeh, boys. Ah'll sing yeh li'l song jes' fresh aout de banjo, an' hope yo'-all laks hit:

"De Good Lawd look in de mohnin'
Aout oveh lan' an' sea:
'Gotter kip dem two ole dry an' wet
Fum a-mixin' up,' sezee—
An' He hum a song,
Li'l wuk-a-day song.

"Oh, des' a song ter go on wid,
Des' a li'l ole rambelin' song—
A song ter hum when de worl' goes right
An' ter shaout when hit all goes wrong—
Des' a humbelin' song—
Li'l wuk-a-day song.

592

"Lawd he hain't no gal to remembeh
  In all de lonesome sky:
But a gal name of Eve widout no clo's on
  Was a-bohnin' by-m-by
    While he hum dat song.
    Li'l wuk-a-day song.

" 'Gotter kip dat wet ole ocean
  Fum a-runnin' all oveh de lan':
Gotter swim lak a 'gater, gotter wuk lak a hoss
  Kip a dry place fo' my gal ter stan' '—
    An' he *boom* dat song,
    Dat wuk-a-day song.

"He spit on he hands, de Lawd did,
  Grab up dat shiny spade,
Mek de black mud fly fum dawn ter dahk
  Twell dat levee hit war made;
    Den he sing nudder song—
    Li'l res'-a-while song."

The lilt and the beat, by this time, had so worked into the bones of
the listeners that they could help somewhat with the chorus:

  "Oh, des' a song ter go on wid,
  Des' a li'l ole rambelin' song—
  A song ter hum when de worl' goes right
  An' shaout when hit all goes wrong—
    Des' a humbelin' song,
    Li'l wuk-a-day song."

"Thet 'ar song," remarked one of the critics, "listens better 'n hevin'
the colic. Whar ye git it, Song-builder?"

"Tuk some an' made some," the troubadour replied indifferently as
he started back toward the levee, plinking at his banjo and still swaying
a little at the hips as he went.

The ancient alliance between Mars and Apollo was evident at once
in the vigor with which the men working at the foundations of the
first battery now attacked their work with a swing. Soon a powerful
tenor soared up from among the Free Men of Color, and a chorus rose
to meet it:

  Li'l David, play on yo' hahp
  Hal-le-loo! Hal-le-loo!
  Li'l David, play on yo' hahp,
    Hal-le-loo!

593

Li'l David was a shepherd boy,
He KEEL Goliath an' he dance wid joy.

Li'l David, play on yo' hahp,
Hal-le-loo! Hal-le-loo!
Li'l David, play on yo' hahp,
Hal-le-loo-hoo!

And then from Plauché's Creoles went up the virile chant:

Allons, enfants de la pa-tri-e!
Le jour de gloire est ar-ri-vé!
Contre nous de la ty-ran-ni-e
L' é-ten-dard san-glant est le-vé!

A horseman came galloping at top speed down the road along the levee, and reined in before a group of officers standing in front of the Macarté plantation. "General Jackson," he panted, "three hundred British have come up Bayou Chef Menteur . . . preparing to attack Governor Claiborne on the Plains of Gentilly."

"I thought they would.—Major Latour, please take two hundred of Carroll's men and reinforce Claiborne. Tell him and Major Lacoste that the battery must be defended and held."

For several minutes the officers stood watching Jackson as he paced up and down, whipping at his tall dusty dragoon boots with a worn hunting-crop. Never had they seen him so gaunt and sallow, or the lines in his face so deeply graven. Only the short blue Spanish cloak flung across his shoulders gave any hint of bulk or breath to his lath-like body. For five days and nights he had not taken off his clothes. He had slept by ten-minute snatches on the hard lumpy sofa in the Macarté house. Fever-and-ague, the incessant pain of old wounds, an ever-growing sense of responsibility, and frantic toil varied by flashes of vituperative wrath, had refined him now to this restless bundle of bone, gristle, sinew, nerves, and tan.

General Coffee, Major Reynolds, Colonel Livingston, and Captain John Donelson gazed at their commander with grave concern. They knew that he had been living for months in the saddle, threading the soggy trails of the Creek country with his left arm strapped to his side, facing down mutiny, eating a few spoonfuls of rice for his dinner, drinking only weak gin and water, sleeping on muddy or frozen ground, often racked by pain, pleading for support from a niggardly

594

government and mostly doing without it, driving his daggle-tail fighters through forest and swamp and heat and cold mainly by the lash of his inexorable will.

Worn down by these pains, toils, dangers, and privations, Jackson was now for the first time in his life facing disciplined forces—a superior body of soldiers, sailors, and marines well armed, well fed, well led, and flushed with the pride of recent and resounding victory. Favored again and again by blind fortune, he had been able to bring against these forces a horde of untrained men hastily gathered up from the northern woods to supplement the local militia and the volunteers from the recent war against the Creeks. Carroll's men had come in already, and in one way or another most of them had been armed. Adair's Kentuckians were understood to be coming, but with no blankets, no tents, no adequate clothing, one rifle to every ten and one cooking kettle to eighty. There were also certain Choctaws under Hold-fast Gaines. There were the Creole companies of New Orleans, the Free Men of Color, a small group of fierce black fighters from Santo Domingo, and the privateers of Barataria. In all, Jackson might have six thousand men, if and when all arrived, but those six thousand would speak in several languages and would be divided by hatreds, fears, and suspicions. They had never fought together before—indeed the Baratarians and keelers were traditional enemies—nor had they been given one hour of common training. With such men, at the fag-end of a weary and disastrous war, Andrew Jackson was preparing to defend New Orleans, the River, and the dear-bought freedom of America.

Not for an instant did the four men who were watching Jackson doubt that he would do it. The set of his long sharp jaw and the clear eager peering of his eyes made doubt impossible.

They stood apart and watched him, leaving him as it were in an atmosphere of his own, a special sunbeam. One and all they would have agreed that there was nothing in the least haughty, distant, or strange about Andy. He was more like them all than they were like one another. He spoke their language as well as he did that other lordly speech of his that came they knew not whence. And yet now he was that totally different person, a leader, a man rapt away by a mission and a high resolve, lonely, and unapproachable. Today they could not call him "Andy." He was now "General Jackson."

Holdfast Gaines came up the bank. His shoulders looked enormous. The collar of his buck-skin hunting-coat lay open, baring the bronze column of his neck. The morning sun glistened on his coal-black hair. They saw him smile—a rare thing with Holdfast—as he gazed down for a moment into Jackson's eyes. The two men spoke scarcely at all, but shook hands. Then Holdfast went down the bank, taking it in two strides.

A sudden roar of field-pieces rolled across the plain from the Villeré plantation. The men working on the ramparts dropped their forks and spades and snatched up their rifles. One of Hinds's dragoons came galloping up. He began to yell from a distance: "Hit's a new gin'ral o' the red-coats jist come in from Lake Borgne. They're a-firin' salutes! Hit must be Wellington!"

General John Coffee, towering above the men of the group by the head and shoulders, spoke one word which might have been a curse, a prayer, or a sarcasm: "God!"

"He'll be welcome," said Jackson with a happy smile, leaving the others uncertain to whom he particularly referred.

Sitting at the table in the parlor of the Villeré house, half an hour after the arrival of Major General Sir Edward Pakenham, General Keane looked a happy man. He had difficulty in keeping the tone of jubilation out of his voice. This Sir Edward might be only thirty-seven, and look still younger, but he was the hero of Salamanca, the brother-in-law of the Duke of Wellington, and one of the most famous soldiers on earth. Perhaps, then, he would be able to make old Cochrane comprehend that land battles required something more than merely getting the weather-gage and then blasting it out yard-arm to yard-arm.

There were four of them at the small deal table—the plethoric and white-haired Sir Alexander Cochrane at one end, Sir Edward Pakenham at the other, and General Keane facing Colonel William Thornton, one of the ablest young officers in the army. Pakenham, who had been hearing and reading reports, was now studying a large map of the district.

"And so they outnumbered you, eh?" said he, without looking up.

"We hear they have twenty thousand sharp-shooters in and about the city, well armed and provisioned, with more coming in daily."

"Who told you that?"

"A prisoner," said Keane.

"Please have him brought in here."

"He escaped!" Cochrane triumphantly shouted. "These blundering asses let him escape!"

"I see.—And have you any corroboration, General, of that prisoner's report?"

"In the night battle about which I told you, Sir Edward, they surrounded us and rushed our lines as they could not have done without being at least four to our one. After that battle they built enough camp-fires for at least thirty-five thousand men."

"Thirty-five thousand patty-cakes!" sneered Cochrane.

"Perhaps, Admiral," said Pakenham, looking up from the map, "it will be as well for me to hear what General Keane has to say all at once, and then we can have your comments."

"You can have my comment now, sir; and in few words. I have never seen a chance of easy victory so shamefully thrown away. The navy, sir, has won by hard fighting a chance for England to win the Mississippi Valley, and, with it, perhaps the whole of America. What has the army done with that chance? Tossed it away!"

A slow flush mantled in Sir Edward's youthful face, but he only said: "And what does the navy suggest?"

"Suggest? Nothing! The navy *demands,* sir, that you attack the enemy at once!"

Keane saw that Pakenham was now looking Cochrane straight in the eyes. "I feel sure," said he, "that I could hear you perfectly if you were to speak in the tone of voice that one gentleman uses in addressing another."

After a moment, while Cochrane was still drumming on the table, Pakenham continued: "We have men enough to meet twenty thousand, if it turns out that they have that many. I find, however, that the troops we have thus far landed are encamped in a most unhealthy position, wading in mud by day and sleeping in ice by night. Our West Indians are dying every night of the exposure. The fogs from the marshes on our right will soon breed fever. We are at the mercy of the enemy's armed vessels in the River because the navy has not brought up any vessels or guns to protect us . . ."

"But, sir, the navy . . ."

"Hear me out, if you please, Admiral.—These present conditions might be endured if there were any prospect of changing them soon. I am told, however, that the enemy has already deepened and extended the ditch marked here on the map as the 'Rodriguez Canal.' That ditch alone would make a formidable barrier to our proposed march against New Orleans. Probably he has also extended his rampart, behind that ditch, from the marshes on his left to the river-embankment on his right. On that rampart he has probably mounted some guns, and he may be bringing up more. Already, as you tell me, his guns have done serious damage to our lines. On our side, the navy has scarcely started to haul guns from the fleet with which to breach his works."

"But, sir, what do you know about their 'works'? We haven't caught a glimpse of them since the night battle, and not much of a glimpse even then. The army hasn't even tried to go and look at them. It's afraid o' that gang o' cavalry they keep prancing up and down in front of us."

"That cavalry, Admiral, has been watching everything we have done. It was sent out, of course, with that purpose. We have no cavalry, and therefore we shall not be certain about the enemy's preparations until we have fought our way through their vedettes and made a reconnaissance in force. Only then shall we be able to plan our main attack."

"Plan our attack!—But we are Britons, sir, and the enemy is before us!"

"I see by this map," Pakenham quietly continued, "that there are five other ways of reaching New Orleans, any one of which appears to be better than the one we have chosen."

"It was Admiral Cochrane's opinion that we should come this way," said Keane.

"So I understand, General; but always in these land operations the army should make its own decisions."

"Hah! Decisions! The army never does make any," growled Cochrane.

"As matters now stand, however, I am inclined to think that we should withdraw the bulk of our forces and renew the attack elsewhere."

"Retreat, by God! You are 'inclined to think' that we should retreat before a handful of ignorant Yankee yokels! And this from the brother-in-law of Wellington, from the man who hopes to be Earl of Louisiana!"

There was a moment of painful silence before Pakenham, still controlling his voice, replied: "It is clear, Admiral, that you and I were not brought up in the same school of strategy."

"No, by heavens; and I thank God for it! The only strategy I ever learned was what the Duke of Thunder told us: 'Get so close to the enemy that you can't miss, and then blow him to hell!'—That's what Lord Nelson said, General Pakenham, and I'm too old to learn anything different from you."

After another and longer silence Cochrane all at once rose noisily to his feet and stood glaring down at one officer after the other. "I've always known," said he in a choked voice, bringing his fist down on the table with a crash, "that there was something rotten in the army. The whole navy's known it. Thus far we've kept still, but unless you march forward from here at once—at *once,* sir—then every man, woman, and child in England shall understand what poltroons you are. If I have to, I'll smash those ramparts myself and take New Orleans with my seamen and marines alone. The army can bring up the baggage!"

INJUN PLAY

(December 27, 1814)

"What 'n hell they wanter post the pore damn fool 'way aout hyar fer?" old McNab was muttering to himself. He didn't wish to seem ungrateful, but the Scotchman in him resented all waste and unnecessary risk, even when it was to his advantage.

Back and forth in the moonlight the British sentry tramped, seeing nothing, hearing nothing, and pausing not at all. He moved, to all appearance, by clock-work wound up for a given time, so that he might as well have left his brain in camp two hundred yards behind. He made a brave and conspicuous show in the moonlight, with his scarlet coat, white cross-belts holding his bayonet and cartridge-box, tightly fitting white breeches and spatterdashes, polished black boots, brass-bound high-peaked helmet, and heavy musket with brass fittings. Wonderfully expensive he looked, and, in a way, beautiful, to the elderly man in soiled buck-skins lying fifty yards off among the cypress shadows. But Jake McNab's aesthetic delight in the sentry was not unmixed with acquisitive interest. Any Injun, he knew, would gladly pay down a hundred beaver-pelts for an outfit such as that.

McNab was lying on his belly with his elbows out-spread for a prop to his rifle, "Honeybee." The stock of the rifle was snuggled against his cheek, and he was squinting down the barrel with a studious eye. As the sentry neared the closer end of his beat McNab brought his foresight to rest between the man's eye-brows. The moonlight glittered faintly on the silver sight-bead and also on the brass vizor of the helmet.

For an instant the rifle-barrel linked and locked the man behind it to the man in front. Then, gently, with a fondling touch, McNab's fore-finger snuggled against the hair-trigger. The report made little noise in the heavy soft-iron barrel as the sentry pitched mechanically forward on his face and, after a moment, lay still, the clock-work having run down.

McNab looked about him, sat up, and laughed without making a sound. By godly, considering how little light there had been, there was a shot to tell Holdfast Gaines about! It wasn't so bad a thing, after all, to be sixty-five when one could still do a clean, quiet, economical job like that one.

After reloading and making sure that no one was coming from the direction of the British camp he began to crawl slowly forward, keeping as much as possible in the shadow of the woods and dropping to his belly whenever he had to cross a patch of moonshine. He meant to get that musket, cartridge-box, and helmet, together with as much of the uniform as he could collect before the guard came out. Perhaps they hadn't heard the shot over there in camp, and even if they had heard it they probably wouldn't think it worth much attention. The British didn't think a man could be really killed unless half a regiment fired at him.

McNab laid the helmet, musket, cartridge-box, and bayonet together so that he could scoop them up if he had to get away in a hurry. The scarlet coat gave him little trouble because the body was not yet stiff. He had to work rather hard at the boots, but they were obviously worth the effort. When the second one came off with a jerk he turned his attention to the dead man's under-garments, and there made at once an exciting discovery. He caught one tantalizing glimpse of red woolen under-wear half a second before he saw the guard approaching to relieve the sentry.

Quickly slinging the cartridge-box and bayonet-straps around his shoulders, he stuck the boots under his belt and clamped his teeth on the vizor of the helmet. Then, with the coat over one arm, the musket in his left hand and "Honeybee" in his right, he made off toward the woods, bending double.

He was too far off when he reached his lurking-place to hear what the corporal and his men were saying, but he could see that they were much puzzled by the sentry's death and his present half-stripped con-dition. Evidently they had heard no shot. They were a long time bend-ing over the body to make sure that the very small hole in the exact middle of the forehead could really have been made by a bullet. They turned the body over several times, trying to find a wound that looked more important. From time to time they glanced across toward the cypress woods, but took no step in that direction. At length a second sentry was posted and the others returned to camp, taking the body and the under-wear with them.

Back and forth, up and down in the moonshine, tramped the second sentry, hearing nothing, seeing nothing, and pausing not at all. Here, then, was another piece of expensive clock-work, newly wound up. In all details he looked the spit and image of his predecessor, recently deceased. The moonlight glinted on his accouterments and trappings in just the same places. He too was dressed as though for an engagement with a very dignified personage indeed. Jake McNab, peering out from the shadows, rubbed his eyes with the grimy back of his left hand. He could scarcely believe that they were actually handing him another complete outfit of musket, cartridges, helmet, bayonet, scarlet coat, white breeches, spatterdashes, boots, and, possibly, red woolen under-wear.

McNab had spent most of his rather long life in buck-skins—too warm in summer, by no means warm enough for comfort in winter, and extremely uncomfortable when, as usual, they were wet. Since his boyhood he had depended mainly upon his rifle for his raiment, and he was quite content to go on doing so with regard to outer garments. Suitable materials for under-wear, however, were apparently not provided by the lower animal kingdom as represented in the American forest, and therefore, as his years advanced, he had given considerable thought to the possibility of someday acquiring an inner suit of red flannel. But red flannel itself was extremely hard to come by. Yankee peddlers and Injun traders never carried it. Red flannel, in fact, was a tide-water thing, a prerogative of rich old men who paid taxes. Yet, being of a sanguine and forward-looking disposition, McNab had never quite despaired.

And now, here was this interposition of Providence, this war, this invasion of men bringing red flannel under-wear from across the sea to him in the wilderness, this reward of faith and long patience! Here, probably, was another suit of red flannel under-wear, ready cut and sewn, offered to him and his "Honeybee" at the price of a little powder and one small pellet of lead! It would cost him no more than the hide of a buck, and far less labor.

At this point in his self-congratulations, however, McNab's Scottish conscience smote him a heavy blow. Was it fair, was it decent, was it moral, to shoot down a helpless man for his under-wear?

601

"But he's not helpless at all," McNab's keen Scottish brain answered. "He has a musket and a bayonet. He would kill *me,* if he could, without a second thought."

"Ah," said Conscience, "if he *could;* but you very well know that he can't. You can see him, and he can't see you. He's walking up and down there as trustful as a baby. And are you a baby-killer, Jake McNab?"

"But look here," countered Brain, "I didn't ask these dunderheaded British to post their sentries right on the edge of the woods. And somebody's bound to shoot him. Somebody's going to get that under-wear. Who needs it more than I do?—Besides, Andy Jackson needs the cartridges and the musket. It's my patriotic duty to get them."

"Huh! *You,* a patriot!—Don't make me laugh."

"I say it's my patriotic duty to get those things for Andy. I tell you it makes my blood boil to think of these twenty thousand British regulars smashing into Andy, just like they used to smash us Scots in the old country! Who asked them to come and camp here, anyhow? Damn their insolent, thieving guts! I need that under-wear; I desarve that under-wear; and, by godly, I'm going to *get* it!"

Finding that his Scottish wit had for the moment overwhelmed and silenced his Scottish conscience, old McNab slowly and studiously brought down the silver fore-sight of "Honeybee" just under the glittering brass vizor of the new sentry's helmet.

"Damn it all, Woodbine," exclaimed Colonel Nicholls, rubbing the sleep from his eyes, "where are they? Did they retreat?"

"I think it was our men who were firing, sir."

"What at?"

"I'm sure I don't know, Colonel. I didn't hear any shots from the enemy's lines."

"And didn't you see anyone?"

"No, sir. It's a strange thing—but I suppose that attack in the dark a few nights ago put our men's nerves on edge."

"Probably.—But don't let the men fire at moonbeams, Captain Woodbine."

"No, Colonel. Goodnight."

"Goodnight, Captain."

"D' ye take the sentry, Zeke, an' I'll 'com'date the corp'ral."

"Okeh, Ezry.—An' 'member, I'm two up on yeh a'ready."

"Like hell, ye be!"

"Wal, anyhaow, 'member we git away 'thout another shot arter they comes aout agin. Jes' let 'em go 'bang-bang' inter woods until they gits tired."

"Colonel Nicholls, how are the men to get any rest if we have this infernal noise every time a sentry dreams he has seen something suspicious?"

"I'm sorry, Colonel Thornton. We thought it was a night attack for certain this time."

"Well, let's not have it happen again, or old Cochrane will be laughing at us for a month."

The heavy red flannel under-wear was warm, dry, and wonderfully comfortable, setting in close against McNab's skin. A strange world it was, McNab reflected, in which a man who had come several thousand miles across the sea for the purpose of killing one should be in fact the person to provide for the comfort of one's old age.

But now, having arranged for himself, McNab began to think about others. He was thinking with special fondness about Maw, who felt the cold more grievously every winter. As she grew older, too, her fever-and-ague seemed to grow steadily worse. No medicine, white or black or Injun, had ever done it much good. What she needed most, no doubt, was red flannels.—Perhaps that third sentry out there . . .

"What in the world are the men up to, Colonel Thornton? General Pakenham will get a strange idea of the army's discipline, being awakened every two minutes by this cursed firing, with never an enemy in sight!"

"They must be using their cavalry, General Keane. I think they come up to the camp on the gallop, shoot down our sentries, and get away again before our men can see them."

"Do you mean to say we haven't even *seen* them?"

"I judge not, General, from the reports that have been brought in."

"Well, then . . . well, but we've got to stop this somehow. Pakenham's piping hot, I can tell you. He's pacing up and down the hall of the house, and says he won't go to bed again. What can be done?"

"You know the game, I reckon, Mad Buffalo," said Russell Bean as the Choctaws crept up at two in the morning to relieve his own men.

"Jest git the sentries an' then lay low while the hornets' nest biles out. When they quiet down, git the sentries agin. Never let 'em see yeh, an' never give 'em a minute's sleep.—Wal, keep yer ha'r on!"

"Okeh!"

"General Keane, this thing is becoming absolutely intolerable! Ten times at least—and that's a conservative estimate—I have been awakened by the men firing at nothing at all—according to your own account, sir, nothing at all! How do you explain it, sir? How do you account for it, General Keane? What are you going to do? An army can't fight if it toils all day in the mud and is kept awake all night by a lot of brainless fools firing their muskets at nothing at all. What do you propose to do about it, General Keane?"

"I can order the men not to fire under any circumstances, General Pakenham, if you say the word."

As the two men stood glaring at each other in the hall of the Villeré house they heard gale after gale of scornful laughter from Cochrane's bedroom.

Having now amply provided for himself and for Maw, McNab was beginning to think about his children, his grand-children, and also those quick-coming great-grand-children with whose precise names and number he no longer even tried to load his memory. He was realizing that a man of means should think not only of his personal comfort but also of the generations to come. Thus one might become a philanthropist, and, by the very magnitude of one's benefactions, avoid all imputation of personal greed.

Deliberately, steadily, and now with a glow of conscious and altruistic virtue, McNab brought the muzzle of "Honeybee" down until the foresight rested for the fourth time right under the brass vizor of a British helmet.

BY THE 'TARNAL

(January 8, 1815)

General Pakenham leaned forward over the map lying on the table between the two candles, his brow pale and puckered, his tones devoid of all feeling, like those of a professor lecturing to a class of earnest students. "And now, gentlemen," he was saying, "let us review our plans for the last time. The first attack is to be made by Colonel Thornton on the west bank of the River. He will capture the guns there and turn them against the main American batteries and forces ranged along the rampart on this side. I shall send up a Congreve rocket telling him when to open fire. At the moment he does so we shall strike at the enemy's rampart between the seventh and the eighth battery. General Keane with twelve hundred men will go forward along the river-road to distract attention from our main attack. The West Indian Negroes will strike through the cypress woods on our right for the same purpose. Colonel Lambert will hold his fourteen hundred men as reserves near the center of the field, to be called upon as the need may arise. General Gibbs and I will lead the main attack upon the two batteries.—Is that all perfectly clear?"

There was a general nodding of heads by the seven or eight officers sitting at or near the little table of deal in the middle of the tiny room.

"Very well. And now, let's get to work. All night we've had nothing but delays, but there's still time to win the battle before the enemy can guess what we're about.—Remember that the rocket from the levee is our signal for . . ."

The door was suddenly thrown open. A young officer, breathless and pale-faced, took two steps into the room and then suddenly froze into the attitude of salute.

"Well, Captain? Is it from Thornton? Has he got across?"

"Yes, sir.—That is, no, sir. Only with . . ."

"Well, speak up, Captain!"

"He has got across with three hundred and fifty men, General, but . . ."

"But that's only a quarter of what he was ordered to take!—Where are the rest?"

"On this side, sir, waiting for boats. The navy didn't bring through enough boats from Lake Borgne."

"Why not?"

"The first boats that got through, sir, knocked down the wall of the canal and blocked all those behind."

Pakenham rose to his feet. His fresh-colored and rather boyish face had gone gray. "Very well," he said curtly to the captain without looking at him. "You may leave us."

When the door was closed he strode swiftly three or four times up

605

and down the room, obviously striving to master his wrath before he trusted his voice.

"It was that cursed mud," said Cochrane, almost apologetically. "I knew it would fall back into the water. I told you . . . Your fellows don't know how to . . ."

Pakenham suddenly stopped in front of the table and impaled the purple-faced admiral on the spear-points of his fiercely glittering eyes. "No!" he shouted down. "My fellows do *not* know how to build a canal that will stand the stupid blundering of your club-footed bunglers. God Almighty would not know how to build a canal that the navy could get through. The army has worked six days and nights, sir, to get that canal ready, and you knock it down in an hour!"

Admiral Cochrane exploded: "I never believed in that canal. I told you so. From the start I've told you that the only way to take New Orleans is to march straight along the levee and—well, by God, *take* it! All this studying of little maps and writing little plans and digging little canals gives me a pain, sir, in a place which I shall not mention. For two weeks, and over, ever since you condescended to come here and take charge of operations, we've had nothing but maps and plans and mud and defeat and delay—which is what you call 'strategy.'"

"No, sir," Pakenham thundered, "we've had something more. We've had boasting and bluster and purple-faced brag from the navy—most of it spoken by *you*. We've had ignorance, bull-headed insolence, empty of brain and devoid of experience, ably represented by *you*.—But from this moment, sir, there are just two things which I, as the commander-in-chief of this expedition, shall require of Vice Admiral Cochrane. One of them is a discreet silence, sir. The other is a decent sense of shame."

Cochrane looked to be on the verge of a paralytic stroke. "Did you say 'shame,' sir?"

"Your sense of hearing at any rate, sir, is still unimpaired. I said 'shame'!"

"By God, gentlemen, can you believe it? He, in the army, says 'shame' to me of the navy—to me, after I've just burned my way down from the District of Maine to the Florida coast to give this man his chance!"

"I said 'shame.' If you in your blatant egotism can't feel it now, then you will if you ever get back to England."

"Hah! England! Do you dare to mention England?"

"Try to talk sense, sir. All that we asked of you was to get those boats down here after dark last night. Here it is at dawn, and you have one quarter of them through the canal, with no more to be expected.—Is that correct?"

"But look here . . ."

"Have you the slightest conception of what it feels like to storm an enemy's battery in broad daylight with three hundred and fifty men when you've been counting on surprising him with fourteen hundred in the darkness?"

"I'm not afraid of daylight," Cochrane shouted back, rising now from his chair and facing Pakenham squarely. "The fact is, I like it, and so do my men. I like to see my enemy, and get close to him. I'm not a 'strategist,' like you. I'm just a man who knows how to win battles."

"You've done everything possible, sir, to make us lose this one," said Pakenham, speaking more quietly but still with intense bitterness. "We have to wait here now until Thornton takes those batteries on the other side with his few men, and in daylight. I hope he can do it, but I don't know. If he does, then we too must march up to the ramparts on this side in broad daylight.—Admiral Cochrane of His Majesty's Navy, you will have the satisfaction today of knowing that you are personally responsible for the quite unnecessary deaths of a good many British soldiers."

Cochrane, leaning heavily on the table and glaring at Pakenham, ground out: "Are you the man to charge the navy with delay? Why, man, you didn't even send an army general here until two weeks after the time fixed upon in our letters from Bathurst! And what was the army doing in those two weeks? Skulking at Jamaica, sir, while the navy did the work! For two weeks you lay there, idling, and in those two weeks our enemy had the opportunity to find out where we were striking, to gather his forces, and to throw up his breast-work. The navy had been here since September. You came on Christmas Day. And yet you have the effrontery to accuse the navy of delay!"

General Pakenham took two or three more turns up and down the room. Then, coming to a stand before the table, resting the fingers of one hand upon it, he said in a quiet voice: "Admiral Cochrane, I do most emphatically charge the navy as you say. Evidently you don't yet know, perhaps because your officers have not dared to tell you, that during those two weeks the army was waiting for the *Plantagenet,* the *Rota,* and the *Carnation* which were bringing General Keane and necessary troops and artillery from England. Those three vessels of the British Navy arrived at the rendezvous two weeks late because they had

607

been soundly and ignominiously beaten in battle by a Yankee privateer of seven guns, sustaining a loss of over two hundred men. They did not arrive because that asinine blunderer whom the navy calls Commodore Robert Lloyd insisted, against the urgent advice of General Keane, upon violating a neutral port. They did not arrive on time because it took Lloyd two weeks to bury his dead, repair damages, send his wounded home, take precautions to keep the news of his blunder from reaching the English people, and then vainly try to capture a few pitiful Yankees who had taken refuge in a convent on Fayal.—When I said a moment ago that the navy had done its best to lose the Battle of New Orleans I forgot one thing. I forgot, in my haste, that this battle may have been lost months ago—and by the navy, sir—in the harbor of Fayal, in the Azores, two thousand miles away."

For some seconds, then, the quiet ticking of the clock in the corner was clearly audible. The gray dawn leaking in at the windows paled the light of the candles.

"Seeing that our plans have been so badly delayed," said General Gibbs at last, "would it not be better, General, to postpone the attack until tonight?"

Pakenham glanced at Gibbs as though about to agree, but the scornful laugh of Cochrane prevented whatever he meant to say.

"Postpone and postpone and postpone!" sneered the Admiral's harsh, taunting voice. "That's all we've heard since you got here. For days we have waited while my men dragged your guns through the canal, and twice your artillerists have failed to blast a way through their miserable rampart of mud. And who has been serving the enemy's guns? From what I hear, sir, a band of pirates brought up from the swamps of the lower River. Those pirates have beaten your gunners in two days' gunfire. Yes, sir! The finest artillerists in the British army have been defeated twice by a party of ruffian pirates! And yet you prate about 'shame'! Good God!

"But now, gentlemen, I'm through with this. I tell you now, and I swear it by the Everlasting Majesty of Heaven, that if the army does not attack within one hour then I will take two thousand of my sailors, armed with nothing but their pistols and cutlasses, and drive these ragamuffin rebels out of their mud-banks and back to New Orleans. I'll do it this morning by daylight, gentlemen. There's my answer to the man who has tried to silence Sir Alexander Cochrane. And when I've done it all the world will know, as you know now, where to point the finger of shame."

608

Once again Pakenham paced the room with his hands behind him and his head bent low. When he returned into the cold light from the windows the others could see that his face was pallid and drawn. He looked fay, like a man who has heard his doom.

"I believe, Admiral," said he, speaking now in a tone of almost compassionate gentleness, "that you really would do the desperate and terrible thing that you threaten. It would not be in my power to prevent you. Against my better judgment, therefore, I must attack as soon as Thornton has had time to capture the batteries on the other bank, if he can do it at all. The rocket which I shall burn telling him to open fire on the American lines will also be the signal for our own advance."

Seeing that the general was buckling on his sword-belt, the other officers rose from their chairs.

"Under these circumstances it is clear," Pakenham continued, "that some of us are meeting for the last time. Let us not part in anger. Each of us, no doubt, has meant to serve England as well as he knows how.—Admiral Cochrane, the world knows you, and I do also, as a gallant and highly successful servant of His Majesty the King. I regret whatever I have said today in which I did not keep that fact in mind."

The officers crowded round him—Cochrane among them—and shook his hand as he moved toward the door.

"And now," said he, " 'England expects every man to do his duty,' as the Duke of Thunder signaled at Trafalgar. Good morning, gentlemen! Success to us all! And—I think I will also say 'goodbye'."

"Thar goes their signal!—They're comin' out!—And now, by the 'Tarnal, we'll *smash* 'em!"

Jackson was slashing his whip hard at his boot-top. His voice was exultant and fierce, like the scream of a hawk when it sights its prey. It made Coffee think of the time when Andy had backed his Truxtun with all he had in the world against the famous race-horse Plowboy. It reminded Carroll of the man who had walked from the dueling-ground with the blood slopping out of his boots, saying: "I'd have killed him if he'd shot me through the brain!" To Russell Bean it recalled a memory older still, and with it came the cry: "Who said ten to one 'g'inst Little David?"

Running down the inward slope of the levee toward the rampart, Jackson and his aides saw that the fog, which had completely hidden the British camp, was rapidly drifting away before the breeze of dawn. It still clung to the ground like a woolen blanket six feet thick, but up

609

from this blanket there bristled hundreds of moving bayonets with a milky gleam. Then, dim at first but soon clear and brilliant, emerged the peaked helmets, the white cross-belts, the red tunics, until, in less than a minute, the field of stubbled sugar-cane was seen to be crowded with marching men, the nearest of them hardly a thousand yards off, all coming steadily forward with a measured tread timed by fife and drum. They were coming in solid columns headed for the seventh and eighth batteries far over on the edge of the cypress woods where Adair's Kentuckians were supporting Carroll's men from Tennessee. For a moment in which the fog seemed to be entirely dispersed their white breeches came into view, and their spatterdashes and black boots trampling the silver-frosted stubble of the cane.

Irregularly ranged and straggling along their wall of mud, nervously fingering their triggers, the men from the northern woods, mostly clad in soiled buck-skins or else in home-spun stained with butternut-juice, stared out astonished at this beauty of disciplined order, this majesty of power controlled. Not one of them had ever so much as imagined such a foe as the huge single body ruled by one will that was moving on many legs so deliberately, steadily, irresistibly forward. Even while they admired and wondered, their hearts quailed. Nothing had prepared them for such enormous congregated might so suddenly emerging from the fog, coming from a country in which there had always been too many men into one where men had always been too few. They were overwhelmed by this final product of the military tradition of Europe, reaching back through the Roman legions to the Macedonian phalanx and beyond, advancing across the frosted field to confront the dream of individual liberty.

Andrew Jackson stopped at the first battery, while Bean and Carroll and Coffee ran on to their posts, to gaze at the oncoming foe. Two or three of the gunners looked up at him as he stood, wondering what effect the spectacle might have upon their leader's courage and purpose. But they saw no change in his face other than a slight hardening of his mouth and jaw and a lowering of the eyelids. For ten seconds he stood very still, no longer switching at his boot. And then, suddenly, almost violently, he turned away and looked eastward along the rampart. His expression changed into an odd mingling of affection and reckless gaiety. For a moment they thought he would break into laughter, so happy he looked. Something in the aspect of that long wall of mud swarming with men ill-clad, badly armed, and untrained must have warmed and cheered him to the heart.

610

"How they usin' yeh, Joe?" he called to one of the men serving the first gun. "Ruther be back home with Aunt Lucy?"

"Not fer ten hosses I wouldn't, Gin'ral!"

"Right ye be! We're in the best place on 'arth this mornin'.—Keep yer ha'r on, boys!"

He moved rapidly along the wall, pausing a few seconds at each battery to say a word of direction, encouragement, or friendly jest. It was as though he were paying calls, and the eyes of the men lit up at his approach. Everyone could see that he had not been daunted, or even much impressed, by the spectacle of the marching British. He scarcely glanced at them as he went along. Evidently that sort of thing was quite familiar to him. Probably he had met and destroyed several such armies, and it was certain that he had definite plans for the destruction of this one.

General Fleaujeac's brass twelve at Battery Six banged out before Jackson reached there, and at almost the same moment was heard the louder roar of the eighteen-pounder at Battery Seven. The other guns held their fire, for now the fog was settling down again.

In the hushed half-minute that followed, while every man on the rampart was peering into the gray, the sound of a distant bugle was heard coming from somewhere near the levee. It was blowing the charge. After a moment the band of the Battalion d'Orleans, stationed behind the rampart, struck into the tune of "Yankee Doodle." Thin, fierce, piercing, like singing bullets, the shrill of the fifes slit the air.

"That's the ticket!" someone heard Jackson say to himself, and he seemed to be laughing.

Two or three British batteries opened fire, lighting up the fog. The balls flew harmlessly overhead.

The men's teeth were chattering with cold and excitement while they waited in the weird half-light. Here and there a rifle yelped from the rampart, let off accidentally by a trembling finger. The strain grew . . . and grew. Five minutes more of it would bring panic.

But then, swiftly, another puff of wind from the River swept all the fog away. The British were advancing in two columns, one of them along the edge of the cypress woods and one directly toward the seventh battery. Their front lines were some five hundred yards off.

Jackson was half-way along the rampart when the fog dispersed. He joined in the cheer, partly an expression of relief and partly of admiration, that went up from Carroll's men and the Kentuckians standing

611

behind. It was echoed by Coffee's Tennesseans to the left and, on the right, by the Regulars, Free Negroes, and Baratarians. From the advancing British ranks there came a cheer in answer.

Then all the eight batteries on the mud-wall gave voice together in one crashing, bounding, bursting, rolling, re-echoing roar. They spoke as though to announce some conviction requiring utmost emphasis. In the first salvo their aim was too high, but with their second and third they began to rip and tear long seams in the British columns, tossing bits of men into the air like rags. The columns closed in and came on. Apparently the marching men did not see their comrades fall, nor hear the screams of the wounded. They seemed to feel that death and wounds were in bad taste. Like a school of sardines into which a stone is tossed, they closed their ranks at once, wherever they were torn, and came on. Their steady advance in the teeth of the thickening fire looked stupid, magnificent, and dreadful.

"Don't waste a shot!" yelled a shrill voice at the riflemen in Carroll's companies. "Make sure o' yer man, every one! Aim above the cross-plates! Fire only at the word of command!"

Closer they were now, and closer! One thousand eyes were squinting down the long barrels. One thousand fingers were trembling on the hair-triggers. Four hundred yards was long for rifle-range and too long for muskets.—Wait.—Now they are at three hundred.—Wait.—Oh, wait! Now at two . . .

"Fire!"

The rampart of mud suddenly became a wall of stabbing, leaping, and flaming death.

Without waiting to see what they had hit, the men of the first line stepped back to reload, giving place to the second.

"Fire!"

The third line stepped briskly forward as the second came back.

"Fire!"

The British were stumbling over their own dead as they came on.

"Fire!"

They were huddling together, their lines buckling, their officers falling faster than the men under the thoughtful selective prod of the rifles behind the rampart. Other rifles were spurting and spraying death from the cypress woods into their right flank. It was almost a pitiful thing to see how fast the officers were going down under the singling, culling, choosing fire of a thousand rifles. Each pellet of lead was going on its own

612

peculiar errand, was finding a special path to the body of one man. It flew along that path of air not to wound but to kill. Where the officers fell they writhed only a little and then lay quiet.

And now that the marching columns had come within easy musket-range the men were falling too, by windrows. Patterson's guns were flinging balls from over the River into their left. From the swamp and the stunted cypress woods on their right the little leaden pellets sleeted in. Just ahead, less than a hundred yards away, the eight batteries of great guns blazed and bellowed down at them from the long wall of mud. Between them and those batteries they could see a long canal, half full of water. They did not know how they were to cross that water, and there were few officers left to tell them. They came to a stand, bewildered. Almost, but not quite, they lost their deeply in-grained habit of standing close together, whatever might befall. Here and there a few of them threw up their muskets as though to reply, but the muzzles were beaten down. That, apparently, was not according to orders. Apparently they had been brought here not to slay but to be slain.

"Where's the Forty-fourth with the ladders and fascines? When we come to the ditch we can't cross it!"

"Gah! Them bloody Irish!"

"I'm saving a musket-ball for that Colonel Mullins. Dear God, let me see him today!"

General Gibbs, leading the main attack on the middle of the American line, saw his men looking at him like lost sheep. Their looks were almost reproachful. He had marched them up to within eighty yards of the rampart in the confident expectation that the Forty-fourth would come with the ladders and fascines at the last moment. Pakenham had assured him of that. But now here he stood in the midst of this wither-ing four-fold fire, and no fascines or ladders were in sight. The only thing to do was to drive his men onward, trusting that some of them would be able to cross the canal on the bodies of those who had gone before. The difficulty was, however, that they would not be driven. Those in front were shamefully striving to hide behind their fellows. The column was disintegrating into a crowd of frantic men. He yelled curses, threats, and encouragement all at once as he spurred up and down the blurring ranks, struggling to force them forward with his horse and then with the flat of his sword. But they would not budge.

613

The looks of reproach were changing to glances of rage. Too many of his officers had fallen. One man alone could not drive on these sullen and bewildered hundreds.

Gibbs suddenly turned his horse and galloped toward the rear. When he had got well behind the last line of his column he paused for a moment and peered back into the still hovering fog. Then, as though bringing good news, he returned to the front ranks with his horse on the dead run. "Here comes the Forty-fourth!" he yelled. "Forward, now, boys! The fascines and ladders are coming! Forward, men!"

"Seven fer me, Ezry! Thet puts me two up on yeh."

"Whatcha mean, two up? Didn't I jest git a major?"

"Majors don't come so high ez colonels. Colonels caounts double."

"Corn-sideration, Zeke! Who told yeh so?—An' anyhow, haow'd ye know he was a colonel?"

"Red nose, didnt he hev? Majors cain't afford red noses.—Betcha he hed the gaout, tew."

As he came dashing at top speed across the field from the direction of the levee Pakenham saw Gibbs's column stagger forward a few paces, like a hog with a butcher's knife at its throat, and then huddle together again and come to a halt. A charge of grape-shot tore into the milling mass. Rifle-fire was melting it like rain on snow.

Closer at hand he saw distracted parties of the Forty-fourth rushing aimlessly about, some dragging ladders and fascines, some firing wildly, and still others in headlong flight.

With the flat of his sword Pakenham tried to drive them forward. "For shame!" he cried. "Are you British soldiers?"

"No, begorrah! Thank God!" cried a voice.

All the other Irishmen whose attention he was able to catch merely laughed at him, or grinned, or snarled something unintelligible.—Ah, well, perhaps it had not been wise to assign the most dangerous task of all to the very men whose discipline and devotion were most in doubt.

General Gibbs galloped up, his face white and his chin uncontrollably trembling. "I am sorry to report, General," said he almost with a sob, "that the troops will not obey me. They expected those fascines, and they refuse to cross the canal without them."

"Refuse, do they?"

614

A bullet had broken Pakenham's sword at the hilt. He threw the hilt away, snatched off his hat, and rode hard toward the few men left before the canal. They were beginning to retreat. "Forward! Forward!" he shouted, waving his hat above his head. "Fourth and Twenty-first, forward, for shame! Remember that you are Englishmen!"

A dozen or fifteen of them, hearing his furious voice and seeing that he cared not at all how he exposed himself, turned and ran head-down toward the enemy. Pakenham watched them splash through the canal. He saw that half of them lived to scramble up the muddy bank on the other side. But not one reached the rampart.

While he was looking back, as though hoping that all the others would follow this gallant example, a heavy ball from the rampart shattered his right arm. He reeled for a second or two in the saddle, and then, glancing down, saw that his hat had fallen to the ground. He dismounted slowly, painfully, picked up the hat, took it by the brim between his teeth, and was just lifting his foot toward the stirrup when his horse fell dead before him, pierced through the eye by a rifle-bullet. His aide, Captain McDougall, rode up at the moment on a black Creole pony. In a few seconds Pakenham, mounted again, was riding after the men now in full retreat, calling to them, cursing them, pleading with them to halt and re-form their lines.

Far over to the British left, near the levee, some unseen bugler had been all this while plaintively blowing the charge.

"Hurrah! Brave Highlanders! Fall in behind 'em, Fourth and Twenty-first. Come on boys! Let's end this thing!"

Onward they came with kilts a-swing, their dirks and claymores glittering. They looked invulnerable, invincible, with their front of a hundred tall men striding shoulder-to-shoulder. They were led by Keane and Dale. William Reid, Keane's secretary, was with them. The shattered Fourth fell in behind, with Gibbs on the right and Pakenham himself on the left. The skirl of the pipes and the steady tread of the marching feet made victory seem certain and near. Pakenham, riding proudly forward with these glorious men, waved his hat over his head with his left hand. His right side was covered with blood. He was shouting he knew not what, but something wildly exultant.

Lieutenant Crawley, at Battery Four, laid his thirty-two pounder point-blank against the head of the advancing column.—Grand men out there, those men in skirts, he had a moment to think. Not one of them was under six feet tall, and not one of them apparently knew the meaning of fear.—Then he dipped his match into the priming.

When the smoke had cleared a little he looked out again. At least two hundred men, he saw, had been mown down by the one discharge of half a keg of musket-balls. Perhaps half of them had been killed. Among the writhing bodies a young officer was running in circles. Twice he stumbled and fell, but he staggered up again, still clutching his sword. When he rose for the second time Lieutenant Crawley caught a glimpse of what was left of the young man's face. Then Lieutenant Crawley looked quickly away, trying with all his might to think about something else.

Pakenham saw that the rampart was like a row of fiery furnaces. Dale was dead. Keane was down. Never had Pakenham seen, heard about, or imagined so deadly a fire. Never had he known the gunners and musketeers of Napoleon to pour out red death with so liberal a hand. It came like a ghostly wind from the sea blowing over an Irish bog. It blew down stalwart and beautiful men as though they were nothing worth. It beat against a man like a tempest in the face and broke his teeth and his breast-bone.

"For God's sake, Tylden, call up Lambert and the reserve!"

Dear God, how the men were falling! Greene there, with his face blown off and running madly in circles! MacLaren down, and his bowels out! And Harrington! Ah, no! But yes! Harrington!

Pablo, the little Spanish powder-monkey at the Baratarian battery, had been greatly surprised when he was told by Captain Dominique You that he must command the gun of Beluche, who was now slightly wounded. It was true that he had sometimes aimed Dominique's gun when the shot had been unimportant, but no one had ever told him that he aimed it well. Yet now the great captain had even been so kind as to slap him hard on the back and to say "Allez, mon enfant! Geeve zee Breeteesh ze hell flamboyant!"—After such trustful words Pablo felt that he must do his utmost.

For the first time in his life he had a sense of power. Backed by the captain, he could make these brawny brutes, the gun-crew, for once do his bidding. At his command they prized the carriage-gun round at a sharp angle so as to sweep the front of the Highlanders. He could see an officer sitting on a black pony over there, vainly flap-

ping his hat and yelling to make the soldiers move forward. This officer had lost his sword, and his right arm hung limp at his side.

So now, finding that the officer was directly in line with the gun-
barrel and that everything was ready, Pablo snatched up the burning
match.

Then he stood still for a moment, considering. He had never killed a
man. In spite of all the din and excitement of this battle, all the many
men he had seen torn and tossed during the last few minutes, he still
thought it a terrible thing to do. And besides, he did not like to think of
hurting the pony on which the officer sat.

There was only a second in which to think. Sleeping Bear might have
told him in a word what to do, but he was not there. In that second,
however, Pablo recalled something that Pierre Lafitte had once said
about how these British soldiers had treated the people, and especially
the nuns, of Badajoz when they had that Spanish town in their power.
Pablo's mother had died in Spain.—Thinking of her and of nothing
else he dashed the match into the priming-powder.

The gun yelled and reared, hurling his frail body to the ground. He
did not hear the joyous shout: "By gar! Vous avez keel le Général
Breeteesh, mon enfant!"

" 'Leven, Zeke."

"Whut 'n hell *fer?*"

"Didn't ye see me git thet gin'ral over thar? Keep yer peepers open!"

"Ye never *did* git thet gin'ral. 'T war them Berryterrians got 'im."

"Zekel, air ye insinivatin' ez I don't allus tell the immackilate truth?"

"Insinivatin'? Suhtingly not, Ezry. I've knowed yeh fer years ter be
a damn liar—an' loved yeh fer it."

"Thet so! Wal, iffen I war a gen'leman I'd be baoun' ter shoot yeh
daid fer them thar words."

"Mebbe; but seein' ez ye ain't no sech useless article, ye c'n jes' lend
me the borry of a chaw o' terbaccer, Ezry."

"Revenge! Revenge! We'll burn the city for Pakenham's funeral!
Forward, brave Highlanders!"

With their bag-pipes squealing and bayonets at the ready they
marched soberly, magnificently on toward the red fury of the rampart.
They came to the edge of the canal, crimson now, and with bodies
floating. They were down among the bodies and splashing through the
crimson, sliding on the mud of the bottom. Some of them, a few, were

struggling up the bank on the farther side, dripping red, and running for the rampart bent double. William Reid, as he ran, heard old Major Creagh shout from behind him: "Come on, lads! The day is ours! Come on, for the glory of Scotland!"

Yes, it was glorious, thought young Reid as he scaled the rampart. This was what the poets must have meant in their talk about the pride, pomp, and circumstance of glorious war. The Scotch had come farther today than any of those thousands of English, living or dead; and he himself had come farthest of all the Scotch. Here he stood now on the top of the rampart, alone, in the very jaws of the battle. He would be a famous man. People would say that he had by no means disgraced the blood of the Bruce.

Standing there on the top, Reid saw just before him, and a little below, lying on the backward slope of the bank, two Americans with very long slender rifles in their hands. For several seconds he stared at them, and they at him. Nothing remotely like these men had he ever seen before. They were unshaven, disheveled, hatless, and their clothing of deer-skin was filthy. Both of them had a hungry look. They were lean, sallow, hard-favored. In these regards they seemed to belong to the lower classes; and yet there was a twitching of restrained humor about their mouths, and something in their quite undeferential meeting of his gaze, which caused him to pause and wonder. They did not pull their fore-locks to him as peasants were supposed to do in the presence of their betters. They did not even offer to rise from their recumbent position. William Reid was puzzled.

But courtesy, he decided, was always in order. Therefore he brought his basket-hilted claymore ringing from its sheath and took a long stride toward them. "Your swords, gentlemen, if you please," he said. "You are my prisoners."

At first these conventional words seemed to have no effect upon the two Americans, unless to increase the strange humorous twitching of their mouths. They looked as though they would have liked to laugh but, for some reason, were restraining the impulse. Not for an instant, however, did their undaunted eyes leave his, nor did the muzzles of their rifles waver in point-blank aim at his bosom. It was for him an uncomfortable moment.

Then one of them said, speaking out of the side of his mouth in a high-pitched nasal drawl the like of which Reid had never before heard from any human voice: "But hell, Zekel, thet hain't right, is hit?"

"Absoloo'ly not, Ezry," the other replied, spurting a copious stream of dark brown liquid into the mud. "Fer one thing, we hain't got no swords. An' then, iffen ye ast me, I'd say he's *aour* pris'ner; an' b' God, I'd fight 'im fer it, tew."

"Wal then, stranger, ye hear whut Zekel says, an' ye see haow 't is. Do ye jes' jump yerself daown hyar in the mud an' make yerself to hum. We hain't got much, but *whut* we got is yournses."

William Reid was not accustomed to such invitations, even when couched in more elegant language. He turned and looked back. Just below him the body of Major Creagh sprawled against the outer slope of the rampart. There was a trickle of blood from the old man's left temple and his white beard was horribly defiled. Farther back lay the others who had crossed the canal—first three together, then seven or eight, and a dozen along the bank. Bedraggled as they were with the bloody water and fixed in the strangest attitudes of complete nonchalance, those bodies looked as though they had been splashed down from a great height. On the farther bank several hundreds of still-living Highlanders stood among the slain. They were neither advancing nor retreating. They were not firing at all. They were only standing there, and then falling, a few at a time. For hours, it seemed, they stood there, and fell, during the seconds while Reid watched. They had no leaders to tell them what they should do except to stand and fall. They were faithfully remembering what their dead leaders had taught them. They closed their ranks as fast as the ranks were torn open, so that the riflemen and gunners on the rampart had no need to change their aim.

But then, all at once, like a flock of starlings which explodes from a tree at dawn without any audible signal, they broke ranks and ran as though they were suddenly stricken with wild horror and amazement. They flung their arms from them. The bag-pipes wheezed down into silence. Their compact unity and disciplined order broke into many scurrying shapes that fled like chaff along a threshing-floor.

William Reid started after them, feeling that he must somehow call them back to their duty; but before he had gone three paces "Hey, you!" a voice sliced the noise-ridden air, "Whar ye gwineter?"

Reid saw that the two long rifles were still leveled at him.—On the whole, it seemed best to return.

"We cain't hev yeh boltin' off thet-away," said one, "jes' when we're a-gittin' 'quainted. 'T ain't mannerable, nohaow. Fack is, we've kinder tuk to yeh, Ezry an' me hez, seein' haow ye clumb thet 'ar bank like ye never heered tell o' bullets."

"Iffen we hedn't liked yer looks we'd a-drilled yeh clean," said the

619

second, "like we done all them others. An' don't fergit ye're the fust damn Englishman Zekel an' me ever sot eyes on 'cep'n' to shoot at, an' we don't wanter lose yeh. C'm on daown hyar an' hev a tell."

"Oh, I'm not English, you know," Reid replied. "I'm Scotch."

"Wal, we-uns never look a gift-hoss in the maouth. C'm on daown hyar anyhaow.—But look aout ye don't slip an' spile yer nice new clothes, even iffen they be a mite red an' dampish."

"Yeah, an' look aout ye don't trip over thet 'ar sword o' yourn. Maought cut yerself rale bad."

Thus reminded of the amenities of the occasion, Reid unbuckled his belt and handed his claymore and sheath to one of his captors. "It's yours," said he.

"Aw hell.—Whut's the damn thing good fer?"

"Give it t' Andy," his companion suggested. "Andy wears a sword, times, when he's gittin' his pitcher done."

"Okeh."

To only one man had the battle been a thing seen, heard, felt, and in some degree comprehended.

Lying beside his friend Mad Buffalo among the Choctaws at the edge of the cypress woods, Holdfast Gaines was closer by hundreds of yards to the blood-soaked heart of the conflict than Andrew Jackson pacing the rampart. The smoke of the batteries on either side did not becloud his view. The cries from the field, the rattle of rifles and muskets, even the grandiloquent rhetoric of the great guns, did not deafen his ears. He looked on without taking sides, suffering with and for both sides, striving to understand the fury and madness of the moment in terms of eternity. His mood was approaching that of a mind in which all personal passion is washed away, absorbed in the presentation on a stage of a tragic drama. In his heart as he watched there was a calm like that of a man on a mountain above the bellow and flash of a thunder-storm.

He saw the march of the British column under General Gibbs sweep past him, and how it crumbled. Then the Choctaws swarmed out like a sudden fury of hornets and came back with many scalps. The kilted Highlanders went striding by with their bag-pipes screaming, and stopped and stood and fell. Pakenham went down in the blast of a Baratarian gun, and little Pablo was crushed by the gun's recoil. For a moment, then, Holdfast put his hand before his eyes; but soon he looked forth again, resolved to see and bear it all.

There were moments of blazing beauty in the battle—moments in which the wave of youth and courage foamed gloriously up and broke in splendor against the toothed granite crags of death. He did not ignore those moments. But then the fiercely lunging guns were once more, suddenly, like so many loathsome lizards sprawled on a rock and darting their red tongues at flies.

"Hobbomok" meanwhile lay quiet and cool within six inches of his right hand. His hand did not move. Out there in the field the invisible Reaper was bringing a sufficient harvest home without any more help from him.

For it was not this present carnage alone that Holdfast was watching. Thirty years and more were cramped into the vision that came and possessed him and passed while the battle raged at its height. He saw the battle extended in time to include all its long preparation, as a single glance at the map takes in the whole vast system of the Mississippi from its lofty mountain cradles to the slumbering Gulf. In the guns that were roaring now he heard the hugely magnified echo of Long Tom's voice shaking the rafters of the night long ago at New London.

If he had fired that night into the second boat instead of the third, or if he had not fired at all, there would have been no wedding at Four Winds Farm, no change of Holdfast Gaines into Sleeping Bear, no Samuel Chester Reid, no Battle of Fayal, no message to Jackson, no help from Tennessee and Kentucky, no cannon and gunners and powder brought in by the Brotherhood of the Gulf, no victory won against tremendous odds at New Orleans, no magnificently unfettered River to water and feed the Land of the Free.

Yes; were it not for that swift decision far back there—and had he really decided, after all?—these hundreds of young bodies now strewn on the field would still be alive, moving, laughing, going forth to beget their kind on the future. What need or call had he to kill any of these men now with his own hand? In a deep, true, and terrible sense he was killing them every one. With this same right hand thirty and odd years ago he had doomed them all to these pitiful, meaningless deaths of theirs, far from home.

For a while, then, Holdfast looked back upon his life with horror. All his years he had striven for peace, yet he had brought to pass little but slaughter—as at Fort Mims, in the Creek War, and here. He had meant to serve Kiehtan alone, but in spite of himself he had done chiefly the work of the Adversary.

621

Ah, there it was again, that insoluble problem! Were the ways and works of those two really different, even separable? Could one of them live, or die, without the other's help? Were they foes, after all? They contended, eternally, but perhaps as friends might do, as partners, as old, old companions.

The wide-spread Indian myth of the celestial twins at their eternal game of chance was apparently enough to satisfy Parson Blandison— an old man, a humorist, and himself an inveterate gambler. To Hold-fast it gave no help. He could not so blandly ignore the stark actuality of good and evil, or the life-and-death contest between them. He was convinced that human suffering and sorrow and loss deserved and demanded a nobler explanation, as human ecstasy did also. He felt that the Parson, like most white men, left out of account the essentially tragic nature of man's life. The Parson did not solve, or even face, the question of divine responsibility. In thrusting every mystery back upon a brainless, soulless, and utterly irresponsible "Goddess Fortuna" he answered no question whatever.

Looking out from the cypress woods across the field of death, Hold-fast Gaines could not endure the thought that all of this devotion and agony had gone for nothing, that the battle had been but a meaningless moment in an everlasting phantasmagoria of raveled fog, or only one play in a game of dice or poker. There came to him, rather, the image of an infinite chess-board over which two evenly matched minds, un-imaginably vast and deep, were brooding throughout the ages. At times they seemed to be slowly working out some plan of an ideal order which could not be achieved unless each of them strove with all his power to win; but then again, for no apparent reason, the board sud-denly became a nightmare of chaotic disarray, as though one or the other had swept over it a violently wrathful hand.

That image was close, was better; and yet Holdfast knew that he had not solved his lifelong problem.

And then came the question: was it for the solving of the ultimate problems that man had been given breath?

Meanwhile, directly across the field and near the River, hidden per-haps among the thick foliage of a certain live-oak tree on the levee, that British bugler was still blowing the charge. He blew it over and over, almost incessantly, as though he could not see or would not believe that he was calling mostly to dead men. He was blowing the notes of victory in the midst of obvious and overwhelming defeat. Leaves, twigs, and even boughs of the tree were shredding down in the storm of lead and iron, but the distant mysterious music rang on through every lull of the guns. To Holdfast, listening more and more intently, it came as the voice of something unconquerably noble which would not, could not die, however these bodies might fall.

Holdfast rose to his feet. For a moment longer he looked out over the stricken field and then spread his arms wide. The Choctaws about him rose also and made the same gesture of salutation and farewell.

"I go now, Mad Buffalo."

"So it seems. Where go?"

"To join our friends and cross the River."

"Ugh! Good!—We go too, Sleeping Bear."

THE CONQUERING HERO

"We should be getting dispatches from New Orleans any day now. I've been hoping to announce our victory to Parliament upon my return to England. It ought to have a salutary effect upon the Opposition."

The rich red wine of Oporto gurgled from the glass decanter as Lord Castlereagh refilled the Duke of Wellington's glass.

"But, Bob, that expedition doesn't make sense. I've been meanin' to speak to you about it for some time, but all these other things kept crowdin' in."

"You mean about the expedition to New Orleans?"

"M'm.—You will remember that when you first mentioned it, and wanted me to go, I thought it was a risky thing. However, you got Ned Pakenham interested, and after that I tried to think as well of it as I could. In fact I may have helped a little toward getting together a larger force than you had thought would be needed."

"That's so, Arthur. And you lent your name—the great name of Wellington."

"Not because I wanted to."

"Perhaps not, but . . . But you've been most helpful all along, considering that you haven't quite believed in it."

"Have I?—But now, what does it all amount to? Suppose we have already won the victory you're so sure of. Let's say that the civil officers you sent over for the purpose are already governing New Orleans. Let's assume that Ned Pakenham has taken the city and the Mississippi, so that now he's ready for that earldom you have as good as promised him. But meanwhile, over here at Ghent, you have signed a treaty of peace with America which gives the whole place back to them. Now I hope you'll pardon me, but—that's absurd.—I thought you were a statesman, Bob."

Lord Castlereagh smiled and sipped his wine. "I'm sorry you feel that way about it, Arthur," he said at length, "because it has looked to me rather a neat thing."

"What do you mean by 'a neat thing'? An expedition that costs England a million pounds, not to mention the lives to be lost, and brings her nothing?"

"No. I mean a thing by which Old England stands to win a huge stake at small cost and little risk."

"I don't understand you. Look here, Bob.—Here's a copy of the treaty, and in the first article of it you stipulate that 'all territory, places, and possessions whatsoever, taken from either party by the other during the war, or which may be taken after the signing of this treaty . . . shall be restored without delay.' Well now, I ask you what you mean, having such a treaty as that in your pocket, by sending Ned Pakenham to capture New Orleans and Louisiana, and by telling him that if he does so he will be made Earl of the same."

Lord Castlereagh was obviously having a good time. "I still feel," said he, "that the thing is rather neat. On the surface it seems to mean that they 'll have to give back whatever little places they may have taken from us."

"But they've taken nothing at all from us! This treaty really means that Ned will have to march his army, empty-handed, right out of the richest city in America the moment he's captured it."

Castlereagh held his glass up to the light. "You said you thought I was a statesman, Arthur; and I hope you didn't mean anything unpleasant by it. Neither do I intend anything insulting when I say, judging from your present remarks, that you must be a—well, a soldier."

"Talk sense, will you? This thing is serious. It isn't, after all, quite the sort of thing you'll want the Opposition to hear about."

"As a matter of fact I am eager to tell them all about it. Now if you will have the goodness to read that treaty with some care you will find that I have referred no less than seven times to the boundaries of the

United States as being the same for the purposes of this treaty as those agreed upon in the treaty we signed with them back in 1783."

"Well?"

"Well!—Oh, Arthur, you *are* a soldier if you can't see the point even now!"

"What is it, then?"

"Why, back in 1783, of course, New Orleans was in *Spanish Florida,* and the whole country that they call Louisiana, west of the Mississippi, was owned by Spain."

"But Napoleon took it from Spain and sold it to America."

"Yes—or so America asserts. But Arthur, is there any particular reason, now that we are the allies of Spain and have beaten Napoleon, why we should respect a transaction in which that Corsican brigand sold stolen property?"

"H'm! Oh! So you mean that Pakenham is not on American soil at all?"

"Precisely! Now you're getting at it. According to the boundaries laid down in our treaty with America in 1783, *he is not on American soil.* Louisiana and New Orleans, according to that treaty and this one as well, simply are not a part of the United States. They never have been, and I've merely been taking steps to make sure that they never will be. In capturing Spanish Florida, the so-called 'Louisiana Purchase,' and all the vast territory from the Mississippi to the Pacific Ocean, Pakenham will only be protecting the rights of Spain, England's beloved but somewhat enfeebled ally."

"And I suppose you hope to persuade Spain to let us 'protect' that land of hers indefinitely?"

"Spoken almost like a statesman, Arthur."

"But that will be more land than all that the United States has east of the Mississippi."

"A good deal more."

"And therefore, when they find out what you've done to their map, we may expect them to start another war."

"Never fear. For months, for years, the New England states have been crying for peace. In Boston they illuminated the State House and roasted an ox in the streets when you defeated Napoleon. I hear, too, that there's a convention in Hartford where they're planning secession. In the West, once we control the Mississippi, we shall have our own way. Cochrane has terrified the Atlantic coast. We have burned Washington. Their treasury is bankrupt. Their main ports are blockaded. We can land an overwhelming force whenever and wherever we please. Pakenham will simply march up from New Orleans, and Prevost will come down from Canada to meet him. Then the West will revolt and the country will fall to pieces."

"Ah. I see. How simple! And so I take it that when you planned this treaty you didn't intend that it should bring all our military operations on the American continent to an abrupt close."

There was a touch of self-satisfaction in Castlereagh's smile as he said: "Just take a look at the date of that treaty, will you?"

"Let's see. Oh . . . ah . . . yes; it's dated the twenty-fourth of December, last.—But, Great God, Bob, by that time you must have known that our forces would be at New Orleans. I say you *must have known it* when you had this treaty signed!"

Lord Castlereagh went on smiling.

"You meant this treaty to blind the American ambassadors to your true intentions. Yes, I see now at least one reason why you've kept them dawdling about here in Europe ever since last summer, putting them off from month to month. You were waiting until the time when you could offer them a treaty of peace with one hand while striking their country the heaviest possible blow with the other.—You said not one word to the American plenipotentiaries, there at Ghent, while you were discussing this treaty, about the really quite pertinent fact that you had already dispatched a great armada to strike their country in its most vulnerable spot. In other words, you told them a silent lie. Is that right? Am I beginning to comprehend what you mean by 'statesmanship'? Is that the sort of thing that you say I've 'lent' my name to?"

"You put it bluntly, even brutally, Arthur, but—well, something like that. I've been playing for big stakes across the ocean there while we've been having all this trouble in Vienna and Paris. Of course the orders have gone through Bathurst and I haven't shown my hand, but now it's becoming clear that we can't lose. The American game is up, as the Yankees will soon learn. We're going to take their country over and run it, as we took India and Canada."

The Duke of Wellington sat back in his chair and surveyed the handsome features of Lord Castlereagh without any sign of pleasure or approval. Two or three times he took up his wine-glass and sipped from it, drumming meanwhile on the table with the fingers of his left hand.

"Keep it in mind, Arthur, that I've given Ned Pakenham plenty of time. According to the eleventh article, this treaty doesn't come into force until it has been ratified and signed by Madison and myself, and the ratifications mutually exchanged. That may take four months, in which time many interesting things may happen at New Orleans and along the Mississippi.—Don't forget that I sent Keane out in September, and Cochrane has been burning his way down the Atlantic coast for months."

Wellington was gazing out of the window with clouded eyes.

"Suppose, if you like," Castlereagh continued, "that the battle for New Orleans is being fought at this moment, while we sit here on this eighth of January, eighteen hundred and fifteen. In that case, fools may pretend that the results of that battle—I mean our victory, of course—are nullified by the treaty you hold in your hand, dated two weeks ago. They 'll be wrong. Our war with America is still going on."

"Well, Arthur," said Castlereagh at length, stirring uneasily in his chair, "what do you think of it?"

"I'm thinking, Bob, how glad I am not to be a statesman. It's bad enough to be a soldier and try to execute the schemes that statesmen think up, but the strain on one's conscience and character is not so great."

"Don't you like the plan?"

"Sir, I detest it!"

"But why, Arthur? Tell me why!"

"Because it's too damned clever. Because it's under-handed—and that ought to mean un-English. Because it uses a peace treaty, which ought to be a solemn engagement of a nation's honor, as a means of deception and fraud. Because it is calculated to make England hated throughout the world—and especially in America, by people of our own kind, upon whom England may have to depend some day for her very life."

"Nonsense, Arthur! England . . ."

"Hear me out! You 'statesmen' have bungled this war from the start. In the first place, there never would have been such a war if you had seen England's true interests and served them. You might have made America our ally against Napoleon. You might have opened our ports to her commerce, and laughed at the French threat of blockade. You might have established a partnership with the swiftly growing American nation which would have made the English-speaking peoples the unquestionable masters of the world for ages to come. But no! No! You 'statesmen' felt that it was more important to maintain your infamous Orders in Council, which were in fact a gross violation of international

627

rights, and to defend our arrogant practice of filching American sailors off American ships on the high seas."

"Yes, but Arthur . . . ."

"Therefore you thrust us into this war, which no thoughtful Englishman or American ever wanted. We have lost many lives, much money, and also the monopoly of the seas—perhaps forever. And what have we gained by it all? According to this treaty of yours we have not acquired one square foot of territory, and we have not established one principle, because we fought for none; and, certainly, we have not gained us a friend."

"Ah, but Arthur, you forget about New Orleans."

"I wish I could! I wish it were not so clear that there too, in that hare-brained scheme, we have the work of *'statesmen.'* "

"Oh, come now! You're getting excited."

"That may be; and it's enough to excite any soldier to hear you talking so easily about Pakenham going up the Mississippi and Prevost coming down it, as though one of the mightiest rivers on earth were nothing but a wavy line drawn on paper. It's often hard for a hostile army to march up and down real rivers, let me tell you. It's hard even after that army has got a foot-hold and won its first battle—and there's nothing to show that we have done that yet. You assume that the battle is won, that the Mississippi is ours, and that therefore we are about to take over the United States of America and 'run them.' You ignore the possibility that those Americans may love their country somewhat as we do ours, and may defend it as fiercely as we should have fought for England if Napoleon had landed on our coast and tried to march up the Thames. I think that before you write any more peace treaties, promise any more earldoms, or send over any more officials to govern the cities of America, you had better wait, sir, for the news."

What a story this would make back in Nashville! What wonderful clothes these women of New Orleans wore—or rather, what clothes they did *not* wear! And how friendly they all were down here, how warm-hearted and hospitable! They seemed to feel that the wife of General Andrew Jackson was as good as anybody.—And of course, in a way, they would be right in so feeling.

But then, to be quite honest with herself, this whole visit had nearly swept Rachel Donelson Jackson off her feet. The city was so big, noisy, and strange. The houses were so different from ordinary houses. People jabbered languages at her that she did not know the names of, and

628

even when they tried to talk English they could scarcely make themselves understood. And then the parties, calls, dinners, and dances! The men had been extremely polite—especially that very handsome and well-behaved Mr. John Lafitte. He had called, he had sent her flowers and wine and books and candy, and even—that had been a queer experience—he had once kissed her hand! Well, what of it? At her age that didn't mean anything.

Still, Mr. Lafitte had been extremely agreeable and polite.—As for all that nonsense about Mr. Lafitte's having once been a pirate, of course it was simply absurd. That was just one of the things that Andrew said to tease her.

However, she must remember as much as she could about everything that went on, so as to tell the ladies back in Nashville. She must try especially hard to remember all the amazing things they were having to eat at this Washington's Birthday Dinner on the second floor of the French Exchange.

Let's see, now. Probably the most important thing was the large ham, completely covered with gold, which Andrew had carved with his own hands for the folks at the head table. Also there had been several quite mysterious kinds of soup, together with fish and game and fowl of which she could only guess the names. It had to be kept in mind that down here in New Orleans they had queer ways of cooking ordinary things which disguised their true nature completely. And yet there were beef and mutton and pork, of course, and baked beans and corn-fritters with maple-syrup. Those things made her feel more at home. Not so, however, the fiercely hot dish which she heard somebody call a "Louisiana gumbo." That burned all the way down and kept on burning after it got there. It made her feel almost foreign again.

Hadn't somebody told her that the word "gumbo" meant a kind of language that people talked in these parts? But now it was something to eat—that is, if you hadn't been warned! Well, it was all very confusing.

And then one mustn't forget the French pastries, which were numerous in kind and good but not very filling. For dessert they had stacks of "pralines" with some kind of nuts in them, and gallons of iced-cream.—Andrew's iced-cream came in the form of a little donkey, most cleverly molded. Just why they had chosen that particular beast for him it would be hard to say, unless perhaps because Andrew was so stubborn.

Well, those things were the main things. They were certainly enough. In fact, one simply could not eat them all. Mr. Lafitte had brought his cook over from Barataria to manage the whole dinner, and he had done it extremely well.

But after the dinner, and also during it, there had been more toasts than anyone could hope to remember—that is, anyone who had drunk most of them herself. There had been at least seven to General Jackson. That she was sure of, even though several of them had been proposed in some foreign language. And she was quite sure, too, that there had been at least one toast to Mr. Lafitte. Others she could vaguely recall had been to Commodore Patterson, to General Coffee, to an old gentleman called Mr. Villeré, to Holdfast Gaines who was not there and perhaps was not even alive, to the noble Creole Militia of New Orleans, to the noble Kaintucks, to the noble Free Men of Color, to the noble Baratarians, and to the noble Choctaws.—Yes; thus far, that seemed to be about all, unless one cared to mention the one proposed by Mr. Lafitte to "Madame la Générale, the charming consort of our hero." And the wines in which these toasts were drunk had been remarkably good. She understood that they had been provided in large part by Mr. Lafitte.

And the ornaments! Such flowers as they had down here, even in winter! Such ribbons and gilt! And those long sheets of clear glass bearing mottoes in gold leaf! The names of "Jackson," "Lafitte," "Villeré," "Coffee," "Patterson," and "Carroll" were lighted up by these transparencies in a way that made them look as though written on the sky. On one of them, in the shape of a pyramid, the names of Jackson and Washington were linked together. She must never forget to tell people about that—modestly, of course. On another, right here at the head table, were the words "Jackson and Victory—They are but One." Andrew, when he saw it, had wondered why they couldn't have just said "Hickory and Victory." Never before had she suspected him of being a poet.

So much for the things she must try to remember. The one thing she could never forget was the way these beautiful and charming women, most of them younger than herself, were petting and adoring her Andrew. Men, of course, had always admired and followed him—at least when they did not hate and try to kill him—but it was something new to see her husband openly courted by women. Moreover, it was something delightful to see how little he really cared for their admiration. Polite he was to them of course, but all his real attention was being given to the plump, middle-aged, and plain-spoken woman from

630

Tennessee who at this moment was yearning for a good long comfortable pull at a blackened clay pipe.

These ladies must never know how she longed for that pipe. None of the ladies down here used tobacco in any way. Madame Livingston had made that quite clear.

And now Mr. Lafitte was standing up to propose still another toast. Oh dear! Ought she to drink it? There had been so many toasts already, and Madame Livingston would not like it if . . .

"Le Général Jackson, le Président futur des États-Unis!"

The words were like a spark that sets off a train of powder and explodes a great gun. Everyone cheered and shouted and whistled far more for this toast than for any of the others. They appeared to be extremely and increasingly excited, as though Mr. Lafitte had found the exact words for what they had all been thinking and wanting. They banged on the tables and stamped on the floor. The handles of the table-knives rang on the tall-stemmed glasses. Mr. Lafitte went to a window and shouted his toast between cupped hands to the crowd in the street below. The walls of the French Exchange seemed to rock with the yells and shouts and pistol-shots of the good Baratarians and all the other friendly folks standing patiently outside.

The full meaning of the last toast had not been clear at first to Rachel Jackson. For ten seconds or more she sat smiling happily, taking the uproar as merely another expression of courteous good will. But then, of a sudden, a chill struck to her heart.—President of the United States! Why, that would take him far away, into an almost foreign country! Would Andrew like that, to leave his horses and stables, the Hermitage, the law office, his cronies at the tavern, Little Andrew, his wife? He had been to Philadelphia as Representative and Senator—and had not liked it. Of course if he really wanted to be President then he would be, but . . . But then perhaps being President wouldn't be so lonely a business as fighting the Creeks and the British and Spanish and all those others. Perhaps she might go with him. Ah, then . . . ! And would they let her smoke her pipe in the White House—at least in the kitchen? Yes, they would, if Andrew said so.

But this time Andrew stood up. He was going to make a speech. That was good! Probably the people of New Orleans had no idea of the wonderful speeches he could make. They probably thought of him as nothing but a soldier. Well!—As a matter of fact it had always been an amazing thing even to her how Andrew could talk to any kind of audience he had before him as though that were the only kind he had ever known. With the grooms down at the training-stables he used their language—which, to be sure, was not always very nice. When speaking in court he used the sober and learned language of the law. When one of his old friends from the Waxhaws or Blue Ridge was with him he slipped easily back into the words and pronunciations familiar to his youth. He could spin a yarn with an old long-hunter in dirty buck-skins as fluently as he could converse with these fine ladies. Every evening, now, he would tell a bed-time story to little Cora Livingston in the words that a child could understand; but then two minutes after she had gone to bed he would be talking like a book to her father. And with Holdfast Gaines, his oldest friend, he talked—well, best of all.

Now that the fighting seemed to be over Andrew was beginning to dress more like a soldier. Very handsome he looked, though terribly thin, as he stood up tall and straight beside her in his new frock-coat with the gold epaulettes. His long narrow face was even more serious than usual. This, Rachel saw, was going to be a speech with no amusing stories or table-talk in it. This was the Andrew that made her feel proudest, and also a little afraid.

"Ladies and gentlemen," he began, "you are doing one man too much honor. It would have been impossible for any general—for Alexander the Great, for Napoleon, or even for George Washington himself—to have won the victory we celebrate tonight without the support of my brave men, my heroic officers, and the loyal citizens of New Orleans."

Tremendous cheers, stamping of feet, and clapping of hands.

"I am also convinced that all of us together could not have triumphed on this field without the help of Powers greater than human. If ever any army has been upheld and strengthened by the Lord God of Hosts, ours has been.

"This you will better comprehend if you consider what our situation was a few weeks ago. After many reverses by land and sea our country as a whole was disheartened. New England, luke-warm from the start in this war, was apparently planning at the Hartford Convention to leave the Union. Washington, our capital city, lay in ashes. Our national government was pitifully, shamefully vacillating. Our national treasury was bankrupt. Our army and navy had been weakened by many defeats and by internal strife. Here in this western country, so far from apparent danger, our vigilance was relaxed, our discipline was weak, we had no military stores, our young men had lost the custom of arms, and

632

there were traitors living amongst us, almost unsuspected, with high honor and emolument.

"Such was our condition, ladies and gentlemen, when we were suddenly and unexpectedly threatened by the chosen troops of the most powerful army on earth. They came down upon us twenty thousand strong in a fleet of fifty great ships of war that bore a thousand great guns. They came with a carefully developed plan which they were able to keep until the last moment a secret. They were led by men born and bred to the art of war, some of whom had grown gray in the habit of victory. So confident were they of conquest that they brought a full complement of civil officers appointed in England for the government of this city of New Orleans. I have heard that their Commander-in-Chief, Sir Edward Pakenham, the brother-in-law of Wellington and the hero of many a hard-fought field, was to have been rewarded for victory by the Earldom of Louisiana.

"But now, behold the result! In less than an hour we passed from fog to clear sunshine, from gloom to victory—or rather, let us say, from the prospect of servitude into an assurance of liberty that shall never end. The glittering host that came so arrogantly against us is limping home now, beaten, shattered, disgraced. Seven hundred of its number will never see the white headlands of England again. Twice that number will never again bear arms. The body of Sir Edward Pakenham, who so confidently expected to be the Earl of Louisiana, is now tossing and tumbling at sea on board His Majesty's Ship *Plantagenet,* preserved in a hogshead of rum."

Wild cheers.

"But let us not boast of this huge slaughter of men. We Americans take no pleasure in killing. Moreover, we know that it was not our courage and skill alone that brought this victory to pass. Let us rather be grateful that in defending the liberty of these our beloved western waters we lost only eight men by death and had only thirteen wounded."

More cheers.

"Let us pause and think of those eight young men who died so that we might live."

For half a minute, while Jackson held up his right hand, the roomful was silent.

"Let it be remembered that in this battle we were fighting on behalf of an America that knew and cared nothing about our danger or the cause for which we fought. From the seat of our national government we have had first indifference and then interference, but all the while complete incomprehension. From the cities of the eastern seaboard, and especially those of New England, we have had for the most part sneers and abuse. From those who should have brought us the aid of American ships and soldiers we have had ignorance, incompetence, and in one signal instance actual treachery. Let it be remembered, I say, that America owes this victory not to Philadelphia, New York, and Boston, but to the men of the West; and not to rich men, not to men in high office, not to professional soldiers such as James Wilkinson, but to Indians, Negroes, Cajuns, Creoles, Frenchmen, Spaniards, Italians, long-hunters in coon-skin caps, trappers in soiled buck-skins, pioneers like my friend Jake McNab with nothing but their rifle-guns between them and starvation, and boys from the plow's tail who until almost the day of the battle had never held a fire-arm in their hands.

"Men and women of the West, you well know that I am not a scholar, yet I make bold to say that in all the numberless pages of history you will not find a clearer example than this of the power of simple, humble, and untrained men to rise to the level of a supreme occasion and need. And I say that the time of those plain men is at hand. They have earned it by doing for ages the world's hardest work for the world's least pay. They earned it again on the eighth of January. No one of you could have walked along that rampart of mud at dawn of that day, seeing those thousands of faces, most of them young, many of them dirty, all of them very tired, without understanding as I did that a new time was coming, a western time, our time. I tell you I saw it as clearly in those faces black and red and white as I see now these two hands. All at once, in that moment when America stood in dreadful danger, I saw what America might be good for. I saw it as the home not mainly of bankers and politicians in broadcloth but of plain folk in buck-skins and home-spun and linsey-woolsey. This I saw, I see it still, and I swear to you by the immaculate and everlasting Majesty of Heaven that while Andrew Jackson draws the breath of life it will never be forgotten."

Huge applause.

"Here has been a triumph of pure will over mountainous might. Here has been a clear and crashing victory of men who had little to help them except the sheer cold knowledge that they had to win. They were ignorant almost utterly of the ancient art of war. They only knew how to win their battle.

"Not for a moment did I doubt that they would win it, yet I confess

634

that when I first caught sight of our enemy ten thousand strong, glittering, disciplined, marching to music across the frosted Plain of Chalmette, led by tried and famous commanders, I felt for some seconds the weight upon me of an almost crushing burden. But during those seconds, if you will pardon the personal reference, there came the recollection of another scene of battle, and of triumph over even greater odds. I saw a tiny red game-cock which had been dragged aside to the barrier and almost given up as dead, first raise his blood-soaked body on one wing, then stagger to his feet, take one step, and finally slay his foe. Forgive me if I say that this recollection only, if I had been given no other help, would have been enough to sustain me.

"But again I say that I did not win this battle, nor did our brave men themselves go unaided. In our gratitude for a miraculous victory, ladies and gentlemen, we must acknowledge the help of a strength and wisdom infinitely exceeding our own. It was no human foresight that sent a seven-gun privateer across the sea to Fayal in the Azores, there to encounter three ships of the squadron coming against us. If Captain Samuel Chester Reid were with us tonight, sharing our celebration of a victory he greatly helped to win, I think he would probably admit that human power alone did not enable him to withstand that vastly superior force of men and guns, and so to maim it that Admiral Cochrane was kept waiting for twenty-six days at Jamaica before General Keane could join him."

"Hurray! Hurray! Samuel Chester Reid!"

"It was during those precious twenty-six days that a member of the *General Armstrong's* crew—a man well known by fame to us all, one of my oldest friends, and one who summed up in himself the best that our country has been and will be—brought certain news of the coming attack, and also summoned from Tennessee and Kentucky the men to meet it. What we owe to that man will never be told in full, but, if I may speak for one who never spoke of himself, Holdfast Gaines did not feel that his great run in six days and nights from Mobile to Nashville was made on his strength alone, very great though we know that strength to have been."

"Hurray! Holdfast Gaines! Sleeping Bear!"

"You are right; but he is not with us to hear you. He was in the battle; I saw him there, and shook his hand, perhaps for the last time. I saw him rise to his feet among his Choctaw friends when the battle was nearly over, and then, after an Indian salute to the fallen, disappear among the cypress shadows. But after the battle he was not to be found, alive or dead. Perhaps his Indian friends have taken his magnificent body away for an Indian burial. Can we blame them?—Or again, as many a talk by the camp-fire and my own hearth leads me to hope, he may have gone back to live with his own people. At any rate, he is lost to us."

Again, for several seconds, the diners sat in silence.

"But when you consider," Jackson went on, "how helpless we were here until Carroll's men arrived, and when you recall that we attacked just three days later, you will see how necessary was that delaying of the British fleet. Had they not been so delayed, had the message from Fayal not reached me in time, had there not been this one man to run north to Nashville—I say, had not some Power greater than ourselves caused these things to happen in this order and in the nick of time, why then New Orleans and the River would be no longer ours, and all the western country, perhaps our country as a whole, would now be losing that liberty which our fathers won for us some thirty-five years ago."

"Hurray! Captain Reid!"

"The *Armstrong*!"

"Holdfast Gaines!"

"All these we had to help us, but even these might not have been enough. We had one other weapon. We had the sword of the River. We fought for the River, yes; but also the River fought for us. It was the River that floated Carroll's boys down from Tennessee. It was the River that rose and sank round the British camp, bogging them down in the mud by day and binding them in ice by night. The push of the River swept Thornton's boats below their landing-place. The River bore the *Carolina* down to the British camp, and the fog of the River shrouded her until she could rake their camp with her guns, just before our first attack. The fog of the River concealed our weakness from the British, and the breath of the River blew the fog away in the battle beginning at dawn."

"Hurray! The River!"

"The Mississippi!"

"Father of Waters!"

"And so, ladies and gentlemen, although the odds against us looked enormous and not to be overcome, yet with such allies as the River, the *General Armstrong,* Holdfast Gaines, all of them mysteriously and unconsciously working together under the Lord of Hosts, no man— not even a lawyer from the backwoods, one who had never before seen a pitched battle between civilized men, even one much given to horse-racing, cock-fighting, and dueling with pistols—no man, I say, could possibly have failed.—I thank you."

*　　*　　*

"Afore I lit aout this mawnin' I et me a good bait o' victuals, but naow I'm hollower 'n a las' year's gourd," said old McNab to Russell Bean as they stood listening below the windows of the French Exchange. "S'pose ye hain't got nothin' on yeh fit to chaw?"

"Chunk o' 'gater-tail I brung 'long," Bean answered, producing it from the bulge of his hunting-coat. "Course she'll be a mite gamier 'n las' week, but . . ."

"Ah! 'Gater-tail! Jes' whut I ben a-honin' fer. Social 'casions like thisheer a feller wants suthin' to set a tooth into, iffen he's got one."

"Yeah. But jes' ye wait a spell, Jake McNab, an' me an' you'll be trompin' into the White House one o' these days to hev dinner with Pres'dent Andrew Jackson; an' then, by the Gre't Horn Spoon, I bet Rachel is a-goin' to git us up suthin' better 'n 'gater-tail or tell us the reason why."

"I'll admire to go with yeh, Russ, iffen ye'll take me."

"Why, suhtingly I'll take yeh, Jake—an' likewise Zekel an' Ezry an' all the rest o' these fellers."

"I s'pose ye don't mean me too, Mr. Bean?" piped the timid voice of Corporal McCuskey.

"I mean the hull damn kit an' bilin'. We-uns 'll jes' nachally camp thar in the White House an' swap yarns with Andy an' smoke our pipes with Rachel. Jake c'n spit amber into the fireplace."

"But mebbe . . ." the corporal began.

"Mebbe, nothin'! Ye won't be no trouble 't all, li'l Corp'ral, an' iffen ye keep yer mouth shet folks won't know ye're thar. 'Sides thet, hain't thet 'ar White House ourn? Hain't we 'arned it fair an' squar? Hain't I knowed Rachel an' Andy f'm way back?"

"Thet's so, Mr. Bean. I s'pose ye'll be a famous man naow, an' Andy'll make yeh a sheriff or suthin'."

"'How wonderful . . .'" began the booming baritone of Russell Bean, almost instantly joined by the cracked tenor of McNab with his mouth full. Ezry, Zekel, the corporal, and a dozen others who already knew the words and tune, chimed in, and then a score, a hundred. Soon a thousand manly voices were shouting over and over to the midnight sky:

637

"How wonderful, how glorious, how marvelous I am!
How wonderful it is to be me!"

*   *   *

Swaying to the pitch and toss of His Majesty's sloop-o'-war *Sophie,*
now homeward bound, the six young officers at dinner in the cabin
sang their boastful and boisterous old song as well as they were able,
pounding and stamping and vociferating, hoping to convince themselves that they were having an excellent time:

> But of all the world's great he-e-roes
> There's none that can com-pa-a-re,
> Singin' tow-row-row-row-ROW, row,
> To the British Gre-e-en-a-diers!

Their dinner had been good enough, and certainly their drink had
been sufficient, yet somehow . . .

Perhaps it was that they were not accustomed to getting along without McWilliams. It had seemed the decent thing to set an empty
chair at the table in memory of him, but the sight of that chair, and
of the drinking-glass turned upside-down on the table before it, did
not tend to enliven the party.

They were finding that it was possible to get very drunk without
McWilliams, but apparently even drunkenness had lost its charm. The
fellow had said the damnedest things, both drunk and sober, and in the
old days it had been a chief pleasure of theirs to howl him down in
chorus whenever he said them, thus asserting and maintaining common sense against the audacious doubter. But now even common sense
itself was beginning to seem a little dull.

Captain Lockyer—red-faced, fat-jowled, pig-eyed—was staggering up
to propose a toast now in what he considered the style of McWilliams.
"Here's to the damn Yankees!" he was saying in a surly voice, staring
hard at his plate. "We don' wan' 'eir country. Go' goo' country of 'r
own. Le' 'em have it. Even if they *was* thirty thousan' strong, they're
damn goo' fighters. Fight like hell. Here's to 'em!"

But no; that was not the right tone and those were not the right
words. McWilliams would have known how to say it much better. He
could have told them how to think and feel about the loss of seven
hundred comrades, including many officers of high rank, and about
the promotions that would certainly follow. He would have known
just what to say about the interesting though somewhat gruesome fact

638

that the body of General Edward Pakenham was going home on the flagship *Plantagenet,* encased and pickled in a hogshead of rum.

And yet for all their sense of loss, they were somehow comforted, they were sustained by a feeling of fitness, in their realization that Mc-Williams—he who had never seemed quite at home in the snug Old World but had been from the start strangely excited by the New—would never return from that vast strange country.

*   *   *

"Ladies and gentlemen, friends and neighbors and guests," said the good-looking young man standing among the musicians on the stairway, "you must not expect a speech from me."

"Why not, Sam," called a voice. "Ye're the hero."—And then the chandeliers shook in a storm of applause and a thousand candle-flames trembled.

"I must ask the good friend who said that—and I think his name is Sam Avery—not to talk nonsense. My heroism, as he calls it, amounts only to this, that I tried to protect a certain piece of private property—and failed."

"Aye, but jes' take an' tell us *how* ye failed, an' what it cost 'em."

"Not now. At present I'm thinking about a banquet that was given to me not long ago by certain officers of the British Navy, at a time when the blood my guns had spilled was scarcely dry on their faces. Tonight, as one of three hundred Americans entertaining these thirty British officers, I have my first chance to return that courtesy in some degree. If New London's court-house had been large enough we should gladly have had a thousand citizens here to meet and to greet not the officers only but every man in the British squadron. Then my grandfather, Colonel John Chester, who planned this reception and ball, would have been an even happier and prouder man than we now see him to be."

"Hurrah! Colonel John!"

"As for heroes, my own notion is that they don't make speeches, but if they do, then we may hear tonight from my old commander and friend, Captain Isaac Hull, formerly of the frigate *Constitution;* from Captain Stephen Decatur, of the frigate *United States,* and from our distinguished guest Admiral Henry Hotham of His Majesty's Navy."

Again the chandeliers shook, and then someone called out: "The Admiral's been waitin' to make that speech for a long, long time."

"True enough," the young man continued when the laughter had

639

died down. "His whole squadron has been waiting for years for a chance to get into New London."

"Yeah—the way they did back in eighty-one," commented an old man's voice.

"I see what you mean, sir," said Reid, "but this time we've made different arrangements. Back there in eighty-one, my grandfather tells me, the British provided all the illuminations. Tonight, we are doing it ourselves. The windows of every house in town, and of every farm-house for miles about, are crowded with candles. Norwich, where my mother lives, at the head of the river, is all agleam. From the hill-top at Four Winds Farm, if we were standing there, we should be able to count a dozen towns and villages with lanterns burning in their church-towers and steeples. Even the old tar-barrel we kept so long on Lantern Hill to give us warning that the British were marching against us is at this moment aflame to show our gladness that they are here."

"Hurrah! British Navy!"

"Hurrah! Cap'n Sam Chester Reid!"

"Therefore we can assure our guests that our present deep interest in them is no new thing."

Laughter, and a voice calling "Not by *no* means!"

"Every sign of growth or shrinkage in their squadron has been important news in New London streets. Every morning for years, before breakfast, my grandfather has taken his spy-glass and climbed the hill behind his house to count the vessels in the British squadron. When he found that there were two or three more than usual he'd go back into the kitchen and say: 'Well, Mother, you'd better cook up every-thing we have in the house. All New London will be here for supper.' "

"Hurrah! Mother Chester!"

"Yes, my friends. Someone here has made mention of heroes, but first of all come mothers. I have known one hero in my lifetime, and I mention him now because the only mother he ever knew was the woman you have just named."

"Who was it, Cap'n?—Is he dead now?"

"Ah, but heroes don't die. They disappear. They come up out of mystery and go back where they came from, so that we can always feel that they 'll return again when we need them. And another thing —usually we don't know them for what they are until they are gone. At any rate, so it has been with Holdfast Gaines."

A murmur of surprise and faint protest swept through the company: "Who's that he said?"—"Holdfast Gaines."—"I remember now. That runner, the strong man."—"Oh, that Mohegan!"—"Oh, yes, I saw him on the street last summer and he didn't know me. Wouldn't speak."

"Ye're doin' fine, Cap'n Sam," called a louder voice. "Jes' keep a-goin' an' ye'll make a speech yet."

"Not if I know it—but I might be prevailed upon to sing you a song in the few minutes left me before the ball begins."

"Yeah, that's the ticket! Sing us Philip Freneau's ballad about the *General Armstrong*:

> " 'In the road of Fayal when their anchors were cast,
>   The British were watching to give 'em a blast;
>   Not far from the port, for destruction sharp set,
>   Lay the *Rota, Carnation,* and *Plantagenet.*' "

"But you seem to know that song already," said Reid.

"That's what we do; an' a good 'un 't is—

> " 'So the *Armstrong* repelled 'em with pistols and pikes;
>   From her musketry fire
>   They by dozens expire!
>   And soon was the work of destruction complete . . . ' "

"Look here, my friend. I said that *I* would sing a song. Your turn will come later, when you've had a little more punch."

"All right, Cap'n. I c'n wait."

"The song I have in mind is a new one. I picked it up at a banquet in Baltimore, while on my way north from Amelia Island. It had been written not long before by a young patriot whose name I did not learn, just after some minor engagement in Chesapeake Bay. He wrote it as a poem, but there at the banquet I heard a man sing it to the old tune of 'Anacreon in Heaven' which, I believe, comes from England. Somehow it seems appropriate that we should have a song tonight with an English tune and American words. Our fiddlers know the tune. In fact they tell me that they meant to play it during the ball for one of our minuets."

"Sing 'er out, Sam!"

"Very well. But please remember that we've had no rehearsal and that my voice has been trained chiefly in trying to out-bawl the wind on ships at sea."

"Wal then, bawl it; but git started!"

641

After an eight-measure introduction by the violins, Reid began, in a fresh and ringing baritone:

"Oh say, can you see by the dawn's early light
What so proudly we hailed at the twilight's last gleaming?
Whose broad stripes and bright stars, through the perilous fight,
O'er the ramparts we watched were so gallantly streaming? . . . "

Except for the violins and the manly voice the room was breathlessly still. Mrs. Rebecca Reid, standing near her son on the stair-case, listened in complete indifference to the fact that many admiring eyes, and especially those of the British officers, were fixed upon her. In a far corner a little white-haired woman smiled with pride and wiped her eyes at the same time.

Reid went through the first stanza of his song without apparent effort, but the closing lines he vociferated as though he were affirming, for all the world to hear, a declaration of national faith:

"Oh, thus be it ever when freemen shall stand
Between their loved homes and the war's desolation!
Blest with vict'ry and peace, may the heav'n-rescued land
Praise the Power that hath made and preserved us a nation!
Then conquer we must, for our cause it is just,
And this be our motto—'In God is our trust!'
And the star-spangled banner in triumph shall wave
O'er the land of the free and the home of the brave!"

While the roomful was still roaring applause, old Colonel Chester hobbled up the stairs to shake the young man's hand.—"And now, folks," said he, turning round to face the company, "ye've heard 'bout them 'broad stripes an' bright stars,' an' I want for yeh to *see* 'em like they're a-goin' to look herearter."

"Hurrah! Stars an' Stripes!"

"We all know how it's ben with our flag. Whenever a new state come in—an' lately they ben comin' thicker 'n spatter—we'd slap on a new stripe an' stick in a new star. Consekence was, the flag was gittin' to look like suthin' the cat brung in. Wal, fin'ly things got so bad even Congress begun thinkin' 'bout 'em, an' one Congressman comes to our boy Sam Chester Reid at thet 'ar bankit they guv 'im down at Richmond an' 'Hyar,' he says, 'ye done so good defendin' the flag, why'n't ye take an' make it look wuth all thet trouble?' An' so Sam he talks it

642

over with his wife Mary, which was a Jennings from out Willington way, an' she goes an' stitches a flag o' the United States like it allus oughter be—an' will be, too, iffen Congress has the sense to vote it in. I brung it with me. I got it hyar in my pocket.—Mary Reid, will ye please to step up hyar an' show these folks what we've ben fightin' fer?"

As the musicians began once more the old tune of "Anacreon in Heaven," playing it softly on muted strings, a dainty little woman, black-haired and bright-eyed, went up the stairs and took from the Colonel's hand a bit of colored muslin. The company, crowding closer, saw that it was no larger than a lady's handkerchief. Just that, in fact, was what it must have originally been, but now, as the result of skillful needle-work, it showed thirteen stripes, alternately red and white. In the union, on a ground of deep blue, were sixteen five-pointed stars arranged in the shape of a larger star.

"Wal, thar ye be, folks. How ye like it? Thar's thirteen stripes fer the thirteen col'nies—an' the top stripe, o' course, is Connecticut. Thar's a star fer every State, with room for a thousan' more—most of 'em made out o' land that was once Connecticut.—Thar's the Star-Spangled Banner, an' long may it wave o'er the land o' the free an' the home o' the brave!"

Mary Reid was still holding up the tiny flag and the violinists were still playing in the midst of uproarious applause when all other sounds were suddenly overwhelmed by a thunderous "Boom!" from the direction of the river. It shook the court-house like a sudden blast of wind.

"Thar's them British agin!" called a voice.

"Come, Mary," said Reid to his wife. "You get grandmother's cloak, I'll find grandfather's great-coat, and we'll go out and watch the salute."

"I don't *want* any great-coat!" the Colonel protested as he started down the stairs, leaning heavily on his cane.

"But you will please to wear it just the same, Father," said Rebecca as he went by her.

A scene of strange and delicate beauty greeted those of the company who gathered at the court-house windows or went out with the Reids and Chesters to stand on the steps. Looking down the slope of State Street toward the Thames they saw that every window within their view was filled, as Reid had said, with burning candles. On the frigates and brigs and sloops in the river every yard-arm was illumined by hanging lanterns and crowded with sailors, dimly discerned, standing at attention. A half-moon, dreamy and serene, laid a silvery luster upon the newly fallen snow in the streets, on the house-tops, and along the earth-works of Fort Griswold across the river.

"Boom!" and again "Boom!" the salute went on at regular intervals of three seconds, giving the echoes that hurried from bank to bank no rest. Just before each crashing roar the watchers saw a spurt of flame, a flash of light, in which the broad bands of white and black on the vessel's side, the masts, the spars, the rigging, and the standing men, sprang vividly forth out of gloom.

"That's the *Northumberland,* my flag-ship," said Admiral Hotham. "She has just fired her twenty-first gun. Now the *Severn* takes up. Captain Aylmer."

"Twenty-one guns!" said Colonel Chester. "That means ye're firin' the national salute, Ammiral."

"Yes, sir; it means just that."

"It means that Old England recognizes a new Power on 'arth."

"She has to. And she's glad to. Let us hope, Colonel, that these two Powers will always stand together! They can wreck the world if they do not, and they can make a better world if they do. Let us pray that every gun they fire in each other's presence hereafter will be a sign, like these we are hearing now, of mutual understanding and respect!"

"Amen!" the Colonel answered in a voice charged with emotion. "Mary, hold up your flag. They can't see it, I know, but it's for that very same blessed flag they're a-firin'."

"Boom!" and again "Boom!" from the *Severn.*

The echoes thronging the air must have reached by this time up to Norwich at the head of the river and down to Jordan Cove on the Sound. Interminable they were, bounding forward and back from hill to hill. Why, indeed, should they ever cease? Why should they not roll out into the western country beyond the Great River, and over the ocean to England?

Sam Avery came out to join the group. They heard the strains of "Anacreon in Heaven" from the violins as he opened the court-house door.

"Dear God," said the Colonel, "what I wouldn't give to have John Reid with us now."

"And Holdfast too!" said his wife.

"O' course, Mother. You an' me don't ever hev to say that. Holdfast started it all. These echoes—he made 'em. This whole salute is only jest the echoes of Long Tom. They've ben rollin' fer thirty-five year. They'll roll forever, I reckon."

"Boom!"

"That's the *Superb*," said Admiral Hotham.—"Is your vessel down there, Captain Reid?"

"No, Admiral. The vessel I last commanded lies sunk just off the town of Horta, in the Azores."

"Ah; a sad thing, that. I've felt it myself. A captain misses a vessel he's lost as he would an amputated arm."

"Boom!"

For many minutes they stood and listened while the *Pactolus* spoke, the *Narcissus*, the *Arab*, the *Tenedos*, and the brig *Despatch*. Slow and evenly measured, the majestic utterance of the great guns seemed to come up out of profound deliberation. It loaded the air with half-guessed meanings that reached back and forth through time.

"The frigate *United States* is answering now," said Stephen Decatur.

They listened to her twenty-one guns and then to those of her prize, the *Macedonian*, after which some of the group turned back toward the door.

"Wait a minute!" said Sam Avery.

They waited and listened. At length four thin popping explosions came up in rapid succession from the water, ludicrously feeble in comparison with the orotund thunder they had just heard.

"What's that?" asked the Admiral, politely covering a smile with his gloved hand.

"That's the *Rebecca*," said Sam. "She carries a crew of ten men and four three-pounders. I told the boys to fire 'em all as fast as they could, so's to make 'em sound more important."

"Does she belong to the United States Navy?"

"Wal, no; not so's ye c'd say she rightly *b'longs,* but, time was, she 's 'bout the only navy we had round hyar. Course, she's a mite old now. Holdfast Gaines and me built her when we were boys.—Same time, she's ben heard from. She's got a right to be hyar."

Then a flash was seen from Fort Trumbull and there rolled up the hill a single magnificent roar.

"They're tryin' to live up to Long Tom," said the Colonel, "but Holdfast Gaines ain't hyar.—Howsomever, that's all we got, Ammiral."

"I do wish," said Admiral Hotham, "that some one would tell me about this Holdfast Gaines I've heard mentioned so many times tonight."

"Why, don't ye know 'bout him?" exclaimed the Colonel. "Prob'ly the greatest man 't ever lived—or so we think in these parts.—Look ye hyar, Ammiral: ye see that leetle light up north thar a piece, on top o' the highest hill? I don't, but with your good eyes . . ."

"Yes, I see it clearly."

"Wal now, thet 'ar's Four Winds Farm, whar I've lived man an' boy fer nigh onto ninety year. Borned thar, an' my father an' granfer afore me. Now I'd like fer yeh to come up so's I c'd show yeh 'round whar Holdfast used to live. We allus keep a candle burnin' in the kitchen winder fer 'im, an' the door unlocked. He mought come 'long by whilst ye're thar. He draps in now an' then."

"Oh, so he's still living, is he? I didn't understand that."

"Livin'! Wal, I reckon he *is* a-livin'. Live forever, that boy will. He ain't the dyin' kind."

* * *

The western sky was piled to the zenith's height with domed and pinnacled magnificence of cloud. Great pinions of gold rushed out from the core of the low-lying sun. The River was one wide glory.

It was hard for an old man's eyes, dimmed by many years of poring over print and dice and cards, to look steadily into the dazzle. Yet minute after minute the Parson stood, with his Indian friends beside him, striving to follow the black dwindling shape that was crossing the River. The beauty and mystery bound him.

"They are steering straight for the sun," said Mad Buffalo.

"And that," said the son of The Breath, "is why we can't see them."

"Sleeping Bear had always the sunset in his face," said the son of the Raven.

"But the rain he had too, and the thunder," said the son of Dragging Canoe.

"Big runner! Big story-teller! Very damn big man!" mused Eats 'em Alive.

The upper sky was fading now and the River was changing his garment.

"We cannot live without Sleeping Bear and the Beloved Woman!" a squaw said, drawing her blanket more closely about her shoulders.

"And we shall not live without them," the old man answered. "They are taking our fire to the Thundering Prairie. They will mingle our flame with the fires that the gods of the thunder have kindled. We shall always sit by their camp-fires."

646

A breeze crisped and darkened the River's hue. The dusk was racing westward after the sunset. It filled every hollow with blue and gray and black.

"They are gone!" said a woman's voice. "They have crossed the River!"

"We shall all cross the River tomorrow," the Parson replied.

There fell through the quiet air, from westward, the cry of some swift and strong-winged bird that could find its way in the darkness.

And then, faint and far, heard or fancied, there came the challenge, the summons of "Hobbomok," like the ghost of an echo, like an end that is also a beginning—"Br-OM-m-m!"

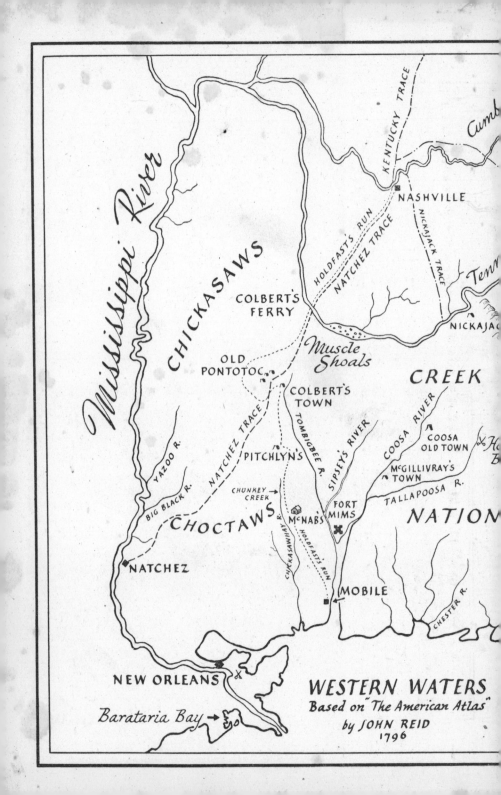

WESTERN WATERS
Based on "The American Atlas"
by JOHN REID
1796